THE JANET BLACK SERIES, BOOKS 1-3

LIBBY KIRSCH

Sunnyside Press

A JANET BLACK MYSTERY

LAST CALL

LIBBY KIRSCH

LAST CALL

Thank you, Tom.
You're so supportive, and I'm so lucky.

CHAPTER ONE

Janet slammed the drawer of the cash register. By the time Cindy Lou jumped at the noise, Janet had her phone out to make a call.

"Hey, darlin'," Jason said when he picked up the line. "I was hoping I'd hear from you."

Janet smiled, in spite of her foul mood, and pushed wisps of light brown hair off her face. Her hand came away damp. She'd been sweating in the Knoxville summer heat since before she even rolled out of bed, and the ancient air-conditioning unit behind the bar couldn't seem to keep up with the soaring temperature. Then she remembered the reason she was calling and frowned. "I just counted—and then I re-counted. Money's missing again." She walked toward the back of the room, away from Cindy Lou and Frank, her bouncer, who'd just arrived for his shift. "This time we're short eighty-two dollars." She couldn't stop herself from turning back to look at her employees suspiciously.

"And?" her boyfriend asked.

"*And* Elizabeth was working last night." She watched Cindy Lou disappear into the back cooler with an empty bucket.

"Anyone else?" Jason asked.

Her lips puckered. Why did he always sound so irritatingly reasonable? "Well, yeah, but I don't think—"

"I'm just saying. Don't fly off the—"

"I can keep my cool, okay?" she snapped, then flushed. She hadn't meant to shout. She lowered her voice to a whisper. "Jason, can you please just check the video? I gotta go." They disconnected, but before she could shove her phone back into her pocket, the screen lit up with a delayed notification telling her she'd missed two calls overnight from the very employee she suspected of theft. She glared at the walls, then realized it wasn't the poor reception *here* that was the problem. She'd been home all night with Jason, and for some reason the incoming calls from Elizabeth were only now showing up.

She tapped a few icons and shook her head. Her youngest staff member hadn't left a message, but the timing seemed suspicious. Janet had learned just days ago that money was disappearing from the register, and now Elizabeth was trying to call her on her cell phone for the first time ever? Did she know, somehow, that Janet knew about the missing money?

Cindy Lou hobbled out from the walk-in cooler, her gait awkward as she wrestled a full bucket of ice behind the bar. As usual, she was dressed to kill—or at least maim. She had poured herself into a bright pink tube top that ended just above a shiny green belly-button ring. Her tight jeans rode so low that her hip bones jutted out, and Cindy Lou had tied her bleach-blond hair back with a teal bandanna. Body parts were spilling from every piece of her outfit.

"You gained a set there." Janet motioned to Cindy Lou's chest. Something had happened when she dumped the ice bucket into the freezer drawer, and her two boobs had turned into four.

"Oh my gosh! They musta come unstuck!" Her twang made the words musical. She bent over and reached into her tube top to rearrange things.

"Come on!" Frank turned away from the bar in disgust and

headed for the far side of the room.

Janet watched him walk off before asking Cindy Lou, "What's under there?"

"It's a silicone push-up thingamajig. Sticks right to my skin and pushes the girls up—but I'm sweating so much, they must've slipped down." She wiped beads of sweat from her brow and then smoothed the fabric of her tube top over her restored figure. "You know, I didn't used to need all this business under here, but after Chip, everything just kind of . . . fell."

Chip, Chip, Chip. It was all Cindy Lou ever wanted to talk about. Janet plastered on a smile when her bartender looked up. "Kids, huh? How old is he now?"

"Seventeen, going on forty." She smiled indulgently. "He leaves for college soon." She turned back to the bar, a towel and spray bottle in her hands, the goofy grin still on her face.

Frank slammed two chairs down from the table in the corner, still scowling. He might not have liked Cindy Lou's methods, but he took his share from the tip jar every night without complaint. Janet only paid minimum wage, but they all cleared more than thirty dollars an hour on a good night, thanks in some part, perhaps, to Cindy Lou's ramped-up double Ds. Their nice pay made it even more frustrating to discover someone had been stealing money from the register, and if Janet's new accounting program was right, it had been going on for weeks. That's why she'd had Jason install a state-of-the-art surveillance system. She was ready to catch a thief.

"Damn gum," Frank muttered, scraping the tabletop with a razor blade.

He fit the job description for a bouncer—tall and strong—but his light brown hair was smashed flat on one side, as if he'd fallen asleep while it was wet, and his eyes were red and puffy.

Was he the sticky-fingered employee? Though Elizabeth, Janet's other full-time bartender, was her prime suspect, Frank was no prize, so if Jason saw him stealing in the surveillance video from the night before she wouldn't be shocked.

But Elizabeth still seemed the most likely culprit, although Janet couldn't articulate why to Jason. She just had a feeling the other woman was hiding something.

"Anything unusual last night?" she asked lightly as she walked back behind the bar.

"Oh, you know," Cindy Lou said without taking her eyes off the two bottles of top-shelf vodka she was combining, "same old, same old. We had to throw poor Ike out just before midnight, bless his heart. Other than that, it was the usual."

"Did he make a fuss?" Janet already knew the answer, since she hadn't been called.

"Nah." Cindy Lou placed the full bottle of vodka back on the shelf and dropped the empty one in the recycling bin.

Frank cleared his throat. "No fuss?" He hefted two more chairs off a table and dropped them to the ground with a bang. "He shouted the whole way out the door, 'The man will always find you—he knows,' not to mention the hail of curse words he spewed at Elizabeth."

Cindy Lou shrugged as she took two bottles of well vodka from the bin and unscrewed the caps.

Janet looked shrewdly at her bartender. "Did we call him a taxi?"

"Yes, ma'am, we sure did, and didn't kick him out until it arrived," Cindy Lou said, unconcerned.

"Well, shit," Janet nodded and shrugged. Really, you couldn't ask for a better outcome.

Cindy Lou raised her eyebrows and looked pointedly at a jar on the counter.

Janet grinned. "Aw, hell, Cindy Lou," she drawled, making a show of pulling not two but three dollar bills out of her back pocket and pushing them into the oversized, washed pickle jar. The swear jar already had five bucks in it from the last hour alone. "I keep forgetting to watch my damn mouth."

Her good humor was tested, however, by Frank, muttering in the corner.

"That's not how you'd have handled it on the force?" she asked.

"It's not a police issue. I just don't know why he's welcomed back time and again." Frank turned away from the women and kept working.

Janet had hired him a few weeks ago, desperate for a bouncer and impressed by his pedigree. She figured a former cop would surely know how to handle the door of her small bar. So far, however, he'd been a disappointment, always ready to escalate a situation and challenge the status quo.

"I suppose you think that kind of behavior is fine?" he asked over his shoulder.

"No, but this is a bar, not a bookstore. It's going to happen." Janet crossed to the back cooler and emerged minutes later with a white plastic bin full of lemons and limes. She looked up at a sudden clattering at the front door. A gray and grizzled man with greasy hair and dirty clothes pulled at the handle. She could practically smell his days-old sweat through the glass.

"Door's broken!" he called, cupping a hand over his eyes so he could see into the bar. "Ma'am? It won't open." He jiggled the handle again, and then, as if he'd expended too much effort, he leaned in, leaving a streak on the glass with his forehead. Janet and Cindy Lou exchanged amused looks, but Frank crossed his arms and stared daggers at him.

"We're not open," Frank said, looking at the man like he was the leftover foam at the bottom of a pint glass.

"Not open?" The man smiled, revealing several missing teeth. "How'd you get in?"

Janet chuckled and looked at Frank. "Take care of it." She pointed to the number for the taxi company nailed to the wall behind her, then waited until Frank picked up his cell phone before she took the empty fruit bin to the back room.

There, Janet caught a glimpse of herself in the mirror on the back of the door. She turned to the side to check her boobs. She was thirty-one years old and had no kids, so they were right where they were supposed to be. She smoothed her black T-shirt with the bar's logo on it and tucked it into her jeans before heading to the desk.

She spent a few minutes going over the books. It was Thursday, which meant they could expect a big college crowd thirsty for deals. She squinted through the window into the back parking lot. If the beer truck didn't show, she'd have to change her happy-hour special, as her inventory of cheap, crappy beer was low.

Janet looked at the clock on the wall and blew out a sigh. She'd check the cooler to see what would make a good replacement.

But first, she decided to call Elizabeth. The call went straight to voicemail, so she left a message, telling her bartender to call in; she wanted to ask directly about the missing money. Her phone chirped—the battery was low—so she laid it on the desk and called Jason on the landline, leaving him a long, detailed message about her plan for Elizabeth.

Despite the missing money, she liked being in charge. It was freeing to think that if there was a problem with an employee, she could fix it.

Buying the Spot a year ago had made her a boss for the first time ever, and she was on a mission to be unlike any crappy boss she'd ever had. She wanted to be calm, be unflappable, and stay the hell out of her employees' personal lives. With a final nod to herself, she logged out of her computer and left the office.

As she cut through the main room, however, her step stuttered and her heart slammed into her chest. What was it about seeing cops that made you feel instantly guilty?

The man and woman in uniform were chatting with Frank by the front door. Cindy Lou was behind the bar, not making eye contact, but Frank looked up defiantly when she cleared her throat.

"Hello, Officers," Janet said. "What's going on?"

CHAPTER TWO

"I'm telling you for the last time, Frank, you either get on board or you get out. Your ninety-day probationary period isn't over, so there won't even be any paperwork to file." Janet spoke low and fast to her bouncer. She'd pulled him aside after gleaning that he'd dialed 911 instead of the taxi company.

"Why do you care if that homeless guy has to spend the night in jail?" Frank's superior smile was almost enough to make her snap.

With a supreme effort, and ignoring the roar of blood rushing in her ears, Janet turned on her heel and marched over to the officers. "More sweet tea?" She attempted to cover her anger with acute kindness. After all, it wasn't the police officers' fault she'd hired an idiot.

The woman shook her head, but the man smiled and held out his glass. After she topped it off from the pitcher on the bar she said, "What are you booking him in on?"

"We got a call for a drunk and disorderly person, but now I'm thinking public intox is a better fit."

Janet shot a disbelieving look at Frank. "Disorderly? He called me 'ma'am' when he tried to open the door. He really just needs a ride home . . . or—or a meal, maybe." She looked out the glass door and saw the person in question huddled in the back-seat of the cruiser. "Cindy Lou," she added, "get him a sweet tea to go." She watched her bartender pull a large Styrofoam cup from an upper shelf. "Y'all don't mind, do you?" she asked the woman cop, purposefully bringing out a little Southern flair.

The officer smiled and held out her hand for the drink, but her partner said, "He *is* getting a ride . . . just not home."

Janet bristled at his attitude. Business would plummet if her bar got a reputation for calling the cops on people who were minding their own business. She shot Frank another dirty look.

"Frank here did the right thing." The male officer nodded with approval. "Public intoxication is a class-C misdemeanor." The two men fist-bumped.

"You two know each other?" Janet asked, looking at the pair shrewdly.

"Frank worked under me for a bit," he answered, then turned to Frank and said, "I still think you got a raw deal, man."

"Thanks, brother," Frank said. He walked the cops to the door.

"He'll spend a few hours in jail, sleep it off, and be on his way," the woman said over her shoulder to Janet as they left.

Janet's expression darkened. She'd have liked nothing more than to fire Frank right then and there, but she couldn't. He'd been the only one to apply for the job when she posted it at the start of summer, so for now, she was stuck.

She had gone over her policy with all the employees many times: if someone was drunk, she would pay for their ride home. The steps were outlined in the employee handbook Jason had insisted she write up when they bought the bar. A bartender took away a customer's car keys and called a cab if they'd had too much to drink. The customer could get their keys back the next day after reimbursing Janet for the cab ride. Sure, they'd had complaints from some customers, but usually only on the night in question. The next day, most were not only apologizing but also thanking Janet for saving them from themselves.

She even had a deal with the local taxi company for a discounted rate for her customers—a system that should have worked seamlessly.

Unfortunately, her newest hire seemed determined to forge his own path at her bar, and it was starting to piss her off.

She spotted a lone lemon lying forgotten next to the cutting board and angrily grabbed the knife.

Thwack.

The blade slammed through the lemon and she shook her head, thinking about Frank's attitude. He was a self-serving, sanctimonious—

"Ouch!" All the air squeezed out of her lungs as the knife sliced right into her finger.

Cindy Lou jumped at the sound and then rushed to the cabinet for the first-aid kit.

After Janet caught her breath, she went to the sink and held her hand under cold running water. The red-tinged water swirled down the drain as Janet's anger swirled up inside of her.

"Am I unclear, Cindy Lou?" she asked under her breath. "Am I not articulating the rules well?" She took the bandage the other woman held out and clumsily unwrapped it with one hand.

"No, you're clear, boss. Clear as a bright, sunny day. He just wants to do it his way."

"When he gets his own bar, he can do that. It can be like the goddamn OK Corral if he wants, with cops there every night. But that's not how we are going to do business *here*." She shrugged off Cindy Lou's offer of help, finally freed the bandage from the wrapper, and then wound the small strip around her left index finger. Cindy Lou lowered her head and looked at Janet through her eyelashes, then put a dollar in the swear jar from her own pocket.

Was she paying for Janet's swear word or swearing at Janet in her head? Janet was surprised enough that she had to fight off a smile. But her good humor faded when she tossed the bloody towel into a trash can. The bin was overflowing—no one had bothered to empty it after closing the night before. Janet pulled the black trash bag out of the waist-high trash can, groaned when her finger pulsed with pain, then tied off the bag and headed for the alley door.

"I sure wish people would share the work around here, instead of their opinions on every damn decision I make," she called to Frank as she pushed through the heavy metal door to the side alley. Within seconds, her tank top stuck uncomfortably to her skin and her jeans felt heavy. The heat of the day was already oppressive.

She took a bracing breath, then heaved the bag up into the Dumpster. Her mouth fell open when she saw several more trash bags on the ground around the other side of the bin. The sound of rushing blood was back, roaring past her ears

"Trash bags go in the Dumpster, not by it!" she shouted toward the bar.

"I put them *in* the Dumpster," Frank replied mulishly at the door, making no effort to come out and help.

"Then why are they on the ground?" Janet glowered at her bouncer. She gestured to the abandoned building next door. "We look like we're competing with old Ben Corker's restaurant!" Foreclosure signs and trash littered the lot, which blended in seamlessly with hers.

When Frank didn't answer, she stalked over and hefted the closest bag up into the Dumpster, then froze when she bent down to get the second bag, her mouth suddenly dry. "What the . . ."

She reached down and gently lifted the lower corner. Nestled underneath the black plastic were what looked like toes. "Whoo," she breathed, and her heart skipped a beat. She took an involuntary step back before recovering her wits. She nudged the bag out of the way with her foot and then swore under her breath when it became clear the toes were attached to a foot and the foot to a man, lying alongside the Dumpster. The exposed skin was bluish white, smudged with dirt that looked as dark as the trash bags.

"Well, shit," she said, staring at the body. "This day can't get any worse."

CHAPTER THREE

A slow, gigantic fly buzzed overhead, and Janet swatted it away. It lumbered toward the Dumpster, joining dozens of others swarming around the body.

"Officers!" she called when she heard a crunch of gravel. But her throat was dry and the word was barely more than a croak. The cruiser was finally pulling away from the bar. Janet waved her arms and called again. "Hey! Over here!"

The woman cop glanced over and seconds later the cruiser stopped with a jerk. She climbed out and headed along the building toward Janet.

"Yes, ma'am?"

As she got closer, Janet turned and pointed to the toes.

"Oh!" The officer hurried forward and moved the final two bags of trash away before pressing her fingers into the neck. "Cold to the touch," she said. "No pulse."

The other cop had honked twice since she walked over, and he finally climbed out of the cruiser and shouted, "Davis, let's go! I don't have all day, here."

Officer Davis muttered under her breath, "We literally have all day—our shift started an hour ago." Louder, she said, "Got a dead body over here, Gale! Our day just changed." She reached up to press a button on the radio clipped at her shoulder. "I've got a ten twenty-nine at the Spot. Body out back." Davis turned back to Janet with a squint. "Do you know this guy?"

Janet shrugged and took a few slow steps toward the Dumpster, ignoring the tightness in her chest. Her eyes moved from the feet, over the light-wash jeans with a belt buckle the size of Tennessee, to a bright, construction-sign-orange tank top. Her eyes finally settled on the face and she pressed her lips together.

"That's Ike Freeman—he's a regular. He—ah . . . he was here last night."

"Was?" Officer Davis said, her eyebrows raised. "Still is." She took out her notebook. "Did you have any trouble with him?"

"Oh no—nothing like—" Janet's throat constricted. The reality of the situation left her momentarily speechless. "Well, I mean, I heard we had to kick him out, but nothing like . . . *that*." She gestured toward the body. When Davis's chin shifted to the left, she added, "We called a taxi. He didn't want to leave at first, but he did."

"No." The officer shook her head and stepped closer to Janet. "He didn't. Do you have any idea why he's here, behind your bar?"

"No." Janet crossed her arms. "I have no idea at all. Like I said, we called a cab."

Officer Davis narrowed her eyes but took a step back. "I'll need to speak to everyone who was working last night."

"Of course."

"EMTs and homicide are on the way," Officer Gale said. He stopped walking when he got to his partner, but his eyes kept traveling until they landed on the dead body. "We need to rope off the area."

Before his partner could reach her hand out for the crime scene tape, a car pulled into the lot. Officer Gale sprang forward, waving his arms as he moved toward it. "You can't park here! This is a crime scene!"

Jason leaned forward over the steering wheel, his eyebrows

drawn together, lips pursed. Janet raised a hand in a weak wave, and he backed up a fraction and then parked near the entrance to the bar. Officer Gale shook his head. "I said it's a crime scene! Back out of the dang lot!"

Jason climbed out of the car, and the cop hurried forward. "Sir, you need to move this car and vacate the premises. This is an active crime scene."

"I'm the co-owner," Jason said through clenched teeth.

Janet felt the weight pressing against her chest release. Jason was here. It would be okay.

He brushed past Officer Gale, and her heart flip-flopped against her ribs, as if she were seeing him for the first time.

Everything about Jason was a study in contrasts. His preppy, short-sleeve, navy blue polo showed off part of the sleeves of colorful tattoos that went from his wrists, over his shoulders, and down onto his back and chest. His dark hair and all-star smile made him a perfect candidate for a lead role in a rom-com, but when Jason turned on his intense, focused gaze, heartbeats accelerated—including hers.

Was Officer Davis panting?

Jason's lips, usually curving up at the corners with a ready smile, were flat and white as he headed for Janet. "What's going on?"

"Homicide's on the way," Gale said, motioning toward the Dumpster. "Until they get here and clear the scene, I'll need everyone—employees and owners—to wait inside the bar."

Janet glanced at the guy in the cruiser and asked, "Does that include him?"

Officer Davis sighed. "I guess it does."

Her partner turned and motioned to Janet. But instead of following him inside, she raised her eyebrows at Jason. His lips hitched up unhappily on one side and he shook his head; her eyes opened wide and she threw her hands on her hips before turning to the cop anyway. "I think we have something that might help."

"What's that?" Officer Gale asked.

"Jason owns a security company. He recently wired the bar from top to bottom with cameras."

"Inside and outside?"

"Mmm-hmm." She turned to Jason for confirmation, but he was rubbing his face. She knew he didn't like the police, but this was a dead customer; he needed to step up.

"I can't."

"Jason!"

"I came here to tell you my whole system is down. I've been hit with some kind of malware attack." But when his gaze swept the outside of the building, his frustration gave way to a new emotion.

"What is it?" she asked, unable to read his expression.

Now squinting, he walked slowly toward the building. "We have four cameras outside and one of them monitors this part of the alleyway."

"We'll definitely need a copy of that surveillance video for our investigation," Gale said before relaying the information into his radio for whoever was arriving.

"I already told you the system is down, but I don't think it matters, anyway." Jason folded his arms over his chest.

Officer Gale took two steps toward Jason and stopped with a wide stance, his chest puffed out importantly. "It wasn't a question, Mr.—what was your last name?"

"Brooks," Jason answered, still distracted.

The officer scribbled that information into his notebook before speaking. "Well, Mr. Brooks, we'll take what we need when there's a dead body to investigate."

Jason's eyes narrowed as he finally turned to face the cop full-on. "It's not a question of whether I want to share it with you." He closed the gap to the building, shook out a folding ladder that had been leaning against the wall, and climbed up until his face was inches from the exit sign hanging over the rear door.

After studying the device for several moments, he said, "It's a question of why I can't share it with you."

Janet was relieved to find that Officer Gale looked as perplexed as she felt.

"I'm sure I'll get to the bottom of the malware attack, but it won't matter: it looks like somebody tampered with the camera."

"Don't touch anything!" Gale said as he took a step closer. "Ah . . . what camera?"

"I have a security camera hidden in this sign, and right now, the lens is covered with a strip of electrical tape."

"Why would somebody do that?" Janet asked.

"One guess," he said, turning to look at the body.

"How many people knew about the camera?" Officer Gale's eyes narrowed as he looked between the co-owners.

"Not many," Jason answered after a pause. He jumped off the ladder. "In fact, I thought it was just me."

The words floated in the air and landed heavily at Janet's feet. Officer Gale's look as he stared at her boyfriend was unsettling. Had Jason just become a murder suspect?

CHAPTER FOUR

An hour later, Janet added ice to a glass and filled it with sweet tea from the huge metal urn on the bar. The cubes clinked and settled under the liquid, and the outside of the glass was cold and wet by the time she raised it to her lips to drink. She almost sighed at the perfect blend of sweet and savory flavors. Cindy Lou was a lifelong Southerner and had named herself Chief Tea Brewer after watching in shock one day as Janet scooped iced tea powder into a glass of water.

So far, the beat officers had given them a wide berth, but Janet had a feeling that was about to change. Two homicide detectives who'd been outside by the Dumpster for the last forty-five minutes had just walked into the bar.

Detective Mark Finch, older, grayer, and heavyset, moved moodily through the space, lifting things with the tip of a pen and looking suspiciously at her staff and her furniture in equal turns.

"He likes to look around first and then ask questions," Detective Patrick O'Dell said, walking up from the opposite side. He was just over six feet tall with broad shoulders, slim hips, disarmingly bright green eyes, and a slight accent. Janet heard a trace of New York just at the end of his sentences.

He gestured to the gunmetal-gray, bottle-shaped refrigerator that sat in the exact center of the bartender's space behind the counter. "Is that a Beerador?"

"Yeah." She looked at the detective in surprise. "You know about them?"

"My granddad had one in his shop back in the day. You don't usually see them this far south."

"It came with the bar when we bought it a year ago, and I know why. It's heavier than a car—I couldn't get rid of it if I wanted to!"

"Still chugging along, though, huh? That's saying something. It must be nearly seventy years old." He eyed the room. "You've got an interesting setup here. Doesn't seem very efficient, ya know?" She squinted back at the man standing in front of her. She'd heard of the good cop/bad cop routine, but this seemed a bit much. He was looking at her pleasantly, as if he didn't have a dead man to deal with. "The square bar top should be good—ya know, more seats for customers on all sides—but then you've got that Beerador blocking vision down the middle, so one bartender can't see the whole room. It doesn't make any sense."

"You're not breaking any news here, Detective. It came like this. We have a plan to make some changes, but we just don't have the funds, yet."

They stared at each other for a moment before he said, "Mrs. Black, have a seat. I have a few questions about last night."

"It's Ms. Black, and please, ask away, but I wasn't here, so I don't know how much help I'll be."

"Where were you?"

"At home."

"Was anyone with you?" He asked the question pleasantly, but her mouth went dry just the same.

"My boyfriend."

"Did you know the victim?"

"Sure. He was a regular here—a pain in the ass, but usually sorry the next day."

"Any idea what happened?"

"Nope."

He leaned back against the seat, his expression unreadable. "Did he have any problems with anyone?"

"Only everyone who got in his line of sight when he was drunk. Like I said, he wasn't a model customer. He drank too much, and we had to call him a taxi to take him home more than once a week."

"So, what happened last night?" O'Dell's eyes were bright, curious, and lightly suspicious as they locked onto Janet.

"I don't know—I wasn't here." Her nostrils flared. Why was he wasting his time with her?

O'Dell nodded and stood, placing his card on the table. "Call me if you think of . . . anything worth saying." He smirked and started to move away.

"Detective, are you sure this was a murder? I mean, couldn't Ike have just hit his head or had a heart attack?"

O'Dell looked down his nose at her. "You don't often die of natural causes and then cover yourself up with garbage bags."

She frowned. "Yes, I know that, but he could have . . . I don't know, decided to cover himself up first . . . maybe for warmth?" Even as the words left her mouth, O'Dell shook his head.

"Sure. The low was eighty-four overnight with ninety percent humidity. It's a possibility, I guess. Also, there was . . . trauma to the body. We'll have to wait on the coroner's report to be certain on the cause of death."

"I'd just rather—" She turned at a clunk of noise coming from the back and looked suspiciously at the office door. Was someone in there? She got up and tried the handle. It was locked, just like it should have been. She reached into her pocket for her key ring when O'Dell cleared his throat.

She heard the clunk again and instinctively turned toward Detective Finch, interviewing Frank nearby. He banged on the jukebox with his fist and the music cut off. He grinned and did it again, and the music started back up.

She blew out a breath and frowned at her own jumpiness.

O'Dell was staring at her intently. "You'd just rather what?"

"I'd just rather it not be a murder," she answered truthfully.

O'Dell tilted his head to one side and finally said, "Yeah. I know." He turned and walked away.

Finch moved behind the bar, picking things up with his gloved hands, searching under shelves and across surfaces.

Jason made his way to her table and slid into the seat next to her. "I hate this," he said, watching as Finch opened the cabinet that held the first-aid kit and the extra dish soap. "What's he looking for, anyway?"

"No idea," she replied.

He took her hands in his. "Are you okay? You found Ike, are you . . . okay?" he repeated.

"Yeah, I'm fine." She started to pull her hands away but he didn't let her.

"Janet, it's a big deal. Some people go their whole lives without seeing that. It's okay to feel shaky or scared, or sad." Jason's eyes were trained on hers and her heart *lub-dub*bed at his gentle touch.

"I promise, I'm fine."

With a sigh that meant he didn't believe her, he squeezed her hands once before letting go. He leaned back and something fell out of his pants pocket with a tiny clink. Janet reached down and picked up his pen from the floor.

"That is the ugliest pen I've ever seen," she said, watching him tuck the neon blue and yellow pen back into his pocket.

He grinned. "I special-ordered it that way. Ain't nobody gonna steal that!" He looked across the bar. "Speaking of special orders, it wouldn't hurt to have everyone wear a uniform." He nodded at Janet's shirt and said, "Even those old bar T-shirts would be better than *that*." His eyes darted across the room. "It would at least look less . . . or, I mean, more . . . hmm."

She scanned the room and found Cindy Lou, sitting alone at a corner booth, stirring a glass of ice water with a small black straw. With the table covering most of her lower half, she looked PG-13 versus the R rating when her full body was on display. If not for the circumstances, Janet might have laughed.

"I don't want to hurt her feelings," she said. "I think she spends a lot of time getting her look just the way she wants it."

"These damn cops rub me the wrong way," Jason said in a low voice. O'Dell had just sat down across from Cindy Lou, his notebook out, pen poised. When Janet looked over at her boyfriend, she expected to see anger. Instead, his eyebrows were drawn together, concern—sliding toward disappointment. He glanced at her and added, "I mean, they're just dying to be suspicious of regular people. I hate that."

Now it was Janet's turn to cover Jason's hands. She squeezed until the tiny creases around his eyes smoothed a fraction.

"Jason—"

"I'd rather you don't talk to each other until we talk to each of you." Finch had apparently finished his work behind the bar. He planted his feet wide, and folded his arms across his chest as he looked between Janet and Jason.

Jason peered up at him but didn't move. "Ask away." He steepled his fingers in front of his face and waited.

"You first." Finch pointed at Janet. "I'll come for you after."

Jason rubbed at his eyelid and shook his head. Janet felt a rising wave of emotion churning inside of him, which was the last thing they needed with cops everywhere and a dead body outside.

She turned so that her lips were a scant inch away from his ear and whispered, "Looks like you're sloppy seconds."

He snorted, then pushed himself up from the table. "I'll be over there if you need me," he said to Janet, pointing to a nearby booth.

"Thanks," Finch said. "I'll be right over."

Jason frowned but moved across the room.

Fifteen minutes later, Janet was appreciating Detective O'Dell's brevity.

Finch was apparently determined to break her by discussing everything about the bar except Ike. Just then, he was honing in on how inappropriately her employee was dressed.

"All I'm saying," he eyed Cindy Lou, "is that nobody wants to see belly button anymore—especially not before dinner."

Janet looked down at her own midriff. Her belly button was completely hidden, but with Finch's attitude, she'd never wanted to show it off more. She'd just opened her mouth, ready to defend her staff, when O'Dell spoke from across the room.

"Finch, leave her alone. Don't you know who her dad is?"

"Brass is going to come down hard on this one—first murder in five weeks. The mayor was just about to hold a press conference about how safe our streets are, and now this?" Finch snapped. "I couldn't care less who her dad is. I'm only interested in solving this murder." He shot Janet a disgruntled look but got up from the table and walked away.

"And belly buttons," Janet muttered, but she couldn't help agreeing with the jerk. She didn't care that her dad was a federal judge, either, and she also wanted to get to the bottom of Ike's murder. The killer was someone who knew about their security system—that much was clear—which meant it was probably someone associated with her bar.

Her eyes swept the room. Someone had gone out of their way to cover their tracks—and the outside camera. The truth was, somebody in this room knew something.

CHAPTER FIVE

By four o'clock, Janet had resigned herself to the fact that she wouldn't be able to open the bar for business. Homicide had only just begun their investigation, crime scene techs were still dusting every available surface for fingerprints, and Ike was still lying next to the Dumpster—although his body was now covered with a black tarp.

Elizabeth's shift had started a half hour earlier, but so far, she was a no-show.

"All I'm saying is it doesn't look good," Frank said to Cindy Lou, unable to contain his glee. "She's not here, and there's a dead body outside?"

Janet turned away from the bouncer; leave it to Frank to be excited about the crime. She stared thoughtfully out the window. She couldn't deny that it was odd Elizabeth wasn't here, though. Her absence was either worrisome or suspicious, and the homicide detectives appeared to be leaning toward the latter, based on the questions they were asking. She tried Elizabeth's cell phone, but the call went straight to voicemail—again.

She disconnected, her finger throbbing in time with her heartbeat. Although Janet had changed the bandage three times, blood seeped through again, and her pain level increased with each passing minute.

"You think she's an intern?" she asked Jason. They sat at the bar, watching an evidence tech use packing tape to lift finger-prints from the section of counter across from them. What the woman was hoping to find was beyond Janet—there had to be sixty different sets of prints from the last night alone. "Are you guys going to be here all night?" she called.

The crime scene investigator didn't answer.

Jason groaned. "What a day. My system is attacked by some malware program, and I'm stuck here, waiting on a detective to tell me I can go back to work. It's just so frustrating!" He grabbed her hand and she moaned, the pain in her wound seared straight up through her elbow. He flinched and released her fingers at once, instead cradling her hand in his own. "Have you called the doctor yet?"

"No."

"Do it now. One of us is going to be stuck here all night, and it might as well be me—I can't do any work at home, anyway; on top of everything else, the Internet chose today to go down, too. Once the police leave I'll set up shop in the office here and try to figure out what's attacking my system."

"What about Elizabeth?"

"If she shows up, I'll tell her you want to talk to her when she's done with the police. I would have said her reaction to the missing money would be telling, but this murder kind of makes anything else seem like no big deal."

Janet stared at him for a moment before she nodded and stood. She bent over to kiss him on top of his head and said, "I'll see you at home, then."

He hooked her arm and stood as she turned away. "Are you okay?"

Nearly nose to nose, they stared at each other. Janet finally shrugged. "I don't know. It's been a . . . well . . ."

"I know," he said, and pulled her close. They stood together for a moment before he smoothed a hand over her cheek. She leaned into him and felt butterflies form in her stomach at his tender smile.

He tilted his face down and gently touched her lips with his own. Heat zinged through her core before he pulled away. "See you later." He squeezed her uninjured hand and she knew his words were a delicious promise.

Finch cut across the space to meet her at the door. "Don't go far—we might have more questions for you, no matter who your dad is." He looked as if he wanted to stop her from going, but his partner called him over, and Finch sent one last wary look over his shoulder. O'Dell winked at Janet, and she felt a puzzled smile form as she walked out the door to the parking lot.

The humidity outside was so thick that she felt like she was cutting through it with every step, and a blast of heat hit her in the face when she opened her car door. She turned the key in the ignition, got all four windows down, cranked up the AC to full blast, and got back out of the car while it cooled down. She had to wipe her sweaty hands on her jeans to tap a number into her phone screen.

After a few rings and a quick word with the receptionist, she was forwarded to the scheduler at her doctor's office, only to find out her doctor was on vacation for the next two weeks.

"That must be nice," she muttered.

"The other two doctors in the office are taking her patients while she's gone," the scheduler said in a bored voice, listing the names with such apathy that Janet forgot them as soon as they were mentioned. "Do you want whoever's first available? We just opened up clinic hours this weekend."

Janet assessed her finger. "First available is fine." She made the appointment for Sunday morning and climbed back into her car. The air blowing out of the vents wasn't cool, but it wasn't hot, either, so she closed the windows and steered her car toward home. In just a few minutes, she pulled up to the duplex she and Jason had bought a year ago.

Newer beige wood siding cut perfect lines along the front of the house. She loved the color—so clean, so fresh—but Jason said it lacked energy. Earlier in the spring, small red and white flowers had filled the planter boxes just under the windows on their half of the house, but they were long wilted and dead from the summer heat, and Janet was glad, despite what Jason said, that she'd planted plastic flowers in the second-floor window boxes.

A moving van stretched across the front of the home; their new tenants waved her over from the other side of the building, but she pretended not to notice. It had been a long day already, and she didn't feel like making small talk with strangers. The two separate entrances were tucked discreetly away from each other, and she walked into her home without a backward glance.

The first thing she saw was a pair of crumpled checks from their new tenants sitting on the hall table: the security deposit and first month's rent.

She took out her cell phone and called Jason.

"I thought you were going to deposit the checks from Kat and Mel two weeks ago—you know, right when they handed them over?"

"I know, and I'm sorry. I thought I did, but then I found them in the middle of a stack of papers in my office. I was going to deposit them today, but then . . ."

She rolled the tension out of her neck and purposefully relaxed her shoulders. "It's fine. I'll do it tomorrow. Is everybody still there?"

"Yep, and regulars are starting to arrive. I wish you could see Nell talk to that idiot cop. It's classic."

"Is she running the conversation?" Janet asked, grinning despite the gruesome topic.

"He can't get a word in edgewise, and last I heard, she was telling him all about her dog's digestive issues."

"You're sending them home, though, right?"

"Yes. I told them that when you open back up tomorrow night, the first drink's on the house. Beer guy finally came—I had him load up the cooler, so you should be set for tomorrow."

"Elizabeth?"

"Nope." She blew out a sigh, and Jason said, "I'm making some progress on the Internet thing, so hopefully I'll be home later," before disconnecting the call.

Janet's finger throbbed painfully, and her head was starting to throb, too. She wandered to the main room and sat on the couch, tilting her head back to stare at the ceiling. As she tried to remember where in town the closest walk-in health clinic was located, her cell phone rang. She didn't recognize the number, and after she answered, she wished she'd let the call go to voicemail.

"Listen, Detective O'Neil—sorry, O'Dell—there's nothing else I can tell you about Ike Freeman, our staff, or our security system. Nothing." O'Dell was the nicer of the two detectives from earlier, but she was too tired to be very polite.

"I wanted to talk a little bit more about Ike. Can you come in early tomorrow? First thing?"

Janet made a face. She didn't like the sound of the invitation.

"I know your dad—well, I know of your dad. When he was appointed federal judge, we helped out with the background check on his family—"

"Yes," Janet interrupted. "I remember it." She and her father hadn't been on speaking terms back then, and she'd successfully evaded the FBI and local police for weeks, not caring to have any part in anything her father wanted or needed. Eventually her father had come to town to track her down, and Janet was more surprised than anyone that it had led to the beginning of a father-daughter relationship, the first she'd ever had.

"I'm not going to pull any surprises on you, Janet, just a few questions I didn't want to ask in front of an audience," O'Dell said. "I'm sure you'll want to do your part to help with this case."

She grimaced, but she heard herself agreeing to go in before she could think better of it. "Fine. I'll see you first thing tomorrow morning."

CHAPTER SIX

"First thing in the morning" was subjective. Janet set her alarm for eleven fifteen, just to be on the safe side, but didn't roll out of bed until shortly after noon.

Her pajamas were rumpled and her hair lay tangled on one side, but as she brushed her teeth, she noticed that her skin was clear. She'd quit smoking about a year earlier and continued to find unexpected benefits.

After taking a quick shower, she spent a few minutes drying her hair and then threw on jeans and a tank top.

She was heading toward the kitchen when Jason called out, "Shoes!" He leaned back to look at her through the open doorway.

She slid her feet into the flip-flops she'd left by the door the night before and walked into the work zone that was their kitchen.

Jason had started renovating it shortly after they'd moved in by tearing the old, dilapidated kitchen down to the studs. A major project had then come in for his security business; another followed, and another after that. They'd been eating out and using the microwave extensively ever since. Now, with the malware attack, Janet wasn't sure when he might get back to working on the kitchen. Just then, he had three laptops spread out on a sheet of plywood over two sawhorses where the island would someday live.

"Did you sleep at all?" she asked, pressing her body against his back and kissing him between his shoulder blades. He turned and draped an arm around her shoulders. His eyes were bloodshot and his hair was rumpled.

"Hi, Janet!" called another voice, this one deep and gravelly. She looked quickly around the room and then at the computers when the voice said, "Down here."

"Wex?" In the lower corner of the left computer monitor, Jason's college roommate waved, live via webcam. His dimples deepened when she asked, "Did you cause this, Wex, or are you fixing it?"

He chuckled and ran a hand through his floppy brown hair. "I'm trying to get Jason to fix it, so I don't have to charge him, and then he'll be able to do it himself next time."

"Oh, please, spare me the learning-experience bullshit and just tell me what to do!" Jason said, only half joking.

Janet smiled at Wex, and then headed through the kitchen into the hallway where the fridge and coffeepot had been relocated half a year earlier. She fixed a cup of coffee and drank it as she made her way back through the kitchen to the front of the house.

"Can I have some?" Wex called as she walked by.

"Stop ogling my woman!" Jason said, and then unplugged the webcam, making Wex's laugh the last thing they heard from him. He followed Janet. "Sorry I'm distracted." She set her drink on the plywood and he pulled her close. "Good morning." She leaned into the hug and felt her body relax into him. He chuckled when she let out a low moan.

"It's okay, you're busy. How are things coming?" she asked his chest.

He stepped back and leaned down, softly touching her lips with his, then it was his turn to moan. "Mmm. I missed you last night. I thought I could lick this thing on my own, but I had to call Wex early this morning. Damn virus." He shook his head. "It's wormed its way into my operating system. Wex thinks he can isolate it before it does more damage, but it's locked up my whole system."

"Are you suspicious of the timing?" Janet asked, suddenly wondering if Ike's killer was a computer whiz, too.

"No," he said, frowning. "Wex thinks it's been lurking on my hard drive for weeks, and something I did, some combination of keystrokes, triggered it into action."

"Wow. Sounds very sophisticated."

"It is," he agreed, running his hands up and down Janet's arms. He cocked his head to the side. "I'm due a lunch break soon."

"How soon?" She ran her fingertips lightly over his chest. Heat flooded her stomach and she pressed her hips closer, nipping hungrily at his lower lip.

His breathing grew louder and it took him a moment of exploring her mouth to answer. "I've got Wex for another hour."

"Ugh!" she moaned. "I'll be at work by then."

Jason's cell phone rang. "Wex," he said, looking at the screen. He tapped a button that silenced the phone, then leaned closer to Janet and planted a scorching kiss on her lips. His phone rang again, and he rubbed a hand through his hair and blew out a loud sigh. "Gotta go. I'll see you tonight!" he said, then jogged back to the kitchen.

Her lopsided, dopey smile remained until she opened the door and a blast of heat melted it off her face.

"Morning!" a cheery voice called from the street.

Janet squinted past the glare of the sunlight and saw a woman carrying a pillow up the drive. Behind her a moving truck was still half-full.

"It's me, Katherine—but you can call me Kat," she said.

Kat had long, wavy brown hair that swung back and forth like a pendulum with each step, and she tossed the pillow up in the air as she approached.

Behind her, her partner, Mel, labored up the driveway with three boxes stacked high in her arms. Mel had short, sandy-blond hair, and wore hiking boots, gray cargo shorts, and a T-shirt. She gave off an air of cool efficiency.

They'd all met three weeks earlier when the two women had toured the open half of the duplex and signed the rental papers.

Janet pivoted and reached back inside the house, her fingers closing around the checks on the hall table.

"I'll head to the bank," she called to Jason, whose only response was a grunt. She turned back to Kat, who was still smiling widely. "I'm, ah . . . I'm running late. You're unpacking, huh?"

Kat hugged the pillow before answering. "Yup, almost done. We want to get the truck back by three, so we can get our deposit back, and I think we'll make it."

"Well . . . great," Janet said. "Welcome!" She barely avoided a hug as she edged past Kat.

In the car, her pulsing finger reminded her that her doctor's appointment was still days away. Blood had continued to seep from the wound all night, and now something else was oozing out as well, something creamy and whitish that definitely didn't belong in a finger.

After a quick trip through the bank drive-through, she headed to the nearest walk-in medical clinic.

The waiting room was packed, and when she signed in, the administrator guarding the clipboard said, "Mornin', sweetie. Looks like the wait is right around two and a half hours to see a doctor."

"Two and a . . ." Janet looked around the room slowly. Despair, pain, and suffering wafted through the air. She didn't have hours to waste *here*.

She crossed her name off the list and headed back to her car. She had bandages and antibiotic cream at home. She'd be fine. She touched the edge of the bandage to wipe away a smear of blood and had to bite her lip at the pain.

It was just a cut, for God's sake!

Janet determinedly headed downtown, ignoring the regular pulsing through the pad of her finger, and turned the music up to drown out the pain.

"You said first thing in the morning," O'Dell said when he came out to the lobby. His eyebrows were knitted together, but he didn't look truly upset. "Oh, and call me Patrick."

Janet squinted up at him, wishing she'd had the foresight to stop for a cup of coffee on the way. "We don't all work nine to five, Det—Patrick."

His eyebrows shot up and he nodded with a half smile. "Well, come on back." He opened the door to the right of the bullet-proof glass that enclosed the receptionist. "My office is through here."

Janet kept a few steps behind him as he wound his way through a maze of cubicles. O'Dell shared one of the very few offices with a door at the far end of the space. Two desks faced each other in the cramped room. He motioned for her to sit in one of the two visitor chairs by the door. The wall facing her was covered in mug shots—a grim row of men and women snarling unhappily at the camera.

O'Dell finally cleared his throat. "Thanks for coming in."

"Sure. I'm not sure what I can do to help, though."

They stared at each other for several long minutes before O'Dell cleared his throat again. "I feel like we got off on the wrong foot yesterday."

"Not you—your partner," Janet said with a frown.

O'Dell nodded. "Mark's very well regarded and is as thorough an officer as you'll find here." When she didn't answer, he added, "He's very . . . enthusiastic."

"Me too," Janet said flatly, and a smile threatened to break out on O'Dell's lips.

"Well, like I said last night, I know your father—well, of your father—and I figured you'd want to do right by him, to do right by this case."

She squinted up at him and leaned forward in her seat. "What does that mean?"

"It just means I know he's good people—you're good people. I hope you'll keep your ears open and let us know if you hear anything about the case, that's all. We rely on the fact that most people are . . . well, good."

She snorted. "Is that all? Did I drive all the way down here for you to tell me that most people are good?"

Surprisingly, he blushed.

"Patrick, I'm not sure about your training or background, but next time you have something similarly urgent, feel free to call or text, okay? You already have my number."

"Sit down." Janet hadn't even noticed she'd stood. "That's not why I asked you to come in." He waited for her to sit, then *he* stood and paced the tiny office. "I wanted to tell you what we know about the victim."

"About Ike?" she asked. "I already know all I need to know about Ike. He came in almost every night, ordered five drinks— three of them during happy hour to keep his costs down—and usually drove himself home, unless he'd had a few drinks before coming in, in which case we'd call him a ride."

"Do you know about his family, though—his history?"

"Well . . . no. I guess not."

"His story is a sad one, but not uncommon. His family is mostly gone, and he turned to drink at some point. We spoke to his only daughter last night to break the news, and she said they'd been estranged since her mother died a number of years ago. She was at home last night meditating. He was all alone."

Janet kept her face impassive. Everyone had a sad story to

tell. Ike's didn't sound more tragic than any of her other regulars'. "Is that all?" she asked, standing again.

His green eyes bored into hers. He seemed disappointed by her disinterest. "For now. I'm counting on you to keep in touch if anything else comes up—especially that surveillance video from your boyfriend. That sure would be nice to have."

O'Dell escorted her through the office to the lobby. "We'll probably come back to the Spot tonight—we need to talk to your customers about Ike and see if anyone remembers anything from Wednesday night."

Janet made a face but nodded. She'd figured the cops would be back. "You and Finch?"

"*Detective* Finch, and it'll probably be just him. Now, now," he said when she groaned, "he's one of our best and has been on the force a long time. Ike deserves that, don't you think?"

Janet didn't answer as she wondered what her now-dead customer deserved.

"Busy day?" O'Dell asked as they stood in the doorway together, looking out onto the hot sidewalk.

"Headed to work. Did you see the news covered the crime last night? With all those live shots from our parking lot, business will be crazy tonight."

"That's grim," O'Dell said.

"It's a grim world."

"Doesn't have to be," O'Dell said.

"You're right," Janet agreed, "but it is, and I want my staff to be ready. Speaking of staff," she said, watching O'Dell's face, "what can you tell me about my bouncer, Frank Ellis?"

"Frank?" he repeated, a little too innocently.

"He said on his résumé that he was a cop here. When I asked him about it after he applied at the Spot, he told me the job wasn't what he expected and he quit, but I think I should have checked that out, you know, made sure it was an accurate reflection of why he left."

"Hmm," he said, and crossed his arms, leaning up against the door frame. "I'll give you the number for HR, they can answer any questions you have about Frank, or any of our employees." She pursed her lips, but he wasn't done. "Oh, we'll also want to talk to that other bartender who was working Wednesday night. Elizabeth? Detective Finch went to her house, but no one was home."

"Mmm-hmm," she said, crossing her arms and smiling at O'Dell. "I'll make sure to connect you with our HR department."

He cocked an eyebrow and the corners of his lips lifted in amusement. "Fine. You want to know about Ellis?" He dropped his arms and moved closer to Janet. "The official release papers say he was honorably discharged after serving eight months on the force to care for a sick relative."

"And?" She tried not to breathe in his aftershave, but it was such a welcome combination of sandalwood and citrus that she leaned toward him while he answered to get another noseful.

"And that's bullshit," he said, his voice dropping. "He was too rough with citizens. He racked up a dozen use-of-force complaints in his first six months. Chief put him on probation, and he didn't slow down. Boss finally told the union he had to resign on his own terms or he'd be fired. He resigned." He looked behind him at the reception desk, then turned back to Janet. "Your turn. Elizabeth?"

"She's scheduled to work tonight," Janet said, distracted enough with O'Dell's new information about her bouncer that she forgot about his cologne.

"What time?"

She shook herself, focusing on the detective. "Seven. She's scheduled to work seven to close."

O'Dell patted her on the shoulder and she pushed through the door, wading through the hot, humid air to get to her car.

So Frank was a liar, and nobody had seen Elizabeth since the night Ike was killed. It was a lot to process so early in the day. Her finger throbbed as she grabbed the steering wheel—and she thought absently that she'd have Cindy Lou cut the lemons from now on.

She put the car into drive and pulled away from the curb. If O'Dell thought she'd help him with his murder case because her father would want her to, he was mistaken. In fact, it only made her want to step as far away from the crime as possible. She wouldn't lift a single finger—throbbing or not—to help.

CHAPTER SEVEN

"Speak of the devil," Janet said, looking at the screen of her phone when it rang. She tapped a button and said, "What do you want?"

There was a beat of silence as her father processed her tone. "I miss you, too, and I love you."

She laughed grudgingly, almost hating the fact that a man she hadn't known for most of her life was somehow able to read her moods as well as Jason.

"What's going on, Dad?" she asked, navigating the streets of Knoxville as she made her way toward the bar.

"We haven't talked in a while, and I wanted to check in to see how you're doing."

"Oh, really?" Janet asked.

"Is it so difficult to believe a father would want to check in on his daughter?"

"This call has nothing to do with the body found behind my bar last night?"

There was a long pause, and Janet cringed when she realized her father might have been telling the truth. Finally, he said, "Well, now I am curious, Janet. Please, do fill me in."

"Uhh . . . It's not a good time. I just pulled up to work." It wasn't exactly true, but she was only a few blocks away and there wasn't nearly enough time to explain a murder.

"Let's talk tomorrow—first thing in the morning," her father said with annoying authority.

"Sure, sure, first thing," she said with a smile, knowing he'd be in the middle of meetings and court hearings by the time she rolled out of bed.

She disconnected the call and, a few minutes later, pulled into the parking lot at the Spot. She pursed her lips when she saw the police caution tape was still blocking off the Dumpster area. "Where are we supposed to put the trash?" she asked the car.

She walked up to the deserted building, unlocked the door, and headed through the dark bar to the light panel near the office to flip on the daytime lights.

Back in the office, she fired up the computer, determined to go over the books one more time. Before she could log in, though, there was a knock at the back door. She looked at her watch; she wasn't expecting any deliveries that day.

She pushed the miniblinds apart and saw the beer truck parked behind the bar, and the deliveryman smiling sheepishly at her through the glass.

She wrestled open the steel door. "Hey, Bud. What's going on?" she asked the burly man leaning against the door frame. Janet grinned. She loved that the man who delivered their Bud was named Bud.

"I shorted Jason a couple cases of the lager yesterday. I only realized it when I was going through inventory this morning and I wanted to make it right."

"I hadn't even noticed it yet," she said, holding up her clipboard. "I was just about to go over the books; things have been . . . busy lately."

"Where do you want them?"

"Straight in the cooler, if you don't mind."

He nodded and headed back outside. Janet turned back to

her computer, but she was distracted by the rolling thunderclap of sound as Bud opened the back of the delivery truck. She scrunched up her face and tried to focus on the accounting figures in front of her while Bud moved through the office with his cart. Cases of beer went in the door and the empty cart came back out. She finally closed her accounting program and waited.

"I broke down these boxes," Bud said, holding the flattened cardboard in both arms. "Do you want me to throw them out back for you?"

Janet grimaced. "If we can," she said, thinking about the police caution tape. She led Bud through the empty bar and out the side door to the alley, and stood there, her hip propping open the door and her arms crossed over her chest.

"Whoa." Bud surveyed the caution tape around the Dumpster. "This is where it happened?"

"Yup," she said. "Did the police talk to you?"

"Nah. The old guy just asked if I knew somebody named Ike. I don't, so he watched me unload and I got right outta here," Bud said.

He tossed the boxes over the yellow tape into the recycling bin, then he adjusted his waistband, and his eyes lingered on the exit sign.

Janet stared for a moment. Did Bud know about the security camera hidden inside? His eyes flitted from the sign to Janet and he grinned, but she didn't know him well enough to say whether the smile was nervous or just a smile.

"Thanks again, Bud."

"No problem." He took a pack of cigarettes out of his chest pocket and tapped one forward. "Hey, sorry again about the mix-up. It won't happen again on my watch." With a final glance at the exit sign, he waved and then disappeared around the back of the building.

Bud had always been friendly, and he'd delivered beer to the bar since she and Jason bought it, but she didn't know anything about him. Why was he interested in the exit sign? She chewed her lower lip as she headed back inside.

"Hey, boss!" Cindy Lou applied an extra coat of bright red lipstick. As usual, she was scantily clad. Today's outfit was a micromini jean skirt and a red tank top with a plunging neckline.

Jason was right: she was going to have to say something before they got a health code violation. She opened her mouth but then felt her eyes glaze over. Who was she to tell someone else how to dress? She didn't want to be *that* boss. After all, Cindy Lou was a grown woman.

"Do you know who's out there?" Cindy Lou asked.

"Oh, it was just Bud, but he's done now."

Cindy Lou cocked her head to the side, and one corner of her mouth pulled up. "No, I saw Bud, darlin'. I'm talking about the lady? She tried to follow me in, but I told her we didn't open for another hour or so. I figured she'd get back in her car and drive away, but she didn't."

Janet walked over and they both looked through the glass door into the front parking lot. Sure enough, a woman was taking a large black trash bag from the passenger seat of an old, beat-up yellow car. She hefted it over her shoulder and headed toward the alleyway. Janet walked through the bar, keeping an eye on the woman through the windows running along the wall.

The woman froze when she caught sight of the police tape wrapping the Dumpster and stood there for several minutes. Janet was just deciding whether to get back to work when the woman finally put her bag down and sank out of sight.

Janet hopped onto the bench seat of the nearest booth and looked down through the window. The woman squatted on the pavement, staring at the Dumpster as she rummaged through her trash bag.

"What the . . ." The woman took out a dozen tea candles, a wooden cross, and wireless speakers. A lighter followed, and within minutes, a mini memorial covered two parking spaces. It wasn't until Janet pushed open the side door that she heard the Christian music blaring from the speakers next to the woman.

"What in the heck is goin' on out there?" Cindy Lou asked from behind her. Janet turned around to see her tying an apron around her waist. The short apron's pockets were only deep enough for a credit card, yet it was still longer than her bartender's skirt. Janet raised her eyes to the ceiling and tried to focus.

Frank came in the front door and joined them at the window.

"Need me to take care of it, Janet? She's on private property, she can't just set up shop here."

"No—thanks, Frank. I'll go talk to her." Janet squared her shoulders and pushed the door open. Her finger gave a sudden throb, and she turned back to Cindy Lou. "Why don't you start prepping the fruit while I deal with this?"

On the pavement outside, the woman now sat cross-legged by the curb, her face and hands raised to the sky as she swayed to the music. Janet cleared her throat loudly and the woman lowered her gaze; the sadness in her blue eyes was so profound that for a moment, Janet couldn't speak. Already, beads of sweat pooled at the woman's hairline; her face was pale and her hands trembled. She looked like she was in her early twenties.

"Peace and greetings," she said in a misty voice. "My name is Larsa Freeman."

Janet's eyes opened wide at the last name. "Are you related to Ike?"

"He was my father." Larsa closed her eyes. "I'm embarking on a spiritual journey of justice and have vowed to sit here in prayer and meditation until my father's killer is caught."

Janet spun around and marched back into the bar, slamming the door behind her. She stalked past Cindy Lou and headed for the swear jar, taking a bill out of her wallet as she walked.

"A twenty? What in the world is that for?" Cindy Lou asked.

Janet shoved the bill into the jar. "Fuck."

CHAPTER EIGHT

Janet knew two things with certainty: Larsa Freeman should have been at home or with family, and Larsa Freeman wasn't going anywhere. She rubbed a hand across her face, trying to find the inner strength to keep from cursing again, when a commotion to her left caught her attention.

"Gosh dang it, Frank! Janet said to stop calling the police every five minutes!" Cindy Lou yelled.

Frank, his voice patronizingly calm, said, "I'm doing my job. That woman is on private property, and if Janet doesn't have the balls to get rid of her, I'll do it."

While her employees fought, Janet snuck another look out the window at Ike's daughter. In the withering heat, her arms were raised again, her lips moved, maybe in prayer. She sat just feet away from where Janet had found Ike. Didn't the woman have anywhere else to go to mourn? Any other family? What if she didn't? The thought pulled Janet up short.

When the argument behind her escalated, she finally turned. "Guys!" She opened her mouth to continue but both of her employees rushed to have the last word.

"Janet," Cindy Lou said, "I told him—"

"It's not your bar, Cindy Lou—" Frank interrupted.

"Enough!" Janet yelled over the pair. "I've had enough. Frank, I told you yesterday to stop calling the damn cops every time someone looks at you crossways. I do not want police here unless someone's dead, and that's final." All three cringed at her word choice, but she plowed ahead. "You need to start listening to Cindy Lou, because, from now on, she's the . . . the assistant manager of this bar. Her word is *the* word if I'm not here."

Cindy Lou's mouth dropped open and Janet noted with satisfaction that Frank's did, as well. But before he could give voice to his sour expression, red and blue lights from a police cruiser flashed across their faces.

"Damn it, Frank!" She certainly wasn't going to let the cops haul away a woman who'd just lost her father!

Stalking past her bouncer to the side door, Janet called out, "Larsa! Larsa, I have a table all set up for you in here, hon. I don't want you getting heatstroke while you wait for justice." She waved to the cop, who was just getting out of his squad car. "I think there's been a misunderstanding. False alarm—no problem here!" She ushered a surprised Larsa in and shut the door without a backward glance.

"Frank, tell the police officer you were mistaken and then get table twenty-one ready for Ms. Freeman while I fix her a drink."

Before Frank could react, Cindy Lou said, "Frank, honey, after her table's ready, I'll need your help changin' out a keg. Thank you." She tried to hide her grin but failed.

Frank huffed out something rude that Janet couldn't quite hear before he stalked past her to wipe down the table and set out some coasters.

"What do you want? Bloody Mary's on special tonight." Janet steered Larsa through the bar.

"Oh, I don't drink," Larsa said in that same dreamy voice. "Alcohol's the devil's work, clear as day. I've been sober for eight and a half years and counting."

"Devil's work. Ah, right," Janet said, fixing Frank with a death stare when she caught him smirking. "Can I . . . can I get you anything? Water? Tea?"

"Well, I guess I'd love a glass of sweet tea."

"Cindy Lou, one sweet tea for Ms. Freeman. First one's on the house."

She left the whole lot of them behind and walked into the office, flung herself into a chair, and threw an arm over her eyes. A teetotaling, antialcohol prayer warrior was going to be taking up prime real estate inside the bar—or causing a scene outside of it—until Ike's killer was caught. As much as she hated to admit it, she was stuck. She would either have to help Detective O'Dell with this case or slowly lose customers until she was out of business. People didn't go to a bar to be reminded of murder, death, and sadness, but to escape all of that. She had to hope the police would find the killer—and soon.

———

By eight o'clock that night, the Spot was standing room only. Customers were four deep around the bar and people hovered aggressively by the tables, ready to jump in as soon as a seat opened up. They were officially over capacity for the first time ever, and Frank had a crowd waiting outside the door.

"Two out, one in," he called to Janet as she passed by with a tray full of beer.

She nodded but didn't slow down, and a moment later, she set the drinks down with a flourish. "Anything else, guys?" They were new customers—their first time there, Janet guessed. They'd asked for some kind of fancy microbrew she'd never even heard of and had then gleefully asked for the menu after she told them their five choices.

"Menu?" she'd said. "There isn't a menu. We have five beers on tap; I don't need to write them down, for God's sake!"

They'd chortled at that and then ordered five light beers.

Now they were drinking them with a kind of curiosity she reserved for the zoo.

"How is it?" she asked, already wishing she hadn't.

"It . . . it just doesn't really taste like anything, does it?" said a man with a pencil-thin beard that rimmed his jawline. "It's not hoppy, it's not malty. What is it?"

"It's light," Janet snapped. On her way back to the bar, she stopped by Larsa's table. The soft flickering glow of her tea candles made the woman look fuzzy. "Can I get you anything?"

"Maybe some more hot water with lemon?"

Janet bustled back up to the bar and grabbed a mug from the shelf.

"Is she drinkin' more free hot water?" Cindy Lou asked grumpily as she pulled two pints of beer at once.

Janet didn't have time to answer—the bar was busier than she'd ever seen it, and they were down a bartender, since Elizabeth hadn't shown for her shift again.

The stack of dirty glasses took up half the lower counter space, and Janet's eye twitched when a nearby customer missed his table and a full glass of beer splashed onto the ground.

"Need some help?"

Janet turned to find Mel, her new tenant, standing opposite. "What can I get you?"

"I'm serious—I used to be a bartender. I can bar-back for you or deliver drinks. It looks like you could use more hands."

"Oh . . . well I, uh . . ."

The cacophony of requests being shouted at her made her agree before she could really consider the offer; soon, Mel was behind the bar, cleaning glasses and pulling pints next to Cindy Lou.

It took three more hours for the crowd to finally thin.

"What's the matter, boss? You look grumpier than a one-handed acrobat!" Cindy Lou grinned. "You'll be able to pay all your bills for the month from this one night!"

Janet frowned. She didn't want to complain, but she didn't

like all the chaos. She'd had to stop those hipster fools from drinking and dashing; the ringleader of the group had nearly come to blows with Frank in the parking lot until she'd stepped in and Pencil Beard's girlfriend finally pulled out a fifty-dollar bill. They'd drained two different kegs before the rowdiest of the crowd had left, and the ice machine couldn't keep up with demand, forcing Janet to institute a three-cube cap around ten o'clock. "We just weren't ready for it, that's all. We need to grow slowly enough that we can handle it. I don't want people trying us out and never coming back because they got bad service," she finally answered.

Cindy Lou turned to look at Janet for a long moment and finally asked, "You all right, sweetheart?"

"Stress," Mel said. "Her eye's twitching from stress." Janet slapped a hand over her eye and Mel said, "I'm taking off. I told Kat I was heading out for one beer," she added with a smile.

"How are you both settling in?"

"Good. We weren't sure it was going to work out, moving in and all, and I wanted to thank you for that, and talk to you about—"

"Frank!" Janet shouted over Mel when she saw her bouncer sipping from a can of beer. "You're not allowed to drink until your shift is over!"

He grumbled but put the beer down on the table next to him. Distracted, she said, "Thanks, Mel. We'll work out what to pay you tomorrow."

Mel didn't move for a moment, but she finally nodded and walked away.

"You haven't heard from our sweet Elizabeth yet?" Cindy Lou asked when Janet took her post behind the bar.

"Nope. You?" Janet frowned when Cindy Lou shook her head. "I understand taking a sick day, but at least have the courtesy to call in with an excuse!"

"Ain't you worried, boss?"

Worried she's got my money, Janet thought darkly, finally dropping her hand from her no-longer-pulsing eye. "No," she said aloud, "I'm not worried. I think she's just taking some time off."

"It ain't really like her, though, is it?" Cindy Lou asked as she topped off the bowls of trail mix from a bag under the counter. "And the timin'? I mean, she's one of the last people to have seen Ike alive. Now he's dead and she's missin'?"

"She's not missing!" Janet said. "She's an inconsiderate employee who couldn't be bothered to tell anyone she was taking some days off." She slammed the cooler lid up and rearranged the bottles inside for something to do. "And it's not the first time, either. Remember a couple of years ago?"

Cindy Lou chewed on her lip but didn't say anything.

"It was the same thing! She took a week off with no word to anyone, then came right back in like nothing happened. No explanation or anything!"

Cindy Lou's worried expression didn't waver, and after a moment, she turned away from Janet, in either resignation or disappointment.

Janet stared moodily at the tap and then shifted her focus to Larsa. "What are we going to do about that?" she asked Cindy Lou.

The other woman shrugged. "Beats me why you even invited her in here."

Janet frowned at the grieving daughter, but when Larsa looked up and they locked eyes, she forced a neutral expression back onto her face. She scooped some trail mix into a clean plastic bowl and headed toward her guest, determined to have a tough conversation about Larsa's future at the Spot.

"Need a snack?" she asked, sitting down across from Ike's daughter.

Larsa blew out a breath before plunging her hand into the bowl and plucking out two cashews. "I know I can't stay here—your bouncer has made that perfectly clear."

Janet's left eye pulsed in warning. "Did he say something to you?" His arrogance was starting to do more than just annoy her.

Her face heated up. This was her bar—she could invite whomever she wanted, and Frank had no business interfering.

"Let's just say I know not to come back."

Janet's temper flared, and before she could stop herself, she was saying the exact opposite of what she'd planned to when she walked over. "Larsa, you are my guest. You will be here as long as you want, and I'll make sure Frank knows that, along with the rest of the staff." Her glare landed on Frank, who was sipping surreptitiously from his beer can again.

"Well, that's so . . . that's just so . . ." As Larsa teared up at the offer, Janet inched away, preparing to stand. "Wait." Larsa hiccupped and took a gulp of water from the mug. "Wait, I'm sorry. It's just, you're being so nice. It means a lot, you know?" Janet stuck one leg out from under the table and shifted her weight, but Larsa laid a hand on her arm. "I know my father was in here a lot. I hope he wasn't too much trouble?"

"Oh, well . . . I mean, he was one of our regulars, that's for sure." Janet tried to stay vague, she didn't want to be the one to tell Larsa they'd had to send Ike home—and suffer his anger and yelling when they did—almost as often as not.

"He wasn't always so hateful, you know. He used to be . . . well, better, I guess."

"Weren't we all?" Larsa's lower lip quivered as she attempted a smile. Janet settled into her seat; she knew a thing or two about dads who didn't live up to expectations. "What went wrong?" she asked, realizing not only that Larsa needed to talk this one out, but also that she might not have had anyone else to turn to.

"Listen, I'm not saying he ever would've won Dad of the Year or anything. He always drank too much, and he was never around as much as he should've been, but he was never the same after the accident."

"What accident?" Janet settled back into the seat and focused on the other woman.

"I guess it was just about ten years ago. He was driving home, probably drunk, and hit someone."

"God, how terrible. What happened?"

"The first cop on the scene drove Dad home. They didn't come talk to him about the, uh, the accident until that night. By then, he'd slept off whatever alcohol was in his system."

"Wow," Janet said. "What happened to the other driver?"

Larsa blanched. "It wasn't—it wasn't another car. It was a guy on a bike." Janet gasped and Larsa said, "He was killed. My dad hit and killed a college kid who was riding his bike to class."

Janet's mouth twisted in shock, but when she saw Larsa's face fall, she racked her brain, trying to find something redeemable about the situation. "Well, I mean . . . maybe the kid wasn't riding with a headlight. Cyclists can be hard to see, sometimes. Maybe it wasn't your dad's fault."

"It was nine thirty in the morning." Larsa's wide blue eyes brimmed with unshed tears. "The boy was heading to an early-morning biology class and my dad was already drunk—or still drunk from the night before. At any rate, he shouldn't have been driving, and he shouldn't have gotten off without charges."

That information startled Janet into silence. Finally, she said, "He didn't get charged at all? He hit and killed a person and didn't face any charges?"

"Not as far as the law went, no, but believe me, there were consequences. He was never the same. He drank more and talked less. He and my mom had a huge fight one night and he walked out. I hadn't really talked to him since."

"When was that?"

"Ten years ago."

"You didn't talk to your dad for ten years—and now he's dead? You must feel . . ." Janet let the sentence trail off, unable to put her thoughts into words.

"Unsettled, like there's no closure. It's just . . ."

"Awful," they said together.

"Thanks for letting me sit here. I don't know why, but it

makes me feel better to think I'm doing something that might help." She dropped her gaze to the mug of hot water between her hands and fell quiet.

Janet didn't ask the other woman exactly how sitting in her bar was going to help. Instead she stood, taking two empty water glasses with her.

On her way back to the bar, she nearly ran headlong into Detective Finch. The frown she had been trying to hold off finally came through. Finch waved off Frank's handshake attempt, nodded briskly at Janet, and then walked toward the bar without a word.

Janet smacked the beer out of Frank's hand as she passed and felt a satisfied grin cross her face when he curled his lips and crossed his arms but remained silent. She dumped the trash into the can behind the bar, set the glasses into the sink, and stifled another smile when she overheard Nell, clearly answering one of Finch's questions.

"I don't know, Officer, I guess I'd say Ike was an insufferable fool who had no friends, no manners, and no idea of how to be a good human—but I'm sure somebody out there is sorry he's dead."

Nell's glasses took up half of her face. The large black frames would have made anyone else resemble a fly, but with her silvery-white hair pulled back into a low bun and dark red lipstick, Nell oozed sophistication, even as she sat on the bar stool drinking well vodka on the rocks.

Janet tried to listen in as she dipped two dirty glasses into the spinning brushes on the left side of the sink and then dunked them into the basin of cold, mostly clean water on the right.

Finch, his voice low, said, "We're trying to find out where Ike's car might be. Do you remember seeing it Wednesday night?"

Janet froze. Of course! Where was Ike's car? In the chaos of finding his body, it hadn't occurred to her that it was missing. Just as she wondered whether the police were thinking it might have been a carjacking or theft gone wrong that left Ike dead, Nell answered.

"No, but I do remember Elizabeth taking his keys. He was fit to be tied when she snatched them off the bar."

"Elizabeth, the other bartender? She had Ike's car keys?" He whipped out his notebook and scribbled down a few words.

"Mmm-hmm." Nell swirled the ice cubes in her glass with a straw. "If I recall, Ike told her to eff off, but he actually said the word, if you know what I mean."

Finch nodded seriously. "Was he often angry like that?"

The brushes on the automatic glass washer spun, cleaning lipstick and sediment from the two new glasses in Janet's hand while she focused on the conversation.

"Every time he got kicked out, he swore it would be his last time here." Nell worried at a bracelet. "He always came back, though—had nowhere else to go, I'd guess."

"His behavior must have made people angry. How did Elizabeth react?"

"She was calm. I mean, it wasn't the first time." Nell took a sip of her drink and winced. Cheap vodka never went down smoothly, but Nell wouldn't spring for top shelf. Instead, she squeezed the wedge of lime that had balanced on the rim of her glass and motioned to Cindy Lou for another.

Finch was quiet until Cindy Lou moved down the bar again. The drying rack was full, but there were still a dozen dirty glasses, so Janet kept at it, glad for the mindless task while Finch was asking questions.

"Was everyone always so calm? What about Janet?" the detective asked Nell.

"Well, Janet doesn't suffer fools. If Ike yelled at her, she yelled back. That's just how she is, though—she doesn't mean anything by it. She'd probably give you the shirt off her back if you needed it," Nell added.

"Did her boyfriend let that pass?"

"Did Jason let *what* pass? He's not going to pick a fight with every jerk here, I mean, that'd be a full-time job." Nell's glass clunked against the bar as she set it down. "Is that all? You're cramping my style tonight. I've got my eye set on that tall drink of water at the corner table—he's new. I think I've got a shot. What do you think?"

Finch's eyebrows arched comically, and his mouth opened but no words came out.

"What, you don't think an old woman's got game? You'd be surprised." She straightened her massive glasses. "You just gotta be direct and tell the man what you're interested in. They almost always bite."

"Oh . . . uh . . ." Finch stumbled back a step in his hurry to get away. "Well, thanks for your, uh . . . candor, Nell."

He hastily walked to the back corner of the bar and looked down at his notebook—maybe gathering his thoughts after the visual Nell had put there.

Janet moved down the bar with a grin. "You had to go there, Nell?"

The older woman set her glass down primly. "What do you mean? If someone's going to ask me so many questions, I'd like them to remember me at the end of the day. Oh, and by the way, you might want to tell your new guest over there to pipe down. She was just regaling some new customers about her sobriety. 'One thousand eight hundred twenty-seven days sober and counting' just seems like a lot of information for a casual customer, you know?"

Janet blew out a sigh at Larsa's tendency to over-share, patted Nell's hand, and moved down the bar until she faced the side door. The condiment container was running low on cherries and limes, so she set to work refilling it from the bin of prepped fruit in the cooler.

As she worked, she pondered the new information from Detective Finch. Ike's car was missing and Elizabeth had taken Ike's keys before he left the building. Now he was dead, his keys and car were missing, and no one had heard from Elizabeth since.

She tried to swallow but her mouth was completely dry.

Where was Elizabeth? Had she killed Ike and left with his car? If she was having money trouble—and Janet suspected something was going on with her if she was stealing from the till —was it too much of a leap to think she might have been desperate enough to kill?

"Would that be okay, Janet?" Nell stood across the bar, her eyebrows raised.

"Oh, sorry, I didn't hear you. What?"

"I was just saying I wonder if you could pour me a sweet tea. The vodka's tearin' me up tonight, for some reason."

"Sure, Nell. No problem."

Before she could deliver the drink, however, Finch approached with more questions.

"Did your boyfriend have any luck with that surveillance video?"

Janet slid the tea to Nell. "No. That's why he's not here helping out tonight: he's been working around the clock, trying to get his whole system back up."

"I'll bet," Finch said, his expression conveying the opposite sentiment.

"What's that supposed to mean?"

"It means it's pretty convenient for your employees that the video's not there. Elizabeth was the last person who talked to Ike and the last person to have his keys, and the one thing that would help solve all the mysteries is mysteriously down. It doesn't look good. Do you see what I'm saying?"

Janet bristled at the insinuation. "All I see is a crime that's not solving itself. I hope you'll put the time in to get justice for Larsa, if not for Ike, instead of expecting someone else to do your job."

Finch leaned across the bar and sneered, his glare burning through her. "Doing my job depends on asking people like you to give a shit about someone besides themselves. Forgive me if I seem hopeless. And tell your boyfriend I've got a subpoena coming soon. Just waiting on the judge to sign off. Tell him we'll have to cast a wide net if he can't get us what we need." He pivoted and stalked out of the bar, pushing past Frank as he left.

Jason would not be happy about cops rifling through his things. He dealt with many high- and low-profile clients, and none of them would like the thought of law enforcement snooping around his computer and files.

Why was Finch hell-bent on blaming someone at her bar? Her eye gave a final, mind-bending pulse, then settled down. She had to find Elizabeth before the police did. If she could only find her bartender, she could solve more than one mystery.

CHAPTER NINE

When Janet got home at close to four in the morning, she found Jason passed out over his desk in the basement. He frowned in his sleep, and the low blue light from his computer monitors cast shadows over his face. She kissed him gently on his shoulder, scribbled Finch's warning onto a sticky note, and slapped it on the largest monitor, then crept back upstairs. She settled on the couch with a blanket, then sloshed some wine into a glass and felt some of the tension leach out of her shoulders for the first time in hours with that first sip. It didn't last long.

After her phone, which had died earlier that night, charged enough to turn on, an alert sounded with a message from Detective O'Dell.

"The coroner's report came in. I thought you might be interested to know Ike was killed with a knife—the same one your boyfriend and Larsa identified as Ike's."

Janet paused the message and pressed the phone against her temple. It sounded terrible when O'Dell said it like that, but they all knew that Ike carried a Swiss Army knife. He would sometimes use the bottle-opening feature at the bar when he felt service was too slow. She frowned and then started the message back up.

"It was a single stab wound to his gut," O'Dell continued, "and the coroner says it would have been a slow, brutal death—it might've taken him twenty minutes to bleed out. She's ruled his death a homicide. Someone was angry, that's for sure. My investigators are going to want to talk with your staff again—especially this Elizabeth person—and your boyfriend. I'm counting on you to keep your ears open, Janet."

She stared at her phone after the message ended. Someone was angry at Ike, but who?

The longer she sat there, the more she thought about Ike's history and how what he'd done in his past seemed a more likely reason for anger than simply his being an obnoxious customer at the bar.

Could Ike's murder have anything to do with the cyclist he'd hit and killed a decade ago? Had someone's anger flared after ten years passed without a single repercussion for the uninvestigated and uncharged crime?

She was sure police knew about the event, but—and this made Janet grimace—what if they didn't? She groaned into the empty room and then pulled the blanket over her head and screwed her eyes shut. She didn't want to get involved, but it was becoming hard not to. With the dead man's daughter now invited to practically live at the bar and police calling with daily updates, as much as she hated it, she was going to have to do something.

Where was Elizabeth? She'd been with the bar for the whole year Janet had owned it, as well as the year before that, when Janet had only been an employee herself. Elizabeth wasn't the most reliable person, but the behavior was still concerning.

Janet decided with another groan that she would call O'Dell in the morning—right after driving to Elizabeth's house.

———

Crrrrrunch. Janet swore at the sound, then backed her car away from the parking block that had just scraped the underside of her car. The front end of the vehicle made an identically awful sound as it scraped back over the block in reverse, and she swore again.

The sun shone down relentlessly as Janet got out of her car. The black asphalt oozed sluggishly under her feet, the tar that covered its cracks mushy already from the morning heat. The slam of her car door was the only sound in the apartment complex, and Janet stood assessing the space for a moment.

Chunks of gray stucco had fallen off parts of the building, but someone had attempted to paint over the holes, even coming close to matching the original color of the outside walls. The freshly mulched flower beds were void of any plants except for some knee-high weeds in one shady patch by the rental office. It wasn't one of the nicest parts of town, but it wasn't bad.

Janet looked down at the paper in her hand to check Elizabeth's address again and then made her way toward number 215.

At the door, she saw some business cards tucked into the frame; they were from both O'Dell and Finch—and that meant the door hadn't been opened since Ike's body was found. Janet frowned, not liking the deserted vibe that emanated from the space.

She knocked, but no one answered. After a quick glance around the property, Janet unzipped a small leather case, then assessed the lock in front of her. As she was deciding which pick to use, the door next to Elizabeth's opened.

"This girl's had more visitors in the last two days than the last two years combined," said an old man with graying brown hair and a frown. "Who are you?"

"Who're you?" Janet shot back, casually tucking her lock-picking set under one of her arms when she crossed them.

"I'm the grumpy old man who don't like all the noise from a half-dozen visitors!" He wore a red plaid robe tied at the waist, light blue pajama pants, and house slippers. Steam curled up from the mug of coffee he held in front of his chest.

"All the noise of six visitors over the last two years?" Janet challenged. "I'd say you're lucky. That's—what? One person knocking every four months?"

"What's that?" He cupped a hand around his ear and leaned toward Janet. She repeated her sarcastic remark a little louder. "No need to shout." He scrunched up his face in distaste. "It's the last two days I'm fed up with. What's everyone want with Elizabeth? Is she in trouble? The other two wouldn't tell me anything—just kept asking questions, and I don't have nothing to say about nobody, you know? I keep to myself and mind my business."

Despite what he said, it seemed like he was dying for a chat. "So, what'd you tell the cops?" she asked, sliding the leather case into her shoulder bag.

"What?" Again, she raised her volume, only to be shushed dramatically before he answered. "Nothing. Just like I said, I got nothing to say about the girl next door." He savored a sip of coffee, then added, "She's a pretty good neighbor, even though she's up until all hours of the night doing God-knows-what with God-knows-who. I bet her mama's rolling over in her grave knowing she dropped out of college to work in a dive bar, but she probably does her best to do her best, you know what I mean?"

Before Janet could unpack everything the gossipy neighbor had just shared, he started up again.

"It's nothing to me if a woman wants to make a living and support herself, but she was planning on going to medical school —or was it dental?—but then she didn't. And I don't see why her plans had to change just because her plans changed, okay?" A small, yappy brown dog barreled around his legs. "Hey, dog, get back in here." He scooped up the small pet and deposited it in the coat closet. The yapping continued, but it was muted behind the door.

Janet cocked her head to the side; she wouldn't have pegged

this guy as a dog person. She shook herself. "So, you've lived next to Elizabeth for a long time, huh?"

"Long?" He scratched his head, still frowning. "Long enough to know her mom wouldn't be happy with her choices."

Parent guilt via neighbor. Nice. "You said her mom is dead? When did that happen?"

"What was that?" She put forth a Herculean effort not to roll her eyes and repeated her question. He winced at her new volume and said, "A couple of years ago. Ah! Vet, that's it! She was going to become a vet, not a dentist! I knew it was something like that." He shook his head sagely and took another sip from his mug. "She dropped out of school and since then, nothing. Just a big lump of nothing."

Janet assessed the nosy neighbor, who seemed determined to judge Elizabeth. "Did Elizabeth drop out of college right after her mother died?"

His brow furrowed and, after a moment, he nodded. "I guess that's right."

"Does she have any family left?"

"Don't know."

"I don't suppose the two events were related, do you?" He lowered his mug slowly, his face taking on the confused look of someone who'd just lost their train of thought. "Like, maybe she didn't have the money to continue her education, or maybe she just lost her spirit or passion or will to learn after her mom died. I don't suppose you checked in on her, made her a cup of coffee, or offered to help in any way?"

The man pulled the belt of his robe tighter around him, but he still didn't speak.

Janet's nostrils flared and she was breathing hard. "Yes, she's an adult, but she's young! I'd say Elizabeth is doing her best to get by after life pulled the rug out from under her by taking her mother before she was ready to be on her own. The girl probably needs more help and less judgment from both her friends and neighbors. Did you ever think about that?" To her surprise, she found that she'd moved closer to the stranger and was touching his chest with her finger. She blew out a breath and took a step back, dropping her hand to her side.

He finally cleared his throat and took another sip of his coffee. "Sounds like you're speaking from experience."

Janet felt blood rush to her cheeks. "You're always too young to lose your mother, no matter your age," she finally said.

"Paul Massie," he said, sticking out his hand. "You want some coffee?"

Janet blinked and then shook his hand. "Janet Black. Elizabeth works for me, at my bar." He held the door open, but she shook her head. "No, thanks. I was just . . ." She looked at Elizabeth's door. "I just came here to check on Elizabeth. So, you haven't seen her?"

"Not lately. She's a good kid. She'll get it together—especially if she's got you on her side." Paul nodded, dismissing her, but continued to lean up against his door frame, watching her, until she turned to leave. She looked back to see if Paul had closed his door, thinking she could try to pick Elizabeth's lock after he was back inside, but he stared at her until she climbed into her car, only closing his door with a final nod after she'd cranked the engine.

Janet wrinkled her nose. Was she on Elizabeth's side? Just days ago, she'd been ready to fire her, certain the bartender was stealing from the Spot. Now the petty theft seemed like no big deal—at least, compared with murder. She didn't like the emotions that were blooming inside her.

Elizabeth was all alone in this world, except for a nosy neighbor and apparently the people she worked with at the bar. Was Janet so heartless and cruel that she couldn't be bothered to care enough to help find her?

With a groan she headed home, knowing what she had to do, but already irritated with her plan.

CHAPTER TEN

She poured herself a cup of coffee and stared at the phone. She needed to make the call. She was going to . . . gulp . . . get *involved* and be *helpful*.

Ugh. She shuddered and dropped down onto the couch, then dialed the numbers; when O'Dell answered, she filled him in on what Larsa had told her the day before.

"A cyclist, huh?" he said.

"I'm sure you know about it already, but Larsa mentioned it, so I just thought . . . I wanted to make sure . . ." She frowned into her coffee. She had to step up for Elizabeth's sake. "It just seems a better motive for murder than anything else I've heard."

"I'm actually just heading out to talk to the victim's family, to let them know what happened," O'Dell said. After a pause, he added, "Why don't you come along?"

"What?" Janet spluttered. Coffee slopped out of her mug onto the table as she hastily set it down. "Why would I do that?"

"I got to talking to your dad yesterday—"

"He was certainly a busy beaver . . ."

"—and he said you have a knack for reading people. He said you're uncommonly good at it, in fact. I just thought, since you're being so helpful, you'd want to ride along."

"Oh, I've got so much to—"

"I'm meeting the family at one thirty. I'll pick you up on the way." He hung up before she could come up with an excuse that would get her out of it.

She was still staring at her phone in disbelief when it rang in her hand. This time, it was the bank.

"Miss Black, we wanted to let you know the checks you deposited yesterday came back insufficient funds."

"What?"

"We wanted to let you know the—"

"I heard you, I just . . . are you sure?" The checks were for her new tenants' first month's rent and security deposit.

"Yes. I wanted to make sure you noted it in your register, so your balance was correct."

Janet disconnected and pressed her hands into her temples. Insufficient funds? She walked to the minibar across the room. Her hand moved past the vodka to the bottle of Kahlúa. She eyed her coffee; maybe just a splash. She sloshed some in and then stalked back across the room to the front door, where she looked out the window at the unit next door and took a long, slow sip of her fortified morning drink.

She thought they'd done a good job of vetting the new renters—she and Jason had even had them fill out a credit report form, and Mel and Kat had both checked out. The money should have been deposited before they moved in, but it wasn't, and now they were stuck with a couple of freeloaders.

There was no movement from the other apartment, but as she stared crossly at the front door, she realized Mel might have been trying to tell her something about their finances the night before at the bar. She felt a light touch on her shoulder and turned to find Jason holding out a plate of scrambled eggs.

"I thought you'd need lunch but would want breakfast," he said with a smile.

"Our renters are broke," she said. She took the plate with a grateful smile and told him what the banker had just told her.

She sat down on the couch and shoved a forkful of eggs into her mouth.

Jason stared out the front window, rubbing his chin. "I don't know, Janet. I get a good vibe from them."

"Is it a broke vibe?" She stabbed a piece of bacon with her fork. It cracked into three pieces, none of them on the tines.

"No, a good vibe. Let's talk to Mel about it and see what she's got to say. We'll take it from there."

"We aren't running a charity, Jason. It's a business! The goal isn't to find people who need a handout." Her feelings of responsibility for Elizabeth had sucked the generosity for anyone else in her life right out of her. She frowned at her boyfriend; he smiled back.

"I know, but let's hear what they have to say. Maybe it's just a misunderstanding." Jason sat opposite her and leaned forward, his elbows resting on his knees.

"You know what the problem is? You're too nice," she said. He snuck a piece of bacon out from under her hovering fork. "Hey!"

"Not *too* nice. *Just right* nice," he clarified. "So nice, in fact, I'm going to help you in the shower today."

"Is that right?" she asked, a grin slowly turning up the corners of her lips.

"Mmm-hmm." He took the plate out of her hands and set it on the table between them.

Her stomach flooded with heat. "I don't have much time," she said, looking at the clock over his head.

"Trust me. You have time for this." He pulled her up and led her to the bedroom.

She stayed in the shower after Jason left, and so did the lovey-dovey smile on her face. Over the last year, she had gotten used to feeling like she was in control of her life for the first time in a long time. She had a steady relationship with a great man and a solid job at the bar she owned. Even though she could feel chaos creeping back into her well-ordered world with Ike's murder and her apparently broke tenants, she needed to remember the good things she had, and protect them.

By the time she toweled off and got dressed, Detective O'Dell was knocking at the front door.

"Are you ready?" he asked when she opened the door. She looked behind her, but the house was empty. Jason must have gone down to his office in the basement.

"Nope," she answered while running a comb through the tangles in her hair.

He laughed as if she'd made a joke and then turned and headed toward his car.

"No cruiser?" She tossed the comb on the hall table and pulled the door closed behind her.

"No, no, my cruiser days are long gone. I drive this baby." He patted the top of his unmarked Ford Crown Victoria with affection and laughed at Janet's horrified face. "It's not so bad once you're in it."

The Crown Vic wasn't brown or tan, but a murky color in between. As Janet pulled open the passenger door, she saw the black leather seats, which would be hotter than an iron against skin in this weather. Luckily, she wore jeans, but she still let out a low groan when she sat as the heat seeped through the denim.

"We get most of our cars at auction. Nobody else would take this beauty, so it's been mine for the last two years."

"Lucky you."

They drove in silence until Janet's curiosity got the best of her. "How's the investigation going?"

"Still lots of questions and not many answers."

"Have you spoken to Elizabeth?"

"Nope—no answer on her cell or at her apartment door. You heard from her?"

"No. Nothing." She tapped her fingers lightly against her

thigh. O'Dell's curious stare was more pronounced this time, and she felt her cheeks heat up under his scrutiny. "These people we're going to see," she said, "do they know why we're coming?"

"Not exactly." He turned his attention back to the road. "But I hear that Margaret and Dan Daniels are sharp people; I'm sure they suspect my visit has something to do with their son."

Janet nodded slowly but kept her eyes trained on the scenery outside. For all her bravado, she wasn't looking forward to getting close to this family's emotional turmoil.

As they pulled up to an average-looking brick colonial in a neighborhood full of average-looking brick colonials, O'Dell turned toward her. "You're just here to watch and listen. You're not a detective, you know?"

"You invited me!" She crossed her arms.

"I know, but leave all the talking to me, okay?"

Janet nodded again and followed him up the front walk. Lush greenery surrounded them on all sides, including a stunning flowering plant bigger than she was. Even the buzzing of the bees seemed louder here. The sound of Detective O'Dell's fist against the door was practically absorbed by the house.

After just a moment, a woman answered. "I'm Margaret. You must be the gentleman from the Knoxville Police Department?"

As O'Dell introduced himself, Janet assessed the woman. She didn't know what she'd been expecting—perhaps some sort of grief-ridden, devastated mother. Instead, a sprightly, energetic, strong, and muscular woman stood before her. Yes, her hair was gray, but she was taller than Janet and far from stooped over; she had the lithe, long, taut arms of someone who practiced yoga for three hours a day. When O'Dell introduced Janet as his associate, Margaret kindly invited them inside.

"Dan!" she called as she motioned for Janet and O'Dell to follow her down the hall. They found a man sitting in a blue wingback chair in the living room. He couldn't have missed them when they'd walked up to his home—his chair faced a huge picture window that looked out over the street—but he looked up, surprised.

His eyes were sad and weary as he stood to welcome them. He shook hands with O'Dell first, then Janet, and when he reached out for her hand, she saw scratch marks on his arm.

"Rosebushes won," he said, then shrugged his cuff down and circled around to his wife's side.

Where she was strong and tall, he was beaten and stooped. Life had chewed him up and spit him out, and it was clear that Ollie's father was only barely hanging on. He had a pasty complexion, and his hair, which according to a family photo on the wall used to be jet-black, was now a shocking silvery white, as if grief had leached all the color from his person.

O'Dell cleared his throat and Janet jumped. "What?"

"I was just telling Margaret and Dan that you and I are both newer to Knoxville. They've lived here their whole lives."

"Yes, that's right. I've been here about two years." When everyone continued to stare at her expectantly, she added, "It's hot."

O'Dell gave her a funny look before clearing his throat again. "Thanks for seeing us on such short notice. I wanted to let you know, in case you hadn't heard yet, that Ike Freeman is dead."

Margaret sucked in a sharp breath and instinctively flung an arm around her husband just in time to guide him back to his chair. He collapsed into it, his shoulders shaking as he sucked in great gusts of air. She looked up and motioned O'Dell and Janet and toward a door before murmuring something into her husband's ear and following them into the kitchen.

"I'm so sorry. We talked last night about how your visit might have something to do with our son's death." Her expression turned dark. "It's always a blow to hear that man's name in this house. My husband has never gotten over it, of course, nor have I."

O'Dell patted Margaret on the shoulder. "I wanted to be the

one to break the news to you, so it wouldn't hit you unexpectedly while you were out and about."

"I do appreciate it, Detective. What happened?"

O'Dell told her about the murder investigation while Margaret bustled around the kitchen making tea. He left out many details of the crime but let her know they hadn't yet arrested anybody.

Margaret nodded, not exactly in satisfaction, but as if she was accepting the inevitable. "I can't say I'm sorry he's dead. He changed our lives forever." She dropped a tea bag into a mug and set it on the counter, then took a pint of milk from the refrigerator. She finally turned to face Janet and O'Dell. "When Ollie was killed, it—it was just awful, you think it's the lowest moment in your life. But then when that man got off without a single charge . . . well, it was like losing Ollie all over again."

"What happened?" Janet asked.

The kettle whistled, and Margaret poured boiling water over the tea bag before answering. "Ollie and one of his roommates were riding to class that morning. This was before everyone started wearing helmets, but I'm not convinced a helmet would've helped," she added, her cheeks flushing red. "Plastic and foam are no match for tons of metal and pints of alcohol." She dunked the tea bag in and out of the water and stared blindly through the window above the sink. "Ollie was in front and had just enough time to yell out a warning to his roommate. Ike missed the other boy by inches—Ollie saved him.

"The rest isn't part of the official record, but it's what we've been able to piece together. A friend of Ike's in the police department was the first on the scene, and he sent Ike home without a Breathalyzer. Ike got an extra eight hours before he was called downtown for questioning. By then, he was sober and Ollie was dead."

She took the tea bag out of the mug, set it in the sink, and poured in some milk and sugar. "I'm going to bring this to Dan. Thanks for stopping by with the news, Detective. Good day."

When they were back in his car, O'Dell asked, "What do you think?"

"I think Ollie's family is still angry."

"With Ike?"

"Well, yes, but also with your department."

"Grief can do interesting things to people," O'Dell said.

"Do you believe them? That a cop kept Ike from getting in trouble that day?"

"I don't know," O'Dell said, starting up the engine. "It's hard to imagine it happening. I'd never help out a friend that way. Would you?"

Janet looked out the window, considering his words. Instead of answering she asked another question. "Have you seen the original police report from the accident?"

"No. But I'll check it out, see who was on the call." Janet nodded and he changed the subject. "Forensics found two sets of fingerprints on the knife that killed Ike: Ike's and someone else's, which are not in the system."

"Do you suspect one of Ollie's parents of killing Ike?" Janet asked, suddenly wondering why they'd really come. "Dan Daniels probably couldn't deliver a deathblow, but Margaret looks tough."

He shook his head. "It's just interesting to know that whoever else handled Ike's knife isn't a hardened criminal. Your boyfriend's never been arrested, either, has he?"

She pinched the bridge of her nose and released it before turning to face O'Dell. "What exactly are you trying to say?"

He eased the car to a stop in front of her house. "Just that it's oddly convenient that a secret, hidden camera that hardly anyone knew about was tampered with before a man was murdered outside your bar. Pretty lucky for the killer, huh?" Janet stared at him, stunned by how baldly and arrogantly he'd stated the accusation. "It's your duty to help us with any information you have about this crime, Janet. Don't forget."

The nerve of this cop. Had today's excursion all been a sham to get her reaction to his baseless claim against her boyfriend?

Her face felt tight. She climbed silently out of the car, then slammed the door with extra force. She was done being helpful —especially if the cops were going to start making wild accusations.

The sound of O'Dell's engine faded away as he drove down the street. She straightened her shoulders and walked slowly up the path to her house, still simmering.

She only had one job—no, make that two—and she was failing at both lately. She ran a bar and she was a landlord. The bar didn't open for hours, but she was going to landlord the shit out of her tenants before she went to the Spot.

CHAPTER ELEVEN

She stalked into the house, aware that she needed to calm down before she spoke to the renters. As much as she hated to admit it, Jason was right: she could easily fly off the handle if she wasn't careful. She headed right for the minibar in the main room and filled a glass with ice before drumming her fingers against the countertop and looking over her choices. She finally pulled a bottle of gin off the shelf, took the tonic from the small refrigerator under the counter, and lined up a lime and a knife on the cutting board. Her finger gave a throb, though, and she hurled the lime into the trash.

"Are you going to get that checked out?" Jason asked. "Oh, and darlin'? It's two thirty in the afternoon. Are you sure you're ready for that?" Janet tilted the glass to one side and assessed her finger. "Is this about the renters?" he asked, nodding at her drink. "Sometimes people just need a second chance, Janet."

She huffed a frustrated breath out her nose. Detectives were zeroing in on this kind man as a murder suspect. It was insane. She didn't want to tell him about the accusation, though, so she latched onto his assumption. "It's not a charity, Jason, it's a business. You're too soft."

"Soft?" he asked, taking several slow, deliberate steps toward her until they were standing toe to toe. "There's nothing soft about me."

Janet gulped as he clasped his hand over hers and slowly lowered the drink to the counter. When she let go, he gently set the highball glass on the table behind them.

Again? her eyes asked, and he smirked. Even though they'd been together for eighteen months, her heartbeat quickened at his expression: it was scalding hot.

With a flick of his wrist, he sent the remaining items on the counter flying into the sink; the sound of the cutting board and knife clattering into the stainless steel basin barely registered, though, as he slowly pressed his body closer to hers.

He walked her back until she was snug between him and the countertop, then he slowly lifted her onto the bar, their bodies rubbing together deliciously, before he settled between her legs. Jason nipped her earlobe as his hands worked to untuck her tank top, and he finally splayed his fingers across the skin of her stomach. The streaks of desire shot all the way down to her toes and fingers.

"I love this bar," he said, undoing the clasp of her bra and sliding one strap down her arm. "It's so convenient."

Convenient. That's just what Detective O'Dell had said about the killer. Janet huffed out a breath and reluctantly stopped Jason's hands from exploring. "We need to talk."

His eyes still smoldered, but he leaned back a fraction. Before she could explain, the doorbell chimed.

"Hold that thought, darlin'," he said as he walked to the door, "because I'm holding mine."

Janet took a shaky breath before sliding off the countertop and reclasping her bra. By the time Jason opened the door, she was leaning against the leather club chair, looking, she hoped, reasonably presentable.

It was Mel and Kat.

"Sorry to intrude," Mel said, looking uncomfortably between Jason and Janet. "We wanted to introduce you to Hazel."

She stepped aside, and Janet gasped as a baby became visible in Kat's arms.

"You have a baby?" she asked, flabbergasted. "Why didn't you tell us?"

"We just got her," Mel said with a slight smile. "Kat is on the foster list for the county, and Hazel was found yesterday. A caseworker came by last night, approved our new place, and another delivered the baby this morning."

"Found?" Jason asked, crossing his arms. "What does that mean?"

Mel frowned and Kat put a hand on her arm. "It's a sad story," she said. "Her mother was arrested. Apparently, she'd left Hazel home alone to run some errands—"

"Errands? She was out buying drugs!" Mel interjected angrily.

"—and got arrested," Kat finished, as if Mel hadn't interrupted. "She didn't want to get in even more trouble for leaving Hazel home alone, so she just didn't tell anyone she had a baby. It took the neighbors two days to call the police about the crying."

"God," Janet breathed, looking at the peacefully sleeping baby with a mix of horror and awe. "She's okay?"

"She is now. She was in the hospital overnight until doctors could regulate her temperature and get plenty of fluids in her little body," Kat crooned. "Now she'll be okay—we'll keep her safe."

"We wanted to let you know some friends are going to drop off a crib," Mel said. "They might block the driveway while they unload—we just didn't want you to think we were being inconsiderate."

"Speaking of inconsiderate . . ." Janet looked meaningfully at Jason, but he just grinned.

"Welcome home, little Hazel," he said before turning and walking into the kitchen.

"Mel, can I have a word?"

"Get Hazel back inside—I'm worried the sun is too bright

out here," Mel said before watching Kat walk to their half of the duplex. Only when the door closed did she turn back to Janet. "I know—you don't have to say anything. I'm working on it."

"Working on what?"

"On getting a job. I came into the bar yesterday to tell you the check might bounce, but I'm working on it. We knew Hazel was coming, and I intend to do right by her, but I just need a couple of weeks to make it work."

She held Mel's gaze for a moment before nodding once. "Two weeks. This isn't a free hotel."

"I know—and thank you."

Janet watched Mel walk into her house and then shivered when she felt hot breath on her neck.

"I knew you wouldn't do it. You talk a tough game, Black, but you're a big ol' softie on the inside." Jason was grinning when she turned toward him. She unsnapped his jeans and lowered the zipper. His smile widened.

"Shut up."

Neither spoke, then, as they picked up where they'd left off on the bar.

————

Hours later, Janet pulled up to the other bar in her life, the Spot. She groaned when she saw Larsa sitting on the parking block by the Dumpster, her candles already flickering and the tinny sound of spiritual music audible over Janet's engine.

She slammed her car into park and cursed under her breath. There it was again, that feeling that things were spiraling out of control. Her chest felt tight; the tension Jason had so kindly worked out of her body at home was coiling back around her. She rolled her shoulders, trying to recapture some of the glow she'd enjoyed just moments ago.

"I hope you're having a blessed day," Larsa said as Janet

climbed out of her car. Listening to her dreamy voice was like eating cotton candy, and it was starting to give her a toothache.

"It's been an interesting one, that's for sure," she said as she walked to the front door. Larsa turned off her speakers, so the only sound was the jingle of Janet's key ring hitting the metal frame as she unlocked the door. She crossed the threshold and paused, took a deep breath and blew it noisily out, then finally called over her shoulder, "Well? Are you coming?"

Larsa quickly blew out the candles but left them on the curb. She shoved the speakers into her oversized bag and scuttled into the bar behind Janet.

"Interesting is good," she said. She was pale and sweating again, and Janet held out a glass of ice water for her when she passed.

"How many days now?" Janet asked, thinking the woman looked closer to five days sober than eight and a half years, or whatever she'd told Nell the number of days was earlier.

"Huh?" Larsa stared back before blinking in understanding. "Oh, today is day two thousand four hundred fifty-eight. I'm so blessed." She took a long pull of the ice water on her way back to "her" table.

Janet's nose scrunched. She was certain Nell had told her that Larsa's sobriety number was in the one thousands.

She took out her cell phone and her free hand clenched when she saw that the Wi-Fi wasn't working again. She checked the computer in the office, and sure enough, the Internet was completely down. She texted Jason, then opened the calculator app on her phone as she walked back out into the bar.

Larsa had originally told her that she'd been sober for eight and a half years.

$365 \times 8.5 = 3{,}102.5$.

But just now she'd said 2,458 days, and now that Janet really thought about it, Nell had quoted Larsa as saying 1,827 the other night. Which was it? In her experience, alcoholics were very precise about that number, sometimes down to the hour of their last drink.

She headed over to ask Larsa, but the other woman spoke first. "What made it so interesting?"

After a moment's hesitation, Janet said, "I went with the police to talk to Ollie Daniels's family." Distracted by her numbers query, Janet suddenly worried that reopening old wounds might jeopardize Larsa's sobriety—however long it had been. Then again, Larsa *was* sitting in her bar, hoping to find her father's killer . . .

Larsa, who had been in the middle of settling into her seat, froze with her arm outstretched, her fingers just hovering over her purse on the table in front of her. She took a deep breath before asking, "And how are they?"

Janet was struck by the real depth of feeling in Larsa's voice. "They are . . . devastated. That's the only word I can think of to describe them. They're still devastated over their son's death all these years later. Your father's death seemed to bring it all back to the surface—especially for Ollie's dad."

"Of course they are devastated. Their family was ruined after the death." Larsa bent her head and Janet got the impression she was saying a prayer.

"It sounds like it ruined your father, as well." Janet kept her eyes trained on Larsa for her reaction.

For a moment, there wasn't one, but finally the other woman nodded slowly. "The fact that he wasn't charged seemed so lucky at first. Of course, it soon became his cross to bear. The death ruined my family, as well."

There wasn't much to say to that, and after a moment, Janet got to work behind the bar, combining bottles of liquor, mopping the floor, and wiping down the ice machine. Larsa finally spoke again as Janet eyed a bin of lemons and limes with distrust.

"I tried to talk to them, the family—Ollie's family—and even with the other boy on the bike, but they just couldn't separate me from my dad.

"My mom killed herself, you know, about a year after the . . . the accident. She couldn't take the notoriety of being associated with it all. Knoxville's growing, but it's still a small town, and everyone knew."

Larsa picked up the sweating glass of ice water and took a long draw, then set it back down and stared at it curiously.

"You know, I don't think she ever tasted alcohol. At least, if she had, she stopped completely when my dad started going down the road he went down. It's hard to live with the knowledge that your husband killed somebody else's kid. She just couldn't do it."

"Larsa, I'm so—"

"I'm not telling you this so you'll feel sorry for me." She took two tea candles out of her bag and lit them carefully. "I guess I just want you to know what he was up against. Of course, he blamed himself for my mother's death, and in my anger at the time, I did, too. In fact, I hadn't talked to him since the night my mother's body was found—until a couple weeks ago, anyway."

Janet looked up from the fruit bin. She thought Larsa had said that she and her father hadn't spoken in years. Janet pushed the bin away and really focused on Ike's daughter.

Larsa's eyes flicked up to meet Janet's before she refocused on her ice water. "A friend let me know he'd been in another accident while driving drunk. My father only had minor injuries, but the car was damaged. I got in touch—I just wanted to tell him to stay off the roads. I really had the best of intentions, you have to know that." She tucked her lighter back into her purse and stared at the candle flames dancing in front of her. "Before I knew it, though, he was shouting at me and I was shouting back. I hung up after saying something awful—just awful," she repeated before falling silent.

Janet said quietly, "What did you say?"

She shuddered. "I said, 'You cannot imagine the guilt I feel for being so relieved that you won't be able to hurt anyone else.'"

Janet's eyebrows drew together. "Because he was going to be charged, finally?" she asked softly. It suddenly made sense—what was driving Larsa's behavior. More than just the sadness of a grieving daughter, the guilt of her angry last words to her father must have been eating away at her. No wonder she hadn't wanted to admit that they'd spoken recently.

Larsa didn't answer, though, as she was folded over in prayer, her lips moving without sound.

Janet decided not to ask about the conflicting number of days Larsa had been sober. The woman obviously had a lot on her mind. What was it to Janet if she couldn't keep her sobriety straight?

She bent over the cutting board, moving a knife through the fruit with caution, but halfway through the first lemon, she stopped, distracted. With all that Larsa had just told her, her mind kept boomeranging back to one thing—person, really: the roommate on the other bike who had watched Ollie die.

Had the ten-year anniversary of Ollie's death reignited the outrage of those who'd been closest to him? She wondered what the other boy on the bike thought about Ike's death. More importantly, she wondered where he'd been the night Ike was killed.

CHAPTER TWELVE

Janet couldn't wait to get out of the bar, and as soon as Cindy Lou walked in, she headed for her car, unsure of where she wanted to go but certain she had to get some distance from Larsa.

How anyone could survive such devastation in their life, Janet didn't know, but even more unsettling was how the other woman's story made Janet think about her own past.

She'd been raised by her mother, a loving woman who more than made up for the fact that her father had walked out on them before she was even born.

Janet's world had been rocked, however, after her mother died several years ago. Her father had tracked her down and shared a completely different story about why he'd been absent for her whole life. He'd had the audacity to blame her mother for not wanting *him* and not even telling him he had a daughter.

It had been a confusing new reality for Janet to come to terms with, and Larsa's story brought it all to the surface. A man Janet had learned to hate in her youth had turned out to be a steady, calm influence in her life—at least, when she let him.

By the time she was able to focus on the road, she was already pulling up to the downtown library. Stuck at a light for a few minutes, she clucked a celebratory cheer when a car pulled out of a metered spot just ahead. "Do I have any quarters, though?" she muttered to herself as she wedged her car into the spot.

She checked the change tray and found just enough to get her a half hour inside.

"Can I help you, ma'am?" an elderly librarian called as she walked through the front door, but Janet waved her off and headed to the computer section. She signed up for a machine and settled in between two elderly people.

It was much easier to navigate on a real computer than on the small screen of her phone, and soon she was reading Ollie Daniels's obituary from the *Knoxville Times*.

Ollie had been nineteen when he was killed. The article also listed the names of his two roommates, Abe and Benji, one of whom had been at the accident. She searched for both online and in just a few clicks she had their information, amazed to find that they both still lived in town. She looked at the clock: it was already after four. Business would start picking up soon back at the bar. This hunt for information would have to wait until the next day.

———

Janet heard crying as soon as she stepped out of her car. She felt her blood pressure increase and wondered what she was going to do with Larsa. It was one thing to sit unobtrusively in a corner booth, but it was completely another to wail and disrupt her paying customers. She pushed open the door to the Spot, prepared to have a come-to-Jesus conversation with the most spiritual person she'd ever met, but she pulled up short when she was met by the tear-stained face of Cindy Lou.

"I—I—I'm so sorry, Janet," she sobbed. "You know Chip is leaving for college in just a few weeks? We just got his first tuition bill in the mail, and I thought I was so excited to get rid of him—I mean, not rid of him, but to get some extra time back —but now I—I—I just don't know how I'll get along without him!"

Janet's eyes widened and she glanced from Cindy Lou to Larsa, who looked guiltily away. She tried to focus on the problem at hand; she couldn't have tears behind the bar, even if Cindy Lou was going to miss her only son when he went away to school.

"Isn't he going to UT Knoxville?" Janet asked. The university was right in town.

"Yes, but he'll be living in the dorms. I might only see him once a week!"

She doubled over in tears and Janet winced; her outfit was so tight and short that drastic movements like sobbing and bending over quickly made the R-rated ensemble teeter toward NC-17.

"I have just the job for you today, Cindy Lou," Janet said, thinking fast. She'd been meaning to organize the cooler for weeks but hadn't thought of it until Bud deposited dozens of cases of bottles and cans. "Did Bud come by while I was gone? You can head into the back and cool off while you organize—"

Instead of calming down, however, Cindy Lou wailed even louder and threw her head back in angst. "No!"

"Okay." Janet instinctively stepped back. "Oh—oh, I've got it! Our renters are fostering a new baby, and I know they must be overwhelmed. Why don't you head over and see if you can help out—give them a break for a few minutes—and come back to work once you've calmed down?"

"A baby?" Cindy Lou sniffled, looking up at Janet with watery eyes.

"Yes, a beautiful baby girl."

Cindy Lou grabbed her keys and turned to Larsa before heading out the door. "Th-thanks for your in-insight, Larsa." She took a loud, shaky breath. "You're right. T-t-time does move too fast!" With another sniff, she was gone.

Janet turned her back on Larsa, exasperated that the woman

had not only put *her* in a funk that day, but had also apparently sent Cindy Lou spiraling out of control.

She ran a hand through her hair, then rolled out the tension in her shoulders. It was time to get to work. The condiment container was full, the ice chest was replenished, and everything behind the bar was clean and sparkling. But they were short two rows of their most popular beer—and Cindy Lou said Bud hadn't been in yet. She depended on him, and he was usually so prompt and consistent, but it had been a solid week of mistakes and missed deliveries. She hoped she wouldn't have to change distributors.

She checked the walk-in cooler to see whether they could make it through the night when the very deliveryman in question knocked on the back door.

Janet opened it, prepared to give Bud a piece of her mind, but for the second time in less than ten minutes, she stopped before she spoke. Bud, usually so open and friendly, looked nervous as he glanced everywhere but at Janet's face.

"Sorry . . . traffic . . . ," he mumbled as he held out a clipboard for Janet to sign, still not making eye contact.

"No problem, Bud. You know where it goes."

He worked faster than she'd ever seen; the usually chatty deliveryman loaded up the walk-in cooler with cases of beer and left the bar without saying goodbye.

She watched him climb into the truck and drive away, wondering what was going on there. Something wasn't right. He'd been acting funny since . . . well, since Ike's murder.

She closed the door and turned the dead bolt, then groaned as pain sliced her finger. Despite her liberal use of hydrogen peroxide and a triple-action ointment, her finger hadn't gotten better. The long-awaited doctor's appointment wasn't until the following day, and the cut had turned a funny shade of green that surely wasn't healthy. The throbbing was like a nonstop low tone in the background, always with her and getting louder by the hour.

By seven o'clock, business was going strong. It was another busy night, and Janet looked around her bar with satisfaction. Her regulars sat in their unofficial assigned seats and were happy to be there after the crowds following Ike's murder.

"It's like church on a regular Sunday compared to Christmas or Easter, ain't it?" Cindy Lou asked. She was back from visiting with the baby and more chipper than before.

Janet grinned. Nell caught her eye and motioned for another round. Janet poured vodka over ice in a shaker, mixed it, filled a clean rocks glass with ice, dropped two limes onto the rim, and poured in the chilled liquid.

The older woman's silvery-gray hair shone under the low lights at the bar, and Janet wondered if she'd ever know *her* sad story. Nell had been a regular for as long as Janet had worked there, but she didn't know much more about her than she'd learned after the first week.

There were other regulars, too: the one-night-out-a-week section, the barflies desperate for contact, and the lonely old people pining for better days. Some might have seen the motley crew as pathetic, but Janet was glad to know they all had a place at the Spot. Sometimes, all you needed was somewhere to call home—to be comfortable and to be yourself—to make the difference between a good day and a bad one.

As the crowd thinned and people filed out of the bar for the night, Janet bused a table by the door and overheard Frank talking to Larsa.

"I'm just saying, if you want one, it's on me."

"I'm pretty sure it wouldn't help," she responded, her dreamy voice flatter than usual.

"I'll bring one over. If you change your mind, it'll be right there."

Janet watched suspiciously as Frank left Larsa's table and headed behind the bar, reemerging moments later with a bottle of beer. She cut him off halfway to the woman's booth.

"What do you think you're doing?" She snatched the beer

from Frank's hand. "She doesn't drink. Why are you bringing her this?"

"Like I told her, it might help her tonight. She seems low."

"So you decided to pressure a recovering alcoholic into having a beer? Her father is dead and she's in the throes of sadness and depression, for God's sake!"

Frank looked unabashedly back at Janet. "Uh-huh."

"Stop talking to the customers and do your job, Frank." She was livid, but softened her tone when she turned to Ike's daughter. "Go home, Larsa. You kept watch tonight; we'll see you tomorrow."

"I just wish I'd taken him seriously," Larsa said gloomily into her water.

"Frank? Nobody takes him seriously—"

"No, not Frank. On the—on the phone? It was just before my father and I argued that last time. All he could talk about was a ghost from his past, and I could only focus on the present. If I had just stopped talking long enough to really listen, I bet he'd still be alive." She pushed up from the table and slung her bag over her shoulder before heading out the door.

Janet watched her walk away, worried for Ike's daughter's mental health. The poor woman was blaming herself for her father's mistakes. What a heavy burden to bear.

She loaded the white ceramic mug onto her tray, along with two empty glasses of water, then handed the beer to a customer at the next booth over. As she wiped down the table, she wondered which ghost had haunted Ike just before he died. It seemed like there were plenty to choose from.

CHAPTER THIRTEEN

"Where have you been?" Janet asked as she watched Jason walk across the bedroom through one slitted eye. "It's the crack of"—she turned her head and pried her eye all the way open to look at the clock on the bedside table—"nine! It's the crack of nine! What are you doing?"

"Janet, a massive virus has disabled my entire computer system. Wex has been here since midnight, and it's going to cost me an arm and a leg, but I can't have my system compromised. I should have had him come here two days ago, but I really thought he could walk me through it."

"Wexford Restin is here?" Janet asked as Jason changed into a clean shirt. She sighed when all his skin was covered up. "If your old hacking buddy is going to do the job for you, doesn't that mean you can come back to bed?" She patted the spot he'd just vacated.

He took an involuntary step closer to Janet before stopping himself with a grin. "No, God only knows what Wex will hack into if he's left alone." He walked to the door and then stopped and turned back. "We'll be in my office for the rest of the morning. Are you headed to the doctor today?"

"Och," Janet groaned, knowing it might be days before she saw her boyfriend again. "Yes, finally."

"Good," he said before disappearing down the hall.

She stayed in bed for another minute and then climbed out to get ready for her own busy day, which would start with tracking down a stranger.

———

The knock echoed in the hallway of the fancy apartment building in downtown Knoxville. Janet had managed to slide in the main door behind a resident, and she bounced on her feet, hoping Benji Watts would answer his door.

With the sudden rattle of the lock and twisting of the door-knob, Janet found herself face-to-face with a bald man who looked like he was caught between two different worlds. A few tattoos crept up from the neck of his dress shirt, and he wore an expensive-looking suit and tie. He pulled the strap of his messenger bag over one shoulder and held a bike helmet in his other hand.

He stopped just short of walking into her, and fumbled with his keys. "Can I help you?"

"Benji?" He nodded. "I hope so." She took a step back to let him out. He locked the door behind him and motioned for her to walk with him to the elevator. "I . . . I guess I'm looking into Ike Freeman's death." She kept her eyes trained on Benji's face to see if the name drew any kind of reaction. It did.

He stopped walking and looked at her again. "Who are you?"

"I own the bar outside of which he was found murdered."

"You're here why?"

"It turns out the police don't have a lot to go on, and I thought it made sense to investigate Ike's past. It sounds like you are a big part of it."

Benji snorted. "You could say that. He definitely changed my life."

"It was a terrible loss," Janet said.

"It *was* terrible—terrible that it happened and terrible that Ike wasn't charged with murder. He's a criminal, but he walked free. It was unbelievable. Still is."

He started walking again, and Janet followed him down the hall.

"I wasn't there, you know, when it happened. I was still at home; my first class wasn't until noon that day. Abe saw the whole thing, though. Right in front of his eyes, his best friend was snatched away. The first cop on the scene drove the man who did it home, like a taxi service." He jabbed at the down button for the elevator and shook his head.

"It sounds like you haven't forgiven Ike."

"He never asked for forgiveness!" Benji said, and his voice echoed in the empty concrete hall. He shook his head and lowered his voice. "You're right: I haven't forgiven him." He blew out a breath and jiggled his keys in his hand. "But the crazy thing is, even if the cops who showed up had given him a Breathalyzer, chances are the same thing would've happened. It's astounding how cyclist rights are trampled on a near-daily basis across this country."

"Cyclist rights?"

"People think cars own the roadways, but it's simply not true. The law gives cyclists just as much of a right to be on the road as motorists, yet time and again cyclists are treated like second-class citizens and literally run down by drivers who think they shouldn't have to share the road. It's ridiculous. I mean, we're people, okay? Some drivers are more careful when they see a dog on the side of the road than when they see a cyclist."

Janet narrowed her eyes and tried to make sense of the man in front of her. "What do you do, exactly?"

"I'm a lawyer at Dystel & Schmatt," he said, naming one of the largest law firms downtown, "but I also work pro bono to represent cyclists who've been injured." They were on the elevator now, heading down to the ground floor. "You wouldn't believe how many *police officers* don't even know the law. Cars have to wait either until it's safe to pass a cyclist or until they have enough room to go wide around them if there's not a bicycle lane. Lots of cyclists get charged with blocking traffic if they take up any space at all on the road, though, like they're supposed to ride through the potholes or something!" He tsked in outrage before the ding of the elevator doors interrupted him; they stepped off together into the wide, open lobby.

"Did you know I was premed in college? I was planning to become a doctor, but then Ollie was killed and rage changed my passion from health to litigation. The fact is that Ike was drunk. He should have been charged with drunk driving and vehicular manslaughter. Instead, he got a taxi ride home, paid for by the city. My goal is to make sure that doesn't happen again to anyone." He slipped a hand inside his briefcase and flicked his card to Janet. "I'm late for work, but if you have any more questions . . ."

She followed him out of the building and watched him unlock his bicycle from a covered rack in the parking garage.

"Hey, Benji! When's the last time you saw Ike?"

He put his bicycle helmet on and clicked the latch together under his chin before answering. "I've actually never seen him in person—only in the papers." He threw one leg over the bike and, with a last wave, pedaled down the street, his unbuttoned suit jacket flapping in the wind.

She felt like scratching her head. Benji certainly didn't seem upset to learn Ike was dead, but she couldn't really blame him. As he disappeared into traffic, she realized she hadn't even asked him where he'd been the night Ike was murdered. God, she'd make a terrible investigator. He had said one thing that stuck with her, though: he hadn't been riding with Ollie the day he was killed. Their other roommate, Abe, had been. She dug around in her purse, finally finding the old receipt on which she'd scribbled their addresses. She wondered if the person who'd watched Ollie die still felt any anger toward the man who killed him.

CHAPTER FOURTEEN

Abe also lived in a nicer section of Knoxville, but his neighborhood was less urban and Janet felt even more out of place. Everything from her car to her clothes to her hair screamed that she didn't belong in this suburban utopia, littered with expensive jogging strollers, luxury cars and SUVs in every driveway, and stucco as far as the eye could see.

It could have been her imagination, but as she knocked, she felt like a couple walking by slowed to watch her. It made her want to turn around and let them know she wasn't going to steal anything.

A beautiful brunette woman wearing tight-fitting yoga pants and a matching tank top and jacket that likely cost more than Janet averaged in tips each night opened the door. "I'm sorry, sweetheart, but we're not interested." The woman's twang was strong; she was clearly a native of Knoxville, or somewhere else down south.

Briefly curious as to what this woman thought Janet was selling, she said, "I'm looking for someone named Abe."

The woman's eyes narrowed. "Who may I say is asking for him?"

"Janet Black." She held out her business card and the woman

snatched it out of her hand then pushed the door closed. Janet heard her yell up the stairs for Abe.

Footsteps pounded down the stairs. The woman pulled open the door again, still assessing Janet through narrowed, now suspicious, eyes.

A man came to stand next to her. "Vanessa?" She shrugged and stared at Janet, so he looked over, too. "Hi, I'm Abe."

He was tall, slim, and muscular, with sandy-blond hair, wire-framed glasses, and long, Nordic features.

Janet zipped up her hoodie, which was at least a size too big with frayed seams at the hemline, and flicked a look at Vanessa before saying, "Is there somewhere private we can talk?"

Abe squeezed the woman's hand, then motioned that he would follow Janet down the walk. Vanessa's eyes disappeared into slits as Janet turned to head toward the street.

"Sorry," Janet said, glancing back, as they reached the sidewalk. "I think she's—"

"Don't worry—my wife is used to it. Patients sometimes show up here. How they find me, I'll never know. Are you a patient?" He stopped walking to look her over, his eyes resting on the white bandage on her finger.

"No! I'm . . . well, I guess I'm looking into the death of Ike Freeman."

"Ah," Abe said, his face scrunched together in not quite sadness, but something near sorrow.

"You heard?" Janet asked.

"I saw it on the news the other night. I was sorry to hear it. Yes, I really was," he said in answer to Janet's surprised expression. "His life wasn't an easy one. It took me years to forgive him for killing Ollie, but I did, and I was sorry to see he wasn't ever able to . . . to get his life on track." He flicked Janet's card back and forth against his hand as he spoke. "I actually became a doctor because of him."

"Really?"

"Ollie and I were both physical therapy majors, but being

there when he was hit and not knowing what to do while I waited for the ambulance . . . well, it changed me. It put me on the path I was supposed to be on."

"What did you think when Ike wasn't charged in Ollie's death?"

"I thought it was a total miscarriage of justice, just like everyone else. You'd think five eyewitnesses would have been enough to challenge the official version of what happened, but it wasn't. I can't make sense of it, but I'm glad it forced me and Benji to rethink what we were going to do with our lives. That's the only good to come from the terrible accident.

"You're with KPD?" Abe asked, finally glancing down at Janet's card.

"Oh, no. I'm, uh, I'm not." She knew Detective O'Dell well enough to know she couldn't pull off impersonating an officer without getting into trouble.

Abe looked down at her business card and frowned. "You own the Spot? What are you, like, a private investigator?"

"Oh, no." She chuckled at the thought.

"What do you have to do with—"

"I'm really just checking facts in a nonofficial capacity," she said with authority.

He squinted down at her. "What does that mean?"

Janet sighed. "It means Ike was found dead outside my bar, and his daughter is having this . . . prayer vigil on my property until his killer is found. So, I guess I'd like to speed that process along."

Abe blinked several times, and then shrugged. "Well, it's been hard on Ollie's family, but I'm sure they're finally feeling a sense of closure. Knowing Ike was out there, living his life, while their son wasn't was difficult for them—for Mr. Daniels, especially."

Janet asked a few more questions but didn't glean any new information, except that Abe's wife seemed the jealous type.

Vanessa glared down the walk through a small crack in the

curtains. Janet's bar-fight radar was running hot, so she held out her hand to Abe to say goodbye.

"It's a felon," he said matter-of-factly.

"Excuse me?" Janet said, affronted. "A few misdemeanor run-ins with the cops when I was a teenager certainly doesn't make me—"

"No—no," Abe said with an uncomfortable laugh, "your finger. The kind of infection you've got is called a felon."

"Oh . . . uh, good to know. I have an appointment scheduled with my doctor for later today, hopefully she can fix me up." She waved before heading down the front walk, feeling like she'd just wasted her morning. Benji and Abe both seemed about as vaguely unaffected as could be expected when someone who had altered the course of their lives ten years earlier finally met what they must have seen as a fitting end.

An idea occurred to her, and she stopped walking and turned back toward the house. "Oh, hey, one last question: when did you last see Ike?" She was thinking about Larsa's ghost-from-the-past comment, wondering if Ike had actually seen a familiar face recently that had sent him over the edge. Abe didn't answer, he was scrutinizing her card again.

"Do the police know you're out here, talking to people about a murder case?"

"As if I'd take on all of this on my own?" Janet asked, arching her eyebrows incredulously. Abe cocked his head to the side and narrowed his eyes, and she decided to leave before he could delve more deeply into how she was connected to the case.

As she drove away, though, she realized he hadn't answered her last question and wondered if that was by design.

CHAPTER FIFTEEN

Janet had just over thirty minutes until her appointment, so she grabbed lunch at a drive-through on the way to the office. But after two bites of hamburger, her stomach clenched.

What was she doing, investigating a murder? It was crazy, and though she hadn't been impersonating a police officer, she hadn't been far off. She'd never felt so out of control! She laughed without humor in the silence of her car, because that was really saying something. Her life had not been the smoothest over the last few years.

Something oozed from under the bandage around her finger; she dabbed it with a napkin and tossed her trash into the takeout bag before putting the car in drive and heading toward her doctor's office. There, she sat impatiently in the lobby, reading an old, torn-up magazine for twenty-seven minutes before her name was called.

She stood, and her finger gave a last, painful pulse, as if it knew treatment was near. But her brow furrowed when she saw that the woman waving her over wasn't wearing cat-and-dog scrubs like the other nurses in the office. Instead, she wore a crisp, black business suit.

"I'm so sorry, hon—I forgot to have you fill out the financial responsibility form, and we'll need to get payment for your services first." She handed a clipboard to Janet over the counter.

"You don't know what they're going to do yet, though. How can I pay for it?" Janet asked, feeling her face heat up. "I know I don't have insurance, but I'm here for a cut finger, not chemo!"

The woman adjusted her glasses. "Yes, well, it's just office policy, hon—nothing to get offended about."

She looked at the clipboard distastefully before pulling out her wallet. "How much?"

"Well, as you so succinctly said, we don't know yet. We'll just go ahead and put a five-hundred-dollar hold on your credit card and then charge you the exact amount when our billing department determines what that is."

"What? That's just . . . that's so . . . it's just a cut!" Janet said.

The woman merely raised her eyebrows and looked pointedly at the forms.

"I don't have five hundred dollars!" she snapped. "I've got renters who don't pay and employees who steal, but I *don't* have five hundred dollars!"

"Well, I'm sorry to say that's exactly why we've got the policy in place," the woman said with a smugly superior expression.

"This is unbelievable!" Janet stared at the receptionist and waited for her to come up with another plan. After all, the customer was always right. But the woman only stared back, and finally Janet, her finger now pulsing in time with her heart, shoved her wallet back into her bag and marched out of the office. She was officially pissed off.

She threw herself into her car and slammed the gearshift into drive, her foot heavy on the gas as she navigated the streets of Knoxville. She'd called Cindy Lou in early to sign for deliveries that morning, so she could get her finger looked at. Instead, she'd chased false leads all over town and nearly gotten fleeced by a doctor's office!

She parked on the street in front of the duplex and snorted in disbelief when she saw her renters—no, her squatters—sitting outside, sunning themselves, as if they didn't have a care in the world.

She climbed out of the car and called to the woman not holding a baby. "Mel! We need to talk!"

Mel headed toward her slowly, clearly sensing a shift in Janet's demeanor.

"You guys can't stay if you can't pay—it's that simple. This isn't a free boardinghouse; it's not a stop on your European vacation where you can run out before having breakfast without paying.

"This rental home is a business for us, and if you want to stay, you need to pay money to live here. If not, you'll need to be out by the end of the week." She resolutely did not look at the baby, suddenly angry that these women were unable to organize their lives.

Mel nodded solemnly, and her lack of reaction somehow stifled Janet's anger.

"Well. Okay then. I'm glad we've got that straightened out." Instead of going into the house, she got back in the car and headed to the drugstore. They were out of bandages at home, and it was clear that she needed a new treatment plan to fix whatever was happening in her finger. The skin was red, tight, and angry looking, with some pearly-white liquid oozing out one end of the cut.

She marched to the back of the store and picked out the biggest box of bandages on the shelf, then grabbed a bottle of hydrogen peroxide and a bottle of rubbing alcohol. She was going to kill whatever was growing in there, no matter how much it hurt—and it was only going to cost her nine dollars.

She pivoted for the cash register and nearly ran into another customer.

"Janet!" Detective O'Dell also had his arms full. He was balancing an eight-pack of toilet paper, a giant red sports drink, a bag of candy, and a value-size container of Tylenol. "I just came in for the Tylenol. I should know by now to always get a cart," he said with a self-deprecating grin.

Janet crossed her arms over her chest and leaned toward the detective. "I have a question about the case."

O'Dell squinted back at her, losing his friendly smile. "So do I."

"Oh?"

"Where is Elizabeth? We're starting to wonder if she really exists." He hitched the package of toilet paper under his arm and looked at her with unabashed curiosity.

She tensed up. "Of course she exists! She's one of my original bartenders at the Spot."

"You mean she was."

"No, she is. I just don't know where she is right now."

"Is that common? Has she missed work like this before?"

"Yes." Janet shifted her load to free up her injured hand. "You don't often become a bartender because you've got your shit together, you know?"

"Why do you become a bartender?"

Janet looked up sharply, but for once, O'Dell wasn't smirking. He seemed genuinely curious.

"It's what you do when you've got great people skills," she deadpanned. O'Dell didn't laugh, and Janet added, more seriously, "It's happened before—with Elizabeth—but it's unusual. It isn't like her, and I'm—I'm worried about her."

"We're worried, too, Janet. It doesn't look good. She's either involved in something or got in the way of something, you know?"

"Well, she's not involved in anything!" she said with conviction she didn't feel.

"That's worrisome, too, isn't it?" O'Dell replied. "Finch checked her apartment—had the manager let him in yesterday afternoon—and said nothing was out of place, but there was no sign of her." They stared at each other for a moment before he said, almost reluctantly, "You had a question for me?"

She took a breath and her shoulders dropped. She no longer felt combative—just tired. "Larsa was at the bar yesterday, again. She said her dad had been in an accident recently. Do you know anything about that?"

O'Dell's eyes widened in surprise. "Well . . . it was a single-car accident maybe a month ago."

Janet's fingers twitched. "What happened?" It was a pain in the ass not to have access to the case file.

"An anonymous passerby called 911 about a car off the road and a man bleeding. Dispatchers sent an ambulance, and EMTs treated Ike for a concussion at the scene. When our officer arrived, he was so drunk that he didn't really remember the details of the crash—his blood alcohol level was over twice the legal limit to drive. He should have been served papers to appear in court a few weeks ago, but there was a filing error, so it just crossed my desk."

"Any idea who this Good Samaritan was who called 911?"

"We're working on it." O'Dell frowned and subconsciously made a humming sound as he blew out a breath. He finally shook his head. "One more for you: I just got a call from Dispatch. They fielded inquiries from both of Ollie's old roommates. Care to explain what you're doing?"

Janet crossed her arms but didn't answer.

"I'm uh . . . I'm late for work, but watch out, Janet. You're not a cop, so don't act like one." He gave her a final stern look before heading for the checkout stand.

She waited until he was out of the store before she moved. As she stared at the shelf of bandages, she honed in on a recurring theme for Ike. How did he get home from his most recent accident? Why had Ike been able to continually skirt the law when he was alive? Was his friend still on the force?

CHAPTER SIXTEEN

"Late for work?" Janet stared at O'Dell twenty minutes later. They stood toe-to-toe in her kitchen and she was furious.

"Yeah," he answered, not taking his eyes off his notebook. "My guys got here fifteen minutes ago."

"What exactly is going on?" She watched a trio of men, wearing navy blue KPD polo shirts, carrying things up to the kitchen from the basement, through the TV room, and out the front door.

He plucked a piece of paper from the plywood island and cursed. "Splinter!" He handed her the paper and then put his finger to his mouth, still wincing in pain.

This was where being helpful got her: with her house being legally ransacked by cops. Unbelievable.

"Look, Janet, I'm investigating a murder, and if that means I have to collect your boyfriend's computer equipment to make sure he's being truthful when he says the crime wasn't recorded on his surveillance cameras, then unfortunately, that's what we're going to do."

"'Collect'? I wouldn't exactly use that term," Jason said as he came up from the basement, his cell phone pressed against one ear. "More like illegally confiscate." Another cop walked past with a large hard drive and Jason said, "Be careful with that!" He turned back to O'Dell. "I have over fifty thousand dollars of hardware down there, and if any of it comes back dented, scratched, or otherwise damaged, you'll be paying—" He broke off midsentence and moved his phone in front of his mouth. "Yes, I'm still on hold for Phil Walderman. It's urgent." He looked over at Janet. "This is going to cost us a fortune." He then stormed back down the steps that led to his office.

"A lawyer?" O'Dell said, recognizing the name of the local attorney. "Save yourself the money. We got a subpoena signed by a judge to take everything. A lawyer won't be able to do anything about it."

"Are you sure? Did the judge know Jason has information on other clients in his system? You can't look through someone's entire office to find information on one case."

"Actually," O'Dell said with an attempt at a conciliatory tone, "we can."

Janet tried to read the piece of paper he'd handed her, but in her anger, she couldn't focus. "Why would we lie? What could we possibly gain by not handing over evidence that would solve a murder? Do you think it's good for business—"

"You said it was yourself! You said business would be crazy the night after Ike's body turned up, and Finch said you were right. Standing room only! I'd say it's been great for business."

"That's—that's just . . . I mean, that's totally off base! Yes, the initial thrust was, but it's not a long-term strategy for growth. How can you—" She was so angry she was spluttering, unable to finish a single thought. Instead, she picked up her cell phone.

"Oh, are you gonna call your daddy now and see if he can get you out of this mess?" O'Dell asked.

She looked up from her phone in time to see his smirk.

"No!" she said, even though that was exactly what she'd been intending to do. "I'm going to text Jason and tell him we'll take out a second mortgage and sell the bar if that's what it costs to get a lawyer down here to make sure you don't trample all over our rights. You can't come in here and destroy a man's business—especially when you have no proof that he's done anything wrong!"

"Good luck."

"What do you mean?"

"I mean good luck finding a lawyer on a—" He stopped, took a deep breath, and then released it slowly. "What is it about you that drives me so nuts?" He shook his head like he was shaking off a swarm of gnats. "This is a murder investigation, Ms. Black, that's it. It's not a personal vendetta against you or your boyfriend."

She stared at him, thinking about what he'd been about to say. A spark of knowledge hit, and she stepped closer, her finger jammed against his chest. "You did this on purpose. It's Sunday, and you must have gotten this subpoena filed when?" She looked down at the paper still grasped in her other hand. "Yes, on Friday, but you didn't act on it until today, Sunday. You knew we wouldn't be able to find a judge to counteract this filing on a weekend!" She looked up from the paper in shock. "You're just as bad as a criminal!"

O'Dell scoffed. "I'm the exact opposite of a criminal. The fact that you can't see that just confirms what we're doing today is the right thing."

Janet stalked past him and yelled down the stairs, "Any luck on Walderman?"

"Still on hold. They'll probably bill me four hundred dollars for this call alone!"

A woman with dark hair slicked back into a bun stepped around Janet, carrying another hard drive. A man behind her gripped two monitors by the stands. Janet watched both walk out the back door and deposit Jason's items into a waiting van.

"Now you're just being punitive," she said, turning to O'Dell. "What are you going to do with the monitors? That's just—that's just plain mean." While keeping an eye on him, she shouted,

"Jason, do whatever we need to do here, okay? This isn't right. Let's make it right."

"Careful," O'Dell said, tucking his notebook under his arm and fixing her with his most irritatingly superior stare.

"Is that a threat?"

"No, just a friendly warning. If you bet on the wrong horse, here, and Jason isn't as innocent as you think, he might just drain your accounts defending himself, and then you'll lose him, this house, *and* your bar."

Janet sucked in a gasp at his audacity, then spun away from him, not wanting to look at his smug face for a second longer. Jason came back up the stairs and she looked up at him, a question on her lips.

"W—" But before she could get Wex's name out, he shook his head almost imperceptibly. Her eyes flicked to O'Dell. "Who else can you call?" she asked, trying to cover up her earlier question.

Jason frowned at O'Dell. "Whoever we need to, to make this right."

She frowned, too. Why was O'Dell so certain Jason was involved in a murder? What did he know? What was she missing?

CHAPTER SEVENTEEN

It was dead.

Janet was halfway through her shift Sunday afternoon and the bar was practically empty. Janet studiously avoided making eye contact with Larsa at her corner booth, and Nell, the only true customer there, sat out of sight on the other side of the Beer-ador, nursing a drink.

She'd left the house in utter chaos with Jason near the breaking point, prowling up and down the stairs like a caged cheetah.

Now she was the one ready to pounce. She paced behind the bar, wondering what was going to happen to his business—to their business—and their home. Sunlight streamed into the dark room when the door opened, and Janet squinted toward the light. "Jason? What are you doing here?"

He grinned. "Figured I might as well hang out here, rather than watch them tear apart our house." He had a bounce in his step that she hadn't expected.

"For someone who was yelling at a lawyer on the phone an hour ago, you sure seem . . . chipper."

His grin widened. "It was a pretty good act, if I do say so myself."

"Act? What are you talking about?"

He straddled a stool across from her and swept a hand through his dark hair. "After you passed on Finch's message about the subpoena, I told Wex what needed to happen. Can you believe he got the problem licked in two hours? That bastard hacked me right past the malware and then sent a line of code back that'll disable the jerks who wrote it for months." He nodded in satisfaction.

"What do you mean? You and Wex were working through the night and all morning. If you weren't trying to fix the virus, what were you doing?"

"Copying everything over to new external hard drives and then wiping my machines clean. If KPD can get past my passwords and into my system, which is doubtful, they won't find a thing."

A shocked laugh escaped before Janet clamped her lips and smacked him on the arm. "Jason, that's going to make you look so guilty!"

"They can't make me guilty just because they want me to be, and lack of evidence in itself isn't evidence. Plus," he shifted in his seat, "I couldn't risk them getting ahold of my files. If word got out that the security guy's computer wasn't secure—" He stopped abruptly with a shake of his head that said he might as well sell pizza for a living.

"Jason," she moaned, "it's all about perception with these guys. If you look guilty, they're going to dig in!"

"Let them," he said dismissively, reaching out to grab her hand. "I'm sorry that I had to worry you, but there wasn't time to explain."

"I get it. I know how important your job is, and I'd never get in the way of that."

"I know. That's one of the reasons I love you."

She grinned at him for a moment before shaking herself. God, she hated feeling so sappy.

Jason laughed, sensing her internal struggle. "I have something for you," he said with a sly smile.

"What?" she asked, suspicious of the change in his mood.

Before he could answer, though, Bud, the beer deliveryman, walked in the front door.

"I knocked around back, but no one answered."

"A Sunday delivery, Bud?"

"Well, Mondays get so busy, I thought I'd get a jump start." His hand tapped out a beat against his leg, and the loose coins in his pocket jangled like a tambourine.

Jason waved her off, slipped off his stool, and walked around the bar to pour himself a glass of water while Janet dealt with the delivery.

"I know Cindy Lou will miss seeing you," she said as she led Bud through the office to the back door. She propped it open and watched him fill his cart with cases of beer.

She counted the bottles as Bud wheeled them into the cooler and then signed the paper on his clipboard. When the truck pulled out of the lot, she went in search of Jason.

She didn't have to go far; he was waiting for her by the alley exit.

"So, mystery man, you ready to spill the beans?" Janet asked.

"Out here." He pushed the door open, then pointed at the eaves of the roof. "See anything different?"

Janet scanned the roofline but didn't see anything out of place. If she really squinted, she could make out the tape still covering the security camera hidden in the exit sign. "You didn't fix the camera?"

"In fact, I have." He crossed his arms over his chest and grinned.

She leaned against the door frame. "Well, then, riddle me this: why does it look exactly the same?" she asked.

"Because I am the top security expert in town and even the cops can't contain me." He wagged his eyebrows.

She rolled her eyes at her boyfriend. "Obviously. But what

does that have to do with *that?*" She pointed at the tape covering the camera. She'd been on an emotional roller coaster for the last few hours and was suddenly tired of Jason's game.

His grin wavered. "I punched a tiny hole in the tape and then replaced it over the lens. Now it looks like the camera's still covered, but it's not—there is a crystal-clear shot of this alleyway." He turned and pointed vaguely to a different part of the roof. "I also installed a second hidden camera a couple of days ago that nobody knows about." He crossed his arms and frowned. "I'm still having some trouble with the wiring for the cameras inside. I'll need a few more days to untangle *that* problem." He paused for a moment, then turned to look slyly back at Janet. "With both cameras up and running, we'll be set for anything that happens out here in the future."

Janet threw her hands in the air. "But what about the past? That's what I'm interested in!" Didn't Jason understand? The police suspected him of *murder* and that meant they needed to find out who'd covered the camera, so the detectives could move on to their next wild guess at who killed Ike!

"I've got some information on that, too," he said, giving her a strange look. Jason held open the door and motioned for her to walk in first. She dropped her head back and groaned but walked into the bar, waved to Cindy Lou as she arrived for her shift, and followed Jason back to the office.

He sat down in the chair and logged on to the computer, then double-clicked on a thumbnail image; the shot showed the empty alleyway behind the Spot, from the surveillance camera they had just seen in person.

"It's from yesterday." Jason tapped another button and the video zoomed forward. Soon, Cindy Lou walked into the frame, and Jason slowed the video to real-time playback. As usual, she had more skin showing than clothes, and just as Janet was trying to decide if her top would be classified as low-cut or high-rise, another person walked into the frame—slunk, really.

"Is that Bud?" Janet asked incredulously.

"The one and only," Jason said with a sly smile.

She looked back at the screen when his grin widened. In the few seconds she'd been looking away, Cindy Lou had lost most of her clothes. With a frantic energy she had a hard time connecting with Cindy Lou, her assistant manager and beer delivery guy were getting it on big-time.

"How does her back bend like that?" Janet asked, but Jason only shrugged.

While Cindy Lou appeared to be completely engrossed in the task at hand, Bud's eyes continued to flick to the hidden security camera often enough that it wasn't coincidence—he obviously knew the camera was there.

"Do you think he's the one who tampered with the camera?"

"Keep watching," Jason said.

"I don't think I can." She scrunched up her face. With her eyes squeezed nearly shut, the images on-screen blurred out enough that she couldn't see actual flopping body parts but was aware when the deed was done. She opened her eyes only after both parties were fully dressed again. "I sure hope she washed her hands before she got back to work."

"Are you watching?" he asked.

"Yes," Janet grumbled, squinting at the screen again. Bud tucked his shirt in and took a step toward the door after Cindy Lou. But before he walked in, he reached right up to the camera and moved his thumb over what he thought was the tape covering the lens. He then nodded in satisfaction and disappeared into the bar.

"I think we found our guy." Jason clicked something that reversed the video. Another tap on the keyboard froze the frame on a close-up of Bud's face.

"But how did he know the camera was there in the first place?"

Jason blew out a short breath. "He came out into the alley with some boxes the day I was installing it. I'd have never guessed he knew what I was doing, but it must have made him suspicious enough that he took a closer look."

"Oh my God!" Janet covered her mouth with her hand. "Do you think Bud killed Ike?"

"Nah." Jason leaned back in his seat and swiveled around to face Janet. "I saw Bud collect a spider in a cup from the walk-in cooler and then set it free outside. He's not the violent type. I think it was just Ike's bad luck that he was killed near Bud and Cindy Lou's meeting place."

The sudden sound of knocking came from both sides of the office, at the back door to the parking lot and the door to the bar. She opened the outside door first and came face-to-face with Bud.

"Is my clipboard here?" he asked sheepishly, peering around Janet into the office space.

She followed his gaze and was immediately distracted by the sight of Cindy Lou standing on the other side of Jason. Her silvery bandeau top was like a sandbar of coverage in the expansive ocean of skin between her eyes and hips, where a micromini jean skirt clung hopefully.

Uniforms. We need uniforms at the Spot, Janet thought dispassionately.

"What's that, boss?" Cindy Lou asked, staring at the computer screen. She looked at Jason and then shifted her gaze to Janet. Before either could answer, her eyes moved again and she adjusted her top with a bright smile. "Oh, hey, Bud! I wasn't expectin' to see you today." She ran a hand through her hair.

Janet swallowed hard and realized this was their chance to get some answers. "We actually wanted to talk to both of you. It seems there's been something going on, and we need to get to the bottom of it."

Bud took a jerky step backward, while Cindy Lou laughed a little too loudly and stepped into the office. She pulled the door closed behind her.

"I guess y'all found us out. I can't believe we kept it a secret for this long, Bud!" Her gaze shifted back to the computer screen and she said, "Seriously, Jason, what the heck is that?"

No one answered, and she looked back to the doorway. "Bud?"

Janet tore her eyes away from Cindy Lou to see her lover's reaction, but the doorway was empty. Seconds later, the beer truck's engine started with a roar.

CHAPTER EIGHTEEN

"Wait!" Jason yelled. He ran out of the office and banged on the driver's-side door of the truck just as Bud slid the engine into gear. The truck lurched and Bud banged on the steering wheel but made no move to get back out until Jason knocked on the door again.

Then he and Jason walked back into the office. Cindy Lou's face, cheerful just moments earlier, had frozen when Bud left. Now tears threatened and her lower lip trembled. Janet said a quick prayer that her assistant manager could keep it together.

Jason closed the door so all four stood in the small office space together. It was silent for what felt like a long time.

"So," Janet said, looking between the pair. "Secret lovers?"

Bud's face flushed scarlet, and Cindy Lou took a tremulous breath before answering.

"Well, I guess it ain't so secret anymore," she said with a brave attempt at a smile. "But, you know what? I'm glad it's out in the open. Now we don't have to sneak around. They don't care, right, Janet? Jason?"

Janet didn't say anything; instead, she inspected Bud, who absently stroked his hand. His left ring finger, to be more specific.

After another few awkward moments of silence, he spoke. "Listen, I don't want any trouble. I mean, this was just for fun, right?"

"Just for . . . just for fun?" Cindy Lou's voice was barely louder than a whisper. Her pale skin flushed scarlet from her cheeks all the way down her shoulders, like beer foam spilling over the edge of a glass.

Bud shifted his weight and said, "I mean . . . I, uh . . . I've got a wife and two kids at home."

Cindy Lou sucked in a noisy breath and her piercing wail flooded the room. "A wife? Kids? What are you talkin' about? I mentioned Chip a dozen times, and how he's leaving for college soon, and I'll be all alone—and you never thought to mention your dang wife? Your k-k-kids?"

Janet's face felt pinched, and she was furious that Cindy Lou had let herself be played so fantastically. What was it with everyone in her life being unwilling to see the truth of things? Jason was so intent on not helping the police that he couldn't see he also wasn't helping himself. Her renters were a mess and had no money and no jobs, yet thought they could sign a lease and foster a baby.

Now Cindy Lou was shocked that secret alley sex wasn't the launching point for a long-term relationship?

"Wake up, Cindy Lou," Janet snapped, glaring at Bud. "You're Dumpster diving with this guy, and you think he doesn't have a secret? Use your head!" She looked down her nose at Bud, who flinched under her cold stare. "That's a man with something to hide."

Her eyes shot over to Cindy Lou in time to see her employee's face crumple completely. The bartender ran, sobbing, from the room. Bud slunk out to the parking lot, and drove away.

Janet bit her lip. The silence coming from the other side of the office was louder than Bud's truck. In her peripheral vision, she saw Jason cross his arms. She could feel him staring at her but couldn't quite bring herself to meet his eye.

"What's wrong with you, Janet? Do you think Cindy Lou needed to hear that from you just now? Where's your compassion?"

"Compassion?" She rubbed her hands over her face and sank heavily down onto the threadbare couch. "Compassion leaves you with broke renters, crappy employees who disregard what you say, and police trying to dig up dirt on you that doesn't exist. I don't think we can afford to be compassionate anymore, Jason!"

Disappointment wafted from her boyfriend like freshly applied aftershave. He grabbed his coat and wallet from the desk, his face taut, his lips tight. "I'm going home," he said. "I have work to do."

He walked out of the office without a backward glance.

"Oh . . . okay," Janet said to his retreating figure. "I'll, ah . . . I'll see you . . ." But she was alone. He was gone.

The phone rang and she answered wearily.

"I can't come in tonight for my shift. I'm sick," a very healthy-sounding Frank said.

"Sick?"

"Yeah, sorry."

"What kind of sick?" Janet asked. Here, finally, was someone at whom she could justify being angry, but she was too tired to expend the effort.

"The kind of sick where I don't feel like working, okay?"

"Well . . . I don't have anyone else I can call to come in—"

"Now that I think of it, I'd better just cancel my shift tomorrow, too. Might still be contagious."

In the background, she heard laughing. Maybe some music, too.

An inner calm took over, and her clenched shoulders relaxed. She took a deep, cleansing breath. "Frank, don't come back. You're fired."

"But—but, Janet—"

She gently placed the phone down onto the receiver before resting her head on her folded arms.

The door opened and Cindy Lou murmured, "I'm sorry, Janet. I'm sorry I'm such a dang disappointment," then slunk back into the bar like a beaten dog.

She scrubbed a hand over her face. Why couldn't she have handled that better? She'd never set out to be the kind of boss who'd make an employee cry. Now Cindy Lou was apologizing to her. Cindy Lou! Apologizing to her! Her most loyal employee, who never called in sick and always had a smile for everyone, had just been emotionally torpedoed by a lover—and Janet had piled on the way Frank would have.

She groaned at her own behavior. Her life had begun to feel like a runaway train, and she was flying off the rails along with it.

In the bar, Cindy Lou slumped over the ice chest, staring dejectedly out at the front door.

Janet leaned up against the cooler too, so they were shoulder to shoulder. "I'm sorry I'm such a bitch." She took her wallet out of her back pocket, then peeled a dollar out of the fold and tucked it into the swear jar. "I've been a hell of a jerk"—another dollar—"but I'm going to own it. I was mad at Bud and took it out on you. That wasn't fair."

Cindy Lou nodded, but her eyes didn't leave the door.

Janet blew out a sigh. "I should tell you that I fired Frank, that asshole." Two dollars that time. "And I will try to stop being such an award-winning cu—"

"Janet, no!" Cindy Lou gasped.

"Okay—bitch"—Janet stifled a grin as she put a fiver into the jar—"for at least the rest of the night so that this shitty day"— another dollar—"can end with enough money in the swear jar for one hell of an extra tip for my employees. I mean, ffff—" Cindy Lou slapped a hand over her mouth to cover a smile. "Ffffuck, it's been a long day." She ended with the final bill in her wallet, a twenty. "Do you forgive me?"

Cindy Lou nodded. "I was a fool, Janet. I know that."

"And I should have been there to support you. Not knock you down even more."

Cindy Lou threw an arm over Janet's shoulders. "You fired Frank?"

"Uh-huh."

"Well. There's one good thing about today."

———

Four hours later, business had picked up and they had a sizable crowd—especially for a Sunday night.

"Watch Jimmy," Janet said to Cindy Lou. "He might need a taxi." The new customer appeared to be on a mission to drink as many happy-hour specials as possible.

Nell had sidled up to him and they were discussing cataracts, with Jimmy boisterously advocating skipping surgery and just going blind. Nell's extra-large glasses turned opaque under the lights as she pondered that idea. Janet grinned, then turned when the door opened and a crowd poured in.

They really could have used Frank that night, so despite their argument, Janet texted Jason, asking him to come in. The bar was nearing capacity, and she didn't have anyone to check IDs at the door, so drink orders were backing up while she and Cindy Lou checked IDs before each order.

A small commotion at the front door caught her eye as she pulled a pint. "What's going on?"

"Huh?" Cindy Lou opened two bottles at once and slid them across the bar to waiting customers.

"Nothing, nothing." Janet opened a tab for someone but scanned the front of the bar until she spotted it. Well, her. Two people moved to reveal a woman slumped against the door, preventing anyone else from coming in. The door rattled, and the woman flipped her head up. Her long blond hair parted, revealing Larsa.

"Larsa, hon, what are you doing?" Janet called. She was so distracted, beer spilled over the side of a pint glass and down her hand. "Damn it!" She wiped off the glass and handed it across the bar. "Cindy Lou, I'll be right back."

"Seriously?" Cindy Lou looked over and swiped the back of her hand across her forehead. When she saw the situation at the front door she nodded. "Get on back here ay-sap, boss!"

Janet hustled around the side of the bar and made her way through the crowd to the front door.

Larsa chuckled when the door behind her pulsed again as someone tried to push it open from the outside.

"Larsa? Are you okay?"

The other woman's eyes opened wide. "Janet. I've had a day, you know?"

"I was wondering where you were!"

"You were?" Larsa drew the hair away from her face and held it back on top of her head, her eyes welling up with tears.

"Well, yeah, sure. Come on up to the bar, away from the door," she added, reaching out to guide Larsa away from the entrance.

Larsa finally leaned forward, just as the door pushed open. The unexpected bump sent Ike's daughter sprawling into a group of people nearby.

A beer from that group flew through the air, spraying a stream of liquid across Larsa's face as the bottle plunged back down to the ground.

Janet and Larsa locked eyes seconds before Larsa's tongue snaked out and tasted the beer dripping down her cheek. Janet's jaw dropped at the move, and Larsa's eyes widened when she realized what she'd done.

"Oh!" she gasped.

"It doesn't count!" Janet said with conviction. "That doesn't . . ."

Larsa mopped her sleeve across her face and tried to stand, but her legs were unsteady. While Janet swooped down to rescue the beer bottle before someone stepped on it, Larsa wailed, "Oh my God!"

"Larsa! Larsa, it's going to be all right!"

But the other woman fell against the wall, shook her head, and pushed back off before stumbling through the crowd of people.

By the time Janet made her way out into the parking lot, Larsa was gone.

She rubbed a hand across her forehead and blew out a noisy breath through her nose. "What in the hell just happened?" She was worried about Larsa, but there wasn't anything she could do about the other woman now. She headed back inside and took her place behind the bar, handing out drinks as fast as people could pay for them.

"Don, Chris, are you ready for another, or are you headed home?" she asked two men seated at bar stools in front of her.

She scanned the room as she waited for their answer, and did a double take when her renters walked into the bar with their baby.

"We have good news," Mel said with a guarded smile. "We found some money to put toward rent. It won't cover everything we owe, but it's a good start."

Janet's eyes narrowed. "Oh yeah?" She dried her hands on a rag tucked into her apron string. "How much?"

"It's enough for this month's rent and half the security deposit. Not perfect, I know, but it's a start, don't you think?" Kat looked hopeful as she held out an envelope; Janet took it and peered inside at a stack of cash.

"Do you think you can pay next month's rent and the other half of the deposit in thirty days?"

Mel stole a glance at her partner before nodding. "Yes."

Kat started yammering on about all of the baby's accomplishments that day, which included things like smiling and touching her toes.

Janet wasn't impressed, but she also wasn't really paying attention. She looked inside the envelope again, then interrupted Kat. "Where did you get this money?"

"Well, the timing just couldn't have been better," Kat answered when Mel didn't. "It's from the state for child support for the baby. We had so much help from friends offering to donate items that we don't need it."

Janet stared wordlessly at her tenants for a moment while she gathered her thoughts.

Hours ago, she might have told them to save the money for the baby, not use it to pay their rent. She might have told them that from what she'd heard, babies grew quickly, needed new clothes every other week, and ran through formula like the people in her bar ran through beer, and they'd likely need the money *for the baby*, as the state intended.

But.

She was a new woman. A more responsible user of words. So, instead, she said, "What about the other half? You think the state's going to cover that for you, too?" But before they could respond, Janet's attention was drawn to a commotion on the other end of the bar.

Jimmy, the customer Janet had recently identified as being on the edge, had officially fallen over it. He leaned over the bar and yelled at Cindy Lou, his finger shaking just inches from her face. Nell scurried off her bar stool and hustled away.

"Cut off? Who are you to cut me off? You don't make the— the—argh!" He'd leaned too far forward on the stool and misjudged where the bar was. His elbow missed the counter completely, and he pitched forward and fell off the side of his stool to the floor, narrowly missing the corner of the bar with his chin as he went down.

He braced himself against the floor and Cindy Lou took the break to call the cab company. She turned to Janet and held up two fingers, indicating his ride was only a couple of minutes away.

In the meantime, Jimmy was gearing up for another outburst. His fingers reached up for the edge of the countertop. Janet could see the wheels turning—albeit slowly—and his face growing redder by the moment.

Her mouth twisted in distaste. With Frank fired, it was up to her to physically remove this unruly customer. "Boy, did you pick the wrong day to mess with me," she muttered as she rounded the corner of the bar. But before she got to Jimmy, another set of hands latched onto the scruff of his neck. He was cut off mid-snarl as Mel literally lifted him off the floor and set him down on his feet hard before propelling him forward.

Cindy Lou, the receiver still pressed to her ear, called out, "His ride is thirty seconds away!"

Mel slammed the idiot down into a seat by the door and pressed her hands against his shoulders in a death grip, keeping him in place until Cindy Lou said, "Now!" and pointed to the door.

Mel hefted him back to his feet and escorted him out into the parking lot. The taxi pulled up in front of the glass door and Mel deposited Jimmy carefully into the backseat. She slammed the door, then tapped the roof and watched the car drive away, her arms hanging loosely at her sides.

The bar had fallen quiet during the scuffle, but when Mel walked back inside the establishment, the other customers erupted in cheers. Mel's grim expression didn't change, but Kat squealed, clapped, and hugged her when she arrived back at the bar.

"So, anyway, what were you saying about money?" Mel asked, as if they hadn't been interrupted.

Janet's mouth hung open again. She had no idea what kind of background Mel had, but that hadn't been learned in a simple self-defense class. Before she could second-guess herself, Janet said, "I was saying you need some—some money, that is—and you can earn it by working for me. I need a bouncer. Are you interested?"

"What kind of hours are we talking about?" Janet glanced at Cindy Lou in disbelief before Mel, her face impassive, said, "I'm just messing with you. Of course I want the job! Obviously, I need it—we need it."

Janet smiled faintly. She wanted to know more about Mel's work history—hell, her life history—but before she could ask where she had learned to kick ass, a man walked into the bar. He rubbed his sweaty hands on his pants, leaving dark streaks behind, then scanned the crowd.

"Abe?" Janet called out. "What are you doing here?"

CHAPTER NINETEEN

The tall, sandy-haired man scanned the perimeter of the space, before his eyes landed on Janet. He nodded solemnly, then walked forward.

"Is . . ." He looked around the room again, zipping and unzipping his light jacket in time with his foot tapping against the floor. He finally brought his eyes back to Janet and tried again. "Is Larsa here?"

"No. No, she's not."

"Oh, I thought . . . I thought you said she was going to be here until the police caught Ike's killer."

"Yes, she was in a bit of a state tonight. I don't know why, she rushed out before I could ask."

"Oh!" His hand stilled when his zipper was halfway down the coat. "Did the police make an arrest?"

She blew out a sigh. "No . . . I don't think so, anyway." She looked at the door, wondering how she could check on Larsa. Until that night she'd thought she might never get the woman out of her bar; now she was worried she wouldn't be able to find her. "Hey, can I get you a beer? On the house." She wanted to know why he was here, and if Larsa couldn't ask, she was going to.

He held Janet's gaze for a long moment before finally nodding. She went behind the bar, pulled two draft beers, and carried them to an empty table in the corner. Larsa's table, she thought with a grimace.

"I see you haven't had your finger taken care of," Abe said as he sat down and shrugged out of his coat.

She plonked the beers down. "I'm going to a walk-in clinic first thing tomorrow," she said with conviction. Her finger had seemed to get worse after she'd treated it at home, instead of better.

Abe took a zip-top bag out of his pocket and set it on the table. "I grabbed a few things from home that might help, just in case you still needed it—and I see you certainly do." He opened the bag and unfolded a large gauze rectangle, a scalpel, a needle, and two small bottles of liquid. He pointed to the smaller bottle. "The iodine will clean out the wound after we drain it." Then he picked up the larger bottle and the syringe.

"Whoa, wait just a minute. You're going to dr—drain it?" She gulped and her heart rate zipped into overdrive. She looked down at her finger, certain that the throbbing she felt would be visible from the outside. It wasn't.

"Don't worry, I'll numb it first." Abe took the very worrisome-looking syringe and drew some liquid from the larger bottle. "Lidocaine," he said while snapping on blue gloves before he held out his hand. She reluctantly rested her hand on his and he got to work. "The first poke is the only one you'll feel." The needle hovered over her hand; she peeled her eyes away from the shiny tip, and as soon as she looked up, Abe struck the needle down into her finger.

"Shh-YOW!" She tried to jerk away, but Abe was surprisingly strong. After a moment, though, the burning sensation faded, and for the first time in days, she didn't feel the constant throb of pain pulsing in her finger.

"See? I told you," he said with a smile. He put the syringe down and picked up the scalpel. "I could tell this was pretty painful when you were at my house." He chatted as if they were at a ball game, discussing how the season was going. She watched him work, fascinated that, even as he drew the blade along the lateral line of her fingertip, she felt nothing.

"Yup, look at that," he said as a yellowish-green liquid dripped from her fingertip onto the gauzy pad below. "That was festering inside you. Time was not your friend—this finger was only getting worse every hour you left it untreated." He poked and prodded around all sides of the cut skin. Whatever he saw made him nod, and then he poured liquid from the small vial directly onto the wound. "The iodine will disinfect anything bad that's still in there. Incidentally, where did you get injured?"

"Back there, cutting lemons."

"Well, next time, I'd just pour some eighty-to-one-hundred-proof alcohol right over the cut. That would do a pretty good job clearing it right up."

She sighed. Surrounded by alcohol, and it had taken her four days just to buy rubbing alcohol at the drugstore. By then, it had been too late.

Abe bandaged her finger with a simple wrap and then set about cleaning up his operating station. Within minutes, he was taking off his gloves and nodding at her hand in satisfaction.

"It should feel a lot better by tomorrow," he said, stuffing the trash back in the bag.

"Thanks." Janet inspected her finger with a wide smile. Abe held his glass out and they clinked before both taking a sip. After a moment of silence, Janet said, "Why were you looking for Larsa?"

Abe blinked. He took another sip of beer before he answered. "I feel . . . I don't know, a strange connection with her." Janet raised her eyebrows and he continued. "Her father irrevocably changed my life ten years ago—and hers, too. Now that he's dead, I feel the weight of the situation. I can talk about it with you and I can talk about it with my wife, but I really feel like I need to talk about it with someone else who feels that same weight."

"Wow." Janet leaned back against the leather of the booth. She had felt many things in her life, but she'd usually wanted to feel them alone. She opened her mouth to say as much when a screech from the doorway of the bar brought the regular din of the crowd to silence. Abe's head whipped around and panic swooped across his face like a sudden storm.

"Who is—" Before she could finish her question, though, Abe stood, an uncertain, tremulous smile on his face.

"Vanessa, what are you doing here?"

"What am *I* doing here?" Vanessa stalked toward Abe and Janet like a mountain lion, her long, dark hair loose and wild around her face. "What am *I* do—" She broke off and huffed out three rapid breaths, blinking in rhythm with her gasps. Finally she snarled, "What are *you* doing here?"

"Vanessa, you remember Janet, the owner of this establishment. Janet, I'm sure you remember my wife." Abe scratched his head as he looked at Vanessa's furious expression.

"I knew it," Vanessa whispered. By now, the crowd had returned to its normal volume, although they were still getting some furtive glances and outright stares from the tables nearby. "I just knew it, Abe Nyack. I knew you were having an affair, but I never thought you'd stoop so low as to mess around with someone like *her*." She jabbed a finger toward Janet and glowered in her direction before turning a venomous eye back to her husband.

"Hey!" Janet said, affronted by the accusation and rankled by the revulsion.

"Vanessa, what are you talking about? I came here to find—"

"Oh, I know exactly what you're looking for, mister, and you know where you're not going to find it anymore? At home. You better pack your bags if you're shacking up with her! You're sure as hell not welcome in my bed!"

Abe opened his mouth, but Vanessa cut him off again, fury turning her face purplish red.

"You know what? You almost had me convinced that you were at work last week when you were out all night, but then your secretary called and said she didn't know how to enter the receipt from the coffee shop into the accounting system. 'Was it business or pleasure?' she asked, and I said, 'The coffee shop at the hospital?' She said, 'No, the one downtown—the twenty-four-hour café.' Now, are you going to try and tell me you worked on a patient at four in the morning *in a café?*" Her eyes cut accusingly toward Janet and then back to her husband. "I guess I don't have to ask what kind of 'work' you were doing!" She hit the air quotes around the word "work" like it was a knockout punch.

"What are you talking about?" Abe asked.

"Are you going to make me say it?" Vanessa asked, her voice rising again to a shriek. "Were you with her Thursday night, Abe? How long has this been going on?"

"No, no—" Janet tried to interrupt to set her straight, but it was like stepping in front of a rabid dog.

Vanessa turned to growl at Janet. "I know exactly what you two were doing, but I am a lady, so I won't say it out loud, you man-stealing *whore.*"

Janet looked to Abe for support, but he stared at his wife, slack-jawed. He looked like a man who'd been caught, but not like a man who'd been caught cheating.

Vanessa was gearing up to launch into falsetto when Janet yelled, "Wait just a minute! I wasn't with your husband that night, Vanessa. My boyfriend and I were home together—at our house."

"Oh, sure. That's a pretty convenient excuse!" Vanessa snapped. "What were you doing?"

"Just about everything," a deep voice rumbled past Janet's ear. "And I'll be honest: we tried a few new things that night that I won't soon forget." Jason's hands smoothed over her shoulders and ran down her arms possessively. "A lady probably couldn't handle the details, though," he added. "A woman could." He squeezed Janet's shoulders and then wrapped his arms around her chest.

Janet leaned into her amazing boyfriend and noted with satisfaction that Vanessa's breathing didn't slow, only now, her chest heaved with anticipation. Abe didn't even look at Jason, just rubbed the back of his neck with one hand and stared blankly at his wife.

The color drained from Vanessa's face until she was as pale as their lightest beer. "I . . . I don't . . . ," Vanessa stuttered, her mind seemingly unable to make the transition from woman scorned to woman stunned. Abe took the momentary silence to press his hand into her back and usher her out the door. Janet heard him mumbling apologies to the crowd as they left.

"Thanks, Jason, I—"

"You're not off the hook—not by a long shot. I just couldn't stand to see that woman try to drag you down. I came in to help out because it's busy, but we've got things to discuss, Janet." He took the beer out of her hand and drained half of it before turning away and crossing to the bar. Cindy Lou gave him a wide berth as he rounded the corner.

Janet didn't want to think about what she'd done wrong, so she thought about Abe instead. If he hadn't been at home with his wife and he also hadn't been at work, where exactly was Abe on the night Ike was killed?

CHAPTER TWENTY

Business stayed strong long after Vanessa and Abe left, and although Jason wasn't talking to her, Janet was glad to have him there. With Mel manning the door and Jason, Janet, and Cindy Lou pouring drinks and clearing tables, they fell into a rhythm that barely kept them from drowning in drink orders and dirty tables.

But as the bar emptied, Janet felt her boyfriend staring at her, disappointed, and a faint throb of guilt bubbled up the walls of her stomach. Watching Abe's wife accuse him in such a broken way had made her appreciate all the people in her life just a little bit more—especially Jason.

Finally, as she bused a table in the corner and he pushed the mop broodingly past, she said, "Okay, all right? I get it. I'm sorry I was a jerk. I—I already apologized to Cindy Lou. Is that what you've been waiting to hear?"

Jason didn't say anything. The only sign that he'd heard her was that he stopped pushing the mop forward and instead worked on a stubborn splotch on the floor.

"I was frustrated." Janet pushed her hair away from her face and stood from the table she'd been wiping down. Although she was feeling contrition, she couldn't help but put her hands on her hips as she said, louder than she'd intended, "I know that's no excuse for how I treated Cindy Lou today, and I'm sorry."

Jason looked up. "It's not just Cindy Lou. What about Elizabeth and the renters? You've been too hard on everyone lately!" She threw her hands up with a groan and opened her mouth to explain, but he cut her off. "See, you're not even really sorry. You're just going through the motions," he scoffed. "Things aren't good, Janet."

"What do you mean?" Janet asked. Her hands dropped from her hips and dangled by her sides.

"They're not good," he repeated, "and I—I need some space."

Her heart stuttered once, twice, then stopped beating all together. "What do you—space?"

"I'm sorry, I just—I have to be honest. I'm really disappointed in you."

Her mouth went dry, and she scooped up a glass of water from the table. It was halfway to her lips when she remembered it wasn't hers—just a dirty glass from a random customer.

She set the glass down hard. "Disappointed? I'll tell you what's disappointing. You've had your security system back up and running since *Friday*, but you haven't told the police? You haven't checked the other outside cameras to see whether we might know who the killer is?"

"Janet, I'm not going to help the police when they're so determined to trap me—"

"You're so busy not helping the police, you've become a target of their investigation, and now I'm getting wrapped up in it, too! So guess what? *I'm* disappointed in *you!*"

Jason's step faltered, and for a moment he looked at Janet with a kind of sad, injured stare that seemed to sink straight into her soul. Before she could take it back, apologize, beg for his forgiveness, though, he backed away.

"I need a break." She nodded mutely, a sudden rush of emotion bringing moisture to her eyes that she had to blink away forcefully. "I can't help with—with *this* anymore, do you understand what I'm saying?"

She looked up sharply at his wording in time to see him wince. "What does that mean?"

"It means I'm going."

"Jason, what are you—"

"Good night, Janet."

She hadn't moved yet when his headlights swept across the room as he backed out of his parking space.

"What the . . ." What had just happened?

She finished clearing the last table and turned to find Mel and Cindy Lou staring uncomfortably at each other.

"Go home," she said, a sudden exhaustion taking over that was so complete, she could hardly stand. "I'll see you both tomorrow. Cindy Lou—"

"I know, boss. You don't have to say anything."

Cindy Lou stepped forward and flung her arm around Janet's shoulders. "You know I love you, boss. So does Jason." She squeezed her shoulders. "See you tomorrow."

Cindy Lou and Mel walked out together and Janet finished closing up the bar, flicking away a tear when she locked the front door. She opened all the miniblinds and turned off the neon signs. Then she pressed down on the light panel, plunging the bar into darkness.

She took a gulp of air, then another, trying to keep it together. But her knees felt weak, and alone in her bar, she sank down against the wall and finally allowed the breakdown to come.

Sobs racked her body. Her frustration, her anger, and even her sorrow and embarrassment came in hot waves. She was a failure. She was a disappointment to her boyfriend. She was a bad boss. The list seemed endless, and she wallowed in it deeply, giving voice to all her insecurities.

She sure as hell wasn't going to do this again, so she might as well get it all out now, alone, when no one could see.

When the tears slowed to a trickle, she took a shaky breath, and then another.

"Damn it, Jason," she said to the empty room, frowning through her tears. She hated when things didn't make sense, and her boyfriend had her twisted in knots. The more she thought about it, the more it didn't make sense. Why hadn't Jason checked the other outside cameras? Why was he leaving her exposed to cops who were determined to see the worst in her—in them?

She wiped her eyes and sat up straighter. Was it possible that *Jason* was the one hiding something? Had she misjudged him from the beginning? She snorted into the quiet room. Maybe her dad was wrong; maybe she wasn't the great judge of character he thought she was.

Under normal circumstances, she'd have driven straight home and confronted Jason, but he'd said he wanted—no, needed—space. And she was going to honor that.

She made up the couch in the office, fumbling with the blanket, her mind racing and frozen in turns.

She'd been alone before, and if she had to, she could handle it, of course she could. But that didn't stop fresh tears from leaking out of her eyes.

Curled uncomfortably on the threadbare couch, she tried to distract herself by focusing on Ike's murder. Alone in the office, staring at the ceiling and listening to the low, steady buzz of the halogen light at the desk, she didn't believe for a minute that Jason hadn't found the video from the night Ike was killed; it would have been the first thing he looked for after Wex hacked him back into his own operating system. Even with the tape covering the back alley camera, other exterior cameras would have captured something about Ike's death. So what was Jason hiding?

CHAPTER TWENTY-ONE

The next morning, Janet awoke to pounding at the office door. She had slept fitfully, tossing and turning on the uncomfortable couch. The pounding continued, and she stood unsteadily, wincing as her bare foot touched the cold concrete floor.

"What?" she yelled—or at least tried to. The word came out like she'd run it through the dishwasher, muddled and wet. She cracked the miniblinds open and winced again as the bright sunlight hit her red, swollen eyes. Detective Finch stood on the other side of the door, flipping his key ring around like a lifeguard with a whistle. "What do you want?" she asked, refusing to open the door.

She'd thoroughly read the subpoena the day before; they had no right to search her office, but she wasn't going to take any chances.

"Janet Black, you look like hell."

"Seriously?" she called back. "You're seriously going to open with that line?"

He barked out a laugh and banged on the door again.

She wrenched it open, and the blast of heat hit her in the face like a nine-iron.

Finch assessed her from top to bottom, with the blanket

wrapped around her, one foot bare. "Have you been crying?" he asked with a deepening frown.

"No," Janet answered mulishly. "Goddamn air conditioner is stuck on, and the wool blanket I found in the closet is irritating my skin, but if I took it off my face, I was freezing."

"Is that right?" He stared past her to a pile of tissues by the couch.

She pulled the door closer. "What do you want?"

"I just wanted to ask, one last time, if there's anything you're not telling us about Ike, about Elizabeth—about anything at all."

"Are you for real? Your department just ransacked my house, accused my boyfriend of a felony, and basically told me I'll lose everything no matter what. You're not welcome here."

"A man is dead!" He stared at her, a sudden heat in his voice. "I don't get the impression that you even care."

"Of course I care," Janet said, wrapping the blanket tighter, despite the hot day, "but I care more that you seem hell-bent on pinning a murder on an innocent person, instead of actually solving the crime, which means whoever's guilty is getting a free pass!" She glared at the cop and stepped back to close the door.

"I don't want any surprises, Black. Do you understand?" The sunlight cast shadows on the wrinkles on his face, making him look older and more haggard than usual.

"Yeah, well, me neither. No more Sunday subpoenas. Our lawyer's going to . . ." Her mind, still fuzzy from sleep, couldn't come up with any kind of credible threat, and Finch snorted when she fell silent.

"Despite what you might think from watching TV, this case is getting colder by the minute. Chances are it will fade away, just like too many others."

She watched him walk across the lot to his car and felt an odd prickle of confusion. Even as O'Dell doubled down on pinning the crime on Jason, Finch seemed to suggest they were out of leads.

Which was it?

Before she could deep-dive into Finch's motivations, her phone jangled in her pocket.

Her heart leapt. Was Jason calling to talk?

She fumbled to answer the call before it went to voicemail.

"Oh," she said, unable to hide her disappointment. "Hey, Dad."

"Jason said you need some background checks on the people involved in this murder. Give me their names and I'll fast-track it for you. I should have the info to you later today—maybe tomorrow if I can't get ahold of the right person."

"What?" Janet stared at her phone as if it were a bug.

"Jason said there's a lot you guys don't know about Ike Freeman's death—and there are a few things Jason can't tell you. So, I'm going to bridge the gap for you. How about that? Your old man coming to the rescue. I like the sound of that, don't you?"

"No," she replied. She actually hated the sound of that. Her voice took on a wheedling tone. "What does he know about this crime that he can't tell me?"

"It's complicated."

"Yeah." She laughed humorlessly. "I guess."

Because she couldn't think of a reason not to, she listed off all the names of the people she'd come into contact with since Ike's murder, including Ollie's family and roommates.

When she finished, her dad said, "I'll get back to you with anything that sticks out. You okay?"

"Sure. I—well, I will be."

"Love you, Janet."

"I, ah . . . I love you, too, Dad."

"I know." He disconnected without another word.

She folded the itchy blanket over the back of the couch, then pulled on her clothes and shoes and stood, staring out the window.

So Jason had secrets. But she didn't think he was the only one. The more she thought about Finch's visit, the less she liked it. Jason had managed to circumvent O'Dell's computer grab in large part because Finch had warned them about the pending subpoena on Friday. Was that a lapse in judgment on Finch's part, or something else?

Now Finch was telling Janet the case was cold, and whoever was guilty likely wouldn't be caught, even though O'Dell had just made a major move against Jason.

What was Finch's game?

Sunlight flared off the back windshield of a black truck up the block as it pulled away from the curb and into traffic, and she scrunched her eyes shut against the glare, but the image burned into the back of her eyelids.

Suddenly, her eyes flew open, and, squinting, she stared at the space where the truck had been.

Surely not, it couldn't be—

"Shit!" She grabbed her keys and took off at a run through the small parking lot, then skidded to a stop at the empty spot a block away. She was at a drab, isolated stretch of street, usually littered with trash and bordered by nothing but the parking lot for the Spot; a run-down, abandoned house; and a city bus bench. She couldn't believe her eyes. Parked less than two hundred feet from the back door of the bar, Elizabeth's car was wedged behind a crappy camper trailer. It had been invisible from the office window until the huge black pickup truck that had obscured it from behind pulled away.

The old, gray Chrysler Sebring was unremarkable, save for the aggressively pink rabbit's foot hanging from the rearview mirror. It was Elizabeth's car.

She tried all the doors, but they were locked. She leaned in close to the trunk and gingerly sniffed, then sank against the car when she didn't pick up any dead-body smells.

She rifled through the handful of parking tickets that were shoved under the windshield wipers. The oldest one was dated the day that Janet found Ike's body. Elizabeth's car hadn't moved since her last shift at the Spot. But where was Elizabeth? The question now seemed more important than ever.

She hit the roof of the car in frustration. According to O'Dell, Finch had checked out Elizabeth's place—and nothing had been amiss. Was that true?

She shivered despite the heat. What if it wasn't? Elizabeth's car had been abandoned and no one had heard from her—including that nosy neighbor—since Ike was killed. She was the last person known to have the keys to Ike's car, which was also missing.

Janet hit the roof again, this time with more force. She'd let Elizabeth down so far, but it was time to correct that. She was going back to Elizabeth's apartment, and she wouldn't stop digging until she found her.

She gulped. Hopefully there wouldn't be any actual digging involved.

———

The apartment manager, a slight, tanned, skinny man with shockingly white teeth named Dale, frowned. "It's an unusual request," he said, scratching his chin, "and I'm afraid it's not allowed."

"I'm just really concerned about her, you understand. She hasn't been to work in days."

"Well, it's against the rules laid out in section one twenty-four of the lessee's handbook." Dale flipped through a three-ring binder he'd just pulled off the shelf behind his desk, then held out the book to Janet.

"I know, and I know you just let the police in, but we still haven't heard from her—"

"Police? The police haven't been on the property since Arty McMaster had a kegger that got out of control about five weeks ago—"

"It's not a secret," she interrupted. "I know they didn't find anything—but I'm still worried." She shot Dale her most ingratiating smile. "I kind of thought, with your help, I could just poke around and see if anything looks out of place."

"I don't know what you're talking about. You're the first person asking about Elizabeth," he said, scratching his head.

"Detective Finch from KPD wasn't here?"

"Nope, and I'd know—I'm the only one authorized to open doors without the lessee's consent. It's right here in the binder," he said, pointing at the book again.

She closed her eyes, glad she'd come, and then opened them wide, her friendliest smile imploring Dale to help. "I need to get into Elizabeth's apartment to make sure she's okay. You can be a hero today or a zero, Dale. It's up to you."

Five minutes later, she skulked in the alcove by Elizabeth's door. Who knew Dale would choose to be a zero? She'd have to work on that smile.

Janet slipped her lock-picking set out of her pocket. With the tension wrench at the bottom of the keyhole, she raked her favorite pick across the top edge until she felt the final pin budge. She cranked the lock over and pushed the door open.

The whole thing took less than thirty seconds, and she dropped her tools back in her pocket before walking into Elizabeth's home.

A burst of color hit her when she stepped over the threshold, and the furniture was unexpectedly floral. She guessed the couch and armchair had been her mother's, because they were well-made pieces that didn't match the other, self-assembled, Scandinavian items in the room. It was like midcentury modern had met a flowery explosion from 1996.

Clothes and shoes littered the main room, as if Elizabeth left things right where she took them off without regard for a laundry basket or shoe rack. Well-traversed paths darkened the cream-colored carpeting between rooms. On the edge of one such path, a huge stain flowered out from under the dining room table.

She hadn't heard a sound since the slow creak of the door when she'd pushed it open. "Elizabeth?" she called out.

There was no response.

She walked through the main room into the dining room and tried again. "Elizabeth? Are you here? It's Janet . . . from the Spot?"

No one answered, and she crouched down to touch the edge of the large stain on the floor, only to snatch her fingers back. It was soaking wet. The wet spot spanned half the room. On the table above lay a broken bowl, a cutting board, and a hammer. It looked like some liquid had spilled out of the broken bowl and poured off the table. An oval-shaped section of the wood finish had bubbled up, ruined.

"What is going on?" She breathed in a smoky smell and, with a mounting sense of unease, moved away from the wet spot and walked through the dining room into the kitchen. "Shit," she muttered slowly. The microwave lay, broken, on the floor; black scorch marks feathered up the cabinet to the counter above. A smoky burnt-plastic smell filled her nostrils.

It looked like one holy hell of a battle had gone down in Elizabeth's home, but who'd been fighting?

Perhaps more important, who had won?

Janet backed out of the kitchen and stared, once again, at the wet spot under the table. Terrible thoughts raced through her mind. The hammer glinted menacingly in the sunlight from a nearby window. Had it been used as a weapon? What had happened to Elizabeth? Was she caught up in a murder? Was the wet area where someone had tried to clean blood? Each scenario she came up with was worse than the last.

She sucked in a breath at a sudden noise from the hallway outside. She had to get out before someone found her here. At the door, she saw both Finch's and O'Dell's business cards lying on the ground—they must have fallen when she'd walked in. She pressed her ear against the metal and started counting. When she got to thirty without hearing anything else, she carefully stepped back outside, then cringed when the door swung shut. The crack of noise echoed in the concrete walkway.

Elizabeth's old, crotchety neighbor's dog barked and yipped up a storm at the sound. She turned and headed toward the parking lot but froze when she heard another door open. The dog's yipping was now louder, a tiny, all-out roar.

"You again?" Paul said when he spotted her. "What are you doing here?" The dog lunged toward her at the end of his lead, barking his heart out.

She turned, her friendliest smile plastered back on. "I thought I'd try Elizabeth one more time, but she didn't answer. You haven't heard from her, have you?"

"No, but I thought I heard a door." He crossed his arms and raised one eyebrow.

"Must have been a car in the lot," Janet said.

He frowned, and the dog lunged toward Janet again.

She wiped what felt like a sheepish smile off her face and said, "Well. Let her know I'm looking for her, okay?"

"You and the rest of the city," Paul said.

"Did you see a Detective Finch Saturday?" Janet asked.

"Nope. Saturday was quiet. Just how I like it." He stared pointedly from Janet to the parking lot with a sour expression.

Instead of saying goodbye, she frowned back at Paul, then sidestepped the noisy pup and headed for her car, and home.

She tapped her fingers against the steering wheel at a stoplight; the sound was like a hammer, pounding nails of worry into her brain. Something bad had happened at Elizabeth's apartment —or something illegal—and Finch had clearly lied about checking on her well-being.

Finding Elizabeth's place in such disarray changed everything. Janet was the only "family" Elizabeth had, and now it was up to her to be there for the young woman. If it was already too late—if Janet's worst fears about what had happened at Elizabeth's apartment proved true—then it was up to her to find out who had done what to Elizabeth and why.

CHAPTER TWENTY-TWO

"Hey!" Mel walked over to Janet's car as soon as she pulled up to the curb in front of the house. "Is everything okay?"

"Sure," Janet answered. Mel raised her eyebrows and she blew out a sigh. "Well, no, everything's not okay. My bartender's missing, now presumed injured or dead; Jason 'needs a break,' whatever the hell that means; and I have no idea what I'm supposed to do—" She'd been about to say "without him," but her throat constricted and she choked out a stuttered breath before saying, "No idea what to do about this whole situation."

When she looked up Mel was staring contemplatively at her own front door.

"I'm sorry—you already have your hands full with a new baby to take care of. How is . . . Mabel. No, no . . . ah, Mazel?"

"*Hazel* is great," Mel said, with a smile that appeared and disappeared so fast Janet wasn't sure she'd seen it.

"Great?"

"Well . . ." Mel ran a hand through her hair. "It's just . . . exhausting, okay, it's freaking exhausting. Kat's got this maternal thing down, but I feel a little lost. And tired, did I say that already?"

"Come on. We need drinks," Janet said over her shoulder as she unlocked her door. "You tell me your problems, I'll tell you mine." She led Mel to the minibar. "What can I get you? I'm having a Bloody Mary."

"Make it two," Mel answered, taking the knife away from Janet and hacking two wedges from the lime sitting on the counter.

"Jesus, what did that lime do to you?"

Mel shrugged and said, "Kat's the cook, sorry."

Janet gathered the Tabasco and Worcestershire sauces, tomato juice, vodka, celery salt, and ice, and soon the women were sitting on the couch with drinks in hand.

"So babies are hard work, huh?" Janet took a long, slow sip. "I guess that's not a surprise, though, really?"

Mel took a sip of her drink and blew out a breath. "Perfect. Just what I needed." She leaned back against the cushion. "No, not a surprise, but knowing that it's going to be difficult doesn't make it any easier when you're living it."

"Amen," Janet said, and the women clinked glasses. "Any idea how long you'll have her?"

"The mother is making her way through the court system. The grandmother's got her hands full with Hazel's brothers and sister, she can't take on a baby, too." Janet clucked and Mel said, "Now all four, including Hazel, are effectively in the system. No telling how long it will be. Could be five more days, could be five more months."

"And then you'll—you'll just give her back? To this woman who seems incapable of making any good choices?"

"Yeah," Mel said, and a heavy silence fell over the room. When both of their glasses were empty, Janet stood. "Another?" she asked, already walking to the minibar. She froze at the halfway point, though, when she glanced into the kitchen.

All of Jason's computers had been seized the day before, yet there, on the "island" plank of wood, sat two monitors, a keyboard, and a hard drive. The monitors glowed in the dark room, and after a moment of shocked silence, she recognized the image on both screens as the back alley at the Spot.

"What is this?" She set the glasses down and walked into the kitchen. "Did you see Jason today, Mel?" She pulled a bar stool close to the computer.

Mel followed her into the construction zone. "Sure. The lights were on over here all night, and then he left . . . let's see, I guess I was giving Hazel a bottle around eight this morning and he waved as he walked to his car. I think he said, 'See you soon,' and then drove away. You haven't talked to him since last night?"

"No . . ." Janet filled her in on what she'd found at Elizabeth's apartment and her concern that something bad had happened to the bartender. "And now I get home and Jason's not here, but his computer is."

"Where is this video taken from?" Mel asked, gesturing to the monitor.

Janet squinted at the screen, wondering the same thing. It was the Spot, all right, but the camera was pointed at her bar from across two parking lots. "It must be . . . Wait . . ." She leaned in for a closer look. "This is taken from—"

"Old Ben's property?" Mel interrupted.

Janet studied Mel for a moment. "How do you know Ben Corker? He sold the restaurant next door long before you came to town."

"It's written down right here," Mel answered, pushing a small pad of paper toward her. "It says, 'Old Ben's place, Wednesday to Thursday.'"

Janet inspected Jason's handwriting, then turned back to the screen. "Jason used to have a security contract with Old Ben," she said slowly. "But when Ben was ready to retire, he couldn't find a buyer for the building, so he shut it down and stopped paying taxes on the property. When the foreclosure notices started to appear, he moved to Florida without leaving a forwarding address."

"Was he still paying Jason?"

"I don't know. It looks like it, doesn't it?"

"And look at that angle." Mel nodded appreciatively. "It shows the whole side lot of the Spot."

"It's lucky, actually. There used to be two big oak trees between our parking lots, but one fell down in a massive hailstorm in the spring, and we had the other one taken out just last month. What a waste of money that was," she grumbled, still incensed at the hefty price tag of that particular maintenance project.

"Janet."

"What?"

"Press play."

Janet snorted when she realized that Mel was right—she was stalling, feeling nervous about what they might see. Suddenly she was glad she wasn't alone. She struck the space bar and the still shot came to life.

Mel's finger snaked out and pressed the space bar again, and the video of leaves blowing across the parking lot froze. "Wait. Should we be watching this, or should we tell the police that we have it first?"

Janet scowled at the mention of cops and turned back to the monitor without answering. She tapped the space bar. According to the time stamp in the corner of the screen, it was just after midnight, early Thursday morning. In less than twelve hours, Janet would find Ike's body. Neither spoke—the gravity of what they were about to watch weighed heavily on them both.

Old Ben's property was up a slight hill from the Spot, so the angle from his security camera gave them a nice overview of her parking lot.

She remembered Cindy Lou saying that it had been a quiet night, and she was right; the parking lot was unusually empty.

A figure came stumbling out the door of the bar. "That must be Ike." She frowned at the screen, "but where's Frank?" The protocol was clear: a drunk customer was supposed to be deposited directly into the taxi by a staff member. On that night, Frank should have been outside with Ike, but he wasn't.

"Didn't Frank tell you he walked Ike to the taxi?"

"Yes," Janet said, incensed that it had taken her so long to fire him. She should have listened to her gut and kicked him to the curb after his first week.

On-screen, Ike stumbled around to the corner of the building by the alley.

"Frank," Janet muttered darkly, knowing her obnoxious bouncer had likely kicked Ike out early just to be rid of him. That move might have cost Ike his life. "Is he—"

"Yup," Mel said with a grimace, "he's taking a leak." They couldn't be sure—the camera was far away and the image wasn't crisp—but Ike stood facing the wall, his back to the camera, thankfully, for almost a minute without moving.

Then, headlights swept over the scene.

"Well, there's his taxi," Janet said, and they watched Ike move away from the building, "but why didn't he take it?"

Another customer with perfect timing came out of the bar and hopped into the taxi.

Ike realized around the same moment Janet did that his ride was leaving without him. He hurried after the departing tail-lights, only to reach down for a handful of rocks to throw at the taxi as it disappeared around the corner. A sudden gust of wind must have blown back some of the gravel and dust, because he doubled over and turned away, scratching at his face.

So there was Ike, drunk and stuck in her parking lot without a way to get home. "Why didn't he just go back into the bar?" she asked.

Mel shrugged.

Back on-screen, Ike meandered over to his car, opened the door, and sat behind the wheel. Apparently, the car had been unlocked, and maybe Ike had planned to sit there until he'd sobered up before going back inside to ask for his keys.

Minutes passed, and Ike didn't move from behind the wheel. "That fool passed out in his own damn car," Mel said.

Janet grunted and then tapped a few keys. The video zoomed forward and the final customers seemed to race out of the bar. When Janet pressed the space bar again, the video slowed to real time, and Elizabeth, Frank, and Cindy Lou left the building, locked the door, and drove away.

Soon, the only car left in the lot was Ike's. It was easy to see how the staff, assuming he had taken the taxi home, wouldn't have given his car a second glance. Janet sent the video forward again, until headlights whipped across the scene.

When she hit play, the time stamp in the lower-right corner of the screen said it was just after three a.m.

Another vehicle, a beat-up SUV, slowly pulled into the lot and parked next to Ike. The driver got out and walked around Ike's car. It looked like the person knocked on the driver's-side window. After a moment, Ike climbed unsteadily out of the car and they faced each other.

It was frustrating to watch, not knowing what was really happening on-screen. Was Ike arguing with the other person? Did he know them? Were they trading recipes? Without audio, there was no way to know.

"Oh, whoa! Did you see that?" Mel exclaimed, watching the mystery driver jab at Ike. Ike struck back, and soon his arms swung around in wild circles.

"Holy—is that—"

"A knife? Yeah." Mel's hand snaked out and hit the space bar. "Didn't the cops say that Ike carried some kind of army knife?"

"Yes," Janet said. "He used the bottle opener a time or two at the bar when our service wasn't speedy enough. But O'Dell told me Ike's own knife killed him. That knife kills him."

She started the video back up. One of Ike's wild swings landed a blow, and the other person dropped to the ground like a keg pushed off a shelf. Ike continued to stumble around, finally falling in a heap next to the other person. Janet stared, unblinking, at the screen for several minutes, but nothing else happened.

She turned to her new bouncer, who looked as confused as she felt, and took her hand away from her mouth. "This is crazy!" She jumped out of her chair, too wired to sit still. "Are the police missing both Ike's car and a second body?"

CHAPTER TWENTY-THREE

"Wait, wait." Mel held her hand out toward Janet. "Didn't you tell me that you found Ike's body by the Dumpster?"

"You're right. Of course," Janet said. "Something else has to happen here." She sat back down and fast-forwarded the video. "What, though?" she asked quietly as the scene flickered past. "What else happens?"

She and Mel watched things unfold with mounting incredulity.

At 3:34, the stranger lying on the ground stood unsteadily, then got into their car and drove away. Just minutes later, yet *another* stranger meandered over to the remaining body lying on the ground. Ike came to and wobbled to his feet, but his arm swung wild circles, and the two moved across the lot and disappeared into the alley, out of view of the camera. Before long, a car pulled into Old Ben's lot. The driver left the car in the side lot and walked to the alley. After about ten minutes, Ike's car started to move.

Janet spluttered, "What—who—"

Mel leaned toward the screen and squinted. "What in the hell?"

Ike's car drove away, but who was behind the wheel? They rewound the video for another look.

"There!" Mel slowed the video. Someone streaked around the front of the building and ran under the eaves until they were even with Ike's car. They'd missed it the first time through because their eyes had been glued to the other side of the screen. The mystery person looked both ways, then dashed to Ike's car. Within seconds, the vehicle—no lights on, merely a dark splotch on the screen—backed out of the lot.

Janet paused the video and turned to her bouncer. "They either hot-wired that car in record time or had the key." Mel gave her a significant look and she started up the video again.

Another ten minutes passed, and then, at 3:56, *two* people emerged from the alley. They paused in the parking lot and one of them flailed their arms, alternately pointing between the bar and where Ike's car had been just minutes earlier. After another minute, they climbed into the waiting car and drove away.

"What just happened?" Janet turned to Mel. The other woman's hand pushed her hair back from her face, pulling her expression unnaturally tight.

"The last person to fight with Ike called for a ride away from the crime, and left his body by the Dumpster."

"But then who took Ike's car?"

Mel shrugged.

Janet turned to squint at the screen. "There are clearly several people with information on what happened that night. I can't believe no one has come forward!"

"The deck is always stacked against the police, but this time . . . maybe more than usual, huh?" Mel said. "Do you think Jason left this out for you—on purpose?"

Janet scoffed. "He probably just forgot it was on the screen. He hasn't been any help in this case from day one."

Mel looked around the kitchen, which was spotless—empty, really, except for the two monitors, hard drive, and keyboard.

"I don't know. Looks to me like he wanted you to watch it."

"If that's true, then why isn't he here with me? Why is he having me do it on my own?"

Mel didn't answer, because there was no answer. The truth was Jason had abandoned her at the worst time possible.

Finally, Mel said, "Well, we just learned a lot about *what* happened, but we can't really tell who all the players are—the camera was just too far away."

Janet scrutinized the screen. Mel was right.

"Maybe my dad will come up with something," she said, and pushed up from the stool.

"Your dad? Does he live here in town?"

"No, but his reach is impressive," Janet said. Mel looked confused, but Janet plowed on. "I'll give him one more day. If he doesn't find anything, then I'll call O'Dell."

"Why wait?" Mel asked. "Why not give this to the police now —let them figure it out?"

"Like you said, the video isn't exactly crisp." Janet paced behind the bar stools. "They might try and make the case that one of the people in the lot was Jason. They've been reckless with facts from the beginning. No way am I giving them evidence they might use against us."

"Yeah, but maybe they can make sense of it all," Mel said, then, when Janet looked doubtfully back she added, "I counted three people in the parking lot between the time the staff left and dawn. That's three people who knew about the body and didn't call the police."

"You're right. I need to track them down."

Mel looked at her like she'd announced a new, all-craft-beer menu for the bar. "You shouldn't be tracking anybody down— those people are involved in a murder. Besides, you don't have time. You need to find Elizabeth."

"Elizabeth?" Janet said doubtfully.

"She must have seen something—that's why she took off. Let's operate under the assumption that she's okay—but in hiding."

"Well how the hell would *I* know where to find her?"

"Put your head into this one, Janet. You've worked with her for two years. Where would she go in a crisis?"

Mel got up to leave.

"Where are you going?" Janet asked, shocked that Mel, too, was abandoning her.

"I have to go help with Hazel," Mel said, looking at her watch. "I told Kat she could nap through the lunchtime wake-eat-nap rotation. But I can't help you now anyway—I've never even met Elizabeth. Use your head. Find Elizabeth and I bet things might start making sense."

After Mel left, Janet sat in silence for over an hour, replaying everything she'd heard, said, or done since she found Ike's body behind her bar.

She thought about Larsa feeling the pull of family obligation after Ike died, and how she was leaning on her father now to help dig up some information.

It would stand to reason that Elizabeth might turn to family if she felt like she was in trouble, and in her case, turning to family was as easy as going to them, where they were: the cemetery.

———

Janet's breath hummed out her lips, and the sound echoed in the deserted room.

The first five cemeteries she'd tried all had automated menus and she couldn't get a live voice on the phone, no matter which buttons she pressed. If only one could search online for gravestone locations. She groaned—it would take days to drive to every cemetery and search for Elizabeth.

Put your head into this one, Janet.

"Goddaaa—" Janet stopped the curse mid-syllable. *God.* In a land of Southern Baptists, Elizabeth was Catholic. Her mother would be buried in the Catholic cemetery in town. The only one.

She looked up the address and grabbed her keys. The oppressive heat hardly registered, because when her finger pressed against the key to unlock her car door, there wasn't a corresponding thump of pain. Hallelujah! She nearly giggled at the normalcy of the movement. Saved by the doctor, and all it cost her was half a beer and his raving lunatic wife shouting at her—not a bad trade, really. Hardly different from any other night at the bar.

Her car was scalding, so she dropped the windows, and the wind whipped her hair around her face as she drove through town. She needed breakfast—and coffee, and, frankly, a toothbrush—but first, she was going to find Elizabeth.

Calvary Catholic Cemetery had been serving the Knoxville area since 1869. Looking at the graffiti-covered sign at the entrance, it wasn't hard to imagine kids from the middle school nearby accepting dares to deface the sign—or worse. The grounds were close to downtown, and though the area was large, it had a city feel to it. She came to a stop at the entrance and looked over the posted map to get the lay of the land.

She had no idea where Elizabeth's mother might be buried, but with the engine off and the heat seeping into her car, the idea that Elizabeth might have been camping out at the cemetery for the last few days suddenly seemed ludicrous.

Okay, so if not outside where her mother was buried, why not *inside* a church?

A quick Internet search on her phone told her that Elizabeth's mother's funeral mass had been held nearby at Holy Ghost Catholic Church.

Janet cranked the engine again and did a U-turn back onto the main road. Within minutes, she spotted the church, but just before she turned the wheel, a cyclist passed her on the right. She slammed on her brakes, fishtailing to a stop on the road, narrowly avoiding the rear wheel of the bike. The cyclist shouted out some curse words and pedaled away. Janet, her heart beating fast, cursed right back.

"Don't pass a car that's turning! I had my signal on, you asshole!"

The curse word echoed out of her window around the church lot and Janet sucked on her lower lip. What an entrance.

She parked and stared at the stained-glass windows, gleaming in the early-morning sunshine. She hadn't been to a church since her own mother died several years earlier. After another minute of uncertainty, she climbed out of the car and walked up to the structure before she could change her mind.

With a deep breath, she pushed open the door and went in.

CHAPTER TWENTY-FOUR

The church was dark and cool, lit only by candles and the sunlight that managed to eke past the colored glass windows. After the initial *whoosh* of cold air hit her in the face, she breathed in the familiar combination of incense and wood polish. It took a moment for Janet's eyes to adjust, but when they did, she wasn't any closer to knowing where to go.

Several people sat in pews, sprinkled throughout the enormous nave, and Janet eyed each of them as she crept down the side aisle. One head of glossy, golden hair stood out among the bluish-white tresses. As Janet got closer, the woman's long hair looked darker than usual, and Janet stopped, suddenly unsure. But when the woman tossed her twisty braid over her shoulder with a familiar flip, she knew it was Elizabeth. She'd been watching her do that hair flip for two years.

Janet crept into the row just behind her and lowered the kneeler. Elizabeth's back stiffened when she became aware that someone was near, but she relaxed a fraction when Janet spoke.

"Feels like the world has been looking for you these last few days, E."

"I've been here the whole time. Go figure, huh?"

"No one's seen you—not even your neighbor."

"Well, that's what I told him to say. He's a good egg—been nice to me since my mom died." Elizabeth's hair was greasy, as if it hadn't been washed in days. When she turned to the side, her face, usually young and fresh, appeared haggard, with dark circles under her eyes. Her skin was pale and drawn. "He even offered to take care of Bitsy until I could come back."

"Bitsy, that little brown ball of hair? She's your dog?" Elizabeth nodded.

Old Paul had played her like a fiddle. She'd have to remember his deaf-and-don't-like-anyone game and use it in the future.

"Why are you here?" Janet finally asked. "What happened the night Ike was killed, Elizabeth?"

"It's . . . I don't even . . ." She shook her head and finally turned in the pew to look at Janet. "I think I'm in real trouble, and there's no one who can help me."

"I'm here—I can help you. I'm on your side, no matter what."

"What about all those messages?" She held up her cell phone and fixed Janet with an unblinking stare. "Why were you calling me?"

"The—the messages?" Janet asked, stalling for time. Now was not the best time to bring up her suspicion that Elizabeth was the one who'd been stealing from her.

"Yes, like this one." Elizabeth tapped a few buttons on her phone and added, "It's from the morning after Ike was killed."

Janet's peeved voice piped out of the phone's tiny speakers, causing an old man two rows away to look over and frown. "Elizabeth, it's Janet. We need to talk, and I'm not jumping to any conclusions, but there's a situation here and I guess you need to come in."

"Oh, that." Janet blanched, scrambling for an excuse. "It was just . . . it was about Ike being dead. I mean, if that's not a situation, I don't know what—"

Elizabeth held up a hand. "The message isn't over."

Sure enough, after a long pause, her voice continued. Janet

apparently hadn't properly disconnected the call. She was now speaking to Jason on the landline in the office, her voice still recorded by Elizabeth's voicemail.

"Well, Jay, I called her, and we'll see if she has the balls to come in or if she just never shows her face here again. Shit. Either way, I guess the stealing will stop, so I don't care which way it goes."

Janet winced as the curse word echoed off the vaulted ceiling, and she realized with striking finality that everyone was right: the cursing had to stop. She sounded like an angry preteen trying out foul language for the first time.

She cleared her throat, stalling. Elizabeth turned back to the altar, letting Janet fumble.

"Elizabeth, I don't care about that now. I care about what happened outside the Spot Wednesday night—or Thursday morning—and why you've been on the run ever since."

Elizabeth nodded grimly. "That's what I thought. You don't care about me, just your business. I figured as much. It's why I've been here. Father Andrew said I could stay as long as I like."

"You want to stay here?" Janet asked, stung by the insinuation, and by the fact that Elizabeth had seen through her so easily.

"No, but I'm not going to trust anyone to help, because what's going down is big and ugly, and it's not going to turn out all right just because I want it to. There are more things at play here than you could possibly imagine, and I'm not sure how all this ends up with me okay—with me . . . not . . . dead."

"Okay, let's not be dramatic—"

"Dramatic? There's a cop out there willing to help cover up a crime—a murder! He's actively keeping a killer safe, and you think I'm being dramatic? I saw him, okay? I saw him."

Janet leaned forward, glad they were finally getting to the heart of the matter. "A cop? What did you see, Elizabeth?"

"Nope." Elizabeth shook her head and moved a few feet down the pew, away from Janet. "See, that's just what I didn't want to say. I don't know anything, because nothing I say is going to make a difference."

"Elizabeth, Jason found some video of the crime. I sort of know what happened—just not who did what."

The young woman turned around and looked back at Janet through narrowed eyes. "Then it sounds like you don't know anything."

Janet grimaced; it did sound like that. "Elizabeth, we have surveillance video from the night Ike was killed. The police don't know about it yet, but the video quality isn't the best. We can see there were more people involved than the police know, but you're the missing link. If you know something, combined with the video, we can give the police a better idea of what happened —of who killed Ike."

"That's just it, Janet. Don't you see? The police are involved. They killed Ike—or at least helped cover it up—and that means it's only a matter of time before I wind up in jail. Or dead."

CHAPTER TWENTY-FIVE

Elizabeth hadn't spoken since they got to Janet's house, save a low groan that had escaped when she stepped under the shower spray. Now Janet listened through the wall to the sound of rushing water as she paced her bedroom just outside the bathroom door. She had to make some big decisions in the next few hours, and she wasn't sure who she could trust.

She walked toward the kitchen to cue up the video for Elizabeth but stopped just short of the doorway. The computer, keyboard, and monitors were gone.

"What the . . ."

Jason was hiding something. She scrutinized the space on the plywood where the computer had been just an hour earlier. Suddenly, his assertion that he needed space didn't add up. He'd left the video out for her to watch, she was sure of it, then he'd taken it away. But why? The fact that he didn't want to watch it with her was telling. She didn't know what it meant, but she knew it meant something.

She raced down to Jason's office in the basement, but it was empty. Where was he?

She leaned back against the wall and raked a hand through her hair, then plodded back up the steps to her room to wait out

Elizabeth's epic shower. The longer she stood there, the more jittery she felt.

According to Elizabeth, someone at the police department was on the wrong side of a murder. Janet herself had more information than she wanted about the crime, and it was only a matter of time before the truth came out. She needed to make sure it all went down on the record, in front of an audience, so no one at KPD could claim they didn't know something important or illegal later.

As Elizabeth's shower entered its fifteenth minute, Janet's cell phone rang.

"It's your father."

"Yes, I know. That's why I said, 'Hi, Dad,'" Janet said. "The name Sampson Foster comes up on my screen, it's not a surprise—"

"It doesn't say 'Dad'?"

"Oh, ah . . ." She scrambled for an excuse. "I guess I put it in there a while ago, before we really knew . . ." She'd been about to say before they knew each other, but they still didn't really know each other.

After a moment, Sampson cleared his throat. "I have some information for you. It's not much, but it's a start. I made some quiet inquiries with an old law clerk who works there in Knoxville, and she says someone was researching Ike Freeman's history recently. A lawyer was at the clerks' office just last week, asking for copies of Freeman's arrest warrant dated July nineteenth, which includes things like his home address and license plate information."

"Who? You got a name?"

"Nope. But I'm waiting on a call from one other friend. I'll be in touch by close of business today."

They disconnected. Ten minutes later the bathroom door finally opened and Elizabeth, her skin red from the long, hot shower, emerged.

"Thanks," she said, toweling off her hair. "I needed that. The church had a lot of things, but not a shower." She dug a comb out of her bag and worked it through the tangles in her hair.

No one else was home, but Janet stood reflexively and closed the bedroom door. She'd filled Elizabeth in on what she'd been up to since Ike's death, but Elizabeth hadn't been quite as forthcoming. In fact, she hadn't said a word about what happened the night Ike was killed. "I need to know what happened, Elizabeth. It might just be you and me together on this. I can't even trust Jason right now—he's telling me not to—so I need to know everything if we're to have any chance of figuring a way out of this."

Elizabeth stared at Janet through the mirror, her expression calculating. She put the comb down and dug around in her bag for a moment before she turned to face Janet, something clutched in her fist. "I left with Frank and Cindy Lou that night —our usual time, probably half past two in the morning. After I got home and changed, though, I realized I still had Ike's car key in my pocket." She shook her head, and Janet could imagine that she was still irritated that forgetting one small detail that night had so irrevocably changed her life. "He left in such a hail of fury that I'd put his key in my pocket, so he wouldn't try to grab it from the basket."

Janet nodded, remembering one recent night during which that very scenario had unfolded, resulting in Frank's tackling Ike and a worker's comp case being filed. She was still paying off the claim.

"I didn't want to come in early the next morning to return the key, so I drove back right after I found the damn thing. It must have been after three—maybe three thirty."

Janet nodded again. So far, her story lined up with the timeline from Old Ben's video system.

Elizabeth continued, "When I got close to the parking lot, though, I could see . . . something. I didn't know what, but there were people there who shouldn't have been. Now, Janet, you know the Spot's not in the best neighborhood. I wasn't going to walk in on a drug deal or a hooker doing her job, okay? So, I circled the block, parked on the street, and crept along the storefronts. I was thinking I'd just sneak in the back door, put the key in the basket, and get on my way."

"Why didn't you just go home?" Janet asked, shooting a suspicious look at Elizabeth. The bartender she'd known only peripherally for nearly two years had never struck her as someone who'd go out of her way to do *anything*, let alone something dangerous in the middle of the night.

"I should have—believe me, I've asked myself that every hour since—but I was already there and had already wasted so much time. So, I was unlocking the back door to get in when I heard what they were saying."

"Who?"

"Well, that's just it: I still didn't know, did I? I saw two people, but I only heard the one. He shouted, 'You killed him! *Ike's dead!* He's dead, and it doesn't matter what you meant to do,' and it . . . it just turned my stomach.

"The man was swearing up a storm, and I was backing up—believe me, I was heading straight back to my car, but then I heard him say, 'This will be my badge, for sure,' and, 'We'll have to burn the body.' Janet, I froze. I—I felt so guilty. Here I'd been the one to take Ike's keys! If he'd had them, he might not be dead!

"I felt this . . . I don't know, sense of responsibility to make sure no one got away with anything. So, when the people were debating what to do with Ike's body, I . . . I hopped in Ike's car and drove away."

"Jesus," Janet whispered.

"I know! What was I thinking? I didn't have a plan—I just thought whatever was happening out there wasn't good—it-it wasn't right—and I wanted to . . . keep them from covering up whatever had happened."

"Where did you go?"

"Well, I called you! Fat lot of good that did me."

Janet blanched. She remembered getting the delayed notification of Elizabeth's call the next day at the Spot, but if she was honest with herself, she probably wouldn't have answered an after-hours call from Elizabeth, anyway.

The young woman continued, her tone fevered as she reached the crux of what had sent her into hiding that night. "I flew out of the lot, I didn't know if they were going to chase me, so I drove hard all the way home and didn't stop for a single red light. I knew I couldn't go to the police—one of them was involved! I was going to just park the car at the downtown courthouse that morning, make an anonymous call or something, and be done with it—but then I was so out of sorts that I nearly rolled over the parking block at my apartment and this fell off." She plunked a small electronic device down on the bed between them.

"What is it?" Janet asked, holding it up to eye level. It was smaller than a belt buckle, and had a smooth front and rounded edges. Or at least, it used to. One side was smashed in, a crack spidered out from the center of the device, and the whole thing looked like it had been melted.

"I researched it when I got inside, and that's when I started running." She looked at the device with mistrust. "It's a GPS tracker. A really powerful one." She passed something else to Janet. It was about the same size but had a hinge on one side and a powerful magnet on the smooth back. "The tracker was inside this case—someone put it under Ike's car. It must have scraped loose when I hit the block."

"So, you were worried someone would know where Ike's car was—where you were!"

"Exactly. So, I dropped it in a bowl of water, microwaved it, and smashed it with a hammer." She grinned at Janet's bewildered expression. "I wanted to be absolutely sure it didn't work, but at the same time, I knew my house had been trackable. I mean, who'd put a GPS tracker on Ike's car?"

Janet didn't answer.

"I'm not sure it makes sense now in the light of day, but then, I was worried it was whoever killed him. So, I dropped my dog off at Paul's next door and took Ike's car to the church. I've been in and out of churches and parks ever since."

Janet felt a gut punch of guilt. This poor girl, all of twenty-five or twenty-six, was all alone with no one to turn to. She certainly wouldn't have thought to turn to her boss, who'd been leaving her angry messages, accusing her of theft.

"Why didn't you come into the bar the next day? We could have sorted it all out together."

"I did."

"What?"

"I came in—walked straight into the office—and I was going to talk to the detectives, but then I heard the voice from the night before—the one who'd been making such a ruckus about moving the body. So, whoever was in on Ike's death is a major player. That's when I knew I had to hide."

Janet sucked in a breath and tried to clear her head. She'd thought she'd heard something in the office when O'Dell was interviewing her. Finch had been nearby, too. So, which cop knew about the murder—or did they both?

They had work to do.

"I think we need to gather all the players tonight—get them all in the same room and start asking questions. We've got the place wired up—"

"Because someone was stealing from the register? Janet, I wanted to say—"

"It's not important now—we have other things to worry about," she said over Elizabeth. "The Spot is wired from top to bottom, though, and if we get people talking, we might shake some information loose. If it's all caught on camera, no one can deny it after the fact.

"I'll invite Benji and Abe to the bar to talk with Larsa, Ike's daughter," she went on. "Abe wanted to discuss something with her the other night, but she wasn't there," she added when Elizabeth raised her eyebrows. "We'll have Detectives Finch and O'Dell sitting on the other side of the bar, listening in."

Elizabeth jumped up, nodding with a spark of something other than fear for the first time that day. "They'll think they're there to witness a confession—"

"But we'll really be finding out which of them was involved. If we're lucky, we'll also find out who delivered the fatal blow. A bar is like a confessional—you never know what might come out when people have a beer in front of them. We can use the TV screens to our advantage, if anybody clams up."

Elizabeth dropped the destroyed GPS tracker back into her bag. "How do we get them all there, though? Abe and Benji won't come if they know what we're planning."

"True, but I have some ideas about that," Janet said.

"Well, what do you want me to do?" Elizabeth asked.

"Head back to the church and keep a low profile. We'll need you in place in the office before we open. Seeing you will be such a surprise that it might help shake some tongues loose." Elizabeth gave her a look and Janet shrugged. "We'll clue in Cindy Lou and Mel, but that's it."

"What about Jason?"

Janet blew out a breath and sat down with a thump. She stared at the door before finally shaking her head. "I have an idea about why Jason's backed out of this one, but I don't know exactly where his loyalties lie. He can't know what we're doing."

Elizabeth frowned. "I guess I have one last question: who's Mel?"

"She's our new bouncer."

"What happened to Frank?"

"He got reassigned . . . to another job."

Elizabeth nodded grimly. "I never liked him."

"Me neither."

"Okay," the young woman said, now pacing the same stretch of floor Janet had trod just a few minutes earlier. "It's going to happen tonight. The Spot opens in just a few hours. Is there enough time?"

"It will be close," Janet said. "But I think we'll make it."

"What about Larsa? Where are you going to find her? You said she was acting odd last night?"

"I have an idea of where to find her, too. Come to the Spot before five. Make sure to park Ike's car around back, so nobody sees it."

Janet sent a text to Jason, telling him what she needed him to do but leaving out the other details. She had to get moving—there were phone calls to make and people to see. She drove away from her house feeling hopeful for the first time in days. She didn't know everything about Ike's murder yet, but she was finally on the right track to finding out.

Would Larsa agree to help her—if Janet could even find her? She had to at least try. But first, she was going to the Spot. She had to get organized for the day ahead.

CHAPTER TWENTY-SIX

The bar was dark when she pulled up, and the building gave off an unexpected abandoned feeling that matched Old Ben's place next door. Cindy Lou was scheduled to open, but not for a couple of hours, so Janet knew she'd have a quiet place where she could make some phone calls to put that evening's plan into motion before going in search of Larsa.

Anxiety crept up her spine as she pulled out her key ring, and when she turned the key, the dead bolt didn't make a sound, because the door was already unlocked.

A quick look behind her confirmed that hers was the only car in the lot. She could taste the tension in the air.

She hesitated at the threshold and pulled the door open wide. It was dark inside, so dark she could barely make out the tables and chairs sitting mere feet away. She glanced to her right and saw that the blinds—which she'd opened and pulled up last night—were closed and lowered. She gulped. Someone had been here.

"Hello?" she called, her voice weak and warbly. She cleared her throat and in a stronger voice said, "Who's here?"

Janet felt around the wall for the baseball bat that always rested right by the door. When her fingers closed around the neck she swung it around, then stalked into the bar—*her* bar. She held her head cocked to the side, ready to pick up any noise that didn't belong, as she made her way to the light panel on the opposite side of the room. Her body betrayed her brain, though, and all she could hear was her own heartbeat thundering in her ears.

Reaching out a hand, she flipped the switches up. Nothing happened. "What the—" Had vandals broken in and cut the power, or was something more sinister at play?

Pressing her back against the wall, she stood frozen until her eyes adjusted to the dark. Still on high alert, she looked slowly over the room, then shuffled along the back wall to the office door. She tried the handle—it gave without resistance. She pushed the door open, then, with a small gasp, gripped the bat and rushed toward the stranger inside with a banshee yell.

Just before she swung, though, Frank said, "Jesus, Janet, what the hell?"

She skidded to a stop and took a few steadying breaths before her shock turned to anger. She swung the bat down to her side. "Frank! What are you doing here? Did you break in?"

He dug a key out of his pocket. "It's not breaking in when you have a key."

She tapped the bat against the concrete floor. "It *is* breaking in when you're no longer authorized to use that key," she said. "And obviously you know that; you lowered the blinds out there to hide the fact that you're in here messing around. I'm calling the cops!" She stalked past Frank to the phone and picked up the receiver.

"Hey, wait a minute. I didn't do anything to the blinds. I'm just here to get a few things I left behind. It's not my fault you left the office unlocked!"

"Unlocked? I didn't leave any of these doors unlocked. And what'd you do to the power?"

"I'd guess you didn't pay the electric bill," Frank answered with a smirk.

"No, you pr—" When she'd turned back to Frank she noticed something was wrong with the door. She set the phone down and tracked back across the small room. In the dark bar she hadn't noticed, but now, with light streaming in through the office window, she saw that the lock had been broken. A large dent bowed in the metal door near the dead bolt. Parts of the lock were flat-out missing.

"What did you do?" she asked. "It was you, wasn't it? Stealing from the register? Here I've been thinking it was Elizabeth, but it was you all along!"

"I wouldn't steal from this hole-in-the-wall bar any more than I'd be caught dead working here. Please. You're not even worth my time." He turned back to the storage cabinet and pulled some items off a shelf. "I just came to get my things."

"What things?"

He held out a small mirror and a comb, and when he shook out a folded jacket, a piece of paper fluttered to the ground. "Ah, sweet," he said, bending down to retrieve it. "I forgot about that."

"What is it?" Janet looked at the scrap of paper. "You broke in to get a shopping list?"

"No. It's the phone number of a girl from the other night. I told her I'd call her, and right now that might be the only thing I've got going for me. The phone number for a pretty girl." He smiled at the paper and tucked it into the breast pocket of his button-down shirt.

Janet looked incredulously at her former employee. "If you think of anything else you left behind, come back during normal business hours, okay? I'll walk you out." She led the way back to the bar.

Coming from the sunlit office, the bar felt darker than it had before. From her new vantage point, she saw that a table by the door was tilted at an odd angle. Two chairs lay on the floor, clearly knocked off the tables in a path directly to the gap in the countertop that employees used to get behind the bar.

"Did you do this?" she asked.

"Of course not," Frank answered. "I swear, I came straight through to the office."

A tiny flare of sunlight from the open office door glinted off the cash register. "You didn't stop to check behind the counter for this precious note? Wait right there. I'm not sure I believe you." Still gripping the bat, she headed straight for the bar, keeping Frank in her sights. She skirted around the counter to the opening. With a relieved sigh, she saw that the cash drawer was in place, locked just as she'd left it. "Do you have any other keys, Frank?" He shook his head and she pivoted slowly again. That's when she saw it.

The circular shelves to the Beerador leaned heavily against the other drink coolers. Her brow furrowed and she crept closer to the appliance, noting as she passed the trash can that it was full—full of whole and broken bottles that used to sit on the shelves inside the sturdy old unit.

"What did you do, Frank?"

He wasn't paying attention, though; he was too busy folding the jacket back into a neat square to hear what Janet had said.

From the side of the Beerador, she gripped the handle and pulled, but the door didn't budge. She blew out a frustrated sigh. All the doors in the bar that were *supposed* to be locked that day had swung easily open, and the one door that was supposed to be *open* was now, inexplicably, locked.

She stepped closer to get a more direct handle on the door latch and turned her focus from Frank to the Beerador, then sucked in a loud breath. "Jesus H. Christ," she breathed, stepping away from the unit.

Detective Finch stared out from the Beerador, unblinking, unseeing. His face was smashed against the glass; a lone streak of blood marred the blue-white skin of his face.

"F-f-Frank!" she stuttered, calling to her former employee.

She stumbled back and almost fell when she bumped into the cooler drawers behind her.

A clash of noise at the front of the bar made her jump.

"Janet?"

She turned, but with bright sunlight streaming in behind him, she could only make out the outline of a man standing in the open doorway.

Suddenly feeling vulnerable, she held the bat aloft.

"Who's there?"

"Janet, it's me, Patrick." She squinted, finally recognizing O'Dell's voice. "I got a text to meet Finch here. Have you seen him?"

She lowered the bat and pointed to the Beerador. "Yeah. Yeah, I think he's been here for a while."

CHAPTER TWENTY-SEVEN

For the second time in as many weeks, crime scene tape surrounded the Spot. However, this time, with a dead active-duty cop in the mix, there were more police brass inside and outside than at the station downtown. Beyond the sea of blue, on the other side of the tape, the press circled the crime scene like hungry dogs.

Janet kept a wary watch across the bar as Frank and a homicide detective huddled in a booth. She didn't trust anything about her old bouncer, and while she couldn't imagine him killing Finch, she also couldn't imagine that he would be completely forthcoming with the police when he was in the middle of a homicide investigation.

"Where's Jason?"

O'Dell towered over her, his fingertips white where they pressed into her table.

She didn't answer, she only had the strength to rest her forehead against her hands. Through her splayed fingers, she saw medics gather on either side of the gurney holding Finch's body. They raised him up to hip height and pushed him out of the bar.

She looked up and found O'Dell staring at her. He rubbed a

hand over his face and sat down across from her. "I talked to Haverfield."

She nodded, barely remembering the cop who'd interviewed her an hour ago. Instead, burned in her mind, was O'Dell rushing into the bar and trying to pull the Beerador open. He'd yelled Finch's name over and over, and had nearly wrenched his arm off pulling at the handle. Janet had finally pushed him away from the cooler and yelled at Frank, frozen by the office door, to call 911. It had eventually taken four firefighters and two steel crowbars to pry the door free, they learned later that the door had been jammed by a metal button on Finch's sleeve. After another conference session, emergency responders finally figured out how to get Finch's cold, stiff body out of the cramped space.

Janet felt sick to her stomach, but she looked across the table at O'Dell and said, "Finch was here this morning. I was rude, maybe even slammed the door in his face."

"And he came here to tell you that the investigation had stalled?" O'Dell looked up from the notebook but couldn't hide his skepticism.

"I know, it sounds like something I just made up, but that's what he said. He asked me if I had any more surprises, and I told him I didn't. And then he accused me of not caring about Ike's death, and said that the case was going to fade away like so many others." She looked down at her hands. "I don't know why he would have come back to the bar. I watched him drive away, and then I left. I'd just come back when I found the bar door unlocked, and Frank in the office."

"Where did you go?"

"Hmm?" she asked, stalling for time. She'd told the first cop that she ran some errands, and he hadn't pressed, but she knew O'Dell would, and she still hadn't decided what her story was going to be. Elizabeth's concerns for her safety now seemed well founded, indeed, and while O'Dell's shock at finding Finch's body earlier had seemed genuine, she truly didn't know who to trust.

"I said, where did you go? What errands did you run today?"

She took a slow, steady breath and made a choice. "I guess they weren't really errands. I . . . I went to the cemetery and then to church."

"Really?" O'Dell said, his surprise evident. "You went to church?"

"Is that so surprising? Doesn't everyone in Knoxville go to church?"

"Yeah, but . . ." He squinted at her and then asked, "Which church?"

"Holy Ghost."

His skepticism turned to disbelief. "I've never seen you there."

"You're Catholic?" she asked, remembering too late that O'Dell wasn't from Knoxville. She should have known the New York transplant wouldn't be Southern Baptist.

"Mmm-hmm. And I go every week."

"Well," Janet said, her poker face back, "I don't. My mom died a few years ago and I've been spinning my wheels for a while. But today I felt . . . called to visit."

"A confession?"

"No," she said, disgruntled at his insinuation. "Just to sit."

O'Dell chewed on that silently for a while, then said, "I had a squad car stop by your house."

"You did?" Her brow furrowed, and she wondered what O'Dell was going to throw at her next. Elizabeth was waiting at the church for their planned showdown. Janet was going to have to get in touch with her somehow—as the plan would have to be delayed, if not outright canceled, because of this murderous turn of events.

"No one answered, and Jason's car isn't there." O'Dell leaned closer. "Where is he?"

"I don't know."

"When did you see him last?"

She gulped, not liking how her answer was going to sound. "Uh . . ."

"Janet. We have a dead cop. Don't play games, just answer the question."

"I'm not playing games, I just don't see how—"

"When did you last see Jason? It's a simple question. What are you hiding?"

"I'm not hiding anything! I saw him last night. Here, at the Spot."

He sat back, looking triumphant. "He didn't come home last night? Or this morning? Where has he been?"

"No—I mean, I don't know for sure, because I didn't go home last night."

That information pulled O'Dell up short. "Where did you go?"

"I . . . I slept here, in the office. We had a fight. Just a dumb fight, but I didn't feel like going home, so I didn't."

"What did you fight about?"

"Me being a bitch."

"Sorry?"

"You asked what we fought about, and that's the answer. We fought about me being mean and rude."

O'Dell nodded but his face was tight. "Excuse me." He walked across away with his cell phone pressed into his ear.

Janet sat there for another ten minutes before she felt too antsy to be still. She stood up and started walking toward the office, thinking she could try Jason's cell phone again, but a hand reached out and landed on her shoulder.

"Miss Black? You'll need to have a seat right there, please."

Janet turned to find a woman in a white uniform shirt with several bars and stars pins surrounding a name tag. "Captain Wiggins, is it? I don't feel like sitting."

"I don't care," the woman answered. Janet stood mutinously for a moment, and the captain said, "You can sit in cuffs or on your own. The choice is yours for the next fifteen seconds. Then the choice is mine."

She lowered herself to the chair with as much dignity as possible and turned her face away from the captain. Several words came to mind, but she bit her tongue, realizing that pissing off the highest-ranking cop on the scene wouldn't do her any good. Plus, this woman's colleague had just been brutally murdered. She likely had more on her mind that Janet's feelings.

She smothered a bitter laugh: she was feeling *compassionate* toward the captain. Not that it mattered, but Jason would have been proud.

"We're going in," O'Dell said, nodding at the captain as he took a seat. She walked away and he leaned toward Janet. "We're going into your house. Judge just signed a probable cause warrant to see if Jason's hiding in the basement."

"What?" Janet said, and a tiny tick of annoyance in the back of her head said, *See, this is where compassion gets you,* but she tried to focus on O'Dell. "Jason's not there! I was home this morning, and no one was there!"

"But that doesn't mean he's not there now," O'Dell said with a superior smile. "And we're not taking any chances. My guys are going in with a battering ram. I just gave them the okay."

"Will you let it rest? Jason had nothing to do with this murder!"

O'Dell frowned. "Then why did we find his pen inside the Beerador with Finch's body?"

CHAPTER TWENTY-EIGHT

Janet sat in mutinous silence across from O'Dell, forcing herself to stay calm. She was surrounded by the enemy, and they all had guns.

"What pen?" she finally managed to ask.

O'Dell shook out a zip-top evidence bag. Sure enough, Jason's customized, obnoxious, neon blue and yellow pen was inside. But she snorted when she saw it.

"Are you kidding me? That's not evidence in a murder. That just shows that your department took all of Jason's stuff yesterday, and Finch apparently wanted to use the pen!" Her temper finally got the better of her. "You call this off right now, O'Dell, I'm serious!"

"Janet, this is happening. Jason was angry, a cop is dead, and we have evidence that he was here at the time of the murder. Or at least right after. That's enough for me."

His words only enraged her more. "That's your probable cause? That Jason was angry and had a *pen*? That's not even true, you asshole, he was *disappointed* in me, okay? Which is worse for me but has nothing to do with you, Finch, or the fact that someone killed him!" O'Dell was maddeningly calm as he sat opposite her, unfazed by her emotion. "O'Dell—call off your people! Just—" She stopped talking and jumped up when an idea struck. "My tenant has a key! You don't have to break down the door! They don't know it's there, but it's hanging on a hook in the cabinet over the oven. Just use the key to get in, okay! A new door is going to cost me five hundred bucks!"

"You don't care if we go in?"

"No. Knock yourselves out—just don't knock the damn door out!"

"You're upset about the cost of the door?"

"Yes—I'm not made of money, and I won't be able to open the bar again tonight. Give me a break!"

"You're not worried we'll find Jason inside your house?"

"No. He told me he needed a break. From me. And since you took all his computer equipment, there's no reason for him to go home."

O'Dell studied her for a moment before speaking again. "I can't get a read on you, Janet, and it's starting to piss me off."

"Yeah, well, it's part of my charm." She leaned over the table. "Will you call your guys? Tell them to knock on the other half of my house—and carefully! They've got a baby over there and don't need you people waking it up if it's finally sleeping."

"It?" He cocked one eyebrow at her.

"The baby." She wrinkled her nose. "It's a *her*, okay?"

O'Dell signaled to another officer and they conferenced for a moment before O'Dell said, "It's done. They'll get the key and search the house. They gonna find anything else I should know about now?"

"No," Janet answered mulishly, though her heartbeat accelerated, thinking about the computer that had sat on the kitchen "island" only hours ago.

"Janet?" he pressed.

"What? I'm worried about Jason is all. It's not like him to disappear like this."

"I'm worried about Jason, too. I think he's involved in this,

Janet, and if I were you, I'd start thinking about how to protect myself."

"I may not know where Jason is, but I know he'd never hurt me. Not in a million years."

"He already has!" O'Dell gestured around them. "He's involved in this murder and in Ike's death, too!"

"That's ridiculous, and if it were true, you'd have already arrested him. Finch was right about one thing: you guys are floundering on the investigation into Ike's murder, and now you've got nowhere to go on this one, either. Don't try casting out random lines just to see what you can catch."

"You have no idea what we've got on Jason, no idea."

She sat back in her chair, frustrated into silence. She crossed her arms and looked over toward the bar when she heard a deafening crash.

Two burly men with hand carts flanked the Beerador. Their white jumpsuits were already marred with dirt and dust, and their hands and feet were covered in plastic gloves and boot covers.

"Again," one of the men said. His partner tried to tilt the Beerador to the right so the other could shimmy his hand cart underneath, but he lost his grip, and the heavy refrigerator slammed to the ground with another crash.

"Ugh!" Janet cringed at the noise.

"I got it," the second guy called triumphantly. He'd managed to slide the lip of the cart under the Beerador, and his partner rushed to his side, ready to help stabilize the huge appliance. With an almighty heave, the cart operator tried to tilt the hand cart back. Nothing happened. His partner reached over and pressed down on the cart. For a moment, the bar fell silent as everyone watching held their collective breath. Instead of succumbing to the attempt to move it out of the bar, however, the Beerador seemed to bear down. The metal hand cart snapped in half, sending the two men tumbling to the ground.

In the shocked silence that followed, Janet looked over to

O'Dell to find him staring, not at the scene in front of them, but at her.

"Are you seriously worried about the Beerador when another man is dead—*dead*—at your business?" Any vestige of friendliness was gone, and O'Dell looked at Janet like she was the enemy. The sight filled her with anger.

"There's so much you don't know about this case it could fill that damn Beerador," she said. O'Dell winced, and Janet flushed, realizing what she'd just said. "That's not what I—" She sighed. "I'm sorry," she said quietly, "but you're all wrong about this case, O'Dell. All wrong."

O'Dell grabbed her arm roughly and led her to a booth in the corner, away from the pack of officers watching the Beerador removal process. "What do you know? Start talking, Black. Now."

She pulled out of his grip. "I'm not telling you anything. Not yet. You're so focused on my boyfriend that you're not in a place to see anything else now anyway. I won't waste my breath."

"Why are you so certain Jason is innocent? Ike Freeman was a nuisance who, according to many of your customers, loved to talk trash to you, specifically, when he was drunk! Maybe your boyfriend decided he'd messed with you one too many times. Mark Finch was screwing with Jason's business, making accusations, and now he's out of the picture. Pretty convenient for your boyfriend."

"You're so wrong it's painful, O'Dell. Painful."

"Listen, Black, you wanna open for business? Then start talking. Otherwise, it might take us weeks to get all the evidence we need out of here. Weeks. It's up to you."

"Unbelievable!" Janet rubbed the spot on her arm where he'd grabbed her. "You do what you have to do, O'Dell. But leave me out of it."

"I wish I could, Janet," he said, looking at her with surprising concern. "I wish I could leave you out of all of this. But you keep turning up right in the damn middle of things."

She sank down into the booth and looked around the room. "What is Frank saying?"

O'Dell lowered himself into the seat across from Janet. "Exactly what you said he told you. That he came in for some things he'd left here and didn't touch anything else."

"Do you believe him?"

"I do," he said.

"Of course you do," Janet scoffed. "You guys always stick together—that's the problem, isn't it?"

"What do you know, Janet? I can't help if you don't let me."

She stared at a tiny nick in the table, torn about what to do. Elizabeth had said that a cop was there the night of Ike's murder, and that cop helped cover up the crime. Was Finch the helper that night, and Ike's killer had decided to tie up loose ends? Or did Finch start asking too many questions and the killer got nervous? And if so, who was the killer? Another cop, or someone else?

"You can trust me, Janet."

She almost opened up—almost told him everything she knew. But something stopped her. She couldn't put her trust in the wrong person, and the only way to know for sure was to continue on with the plan she and Elizabeth had come up with— God, was it only a few hours ago?

She looked up from the table. "How much longer is this going to take?"

He broke the eye contact first and frowned. "Could be hours, could be all night, Janet. It'll depend on those guys." He gestured to the men—now numbered at four—who surrounded the Beerador.

"Go," one yelled, and two men together pushed against the side of the heavy appliance, with the other two bracing it from the opposite side. They finally tipped it up enough so that one could slide the edge of a fortified, heavy-duty rolling hand cart under the bottom edge. With a crash they let go, and then with one dragging the cart and the other three surrounding the Beerador, supporting it with their arms, they pulled the refrigerator out from behind the bar.

A flurry of detectives and patrol officers flung tables and chairs out of the way, clearing a path to the door.

"Now what?" Janet asked, watching them drag her property off like a prize. With a pang, she realized she was going to miss that giant steel and aluminum bottle.

"Now they take it apart and see what evidence is hiding inside." He leaned in, forcing Janet to turn and face him. "You can trust me, Janet. I'm here for you."

His eyes were clear and convincing, but he seemed to be looking for something from her that she couldn't give him. At least not yet.

"We'll see, O'Dell." She stood and headed for the door.

CHAPTER TWENTY-NINE

Janet's joy at finally being allowed to leave the Spot was quickly overshadowed by the wall of sound that hit her when she stepped foot in the parking lot. She looked over the crime scene tape that circled the lot in shock. A bevy of reporters, some standing next to the unblinking eye of news cameras, others holding out tape recorders, lined up and pressed in, yelling questions they couldn't possibly have expected her to answer.

"What did you do?"

"Did you kill Detective Finch?"

"Who else is in there?"

"Are you guilty?"

"Are your customers all targets?"

Exasperated, she'd just opened her mouth to answer that last one when a nearby officer standing guard at the perimeter shook her head.

Janet realized with a start it was Officer Davis—the same cop who had been there when she'd found Ike's body.

"Where are you headed?" the officer asked.

"Home, I guess. Looks like we won't be able to open tonight."

"No, I'd say not," Davis agreed. "You be careful. Someone's angry. Hard to guess who."

Janet nodded slowly and climbed into her car without a word, chewing over the policewoman's words. *Someone's angry.* Until a couple of hours ago, she'd have said *Finch* was angry. Now he was dead.

But the list of angry people seemed long and noxious. Frank was angry about getting fired from his last two jobs. Abe's wife, Vanessa, was angry, convinced her husband was cheating. Benji the lawyer was angry that Ike had gotten away with murder so many years ago. Ollie's parents were angry that the police were complicit in protecting their son's killer. Was Jason angry? She started up the engine, mulling that over. If she was being honest with herself, sure, Jason was angry with the cops for messing with his business. But she'd have guessed he was more angry at O'Dell for serving the subpoena than Finch.

Of course, she couldn't know until she spoke to Jason. She picked up her phone and dialed his number using the keypad, instead of tapping his name, as if the process of pressing each number might make him more likely to answer. But once again, the call went straight to voicemail. She left Elizabeth a message, only advising her that the plan had changed, and that she should stay put at the church for now.

She stared out the windshield, barely noticing her route as she wondered why her boyfriend wasn't answering his phone. What was he hiding?

Ten minutes later she pulled up to her house in time to see the SWAT team loading up their trucks, ready to depart.

"You Janet?" one asked, swaggering up to her car.

"Yes."

"Here's your key. It wasn't as much fun as the battering ram, but I guess they can't all be fun."

"So no one was inside?"

"Nope."

"Did you guys take anything?" Janet checked the trucks

behind him, wondering if they were going to call her TV evidence and haul it away.

He pinched his lips together. "We're not thieves, we're law enforcement."

She nodded. "Mm-hmm. Right. So, did you take anything?"

"No," he said, before turning with a sneer.

The engines growled to life and all three SWAT trucks pulled away.

Janet stared uncomfortably at her house. It hardly seemed like home just then. Her boyfriend was gone and the police had been there more than she had in the last two days. Before she could shake the feeling of discomfort, Mel waved from the porch.

"Everyone okay?" Janet called, glad to have a reason not to go in her half of the duplex. "I hope they didn't scare the baby!"

"Not as much as they would have if they'd rammed in your front door! What were they looking for?"

"Jason," she answered, then said in a low voice, "Aren't we all looking for Jason."

She filled Mel in on the latest from the Spot, and the other woman whistled under her breath. "So . . . Now what?"

"Now we wait for the police to finish their investigation, I guess." They stared at each other for a moment before Janet turned toward her half of the structure.

"You wanna stay here tonight?" Mel asked, and Janet felt a sudden urge to cry at the offer. But before she could even consider it, Hazel let out an almighty yell that shook the entire first floor. Mel chuckled. "I'm not saying you'll get any rest, but you won't be alone at least."

"Thanks, Mel. I'll be fine."

"Don't—" Mel cut herself off. After a moment she said, "Just be careful." She shook her head as Janet turned to walk back to her car.

Maybe Mel knew that she wasn't going to wait on the police.

After all, they'd been wrong about just about everything so far. So she was going to get to work.

Finch's murder felt personal, and Janet was determined to get to the bottom of things, even if that meant starting back at the beginning.

Margaret, Vanessa and Abe, and Benji—she wanted to talk to all of them again, but on her own this time, and she'd start, she decided on the fly, with the doctor and his wife.

———

Abe's house looked much the same this time as the last, and Janet felt just as out of place as before.

Curtains fluttered at the house across the street and Janet knew she was on display as she walked up the path to the front door. She raised her finger to the buzzer, but before she pressed it, Vanessa flung the door open from within.

"What?" Gone was the matching athleisure wear from before. Instead, Vanessa wore designer jeans, a form-fitting sweater, and high-heeled booties.

"I'm sorry, are you headed out?" Janet asked, stepping aside to let her pass.

"No," she snapped, her face twisted in dislike as she stared at Janet.

"Oh." She'd never met anyone who dressed so meticulously to sit at home.

"What do you want?" Vanessa narrowed her eyes. "If you're looking for Abe—and you shouldn't be, if anything you were a small, disposable distraction for him—but anyway, he's not home." She stepped back and made to move the door.

Janet stepped across the threshold, blocking the other woman. "I actually wanted to talk to you."

Abe's wife was so surprised, she stopped pushing against the door. "About what?"

"About the other night. In my bar." Janet used her most supe-

rior tone, and it worked. The manners bred so strongly into
Vanessa came out, and she looked abashed at the memory.

She leaned against the wooden door frame. "Oh, that. Abe
insists I got everything wrong that night."

"Not everything," Janet said, hoping to shock Vanessa into
letting her in. No one in this kind of neighborhood wanted an
ugly scene outside. "Can I come in?"

Vanessa frowned but pulled the door all the way open.

Janet stepped into a massive entryway, about the size of her
entire house. An actual crystal chandelier hung from the vaulted
ceiling, and a curved staircase wound its way up to the second
floor. She followed Vanessa through to the kitchen, a room so
immaculate she was convinced they did as much home cooking
there as she and Jason did at their place.

"Wow," Janet said when they were both sitting at a claw-foot,
round cherry table surrounded by a wall of windows. "Great
place."

"Cut to the chase. Did you come here to tell me that you are,
in fact, sleeping with my husband?"

"No! I've only met Abe twice. Once here, and again at my
bar. He wasn't there looking for me, though. He was looking for
another woman."

"Oh, well now I feel completely at ease," Vanessa said with a
scowl. "Thanks for coming." She pushed up from her chair and
made to move past Janet.

"Sit down, Vanessa. After I've had my say, then you can act
shocked, or appalled, or whatever emotion comes to mind in
your designer booties. Until then, shut up."

Vanessa's mouth opened and closed twice before she finally
sank back into her seat. She had the impression Abe's wife was
grappling with how to deal with a rude person in her own house.
Her every instinct must have been telling her to offer Janet a
drink or hors d'oeuvres. She was trying hard to ignore those feelings and settled on looking over Janet's head at the far wall of
cabinetry.

Now that she had Vanessa's attention, Janet took her time. "Did you know that Abe's college roommate was hit and killed by a drunk driver?"

Vanessa didn't answer, and Janet waited. Finally, she blew out a sigh and said, "Yes."

"Did you also know that that man, Ike Freeman, was recently murdered behind my bar?"

A flicker of unease in Vanessa's eyes put Janet on high alert.

"Yes, I—Abe did tell me that, yes."

"What did he say?" Janet asked, curious as to what was making Vanessa so uncomfortable.

"He said that Ike Freeman was dead, that's all."

"Did you know that the murder happened the same night that Abe wasn't here at home, and wasn't at work like he'd told you?"

"No, I'm sure that's not—"

"The very same night. You told him at the Spot yesterday that his administrative assistant didn't know how to code the receipt from that twenty-four-hour diner. I did some digging, and it turns out there's only one twenty-four-hour diner in town. It's not by the hospital." Vanessa fiddled with her hair, her eyes now magnetically attached to Janet. "Do you know where it is?"

She shook her head.

"It's about two blocks away from the Spot."

No response from Vanessa, save a line that formed between her drawn eyebrows.

"Why would Abe have been near the Spot the night that Ike Freeman was killed?"

"He . . . he took a shower right when he got home. That morning?" Vanessa stared over Janet's head again. It was almost like she was talking to herself, except that her eyes occasionally flicked over to her guest. "And I found his clothes from that night in the outside trash can the next day. Not the kitchen trash can or the bathroom trash can. He'd taken them all the way outside. So I wouldn't find them. I thought it was because—because he'd been with another woman."

They sat in silence for a few minutes and Vanessa's countenance seemed to improve with each passing second. She finally looked over at Janet with a victorious smile. "So, you're telling me there's not another woman?"

"Well, no—not another woman, but a *murder*, Vanessa—"

"But not another woman! All right. I can work with that." Vanessa clapped her hands and stood up with markedly more spring in her step than when Janet had first arrived. "You've got to go. I've got things to do!"

"What things? You do realize that I'm telling you your husband may have been involved in another man's—"

"Oh please. Even if that's true, which I don't think it is," she added hastily as she steered Janet to the door, "I'm still not worried. All the lives Abe has saved in his career? And some old drunk who killed someone is dead now? My husband's karma is just fine."

Before Janet could think of a counterargument, she was alone on the front porch, her only company the echo of the front door slamming.

"Rich people are strange," she said out loud as she headed to her car. *She* wasn't ready to cross Abe off her list; in fact, he sounded more guilty than ever based on what his wife had said.

She circled his name on the list she'd made earlier and pointed her car across town. Time to check in with Ollie's parents. It had occurred to her this morning that Detective O'Dell hadn't asked them where they'd been the night Ike was killed. They had the strongest motive of anyone she'd met so far. Time to get some answers.

CHAPTER THIRTY

Though Janet had been there only days ago, she was surprised to find the house looked the same. So much had happened over the last week, it felt like months, maybe even years, had passed. But the flowering shrub by the door had the same endless number of blooms, and she admired the plant as the door opened and Margaret walked out.

"Crepe myrtle. Dan loves them, he just planted two more out back. They never stop blooming."

Janet reached out to touch the nearest flower. "The red is stunning."

"Blood red." Margaret walked down the steps to join Janet. "They're hearty, and the blooms last. It's a great combination. Janet, right?"

"Yes," she said, startled that the other woman almost seemed to have been expecting her. "I wanted to ask you a few questions. Do you have a minute?"

"More than a minute. Why don't you come in for some tea?" She turned and walked into the house without waiting for Janet to answer.

With only a cursory concern about walking into the house of

a woman she hadn't yet crossed off her suspect list in two murders, Janet followed her in.

The house was still and quiet. "Is Dan home?" she asked as they made their way into the kitchen.

Margaret put the kettle on the stove and went through the same methodical process of preparing the mugs. By the time the teakettle whistled, she still hadn't answered Janet's question.

"Dan always likes milk and sugar in his tea, but I think that masks the real flavor. You might as well just have chocolate milk at that point." She looked up from the mugs. "How do you take it, Janet?"

"Plain," she answered, the first prickle of unease touching her stomach. She took the steaming mug from Margaret and set it down on a coaster in front of her. It was just shy of one hundred degrees outside. She wanted a hot cup of tea like she wanted another dead body on her property.

Margaret blew on the surface of her tea and took a small sip before placing her cup on the table, too. "Perfect. What did you ask?"

"Ten minutes ago?" Janet stared at Ollie's mother over the curls of steam between them. "I asked where your husband is."

"Ah. Yes, Dan. Where is Dan. You're not the only one asking that question."

"What do you mean?"

"Well, I haven't seen him since yesterday."

"What are you saying? He's missing?"

"No, not missing. He left a note. Says exactly where he is going."

"Which is where?" Janet asked, perplexed by Margaret's demeanor. The woman was edgy and nervous, and kept looking out the window to the backyard.

"Well, it's not that specific. He just says he needs a break and is taking some time for his health." Margaret picked up her mug again and cradled it in both hands, like she was cold and needed the warmth. "It's not the first time it's happened. Dan doesn't deal with things as well as he used to. This business about Ike Freeman, it just ate away at him after you and that handsome detective were here. He needed an escape, and I understand that, I really do!" She ended with such force that tea slopped over the side of her mug and she set it down without taking a sip. "This house has been an absolute hive of activity these last days. Reminded me for a moment of having a teenager at home."

"What do you mean?"

"Just so many visitors. On Sunday it was Larsa."

Janet leaned forward. Now she knew where Larsa had gone after she'd left the Spot. "What did she want?"

"What she did was make my poor husband upset. What she wanted? Who knows. She was a rambling, incoherent mess."

"And it upset Dan?"

"Just all the talk, all the discussion about that day—the day Ollie died. You think you've forgiven everyone involved, and you spend a lot of time praying about the right thing to do, and you think you're there! You think you've made it to this kind of holier-than-anyone-can-imagine space, where you still miss your son but you've done what you're supposed to do. You've forgiven his killer. And then you realize, quite simply, Janet, that you haven't. You haven't forgiven the man who took your son, you haven't forgiven the ones who helped him get away with it, and you're in fact as angry as you were the day it happened."

"So . . . *Dan* was upset?" Janet asked, taking stock of Margaret's heavy breathing, red face, and glistening eyes.

Ollie's mother pulled a wadded-up tissue from her sleeve and dabbed at her eyes. "Fair enough. We were both upset."

"At Ike?"

Margaret agreed.

"At the police?"

Another grim nod.

"At Larsa?"

Margaret froze. "No. That poor girl is worse off than us. We, at least, had each other to lean on. She had no one. Nothing."

"How did she leave? Did she say anything?"

"Well, that's just it, that's what got Dan so upset. Her visit was difficult enough—but then she . . . Well, she must have been drunk is all I can guess. A rambling apology turned rude and confusing and we finally asked her to leave. She grabbed a branch of the crepe myrtle on her way out the door and snapped it clear off. Dan spent the next two hours working on the shrub, pruning it, cutting it, cleaning it up." Janet raised her eyebrows. "We planted it to memorialize Ollie. It's a very special plant to us. The blooms remind us that Ollie's love will live on through us, even if he's not here physically." She teared up again, and Janet looked down at her tea, unsure what to say. In the backyard, she saw two more flowering crepe myrtles. Mounds of dirt at their bases made her think they'd only been planted recently.

After a few moments, Margaret seemed to compose herself. She sniffed, and the tissue came out of her sleeve again. She got up and threw it in the trash, tucking a clean one into her sleeve before leaning against the counter by the sink.

"Well, I've taken up enough of your time," Janet said. "Thanks for the tea."

"If you can apologize to your friend—tell him I just wasn't in a space to chat earlier," Margaret said absently as they walked to the front door.

"What—what friend?"

"Your friend with all the tattoos? He was here earlier, said the two of you were working on something and he had some questions. But I just—I was just a mess earlier," Margaret said. "He said you'd be by later and it was no problem. Very nice gentleman. Very friendly for all those tattoos."

"Jason?" Janet asked, looking back at Margaret and then losing her footing on the last two steps down to the front walk. She managed to catch herself just before falling, face-first, onto the concrete.

"Yes, that's it!" Margaret said, tenderly touching a bloom on Ollie's plant. She hadn't noticed Janet flailing and turned back into the house before Janet's mouth had closed from the surprise of Margaret's last revelation.

She climbed back into her car. What an eventful twenty minutes. Larsa was possibly off the wagon, making rambling, confusing statements to Ollie's parents. Dan had been so upset with the police yesterday that he'd disappeared, mere hours before Detective Finch was murdered, and Jason was asking the same questions she was—had told Margaret they were "working together."

Funny, it didn't feel that way.

She took one last look at the crepe myrtle as she drove away, and a startling thought entered her mind. If they'd planted it after Ollie died, were they memorializing two other deaths with the new plants behind their house?

CHAPTER THIRTY-ONE

At a red light, Janet drummed her fingertips on the steering wheel, thinking. A cruiser drove by, going the opposite direction, and she instinctively turned her face away. She hadn't felt this on the run since she'd left Montana several years ago after her mother had died.

A horn blared and she took her foot off the brake, easing through the intersection and giving a single-finger salute right back to the driver behind her.

She needed to think about Benji, Ollie's old college roommate turned bicycle-rights lawyer. She was headed toward his downtown condo, but she suspected that he'd be much harder to press for information than anyone else on her list. As a lawyer, he would likely be adept at keeping interesting things to himself.

But instead of focusing on how she could get Benji to open up, all she could think about was Jason. What was he hiding? And was he trying to help Janet now or make her job more difficult?

Her stomach growled. It was after five, and she realized with a pang that she hadn't eaten anything all day.

Benji's brick building was an imposing structure—an old

candy factory from the 1920s, with high windows and weathered brick. She drove slowly past, her eyes trained on the entrance. The main door was in an alcove, set back several feet from the street. It looked dark and dangerous. Despite the sun still shining down outside, Benji's building resembled the opening scene from a movie where you'd yell at the stupid girl for going in anyway.

She wanted to talk to Benji, but her gut was telling her to keep driving. So that's what she did. She needed to get Elizabeth. She had to break the news about yet another homicide.

———

Janet saw Ike's car parked by the Dumpster at the church. She parked nearby and then headed up the stairs and pulled the door handle. It didn't budge.

She stepped back for a moment, unsure of the proper protocol. Should she knock at the house of the lord? Sounded like the title to a song you'd find in the hymnal. Before she could take action, though, the clunky lock turned over and Elizabeth pushed open the door.

"We watched you pull in." She stepped back to let Janet enter, then locked the door behind her and led Janet up the aisle, to the side of the altar, and through a door to a surprisingly normal-looking office space.

"I thought churches were always unlocked," Janet said once they were sitting at a small table by the door.

"Strange times, huh?" Elizabeth's eyes darted back to the exit. "Father Andrew thought we should be careful tonight." Janet nodded, and Elizabeth turned her worried brown eyes to her. "What happened? Why aren't we going through with the plan?"

"There was an . . . an accident." Janet looked down at her hands. "And I can't open the Spot tonight while police investigate."

"Why are police investigating an accident?" Elizabeth's focus on Janet was now razor sharp.

"Well, it wasn't exactly an accident. It was . . . ah, hell. Detective Finch is dead. Murdered, by the look of things."

"What? Killed at the bar?" Elizabeth fell back against her seat and all the color drained from her face.

"Yes. I'm not sure how it happened, but I—I found his body. It was shoved into the Beerador."

"Oh my God!"

"Who is calling for God?"

A young man walked into the room. By his dress, jeans and a T-shirt featuring some rock band she'd never heard of, she guessed he was an older altar server. "I'm sorry, sweetie, we'll just need a few more minutes here, okay? Or did you need the phone to call your mom or something?"

Elizabeth continued to stare blankly at Janet, but the altar server grinned and pointed to himself. "Me? Call my mom? She'd probably appreciate that, but we usually talk on Wednesday nights. I'm Father Andrew. You must be Elizabeth's friend Janet."

"Father?" Janet stared at the boy in shock, and before she could stop herself she said, "You look like you're fifteen!"

"Well, I'm not."

"I'm so sorry, I—I've never, I mean, I guess I've only ever seen old-man priests. Gray hair, potbelly, the whole bit. You look like you should still be in school—and I'm not talking about college. I mean high school or something." Then she added under her breath, "Maybe even middle school!"

"Long out, I'm afraid. Well, I graduated the seminary several years ago, but I guess in reality you never stop learning in the school of life, right?" She raised her eyebrows and he smiled again.

He held out a hand and she looked at it like it was an alien.

"You can touch me, you won't burn in a fury of hellfire, I promise."

"I'm sorry—I just never . . . it's strange to say it, but I've never actually talked to a priest before. I mean, except for confession, which is so painful, and you're not actually looking at each other, you know?" She reached out her hand and they shook.

"How was it?" he asked, dimples forming.

Janet smiled back. "Just like anyone else."

"Well, good. Now that we've established that I'm human, and not fifteen, let's check on Elizabeth." He turned. "You don't look so good."

Elizabeth shook her head and blinked a few times. "This is— it's just what I was worried about. I don't think it's safe here. I should go, but I don't know where . . ."

"You're coming home with me. That's why I'm here. We'll stay together and figure out what to do next. Come on." She stood and nodded at Father Andrew. "Thanks for your help, Father."

"You don't have to go, Elizabeth. This is a safe space, and we've made it even more so tonight for you, by locking the doors and keeping this monitor of the parking lot and entrances here for you to watch." He motioned to a small TV set on the desk nearby. "And I don't think you have to worry about visitors, anyway. Monday nights are very slow. Sometimes old Mr. Jones comes to light a candle for his wife, but that's not every week."

They all looked at the monitor as he spoke, and Elizabeth let out a moan when a pair of headlights swept across the lot.

A car pulled up to the main entrance and Janet moved closer to the TV, drawn to the monitor when she recognized the make of the car. "That's a Crown Vic," she breathed, wishing the screen was bigger. "Is that—" She bit down on her cheek to keep from gasping. She didn't want to alarm Elizabeth, but she grabbed her arm and pulled her up. "It's time to go. Let's go."

"Oh," Father Andrew said with a smile. "Well this is a nice surprise. It's one of our Eucharistic ministers. This is an unusual time for a visit, but I'll go let him in."

"Wait!" Janet blocked his path. "Patrick O'Dell can't know that we're here, okay, Father Andrew? Just keep him busy out front, and we'll head out the back door."

"I think that's a mistake. Patrick might actually be just what we need tonight. You know, he's a very highly regarded detective with the Knoxville Police Department. Maybe he'll know what to do."

"Or he'll try to kill us," Janet said, and Father Andrew snorted, then sobered quickly at her expression.

"I just came from my bar, where I found his partner dead. Elizabeth knows that a cop was involved somehow in Ike Freeman's death last week. I'm not saying Patrick is involved, but he's coming down mighty hard on my boyfriend with no evidence, his partner's dead, and now he shows up at the very church where the only woman who can tie a cop to Ike's murder is hiding out?" Janet glared at Father Andrew. "I'm not taking any chances. Now, we need to get out of here, and you don't have to help us, but you'd better get out of my way."

She grabbed Elizabeth's arm and pushed her out the door in front of her.

"Janet, Elizabeth, wait!" Father Andrew called. "You're going the wrong way. I'll hold O'Dell off by the sacristy. You head out the Epistle side and get directly into your car." At her blank stare he pointed. "That way. Wait until you hear me unlock the door." Janet nodded and he said, "Godspeed," then disappeared.

She would have laughed at the absurdity of the conversation if it didn't feel like their lives were on the line.

CHAPTER THIRTY-TWO

"Was he coming for us?" Elizabeth's voice shook as they made their way through town. The heat was still oppressive, and the long summer days meant the sky was still bright at quarter to seven at night. "Should we have left Father Andrew alone with O'Dell? Oh my God, if anything happens to him, I'll never forgive myself!"

Janet felt shaky for another reason entirely. "I know this is bad timing, but I need to eat." She pulled into a drive-through. "Do you want anything?"

"N-n-no," Elizabeth answered, "I can't eat now! I can't even think, to be honest."

Janet ordered a double cheeseburger, fries, a large soda, and a cookie. "You sure? I'm buying," she clarified, remembering that Elizabeth might have been stealing from the till at the Spot because of money trouble. Her bartender shook her head again, and Janet shrugged. "Suit yourself." When the drive-through employee handed over a bag of food, Janet dove straight into the bag of fries, shoving four into her mouth at once and reaching right away for more. Meanwhile, Elizabeth covered her face.

"Erf gow be aw-ight," Janet said around a mouthful of food.

She glanced over and slowed her chewing. Elizabeth was more than pale. Her face had taken on a greenish hue.

"Pull over! I think I'm gonna be—"

The rest of her words were cut off by a screech of tires. Janet wrenched the wheel over, and Elizabeth just got the door open in time. After two more heaves, she sat up and wiped her sleeve across her mouth. "The smell of that food—it just turned my stomach."

"I know the feeling," Janet said, chewing what now felt like a wad of wet concrete. She rolled the top of the full bag of food and tossed it into the backseat. Hard to keep your appetite with the smell of vomit in the air.

"I'm sorry."

"Let's go back to my house so you can clean up. It's going to be okay, Elizabeth. We're going to get through this."

"How can you say that? If that O'Dell guy *is* behind every-thing—he's got a badge. He can do whatever he wants and we can't stop him." She crossed her arms over her stomach and slumped against the door frame.

"I don't—I don't know who's behind this, but no one has that kind of power, Elizabeth. And eventually, the killer's going to screw up. Hell, they probably already did, we just don't know about it yet. They need to start laying low. I mean, you can't get away with too many crimes in a row. So at least we have that going for us." Janet smiled, realizing her words were true. They were only a block from home now, and she relaxed her grip on the wheel. "You mark my words, Elizabeth. I think we've turned a corner, here, and everything's going to be all right."

She pulled up to the curb, not realizing there was a problem until Elizabeth said, "Oh my God."

"Wha—" She saw it as soon as she turned toward the other woman. A message was spray-painted across the front of Janet's house.

Mind your business. Stay home.

"Well how can I stay home if you're targeting my house?"

Janet asked, trying to break the increasing tension in the car, but Elizabeth didn't smile.

"This was the killer, Janet. They're telling you that you're next!"

———

"I didn't see anything," Mel said. She frowned as she patted Hazel's back and adjusted the baby's head so it was squarely over a burp cloth lying across her shoulder. "I've been home all night. Kat's asleep, so we've just been sitting on the floor, talking about life." Janet shot a disbelieving look at her bouncer. "You have no idea what happens when you're alone with a baby for too long. You really do start talking about life. It's crazy."

"But didn't you hear anything unusual?" Elizabeth pressed, looking past Mel to Janet's front door.

"Nothing. I mean, what would I have heard, though? Someone pressing the nozzle on a can of spray paint? Graffiti's not exactly noisy, is it?"

"Pretty brazen, wasn't it? I mean, it's not even dark yet. Anyone driving or walking by would have seen them do it." Janet inspected the graffiti up close. Paint dripped down from each letter, as if the person was using spray paint for the first time that night and didn't know how far away to hold the can from the house.

"Do you think it was O'Dell?" Elizabeth asked. "He could have stopped by here on his way to the church."

Janet shook her head. "Graffiti seems pretty childish to me. Not something I'd expect from a cop."

"Then who?"

"Could have been a random teen," Janet said. Though she was still staring at the letters, she heard Elizabeth's irritated sigh.

"It's not a coincidence. Who did you talk to today? Who's angry?"

Janet barked out a laugh. "Who isn't angry is probably the

shorter list." She turned to find Mel and Elizabeth staring at her. "Oh, okay, let's see, I spoke to Abe's wife, Vanessa; Ollie's mother, Margaret; and then a bunch of cops at the Spot—"

"Including O'Dell!" Elizabeth interjected.

"Yes, including O'Dell."

"Anyone else?" Mel asked.

"No, but I tried to talk to Benji." She felt her face flush at the semi-lie. She'd driven right past his apartment without stopping, which wasn't much of an effort if she was being honest. "He wasn't, uh, he wasn't home. And I *need* to talk to Larsa," she hastily added, trying to cover her embarrassment. "Still no sign of Jason?" she asked, looking at her neighbor.

Mel shook her head. "Sorry, Janet. I haven't seen him, either."

Janet turned away to hide her frustration. She and Jason hadn't spent more than a day apart since they'd met. This behavior was unusual and, if she thought too hard about it, worrisome.

"Do you think he's on the run from the police?" Elizabeth asked. "They sure are putting the screws on pretty tight." Janet shrugged. "You don't think . . . you don't think he did anything, do you?"

"Oh, please," Janet said, glaring at Elizabeth and Mel. "There's no way. Like I told the cops on day one, Jason and I were here the night Ike was killed."

"Kat and I were loading up the moving truck that night." Mel eased into the lone chair on the porch. Hazel stirred sleepily, then fell quiet again. "Hard to believe how much life has changed, huh? New house, new job, new baby."

Janet tried to smile at Mel, but she felt the blood drain from her face at a sudden memory. She and Jason had been watching a new TV show the night before she'd found Ike's body. It was a remake of the old show *This Is Your Life*. Janet had fallen asleep on the couch right after it started and hadn't woken until the next morning. She'd slept for thirteen hours.

But now, with two dead bodies and a missing boyfriend, she

had to face facts, at least to herself: who was she to say where Jason had been all night?

"But what about Finch?" Elizabeth asked in a small voice. "I mean, you don't know where Jason was this morning, right?"

"But he wouldn't have needed to break the locks at the Spot!" Janet shouted triumphantly. Both women jumped, and Mel shot her a dirty look when Hazel let out a cry, but she hardly noticed. "Right? He wouldn't have needed to break the locks, he'd have just used his key. Jason is innocent." *Of killing Finch, at least*, she added silently.

CHAPTER THIRTY-THREE

"What is this place?" Elizabeth asked, gingerly stepping out of Janet's car and looking at the building in front of them.

Mel climbed out cautiously, too, but for another reason. "There's something gross on your car over here," she called, using her elbow to slam the door. "It's kind of smelly. And chunky. You don't think the spray-painter got your car, too, do you?"

"Oh, yeah, sorry about that," Elizabeth said, looking back at the door with a grimace.

"Onward," Janet said, walking forward with purpose. "The Wheelbarrow is the closest competitor to the Spot. And I mean in distance, not quality," she clarified as she pulled open the door. It was like walking into a smelly barn.

"The Wheelbarrow? Oh, I get it, Wheel-*bar*-row. I guess it's clever?" Elizabeth said, staring at the sign.

"It's more like trying to be clever and failing," Mel said. "If your goal is to get the word 'bar' into your name, surely there are better choices?"

"Like *Bar*bershop?" Elizabeth offered. "It's already known as a good place to meet up for dudes."

"Or *Bar*racuda?" Janet said. "Angry, fast fish you don't want to mess with."

"What about Em*bar*go?" Mel said, and Janet and Elizabeth nodded appreciatively.

"I like that," Elizabeth said. "You get both 'bar' and 'go' into the name. It's almost like some kind of sneaky mind-control thing."

"How did you end up with 'the Spot' as the name of your bar?" Mel asked, leading the way to three open seats at the counter.

"Oh, we didn't pick it. That's what it was called when we bought it, and it was too expensive to order a new sign. First round's on me, ladies." She motioned for the bartender.

The Wheelbarrow was as dimly lit as the Spot but had fewer tables, more shady characters, and not as many friendly faces— although that likely had more to do with the fact that they were surrounded by strangers, and were, perhaps, on the run from a killer.

They ordered their drinks, and then Mel lowered her voice.

"Assuming Jason is innocent of both murders—"

"He is!" Janet said.

"Then what are we going to do to prove it?" Mel asked.

The bartender slid drinks in front of the women and Janet downed half of hers in one sip. "The morning Ike died—"

"Ike Freeman?" the bartender asked, leaning against the counter. "I heard about that. Sad business, huh?"

Janet wrinkled her nose and took another sip, smaller this time, before looking up. "Who're you?"

The first rule of being a bartender is stay out of the conversation unless you're asked to be a part of it, but this guy seemed to be settling in for the long haul. He picked up a glass of beer from a lower shelf in front of him and took a sip. "I'm Carl. Longest-serving bartender here at the Wheelbarrow."

Mel rolled her eyes and leaned toward Janet and Elizabeth,

attempting to cut Carl out of their conversation. "What happened that morning, Janet?"

"I remember it well." Carl rested both elbows on the bar top, and leaned closer still to the group of women. "His daughter had been in here just the night before. We haven't seen her since. I'm sure she's right torn up over it all."

Elizabeth rolled her eyes, but Janet's stomach rolled over at his words and she leaned toward him. "Ike Freeman's daughter was here the night he was killed?"

"Well, yeah, I guess that's right. She used to come every night, though, so that's nothing newsworthy."

"Larsa Freeman?" Janet asked, just to make sure Ike didn't have another daughter she'd never heard about before.

"Yeah, you know her?"

"Sure," Janet answered. "Long, flowing hair? Drinks hot water with lemon?"

"Nah—well, she's earthy, sure, I'd even say kind of granola-y if you know what I mean, but she drinks straight-up gin. Sometimes with a squeeze of lemon. Mean as a snake, but a good tipper, which is more than I can say about most," Carl said, looking darkly around the room. "That guy, in particular." He pointed at a bearded man lurking at a corner booth. "I'm lucky if he leaves the penny behind on a five-ninety-nine drink special!"

Elizabeth stared at Carl in shock, but before any of the women could speak, a whiny voice rose from the far end of the bar.

"Can I getta beer over here or what? Carl? Can I getta—"

"Sorry, ladies, duty calls," Carl said, excusing himself and heading down the bar.

The three women put their heads together.

"Have you ever heard a bartender flap his lips like that before? Like a bird taking flight?" Elizabeth shook her head. "How is he still a bartender?"

"I don't care about that," Janet said. "Do you believe him?"

"No reason for him to lie," Mel said.

"So why did *Larsa* lie?" Janet asked. "She told the police she'd been home praying the night Ike was killed. She's also said, over the last week, that she's been sober for anywhere from one to three thousand days." She looked at Carl, who was now pulling a pint of beer for the other customer. "But she was here the night Ike was murdered."

"Drinking," Elizabeth added.

"Drinking very close to the Spot," Mel said. "What do you think? Four blocks?"

"Three," Janet said.

"Much closer than *your* home, at any rate," Elizabeth said.

Janet turned toward her bartender. "Did you see or hear *anything* at all from the other person that night? The one the cop was helping to move Ike's body?"

Elizabeth shook her head. "Not a thing. I guess I should have stuck around, tried to see who else was there—"

"Don't be ridiculous. You might be dead now if you'd done that!" Mel interrupted.

"And you did enough. You got Ike's car and got yourself out of there. There's nothing to feel bad about!" Janet added.

"Who's your money on?" Mel asked.

"For the killer? It seems murkier now than ever before!" Janet stared broodingly into her drink. "Abe, Benji, even Ollie's father all seem like possibilities. Now you add Larsa to the mix? Ugh."

"What about O'Dell?" Elizabeth asked after taking a fortifying sip of her beer. "He's so committed to proving Jason guilty. Isn't that suspicious? What if he's the one I heard, and Finch started asking too many questions?"

"I don't know. You didn't see his face this morning when he saw Finch's body. I'm not sure anyone, even in Hollywood, is that good of an actor," Janet said with a shudder.

"Suspicious, or just choosing the most likely suspect," Mel answered, stirring her cosmopolitan with a tiny red straw. "Sometimes cops just get stuck in a groove and can't see the forest for the trees, ya know?"

Janet looked at Mel. "What does that mean?"

Mel looked up. "Tell me this: does Jason have a record?"

"A what?"

"A criminal record," Mel said. "Of any kind."

Now it was Janet's turn to stir her drink. She finally heaved out a sigh. "Yes. A hacking conviction. He got a five-year suspended sentence when he was a teen. It was juvie court, and it was ages ago. He's been off probation for years."

Mel nodded sagely. "And that's all it takes, sometimes, for a cop to turn their focus on someone. He's probably the only one at the Spot with a criminal record, and that's what made him a suspect in O'Dell's eyes."

"Even Ike didn't have one!" Janet said with a bitter laugh. "Where did you work before the Spot, Mel?" she asked. Elizabeth looked over with interest.

"Nowhere," Mel answered, taking a small sip of her pink drink. "Nowhere worth mentioning."

Janet narrowed her eyes, but she dropped it. She didn't have time for another mystery just then.

"We're going to go ahead with our original plan, Elizabeth," she said, sitting up straighter on the stool. "It happens tomorrow night at the Spot. We'll call it a memorial for Finch and we'll see what shakes loose when we have all the players—all together."

CHAPTER THIRTY-FOUR

After a restless night of sleep at her graffiti-covered home, where every noise made her pick up her baseball bat and rush the door, Janet padded through the kitchen to the makeshift coffee station parked just outside the bathroom door. She caught sight of herself in the mirror—dark circles under her eyes, frizzled hair, pale skin—and decided an extra-strong brew might help her feel human again. She reached for the pot and grabbed air. Looking down she muttered, "Those assholes."

"Which assholes?" Elizabeth asked, coming from the guest room on the other side of the bath.

"Cops must have taken my coffeepot along with Jason's computers as evidence on Sunday." She shook her head at the injustice. What kind of unlawful activity could happen with a coffeepot? She was going to reread that subpoena. Just as soon as she was awake.

"That's just mean," Elizabeth said, opening the refrigerator. "When's this renovation supposed to wrap up?" she asked, motioning to the empty room behind them that used to be the kitchen.

"When will it *start* seems to be the more appropriate question."

"Juice?"

Janet sighed but took the cup Elizabeth offered.

After a shower and another quick conference with Elizabeth and Mel, Janet set out to find Larsa, but not before sending a text to Jason with a very specific request. She didn't know why he had taken himself out of the mix, but the fact that he'd been to Ollie's parents' house reassured her. If he wasn't on her side anymore, he'd have been long gone. Instead, he was lurking, asking questions, just like she was. That meant something. It meant she could trust him.

She drove directly away from civilization for fifteen minutes, from bright highways to shaded, two-lane country roads. She hadn't passed another car for five minutes when she finally slowed to make a sharp turn onto a small driveway. The contrast between this cemetery and the one downtown was sharp. Though marked only with a plastic banner stuck into the ground like a For Sale sign, the Descendants of Valor Cemetery was naturally beautiful this time of year. Wildflowers burst from the ground, not yet wilted with the afternoon heat.

She didn't know exactly where Ike was buried, so she slowly drove down paths in a haphazard manner, meandering this way and that. She passed old tombstones and newer graves still mounded with fresh dirt. The parklike setting was peaceful and quiet.

When she rounded the fourth or fifth bend in the road, she saw a lone figure among the grave markers and slowed to a crawl. The woman's arms were raised, scarves circled her neck, and rosary beads swung from one hand; with the window down, Janet could hear strange, organ-heavy monk-chanting music rise above the sounds of nature.

She parked her car and cut the engine, then raised her hand in greeting when Larsa looked over.

The other woman pulled her scarves closer around her neck before reaching for the bottle of water at her feet.

"How are you?" Janet called, not sure she wanted to get out

of the car. The cemetery was deserted, and who knew what Larsa had in that big bag of hers?

Larsa looked down at the speakers and reached over to lower the volume. Without the music, the sound of twittering birds and chirping crickets swelled like an orchestral crescendo.

"I'm finding it far more peaceful here than at your bar," Larsa said with a small smile. "Leaving that sin-soaked, booze-infested structure was probably the best thing I've done since my father died."

Janet stepped out of the car and stopped a few feet away from Larsa. "Are you okay?"

"I'll be fine. I always manage to be just fine."

Larsa attempted to regain some of her serenity and raised her face back up to the sky.

Janet bit her lip and considered the best way to approach what she'd come here to say. She needed Larsa's help to pull off her plan that evening. Silence extended between them, with Larsa raising her hands skyward again and Janet trying to figure out how to proceed.

"There are . . . new developments in your father's murder."

Larsa's eyes slowly opened and she lowered her hands. "What kind of developments?"

Janet filled her in on Finch's death.

"Do they have any suspects?" she asked, studying Janet intently.

Was that true concern, or something more sinister behind her eyes? Janet didn't know—she didn't trust her own impression of Larsa anymore. "No," she answered. "As far as I know they're still collecting evidence."

"Well, you know what the police say about that," she said, almost to herself. "Evidence will only get you so far."

"What does that mean?" Janet asked sharply.

Larsa smiled slightly and turned her music back up. "It just means evidence is amazingly accurate. As long as the police have something in their system to match it to. And I certainly hope they do this time. That's all." She looked quizzically back at Janet. "Is there anything else?"

"I've invited some people to the bar tonight." Larsa raised her eyebrows and she continued. "I was trying to figure out a way to help bring you closure," Janet said, skating close to the truth so she could really sell the story. "I called some of the people you said you wanted to talk to—to apologize to—for your father's actions. They want to talk to you, too. Maybe you could finally set down this burden your father left you with. Cross it off your list, you know? Ike's problems shouldn't follow you for your whole life."

Larsa closed her eyes. Janet was slightly downhill from the other woman, and the sunshine shimmering off her hair created a halo effect, a stark contrast to the tension Janet felt emanating from her.

"I'm not sure I'm strong enough," Larsa said after a long pause. Janet didn't disagree. It would have been a difficult encounter for anyone, but Larsa's hands shook slightly, and despite the cooler morning air, her temple was wet with sweat.

"It might be uncomfortable, that's true," Janet agreed, "but I think it's the best way to finally get peace. You don't have to come tonight, but it might help . . . lighten the load."

Larsa was quiet for a while before finally nodding. "What time should I get there?"

"Around eight o'clock."

She didn't answer. After a few moments, Janet backed away and climbed into her car.

One down, two to go.

She had an idea of how to get Abe to the bar, but she wasn't sure how she was going to entice Benji—if she could even find him.

There was no time to worry about what-ifs, though. She had a lot of work to do, and the clock was marching steadily toward eight.

CHAPTER THIRTY-FIVE

Janet swiped a dishrag across a pint glass as she stood behind the bar, staring at the door. She felt jittery again but shot Cindy Lou a dirty look when her bartender muttered, "It ain't gettin' drier than dry." Janet set the clean—and dry—glass on the shelf and took another off the drying rack while Cindy Lou handed two bottles of beer over the counter to a customer.

"That'll be nine—" Janet started before the customer cut her off.

"I just paid!" He shot a confused look at Cindy Lou, who nodded in agreement, and then turned to take his drinks back to his table.

"You'd better just settle right down, boss," Cindy Lou said before walking to the other side of the bar to help another customer.

Janet knew she was right, but it was nearing nine fifteen; Larsa was supposed to have shown up at eight, and Abe and Benji shortly after.

Mel caught Janet's eye from the door and shrugged before she turned back to check an ID.

"Is this happening or not?" O'Dell asked from a corner seat at the bar right across from Janet.

"I know Larsa wants to pay her respects," she said, glancing over at the detective. Earlier that day, after speaking with Larsa, Janet had called O'Dell. He'd reluctantly agreed to come to the bar for the memorial candle lighting but clearly wasn't happy to be kept waiting.

Dressed in plain clothes, he hunched over a glass of sweet tea, looking hulking and out of place at the bar. Not only did he take up enough real estate for two people, but he was dressed more formally than her other patrons, and his sports coat hung open, revealing an underarm-holstered gun and handcuffs hanging from his belt loops.

Janet couldn't decide whether she was relieved that the other people she'd invited appeared to be no-shows. It was one thing to *talk* about getting all the kindling together and hoping for a spark. It was another to wait for the fire.

"Any news on the . . . on the case?" she asked, and they both looked at the empty spot where the Beerador had stood. Janet rubbed some lingering fingerprint dust off the liquor shelves nearby with a bar towel.

O'Dell grunted and took another sip of his tea.

"Excuse me," Nell said. O'Dell had to shift sideways to make room, and the older woman brushed against his arm as she squeezed into her regular seat at the bar. Her eyes lit up at the contact.

Janet bit back a grin, then turned away to fill an order from a persistent customer. Business wasn't booming as it had right after Ike's murder, but it was busier than a usual Tuesday night.

She lost track of time busing tables, keeping on top of dirty glassware, and filling drink orders. Eventually her phone vibrated on her hip.

She reached down and read the incoming text from her father. Her breath caught in her throat. It was a lot of information—mostly screenshots of heavily redacted files from the old Knox County courthouse.

My source went down to the file room personally and pulled the case file. You're welcome.

It wasn't a smoking gun, but it was close.

It was certainly enough to change everything.

She tucked the phone guiltily into her pocket when O'Dell spoke.

"So much for a memorial. Makes me more depressed than I was before. Does no one care?" He nodded when she motioned to his glass and she refilled his tea. "How late are you open?"

"Supposed to be two a.m., but I'm going to call it early." She felt the weight of O'Dell's disappointment added to her own, that her plan, however tenuous it had been, was a complete failure. Janet rang the cowbell hanging above the cash register and Nell groaned.

"Last call!" she shouted, then rang the bell one last time, just to make sure no one could claim not to have heard it later.

Nell put two fingers out, so Janet lined up two drinks in front of her, then helped a customer cash out before her impatient fingers ran out of things to do. Just as Cindy Lou started to run dirty glasses through the washer, Mel made a funny "hup-hup-hup" sound at the door.

Janet looked up to see a long, blond, frizzy head of hair sail past the bouncer. Larsa's eyes scanned the space before locking onto Janet, and she headed, unsmiling, toward the bar.

"I almost didn't come, but in the end, I thought, *I want to hear what Abe has to say*," Larsa said. "Do you know I've decided he must be guilty of something? I'd like to have the chance to ask him some questions."

"I . . . I would, too," Janet said, taking a deep breath, hoping O'Dell didn't jump up from his seat too quickly.

"Uh, yeah, we'll take two frozen margaritas and some kind of loaded fries basket." A man wearing jean shorts and a bright orange tank top had scooted right in front of Larsa and plopped down in the seat Janet had been saving for her.

With a frown of distaste on her face, Janet said, "We don't

serve frozen drinks—or food. Do you want it on the rocks? Cindy Lou?" She motioned for the bartender to take over.

"Hon? On the rocks?" he called back to his date. What ensued was a loud and lengthy back-and-forth conversation on whether a bar could choose to not serve frozen drinks.

"Sir, if I can have you move away from the bar until you're ready to place your order—now," she said with a look that brooked no argument. Larsa stepped up to the empty seat and smiled when Janet placed a glass of fizzy water in front of her and slammed a lime wedge onto the rim. "They should be here any moment."

"They?"

"He, I mean—Abe."

"Okay, what about a frozen spritzer?" Orange Tank Top Guy was back.

"Oh, a frozen spritzer? Let me check." She stared at the man without moving. "Nope, we're fresh out of frozen spritzer." She sent him scurrying back to his date with a glare and Larsa sat down. Before she could say anything, though, the front door opened again, and this time a tall, lanky man walked in, waving off Mel's attempt to card him. He stalked directly to Janet at the bar as if he'd spotted her from outside and knew just where to go. He stopped behind the row of chairs, towering over Larsa.

"Don't do that again, Janet. People at the office are starting to talk—asking questions that I can't exactly explain to Vanessa."

I'll bet, Janet thought, a grim smile on her face. "You wanted to talk to Larsa, Abe. Here she is," she said, motioning to the woman just below him.

He froze and stared at Janet for a moment before his eyes traveled down to Larsa's golden crown of hair. "Oh. I, uh . . . oh."

"Have a seat, Abe." Janet pulled a pint of beer for him and plunked it down next to Larsa. His face was still slightly stunned as he picked up the beer without taking his eyes off Ike's daughter and gulped half the glass down. He finally tore his gaze away and looked reproachfully at Janet.

"I'm serious. You don't know what my office is like. You can't go in there telling my receptionist to have me stop by 'late night' to discuss things. It sounds dodgy. She'll tell Vanessa, and I'll never be able to explain things, especially lately, she's off her rocker, you saw her—"

"I don't plan on visiting you again, so I think we're all set on that front," Janet said drily.

Abe nodded and took another bracing sip of beer.

"Janet told me you wanted to talk. About what?" Larsa asked in her dreamy way.

On the other side of the bar, O'Dell fidgeted with his wristwatch.

"Just wait," she muttered, and plunked a bowl of trail mix down in front of him.

She hoped he would stay put. No one had noticed him yet, and she wanted to keep it that way for as long as possible.

"What's—"

"Just wait. And listen." She tuned back into Abe and Larsa's conversation.

"I—well, I just wanted to say I'm sorry for your loss. Sorry about your dad, I mean," Abe said.

"You are?" Larsa fixed her large, bulging eyes on him.

"I am. He changed my life. I don't thank him for it, but at the same time, I guess I do."

"Hmm." Larsa turned back to her drink, stirring it with the tiny black straw before taking a sip. "I think you brought nothing but heartache to my dad—especially at the end."

"I brought heart—what? What do you mean?" Abe asked, incensed.

"Were you there at the end?" Larsa asked.

"No—that's not what I—I just came here—I wanted to talk to you because I know what you must be going through, and I . . . I . . ."

Larsa ignored his stuttered excuses. "Did he say anything—at the end, I mean?"

Janet stole a look at Detective O'Dell. Larsa was a better interrogator than he was. O'Dell had pushed his drink aside and stared, captivated, at Abe and Larsa.

Meanwhile, Abe's face had turned ashen. His mouth opened and snapped shut wordlessly before opening again. It was another voice that spoke, though.

"As a lawyer, I recommend you not say anything else, Abe."

Janet had been so focused on Abe and Larsa that she hadn't even noticed Benji sit down on Abe's other side.

"Benji," Abe said, but not with relief—more like accusation. "I think it's fair—it's right for her to know—"

"There's been nothing fair about this family since they first crashed into our lives, Abe. Like I said, I think it's time for you to shut up and for us to walk out of this bar and never look back —not at the bar or at that family." He spat the last word out as if it were a curse. His face was twisted in dislike as he looked at Larsa.

Larsa blanched at his tone, but Janet, sensing a pivotal moment in the evening, jumped in. "It's not fair to bleed out alone on the asphalt," she said. Larsa cringed and Abe looked down at his beer. She held up a hand to cut off Benji's response. "What happened to your friend Ollie wasn't fair, either." She fixed Benji with a stare. "Wouldn't you agree?"

"It's not that I don't agree," he answered in a measured tone. "But sometimes, when shit happens, it happens for a reason."

Janet looked reflexively at the swear jar before saying, "Did it happen for a reason anyone here can say?" She looked pointedly at Abe, who was now staring at his drink as if it were an escape potion.

"I—look, I don't know what happened, but I was there— here—at the end," Abe said. "I don't know who killed your father, though, Larsa."

Larsa didn't say anything, so Janet leaned in to cut Benji out of the discussion. "What do you mean you don't know? You just said you were here—*that night*! Who else would know?" Abe shook his head, and Benji stood, trying to pull Abe up by the elbow. "Why were you here, Abe?" Janet demanded. "And more importantly, why did you put this GPS tracker on Ike's car?"

Abe gasped when she placed the small, magnetized device onto the bar in front of him. "How did you—where did that . . . Wait, what happened to it?"

Janet was ready with a follow-up question, but before she could get it out, Benji said, "Okay, folks, I think that's enough for the night." He put his hand on Abe's shoulder. "Time to go. As your friend, I'm telling you to get a lawyer before you do or say anything else."

CHAPTER THIRTY-SIX

"I don't need a lawyer." Abe shook his friend's hand off and drained the last of his beer. "At least, I don't think so."

"As a lawyer, I can tell you that everyone here needs a lawyer." Benji motioned to the group of people listening raptly and then in an undertone, he said, "And if you think you don't, I'm almost certain that you really, really do." But despite his own plea for silence, Benji seemed unable to stop himself from adding, "It's tearing you up, isn't it?"

Abe nodded sharply and then held his glass out to Janet. She pulled him another pint. After he took a slow, steady sip, he carefully placed the glass down in front of him.

"I think about the accident a lot. Did you know that?" Abe looked up from his glass to meet Larsa's gaze. "Not just in the last week, either. I mean, I think about it all the time, ever since . . . ever since Ollie died." He looked away when a tear rolled down her cheek. "I don't say that to make you feel bad— it's just how it is. I think about the squeal of the tires, hear the crunch of metal as Ollie went down, and the sound of his head— God, the sound of his head hitting the pavement." His breath stuttered and he took another drink before looking back to

Larsa. "You don't know how the nurses make fun of me—I tell everyone to wear bicycle helmets. A patient will come into the office asking about a blister on their ass, and I make sure to tell them to wear their helmet next time they ride anywhere before they leave my office. I just can't stop thinking of that awful sound."

He took another shaky breath. "I was always so surprised that I never saw your dad again after Ollie died. One minute, he was there, asking in a slurred voice what he'd hit, and the next, he was gone—ferreted away to safety while I waited with Ollie for an ambulance.

"Knoxville's small, you know?" he said to Janet. "It's a small, big city. Odds were I'd run into him again at some point. I always knew what I'd say—worked on my speech of forgiveness all the time." He turned back to Ike's daughter. "It's not that I wanted him to suffer, but he never apologized, you know? And not just to me! Not to Ollie's own family, either."

When he lapsed into silence, Janet prompted him. "But then you did see him?"

Abe barked out a laugh. "I didn't just see him—he hit me with his damn car!"

Janet sucked in a breath. "What? When?"

"A few weeks ago. I was coming home from a late shift at the hospital—I fill in sometimes in the emergency department. I was tired as hell, just trying to get home to sleep, when a car came out of nowhere and sideswiped me. I was able to keep control of the wheel, but the other car went careening off the road and slammed into a pole." Abe ran a hand over his forehead and said, "Of course, I stopped right away to check on the other driver—had the phone to my ear to call 911 when I recognized him. He must have recognized me, too, and started ranting about ghosts from his past. Well, once I realized he wasn't seriously injured, I—well, I read him the riot act and told him to get off the roads and stop drinking—or at least stop drinking and driving." His voice had risen over the din of the crowd, and some patrons nearby looked over to see what the fuss was about.

"You were angry," Janet said.

"No, no, no," he laughed, but the sound wasn't happy. "'Angry' doesn't begin to describe it. I was livid! He killed my roommate ten years ago and could have killed me that night if I hadn't moved my car at the right time. Did he learn nothing from Ollie's death?"

Janet looked over to see how Benji was reacting. His face was closed off, but he said, "So, you called 911 like any good citizen would have done. Abe, I think that's enough."

Abe shook his head, though. "Don't you see? It wasn't enough. He was out there, drinking and driving again! When I saw the ambulance in the distance, I left—didn't want to stick around and watch him act the victim. I scoured the papers for the next few days and couldn't believe there was no sign he'd been arrested—or at least charged with DUI."

"That's why you had Benji call and check his record?" Janet asked, remembering her father had told her a lawyer was recently digging into Ike's history. She was desperate to keep the conversation going.

"Yes! I don't understand why he was able to keep wriggling out of being held responsible!"

Larsa finally spoke. "What did you find out?"

Benji shook his head. "Abe, I think that's enough. We don't owe anyone here anything, and that includes this woman."

Janet held the GPS tracker out to reclaim Abe's attention. "So you took matters into your own hands and contacted the best security expert you could find." Janet almost smacked herself in the head when she realized what was going on. Jason must have recognized Abe when the doctor came into the Spot and fixed Janet's finger. Abe hadn't spared Jason a second glance, he'd been so worried about Vanessa's assumption he was cheating on her, but Jason must have known at once that Abe was somehow involved in Ike's death, and that was why he'd disappeared. "Is your car damaged?"

"Hell yes it's damaged! The whole driver's side is smashed in."

Janet nodded. Jason's absence finally made sense—Abe was his client, and Jason was doing his best to protect him. But Abe was nothing to Janet, and she wasn't about to let him off the hook now, so she pressed on with another question. "You wanted to keep track of Ike at all times. Why? What were you planning?"

"I thought I could keep him from drinking and driving—or at least make sure he was arrested if he did it again! I figured if his car was at a bar for longer than an hour and then started moving again, that meant that he was drunk and shouldn't be on the road. I was just going to keep track of him, so I could tip off the police. He shouldn't have gotten another chance to kill someone! Why am I the only one who seems to feel that way? He was dangerous—and you know what? I'm not sorry he's dead. Now I can sleep easy at night, knowing the rest of us are safer for it."

Janet looked at Larsa. Ike's daughter stared into her sparkling water, her eyes sparkled with unshed tears. Janet reached out to touch her hand, but Larsa pulled away, shaking her head violently. "No," she said, finally looking up at Abe. "That's not true!" She banged her hand down on the bar to emphasize her anger, but then she clamped her lips and fell silent.

It was Janet who spoke next. "That's a nice story, Abe, but it doesn't explain why you were here in the dark, deserted parking lot of the Spot on the night Ike was murdered."

"There's a lot I can't explain," Abe said, staring over Janet's head at the back wall of the bar.

Larsa wiped away a stray tear that had streaked down her cheek. She mumbled something, and when no one answered, she cleared her throat and said it louder. "Try. You'd better try to explain why you were here the night my father was killed."

Abe fell quiet, though. When Janet looked to Benji, she was surprised to see him looking at Abe with a mixture of surprise and concern.

"Abe, I agree with Larsa. Try."

CHAPTER THIRTY-SEVEN

Abe lifted his glass to his lips and then looked surprised to find that it was empty again. He started to hold it out to Janet, but seemed to think better of it and instead set it down carefully on the coaster in front of him.

"I can only tell you what I know—and things get hazy at a certain point."

"Hazy when you killed my father?" Larsa's voice was oddly triumphant, and O'Dell sat forward in his seat, staring not at Abe, but at Ike's daughter.

"No, hazy when he nearly killed me—again." Abe swirled the foam around at the bottom of his glass and then slammed it down on the counter. "God dang it. *Again!*" He picked up the GPS tracker. "Yes, I bought this from a security expert here in town and slapped it under Ike's car one morning. I was on my way to work and made a quick detour to his house—figured he'd be sleeping off whatever hangover he had from the night before and no one would notice.

"I was mad—just furious—that Ike kept getting away with things. He killed Ollie and suffered zero repercussions, and then he ran me off the road and somehow, instead of getting booked into jail, got a ride home—again. When Benji told me there weren't any subpoenas or arrest warrants in the system for him, I decided to track him at night, and tip off police when he was at a bar."

"That's not an easy job," Janet interjected, thinking about how Jason could track someone with all of his specialized equipment and how different it would be for an average joe.

"Yes, I realized that the first time I tried to see where Ike was. That's why Vanessa thinks I'm cheating—I'm online all the time, looking up GPS coordinates, trying to see if there's a bar nearby."

"Why didn't you tell her, man?" Benji asked. "She'd understand."

"No, she'd tell me to move on, and I just—I couldn't. I needed to see justice served *just once* when it came to this guy."

Benji rubbed a hand across his jaw, but he finally nodded.

"So, last Wednesday night, I was working late but checked to see where Ike's car was before I left the hospital for home. It was after two in the morning, and there it was, parked right in the lot of a bar. The bar was closed and his car was there—I figured he must have drunk too much and left his car. I thought maybe he had finally learned something." He looked up. "And I also realized I was being stupid. A GPS tracker on his car? What had I been thinking?"

He looked at Benji, who shrugged, but Janet nodded. She got it. If someone in authority lets you down—in Abe's case, the police had, time and again—then you take care of it yourself.

"I decided to take the tracker off his car. I mean, it was an extreme idea in the first place, and Vanessa was getting hysterical about things . . . it just wasn't practical. But when I got there—got here," he corrected himself, "I found Ike, passed out in his car, drunk. I just . . . I couldn't believe it."

O'Dell, who'd been leaning forward with increasing interest since Abe started talking, was unable to stay out of the conversation. Only Janet heard the scrape of his bar stool as he pushed out of his seat, but when he approached, Benji sucked in a breath, clearly recognizing him from an earlier interview.

"So, you stabbed him—decided to exact your own street justice? Is that what happened?" O'Dell said, towering over the group of suspects.

"No!" Abe said, clearly upset. "Well, I don't know exactly what happened next."

"Because you blacked out in a fit of rage," Larsa said with conviction, "after you stabbed my dad."

"No, that's not what happened. I mean, I don't think . . ."

Benji left his own bar stool and wedged himself between Abe and O'Dell. "You're in it now, friend. Tell us everything you know. Now is not the time to leave anything out."

Abe took a deep breath and turned to Janet, the only one not staring at him with contempt or judgment.

"I confronted him, yes. He was passed out behind the wheel —why wasn't he in the backseat, for God's sake? So, I knocked on the window until he came to. I was just going to talk some sense into him, I swear, but he came up swinging. He thought I was some kind of ghost—someone there to punish him—"

"Weren't you?" Larsa said combatively with a strange look on her face.

"No. Well, yes, but not like that. I wanted him to stop drinking and driving, and I was angry, yes, but then he took out a knife and came after me. I barely dodged his first swipe, but then he dropped the blade. We both dove for it, and that's the last thing I remember."

"What a load of crap," Larsa said, glaring at Abe. "You're going to claim you blacked out and don't remember killing my father? Officer, arrest this man. He as good as confessed to murder."

O'Dell didn't move, but Benji did. He turned to Abe and said urgently, "What's the next thing you remember?"

"I came to maybe an hour later. Ike was lying next to me, but he was breathing—he was alive, I swear—and the knife was still in his hand. I didn't want to risk getting hurt even more, so I took off. I just got in my car and drove to a twenty-four-hour café to clean up, get some coffee, try and recover my wits. Then I went home. I swear, he was alive when I left!"

"Were you safe to drive with what I'm guessing was a fresh concussion? Doesn't sound like someone who should've been behind the wheel!" Larsa snarled.

Abe blanched but nodded slowly. "I agree. I wasn't thinking clearly—fear drove me from that lot. I didn't know what had happened."

"Why didn't you call the police?" O'Dell asked.

"I was going to! I got home, fixed myself up as best I could, and was going to call and report the crime—I mean, Ike had assaulted me! But then I saw on the news that he'd been killed, and I knew it didn't look good."

"Of course it didn't look good! It still doesn't! It looks like you're the one who killed him!" Larsa raged.

"Wait just a moment," O'Dell said before Abe could respond. Janet had been so engrossed in hearing Abe's version of events that she'd almost forgotten the homicide detective was standing right there. He turned his piercing gaze on her and said, "Janet, you've been holding out on me, but that stops now. I need to know how you got that GPS tracker. Where is Ike's car?"

CHAPTER THIRTY-EIGHT

The room seemed to contract, to heat up, and Janet felt cramped behind the bar. She hadn't been planning on revealing any of her secrets—at least not yet—but with O'Dell staring her down, she decided to put phase one of her plan into action.

"Cindy Lou?" she called. Her assistant manager scurried back to the office. "Hold on," Janet said, looking up at the TV monitor closest to her. The replay of a favorite UT Knoxville football game cut off mid-down and the screen went to black. Several customers shouted out in protest. "Oh, please," she muttered, "Y'all have seen that game a dozen times. Spoiler: UT wins!"

"Janet?" O'Dell's fingers tapped against the handcuffs clipped to his belt. His impatience was palpable.

"Just wait," she said, crossing her arms over her chest. "Ah, here it is." Cindy Lou had changed the TV input from cable to Janet's computer system. Old Ben's surveillance video played on every television set in the bar. Earlier that day, Janet had asked Jason to cue it up to the struggle over the knife between Ike and Abe.

"Ooh, I bet that really hurt. Did you need stitches?" Cindy

Lou asked when she walked out of the office just as Abe went down hard on-screen.

"Probably should have gotten two or three, but I didn't," he answered darkly.

"What the hell is this, Janet?" O'Dell asked. "You said there wasn't any surveillance video. We subpoenaed your boyfriend and he said that it was gone. Plus, we took all of his computers. So where'd you get this?"

"This is from our neighbor's camera." Janet explained about the abandoned building next door, and O'Dell swore loudly.

Larsa's eyes were locked in on the screen, and one hand covered her open mouth. O'Dell's laserlike focus shifted and he assessed her with new eyes. Janet felt a surge of hope that O'Dell wasn't in on the crimes.

"Larsa," Janet rested her elbows on the bar top and leaned forward, "why don't you tell us what happened that night— before you called your uncle in for help." She hated to admit it, but this evening would likely have gone off the rails just then if not for her father's text.

"Uncle?" Benji asked, shifting his gaze from Larsa to Janet. "Who's her uncle?" In that moment, Janet could easily picture him in the courtroom, both his tone and stance demanding answers.

"Step-uncle," Janet clarified, "but same thing, really. You knew Finch practically your whole life."

"And he failed me every step of the way, just like my father did," Larsa whispered. "It's his fault—all his fault."

"Finch? What's going on?" O'Dell's eyebrows knitted together, his frown equal parts disbelief and anger.

"Why do you think it was me?" Larsa asked Janet, ignoring O'Dell completely.

"It was something you said last week. You were telling me about that last conversation you had with your dad on the phone. Only, what you said wasn't something you'd say to someone still alive—it was something you'd say to someone already dead."

Larsa looked confused for a moment, but then her face cleared. "I was so relieved he couldn't hurt anyone else. I did say that to him . . . after. Does that make me an awful person? I felt no remorse that he was dead—only that I'd killed him by accident."

She looked furtively around the room, her eyes finally landing on the tap in front of her. She held her glass out for Janet. "Fill me up first, okay?"

"You don't drink!" Janet said, refusing to take the cup.

"I . . . I only quit last week—Thursday morning, as a matter of fact—but it's not going so well." Her hand shook. What Janet had mistaken for overwhelming emotion last week now looked more like withdrawal symptoms.

Janet still didn't move, but Elizabeth, drawn from the office by the spectacle unfolding, reached past her and took the glass. Larsa's brow furrowed for a moment, and then she licked her lips in anticipation as the alcohol flowed. When the glass was in her hand, she took a long, slow sip before speaking again.

"It wasn't supposed to happen, you know. I just came here to talk. I knew this was Ike's hangout—he'd been coming here for years."

"You just happened to be in the neighborhood after the bar closed?" O'Dell asked. "Where were you coming from?"

She took another slow sip, then she and Janet said together, "The Wheelbarrow."

"Where?" Abe asked.

"The dodgy bar down the street," Janet answered.

"That's a bit rich, coming from you," Benji said, looking around the Spot with a frown.

Janet bit back a retort and tried to focus. She wanted Larsa to share everything.

"I've been battling demons for a while now," Larsa said, swirling the cheap draft beer like it was a fine wine.

"So you were drunk and came to talk to your drunk dad?" Abe interjected. "What a great plan. What did you want to tell him that couldn't wait?"

"My uncle had told me about Ike's recent accident, and I was upset. Dad ruined our family when he killed Ollie. I know you think he got off easy by not facing charges," she said, turning to Abe and Benji, "but it was the worst thing, in the end. If he'd have gone to jail, he would have been forced to sober up. He might have come out a new man. Instead, he drank more. The guilt nearly killed him, and it did take my mother. Without her, I was lost. In the end, I turned to the same thing that ruined my father." She took a drink of the very thing she professed to despise.

"Need another?" Janet asked angrily, motioning to her empty pint glass.

"God, yes," she said, holding the glass out.

Benji smashed it out of her hand, and Larsa flinched at the crash of breaking glass. In the silence that followed, Janet looked up, shocked to see that the bar was empty, save for the people involved in the investigation. Mel was ushering the last patron, Nell, out the door. Then her bouncer turned back, her stance wide, her eyes narrowed as her gaze swept the room.

"Enough!" Abe shouted. "Just tell us what happened, Larsa. Stop blaming other people and tell us what you did."

Larsa was startled for a moment, then another tear streaked down her cheek. She roughly wiped it away. "I got here too late —the bar was closed and the parking lot was empty. I was going to head back to my car—I mean, walk home," she corrected herself when Benji gasped in anger, "when I saw Ike lying on the ground. He was alone, so you must have already left," she said to Abe. "I tried to wake him up—I—I was angry. I mean, who passes out on the ground? Jesus. He woke up swinging that damn knife of his, though. I shouted at him—told him he was an embarrassment to our family for his behavior. He didn't disagree, but then I fell back against the curb and he tripped over my feet and landed on the knife right by the Dumpster. I rolled him over . . . it was too late. I called my uncle, but by the time he got there, Ike was dead."

"Why didn't you call 911?" Janet asked, not sure she could buy Larsa's story completely.

"Uncle Mark said it didn't look good for me. He... he didn't want me to take the blame. He'd risked so much for my family already."

"What does that mean?" O'Dell asked, staring intently at Larsa.

"He was the first on the scene when . . . after . . . when Ollie died. He drove Ike home that morning and didn't pick him back up for a Breathalyzer for the whole shift. He was trying to protect us," she said, her eyes filled with pain as she looked at O'Dell. "But he only made it worse for us."

"W-worse for you? You p-people still don't get it! You never think about anyone else," Abe stammered. "Ollie's family was broken by his death and again when Ike wasn't charged. Didn't Finch know that? How could he have done that to them—to us?"

"Family," Elizabeth said with a shrug, as if that explained everything. Maybe it did.

"That certainly explains why the paperwork for Ike's recent DUI didn't get filed," Benji said, sitting down slowly. "Finch buried the report so Ike wouldn't get charged."

"Sounds like something he'd do," Larsa agreed.

"You tell a nice story, Larsa," Janet said, "but let's not forget there's another dead body to discuss. And Mark Finch's death was no accident. So what happened?"

CHAPTER THIRTY-NINE

An uncomfortable silence fell over the group. Larsa took small, savoring sips of her beer. O'Dell's piercing gaze moved down the line of people. Abe shifted uncomfortably in his seat. But no one spoke.

After a few more minutes Janet cleared her throat. "Cindy Lou, do you know how our security system works?"

The bartender looked up from the glass she was wiping, her face blank. "Huh?"

But Abe snapped to attention. So did Benji.

"I asked if you know how our security system is set up. How the actual cameras work."

"Oh, uh . . . no, boss. I have no idea."

"Well, it turns out a few weeks ago, I started to suspect that someone was stealing money from the cash drawer." She locked the drawer, then pulled the key out, tucking it into her pocket for safekeeping. "I asked Jason Brooks—my security-expert boyfriend," she added, talking over Abe's gasp of recognition, "to wire the place from top to bottom. Top," she said again, pointing to a tiny disc embedded in the ceiling above the cash register, "to bottom." This time she pointed to the bottom edge of the front door.

Mel, surprised to suddenly be in everyone's line of sight, stepped away from the door.

Silence fell again while the group looked at the door, perplexed.

"In the cooling register cover?" Mel said, inspecting the brass plate.

"Yup," Janet said. "Right there in the corner. It's practically invisible. But the camera is all-seeing. Gets a great shot of anyone who's leaving the bar through the front door. Then a camera right over . . . there"—she pointed to the space above the office door—"can capture anyone walking toward the back of the bar. So," she said, looking back at the group, "coming, going, and being here"—she pointed back up to the ceiling—"all recorded. And the best part is, it's not on a timer, it's motion activated. So *whenever* someone's moving around in the bar, it starts recording."

"That must take up a lot of computer space," Benji said. "How many hours can you keep at a time?"

"I have terabytes of storage."

"Terabytes? That's—that's enough for—"

"Days—no, weeks of video. It's got 1080p high-def resolution, night vision, a huge field of view—" She noticed that Cindy Lou looked lost and said, "It means the camera captures a wide shot of the room, doesn't miss anything. Oh, yeah, and it records sound, too."

"Wow," Abe said.

"My man is thorough," Janet said with a shrug. "What can I say?"

O'Dell stood up, his face red again. "Are you saying you have video evidence of the murder of a police officer and haven't yet offered it up?" He breathed in and out noisily a few times, like he was trying to control his temper. "Janet Black, I should arrest you right now for obstruction of justice. That was my partner who was shot and shoved into a damn refrigerator like a piece of meat yesterday, killed in cold blood"—the group cringed at the expression, but O'Dell plowed on—"and you couldn't bother yourself to let anyone know?"

"What I'm saying, O'Dell, is that the person who killed Finch has nothing to gain by remaining quiet. In fact, they'd better come forward now. There's no hiding anything here." She looked darkly at the group. "Not when every little step and sound you make is being recorded."

She narrowed her eyes at Abe. Just behind him, a police officer slipped into the room, then another. A third led Mel outside. Janet started to lose focus. What was going on?

"Abe?" she said, watching the other man fidget with his watch. "Now's the time."

"Time for what?" he said, looking up. "I didn't kill anyone. I —I mean, yes, I should have called 911 when I found Ike drunk and passed out behind the wheel, but I don't think those are technically crimes, isn't that right, Benji?"

Janet looked to his old college roommate and friend for confirmation, but he was staring at the camera above the cash register with barely concealed rage.

"I can't believe it's going to come down to this," Benji said, shaking his head.

"Down to what?" O'Dell asked, carefully putting some space between himself and the rest of the group. Janet heard soft muttering, maybe from a walkie-talkie, and O'Dell seemed to be readying himself for something.

"Ending in a bar. I just can't—I can't believe it. You know, I never meant for this to happen. I came here to talk to *you* yesterday!" He pointed accusingly at Janet. "I wanted to let you know about Ike slipping through justice's fingers *again*. But you weren't here. Finch was. And we got to talking, because frankly, I wanted to know why the police continued to let this guy get away with shit. Even though Ike was dead, I wanted someone to be held accountable, you know? Someone let him off the hook twice— twice that *we* know of—when he was alive, and even though he's dead now, they shouldn't get away with that.

"Finch starts giving me a song and dance about how Ike Freeman needed a second chance. Well that's bullshit!" he exploded, leaping up from his seat. "He got too many second chances. That guy deserved a second chance like Ollie deserved to die!

"And I don't know, maybe he was feeling guilty or sorry, because then he told me that he and Ike were brothers. Step-brothers. Had grown up in an awful house together, and Finch just wanted to protect him, he was the big brother, it was his job. But instead of calming me down, it just pissed me off more.

"I asked him, I said, 'Did you let Ike off—did you help him get away with murder all those years ago?' And do you know, he just nodded his head and said, 'Yes, that's what family does.'" Benji shook his head, still in disbelief a day later. "No remorse at all—and in fact, said he'd do it again if he had to."

"And you snapped," Janet said.

Unnoticed by Benji, O'Dell and the patrol officers behind him moved into place. Sweat rings bloomed out from under Cindy Lou's arms and Larsa reached over the bar and refilled her own beer.

"Damn straight I snapped," Benji said. "I—I keep this gun for safety when I ride," he said, whipping a tiny, purse-size gun from his pocket and setting it on the bar top. Abe gasped and Cindy Lou stumbled back into the liquor shelf, sending at least two bottles clanking loudly to the floor.

"When you ride your bicycle?" Janet asked. "How does that work?"

"I bought it after I got run off the road the last time. These cars, they think they own the space—that I shouldn't even be allowed on it! Do you know how many times I've been nearly killed? Last time was close—a car pushed me into a fire hydrant. I nearly broke my arm! I decided if they have a deadly weapon—their car," he clarified when he saw Janet's confused expression, "then I should, too. I carry this now when I ride, so I'm ready. Just in case.

"And you were ready yesterday. Did Finch try to run you off the road?"

"No, but he railroaded the justice system ten years ago, and then again just a few weeks ago, when he made sure Ike didn't face charges for sideswiping Abe. *He was enabling a killer*, don't you see? I couldn't stand for it. He was getting back in his car, trying to leave the scene of the crime. So I—I shot him."

A cop grabbed Benji's arms from behind. A second officer took the gun off the countertop and dropped it carefully into an evidence bag.

"But why the Beerador, Benji? Why go to all that trouble?" Janet asked, even though he was being led away in handcuffs. O'Dell stepped closer and Janet frowned, not liking his expression.

Larsa finished her beer. "Now what?"

"Now I take you downtown," O'Dell said to Larsa. He turned and pointed at Janet. "You too."

CHAPTER FORTY

Janet's foot tapped out an uneven beat against the concrete floor of the interview room. She wasn't nervous; she *was*, however, tired, hungry, and a little chilly, if she was being completely honest. She was glad to be wearing a boxy black T-shirt instead of a tank top, at least.

"Coffee?" O'Dell asked when he stepped into the room.

"You know, when we first met, I had you pegged as the good cop. But after sitting here for two hours, I'm not so sure anymore."

He took a sip of the very coffee he'd just offered her. "I wasn't going to give you the coffee, even if you'd said yes. So I guess I am the bad cop." He sat down opposite Janet. "You pulled a very risky move back there, Janet. And if I could have my way, I'd charge you with so many offenses your head would spin."

Janet scoffed. "I don't have the video of Finch's murder! I made that whole thing up to get *Abe* to confess! I had no idea Benji was the killer."

"You don't have the video?" O'Dell said skeptically.

"No, god—*bless* it, Jason didn't give me a fifty-thousand-dollar security system! We were trying to catch an employee who'd stolen a couple thousand bucks! Plus, his system really has been down since before Ike died. He's finally getting it back up and running, but his priority was his paid clients—not me."

"I doubt that," O'Dell said.

Janet grinned despite her circumstances. "Okay, fine, you're probably right, but regardless, my system isn't back up yet."

"Actually, it is. Why do you think all those officers showed up tonight?"

"Didn't you call them?"

"No," O'Dell said with a rueful sigh. "I've been blind when it came to this case from day one. I've gotten everything wrong, pinned the blame on the wrong people, didn't trust the right ones," he said, staring at Janet. "But Jason called 911 as soon as Larsa confessed. He was watching the whole thing go down from a computer at a 'secure location,'" he added with a sour expression.

"What secure location?"

"Wouldn't I love to know."

"You don't?" Janet asked, now thoroughly confused.

"No. He won't tell me. I just finished talking to him in the next room."

"What?" Janet leapt up from her chair and took a step toward the door. Then she remembered she was stuck in this room for now.

"He came in on his own—wanted to tell us what he recorded and what he didn't."

"What did he record?" Janet asked, crossing her arms and staring at O'Dell, incensed.

"He recorded everything tonight, from the moment Larsa walked into the bar. He said he knew that you were going to get to the bottom of things, and he wanted to make sure that he captured any confession that came out on camera. That's why he had Mel empty the bar."

"Jason had Mel—wait, what?" She suddenly felt like Cindy Lou: totally clueless.

"She says he called her cell phone and asked her to get everybody out so the microphones would pick up anything important, and to keep the customers safe. He wasn't sure what might go down when the killer was cornered."

Janet flinched. Why hadn't she thought of that?

"Does that mean that you have the whole thing on tape? Larsa's claims, Abe's involvement, Benji's confession—all of that is on camera? Is it admissible?"

O'Dell steepled his fingers under his chin. "I think so. We'll let our prosecutor have the final say, obviously, but Benji's already claiming coercion."

"Bah," Janet muttered.

"Exactly. A regular citizen can't coerce someone to confess to a crime. He's grasping at straws."

"What about Larsa? What's going to happen to her?"

O'Dell took a long, slow sip of his coffee and Janet licked her lips, wishing she'd grabbed the cup from him when he walked in. Now that she thought about it, she was parched.

"I'd like to book her on murder two," he said, "but I know the prosecutor's not going to try for a court conviction. There's no one to counter her claim that it was an accident. Patricide is pretty rare, hard to get a conviction when you consider her sad story. Jury'll be very compassionate toward an orphan with an unhappy childhood."

"Do *you* think it was an accident?" she asked.

He swatted the question away with an irritated hand. "I don't want to think about it. It doesn't make a difference what I think, anyway. Prosecutor does what she wants to do."

"Huh," Janet said, slowly sitting back down. "Kind of like homicide detectives, then."

He looked up sharply, then nodded. "Fair enough. I zeroed in on Jason on day one. I didn't like his attitude, and he had that juvie conviction. Not hard to see him snapping at an obnoxious customer. I was wrong."

"So how did Jason's pen get into the Beerador with Finch's body?"

O'Dell's face flushed, and he looked uncomfortable for the first time that night. "Rebecca, one of our evidence techs, says she remembers Finch using the pen yesterday. He must have picked it up from the evidence we gathered at your house by mistake."

Mistake? She'd file that one away with *Where the hell is my coffeepot?* and move on. Now that she knew Jason had been watching over her for the past twenty-four hours, she felt warmer and fuzzier toward him than ever. "Any idea who spray-painted my house?"

"Someone graffitied your house?"

Janet shook her head. "Never mind. Can I go?"

"I just need to ask you a few questions and then we'll get you on your way. Your boyfriend is in a barely concealed rage in the waiting room; be sure to tell him we treated you nice."

Her eyebrows drew together. "Jason's still here? Why?"

"I knew you'd need a ride home—and, contrary to popular opinion, I *am* the good cop." He smiled lightly and then looked down at his notebook. "Did you ever consider telling me anything you knew when you knew it?"

"No." He grimaced and she said, "I answered one, now it's your turn. Why was Larsa so involved after Ike died? You'd think she'd have had a better chance of getting away with an 'accident' she had her uncle help cover up if she'd just laid low and stayed out of the way."

"Maybe she knew he didn't end up knocked out on the gravel by himself that night. Maybe she wanted to get to the bottom of who put him there. I think she blamed them for his death as much as anyone else."

"That's grim," Janet said, quoting O'Dell from what felt like a lifetime ago.

He shrugged. "But true." He blew out a breath before

looking back up at Janet. "I would have helped you. I would have helped Elizabeth."

"Before or after charging my boyfriend with murder?"

He didn't say anything for a moment, just nodded slowly. "How'd you find her, anyway? It seems like she was the missing link to figuring everything out."

"Family," Janet said. "It always comes down to family."

O'Dell frowned. "You'll need to write it all down in a witness statement." He pushed a pad of yellow legal paper toward her and motioned to the pen on top.

She crossed her arms and leaned back in the uncomfortable metal chair. "My dad told me not to say anything until he gets here."

"No, no, you don't need a lawyer. This is just your chance to—"

"I have knowledge of a police cover-up of a debatably 'accidental' homicide," Janet said, staring stonily across the table at O'Dell. "I'm pretty sure I'm going to need a lawyer."

"Larsa has already confessed—to her version of events. And Benji will. It's only a matter of time."

"Sure, and you have to tell me the complete truth in this room, don't you? Cops *never* lie in the interview room." Janet looked suspiciously in the corners for hidden cameras. "No way. I'm waiting for my dad."

O'Dell made a face. "I guess you can wait at home, then. Come back when he gets here," he said, "and we'll get you sorted."

They both stood, and he opened the door for her to leave. "Hey, you did good," he said, all the flip attitude gone from his voice. "This would have taken years to get to the bottom of without your help—your boyfriend's help, too. I was wrong about him and you."

"Gee, thanks," Janet said drily. "It's always great to hear someone assumed you were crap until you proved them wrong."

"That's not—you know what? Fine. You're welcome."

She smiled to herself as she walked down the hall. He was fun to tease—she'd miss that.

O'Dell pointed to the exit, then continued walking down the hall with a wave. "As soon as your father gets here, Janet. Don't make me come find you."

Her lips flattened. How could he still be issuing her orders after the night they'd just had?

When she pushed open the door to the lobby, she stumbled right into the one person she wasn't yet prepared to see.

CHAPTER FORTY-ONE

"Janet!" Jason rushed forward, his expression a mixture of relief and concern. "God, what took so long in there?"

"Power," she said, knowing it was true. The powerful could take as long as they wanted.

Jason pulled her into a hug. "I'm sorry," he said, rocking her back and forth, not letting go. "I'm so sorry. You know why I couldn't be involved, but it was tearing me up inside. I knew you'd figure it all out; that's why I left Old Ben's video out. You're so good at reading people, I knew I didn't have to worry about you, but man, I worried about you!"

She breathed him in, getting scents of mint and vanilla as usual before steeling her nerves and pushing away. "Mmm-hmm, I can imagine. So very worried that you cut off all contact with me."

He flinched. "Don't be like that—it was a client! You know I couldn't help police investigate a client."

"Right, and now I know that in a time of crisis, I can lean on Cindy Lou, Elizabeth, and Mel, but not my boyfriend if his job happens to get in the way!" She turned her back to him. "I don't even know Mel, but she was there for me tonight and you weren't."

She wanted to make him sweat, just like he'd made her do.

"How about some new intel I got tonight?"

"Nice try. I know everything that happened tonight. I was there—you weren't—and O'Dell filled me in on the loose ends."

"I'm not talking about the murder or the confessions. Yes, yes, I saw all of that—and you were great." He stopped to look admiringly at her. "I'm talking about something else."

"What *else* could possibly have been going on at the Spot tonight?"

"While you were yammering on and on about Ike and Ollie, Larsa and Finch, the bar thief struck again, right under your nose. You were so busy, though, that you didn't notice."

"What?" Janet swore loudly. "Elizabeth is back one day and she's taking more money from me? Unbeliev—"

"Not Elizabeth."

"Not Eliz—" Janet dropped her facade of anger at Jason and popped a hand on her hip. "Then who?"

———

Nell took a sip of her screwdriver and carefully placed the highball glass on a cocktail napkin.

"Can I get you anything else?" Janet asked sweetly, making a note on a nearby pad of paper with Jason's god-awful, ugly pen that they needed more cocktail straws. When Nell shook her head, she loaded up a tray and walked around the bar to a table in the back.

"Don't forget about us, here!" she said, putting a sweet tea in front of Chip and handing the other to Cindy Lou. Janet's eyes twinkled as she added, "When you're away at school, we'll be thinking of you."

Chip's eyebrows knitted together and he looked at his mother. Cindy Lou laughed, swatting Janet's arm with good humor. "Oh, stop. I know I've been a mess lately. You just have no idea how fast it all goes," she said, motioning to the space around her son. "Watching you grow up has been the longest and the shortest stretch of time I could imagine. Yes, at the same time—it's true," she added when Chip shook his head.

"Mom, I'll be down the street. Seriously, my biology lab is less than a mile from here." The deep timbre of his voice didn't match his young face and scrawny arms.

"Did you ever find out who spray-painted your house?" Cindy Lou asked, taking a handful of trail mix from the basket Janet had just plunked down between them.

Janet chuckled. "Can you believe it was Jason?" When Cindy Lou gave her a blank look, she explained. "He's never liked the color of the house and saw this as his chance to force a paint job ahead of the kitchen remodel."

"With all that was going on, he thought it was a good time to—"

"I'm pretty sure with all that was going on, he thought he could slip one by me," Janet interrupted.

"Not a chance," Cindy Lou said.

"Nope, not a chance," Janet repeated under her breath as she walked back to the bar. Nell motioned for another lime wedge, and Janet—her finger both bandage- and pain-free—happily took one from the container.

"So, right after Mel hustled me out of the bar—very unceremoniously, by the way—the lawyer confessed to killing Detective Finch?" Nell asked.

Janet nodded. "Just two seats away from where you are right now."

"Can you imagine carrying that kind of anger around for so long? That kind of rage? Mmm." Nell dug around in her small clutch. A moment later, a tube of lipstick was in her hand, and her ruby-red lips got a touch-up. "I can't believe I missed the grand finale. Sounds like Elizabeth really saved the day by taking Ike's car."

Janet nodded. "And to think I almost fired her!"

"Why? She makes the best vodka-soda—gets the ratio just right." Nell looked up quickly and added, "No offense."

Janet shrugged. "None taken." She leaned in closer. "I thought she'd been stealing from the register. Money's been missing." Nell's back stiffened and Janet lowered her voice as she said, "And I can't have that, now, can I?"

The older woman pursed her lips and kept her eyes trained on her drink. "Well, she has to go, then. No second chances, that's what I say."

"What if there was a good reason, though? I don't want to throw someone out if they're just in a bad fix. I'd want to help them," Janet said, keeping close tabs on Nell's face.

"She's too old—she should have known better," Nell said, and Janet knew the other woman wasn't talking about Elizabeth. She drained the last of her drink and pushed her chair back with finality. "Goodbye, Janet. Thank you for—"

"No."

Nell primly fixed a flyaway hair, her face impassive. "What?"

"No, you're not walking out of here. You owe me at least two thousand four hundred twenty-nine dollars, and that's just from the last three weeks. What gives, Nell? Why have you been stealing from me? I thought we were . . . friends?"

Nell straightened her shoulders defiantly before sinking back down onto the bar stool. "I don't honestly know why. I've got a problem. I, uh, I take things that aren't mine. I just can't stop myself."

She opened her purse and took out a fat wallet stuffed with cash. "I didn't need the money—didn't spend a dime. I just like knowing I can do it." She unfolded her wallet and turned it upside down. The money was so jammed in that nothing fell out. She huffed out an irritated sigh and then forced her fingers around the edge of the wallet, freeing the wad of bills.

"It's just under one thousand. There's some change, too, but it was too heavy for my clutch. The rest of it is back at home."

Janet stared in disbelief at the mound of money between them. Her eyes flicked to Nell's open purse. "Is that my pen?"

"Oh." Nell's cheeks colored and she took Jason's pen out and handed it over.

"How long has this been going on?" Janet asked. She obviously needed a new accounting program.

"About a year."

Janet's jaw dropped, but she shut it quickly when Nell finally looked up.

"You don't have to say it—I'll go. I've lost a lot of people over my lifetime because of it, but I just can't . . . I can't make myself stop." She slid a smooth piece of sea glass across the bar. "This is Cindy Lou's. I just took it from her back pocket twenty minutes ago."

Janet stared at the aqua glass in surprise.

The older woman stood once again, slower this time, and took a step toward the door.

"Nell, you're still welcome here. You're just not allowed to sit by the cash register anymore."

The other woman looked uncertainly at Janet before smiling. "Really?"

"Like, far from the register, okay?"

Nell glided over to the opposite side of the bar and settled onto a new stool, her old smile back in place.

Janet wiped down the counter and looked at the clock; Elizabeth would be in for her shift any minute. Janet would have to rearrange the schedule soon to accommodate Elizabeth's new semester of classes at the community college. Mel had the day off so she and Kat could attend an adoption hearing, but Janet wasn't expecting any trouble at the door that night, and if there was, Jason was in the office, ready to spring into service if needed.

Her father, as much as she wasn't looking forward to it, was due at the airport first thing the following morning. He was going to help her write out a statement for the police, and—if she knew him at all—give O'Dell one hell of a talking-to.

She hummed to herself as she worked, giving the cutting board and lemon knife a wide berth. Not long ago, Janet had been all alone. Now she'd reconnected with a father she once didn't know existed, her boyfriend had her back, and the truth was that everyone at the Spot was a part of her family, too.

"Another one, sweetie?" Nell asked, pointing to her empty glass.

Janet nodded and pulled a glass from the shelf. Sure, they were a bunch of nut jobs and kleptos, but they were hers, and that's all that mattered.

A JANET BLACK MYSTERY

LAST
MINUTE

LIBBY
KIRSCH

LAST MINUTE

CHAPTER ONE

Janet Black stood back and looked at a spot on the floor near the bed critically for a long moment, then finally nodded at her boyfriend. "You know what? I think you're right."

Jason Brooks raised his eyebrows. "Well, darlin', let the record reflect that on September fourteenth, at three forty-seven in the afternoon—"

"Oh, shut up and get a stool! That should take care of the problem."

Jason's eyes lingered on her before he turned and left the room. Janet adjusted her garter belt and tapped the heel of her stiletto against the wood floor. *Ta-ta-tap. Ta-ta-tap. Ta-ta—*

"Something like this?" Jason was back, his expression betraying his opinion that it would never work.

"Yes!" Janet grabbed the stool and then eyed the bed before placing it on the floor about two and a half feet away from the edge of the mattress. "If I stand on the stool and then do a back-bend to the mattress, everything should line right up—"

"What kind of tread do those heels have?" Jason's eyes narrowed and he nudged the stool closer to the bed by a few inches with his toe. "I don't know . . . if your hands slip, you'll fall to the floor." Jason crept toward her, despite his objection.

"Well, you won't just be standing there, will you? You'll be holding on to my hips!" Janet tossed her shoulder-length light brown hair back and pushed her chest out while batting her hazel eyes. At five foot six, she was too short for her original idea —but the step stool and heels combined more than made up for the height difference. "I know you won't let me fall."

The colorful ink on Jason's arms rippled as he crossed them and considered Janet's plan. He'd shed his shirt earlier and the top button on his jeans was undone. Janet licked her lips as she watched him think about doing what she wanted him to do.

She wiggled her hips and he finally reached for her.

Ring, ring.

"The phone," Jason murmured, stepping close. His day-old whiskers tickled her neck.

"Let's ignore it," she sighed, and ran her hands down his arms.

The phone went quiet, and his lips moved across her neck and up her jaw until he finally parted her lips with his tongue. Heat licked up from her core. Her legs felt like jelly.

Ring, ring.

"Damn it," she moaned, reaching back blindly for the receiver on the nightstand. "What?" She sucked in a gasp when Jason knelt in front of her, nibbling at sensitive skin.

"Uh, boss?" The woman's twangy, uncertain tone made it clear who was on the other end.

"What is it, Cindy Lou?" Janet focused on not moaning as she shifted her body to the right. Jason grinned and kept working his way up her leg.

"I think you better come in," the bartender said. "We've got —well, cops are here, and I don't know what to do."

Janet pushed back from Jason and thumped down on the bed, worry edging away all other emotions. "What do you—wait, never mind. I'll be right in."

She dropped the phone back onto the receiver. "Cops are at the Spot! I've got to go."

Jason's eyebrows knitted together. "I'll come, too."

"That's sweet, but you don't have to—"

"Janet! Of course I'm coming." He hopped up with a scowl and snagged his shirt off the ground as he stalked out of the room.

She blew out a sigh. Somehow he'd taken her offer for him to stay home as an insult.

She slipped out of the lingerie and got dressed in her usual bar "uniform" of jeans and a T-shirt. So much for being spontaneous. She picked up an envelope off the dresser and left the room. Jason's dad's mail had inadvertently been mixed in with hers, and she tossed it on the hall table on her way to the front door.

William Brooks had moved in with them over the summer, after he and Jason's mom argued their way through a messy divorce. The situation was not ideal, but Jason felt bad; his dad had nowhere else to go, so they'd been making the best of it.

On the plus side, William had been working on their kitchen remodeling project. In the minus column, he spent a lot of time moping around the house. Janet struggled to feel empathy for the man; after all, you can't cheat on a woman and then be mad when she leaves you!

"Ready?" she called to Jason.

"Let's go." He swept past her and she frowned. Every time she tried to do something nice, Jason took it as dismissive. William Brooks had brought his bad mojo from Memphis and Janet couldn't wait for him to leave.

"Bye, William. We'll be home later."

"Everything okay, Janet?" He stuck his head through the open kitchen door; drywall dust covered his hair. "I forgot to tell you I called an arborist to come to the Spot. Those ash trees need to come down—they're being devoured by emerald ash borers—"

"Fine, William, thanks so much." She turned and walked out of the house, a stiff smile plastered on her face. He needed to get his own home and business to worry over, and leave hers alone.

———

Janet stood frozen in the parking lot. The bar's Beerador, a massive seven-foot-tall, bottle-shaped refrigerator, stood guard by the door. The unusual appliance had come with the bar when Janet and Jason had bought it years ago, but it had been taken during a murder investigation several months earlier. Why was it back?

She shuddered slightly, remembering the body she'd found, staring lifelessly out the Beerador's window all those weeks ago. A quick look behind her confirmed that Jason was still on the phone call that had just come in when he parked. She waved when he looked up, then turned and strode into the Spot. It took a moment for her eyes to adjust to the low lighting inside.

Her bar looked like it had been ransacked.

Someone had cleared a path from the door to the center of the room, forcing tables and chairs aside in an uneven mess.

Janet made her way behind the bar to Cindy Lou.

Her assistant manager, and most faithful bartender, was channeling Rosie the Riveter that day; her bleached-blond hair was tied back in a red bandana, and a short denim jumper with a plunging neckline replaced the blue jumpsuit from the poster.

"What's going on?"

Cindy Lou stared pointedly across the bar but didn't speak, only continued to prep a pile of lemons for the night ahead, her knife making *click, clack, clack* sounds against the cutting board.

"I should charge you extra for the door-to-door delivery, but I won't." The deep voice came from Janet's left. Detective Patrick O'Dell grinned from a bar stool, his green eyes sparkling mischievously. A sports coat hung off the back of his chair, and his white shirtsleeves were rolled up to the elbow. One of her regulars, Nell, an older woman with silvery-gray hair, waved, but Janet could only stare at the cop, her mouth open.

His resulting chuckle shook her tongue loose. "You're giving it back? I mean, shouldn't it go to . . . I just assumed it would be disposed of, or something—I . . ."

Janet eyed the Beerador suspiciously. She'd thought—hoped —she'd never see it again.

"Would have cost the city too much to bring it to the dump with the fees and everything," O'Dell said. "Where do you want my guys to put it?"

"Ahhh . . ." Janet grimaced. "Has it been cleaned or anything?"

"Nope."

"Son of a—"

"Biscuit!" Cindy Lou interrupted with a sharp elbow in Janet's side. "It can be just as satisfying if you say it right," she added out of the side of her mouth.

Janet snorted. Nothing could be as satisfying as a real curse word, but she bit back the one that had been on her lips, crossed her arms, and glared at the refrigerator. She'd once considered the Beerador fun—campy, almost—but now . . . Now it was a tainted vessel of death. "What am I supposed to do with it?"

"Clean it out, I guess, hon." Cindy Lou wiped her forehead with the back of her hand, then pointed at the offending appliance with her chef's knife. "I'm gettin' dirty just looking at all that fingerprint dust! I bet if we use a mixture of bleach and baking soda—"

"We'll blow up the building?" Janet popped a hand on her hip and scowled at the Beerador.

"Everything okay?" Jason edged past the Beerador at the front entrance, then stopped short when he saw O'Dell. "Oh." He crossed his arms over his chest and walked up to the bar.

O'Dell forced a grin. "Jason. Good to see you, man."

Just beyond O'Dell, Nell leaned in, her eyes flicking from O'Dell's wallet to his hand resting just inches away. Nell's dark, quick eyes—magnified through the enormous lenses of her bold, black eyeglass frames—were even then calculating the distance between his wallet and her handbag.

Janet stifled a groan; the last thing she needed just then was for their resident klepto to strike against Knoxville's lead homicide investigator. She cleared her throat. "Nell, did you need another round?"

Nell dropped her chin to her chest and tucked a stray gray hair back into her tidy, low bun. "All good here, Janet."

Janet smiled to herself, then racked her brain for how to solve the larger problem in the room. "I think . . . we should . . . turn the Beerador into a coat closet."

Cindy Lou's nose wrinkled, and her head tilted to one side. "I don't know. It wouldn't hold that many coats, would it?"

Jason didn't smile. With a scowl still etched firmly on his face, he said to O'Dell, "Now that it's here, I guess you'll be on your way."

O'Dell slid off his bar stool and laid a few bills from his wallet on the bar for Cindy Lou, then all six foot one of him tried to move past Nell. The older woman closed her eyes and leaned into the empty space between them, her puckered lips tilted up as he brushed past. Janet almost laughed out loud. Nell hated cops, but even she couldn't ignore O'Dell's broad, muscular frame and boyish good looks.

Janet met O'Dell on the other side of the countertop. "Can your guys move it out of the doorway, at least?"

"Sure." O'Dell grinned at Jason as he rested a hand on her shoulder and squeezed. "Anything for you, Janet."

Jason's chest puffed out and Janet stifled a groan. These two grown men were acting like possessive peacocks.

O'Dell tapped something into his cell phone and soon four burly men walked into the bar with a heavy-duty hand cart.

As they surrounded the Beerador, O'Dell asked, "Where do you want it, Janet?"

"Jason?" She turned to her boyfriend, but he was beyond

being able to help. Waves of irritation rolled off his body like freshly applied aftershave.

She locked eyes with Cindy Lou. Her head bartender lifted one shoulder and dropped it back down, then motioned behind her. "I always did like having the bottles in there."

Janet raked a hand over her face. "I guess back behind the bar, O'Dell. We'll deep-clean it and see if it still works." Could you get the smell of murder out of a refrigerator? Seemed like a Clorox wipe just wasn't going to be enough.

As the men navigated through the bar with the heavy load, the front door opened, and a beam of sunlight sparkled beautifully off the Beerador's curved glass door.

Cindy Lou gasped, and new emotion multiplied the twang in her voice when she said, "I think she's glad to be back home, y'all!"

Janet suppressed a snort and turned her attention to the newcomer. "Come on in, don't mind the mess. Can I get you a drink?"

But the man, wearing a herringbone sports coat over khakis and a blue button-down, beelined for O'Dell. A golden badge glinted at his waist. "O'Dell. What are you doing here?"

"I'm giving that back to its rightful owners." He pointed to the Beerador, which came down off the dolly with a crash behind Cindy Lou. "I thought you were heading to a dead body call-out, Rivera?"

"I did." Rivera scanned the bar. "Now I'm here to find Nell Anderson. Do you know her?"

Janet leaned in when O'Dell asked, "What's going on?"

Rivera blew out a sigh and lowered his voice. "I just came from her daughter's house. She's dead."

CHAPTER TWO

"Oh my gosh, I mean, have you ever heard anything so terrible?" Cindy Lou said for at least the ninth time.

Janet dumped her tray onto the bar and took the dirty glasses to the sink. While Cindy Lou yammered on, she thought back to Nell, and the way her shoulders had slumped and her eyes—usually bright and sharp—had dimmed, turned dull and lifeless, when the homicide detective broke the terrible news.

Detective Rivera had said that Nell's daughter, Liv, had taken a "spill" down the stairs while carrying a huge load of laundry. It looked like a terrible accident, but they needed Nell to go to the house. She had to be there for Liv's husband and children.

Three children! Motherless now, because of laundry and a missed step.

Cindy Lou couldn't stop talking about it, and even though she was trying to tune her bartender out, Janet couldn't stop thinking about it, either.

Rivera had led Nell out of the bar. For the first time, Janet wasn't sure how old Nell really was. She'd always guessed her most steadfast customer was in her early sixties, but that afternoon's news had aged her considerably.

"O'Dell, you need another?" She pointed to the homicide detective's sweet tea.

"Nah, I gotta get back." He took another leisurely sip and made no attempt to move.

"Why is homicide involved when they think Liv slipped on the steps?"

"Standard operating procedure, Janet," he answered self-importantly. She leaned forward over the bar and rested her elbows on the countertop, staring at him expectantly. "They won't know the actual cause of death until the coroner does the autopsy." O'Dell shook the ice cubes in his glass and drained the last of the liquid. "Homicide goes to all calls with a dead body—we collect evidence, just in case."

"In case?"

He nodded, his lips pressed into a flat line. "In case it wasn't an accident. I mean, really, how many women in their thirties slip down the stairs and die?"

Janet's eyes opened wide. "Do you think—"

"I don't think anything, sweetheart, because I wasn't there, I didn't see the scene. I'm just telling you why Rivera's there, and why he's probably suspicious."

She nodded and swiped his empty glass off the bar. A throat cleared near her and she turned, then had to stifle a gasp when she found Jason on the floor in front of her, down on one knee.

"Oh my God!"

"I have a question." He leaned forward and looked up at Janet.

"Jason, don't—" She choked on the last word as panic crept up into her throat, constricting her airflow.

"Can you pass the bag of trail mix? I thought it was under here." He gestured to the cabinet by his bent leg, "But now I see it's up there by the cash register."

"Oh." Janet's face flushed and she handed him the bag. He grinned, then stood up and walked away.

Janet grabbed a piece of paper from the countertop and

fanned her neck. Was it hot in here? Even the tips of her ears pulsed with heat.

Cindy Lou handed her a glass of iced tea. "You look like you've seen a ghost." She propped her hip against the nearest cooler and crossed her arms under her ample chest.

Janet took a long pull of the tea while she watched Jason top off the bowls on each table. "I thought—I mean, I worried that . . ." She tried to laugh lightly, but it came out sounding choppy and forced.

"He wants to," Cindy Lou said, tapping a finger against her teeth. "I don't know if he has the ring yet, but he's ready for the next step."

Janet turned to her assistant manager; the skin around her eyes and mouth suddenly felt too tight, and she could barely move her lips when she asked Cindy Lou, "What? Did he say something to you?"

"Yup. Asked if he should do it here at the bar or somewhere else."

When Cindy Lou fell quiet, Janet prompted, louder than she'd intended, "And? What did you say?"

The other woman jumped. "I told him that you weren't ready, of course! That it was too soon. I said that it'd be like asking for the Grey Goose after the well vodka—timing's all wrong!"

Janet felt her eyebrows knit together. "And then what did he say?"

Cindy Lou shuffled her feet. "Well, I mean, I wasn't takin' notes—"

"Cindy Lou!"

"Okay! He said, 'Sometimes you don't know you're ready until it happens.'"

Across the bar, Jason turned and winked, then stopped to talk to a customer with an easy grin.

He was perfect for her, no doubt about that. Jason was smart, funny, adventurous—but also low-key, relaxed, and easygoing. In short, none of the things that Janet could say about herself. But engaged? Married?

Janet shuddered. Thank God for Cindy Lou. She was right—Janet wasn't ready. Not for a proposal or for anything that came after. Hopefully Jason had listened.

The bartender grabbed a cloth and wiped down the bar. Then, in a quiet voice she said, "But that was months ago that he asked me about it. So maybe he . . . Well."

Janet drummed her fingers on the counter. Cindy Lou had just sent her only son off to college after raising him alone. Divorced for more than ten years, tonight she was dressed, as usual, to meet Mister Right Then. Her low V-neck and short skirt screamed, "Try me out!," not "Let's settle down."

"I can't think of a single happily married couple," she said to Cindy Lou. "Not one. Can you?"

The bartender's lips puckered while she thought, but it was O'Dell who answered. Janet had forgotten he was still sitting there until he spoke.

"My parents. Going on thirty-five years and most of them blissful—and those are their words, not mine."

"Yeah?" Janet asked.

O'Dell grinned when he heard the doubt in her voice. "Yeah. High school sweethearts, got engaged in college. Never been apart more than one night in a row. They're pretty great."

Janet tilted her head to the side as she considered being with the same someone for almost forty years. She frowned and plunged two dirty glasses into the automatic washer in the sink.

"What about you?" Cindy Lou asked. "You ever come close to finding Mrs. O'Dell?"

Janet's ears perked up, and when he didn't answer, she looked over, only to find him staring at her.

Before O'Dell could answer, an official-sounding voice at the opposite side of the bar rang out. "Janet Black?"

She pulled her eyes away from O'Dell and turned, only to find a nearly identical copy of him facing her. The stranger was also tall, with short, brown "cop hair," not quite buzzed, but nearly. He was attractive and well built but didn't have O'Dell's bright green eyes. Instead, his brown eyes squinted at her suspiciously.

"What?" She propped her hip against the cooler and raised her eyebrows.

He looked over her head and his frown deepened. "O'Dell."

"Donaldson?" O'Dell's voice was tinged with surprise. "What are you doing here?"

Donaldson's head ticked to the side and he brought his eyes back to Janet. "I am Gary Donaldson, the chief enforcer with the Tennessee Department of Commerce and Insurance." He stopped and gave her an imposing look.

"Cool." Janet motioned to the nearest bar stool. "Welcome, Chief Enforcer. Do you want a beer or a shot?"

He sneered. "Neither. I am here to issue you a verbal warning that an anonymous complaint has been filed with my department, and we are launching an investigation into you."

"A complaint?" Jason walked behind the bar and stood on Janet's right, between her and Donaldson. "Where did you say you worked?"

"The Department of—"

"What's the basis of the complaint?" O'Dell interrupted, moving from his bar stool to stand on Janet's left.

Donaldson pinched his lips together, and for a moment he looked as if he wasn't going to answer, but finally he said, "Operating as a private investigator without a license."

CHAPTER THREE

Later that night, Janet fumed silently about the inquiry with the state. Donaldson had—gleefully, in her opinion—handed over a stack of forms she would need to fill out within thirty days to refute the anonymous claim. She hated paperwork, but she hated the government's overstepping its bounds even more. The stack of papers now sat prominently on the bar by the cash register, to remind her of what needed to get done.

Cindy Lou sidled up to Janet and picked up the papers. "If you ask me—"

"Nobody did."

"—there's somethin' funny goin' on between that guy from the government and O'Dell. Did you see the way they glared at each other?" She tapped the edge of the stack against the bar until the corners were perfectly aligned, then set the papers back on the counter.

"I don't know, I mean, they're kind of on the same team, right?" Janet poured bourbon, fresh lemon juice, and simple syrup into a shaker, added a scoop of ice, and shook it more aggressively than usual. Then she strained the whiskey sour over an ice-filled rocks glass. "What I can't figure out is, who'd have filed a complaint? I mean, I may have looked into a homicide over the summer, but nobody paid me to do it. Wouldn't that be a key part of acting as a private investigator? Exchange of money for services?"

Cindy Lou looked blankly back, her mouth hanging slack, then blinked slowly and cleared her throat. "Sorry, hon, I'm downright exhausted! Been trying to go to Chip's club hockey games, but they play at eight in the mornin'! Might as well be in another country, it's that hard to get my butt outta bed at that hour." She shook herself. "Any word from Nell?"

Janet threaded a cherry through a toothpick and laid it on top of the rocks glass, then passed the drink across the counter to a customer. "No. I'll check on her tomorrow. Give her some time tonight to be with her family."

"Where's Jason?"

"He had to go home. Big account just came in from the west side of the state. He'll be busy for the next few weeks, getting everything set up."

It was eight o'clock, and the after-work crowd was thinning out. Janet wiped down a sticky splotch on the counter by the condiment tray. The only thing that could distract her from thinking about the inquiry from the state was Jason, and the more she did, the less she liked it. Jason had asked Cindy Lou about proposing to Janet months ago, but lately, he seemed reserved, almost like he was pulling away from her.

She thought back to their near-tryst in the bedroom that morning. Things had been tense since their long-term house mate moved in a month ago.

As if Janet had spoken out loud, Cindy Lou asked, "How much longer is William going to be with you all?"

Janet's lips puckered. "I guess until the houseboat situation clears up."

Cindy Lou frowned. "He'll be with you until spring?"

Janet heaved a long-suffering sigh. "God, I hope not."

"He just didn't understand how the drawdown works?"

Janet shrugged. The Tennessee Valley Authority was a well-known entity in all of Tennessee. The government agency drastically reduced water levels in lakes and waterways across the state to keep dangerous floods away over the winter months. This turned some houseboats into plain old houses, with the rectangular platforms that supported them resting at odd angles against the uneven lake bottoms until the water levels were raised again in the spring. The structures that counted on the lake water below them for plumbing were out of luck from September through March.

"William didn't realize Douglas Lake got so low when he bought the house. Anyway, he's with us now."

"What about Jason's mom?"

"We haven't seen her since William moved in. I think she's still pretty angry about the divorce, but Jason won't really talk about it, so . . ." She shrugged again and turned away from Cindy Lou, effectively ending the conversation.

The truth was, she didn't know any particulars about his parents' divorce, only that Jason refused to share his feelings about it, and William couldn't seem to stop. Janet knew every thought that entered William's head about how unjust the law was about splitting assets. And every time he opened his mouth, Jason retreated farther away. He'd barely spoken to his mother, but according to William, she'd taken everything in the divorce settlement, including the pet fish.

William was angry, Jason was reserved, but Janet, for one, was delighted. Women had to be proactive about protecting themselves, because God knew no one else was going to look out for them.

She filled a bucket from the ice maker in the walk-in cooler and lugged it out to dump into one of the beer chests. The Beerador gleamed ominously in the corner behind the bar. She'd gone over the outside of it with some cleaning wipes but hadn't yet opened the door.

"Maybe some stainless steel cleaner?" Cindy Lou said.

Janet nodded and made a note on the pad by the register.

"I'll take a strawberry margarita," a man's deep voice said off to the side. "Make it frozen."

Janet's lips pressed flat, but she couldn't bring herself to look over at the customer. A frozen margarita? And a strawberry one at that? Where did this guy think he was, Applebee's?

"Sorry," she said as she wiped a nonexistent spot on the counter vigorously, "but we don't do *frozen* drinks—O'Dell!" She laughed out loud when she looked up to find him grinning ear to ear. "What are you doing back here?"

"Just got off my shift, and thought I'd come have a beer for once, instead of a sweet tea."

"You drink?" Janet leaned her elbows on the now-clean counter between them. "I pegged you for a teetotaler."

"Please. I'm a Catholic boy from Jersey. I started sneaking beers when I was thirteen."

She smiled and took his order. She poured herself a beer too and they clinked glasses.

"Long day?" He set his beer down neatly on a coaster after taking a sip.

She thought about Jason's pulling away, a favorite customer learning that her daughter was dead, and the new investigation into her supposedly illegal activity by the state and grimaced. "Sure feels like it. Anything new on Nell's daughter?"

"Nope. Homicide cleared the scene. Now we wait."

"On the autopsy?" O'Dell nodded. "Huh." She shuffled her feet. Cindy Lou hip-checked her from behind. After she caught her balance, she glared at her assistant manager, but the other woman looked pointedly at the stack of papers, then motioned toward O'Dell with her chin. Janet sighed but turned back to the cop. "So . . . what's up with that Donaldson guy?"

O'Dell spluttered into his beer. After he stopped coughing, he wiped his chin with a cocktail napkin and grinned sheepishly. "What do you mean?"

Cindy Lou snickered nearby and Janet smiled, too. That was

a guilty reaction if ever there was one. "It just seemed as if you two knew each other."

O'Dell frowned. "I know *of* him. He's worked at Commerce for years. But we don't know each other well."

Janet tapped her fingers against her pint glass. There was more to that story, but O'Dell turned to the customer seated next to him and struck up a conversation. Janet watched him for a moment, then moved down the bar.

While she filled another order—a cosmopolitan, which was at the absolute outer limit of snobby drinks she'd mix up—she overheard O'Dell talking into his cell phone.

"Family's not taking it well, huh? Well, you just never can tell who's doing what these days. I guess it shouldn't be a surprise."

Janet unconsciously moved closer. When he tucked his phone back into his pocket she pounced. "What's going on?"

"Early notes from the investigation are in for the Birch death." When Janet raised her eyebrows, he added, "Liv Anderson Birch."

Janet nodded. Nell's daughter.

"Looks like drugs were involved. Heroin."

CHAPTER FOUR

Janet unlocked the main doors of the bar Friday morning and headed straight for the Beerador. She had to balance the books before any customers came in, but then she was going to make time to clean that god-awful refrigerator if it was the last thing she did. She planned to drop off the bucket and mop that banged against her leg with every other step and then head to the office, but before she made it behind the countertop, a jingle let her know her first customer had arrived. She turned around, surprised to see Nell making her way through the space.

The older woman's shoulders hunched forward and she crept to her regular spot at the bar. Without a word she held up two fingers. Janet shoved the cleaning supplies under the counter, clicked on the light switch behind the bar, then mixed up two vodka sodas. She fumbled with a lime, hacked off two wedges, slammed them onto the rims of the glasses, and then slid the drinks in front of Nell.

Some people didn't know what to say when a friend suffered a tragedy. But Janet was rarely at a loss for words, so she rested her elbows on the bar and waited until Nell looked up.

"I'm so sorry, Nell." The tiniest motion let Janet know the older woman had heard her, but Nell didn't speak, only raised the glass to her lips and downed half of it in one smooth gulp. "Talk when you're ready. Drink until you are."

Before she got more than a few steps away, Nell had drained the first glass and reached for the second. Janet wanted to stay close, so she decided to postpone her accounting work until later. Instead, she got her cleaning supplies ready. While the bucket filled with water in the sink, she watched Nell out of the corner of her eye.

The older woman took small sips of her drink and stared at a knot in the shiny wooden countertop.

Janet turned away and assessed the Beerador. The round shelves that were supposed to go inside the unit instead leaned up against the liquor shelves. She'd deal with them later. Her plan was to scrub the inside, then the outside, then somehow hose down the shelves with bleach before putting the whole thing back together and plugging it in.

She hefted the bucket out of the sink and carefully set it down on the floor, then plunged the mop into the warm soapy water. She wrung it out, then held her breath and opened the Beerador.

She took a tenuous, tiny breath in through her nose, expecting to smell decaying flesh or rotten blood. Only the faintest, chalky scent of ink and a light yeasty beer smell came out.

She'd just taken a deep breath and begun to lift the mop out when Nell cleared her throat. Janet dropped the mop back into the bucket and turned to face her only customer.

"Damn cops have the gall to say my daughter was using *drugs*." Nell swirled the small black cocktail straw through the ice cubes in her nearly empty glass.

Janet walked forward until the women were eye to eye and asked the question she hadn't thought to ask O'Dell the night before. "How do they know that? I heard the coroner's report won't be in for weeks—maybe months."

Nell stopped furiously stirring her drink. Her eyes clouded

and she set the glass down gently on the bar. "They found a fresh puncture hole in her arm. I guess you don't . . . you don't shoot up a prescription, right?" Nell stared straight ahead, and Janet couldn't quite read her expression.

"Do they know what kind of drugs?" Janet asked carefully, not wanting to offend her favorite regular. O'Dell had said heroin the night before, but she didn't understand how anyone could know that without the toxicology report.

Nell's shoulders pulsed slightly, and she took another sip. "I guess—well, they guess it's heroin, based off some powder they found on her—" Her lips trembled and she set the glass down and swallowed hard. "On her body."

"Does that . . . surprise you?"

Janet hadn't known that Nell even had a daughter until she died, so she didn't want to assume anything about Liv.

"I guess you never really know anyone after they reach adulthood. And certainly Liv and I weren't the kind of mother and daughter to share secrets." Janet raised her eyebrows. Nell looked down at her drink again and lowered her voice when she said, "We grew apart because of my . . . Well. She didn't like that I was taking things, and I couldn't . . . well, you know I can't just stop." Nell pressed her lips around the tiny black straw. She vacuumed the final drops of liquid from the bottom of the glass. "But I can't help but wonder why you would carry a load of laundry down the stairs after shooting up heroin. Doesn't make much sense to me, you know?"

"How do you know—"

"Clothes from the basket had dumped out everywhere."

Two splotches of pink spread across Nell's cheekbones.

Janet leaned over the bar again to get closer to her friend. "This kind of stuff is happening from suburban homes to inner cities to mansions up on the hill. I didn't know Liv at all, but—is there . . . is there a chance that she—"

"I'm not saying my family is immune to trouble," Nell interrupted, motioning for another drink. "Certainly I've proven that!

Here I am, an old lady, completely and totally addicted to stealing. And not because I need anything—God, I could paper this bar with cash from my savings account. I steal because I love the rush involved in it." She flicked her head and pressed her lips together so tightly that a white line formed in the middle of her mouth. "But my Liv? She's never done laundry a day in her life."

Janet's nose wrinkled. "What? Didn't you say she's got kids? What do you mean she never—"

"Three kids! And not a single load. That was Eric's job, and she made sure of it! She would buy new pants for her waitressing job before washing a dirty pair herself." Nell went back to stirring her ice cubes. Janet walked around the bar. As she slid onto the stool beside her friend, she tried to choose her next words carefully. An unusual move for her, but this was an unusual situation.

"Nell." She waited until the other woman looked up. "I didn't have the chance to know Liv, so I can only guess here, but with a gaggle of kids and a stressful job—I mean, she sounds like someone who could have been trying to escape. Is that—is that impossible?"

"Escape. Escape from what?"

Janet bit her lip. "Look, I'm just saying, sometimes I want to escape from life. I'm so tired of finally feeling like I have things under control and then they go and flat-out change without warning! And I can't even imagine the pressure, the added strain of a big family to provide for. Could it be that Liv needed to escape?"

Nell shook her head. "Oh, Janet. Don't you know? Life *is* change, honey. To live is to be ready and willing to accept those changes and figure out how they make your life better. And if they don't, then be ready to change again. My Liv knew that better than anyone."

Janet felt a stab of uncertainty at Nell's words that pierced into her chest with surprising pain. Life was change? No, that couldn't be. Life was about getting to the place you wanted to be and then fighting to stay there, at all costs! Before she could say as much, Nell spoke again.

"Liv and Eric weren't doing well. Their marriage was on the rocks. She told me that he'd been cheating on her—and she wasn't going to take it, no ma'am. She embraced the change. Kicked him out of the bedroom and was making plans for her future."

"Maybe it was all too much for her," Janet said.

Nell shook her head. "No. She knew it was going to be a challenge, but she told me that it was one worth embracing. That's why I'm left thinking, my daughter, who's never done drugs in her life—has never done laundry in her life—all of a sudden is dead at the hands of laundry and drugs?" Nell shook her head. "No ma'am."

Janet pushed herself back away from the bar and rubbed a hand up over her temples. "What are you saying, Nell?"

Now it was Nell's turn to lean forward, and for the first time since she'd gotten the terrible news that her daughter was dead, her eyes glittered like freshly broken glass. "What I'm saying is that someone murdered my daughter. And there's only one person who would have done it: her husband. I think Eric killed Liv."

CHAPTER FIVE

Sunday morning dawned earlier than usual at the Spot. For the first time in Janet's memory, sunlight streamed in through the windows.

The extra visibility inside the bar had necessitated a last-minute deep clean that morning, and Cindy Lou and Elizabeth, another bartender, had agreed to come in early to help her get ready for Nell's daughter's memorial. Not only had they scrubbed the floors, but they'd also had time to polish the table-tops and the kick plate of the bar.

Mel, her bouncer, manned the door like always. Only this morning, instead of checking IDs, the gruff woman directed guests to the sign-in book, pulling an endless supply of pens from the pockets of her cargo shorts when needed.

At home in any situation, Mel had traded her flannel shirt for a long-sleeve, black button-down. Her short blond hair was neat and tidy, and she nodded soberly to everyone who entered the space.

According to the obituary, Liv Anderson Birch was thirty-six years old and had died ten days ago from an unfortunate accident at home. She was survived by a husband, three children, and her mother.

Was that husband a killer, like Nell suspected? Janet had been watching him all morning. He didn't look suspicious, only sad. His brown eyes were watery and red rimmed, like he'd hardly stopped crying since Liv died. His children were much the same. Though his oldest, a girl, seemed more angry than sad. Janet didn't blame her.

"Terrible business." O'Dell came to a stop next to her, a sweet tea in one hand and a prayer card in the other.

"I'm surprised to see you here." Janet tilted her head back to look him in the eye. "You didn't know Liv, did you?"

O'Dell shook his head. "No, but it's always interesting to see who shows up to these things."

"Huh." She narrowed her eyes at the detective. "Are you saying you're investigating?"

"I'm not saying anything." His eyes scanned the room as he took a casual sip of his tea. "But we were sure interested to learn that the washing machine at Liv's house had been broken for a few days before she died."

"So why was Liv bringing laundry downstairs?"

"Exactly."

Janet raised her eyebrows. "Who told you about the machine?"

"The husband." O'Dell drained the tea and set the glass down on the closest table, then tucked the prayer card into his back pocket.

Janet shifted her weight from one foot to the other and crossed her arms. "So what's the next step?"

"Wait for the coroner to make a ruling, and that could take weeks—months even, when you're waiting on Toxicology."

"Can't your department fast-track it for something like this?"

"Maybe. Prosecutors are making drug overdose deaths a priority lately. So we'll see if he can push it through. But you know how it is, the lab is always backed up." O'Dell had been surveying the crowd along with Janet, but he turned to her with a pointed gaze. "Anything else?"

Janet shrugged. "Nell just can't see her daughter on drugs. Or doing laundry."

It was O'Dell's turn to shrug. "Drugs can take a lot of people by surprise. Family, especially, don't always see it coming." He started to walk away. When Janet reached out, he looked down at her fingers resting against his arm and stepped closer. "What?"

"I hate to bring this up again, but I get the feeling that there's some history between you and that Donaldson guy from the state. What gives?"

O'Dell raised his eyebrows, a "Who, me?" expression on his face that Janet didn't buy entirely. "We've both been working in Knoxville for five or six years; what can I say? We're not best friends. Just colleagues."

"I can't believe someone can file a complaint anonymously like that," she grumbled.

"Call your representative," O'Dell said, and his words were like a verbal shrug. It irritated Janet enough that she snatched her hand back.

O'Dell melted into the crowd with a small smile just before strong, steady hands wrapped around her shoulders and pulled her close. Jason murmured into her ear, "Need anything?"

She turned around and stood up on her tiptoes to kiss Jason on the cheek.

"I think we're good. I just asked Cindy Lou to refill the tea pitchers. The food seems to be holding steady."

Jason looked over the covered dishes and Sterno pots warming food on the bar and nodded. "I'm still surprised they wanted to have it here."

"I think it was easy—and that made it perfect." Janet had offered to host the memorial right after Liv's body was returned to the family, and Nell said Eric had jumped at the idea.

"Did you meet the kids?" Jason asked, lowering his voice.

Janet's face felt pinched when she nodded. The oldest was the angry girl, twelve, who had the knobby knees and wiry arms of someone who'd just grown too many inches in too short a time. Then there was a boy, eight, and another girl. She'd said she was six when Janet asked, holding up seven pudgy fingers, but based on her size, she couldn't have been more than two.

Liv's children stood in a group off to the side of the room, hovering near their father as the line of friends and family slowly shuffled past. Nell stood a few feet apart from them but shot furtive glances at her family. Janet could feel the distance between them was more than literal.

"Who's *she*?" Janet motioned with her chin to a woman taking more than her fair share of time with Liv's husband and children. She had piercing blue eyes, made even more striking because of her dark brown, almost black, hair. The woman smiled at something Nell's grandson did and tucked a lock of hair back into her sleek bob. She seemed to know the children well, and took turns hugging each of them and whispering into their ears.

"Summer Hughes," Jason said. "I met her right when she walked in. She said she was school friends with Liv."

The woman was sophisticated in a way that didn't match the rest of the crowd. Liv was a waitress; her husband worked in a mechanic shop. Nell was a drunk thief happy to have her daughter's last gathering at a dive bar. The crowd that filled the room matched what you'd expect, but this woman, this friend, wore a suit and fancy heels.

"What's she do?"

"I heard her mention a family counseling practice, but I didn't catch the name." He chuckled. "She's wearing some kind of flowery perfume and it's so strong, I had to move away."

Janet turned to look at the kids again, just as Nell brushed past her son-in-law and the friend. Summer's purse trembled and Janet groaned.

"You've got to be kidding me. At her own daughter's memorial?"

Jason looked over, a ghost of a smile on his lips. "Nell just struck?"

Janet nodded. "I'll be right back." She cut across the room toward Nell, who was walking nonchalantly toward her own purse, hanging over the back of her regular bar stool. "Freeze."

Nell turned with a clear, innocent expression. She raised a hand to brush a stray silvery hair from her face and looked around the space. "Thank you, Janet, this is more than I could've hoped for. I really do appreciate you opening the bar early for us."

"Nice try," Janet said, stepping close. "What'd you take?"

"Hmm?" Nell blinked a few times, her eyes wide.

Janet had to hand it to her; she looked as innocent as a child. "I couldn't tell—was it from her purse or her pocket?"

Nell's eyes flicked to the ceiling and she blew out a slow breath. "Purse. But it's nothing." She shook her head. "Just some fancy pen."

Brendon, Nell's only grandson, stared at them from across the room, and Janet pulled her closer. "Why did you take it?"

"Why wouldn't I? I need something to take my mind off this awful day."

As Janet patted Nell's shoulder, another woman approached. "Mrs. Anderson?"

Nell pasted on a wan smile. "Yes?"

"You might not remember me, I'm Skylar Rowen? I went to school with Liv? I'm so sorry for your loss." The slight woman looked up at Nell through a curtain of long, stringy, greasy brown hair.

"Skylar? Lord in heaven above, I haven't seen you in years! So nice of you to come out today for my Livvie."

As the two women caught up, Janet couldn't take her eyes off of Skylar. She looked like the "before" picture in a drug treatment advertisement. Her pockmarked face was somehow flushed and pale at the same time, and her cheekbones cut sharply into her too-thin face. When the women said goodbye, Skylar headed right for the door.

Janet turned on Nell immediately. "You should give it back, even if it *is* just a pen."

"And *you* should mind your business."

Before she could argue the point, an older gentleman tripped over a table nearby.

"Ger-outta my way, ya dumb table!" He pushed the table roughly and several glasses and bottles slid off as it tilted dangerously to one side. He tripped again when the table crashed back down onto its heavy pedestal base, shunting him to one side.

Shards of glass crunched when he walked over the broken bottles on the floor.

Mel moved in with precision. "Sir, step this way, please." She clamped her hands around his upper arms, propelling him forward with apparent ease, then placed him in a chair at an empty table and somehow held him down without breaking a sweat.

"Oh, Sumpter, get ahold of yourself." A woman matching Sumpter in both age and demeanor stalked over and grabbed him under the arm. "Tables don't fight, you big oaf. Only drunk men do!" She led him out into the parking lot.

"Who was that?" Janet asked.

Mel read down the guest book names. "I think that was Sumpter Hamstetter and his lovely wife, Lorelai. Look like friends of Eric's."

"You need to teach me that. All of us, actually."

"How to read the guest book?" Mel asked with a grin. She straightened her collar and then rearranged the pens around the book.

"No, that bouncer stuff. Most nights we have an all-woman staff. We should all know how to remove unruly customers."

"Anytime, Janet. Every woman should know self-defense."

"No . . . What you did was more than that."

Mel grinned. "True. It's really offense. Sometimes you've got to go on the offensive to avoid trouble." She turned back to the door when it opened and directed the new guests to the sign-in book.

Janet sized up her bouncer. She didn't know much about Mel, except that the woman had secrets, and that was fine with Janet. After all, who didn't?

CHAPTER SIX

Monday morning dawned cool and bright, and Janet was glad she'd worn a coat. The downtown structure she approached was notable only for its lack of character. Many of Knoxville's government buildings were impressively old or impressively maintained. However, the Tennessee Department of Commerce and Insurance had been stuck in an overflow office, a nondescript, white concrete, eleven-story block that housed some government agencies, some law offices, and even a few Realtors. The space was so generic, it could have been the headquarters for a local bank. Or a white-collar prison.

Janet made her way to an office on the fifth floor.

A woman with red hair and rouged cheeks looked up from her computer screen when Janet walked in. "Can I help you?" Her voice was thick with the same Southern accent nearly everyone in town had.

"I'm supposed to turn in some paperwork in response to an anonymous complaint—"

"You must be Janet Black?"

"Oh." The corners of Janet's mouth pulled down. "Yes, I am." She looked at the other woman with a question in her eyes.

"It might be a big building, but we're a small office, dear. I heard Gary mention something about the complaint. It's pretty unusual to have an anonymous filing in the first place."

Her accent wasn't the only thing that marked this woman as a true Knoxvillian. She looked like she wished they were chatting on a front porch over iced tea as she leaned forward, her expression curious. It wouldn't take much to open the floodgates.

Janet smiled. "Gary Donaldson? Is he here?"

She laughed. "No, hon, he's not. I'm sorry, I'm Rachel, the admin here. He takes his lunch break every day from noon to one without fail. He'll be back at one on the nose if you want to wait?"

Janet shuddered. "Gah, no. I just had a few questions about the forms he gave me—maybe you can help?"

"Sure, hon, set 'em up here." She tapped the raised countertop and then flipped through the forms and stopped at the page Janet had dog-eared. "If you sign this one here, you're confirming that you had nothing to do with any criminal investigation, and then you have to have it signed by a notary. You know . . ." She looked up at Janet over the forms, a small smile on her face. "The best way to get rid of this whole thing?"

Janet rested her elbows on the counter and looked down at Rachel. "How?"

"Just become an actual private eye. Look, the test isn't very difficult, and as long as you have no criminal record, all you have to do is pay a hundred bucks—which is half what you'll be fined if the board were to find you guilty."

"But it wouldn't matter if I become a PI now, would it? The complaint was for something that happened this summer."

She patted a stray lock back into her French braid. "Retroactive, hon. Just apply for retroactive status. All you need is a character reference from someone upstanding in the community. You know any of the local commissioners, maybe a judge?"

Janet frowned. "How about a homicide detective with KPD?"

"Perfect. Yup, that'll work." She added some pages to the

stack, then handed them back over the counter. "It's all pretty straightforward, but if you have questions after reading over the application, just come on back in. If I were you, I'd try and take the test before the commission meets again. Then, instead of voting on if you should be fined, they'll vote on whether to allow you to get a license with retroactive status."

Janet stepped back and considered the woman in front of her. "Thanks for the advice."

"You'll have to apprentice, but that's no big deal. Just a few months with an established PI to learn the ropes. Of course there's the annual CE—" The admin picked up a ringing phone. "Thanks for calling the Department of Commerce and Insurance, please hold." She put her hand over the mouthpiece and smiled at Janet. "Anything else?"

"CE?"

"Continuing education. PIs need twelve hours every year."

Janet stifled a sigh. This sounded more involved than she really cared to get, in a field she had no interest in pursuing. "Do you know where the business licensing office is?"

"You won't need that for the PI license. It's all part of the—"

"Oh, I know. It's for another matter."

Rachel sat back. "Oh. Well, sure. It's down two floors. Office three seventeen."

"Thanks." Janet waved and headed back to the elevator. When the doors opened, she gasped. "Dad? What are you doing h—"

Her final word was muffled by Sampson Foster's chest when he pulled her into a hug. "Janet! I was going to surprise you down at the Spot later today after my conference ended, but you found me first." He pulled her back and inspected her face. "How'd you do it?"

"It—it actually wasn't planned! I have errands for work—I had no idea you were here."

His bald head gleamed under the fluorescent lights, and in just that first glance, she could tell he'd lost weight. The paunch that used to envelop his midsection was gone, and he looked taller somehow because of his newly slimmed-down waistline. He pulled her against his side and pressed a button to close the elevator doors. "Never mind, never mind. What a great surprise! What floor?"

"Three. What are you doing in Knoxville?"

"I'm attending a weeklong conference right in this very building. I thought I'd stay through the weekend so we can visit. It's been too long."

"Sounds great, Dad. I'll let Jason and his dad know."

"William's still staying with you?"

She kept her smile plastered on. "Yes, and he's almost done laying the cork floors in the kitchen."

"Well, at least he's earning his keep, huh? Don't worry, I'm booked at a hotel downtown."

The elevator doors pinged open. "This is me. So . . . Dinner tonight?" She stepped off the car, relieved to escape any probing questions.

"Not so fast, young lady. What are you doing here, anyway?" Sampson's foot wedged into the path of the sliding doors and he scrutinized her face.

"Uhhh . . ."

"I could ask tonight, but I'm thinking you might not want everyone to know?"

She smiled. How was her dad so observant? "Well, to be honest, I'm looking into buying Jason's share of the Spot. I wanted to find out how the liquor license transfers. Tennessee is so weird about alcohol, you know?"

"Does Jason want out?"

"Not exactly . . ." She raised her eyes to his and they smirked at the same moment. "I just thought it made sense to own my own business. Jason owns his security business, why shouldn't I own mine outright, too?" She took another step away from the elevator when an alarm sounded. The doors had been open so long, they tried closing again over Sampson's foot.

"We'll talk more about it tonight over dinner." She grimaced and he added, "Or maybe not?"

She nodded. "Bye, Dad."

The alarm cut off when the doors finally met in the middle. Janet turned and took out her phone when it pinged and deleted some spam emails, then looked up to get her bearings. A massive, impressive set of oak doors was straight ahead.

The sign above read, *Law Offices of Thornton & Brown*, and a commercial jingle immediately popped into Janet's head: *"Need a divorce, don't stray from the course. Thornton & Brown attorneys!"*

Janet backed away from the office and frowned—it was kind of depressing to think of a company making all their profit off of other people's failed relationships. She turned and walked right into a huge potted fern. As she stumbled back, she heard a familiar snort.

"What's happening here? You interested in gardening all of a sudden, darlin'?" Jason grinned and moved a frond of the fern away from her face. "Why do you look so guilty, though?" His eyes narrowed and he stepped back. "What's going on, Janet?"

CHAPTER SEVEN

Janet forced her eyes forward and tried to focus on her boyfriend, but what she wanted to do was look around to see if anyone else she knew was lurking nearby. How many other people could possibly be in this random municipal building at lunchtime on a Monday?

When Jason cleared his throat, she stuttered out, "H-how did you know I was here?"

"I didn't. My dad said you headed out to run some errands. I just tried calling you, but it went straight to voicemail. Then— the strangest dang thing—I saw your dad in the lobby, and he said you were on the third floor. And you are." His smile was stiff and not entirely happy. "Did you know he was coming to town?"

Janet's heart clenched at his expression. Was he mad again? "N-no! I mean, not until just a few minutes ago. I saw him in the elevator. I told him we'd all go to dinner tonight."

Jason nodded. "Sounds good, sounds good. So then . . .what are you doing up here, anyway?"

She looked guiltily at the door for the business licensing office and her throat constricted. Suddenly the idea of telling Jason she wanted to buy his share of the bar seemed impossible.

"What's going on?"

A flush of color warmed her cheeks and she shifted on her feet. Now was as good a time as any to start the conversation about buying the Spot, and she tried to ignore the flat feeling in her chest. It was exactly what she wanted, so why did her stomach suddenly feel like it was on the last loop of a never-ending roller coaster?

She opened her mouth, but no words came out, so she finally held out the sheaf of papers. "I just had some questions about the investigation, so thought I'd stop by Gary Donaldson's office."

Jason took the stack and rifled through the top slips. "Is this an application?" He looked up incredulously. "Are you going to become a private detective?"

Fumbling, she took the papers back, and sure enough, the PI application was on top, not the complaint.

"Oh, I don't—I mean, it probably wouldn't make sense—" But as her eyes scanned the sheet she laughed, interrupting herself. "For God's sake, they recommend reading *Private Investigation for Dummies* to prepare for the test." She crowed again. "How completely ridiculous."

Jason motioned to some nearby chairs and as they dropped down into the seats a grin relaxed his face. "So ridiculous that you look like you're about to order the book from your phone and read it cover to cover?" He draped an arm across the back of her seat and squeezed her shoulder.

She tore her eyes away from the application. "Why are you here, anyway?"

Suddenly it was Jason's turn to shift uncomfortably in his seat. He rubbed his jaw and looked over her head. "Oh, I—I'm looking into buying old Ben Corker's restaurant."

She dropped the papers down into her lap and turned to focus completely on her boyfriend. "What are you talking about?" The abandoned building sat adjacent to the Spot and had been empty as long as Janet had lived in Knoxville.

"It's going up for auction at the end of the month. My dad's interested in opening a restaurant."

"Right next door to us?" Janet's smile froze on her face, but Jason saw through her attempt at happy.

"Well, he, ah—he needs something to do, and he's worked in the food industry before. I don't know, it's just something I said I'd look into."

She hesitated. "This is a . . . a bad idea."

"I know, you're ready to be done with my dad—I get it. But he's—he's here for a while, it seems. And he can't work on our house forever, God knows."

How could she nicely say she didn't want Jason's father operating a business next door to her bar? She wanted William and his bad mojo to go far away. Instead she asked the obvious question. "But how can he afford to buy a business?"

"It's an auction, so he'd only bid what he can."

She fixed Jason with an unblinking stare.

He leaned forward and rested his elbows on his knees, staring at a spot on the floor about a dozen feet away. "And I can help him out. Just a little, you know, if he needs me to."

Janet rubbed the bridge of her nose. "But then he's got to operate it—buy equipment! Tables, chairs, cash registers, serving trays—"

"But there might be stuff already there, who knows what old Ben left behind? I wanted to stop into the tax office to find out."

"But . . ." Her shoulders drooped. Would they never get rid of his dad?

"So, dinner with our dads tonight, huh? Sounds fun." Jason's forced smile stayed on his face as he stood and walked the few steps across the space to the tax office. He pulled the door open and waited for her to walk through.

She hung back and let him get the information about the real estate auction, trying to work through why she couldn't seem to talk to Jason about something so important. She wanted—no,

needed—the security of owning the Spot. Jason would understand, surely.

Or would he misconstrue her intentions and be hurt, just like
he'd been when she offered to let him stay home while she investigated why cops were at the bar?

After he got the forms about the upcoming auction, they
stood in the lobby by the elevators.

"You heading out?" Jason tapped the button for the elevator
and looked up at the floor indictor before tapping the button
again.

"No, I—I . . . Jason, wait."

He turned and looked at her expectantly.

"Well . . ." She didn't know how she was supposed to talk to
Jason about a life-changing decision, a major change to the way
they operated as a business—as a couple—when he was staring at
her like she was a scorpion about to strike. "I—I'm going to look
over these forms the receptionist gave me." She held up the
stack of papers. "That way if I have any questions, I can go back
in and ask. I guess I'll be home later."

Jason pressed a kiss to her cheek, then stepped inside the
elevator with a small wave. When she was alone again she
breathed out a sigh and shook her head. What a wuss. She didn't
deserve security if she couldn't even handle a difficult conversation with her boyfriend. But her brow furrowed and she dug her
cell phone out of her bag. The screen was blank. No missed calls.
Had he really intended to tell her about the restaurant? Maybe
she wasn't the only one in this relationship who was trying to
avoid difficult conversations.

———

Too jumpy to sit still, Janet headed to the Spot. It wasn't time to
open, but the Beerador needed tending to, and she'd put off
cleaning it for too long.

But as she reached out with her key to unlock the main door, a car pulled into the parking lot. Janet turned and waited to see who was behind the wheel.

The driver's side window of the sleek, shiny black sedan lowered, and a dark-haired woman smiled tentatively. "Janice, right?"

"Ain't nothing *nice* about me, hon. It's Janet."

The other woman's face flushed pink. "Of course, I'm sorry. I'm Summer Hughes—Liv's friend? We met at Liv's memorial."

"Oh—right, hi." They hadn't met, not really, but she remembered pointing the other woman out to Jason. Janet scrutinized Summer's car, from the shiny rims to the perfect paint job. "That's quite a ride."

Summer's dark sunglasses masked her eyes, but a small smile tipped the corners of her lips up. "I was in a car accident years ago. I understand, in a way few others do, that a safe car is a worthwhile investment."

Janet glanced around the deserted lot, then trained her eyes back onto Summer. She held a hand up to block the sun from her eyes. "We're not open yet."

"Oh—no I don't want to go in." The gravel lot absorbed the counselor's tinkling laugh as soon as it left her mouth. She propped her head against her hand and a friendly smile stretched across her face. "But I *was* hoping to find you here."

"Me?" Janet's confusion prompted Summer to take off her sunglasses and tap a button on her steering wheel that cut off the radio. "I don't suppose—I mean, you look busy, but I just thought I might be able to take you to lunch today."

"Oh—I—well . . ." The invitation was so unexpected that Janet was at a loss for words. Sitting down for a meal with a stranger was the last thing she wanted to do, but apparently her mouth didn't get the message from her brain, because suddenly she heard herself say, "I'd love to. Thanks."

CHAPTER EIGHT

"Thank you." Summer smiled at the waiter when he placed a steaming mug of hot water in front of her, and once again, Janet was struck by the contrast between the other woman's dark hair and cornflower-blue eyes. Summer unwrapped the tea bag and dunked it down into the cup. The warm, heady scent of cinnamon apple wafted up but didn't quite win the battle with her heavy floral perfume. "What a gorgeous day." Summer held the mug in front of her face with both hands. "I walk the square all the time when I need a break from the office, but I don't stop to enjoy it enough."

Janet glanced up from the menu and had to agree. Even on this chilly fall day, Market Square was hopping with activity. A half-dozen trees broke up the sea of concrete nicely and offered good shade during the hot summer months. Now wind rustled through the leaves, soothing patrons at the handful of restaurants with outdoor seating that faced the square.

"I wonder what's happening there?" Janet motioned to a tree farther away. Men in orange were blocking off part of the sidewalk, moving a cherry picker in. Another crew member marked a giant X on the tree trunk with red spray paint.

"Emerald ash borer." Their waiter was back, his order pad

held at the ready, a bored expression on his face. "All the trees have to come down. They'll replant in time for the spring concert series, but the shade'll be cut in half until the new trees can grow in."

"Such an invasive insect." Summer wrinkled her nose at the trees.

"Should I come back, or . . ."

Summer nodded and he walked away, muttering under his breath.

"You said your office is nearby?" Janet asked. Summer nodded. "And you're a counselor?"

Summer nodded. "That's right—now, don't do that! You just pressed your lips together!"

Janet unpeeled them to laugh.

Liv's friend took another luxurious sip. "Don't worry, I'm off the clock. And no one *has* to talk to me. But sometimes people need help figuring out how to talk—either to themselves or each other. You ever feel that way?"

Janet shrugged. She had felt that way, in fact, less than an hour ago with Jason.

"For example," Summer went on, "often couples need help churning through their differences and figuring out how they can make them work to their advantage."

Janet leaned forward despite herself. "What do you mean?"

"Well . . ." The other woman took another sip of her tea before focusing on Janet. "Each case is different, but any change in relationships can cause challenges—that's true for new parents welcoming a baby, or couples taking their relationship to a new level. Open communication is key!"

Janet's lip curled as she thought about how closed off she and Jason had been with each other lately. She looked away from the successful, polished woman sitting across from her, who probably had never struggled with anything in her life and her expression hardened. "Then again, other times it's best just to shut up, and not rock the boat."

Summer winced and sat back. "Well, if you ever need to talk . . ."

The waiter was back and they both placed their orders. After several long moments, Janet tried to relax her shoulders. It wasn't Summer's fault she and Jason weren't talking to each other about important life events. She cleared her throat. "So . . . how are Eric and the kids?"

"There's someone else who doesn't want to talk," Summer said, almost to herself.

"Excuse me?"

"Oh, Eric. He's—well, he's really struggling with things. The kids are, too, I mean, of course they are! He lost his wife, his life partner! The kids lost their mother. But Eric . . . well, I'm just not sure what to make of him." She turned her bottomless eyes on Janet.

"Are you—you're helping out at the house? Nell and I are headed over there later today." She bit her lip, hating that Summer had somehow coaxed her into volunteering information.

Summer's head dropped and she cradled her mug for a moment before answering. "I wish I could do more, but between work and life—you know how it is. To be honest, it's hard to be there. I can hardly stand to look at Eric."

Janet set her glass of tea down with a jolt. "Why?"

"It's no secret he cheated on Liv. I'm not one to judge, but, I mean, of course I was on Liv's side, and she was furious! Wanted him out of the house, out of their lives. And now this . . . I mean I'm sure Nell blames him for her daughter turning to drugs. If it weren't for the kids, I'd probably never see him again. As it is I'm trying to be supportive for their sake."

Summer looked up through her eyelashes. "It's too bad Nell can't be there more. The kids just light up when she arrives. Then again, I get the impression she wasn't over a lot before Liv died? Something about a stealing problem?"

Janet made a mental note to never see Summer in a professional capacity. She was like an open tap you couldn't close down. She had to remind herself that she was in the South, where talking to strangers was an art form. But she wasn't going to be the one to parse her friend's fraught relationship with her dead daughter's family with a near stranger, so she shrugged and said, "What do you mean?"

"Oh, Liv mentioned something weeks ago, she felt frustrated, that's all. And then some little things I've been picking up at the house from Eric and the kids. I thought you might be able to shed some light on their relationship."

The women locked eyes and Janet's narrowed. "Sorry, I don't know anything about that."

Their food arrived and Janet was happy for a reason to stop talking. They fell silent while they ate, but when Summer set down her fork and took another sip of her tea Janet braced for more probing questions.

"Sorry," Summer said, taking in Janet's stiff shoulders and frown. "Job hazard. I can be charming when I think about it."

Janet snorted. "I know all about job hazards, believe me."

"Thanks for keeping me company today." She swept the bill up in one hand and stood. "I won't ask you any more questions, you're like a lockbox, and I do wonder why that is . . ." She narrowed her eyes and studied Janet before continuing. "I don't know your relationship situation, but I'll leave you with one piece of advice I give to all the couples who come into my office. If you can't be honest with your partner, you're not only doing a disservice to him, but to you and your relationship as well. If you love each other, you can find a way through almost anything."

"Almost? Well that's disappointing," Janet said, standing too.

"Everyone has a red line, Janet. Do you know yours? Your partner's?"

Summer offered a small smile and turned away. Janet watched her take care of the bill at the front desk and walk out into the cool, cloudless day.

People joked that bartenders were as good as counselors, but she was rethinking that after an hour with Summer. Just a few words from Liv's old friend had her reassessing multiple things in her life, and frankly, she didn't appreciate it.

"Red line? I'll give you a red line. Getting too personal with strangers, people prying into things they don't have any business prying into—those are *my* red lines."

"Excuse me?" The waiter was back; Janet had been so caught up in her own worries, she hadn't noticed that he was clearing the table. Now he was frozen with a plate halfway to his tray, his expression alarmed as he stared at Janet.

She headed away from the table but stopped to watch as a chain saw spluttered to life, then tore into the first of the infested trees on the square right at the red lines crossing the trunk. Sawdust flew up into the air and a fine layer of it settled onto the closest tables and chairs.

Janet rubbed her temples and turned her back on the red lines, the destruction being wrought, the mess. She would ignore it completely for now. Instead she took out the paperwork and her heart seemed to speed up, beat faster, as she read over the steps to become a PI. Here, at last, was something under her control.

She smiled as she walked to her car and ordered a few books from an app on her phone before she cranked over the engine. The books would be here by the weekend. Plenty of time to soak up all she needed to know to ace the test.

CHAPTER NINE

Janet pulled up to the small house on Knoxville's east side and tapped her horn.

Beep beep.

It sounded low and sad, but maybe that was Janet's imagination, knowing who she was picking up and where they were headed.

Just as Janet was deciding whether she should properly park the car and get out, the front door opened and Nell emerged. The older woman buttoned up her overcoat, then set a small purse primly on her arm before turning around to lock the door.

"Thank you so much for doing this," Nell said as she pulled the door open. After buckling up, she turned to Janet. "I hate that I don't want to go over to the house on my own, but I just don't trust Eric."

Janet eased the car away from the curb and snuck a glance at her companion. Her conversation with Summer had piqued her interest on several fronts. "What was your relationship like with Liv and her family before she died?"

Nell pressed her lips together and stared out the window before answering. "We managed." Her eyes flicked over to Janet. "Liv wanted me to get counseling, wanted me to stop the stealing, but I . . . I just couldn't do it. And things were strained because of that."

"How so?" Janet turned to look Nell full in the face at a stoplight.

Nell's cheeks pinked slightly and her lips pressed together again. "She never said as much, but I think she worried that I would be a bad influence on the kids. As if I'd steal from my own family!" Her eyes flicked over to Janet's again, and she flushed a deeper shade of red.

"Not once?" Janet asked. "You never once stole from Liv, her husband, or your grandchildren?"

"W-well, I mean nothing important." Nell turned her face away from Janet. When she spoke again, her voice was softer, all the defensiveness gone. "I should've listened to her. She thought getting help would be good for me, not her. She had my best interests at heart, and I should've listened."

A different person would have reached over to pat Nell's hand, but Janet just drove, and she hoped that Nell knew there was no judgment in the silence.

"Make a left up here." Nell pointed the way, then turned in her seat to face Janet. "You know, there's one more thing that's been bothering me. About the drugs? So let's say Liv was using. Let's say my straight-as-an-arrow, always-do-the-right-thing daughter was using drugs. Where did she get them?"

Janet shrugged. "Where does anyone get drugs? Corner store, someone at work, family member?"

Nell nodded encouragingly. "Exactly. But not just any family. I mean, those damn police didn't find any other drugs in the house. No sign of previous drug use, no pills, no hidden stash of anything anywhere." Nell shifted in her seat to face Janet. "And as far as I know, they didn't even find the needle she'd supposedly used that very day. And why not?"

Janet raised her eyebrows and her shoulders.

"Because Eric covered it all up, that's why! *If* she used drugs, it's because of him! He's responsible for my Liv's death. I can't stand to look at him!"

Janet flicked on her blinker and changed lanes. As far as she was concerned, there wasn't an "if" about it. The police had found trace amounts of heroin on Liv's body, found the puncture hole where she'd used the needle. All they were waiting on was confirmation from a blood test. But Janet set that aside for now as she turned to face her friend. "Nell. That's a very serious accusation to make about the father of your grandchildren, and you have no evidence to back it up."

"Yet."

"What do you mean?"

"I mean I don't have any evidence yet, but I'll be looking. I did some research online last night. If Eric is the one who brought the drugs into the house, he can be held liable for Liv's death. Legally, he can be charged with a drug-induced homicide." She looked triumphantly at Janet. "And that's why he got rid of everything before calling the cops when Liv died." She turned to face forward again, her shoulders set resolutely. "So I just have to prove that Eric brought the drugs into the house."

Janet's right eye started to twitch and she pressed the heel of her palm down on the socket. "Even if that's true, the police didn't find any evidence. What makes you think that *you* can find—"

"Slow down."

The women had been getting louder to talk over each other, and Nell's last words echoed in the small car. Janet pulled over, took a deep breath, and lowered her hand from her face. "I'm not the one jumping to conclusions, here, Nell, you are."

"No, I meant slow down the car. That's their house. We're here." She pointed across Janet's line of sight. "Let me do the talking, but keep your eyes open." The older woman climbed out of the car and strode across the street. "The black truck is Eric's, that old Taurus was Liv's, but I don't know who owns the red Firebird. It seems indecently happy at a time like this." She drew her eyebrows together and glared at the car before squaring her shoulders. "We are about to find out though." She buzzed up the front walk and knocked sharply on the door. Brendon answered.

"Hey, Grandma Nell."

"Brendon. Why are you home?"

The boy only turned to yell over his shoulder, "Grandma Nell's here!"

Janet followed Nell into the house but hung back in the entryway, taking in the children's artwork hung crookedly on the wall with blue painter's tape as Nell continued to fuss over the boy.

"Give me a hug, Brendon. Have you eaten today?" Brendon only grinned self-consciously, and she tried another question. "Your dad home?"

"Yeah, but he's napping."

"Then who's cooking chicken?" Nell raised her nose in the air and sniffed delicately. "Smells like my recipe, too."

Brendon ducked away from Nell and backpedaled to the couch. Two women walked out of the kitchen, ignoring everything but each other, their voices raised but controlled.

"I think it's time you left, Skylar."

"Like I said, I'll wait for Eric."

Summer's face was tight, but she forced a smile when she saw the new guests. "Oh, Nell, Janet, hello. I was just telling Liv's old friend Skylar that Eric is sleeping, and it's probably best she be on her way."

Skylar shook out of Summer's grasp. "I brought a casserole over for the family. I just wanted to make sure it makes it *to the family*."

Summer scowled. "I'll make sure it does. Thanks so much for stopping by." She looked pointedly at the door and with a huff, the other woman stalked through the room.

"Mrs. Anderson." She nodded stiffly as she passed. Nell tried to reach out, but Skylar slipped by without a backward glance, her body rigid. The drawings taped to the wall danced in the wind as the door slammed, and Janet's hand shot out to catch one piece of paper as it fluttered down toward the ground.

She pressed the tape back against the wall and smoothed out the sheet. A strange jumble of letters written in bold black print filled the page—it must have been written out by the youngest child, because there wasn't a single real word, just a series of letters grouped haphazardly together, though the writing was sure and steady. Strange. Janet turned when Nell spoke.

"What happened?"

"Oh, that woman just makes my blood boil!" Summer said, still breathing hard. "Coming in here, after the way Liv d—" She blanched, then cleared her throat. "Brendon? Why don't you wake up your dad, tell him your grandma's here." After Brendon bounded away, Summer cleared her throat again. "I don't think Liv would want that woman coming here. She's still using by the looks of her, and she needs to get her own life together before she comes knocking into their lives." She pressed her fingertips into her temple.

"Using?" Nell asked. "Skylar Rowen? Never."

Even Janet had to force the look of disbelief from her face. "Oh, Nell. She's in a bad way, and has been for a while by the looks of her."

Nell harrumphed and then took a step toward Summer and lowered her voice. "Why isn't Brendon in school? I thought it might be a good distraction for him to get back there."

Summer shrugged. "He thought he needed some time at home, and Eric said it was okay." She dropped back a step and led the way into the kitchen, holding the swinging door open for the other two women.

Janet paused when she saw two overflowing laundry baskets of dirty clothes leaning next to the couch, and a third by the steps that led down to the basement.

The steps.

Janet couldn't blame anyone in the family for not wanting to tackle the exact thing that had led to their mother's death. Was the machine fixed finally? Would Summer start up a load after she cooked the chicken?

"It's been stressful, of course it has been," Summer said, and Janet snapped to attention and slipped into the kitchen after Nell. "But these kids are resilient. You always read that that's the case, and I'm watching it in real time. They're just amazing."

A pan of hot oil shimmered on the stove, and steam rose up from a paper-towel-covered plate of fried chicken. Summer saw her studying the food and smiled. "I know we just ate a few hours ago, but I'm starved again, what about you?"

Before she could answer, Eric banged into the small room, rubbing sleep from his eyes. His well-worn jeans hung from his thin frame. In the main room, Brendon leapt from a chair to the couch, and over to another chair.

Nell's hands fluttered between the water Summer had set in front of her and her lap, her lips set in a thin line—angry, but unsure how to proceed. She suddenly stood. "Excuse me, I have to use the bathroom." She sent a knowing look toward Janet, but before she could sweep out of the room, Summer cleared her throat.

"Nell, you'll need to use the upstairs bathroom. Somebody decided to see how many Crayons they could flush down the toilet." Summer frowned. "Five was too many, in case you were wondering, too."

Nell shot a victorious look at Janet before she disappeared behind the swinging door and Janet had to bite her lip to keep from smiling. Having a legitimate reason to go upstairs was much better for snooping around, and Nell was delighted with the unexpected news.

Eric groaned and then dropped down into the open chair next to Janet. "Do I need to call the plumber?"

"I already did," Summer said.

"Thanks."

Summer nodded, then after a moment, he turned to Janet with red, watery eyes. "Who are you?"

"You remember Janet, Nell's friend from the bar?" Summer said.

Eric grunted out a greeting and dropped his head into his hands.

"Eric told me that Bonnie's just been sleeping terribly these last weeks." Summer pulled a bag of corn from the refrigerator and started shucking it over the sink. "Long nights make for long days, that's what Liv used to say, anyway."

His head nodded in his hands and he muttered, "It's nothing new, I'm just not used to dealing with it."

Janet's lips pursed. He'd been a father for twelve years but wasn't used to dealing with kids waking up at night? She guessed that meant that Liv had been on night duty for more than a decade.

"Anything else keeping you up?" With Nell gone, it was up to Janet to ask probing questions, and she was ready.

Summer's eyebrows shot up and she stopped mid-shuck to look over, but Eric didn't seem to catch her tone.

"Just everything. And nothing. That's the worst." Eric shuffled to the fridge and pulled out a soda. "Everything and nothing." Air shot out of the can when he pulled the tab. He took a long drink.

Brendon streaked into the kitchen to grab a bottle of water. He ran back out in time with the door swing and, once again, leapt from the floor to the chair. But this time, when he skipped over to the coffee table, the surface quaked, and all the adults froze at a splintering crack of noise.

"Brendon! What did I say about jumping on the furniture?" Eric roared. He flung the door back open. Brendon stood frozen on the tabletop. He took a tentative step, then another. When the table didn't collapse, he breathed out a sigh. "Sorry, Dad!"

He landed on the carpet lightly and then threw himself onto the couch and picked up the remote.

Eric's hand fell to his side and the door swung toward him, faster than he'd been expecting. He caught it just before it smacked him in the face as Nell marched into the kitchen, a small, round plastic trash bin in her hands.

"What is this?" Her eyes locked onto Eric's, the trash bin held out between them, her body stiff, a red flush creeping up her neck.

"A trash can." Eric's brow furrowed and he stepped away from his mother-in-law.

"Not the can, what's inside it? Huh? Where did it come from, Eric?" Nell's voice shook with emotion, and Janet leaned forward to get a better look.

But when Eric squinted over the rim, his whole body went rigid. "I—I don't . . . I mean, what . . ."

Nell's lips turned down into a disgusted frown. "How long have you been using, Eric?" She slammed the trash can down onto the table. "Did you pressure my Liv to use? But why? Why would you do that? She was a good girl, she didn't deserve any of your crap—not your cheating, not your drugs, none of it!"

"It's not—it's not mine, I swear it!" Eric stumbled back a step and reached behind him for a chair. "Where did that come from?"

"Where did it—what do you mean where did it come from? It was sitting right there in the bathroom where *you* must have put it!"

"But the kids—the kids use that bathroom all the time!" Eric gasped, passing a hand over his face. "What if they'd—"

"Not the kid's bathroom—this was your bathroom! The master bathroom!"

Eric's face twitched as he considered that Nell had been in his room. Janet stood to lean over the plastic receptacle. Peeking out from the bottom folds of the plastic liner, a small, silver hypodermic needle glinted in the overhead light.

After a beat of silence, Nell peppered Eric with more questions.

"Who's your supplier? How long have you been using? How in God's name did you convince Liv to try it?"

Eric's eyes hardened and he clenched his jaw so tightly that when he answered Nell, his lips barely moved. "I'm telling you that's the first I've seen of it."

In an instant, the atmosphere in the small kitchen changed. The exhaustion and irritation that had been exuding from Eric was gone, replaced with a simmering anger that left Janet breathless. She moved away from the table; even Summer dropped the ear of corn she'd been holding and stepped back.

The hot oil on the stove popped and the older woman dropped her voice. "*Whoever* this belongs to"—her tone made it clear she thought it was Eric's—"it should be sent to the police. They'll want to test it."

"I agree. They've been asking questions about Liv's habits, and frankly, I didn't have any answers for them. I'm sure they'd like to test it. I'll call them about it right now. I'm sure you can see your way out." He stormed out of the room and they heard him pound up the steps.

Nell's shoulders slumped and she swayed unsteadily on her feet, then leaned against the table, and her hand trembled when she reached up to rub her eyes. "It's time to go."

They left Summer standing, frozen, in the kitchen, and made their way through the family room. Janet's only concern was getting her friend into the car before she collapsed.

However, as they walked down the path toward the street, she turned to look back at the house. Framed in an upstairs window, Eric clutched his chest. The only word that could describe his crumpled face was "anguished". Though it seemed that he had lashed out at Nell in anger, maybe the emotion that came through was powered by something else. Because the person she was staring at now was a devastated man. Maybe seeing the needle in the trash can had made him angry at Liv—for using, for leaving him alone, for dying.

How could she, or Nell, ever know the truth of what had happened?

CHAPTER TEN

"Ready, Janet?"

She jumped, then shook herself and flicked a stray wisp of hair from her eyes. "Yup, let's go!" She turned from the hall mirror and joined Jason at the front door.

Jason squinted briefly, and Janet thought he was going to say something, but he only held the door open. "My dad's going to meet us at the restaurant, he's wrapping up some business downtown."

"What kind of business?" She waved to Kat, Mel's partner, just returning to their half of the duplex from the grocery store, and a surge of excitement flooded her veins. "Now that he's done with the kitchen floors, is he going to move on to cabinetry?" They'd been without a kitchen at the house since they moved in over a year earlier. Janet was no chef, but she longed to make coffee without having to partially fill the carafe under the short bathroom sink twice in order to brew a full pot. Even home-boiled pasta would be a nice change from their daily fare of takeout and microwavable meals.

"It's about his restaurant."

"His restaurant?" Janet tried to keep her voice pleasant, but

Jason's shoulders tightened at her tone. "Have things moved forward since this morning?"

"I guess I should just tell you. He was in talking to Cindy Lou about coming on board as his manager."

"*What?*" Jason's jaw clenched, but Janet pressed him. "He's going to steal my employees without even having the courtesy to ask me first?"

"*Our* employees," Jason corrected her, but frowned. "And I know. I talked to him about boundaries."

"Did he hear you?"

Jason shook his head. "Probably not. He's like a dog with a bone with this new idea."

"Well he can't take Cindy Lou." She climbed into the truck and slammed the door, fuming.

"It could actually be a really good move for her." Jason got into the car and kept his eyes on the road as he backed out of the driveway. "Better hours, probably better pay—I mean, she'd draw an actual salary, wouldn't be so reliant on tips."

"That's just—I mean, she'd never—how can you even—"

"Calm down. Nothing's happened yet."

She turned away and glared out the window. This was exactly why she wanted to be the sole owner of the Spot. You just couldn't trust anyone anymore, including your own boyfriend's family. Hiring employees right from under her nose! Ridiculous. She cracked her knuckles, then flexed her fingers and turned back to Jason. "What did *she* say?"

"She said she was going to talk to you about it."

"Well she hasn't!" She huffed out a breath and crossed her arms over her chest.

"Wonder why." His eyes flicked over to her but he held his tongue, and they drove in silence the rest of the way to the restaurant. After Jason thanked the valet he reached for her hand. "Can we just have a nice dinner with our dads tonight? Figure this out tomorrow?"

She didn't answer. He held the door for her, and she breathed out a sigh when her father stood up from the bar to greet them.

"Janet, Jason! Lovely to see you both."

Sampson stepped back, surprised, after she gave him a particularly warm hug. Hating the misty feeling that tickled the back of her eyeballs, she turned to the waiting bartender and ordered a drink.

In the mirror, she saw Jason and Sampson exchange a look, and she hurried to sit between them. Sampson was *her* father. Even though they'd only known each other for a few years, she was confident that he'd be on her side.

"How's the conference?" She turned her back on Jason to focus on her dad, still amazed, three years after connecting with Sampson, that she had one at all. When Janet was growing up, her mother had claimed that her father left when he found out she was pregnant with Janet. Sampson had tracked her down several years ago, insisting it was her mother who'd left *him*, and had never even told him she was pregnant. By then, her mother—the only one who could refute his story—had been dead for years, and Janet had slowly adapted to—and secretly loved—the new reality of her family.

"It's great, really interesting stuff on tort reform at the federal level. I won't bore you with the details, but I'm glad to see such interest from a broad range of federal judges in attendance."

"Hey, y'all! Sorry for the delay!" William squeezed between Jason and Janet and motioned to the bartender for another round.

Sampson canceled the order for his drink refill. Janet, meanwhile, downed the rest of her existing drink in one gulp and reached for the second as soon as the bartender set it down.

Ignoring Jason's pointed look, she turned to look his father square in the face. "William, I heard you're trying to hire Cindy Lou out from under me?"

William ducked his head good-naturedly. "I got found out,

huh? All I did was talk to her about the idea of coming to work for me, just to gauge her interest."

"And?"

"She didn't leap at the offer, but she didn't send me packing, either. I think she wanted to talk to you before she really considered it."

"It does seem the appropriate order of things, doesn't it?" She glared at William over the rim of her glass.

His brow wrinkled, but before he could answer, Sampson broke in.

"What's the new business going to be, William?"

Janet ignored Jason's peeved expression and focused on her drink. If he wasn't going to keep his father in line, she had no problem taking the reins.

"I'm thinking about opening a restaurant next to the Spot. Just small at first, with the ability to expand as business does."

"Restaurants are hard work. Very difficult to turn a profit."

"You sound like my wife." William waved his hand. "It's all a matter of proper planning and good employees . . ."

Janet's mind wandered as William recited his business plan. Liv had probably thought she'd planned well, but she'd been one cheating husband away from having to figure out custody arrangements and alimony. Jason's mother had had to take her ex to divorce court to protect herself when the schnapps hit the fan after twenty-two years of marriage.

She smirked to herself; now she was fake-swearing in her own head! Cindy Lou would be proud.

Her lips pressed together and she swallowed hard against a sudden aching in her chest. Janet didn't want to find herself in the same situation. One breakup away from the welfare line, no control over her own life. She would find a way to make Jason see her side; her desire to own the Spot had nothing to do with him—it was all about her taking care of herself. How could he not understand that?

She tuned into her father's conversation with William again, only to find Jason staring at her, his expression unreadable.

She smiled thinly as William said, "I just think you miss the signals, and all of a sudden you're out on your ass, without a leg to stand on legally."

"Well, I'm not sure about that." Sampson grimaced, then motioned to the bartender for another drink. "There are plenty of laws in place to protect everyone's rights in a divorce. Then again, Tennessee is an 'at-fault' state. So if you cheat . . . well, all bets are off."

The bartender set Sampson's new drink down and smirked when William said, "One random lay hardly constitutes losing half my 401(k), though, right?"

Sampson took a long pull of his new drink instead of answering, then the bartender was back, this time with a sizzling appetizer for the group. He lowered the platter onto the counter in front of Janet. Delighted to have something else to focus on, she smiled and scooped up some of the seven-layer dip with a sturdy chip, then looked up when Jason chuckled.

"What?"

Jason only shook his head.

"Another round?" William asked, his hand already waving for the barkeep's attention.

Her father looked just as relieved as she felt to end the conversation.

CHAPTER ELEVEN

"Okay, crew. I want everyone to face me, wide stance, hands out." Mel's white sneakers stepped apart and she waited for the rest of the bartenders to mimic her.

Cindy Lou yawned but set her glass of tea down and bounced slightly on the balls of her feet. Her yellow hair was curled and ready for a night out, not a hands-on tutorial on taming unruly patrons, but that was Cindy Lou's way. She'd wear high heels to the gym.

Elizabeth, meantime, had pulled her long blond hair back into a ponytail and set a textbook down reluctantly on a nearby table.

"Janet?"

Janet jumped. She'd been so busying studying her employees, she was holding up the demonstration.

"Wide stance. Got it."

Mel surveyed the small group of women. "Great. Now, what you want to do is be ready with quick fingers"—she wiggled her outstretched digits—"to call the police."

Cindy Lou groaned and Janet crossed her arms. "Mel."

Janet's neighbor raised her eyebrows. "Ladies, let me be clear. Getting involved with a drunk, combative person is not a good idea. Your first line of defense should always be to call the cops if someone is acting dangerous or violent."

Janet perched against the nearest table. "Mel, no one is under the delusion that Cindy Lou—or I," she added hastily when Cindy Lou glared at her, "are going to take out a three-hundred-pound drunk, belligerent man. What we need to be able to do is neutralize the threat before it gets to that stage."

Mel frowned but nodded and pushed back her sleeves. "I agree, which is why I'm here. But I want to impress on you that I've had years of training, and even I—"

"Where?" Cindy Lou cocked her head to the side and fixed Mel with an unblinking stare.

"Huh?"

"Where did you have years of training?"

Elizabeth focused fully for the first time on the meeting and even Janet leaned forward with a finger tapping her lips. Mel was a mystery, and even the tiniest nugget of information would double what they knew now.

"Everywhere," she answered with a small smile. "But the main takeaway in all my training was always try and deescalate first. If that fails, then take 'em out." She stepped behind a table like it was a podium. "To deescalate, you want to try several things. First, be friendly and confident. These assholes can smell fear, and you don't want to give them a reason to prove their power. Always approach from the side—never give them a direct line of attack from the front. Your advantage in this bar will be that you're sober and they're drunk! Don't lose that advantage by giving them a clear shot . . ."

Elizabeth paled at the words, but Cindy Lou's eyes narrowed and her head bobbed, like she was soaking it all in to try out later.

Suddenly Janet wasn't sure this training was a good idea. She bit her lip just as Mel called everyone up to the front to do some practice moves.

After an hour of learning about elbow strikes, bear-hug holds, and other basic safety moves, the group broke apart.

"Pressure points, huh?" Janet grinned up at Mel.

"Cindy Lou will have the advantage on all of you there."

"What do you mean?" Janet's nose wrinkled. She was certain she could take someone down. As long as they were smaller. Or already passed out.

"A foot stomp, with those heels? She'll lay anyone out flat and break about ten bones in their foot. Look out."

Cindy Lou grinned and took a sip of her sweet tea. "Thanks for the lesson."

Mel's smile faded. "Honestly, we'd probably be better off arming everyone with pepper spray, but it's always good to know the theory behind the moves, at least." The bouncer looked doubtfully at the staff and Janet frowned. She hoped Mel wasn't lumping her in with Cindy Lou and Elizabeth.

"I've got to jet, Janet!" Elizabeth called from the door, her backpack heavy with textbooks.

"We miss you, E. How are classes going?"

She leaned against the door frame. "They're good. I just have to finish up these core classes before I can apply for a transfer to UT. I'll be able to pick up more shifts after the fall semester ends."

"You just let me know when. We can always use more help behind the bar."

The young woman headed out and Janet sighed. She was glad Elizabeth was getting her studies in order. She wanted to become a veterinarian, but Janet hated to think about hiring a new bartender to fill the hole in her schedule with Elizabeth's class load taking priority. She mentally added "post job opening online" to her to-do list.

Cindy Lou draped an arm across her shoulder. "I miss her, too."

Janet turned to look at her. Would she have another spot to fill if Cindy Lou left? Her assistant manager dropped her arm and her cheeks flushed, but she stayed quiet. Janet sighed and pushed a spray bottle toward her. "Let's clean this mess up before the regulars get here."

Cindy Lou fiddled with her dangly earrings and opened her mouth, but then snapped it shut when she met Janet's eyes. "Whatever you say, boss."

———

Janet dunked a rag into a sink full of clean soapy water, then wrung it out before approaching the Beerador. Cindy Lou had finished deep-cleaning the outside of the refrigerator unit, and now Janet had to tackle the inside.

She cracked her neck and mentally rolled up her sleeves. It was just a refrigerator. If you thought about it, what she was doing was nothing new. Really, blood had to be cleaned out of refrigerators all the time—if a package split open and liquid seeped out. She gulped. It was just usually blood from *animals*.

But just as she reached for the handle of the Beerador, the bell over the main door jangled.

She frowned at the happy sound and dropped the dishrag down to her side. It had been Cindy Lou's idea to put the bell over the door, so of course it was cheerful. She wished there was a different-sounding bell they could get. One that was less "Hey, y'all, thanks for coming" and more "You sure you're supposed to be here?"

She plastered a smile on her face to welcome the customer and it turned cautious when she recognized the new arrival. "Hey, Summer."

Liv's friend strode toward the bar and dropped her bag onto a barstool, her expression distressed. She had appeared just as shocked as anyone else at the turn of events in Eric's kitchen the day before, but Janet wasn't sure where her loyalties really lay, or why she'd come to the Spot now.

"Such a disaster at the house yesterday. What are we going to do? How is Nell holding up?"

"She's—well, she's pretty torn up about it all. Eric called her after we left—told her not to come back to the house again. I mean, I know he's angry, but I don't know what he's thinking! He's got to work full time; how's he going to take care of the kids without Nell's help?"

Summer sighed. "He asked me to step up, but I'll be honest; it's more than I can really handle at this point. I mean, I've never had kids—even an hour with them is fairly exhausting."

"I feel that way about ten minutes in," Janet said.

Summer's smile at Janet's words turned indulgent. "They're amazing, though. I try and think about their future when I get overwhelmed. They're going to have great lives, those kids."

Janet absently wrung her cloth out over the sink. Tiny droplets of water dribbled down and hit the metal basin with a quiet *tap-tap-tap*. "You're there at the house a lot—do you think Eric's using? Or do you think that was Liv's needle and the police just missed it?"

Summer's hand fluttered to her neck. "I've been asking myself that very question since you and Nell left yesterday. Liv mentioned that finances were tight, and I'm sure that's stressful, but stressful enough for that? From him? I just . . ." She blew out a sigh. "I don't know what to think."

"Well, I mean, how well do you know Eric?" Janet asked.

"I met him in college but didn't really know him well."

"Eric went to college?" He was a mechanic; Janet had imagined he'd gone to trade school, not college.

"Well, he started, anyway. That's where he met Liv."

Janet dropped the rag down onto the counter and leaned forward. Finally some backstory on all the players. "Were you all friends back then?"

"No, Liv and I just realized the connection recently. We all started at Community around the same time, but none of us finished there. I think I'm the only one who got my bachelor's."

Summer turned away from Janet and her eyes wandered the bar again. "Well, I've got to go, I'm running late. But I just wanted you to know that I'll talk to Eric today about letting Nell back into their lives. Something's going to have to change." When she reached the door, she stopped and turned back, one hand behind her resting on the handle.

"I almost forgot—is there any chance I left a pen at Liv's memorial?"

"A pen?" Janet remembered the nice fountain pen that Nell had lifted from Summer's purse at her daughter's memorial gathering, but she kept her expression flat. Pointing out Nell's problem to the one woman who might have influence with Eric didn't seem right. She opened her eyes wide and said truthfully, "Nothing's been turned in."

"No," Summer said slowly, "I wouldn't expect that it would." She let out a loud breath through her nose just as Jason walked out of the office, the sleeves of his shirt stretching tight across his biceps.

"I'll stay through the beer delivery," he said to Janet, "then I've gotta head home to get some work done."

Janet smiled at Jason, then her grin widened when she caught Summer standing halfway out the door, staring at her man. "Well, nice to see you again, Summer. Have a good day!" she called, watching with satisfaction as Summer jumped guiltily.

"Oh, ah . . . Yup. Yes, I'll talk to you soon." She smiled brightly at Jason and left.

"What was that all about?" Jason asked, resting his elbows on the countertop and leaning across the bar toward Janet.

Janet explained what Summer had been looking for, and they laughed together for the first time in days. A knot she didn't even know had been wound tightly in her chest relaxed just a fraction at the normalcy of their interaction.

"Wonder if Nell still has it." Janet shrugged and he reached across the bar to tuck a stray lock of hair behind Janet's ear. His fingers trailed slowly down her jaw, his eyes never leaving hers. "Are you happy?" he asked.

Janet's brow furrowed. "Aren't you?" She tilted her head to the side and stared into Jason's soulful brown eyes. There was some emotion reflected back that she couldn't name: not quite worry or concern, but something wasn't right.

Instead of answering, he asked her another question. "Do you ever think about starting a family of your own? Of our own?"

She took a calm, steadying breath and ignored the urge to run screaming from the room. Instead, she laced her fingers through Jason's. "I think that sounds nice, someday. But I'm not ready for it today." She hesitated, then asked, "Are you? Ready for it today, I mean?"

He looked past her, but Janet didn't think he was seeing the rest of the bar.

"Your dad coming in today?" he asked mechanically.

She must have stopped breathing for a moment, because the next sound she heard was her own sharp inhale. He'd avoided her question, just like she'd avoided his a moment earlier.

Was neither of them prepared to have a real discussion about their relationship? Were they both worried it would end if they did?

He finally brought his eyes down to meet hers and she attempted a smile. "Not sure. His conference wraps up with some kind of dinner tonight, but he's being cagey about what he wants to do this weekend."

"Cagey, huh?" He smiled, but it didn't quite reach his eyes, and Janet felt an underlying edge to his words.

"How's your mom? Have you talked to her lately?" In the divorce, Faith had gotten the Memphis house, the fish, and a major anger problem when it came to her ex. "I mean, have you talked to her at all?"

"She's not happy that Dad's here, you know? She feels like I picked his side."

"Did you tell her you didn't?" He dropped her hand, and she

pressed it to her chest. The knot was back and tighter than ever. "Is everything okay?"

"It will be." He pushed back from the bar. "I think I hear the truck." He headed into the office to sign for the beer delivery, and Janet stared after him long after he'd left.

After the driver carted the cases into the walk-in cooler, she waited for Jason to come back in. Instead, she saw his pickup truck drive past the front window.

She tossed the rag she'd been clutching into the sink and let out a breath she didn't even know she'd been holding in, then kicked the Beerador. The huge, heavy appliance didn't wince, but she did. "Daa—" She grimaced, trying to think of a good word to substitute for the one she wanted. "Daiquiri!" But as the bar settled into quiet and her toe continued to throb, she slumped into a stool and dropped her head into her hands. Why did life always have to throw curveballs? Couldn't there be one or two easy pitches over the plate?

CHAPTER TWELVE

"Any update on your grandkids?" Janet slid a drink across the bar to Nell. "Are they all back at school finally?"

It was three thirty on a Saturday afternoon—more than a week since Eric and Nell's showdown—and customers crowded in for the happy-hour specials. Nell wore all black, as she had since Liv died. Today a black scarf wrapped around her neck, blending into her black button-down top and black leggings. The only bits of color were the sparks of light that glinted off Nell's silver hair.

"I don't know." When Janet raised her eyebrows, Nell looked down at her drink and swirled the ice around clockwise twice, then counterclockwise, before answering. "I haven't spoken to Eric or the kids since . . . since last week."

Janet frowned, remembering how shaken Nell had been when she'd discovered the needle. "Do you think he called the police after we left?"

"Doesn't matter."

Janet leaned close, studying Nell's satisfied expression with confusion. "Why not?"

"Because I did. Rivera was very interested to hear what I found and said his people had specifically checked all the trash cans the day Liv died, and hadn't found anything. He said they would send someone out to the house to collect the evidence and run some tests, but I haven't heard anything since."

"You think it wasn't there the day she died?"

Nell set her drink down onto the bar and leaned closer. "That's exactly what I think! I think Eric's the drug buyer and main user in that house, and if my Liv used, it's because she got the drugs from him!"

"I don't know, Nell—"

"And then he tried to cover his tracks!" Nell interrupted. "It makes sense! After Liv died, Eric realized he could get in trouble! We've all seen those officials talking tough on the news lately; about how they're going to crack down on suppliers! So Eric got rid of the evidence and then hoped no one would notice the heroin in Liv's system, but they did. After it came out that Liv had the puncture mark on her arm, he realized he'd made a mistake, so he put the needle in the trash can for me to find."

Nell had gone from abstract, baseless claims to very specific ideas on how her daughter had died. But were there any facts to back them up?

"If he's using, it could just be another needle, though."

"Rivera said they can run tests on it—see who used it. And then we'll know. *Then* we'll have some facts." Nell pursed her lips and looked away.

Janet grabbed a glass off the shelf and filled it with ice. "Also, other people have been at the house between Liv's death and when you found the needle." Nell waved her hand dismissively but Janet pressed on. "Skylar." She tilted her head to the side and waited until Nell looked back over. "We know Skylar's using, and she's been at the house. Why are you so sure it was Eric?"

"Eric found Liv in the basement. Eric called the cops. Only Eric had a reason and opportunity to hide the needle."

"He doesn't *look*—" She'd been about to say that he didn't look like he was using drugs, but the words died on her lips. He was skinny—too skinny—and had ever-present dark circles under his eyes, stark smudges against his sallow skin. Janet had chalked it up to grief over Liv's death, stress from single parenting. But what if it was more? What if he *was* using?

"Aha! Coming around, finally?" The small, victorious smile that had lifted the corners of Nell's lips flatlined within seconds. The older woman turned to the side and rested her elbow on the bar, so Janet could only see her profile. "I know Eric had a hand in what happened to my daughter, and I will make sure he pays for it."

Janet sighed and poured vodka over the ice in Nell's glass, then swiped a lime wedge across the rim. "So what happens next?"

Nell's shoulders relaxed marginally and she turned back toward Janet, but the vigor that had powered her words earlier had left her body. She slumped over the bar, her glass dangling from her fingertips at eye level, her face pale. "Rivera said they'll be in touch if there's anything to report."

"And until then, you don't get to see your grandkids? Oh, that just really burns me—"

"Nell? I thought I'd find you here." Liv's widower, Eric, sat down next to Nell. Those dark circles lay under his eyes like crescent moons, and his wrinkled clothes had grease stains down the front.

"Eric." Nell barely inclined her head in greeting, and she tucked her elbows into her body, her frame rigid, her back straight.

"Nell, I'm sorry about—about everything." He stared at the edge of the countertop. "I got upset at the house, and I shouldn't have lost my temper with you." He looked up and searched Nell's face. "You have to know I never wanted any of this to happen."

"Nor I." Nell focused on her drink. The set of her lips let Janet know she wasn't about to help Eric with an encouraging word.

"I know you're upset with me, and I—I can't blame you."

"Eric, you cheated on my daughter, you are responsible for

her death, and now you've cut off access to my only grandchildren. You have no idea what I'm going through. You—you didn't love her like I did."

Eric flinched, but leaned toward Nell and dropped his voice. "I did love her, Nell. We'd just been going through a rocky patch. I knew we'd work it out, it was just going to take some time. The other woman—she meant nothing to me. It—it was a mistake, and I knew it. I was working for forgiveness. There was hope for us, there was."

Janet pressed her lips together but slid a beer to Eric across the bar. He grabbed it like it was a lifeline and swallowed a few gulps before turning back to Nell. "The kids—they miss you."

"How are they?" Nell asked, turning to look Eric in the face for the first time.

"Brendon seems to be bouncing back. And the baby is confused, but she'll be okay. It's Andrea I'm worried about. She heard about the drugs, and she just can't make sense of it."

"That makes two of us," Nell said archly.

"Three of us," Eric said, lifting the bottle to his lips.

Nell shook her head in disbelief, but Janet jumped in with a question before the other woman could ruin the possibility of a truce and a chance to see her grandkids again.

"Has anyone found where she kept the drugs?"

Eric looked up when he realized that Janet was talking to him. "Excuse me?"

"Nell's been telling me about the case. I just wondered, where did Liv keep her needles? The drugs? Most people don't start with heroin. What else was she using?"

"Nothing. She was perfect. She always was."

Nell shook her head. "When I searched the bathroom, except for what was in the trash can, I only found hairbrushes and makeup."

Eric frowned. "It must have been her first try. It doesn't make sense, but it's all I can figure."

Nell's mouth pressed flat. "How does a first-time user even know where to find heroin unless it's already in the house?"

Eric flinched again, and again Janet tried to stave off an argument with another question.

"Didn't you pick up anything in the weeks before her death? Did she seem depressed? Sad?"

"She'd just found out I cheated on her. We weren't really on regular speaking terms."

Nell fixed Janet with a meaningful look, then pushed away from the counter. Her chair screeched against the tile floor as she stood. "I have to go. Janet. Eric." She carefully set her purse on her arm and tottered out of the bar.

Eric took a long, deep breath after she left and drained his drink in one gulp. "Another," he said, then added, almost as an afterthought, "please."

Janet assessed him over the taps as she pulled another draft. "Was it Summer?"

He spluttered into his drink. "What?"

"Your affair. Was it with Summer?"

"Oh, God no. Summer was Liv's friend. I actually don't think she likes me very much—but she's been a huge help since Liv . . . since she . . . Well." He cleared his throat and took another sip, slower this time. "She spends as much time with the kids as I do these days. But no . . ." He stared at the lip of the bottle. "It was a mistake. Just a dumb mistake with a near stranger, and I . . . Kids are hard, you know? Don't get me wrong, they're amazing, and life changing—but they're *life changing*! You're tired all the time. Do you have kids?" Janet grimaced and shook her head as she set his beer on a coaster in front of him. "Then don't nod like you understand. You don't. You can't! It's bone-weary exhaustion. And you stop communicating as a couple and just talk to the kids, and soon you're living separate lives and sleeping with a customer who needed a new fender."

"Wow." Janet slid two dirty glasses into the dishwashing sink. "How did Liv find out?"

"I told her. I—I had to tell her! She didn't say a word. Just took the kids and left. I—I didn't know if she was going to come back when I left for work that day. And when I came home she was there, but I was on the couch. She didn't talk to me again. Not a word. She didn't even let me explain—not that there's any explanation! But she wouldn't even let me apologize, and I was gone. Out of the bedroom, out of my own life as I knew it . . . out of my mind, really."

The spinning dish brushes buzzed through the soapy water and then Janet dunked the glasses into the cleanish water in the next sink over.

"I didn't give drugs to my wife."

She looked up to find Eric's penetrating glare fixed on her.

"I know that's what Nell thinks, but I didn't. I don't—I wouldn't even know where to start with buying drugs. But it is my fault she's dead."

"How do you figure?"

"The affair, the way I handled it? It must have driven her out of her mind. If she used drugs like the cops are saying—then it's because I drove her to it. And I'm angry—so damn angry when I think about it, and then so s—" He broke off, his eyes shone brightly, and he shook his head hard, as if to shake off the sudden emotion. He looked away from Janet and cleared his throat. "I'll never forgive myself. Never."

His words had the ring of truth to them, but it wasn't her job to absolve him. He drained the beer and made to stand up, but Janet had one last question.

"What happened to the other woman?"

He snorted. "I have no idea. I don't even know her name." He rummaged through his wallet and Janet struggled to make sense of the situation. She didn't know him well, but he didn't seem the type to pick up a stranger without even knowing her name—only to tell his wife about it right after. There was something else going on, but she didn't know what.

He tossed a twenty down on the counter, then snorted again. "I'm a mess."

"I'm sure it seems that way now, but things will work themselves out." She was thinking that if he had killed Liv, he'd eventually pay for his crimes, but he seemed to take solace in her words.

"Thanks, but I mean literally, I'm a mess. The washer's still broken. No one's done laundry since Liv died." Air snuffed out his nose and he held up his arm: a streak of grease ran from his wrist to his elbow. The stain wasn't new; the edges were lighter, the fabric stiff. "It's not so bad for the kids, but I'm a mechanic. This is my last clean shirt, and it ain't so clean anymore."

"I'm guessing it's just as bad for the kids. How old is Andrea?"

"Sixth grade."

"Old enough to be worried about clothes." Janet sensed an opportunity. "I can . . . I mean, I'd be happy to take it all to the Laundromat. I could probably get all the loads done in an hour." She didn't know why Summer hadn't offered, but she didn't care. She was going to help Nell find her way back into her grandkids' life in spite of how she felt about her son-in-law. And if that meant doing ten loads of other people's laundry, it seemed a small price to pay. "Why don't I follow you to the house, and I'll just load it all up in my trunk. Nell will make sure it gets back to you in the morning. Then she can take the kids to the park and give you a break."

"Oh, no, I'm sure we'll—"

"Does anyone have any clean clothes left at all over at your house?" Janet asked.

Eric had the grace to blush. "Well, no. Andrea tried to do it the other day; poor thing didn't know the washer was broken and ended up crying in the basement, laundry in the machine, nothing working. Summer's done so much, I just hate to ask her, and honestly by the time I get home from the shop and take care of the kids, I'm done. We aren't quite sure what to do without

Livvie. She was the happy one, you know? The solid, caring, giving one. The one—"

"So I can come get it right now," Janet interrupted. She didn't want to hear a posthumous love story from a definite cheater and possible killer.

Eric's eyes glazed over, and Janet bet he was still thinking about how Liv had been the lifeblood of his family, but he nodded and pushed his stool back. "Okay. Yeah. Thank you."

Janet motioned to Cindy Lou that she was leaving. The other bartender gave her a look that meant she'd have a lot of explaining to do later.

Janet gave the same look back to Cindy Lou and the other woman flinched. Her assistant manager hadn't yet mentioned William's employment offer. Janet had given her enough space and time to make Jason happy, but the clock was ticking. She would bring it up on her own terms soon. Apparently, she'd have the time to figure out when to confront Cindy Lou while she was at the Laundromat.

CHAPTER THIRTEEN

Eric carried a stack of laundry baskets out to her car, then with a sheepish grin said, "Give me a few minutes, and I'll bring out the rest."

"The rest?" Janet muttered under her breath, unsure where any additional laundry would fit.

By the time she drove away, there was barely room for *her* in the car. She made her way through town to a Laundromat she'd passed before.

At four thirty in the afternoon, thankfully business was slow. Janet hauled in all the baskets, set them on top of a dozen washers, and inserted a twenty-dollar bill into the change machine. The initial surge of excitement that hit when the quarters rained down ended when she counted the coins. "Shorted a quarter already?"

"Fancy meeting you here," a deep voice said as a hand touched her lightly on the elbow.

She bit back a smile as she turned around and then narrowed her eyes at Detective Patrick O'Dell. "I'm beginning to think that you're following me." He grinned sheepishly and she added, "I'm pretty sure that's against the rules in detective-land."

"I was thinking the same thing of you," O'Dell said. "I've been coming to this Laundromat for four and a half years and never seen you here. What gives?"

"It's kind of a long story."

He grinned charmingly. "I think we'll have twenty-seven minutes to kill as soon as your baskets are in. And your story sounds better than this old magazine I found on the table over there." He held up a sports magazine, at least three years out of date.

She nodded and said, "I'll meet you at the vending machines in . . ." She looked at her wristwatch. "I'm betting it'll take me ten minutes to get all these machines up and running."

O'Dell lifted his own laundry basket from the ground and nodded. "It's a date." They locked eyes and he turned and walked away with a grin on his face.

Don't be stupid, Janet told herself. She had a good thing with Jason; just because they were having trouble now didn't mean it was time to cut and run, and take off with someone else. Nevertheless she found herself humming a happy tune as she put quarters in the first machine.

By the sixth machine that happy feeling had disappeared entirely. Two machines had eaten her quarters, and a third one just flat-out didn't work, which, of course, wasn't clear until *after* she loaded the laundry and detergent into the machine. When she tracked down the manager he shrugged and said, "Oh yeah. That one's broken."

Another twenty in quarters later, she finally closed the last lid, then hurried down the line to check her first one. She had eighteen minutes until she'd start all over again with the dryers.

She glanced over at the vending machines and gulped. O'Dell waited at a table, a soda and chocolate bar beckoning from the empty seat across from him.

Her stomach felt pleasantly hollow as she walked across the room, his eyes taking in her every step.

This was clearly not a good idea.

Janet sat down with a smile.

"Dinner of champions," he said with a grand gesture at the food. "I tried for the pretzels, but the machine ate my quarters."

"I know the feeling." Janet looked darkly at washing machines seven and nine.

O'Dell shifted on the hard plastic bench. "So what's with all the laundry?"

Janet filled him in on Nell's family situation. When she finished, he whistled low.

"Sounds like a lot of drama."

She leaned forward. "Any new developments with the case?" O'Dell's open face shut down almost imperceptibly, so Janet leaned closer still. "Nell told me she called Rivera about the needle and he can't figure how his people missed it the day Liv died."

The cop looked at his watch briefly, then leaned toward Janet. "Rivera had the needle tested, and here's where things get strange. It had been wiped clean."

Janet's brow wrinkled. "What—no fingerprints at all?"

"Exactly. Rivera asked Eric to submit to a drug test but he missed the appointment at the lab. But if we take him out of the equation, and go with the theory that Nell found Liv's needle, the needle that delivered a fatal dose of heroin, then we're supposed to believe that she shot up, then took the time to wipe down the needle before heading downstairs to do laundry?"

"Doesn't make sense."

"No, it doesn't," O'Dell agreed. "That's someone else's needle."

"So what are you doing about it?"

"Rivera is out sick with the flu. He asked me to clean out Liv's locker at work. You want to come along?"

"When are you going?"

"Right after we're done here. You should join me." As the

words left his lips, his gaze deepened, and Janet felt heat rush to her cheeks. *Pfffft.* She looked away as she cracked open the can of soda, then took a long, slow sip, and only when the cool liquid reached her belly did she turn back to the Knoxville cop. His hand rested an inch from hers on the table. If he moved even slightly, their fingers would touch.

She gulped. "I wouldn't miss it." They held each other's gaze for a long moment. Things were about to get interesting.

———

When the dryers were full and another fistful of quarters gone, the pair sat back down at the table.

"How are you, Janet?"

She tried to smile but could only force one side of her lips up. Everyone was asking that lately, but no one really wanted to know the answer.

"Great. Your name came up the other day."

"Why's that?" he asked, looking pleased.

"Turns out the best way for me to avoid this whole investigation of your pal Donaldson's—"

"He's *not*—"

"—is for me to become a legit PI. And to do that, I'll need a character reference." Janet leaned forward with a grin. "Guess who'd be perfect for the job?"

"Me?" O'Dell chuckled. "Oh, boy. That would be a challenging letter to write."

"Hey!" Janet said, but laughed. They fell silent and stared at each other until Janet looked away.

O'Dell leaned forward. "But really, how are you?"

"Fine. I'm fine, thanks."

His eyes narrowed. "I can tell things are tense for you at . . . at work, and I just wanted to make sure you're okay." Her lips pressed together and he chuckled. "Don't make that face at me. I'm worried."

"Oh, you're worried, huh?"

"Okay," his gaze intensified. "I'm interested and worried."

She sat back and folded her hands together on the table. "O'Dell, I'm not who you're looking for."

He leaned back too and tried to look casual, but his words cut to the heart of the matter. "What if you are?"

"I guarantee I'm not. You're looking for steady, consistent, law-abiding . . . and probably kid-loving?" His face remained impassive. "I'm—" She struggled to find the right words. "I'm in my first long-term relationship in my life and I'm thirty-one. And I'm still learning. You probably had your first serious girl-friend when you were twelve."

She raised her eyebrows and waited until he made eye contact. "Thirteen." He grinned sheepishly.

"Exactly! I know what you're looking for and it's not here."

He frowned but ignored her last statement, asking instead, "What do you mean you're still learning?"

"Oh." Her cheeks flooded with heat and she looked away, under the guise of checking the time on her machines, but when she turned back he was still waiting for an answer. "Well. It's a tricky balance, isn't it? Between the you that's alone, and the you in a couple?"

"Tricky? How so?"

She fiddled with the pop top on her can. "I mean, I can barely make 'me' work, so how in the world can I make an 'us' work?"

His eyebrows drew together and a lopsided smile crossed his face. "If the relationship is good, then whatever makes you great also makes the couple great. The two things aren't mutually exclusive! Just the opposite. A relationship succeeds because both halves benefit the whole."

Janet's nose wrinkled and she stood. "That's my machine." She unloaded the warm, dry clothes and got to work at the folding table, keeping her eyes resolutely on the job at hand, but she felt the weight of O'Dell's stare until his own machine buzzed.

If being stronger on her own was supposed to make her relationship with Jason stronger, then she was doing something wrong. Because it didn't feel that way at all.

CHAPTER FOURTEEN

O'Dell parked at the far edge of the parking lot.

Janet cleared her throat. "You got a problem with any of those closer spots?" She pointed to the hundred spaces between them and the door of the restaurant.

"I'm not getting boxed in over there. We can walk." He climbed out and slammed his door. He might have chuckled, too.

It was dark now, and cooler. Janet wrapped her sweater around herself and crossed her arms over the light fabric to keep it tight. O'Dell stepped closer, and her body warmed considerably.

She knew she should step away.

She didn't.

"Are they expecting us?" she asked as they approached the main door to Plaza Eats.

"Rivera told the manager not to touch her locker until we got here, so in a way, yes, they're expecting us." He pulled open the door. "After you."

She walked in first and blinked in the sudden light. The diner-style restaurant had dark coverings over its windows, but the fluorescent lighting overhead was like daybreak on the beach in North Carolina—blindingly bright.

A chipper young girl behind the hostess stand pulled menus from a slot on the wall. "Hi, welcome to Plaza Eats. Table for two tonight?"

O'Dell flashed his badge. "I need to speak to your manager."

The girl's eyes opened wide and she yelled through the open kitchen door without looking away. "Dad! I got some cops out here to see you!" She leaned against the stand and lowered her voice. "Are you here about Liv?"

Before O'Dell could answer, a burly, bald man walked out of the kitchen, his apron tied haphazardly around his expansive middle. He stared pointedly at his daughter. "Poppy, didn't I ask you to walk over and *get* me if you need me? The customers don't need to hear you screaming across the restaurant, do they?"

He turned, wiped his hand on a white towel that was folded over his apron string, and then stuck it out toward O'Dell. "Paul Monte."

"Are you the manager?"

"Manager, owner, cook, sometimes busboy, yes to all of that."

"I'm Detective Patrick O'Dell, Knoxville PD. I need to clear out Liv Birch's locker."

Paul shook his head. "Bad business, real bad business." He looked past Janet and O'Dell, and in a more cheerful voice, said, "Welcome to Plaza Eats, folks. Poppy here will get you a table." Then he turned to O'Dell. "Follow me."

He led them through the kitchen into a small employee area by the dishwashing bay. A short, pale, skinny man barely glanced up as they passed, too busy sending a plastic crate full of glassware through the large, steamy dishwashing machine.

"Mrs. Trestle was in. Make sure you get that lipstick off her glass," Paul called as they walked past. The dishwasher grunted, and Paul raised his eyes to the ceiling. "Good help! Hard to find. And even when you think you've got it, they go and die on you.

Poppy said Liv was doing drugs?" Paul frowned and looked at O'Dell for confirmation.

"How did Poppy know that?" Janet asked. The girl didn't look more than fifteen years old.

"She used to babysit over there. I'd have never let her if I thought . . . Well. Poor thing was all torn up, I mean, of course she was, but heroin?" He shook his head. "It's everywhere these days. I had to call the paramedics just a few weeks ago, some yahoo passed out in the bathroom here. Damn needle still in his arm."

"Did he die?" Janet asked.

"Nah," Paul answered. "Paramedics showed up and revived him with that naloxone stuff. What an idiot, though, shooting up in a restaurant bathroom? Jesus, what is the world coming to?"

O'Dell cleared his throat. "Which one was hers?"

"Top right. She'd been here the longest—well, except for me." He smiled wistfully. "She's going to be hard to replace. She was a great employee. Knew her customers; they came back just to see her, some of them anyway." He shot a dark look over his shoulder at the dishwasher. "Not everyone is so dedicated to their job."

The dishwasher mimed a guitar riff to match the solo he was singing along with from an old nineties song, which was playing so loudly through his headphones that Janet could hear every note. She recognized the tune but couldn't name the song. A crate of steaming, clean glassware neared the end of the conveyor belt.

"Oy!" Paul shouted. "Dave! The dishes?"

The dishwasher grabbed the plastic crate just before it would have tumbled over the edge.

Paul grimaced. "He's lost four crates of dishes since I hired him a month ago. Idiot."

"Thanks, Paul. If you can just unlock the locker door here,

then I'll let you know when we're done," O'Dell said, dismissing the owner.

Paul reached forward with a key.

"Anyone been in here since she died?" O'Dell asked when the small door swung open.

"Nope. I have a master key for all the lockers, but each employee makes their own code with the dial."

O'Dell snapped on a pair of blue latex gloves as Paul walked away. At first glance, the contents looked pretty basic: a can of hairspray, a mirror, some makeup items. While O'Dell started sifting through everything, Janet turned and saw the dishwasher looking their way with interest.

She walked over. "What are you listening to?" She read his name tag, then pointed to his earphones. "Dave, is it?" From afar, she'd pegged him as a twentysomething, but as she got closer, the crow's-feet around his eyes and mouth came into focus. He looked like he was about her age but dressed like he was a decade younger. His entire rear end—covered with blue, paisley-print boxer-briefs—was exposed above the belt that cinched his jeans tight against his thighs.

He pushed his headphone away from one ear. "Just some old hair band. You a cop?"

"Nah, just hanging out with one tonight." She wrinkled her nose. "Paul said you've lost some dishes?"

"One slippery crate when I first started and you'd think I damaged a Picasso." Dave rolled his eyes. "Paul ain't happy unless he can shout at someone."

"Is he mean?" she asked.

"Nah. He's cool." Dave shrugged. "Just loud, ya know?"

Janet nodded. She'd known some yellers in her time working at bars and restaurants. She glanced over her shoulder. O'Dell had pulled a small metal table close to the lockers and was cataloging all of Liv's belongings in an orderly fashion. "Did you know Liv at all?"

"The dead lady? Sure." Dave pulled at his waistband, then moved another rack of newly cleaned dishes off the machine's conveyor belt. "She was nice." He started loading dirty dishes into an empty rack but looked up at Janet. "I didn't know about the lipstick thing at first." At Janet's blank stare, he elaborated. "I mean, this machine gets everything hotter than hell, but it don't touch lipstick. You gotta scrub that shit off by hand." He held up a water glass with a smattering of rose-colored lip prints. "I didn't notice that at first, so Liv had to bring a bunch of glasses back. But she was real nice about it. She told me to remember that rain don't wash everything away, only the stuff on top, you know?"

"Did you know that she was using?" Dave pressed his lips together. His eyes flitted over Janet's head and she stepped closer. "Did you see something?"

"Hello, officer. How are you tonight?" Dave said very formally, looking to Janet's right.

O'Dell stood by her elbow, looking at them critically. "Janet? I'm done here. Did this kid know Liv?"

"Nah. I mean, do you really know the people you work with? I'm just passing time here until I can afford college, right?" Dave slid his headphones over his ears and turned his back on them both.

"That's gonna take a long time," O'Dell muttered.

"What'd you find?" Janet asked as they made their way back through the kitchen.

"No idea, yet." O'Dell patted a bag at his side. "But there's plenty to look through at the station."

Janet glanced back and found Dave staring at her, his expression tinged with concern. He knew something but didn't want to say it in front of O'Dell. She wondered if it was important. She'd have to come back alone and find out.

Poppy's eyes followed them as they walked through the main restaurant. "Did Dad tell you that Liv was interested in buying the restaurant from him?"

"Poppy!" Paul stood up from behind the counter and glared at his daughter. "Go clean table twenty-two."

She flounced off in a huff.

"Is that true?" O'Dell asked.

Paul sighed. "Yes and no. Liv wanted to buy into the restaurant—a fifty percent stake."

"When?" Janet asked. "When did she tell you that?"

Paul leaned in and lowered his voice. "It was right when she found out that Eric had been cheating on her. Said she'd been saving up to help him open a mechanic shop, but—well—things change."

"Were you going to do it? Sell?" O'Dell asked.

"I was considering it. We took a hit when this strip mall changed ownership last year. Never really recovered after the Target moved out. Liv said we couldn't do it until the divorce was finalized, otherwise Eric would own half of her half, ya know?" He shrugged, then crouched back down behind the counter, rearranging cleaning supplies.

O'Dell pulled the door open for Janet. She walked backward toward his car so she could keep her eyes on his face. "Sounds like Eric was about to lose more than his marriage, huh?"

O'Dell lifted one shoulder. "Maybe. But we don't know if he even knew about Liv's plan."

"You going to ask him?"

O'Dell's shoulders lurched back and his chest swelled. "Yes I'm going to ask him."

CHAPTER FIFTEEN

O'Dell insisted on following Janet back to the Spot after he brought her back to her car at the Laundromat.

"I need a beer, anyway," he said, trailing her into the bar.

Mel waved them through the crush of people by the door and Cindy Lou shouted, "What is going on?" when she saw O'Dell. Janet forced her way through the standing-room-only crowd and leaned over the bar.

"Shut it," Janet said from between mostly closed lips.

"Jason is here," Cindy Lou replied from a similarly clenched jaw.

"Shit," Janet muttered.

Cindy Lou furrowed her brow, then her eyes lit up and she said, "Shiraz!"

Janet started to laugh, but it died on her lips when she saw Jason's expression as he walked out of the office.

"Gary Donaldson has been waiting for you. We didn't know you were with O'Dell." He frowned at the police detective. O'Dell grinned carelessly back.

"I wasn't *with* O'Dell," she said, recognizing the lie only after it left her lips. "I was at the Laundromat."

"Why?" Jason asked, momentarily sidetracked. "Are our machines broken?"

"No, I—I offered to do Nell's grandkids' laundry."

Whatever Jason had been expecting her to say, it clearly wasn't that, because he stared at her wordlessly for a moment before shaking his head and motioning to Donaldson.

"Well, here she is. What did you need to say?"

Donaldson couldn't tear his eyes away from O'Dell. Finally, he cleared his throat, but it took another moment before he spoke.

"I am required to inform you, via section eleven seventy-five dash oh one of the Tennessee Private Investigation and Polygraph Commission, that the review board has voted unanimously to move forward with investigating the complaint filed against you."

"What?" Janet exclaimed. "My thirty-day response period isn't even up yet!"

Donaldson's gaze moved from Janet to O'Dell and then over to Jason. His jaw tensed, and he shook his head as if he'd reached some internal decision. "You'll need to attend the next meeting to answer questions from the board. It's on the first of the month, or the next Monday if it falls on a weekend." He sent one final glare to O'Dell before turning on his heel and stalking out of the bar.

Jason crossed his arms and stepped between Janet and O'Dell. "I think it's time you leave, too, O'Dell. There's nothing for you here." A casual listener might have assumed he was talking about the menu, but Janet knew otherwise, and she was incensed.

"Jason! Don't be ridiculous. You can't kick out a customer for no reason!"

"No reason? N-no reason?" Jason spluttered. "Janet, this guy's got to go. *Now.*" His jaw, shoulders, and fists clenched; his entire body was strung tighter than a harp.

"Jason—"

"I'll go. It's not as relaxing in here as I'd wanted, anyway." O'Dell stepped around Jason and lowered his voice. "Donaldson's crossing lines. You need to get the city code, make sure he's following the law. He can't skip steps in this process." He put his coat on and touched Janet's elbow. "It's not fair for Donaldson to target you like this, Janet. I'll see what I can do on my end. I promise I will."

Jason smacked his lips together in disgust, but Janet nodded.

When he was gone, Jason dropped his arms. "I canceled the trip to Blackberry Farm. It doesn't seem like the right time to go, you know?" He pivoted and walked back to the office.

Janet stood shell-shocked for a few moments before Cindy Lou tapped her arm. "Uh, boss? You okay there?"

"Uh-huh."

"When were you supposed to go to Blackberry Farm? Isn't that the place down in the Smokies? The really fancy one?"

Janet cleared her throat. "Uh, yeah. We'd planned to celebrate our anniversary there, but . . . it's—I mean, he's right, it's probably not a good time."

Cindy Lou propped her hip against the cooler and studied her nails. "I've heard of so many people getting engaged there."

"Really?" The last thing she wanted was to get engaged, so why did her stomach drop uncomfortably when the office door slammed and Jason disappeared from view?

"It's all for the best," Cindy Lou said, parroting Janet's own thoughts, as she swiped at the outside of the Beerador with a towel. "You said you weren't ready to get engaged anyway, right?"

Janet nodded woodenly and walked blindly down the bar toward the beer taps. She pulled herself a pint and leaned against the counter. Jason was slipping away, and she didn't know why.

She was used to relationships ending—in the past, because she'd dated unsavory characters who weren't smart enough to hold her attention. Jason was different, and it would be hard to let him go, especially because she didn't really understand what was happening between them.

She shook herself. The time to dissect her relationship with Jason was not now, in the middle of her bar during a busy night with customers crowded around the countertop shouting drink orders. She squared her shoulders and took one order, then another.

Janet shoved a twenty into the cash register and as she mentally counted out the change, she was distracted by Cindy Lou's low muttering nearby.

The other woman poured liquor and mixers into a shaker, her eyes glued to the task, her voice oddly singsong as she muttered at the stainless steel. "Sounds like he just saved you from having a difficult conversation, huh?" She clapped a glass over the shaker and rattled the drink back and forth, then continued muttering as she poured the liquid over ice in two waiting glasses. "And we all know you don't like those tricky chats, just not your cup of tea, right? So when people think about moving on, you'd rather just let them think about it on their own terms instead of trying to convince them to stay, ain't that right, sugar?"

Janet frowned in confusion, but just as she reached out toward her assistant manager, Cindy Lou passed the drinks across the bar and took another order.

Janet blinked. Was Cindy Lou upset that she hadn't confronted her about William's job offer? The only reason she hadn't was because Jason had told her to give the woman some space. Her eye twitched and she felt like chugging liquor directly from a bottle.

Instead she grabbed the ringing phone behind the bar.

"The Spot, we're open." Janet tucked the receiver between her shoulder and ear while she took change out of the register and passed it to a customer.

"Janet? It's Nell."

She pulled out two beers and slid them across the bar, then turned away from another customer shouting his order to press the phone tighter to her ear. "Nell! Where are you?" Even though the woman was on the phone, Janet glanced over to her usual spot and saw that her seat had been taken by a regular named Bill, an older man with a beer belly and twitchy hands.

"I'm at home, but the strangest thing happened today, Janet. I'm coming straight in. Will you wait for me?"

CHAPTER SIXTEEN

Business was so brisk that Janet didn't think of Nell again until the older woman tottered into the bar over an hour later. Nell stalked to her seat and stared at the gentleman sitting there for a good thirty seconds before he turned to her with a question in his eyes.

"Yes, thank you, I do need to sit." Nell leaned against the back of the chair. When the surprised customer didn't budge, she stepped in between him and the bar and set her purse down on the countertop, pushing his beer out of the way. Janet rubbed a hand across her forehead when her favorite regular customer then proceeded to back into the still-occupied seat. She hefted herself up onto the lower rung of the stool, and when her hindquarters came into contact with the seated man's belly, he scrambled off the stool with a surprised, "Hey!"

"Thank you, dearie, my back is just killing me tonight." She looked up at the stranger. "You know, they say that Southern manners are dead and gone, but look at you! Gave up your seat for a little old lady. Your mama'd be proud."

His stunned face softened a bit at her words, and Janet said, "Next one's on the house, Bill. Back booth is open. I'll have Cindy Lou bring you another round."

He smiled, and his buddy slid off the stool next to Nell and they trooped to the back of the room.

"You know that isn't *your* seat. If someone else is there, you have to pick another spot."

Nell flicked her head. "You'll never guess what happened tonight!" She dropped her voice and leaned in close; her lips smacked together and she eyed the wall of liquor behind Janet. "Can I have a vodka soda, hon?"

Janet stifled a laugh and poured Nell a drink. After the older woman took a pull, she carefully set the glass down on a cardboard coaster and motioned Janet closer. "Eric called earlier tonight, just after you picked up the laundry, in fact, to see if I could help with the kids." Nell's eyes narrowed. "And something became so clear to me when I heard his voice. He took my daughter from me. I'm not going to let him take my grandkids, too! I'm going to take whatever time I can get with those kids and let the police worry about Eric. And if I happen to find something that they would be interested in, I'll be in an excellent position to pass it right on to investigators . . ." She stared into her drink with a grim smile, then shook herself. "Anyway, I went over, and the kids were doing what kids do—" At Janet's blank look, she added, "You know, faces buried into their devices, blindly eating chips out of a bowl—when I saw a huge pile of mail on the table." She lowered her head with a small smile. "I was just going to toss all the junk mail, really, but when I saw this...well..." She dug into her purse, pulled an envelope out, then plucked a paper from inside and slapped it onto the bar between them.

Janet wiped her hands on a towel. The letter was addressed to Eric Birch. "You took Eric's mail? I think that's a federal offense."

"Nonsense. It's about my daughter, and I was at their house watching their kids. I think I can look at something about my own daughter!"

"What is it?" Janet asked.

"It's information about her new, huge life insurance policy." Nell's bitter voice broke and she cleared her throat and leaned in closer. "I'm telling you, Janet, Eric must have decided she was worth more dead than alive."

A single tear streaked down Nell's pale, wrinkled face and she didn't even wipe it away, just took a long, slow pull from her drink and set the glass down on the coaster carefully.

Janet slid a pen under the corner of the paper to turn it around so it faced her. She wasn't taking the chance of getting her fingerprints on a piece of stolen mail, especially with a PI test coming up.

"A million dollars? That's—well, I agree, it's certainly a lot of reasons to kill . . . but, I don't know. He seems pretty torn up about Liv's death. Not like a man who knows he's on the verge of easy street!" Janet looked over the letter from the insurance company. It explained that since the children were the named beneficiaries, the payout would go to the parent or guardian of Liv's children after the investigation into her death wrapped up.

"Then why don't the police know about this? No. He's a dirtbag," Nell said with finality.

Janet crossed her arms. Family life at the Birch house had been strained in the days before Liv's death. If Liv had taken the policy out recently—say, after finding out Eric had cheated on her, and while she was planning on leaving him, as her former boss had explained—would she have told him about it? Would Eric even know about the policy?

One look at Nell told her that the older woman, at least, considered this piece of information to be the smoking gun that would convince the police there had been foul play.

Eric seemed genuinely distraught over his wife's death, but . . . She shook off a sense of horror at the thought that Eric would have killed the mother of his children for money.

Jason moved past her. "Love all this business!" He grabbed six bottles of beer from the fridge and headed back around the bar with a grin. She tried to smile back, but the expression got stuck halfway, her lips settling into a straight line.

You never knew who you could count on or for how long. Best to take care of yourself first. Always.

CHAPTER SEVENTEEN

An hour later, the bar was quiet. Only a few patrons remained, spread out across the space, and Cindy Lou and Mel had already started the closing routine.

"Janet?"

Janet stopped scrubbing the inside of the sink basin to look up at Nell. The older woman hadn't moved more than her arm since tucking the insurance letter back into her purse earlier that night. Now the older woman shook her empty glass and Janet slid a cup of ice water over. Nell grimaced but took a sip through the straw.

"There's something else."

Janet looked up again, this time dropping her sponge and crossing her arms over her chest, waiting. Nell's prolonged silence piqued Janet's interest, and she looked critically at her friend. Under the increased scrutiny, Nell's eye twitched. "Nell, what did you do?"

"Nothing illegal."

"I guess that's a good place to start."

The older woman blew out a huffy breath and looked away. "I *might* have taken something—but I wouldn't even consider it stealing. More like pre-cleaning, really, so I'm sure he'd thank me in the end."

Janet waited and Nell's cheeks colored slightly. "It's just a scrap of paper."

"Oh." Janet barked out a laugh. She'd been expecting something more dramatic—a diamond ring, Eric's driver's license. "Well. What's the big deal about that?"

Nell frowned. "Eric said he'd been relying on Summer too much, and he felt bad, that's why he asked me to watch the kids tonight. But I slipped this out of his wallet after he came home tonight." Her eyes opened wide. "What? He set it down on the counter right next to me and then went to check on the kids! It's almost like he was inviting me to go through it . . . so . . . when I saw this note scribbled down, I thought it needed looking into."

"What's on the paper? Let's see it." Janet held out her hand with a "Give it here" motion, and Nell handed the scrap across the bar.

A phone number was scrawled across the page in red pen, along with the words *Dino can help*.

"You took this out of his wallet?" Nell nodded. "Who's Dino?" A shrug this time. Janet picked up the phone in the bar. "The Spot's number is private—comes up 'unavailable' when we call out." When Nell nodded, she punched the digits into the phone.

It rang twice and disconnected.

"That's weird." She dialed the number again, and, again, the line disconnected on the second ring. Rolling up her sleeves, she punched the numbers in one last time. When she looked up, she found Nell staring at her. "Third time's the charm," she said with a smile.

"It sure is," a man's voice answered back. The phone hadn't rung on her end at all, so she was momentarily confused. Then the voice said, "You got me, now what can I get you?"

Janet frowned. What the hell was going on? Intrigued enough to keep the conversation going, she said, "How . . . uh, how much you got?" Nell gave her a funny look, and she shrugged.

"Why is every bitch bein' so crazy tonight! You want it or not? I ain't got time for games."

Indignant, Janet snapped, "Then, bitch, I ain't got time for you!" In her peripheral vision, she saw Nell's jaw drop.

After a long pause, the man on the other end of the line chuckled. "Touché, bitch. It's late. Tomorrow okay?"

"Sure." Janet wondered what she was agreeing to.

"Text me an address tomorrow. I'll meet you at . . . eleven a.m. okay?"

"Uh-huh."

He disconnected and she looked up at Nell. "I think I just made plans to buy drugs tomorrow morning at eleven."

Nell gasped as Janet dropped the receiver back in the cradle. She rested her chin on her palm as she leaned across the countertop.

"I knew it!" Nell pushed her glasses up her nose and thumped against the back of the bar stool. "I knew he was using." Her eyes narrowed. "But now we *know* it!"

"Do you want to call the police?"

"No!" Nell covered her mouth and leaned back toward Janet. "At least not yet. We need to investigate this ourselves, first. I mean, if Eric's involved with a drug dealer they might—they might try to take the kids!"

Janet's face softened. "Nell, honey, if he's convicted of providing your daughter with the drugs that led to her death, that's going to happen anyway."

Mel stopped pushing the mop and leaned against the handle. "If the state gets involved, the kids could be in government custody for weeks while they sort out who gets them. That's what happened with Hazel, anyway."

"Have you seen her lately?" Janet asked. Mel and her partner had fostered a baby for several months earlier that year.

"Nah. The birth mother isn't too happy with how things went down."

Nell drew herself up. "That mother should be kissing your and Kat's knuckles! You stepped in and saved her child when she couldn't do it herself!"

Mel frowned. "Not everyone can be a good parent all the time. Kat and I were glad to be there to help when the state came calling—but you know not every child is so lucky." She laughed bitterly. "And some would probably question whether Hazel *was* lucky—sent to live with a lesbian couple? Some Bible beaters down here would think that's a fate worse than death!"

"That child probably had the best two months of her life when she was with you," Janet snapped.

"And how sad is that?" Mel's eyes grew bright. "And how sad to sit by now, idly hoping her mom stays clean—and if she doesn't that she thinks to bring Hazel to us?" She pushed the mop forward. "When all goes according to plan, the kids stay safe, they stay together. But that doesn't always happen. Did Liv have a will?"

Nell's face paled and she leaned unsteadily against the counter, her eyes trained on Mel as the bouncer mopped her way across the room. Finally, she turned to Janet. "We haven't found a will. What's going to happen to the kids? What are we going to do?"

"I guess we're going to meet with a drug dealer tomorrow at eleven a.m."

Nell nodded. "We can ask him some questions—find out how long Eric's been using, if he sold Eric the heroin that killed my Liv."

Janet frowned. "I don't think this guy's going to sit for an interview, Nell."

"Well we have to at least try! For Liv's sake!"

Nell was clearly shaken, and when her glazed expression didn't clear, Janet said, "Do you want me to call you a taxi?"

"No, dear. No. I'm fine. I'll see you tomorrow."

Janet watched her walk out, then turned when she heard Cindy Lou tut-tut under her breath. "What?"

Her bartender patted the sides of her hair and tucked a stray yellow strand back into the loose French twist. "What *the fudge* is Jason going to say when you tell him you're going to meet with a drug dealer tomorrow morning?"

"Why in the fudge would I tell him?" Janet said, avoiding Cindy Lou's glare and wiping down the counter. Despite her glib response, she was unable to shake off a sense of foreboding that slid down her spine and settled into the base of her belly. But what could she do? Nell had to protect her grandkids and her daughter. Liv certainly deserved as much.

CHAPTER EIGHTEEN

Janet held a perfect plank position in bed over Jason. He murmured in his sleep, and she lowered herself down slowly and shifted, until her body pressed against his side. She draped a leg over his lower half, ignoring the way the thin strings of her lingerie dug uncomfortably into her waist. It would be worth it when she saw Jason's face.

One eyelid blinked slowly open. He moaned. "Wicked, wicked woman!" After thoroughly exploring the lines of her slinky garment, he saw the clock. It was just before nine. "I love that you woke me up this way, but why in God's name are we up so early?"

"Are you saying it's too early for this?" Janet moved his hand to her chest and sighed.

"You know it's never too early . . . or too late . . ." Jason's hands roamed lazily over her body and she sucked in a sharp breath when they reached under the G-string and lingered. "But it seems lately you're more disposed to sneak out of the bedroom than wake me up to make love."

Janet moved his hand to the left and moaned, "I don't sneak!" She flopped back against the pillows. Jason propped himself up on his elbow and a slow grin came over his face while he cataloged her body. She sighed. "I don't think we've ever had trouble connecting, Jason Brooks."

"Mmm," he agreed, and ripped his boxer shorts off in one swift motion. "So true."

———

Janet crept out of bed and showered off, then pulled her clothes on and tiptoed toward the bedroom door.

"Busted."

She stumbled back at the sudden sound. "I thought you were asleep, I—I didn't want to wake you."

Jason threw an arm over his head and assessed Janet from the bed. "You didn't seem to mind waking me an hour ago."

She grinned. "True. But that was for fun. I thought you could use some recovery sleep."

He chuckled. "Where are you sneaking off to, Janet? Bar doesn't open for another few hours."

"Oh, uhhh . . ." She looked sideways at the door. "Just . . . uh . . . I told Nell I'd help her with something this morning."

"Not laundry again?" Jason's eyes narrowed as he asked, without asking, if she was going to see O'Dell.

"Nope. Something else. I'm supposed to pick her up at ten thirty, so I've really got to get a move on." She smiled and took another step toward the door.

"Why don't you let me help?" He jumped out of bed. "She's my friend, too, you know."

"Oh . . ." She watched him pull on his jeans and bit her lip. This wasn't going according to her plan at all. "This should probably just be me and Nell.

Jason stopped the search on the ground for his T-shirt and stepped closer to his girlfriend. "What are you up to, Janet Black?"

"What do you mean?" Her eyes widened, but Jason wasn't buying it.

"Now I know something's going on. Spill it, darlin', before I fill in the blanks with something much worse."

"Okay, but it's not a big deal, so don't act like it is, okay?"

Jason stepped closer and rubbed his hands over Janet's arms. "Officially worried now. But go ahead. Tell me." It was almost a command, and his hands were obviously placed with precision, keeping her locked in his grip.

Because she had no other choice, she told him about the scrap of paper, the phone call, and the plan to meet at eleven. Each time his expression darkened further, her voice grew harder, tighter, and she could barely snap out the final words.

"You're meeting with a stranger?" Jason asked incredulously. "A stranger that you believe—with good reason, I might add—is a drug dealer? Janet!" He dropped his hands like she was suddenly too hot to handle. "What are you thinking? And Nell is on board with this?"

She nodded silently. There wasn't really anything else to say, but she stood there as if she were waiting for Jason to approve of the plan. Not likely.

"Why not call O'Dell?"

The words were so unexpected that Janet's shoulders dropped from their tense position and she said, "What? Why?"

"Don't you think he could find out who the guy is? Surely he's got friends in the drug unit—they could trace the number somehow."

At first, Janet couldn't believe she hadn't thought of that, then she cringed anew, imagining O'Dell's reaction to the plan.

"Aha. You don't want O'Dell to know you're acting like an idiot either, huh?" He crossed his arms over his chest and nodded. "How could you consider doing something so rash without discussing it with me?" She didn't answer, and her silence seemed to galvanize him. "Are we or are we not a couple? Are you willing to entertain the idea that we are together, or is even *that* too much of a commitment for you?"

"Jason, of course we're together! We live together, we own the Spot together. We have sex together. Yes! We're together."

He took a step back. "Is that how you'd describe us?"

"No—I was just—I was answering your question! Jason, this has nothing to do with *you and me*. It has to do with me. This is something I can do. I don't need anyone else's help."

Her answer did the opposite of satisfy him. "Something you can—what are you talking about? No, darlin', you can't investigate drug dealers—and you *shouldn't* investigate drug dealers."

His words echoed in the small space. They'd both been shouting.

She unclasped her hands and stepped back toward the door. In a quiet, controlled voice she said, "I'm going, Jason. I'll be careful."

He snorted and threw his hands up as he stalked to the door. "It's nice to know where I stack up for you, Janet. My feelings come somewhere after Nell's and O'Dell's, but before . . . uh, that's right, I'm not sure who I come before. Huh." He headed through the main room, muttering about his "stubborn damn woman," and disappeared into the kitchen. Footsteps pounded down the stairs to the basement and his office door slammed with finality.

She took a moment to compose herself, then stepped out of the bedroom. William leaned back from his work station in the kitchen.

"Morning, uh . . . morning there, Janet." His expression was pained, as if he was embarrassed to have to talk to Janet after hearing her fight with his son.

"Morning, William." She didn't even try to sound happy. This was her house, and if she wanted to be morose, it was her damn right!

She shuffled past the kitchen and slipped her feet into her shoes. She didn't intend to say anything, but she could feel William staring at her; his eyes bored holes into the back of her head.

"What?" she said, feeling only slightly guilty when William flinched at her tone.

"I just wanted to say, hang in there. You're like a magnet to him, he just can't stay away."

The slightly encouraging words were tempered by his disapproving expression. It was almost enough to break her. Before she could turn away, he pushed up from the floor, his bones and joints creaking and popping painfully. "I know it's not easy having a houseguest, and I'm going to make some changes so this doesn't happen again, you know, during the drawdown next fall."

She swallowed hard. This was William's not-so-subtle way of telling her he was going to be with them until the spring, when the TVA would raise the water levels and his houseboat would be floating again. She had to work hard not to break down in tears at the news. "We're glad to have you, of course, William. I just wish . . ." This was her chance to flesh out some information on Jason's mother, and even though she was running late and emotionally wrung out, she had to ask. "I wish Jason's mother wasn't so upset about you being here."

"Pfft." He flicked his hand and smiled. "She'll be fine. A divorce is hard on everyone, but at least she's got all of our stuff to keep her company." The bitterness in his voice couldn't hide behind his lopsided smile when it was just the two of them.

"What *really* happened between the two of you?" Janet asked, picking up her car keys from the hall table but keeping her eyes on his face.

This time he flicked his head dismissively and turned back to the kitchen, picking up the drill and engaging the trigger. The tool whirred, then stopped. He knelt back down by the base cabinet he was placing and said, "Someone's got to be in charge in a relationship. I don't care what everybody says nowadays about fifty-fifty. That doesn't work. Never has." His head disappeared into the cabinet and the drill spun to life again.

Janet stared at his feet silently, waiting for a more forthcoming explanation. Just as she gave up and turned to the door, though, his voice floated out of the cabinetry.

"If you're the one who's in charge in a relationship, you gotta stay in charge. Can't go changing the rules halfway through the game is all I'm saying."

She frowned as she walked through the door into the crisp fall day outside. It sounded like Jason's father had wanted life to stay the same, and his wife had wanted something to change. Was that so bad—to want things to stay the same? Much as she hated to admit it, she understood William better than she liked after their short conversation.

Her shoulders drooped. If only she could understand her Jason as easily. Something was going on with him, and she couldn't figure out what. They would have to talk later—if she had to force the issue, she would.

It wasn't until she climbed into her car that she realized Jason was gone. He must have left through the basement door after their fight and driven away. Maybe they wouldn't talk later after all.

CHAPTER NINETEEN

Janet pulled away from the curb too fast and had to slam on the brakes at the stop sign at the end of the street. Her car swerved and a woman swore loudly from her porch that Janet should slow down. She did, but not before swearing back at the woman.

Using an actual string of curse words instead of Cindy Lou's fake ones put a smile on her face, and she drove with more restraint the rest of the way to Nell's house.

She tapped the horn when she pulled up to the small structure, and Nell popped out the front door. Janet smothered a laugh.

Nell wore a prim black headband in her silver hair, a black turtleneck sweater, and black leggings. A pair of black Keds finished the outfit, and her usually jaunty, colorful, beaded bag had been replaced that day with a nondescript black backpack.

"Oh, good, I think we'll fit right in driving your car." Nell tapped the hood of Janet's beloved, beat-up clunker with a satisfied smile. When Janet climbed out of the car she added, "I see you dressed for the part, too."

With a frown, she turned away from Nell and pulled the first of the baskets of clean and folded laundry out of the backseat. She'd done no such thing—she was just wearing her usual jeans and a navy blue T-shirt—but supposed that Nell didn't need to know that. "Is your car unlocked?"

She shuffled the baskets into Nell's car, then climbed back into her own.

As she backed out of the driveway Nell said, "So what's the plan?"

Janet, still stung by Nell's assumption about her outfit, took her time answering. "We'll meet the owner of the phone number. If he is who we think he is, then we'll pump him for information."

"I'm certain he won't know my Livvie. No," she said with certainty, "he knows Eric."

"But here's the thing, Nell. Why would Eric have his number written down? Wouldn't he just have it stored in his phone?"

Nell harrumphed and they were quiet for a few blocks. "Well, it's not her handwriting," Nell said slowly.

"What?"

"On the scrap of paper. That's not Liv's handwriting." She took the paper out of her handbag and held it in front of her face. "It's not . . . it's not Eric's chicken scratch, it's not Andrea's beautiful script, it's not Brendon's terrible penmanship, and it sure as heck isn't Bonnie's. So who wrote down the number?"

Janet bit her lip. "Maybe the dealer did? I don't know."

Nell's eyes narrowed. She opened her mouth but snapped it closed before she said what was on her mind.

"We'll find out soon, anyway," Janet said, motioning to the clock on the dash.

Nell sniffed loudly and looked out the window. She swiped at her face roughly with a tissue. "We are going to get some answers."

Janet's stomach clenched. Couldn't Jason tell that this was important? Helping Nell wasn't the same thing as putting him last. She could be his girlfriend and a good friend. It didn't have to be either/or.

"We're here."

"Why are we at the Spot?" Nell said suspiciously.

"I told him to meet us in the parking lot. The bar's not open yet, so there shouldn't be any prying eyes, and it's a dodgy enough area, I figured we'd blend in."

Nell guffawed and settled into her seat. "So. I guess now we wait." She took a set of knitting needles out of her bag. "I told Bonnie that I'd make her a blanket for her lovie. Might as well start now." Soon, the only sound in the car was her needles' clacking in a regular rhythm.

Janet tapped her finger against the steering wheel, her eyes constantly scanning the street. Should be any minute now.

"Do you think I'm a bad influence?" Nell asked.

Janet turned to look at the older woman. "What do you mean?"

"Oh, it's just . . . you know, now that I'm spending more time with the kids, I guess I just worry . . . that I'm not good enough."

"What's got you talking such nonsense?" Janet took off her sunglasses to look her friend in the eye. "Did something happen?"

"No . . . well . . ." Nell set her knitting needles down and sighed. "I like to think that no one knows when I take little things."

"You're smooth, no doubt about it, Nell."

"But last night, for example, as I was putting the kids to bed, I may have collected some . . . items."

"You mean apart from the phone number and mail?"

Nell's cheeks flushed. "I wasn't really going to take anything else, but sometimes I just slip things in my pockets, and then into my bag. Just because."

"So what happened?"

"Well, after I'd cleaned up the kitchen and sat back down, everything was gone."

"Gone from where?"

"From my bag."

Janet bit her lip. "Are you saying one of the kids is stealing from you?"

"Here's the crazy thing: everything I'd taken was back in its proper place in the house."

Janet grinned. "One of the kids is recovering items from you?" Nell's eyebrows drew together but she nodded. "I think you can file that under the 'good influence' column. Someone knows that taking things is wrong, and they're trying to keep you in the right column."

Nell smiled and picked up her needles again. Just as the urge to chuckle almost overcame her, Janet saw movement on the street. "Here we go."

A low-rider Chrysler Sebring crept into the parking lot and pulled up next to Nell's open window.

A deep voice said, "You looking to score?" Extra-large wheels with blindingly bright, two-inch whitewalls pumped the other car up enough so that Janet couldn't see the other driver through the open window. She didn't want to blow their cover by looking overly interested, so she let Nell do the talking.

"Mm-hmm. Are you Dino?"

The dealer chuckled. "Not Deeno. They call me Dynamite, Dino for short. How much you want, Gramma? I got a ten or a twenty." He spoke with a slight lisp on his T sounds.

"H-how much?" Nell asked, her fingers still working the yarn in her needles.

"Yo, this is some crazy shit right here." He leaned closer and his lower jaw came into view. He rubbed it and grinned. "I am freaking out right now. Old lady needs heroin. I just can't *even*."

An old nineties rock song wafted from his speakers into Janet's car. It was the second time she'd heard it in two days.

Janet lowered her head to get a better look at the driver and gasped. "Dave?"

The driver squinted. "Who's askin'?"

"Dave, the dishwasher from Plaza Eats?" Janet leaned over

Nell's lap so that she could see him better. "What are you doing out here selling drugs?"

"I—I'm not—is this some kind of sting?" He glared at Janet. "You said you weren't a cop! I thought you were cool, man!"

"No—no cops." She motioned behind her. "This is my bar, not a sting. We're totally coo—" She looked at the knitting needles and bit her lip. "We're cool," she said with conviction. "What are you doing out here, what about college?"

"I don't give my permission to be recorded!" He craned his neck around so he could look into Janet's backseat.

Janet looked at him critically, the gold chain around his neck, a gold front tooth that hadn't been there before. "You look like you watched a movie on how to be a drug dealer and then copied it. When'd you get a gold tooth?" Janet looked accusingly at the dishwasher.

"Yo. I ain't need your permission—"

She raised her eyebrows and he frowned, then spit something out of his mouth into his hand. He held it out through the open window. It was a gold tooth cover. "It makes me look legit. That's all it takes for some people to not screw you over, you know?"

"If you say so."

"If you ain't stinging me with the cops"—he looked warily around the parking lot—"then why did you call me? Old lady don't look like my regular customer. Neither do you, at least, not really."

"I am not an old lady," Nell said, bristling. "And I could certainly do drugs if I wanted to."

"Do you?"

"Yes," Nell said. She threw a twenty into his car. "How much can I get for that?"

He laughed. "A hit. You really want a hit?" Dave looked at Janet. "She really want a hit?"

"Don't talk over me, boy. Just give me the goods."

He chuckled again and then wrapped something into a package and handed it to Nell.

Janet frowned. "Liv died from a heroin overdose. Was she your customer?"

Dave tsked. "Shit, no, she wasn't my customer. I don't deal at work, okay? That's separate."

Janet raised her eyebrows. "Do you know Eric?"

"Who's Eric? He dead, too? Look, just because Liv died of an overdose doesn't mean it was from *my* smack." He put his car back in gear and it lurched forward. "My shit is good, okay? She musta got some bad shit." His car crept forward a few inches.

Janet was struck again by the endless contradictions that made up Liv's coworker. He didn't want to care about anything, but something was bothering him about Liv, she could tell. He acted young with his pants and his music, but he was Janet's age or older. He spoke of college—but likely it was just a place to do market research for his drug business.

Before he rolled out of sight, he slammed on the brakes and backed up. "Hey, how'd you figure out my password? Who gave you my information?"

Janet looked at Nell and both women shrugged. "What password?" she asked, avoiding the last question.

"You know, call twice and I hang up, then on the third time you say, 'Third time's the charm.' Who you been talking to?"

"Your *password* is to have someone call you three times, then say 'Third time's the charm' when you answer? It was dumb luck." He looked at her uncertainly. "You should make the secret phrase 'First time's the charm' on the third try. That way no one will accidentally say it."

"Yo, but that shit don't make sense!" Dave glared at her.

"Exactly."

He peeled out of the parking lot, leaving a cloud of smoke and the smell of burnt rubber behind.

"That was a waste of time," Nell said, putting her knitting needles away.

"It was worse than that. Now we have heroin in our possession, and you're out twenty bucks."

"You take it, Janet. I don't know what to do with it. I just couldn't have him calling me Grandma, like I couldn't handle heroin."

"But you can't! You can't handle heroin!" Janet exclaimed. "And that's nothing to be ashamed of. I mean, no one can!"

"But he didn't have to say that to my face!" Nell set the tiny blue balloon full of heroin down on Janet's dashboard and climbed out of the car. "Come on, can you open early today, Janet? I need a drink."

Janet looked at the contraband on her dash and dropped her head. No kidding. So did she.

CHAPTER TWENTY

When Nell was settled with a drink, Janet called her boyfriend. At least, she hoped Jason was still her boyfriend. He didn't answer, so she left a message explaining that she was still alive, then stared glumly at the phone for several long moments before picking up the receiver again. This time, she dialed O'Dell.

"You did what?" His next series of swear words was muffled, and Janet could picture him putting the phone down and walking away during her explanation of the events that had taken place that morning. "Jesus H. Christ, Janet! What were you thinking?" His voice vibrated the phone, and it rankled Janet enough that she started shouting, too.

"We thought we might get some information, O'Dell, that's what we were thinking!"

"Information on what? How to buy drugs?"

"No, on Liv's death!"

A noisy sigh echoed through the line, and when O'Dell spoke again he'd lowered his volume, but his voice had no less venom than before. "I should arrest you. God, I only hope you didn't buy yourself a felony."

"First of all, *I* didn't buy anything, okay? Second of all, your department isn't doing anything about Liv's death! What are we supposed to do? Just . . . wait?" She snorted.

O'Dell pounced. "This isn't a joke, Janet. People die at the hands of these dealers. Liv did. Now you're putting an old woman—a grieving mother, the only granny those kids have left —in harm's way, too? I—" He sighed again, then said with finality, "I thought you were smarter than that. You mentioned a reference letter? Never."

Click.

He'd disconnected.

Shit. What was she supposed to do with the drugs?

She rubbed her chin and stared at the bar, then resolutely snapped on a set of disposable latex dishwashing gloves and marched the balloon to the bathroom. Over the toilet she snipped open the edge and watched the brownish-yellow crystallized powder sprinkle down to the basin.

Water swirled down the bowl with a whoosh. She pushed the lever a second time, then got out the toilet cleaner and scrub brush for good measure.

She took off the gloves and stared at them uncertainly. They might have heroin residue on them, but how to destroy the evidence?

Nell pushed open the door, and before she could react, the older woman grabbed the gloves, threw them in the toilet bowl, and pushed the handle down to flush.

"Wait!" Janet lunged toward the toilet but stopped short of reaching into the water to retrieve the gloves. She held her breath, hoping the gloves would make it out of the bowl and down the pipes without blocking the line and causing a backup.

They disappeared with a gurgle.

"That toilet is twenty years old! They don't make 'em like that anymore. You could probably flush an entire pint glass down without a problem." Nell brushed her hands off on her pants and left Janet gaping after her.

After she drove Nell home, all she wanted to do was get to Jason and grovel, apologize, beg for his forgiveness. But when she was finally alone in the car, her dad called.

"Hey, kiddo. Can you still pick me up? I—I have a bit of a deadline—can call a cab if you're not going to make it."

She clapped a hand to her forehead. Her dad! She'd forgotten that they'd made plans to see each other that day. "No—sorry, Dad, I'm on my way. Be there in ten minutes."

She spent the drive downtown rewriting the last day of her life. Even after Jason's silence and O'Dell's anger, if she could have done it all over again, she still would have brought Nell to meet the dealer. She only wished that she'd pressed Dave for more information. He knew something.

When they'd first met at the restaurant, she thought that he was on the verge of telling her something before O'Dell butted in, and then today there had been a spark of . . . "guilt" wasn't the right word, but maybe regret. When she'd mentioned Eric's name some emotion had crossed Dave's face that she needed to explore further. And she was going to. Right after she spent some quality time with her father.

———

"Janet!" Sampson Foster crossed the sidewalk and had the door open and his seat buckled before she'd really come to a complete stop.

"Where to, Dad?"

"Head south on the Alcoa Highway." He fidgeted in his seat so much that Janet checked to make sure the seat heater hadn't accidentally flipped on.

"Down toward the airport? Where are we going?"

"There's a nice little walking trail I thought we could manage, and . . ." His eyes flicked to her face before he cleared his throat. "Kaylee flies in later this afternoon. I want you to meet her."

She stared at him for so long that Sampson grabbed the dash. "Watch the road!"

"I am," she said, still leveling him with a stare. She blew out a loud sigh and pulled her eyes away from her father. Kaylee. Sounded like a four-year old, not the name of a grown woman close to retirement age. "How'd you meet her again?"

"We've run in the same circles for years. Finally connected."

"What do you mean 'finally'?"

He shifted in his seat and stared ahead. "She got divorced recently, and—"

"Dad! Did you break up her—"

"No-I-did-not-Janet-Black-now-keep-your-eyes-on-the-road."

His admonition came out sounding like one long word and it was enough to make her smile. "You really like her, huh?"

He didn't answer, and when she finally risked a peek to see why he was so quiet, she found him inspecting the dash of her car. The exact spot where the heroin balloon had rested just hours ago.

Did her father somehow know? Rationally she knew there was no way he could, but when he reached out to touch the surface, her stomach clenched. That was dust on the dash, wasn't it? Just regular dust?

"Janet," her father began, an underlying edge to his voice that was impossible to ignore. He dragged a finger across the dash. "Listen here, kiddo—"

"Dad, I messed up, okay?" The whole story poured out of her: Nell's daughter's death, the insurance policy, the motherless kids, the cheating husband, the broken washing machine, even the drug buy that morning.

When she finished, her father reached over and squeezed her shoulder. "Janet, pull over. We'll figure all this out, but not if we die because you're not paying attention to the road."

She took her foot off the gas and eased to a stop along the shoulder. "How did you know?" Janet asked, wiping her nose on her sleeve.

"I was going to admonish you for letting your car get so dirty. There's a layer of dust on the dash so thick my allergies are already acting up. But that's just dust, Janet. Not heroin. Thank God."

Even though she and her father were barely more than strangers, she was glad he was there. She was glad to have someone firmly on her side.

She calmed down and started driving toward the hiking spot again. Sampson cleared his throat. "I want to hear more about the case, and more about your plans moving forward, but I also want to say that you're being reckless." He held up a hand to stop her from interrupting. "It's okay to take chances, but you have to weigh the risk with the reward. Did you get valuable information you need from this Dave character? Yes? Then it was worth it. But, Janet, aside from being reckless with the drug dealer, you were reckless with Jason and his feelings, too. If you're not careful you'll end up just like me. Or even worse—" His face scrunched distastefully. "—you'll end up like William."

Janet bit her lip. The turn to personal matters was so unexpected, she had to force herself to keep her eyes on the road. "End up like you?" she repeated. "Sign me up. A successful federal judge with the respect of an entire community and job security you can't even buy anymore?" She smiled wanly. "Yes, please."

"No, Janet." She looked over in time to see Sampson smile ruefully. "You'll end up sad and alone, pining for the family you never got to enjoy."

"You're sad?" she asked, his words wedging down into her heart in a way she'd never experienced before.

"I was. But Kaylee . . . well, one of the reasons we planned this trip is because I want you to meet her. She makes me happy in ways I never thought possible. And . . . well, I guess there's no reason to keep it from you. We're engaged."

Janet forced herself to smile and say the proper words at her father's surprise announcement, but inside she crumpled a little, because her sense of security had just been blasted apart in seconds. Her dad wasn't there to save her. He was there to tell her he was moving on, and she was on her own after all.

CHAPTER TWENTY-ONE

"You want another layer?" Cindy Lou asked with a barely suppressed smile.

Janet wore her usual work clothes, which consisted of jeans and a black T-shirt, but then, because of the task at hand, she'd added a long-sleeve T-shirt and two layers of rubber gardening gloves, and topped the whole thing off by pulling her hair back in a ponytail and then covering her head with a baseball hat.

"I thought an oxygen mask would be overkill." Janet stood halfway inside the Beerador with a spray bottle of cleaning solution and a sponge. A box fan pointed at the entire setup to carry away the fumes. "Why don't you get the outside one last time. I thought I still saw some black smears by the side window." Cindy Lou grumbled and Janet smiled. Served her right for mouthing off.

After her near breakdown in the car with her father, she'd begged off going to the airport with him to pick up Kaylee. Instead she'd dropped him off, with assurances that it was no problem for the pair to take a taxi back to the hotel and meet up with Janet later at the Spot.

With unexpected time on her hands, she was determined to get the Beerador up and running. Before she'd suited up, Janet had topped off the drinks of the two customers in the bar, and now she and her assistant manager worked quietly. Cindy Lou hummed a nameless tune, and Janet's mind wandered to her relationship with Jason.

She and Jason had been dating long enough now that they'd worked through all but a few of their issues. She supposed that was how it went in any long-term relationship. You came to accept most things about your significant other, but one or two things would always irritate you. For her, that seemed to include Jason's desire to talk about every damn thing she wanted to do, and for him, it was her need for independence and reluctance to report everything she was doing to him.

Really, they were two sides of the same issue. Could there be any way to resolve it?

She was delighted when the bell over the door tinkled, saving her from scrutinizing her own shortcomings. She dropped her spray bottle and stepped out of the Beerador, coming eye to eye with Cindy Lou.

"I've got it—"

"You keep working, I'll—"

They burst out laughing, and Cindy Lou snapped her gloves off first. "I'm on it, boss!"

But as Janet picked her spray bottle back up, Cindy Lou groaned. "Never mind. You take it. He's here to see you, anyway."

Janet's heart leapt. Jason! She looked over with a smile that froze on her face when she came face to face with O'Dell. "Oh. It's you." Disappointment slid down her throat like bitter beer.

He crossed his arms. "Not you, too? I expect that greeting from others here, but not you."

She shook her head and remembered her last conversation with O'Dell. "What can I get you?" she asked woodenly.

"Now, don't be like that. I came to—well, not apologize, really, because I stand by what I said on the phone. Did you take care of it?"

"Yes." She set the spray bottle on the bar and snapped off her gloves. "I just—"

"No, no—nope." He covered his ears. "I don't want any details. At all. I just want to know that it's gone."

Janet nodded mutely.

He blew out a breath. "Good, good. Okay, then." He tilted his head to the side. "Like I said, I'm not going to apologize, and I'm certain you're not either, so let's just move past it. We can have disagreements and still be friends. Right?" Most of what he said sounded like a rehearsed speech, but his last word came out as a real question.

Janet relented and smiled faintly. "Of course. We're fine, O'Dell."

"Okay." He smiled too. "Okay if I stay and have a beer?" She nodded and pointed to a stool, then cocked an eyebrow. He drummed his fingers on the bar and said, "I'll take that new one you've got on tap."

When he was settled, Janet got back to work. After another fifteen minutes, she decided the Beerador was as clean as it was ever going to be.

She climbed out, pulled off her gloves, and wiped her forehead with the back of her hand. Cindy Lou handed her a tall glass of sweet tea, and Janet smiled at the other woman before taking a long sip. The sugar, caffeine, and cooling ice had an immediate impact on her outlook on life, and she felt herself perk up.

"Let's get those shelves back in and we'll be ready to load her up," Janet said. She and Cindy Lou wrestled the heavy, circular metal shelves back into the unit, then started loading beer bottles into the refrigerator.

Janet was so focused on the task, she'd blocked out all the other noise in the bar, but when the dull job of adding bottles to the shelves was nearing an end, she heard O'Dell talking with someone about an old case. She glanced over. Detective Rivera sat on his right with a beer. They must have planned to meet up .

"I just hope she can do it, man." Rivera ran both hands down the sweating glass in front of him. "You know that not many cases really stick with you, but this one did."

O'Dell popped a pretzel in his mouth from a nearby bowl of trail mix and grunted. "Those are the worst. And the best, huh?"

Janet gently lined two more bottles up next to each other on the second shelf from the top, eavesdropping on the cops without remorse.

"Exactly." There was a long pause while both men drank. Janet continued to move bottles around, although now with much less thought behind the process.

She willed O'Dell to ask about Nell's daughter. It was as if he knew what she wanted, because he said, "Autopsy back yet on the Birch case?"

Rivera grunted. "Yup—we asked them to fast-track it because of that thing I mentioned earlier."

Janet grimaced. What thing? She turned her head to the side to hear better.

"It was heroin laced with fentanyl in her system, like we suspected. She probably died minutes after it entered her system. So glad we rushed through the tox screening. You just never know these days."

"No kidding," O'Dell said. He lifted his beer to his lips, then pulled it back without taking a sip. "Homicide?"

"Coroner hasn't finalized it yet," Rivera answered. "But pros-ecutors'll want us to go all out, find the dealer, see if they can make charges stick."

O'Dell's eyes drifted up to meet Janet's. "Family thinks a few things don't add up."

Rivera rooted around in the snack bowl, finally plucked out a cashew, and popped it in his mouth. "They're right about that. We'll probably bring the husband in. See what he *really* knows. He's skipped two drug tests now. All voluntary, but still. Looks bad." He wiped his hands on a napkin and turned toward O'Dell. "You know how these things go. It'll be hard to prove she didn't buy the drugs herself. These idiots mess around with heroin . . . I mean, they kind of know they're playing roulette, ya know? Roulette with a syringe, and everybody loses."

Both men fell quiet, and Janet turned to get two more bottles to add to the Beerador. She glanced at O'Dell and he lifted his eyebrows. Had he asked those questions just for her? She smiled slightly and he nodded, then turned to Rivera. "How 'bout that game last night?"

Janet finished filling up the Beerador and then grabbed Cindy Lou's hand. She held her breath as she plugged it in. The lights across the bar dimmed, then came back up to full as the old refrigerator sucked wattage from the entire building to start up. The unit hummed and Cindy Lou patted it on the side with affection. "This crazy thing is glad to be home, ain't that right, baby?"

Janet's mind buzzed, too, as she took off her protective layers and pulled her hair out of the ponytail. Heroin laced with fentanyl. A killer dose. And not long after Liv died, her mother had found the phone number for a heroin dealer scrawled on a scrap of paper in Liv's husband's wallet.

Who was responsible for Liv's death? Dave? Eric? Or Liv herself? Her phone buzzed in her pocket and she checked the screen. A stab of dread hit her in the stomach when she read the text from Jason.

Meet me at our spot in thirty minutes. We need to talk.

She gulped. It wasn't as bad as a breakup text, but it didn't seem far off. Was he asking her to meet him at their favorite fountain at the park so he could break up with her? No way, not on her watch. She texted him back one word, *No*, and then resolutely turned off her phone.

She must have made a distressed sound, because when she looked up, O'Dell stood in front of his stool, one hand extended toward her. "Are you okay, sweetheart?"

Before she could answer, another voice called her name. Mel strode over, a folded piece of paper in her outstretched hand.

"Some guy just dropped this off for you." She nodded to O'Dell and slapped the note down on the bar.

"What is it?" When Mel shrugged, Janet dragged the slip of paper across the counter and unfolded it. *Meet me tonight in the alley behind Plaza Eats. 8 p.m. Dave.*

She gulped, and her heartbeat quickened when she looked up at the two Knoxville cops sitting nearby.

Mel noticed O'Dell's interest and leaned in and lowered her voice, effectively cutting the cops out of their conversation. "The guy was nervous. Said it was important that I get that note to you immediately. Is everything okay?"

"I don't know." Janet looked at the door and grimaced. "I guess I'm about to find out."

CHAPTER TWENTY-TWO

If meeting an unknown drug dealer in broad daylight outside of her own bar had sounded insanely dumb to Jason, she hated to think of what he would say about her current situation. She eased her car next to the Dumpster in the alley behind Plaza Eats and turned off the engine. It was dark, but a low-wattage bulb over the back door of the restaurant cast a faint glow over the alley—until it clicked off without warning, plunging the area into complete darkness.

"Well, shit." She sat as still as a statue in her seat, feeling very much like a bunny frozen when a predator is near, hoping the threat would slide by without noticing her existence.

A gentle tap on the passenger window might as well have been a gunshot for how she jumped. Dishwasher Dave's mouth moved, and his muffled voice came through the glass.

"You gonna let me in, or what?"

Cold fingers of fear scraped at the sides of her stomach, and she nearly said no. Instead, she reached across the passenger seat and unlocked the door.

She inspected Dave from head to toe as he climbed clumsily into the car. His gold tooth was gone; so was the gold chain. He smelled of lemon-fresh dish soap and tangy sweat, and despite the cool night, he wore only a short-sleeve T-shirt and the same style of low-rider, baggy jeans as he had on their first meeting. A sweatshirt dangled from his hand, and he shoved it down on the floorboard as he climbed in. He could have been hiding a gun, but it wouldn't make sense to kill Janet tonight. Not with Mel's knowing about their meeting.

"Didn't think you'd have the balls to come," he said, sucking on his teeth.

"Didn't think you'd be dumb enough to ask me to." He flinched, and Janet knew that she wasn't the only one worried.

"I've been thinking," he said.

It wasn't the start of a thought, it *was* the thought. Janet waited for more to come, and after several long minutes, she prompted him. "About anything in particular?"

"Yes. There was a bad shipment." His eyes flitted to Janet's, then back out his window. "It was a while ago. But there were some deaths."

She searched back in her mind, remembering a news story. "Eight, ten months ago? The two men at the library?"

"Mmm."

News coverage of the deaths and investigation had been thorough. Two men, less than two days apart, had been found dead in study cubicles in the back of a little-used area of the downtown library. The employees had been heartbroken and the city passed a resolution to provide staff at all city buildings with naloxone, a drug that could reverse the deadly effects of heroin if administered fast enough. After one day of celebrated news stories, the backlash struck, with a minority of the library board of directors against the plan, as they worried about the risk to their employees of trying to treat drug-addicted, unpredictable people in crisis.

"That was you?" Janet turned to look Dave full in the face for the first time.

His breath came out heavy and loud. "It wasn't *me*. It was a bad shipment, okay? Once I found out, I contacted all my customers. Got most of it back. Everyone got a freebie for the mistake."

"Oh, well, that was nice of you," Janet said drily. "The customer's always right, unless they're dead, something like that?"

He hissed and moved farther away from her in the seat. "Do you want to hear this or not?"

"Yes, please. Go ahead."

"Obviously I didn't get it all. Some people didn't call me back—and I never heard from them again. Don't mean they're dead," he added defensively. "Just means they left town, or got clean or whatever. But I wonder if someone saved some. Somehow gave it to Liv." He'd slowed down by the end of his thought, so that the final words came out like a funeral dirge.

"Who would do that?"

He bit his lip and looked out the window. Something was holding him back from sharing everything he knew with Janet. Something—or someone.

She took a different tack. "How did you know it was yours back then, anyway?" Janet turned to look at the dealer.

He squirmed uncomfortably in his seat. "I always thought I'd want to know if my shit was bad, okay?" His words spluttered to a stop. Janet leveled a glare across the seats, and he coughed and started back up again like an old motor on its last ride. "So I tinted my product."

"What do you mean?"

"It's a simple process, just a drop of this, a bit of that," Dave said dismissively. "But my point is, back then, I tinted it orange." He looked beseechingly at Janet. "Do you know if the heroin Liv used was . . . was it orange?"

Janet shook her head. "I'm sorry, I don't know." Her eyes narrowed. "But the drugs I flushed down the toilet today were brown."

He rubbed a hand across his jaw and turned to stare out the

window. "Yeah, well I don't tint mine anymore. Turns out I don't want to know if it's mine."

Janet's eyebrows drew together as she looked at Dave. This drug dealer, who must surely have delivered people to their final moments on a weekly, if not daily, basis, was racked with guilt.

"There's something else," Dave said when Janet remained quiet. "Liv's husband was in tonight."

The way he said "husband" pulled her out of her own head.

"You don't like Eric?"

"You know, a restaurant is like a big family. Liv was pretty torn up when she found out he cheated on her. She lost some weight, seemed to really be out of sorts just before she died." He turned back to look out the window. "Anyway, he came in to clear out her locker. Really lost his shit when he found out the cops had been there first."

The news surprised Janet. "Why?" she asked. "What was his problem?"

"I don't know," Dave said, turning to Janet. "But he ripped through her things like something was lost. Like something important was missing. Then he threw out almost everything."

Janet blew out a sigh and then looked at her watch. It was too early to feel as tired as she did just then. She saw movement from the corner of her eye, and when she looked over, Dave was polishing a silver compact mirror with his thumb. "What's that?"

"She used it to touch up her lipstick every night. Hey, I took it out of the trash, okay?" Janet bit her lip at his defensive tone. She hadn't meant to look at him with judgment. "It's real silver. Probably worth a lot of money," he added in a harder tone, but Janet didn't miss how he carefully placed it in the breast pocket of his T-shirt and patted it, before pulling his sweatshirt from the floorboards and shrugging into it.

"Let me know if you find out anything." He climbed out of the car.

"Hey, Dave," Janet called, and the drug-dealing dishwasher turned to look down at her. "Stop dealing. If Liv did die from your drugs, she's certainly not the first and won't be the last. Do good, okay?"

He frowned and looked down his nose at her. "Who are you to talk, lady? You run a bar, right? You're serving up alcohol to people to numb the pain from their sad lives. I do the same thing, you're just making them suffer a slow painful death."

Janet flinched when he kicked her door before turning away. She sat in the dark for a while, then finally turned her phone back on. It vibrated with notifications of four voicemails and a text from Jason.

Don't avoid me, Janet. I'll find you.

Nell's son-in-law might have killed his wife to cash in on her insurance policy. Meanwhile, here she was, hiding in an alley at night to avoid having Jason break up with her.

She started up the engine and flooded the dark alley with her headlights.

Ain't love grand?

CHAPTER TWENTY-THREE

Janet drove back to the Spot. She certainly wasn't going to risk running into Jason at home—the quiet privacy of their house was too scary a proposition just then. Surely Jason wouldn't break up with her in a crowded bar, their place of business? Yes, the Spot was home base that night—safe for Janet while she figured out what she was going to do.

She stepped inside, and when her eyes adjusted to the low lighting, she recognized her father at the bar. To his left an older woman looked nervously around the space. Could it be the dreaded Kaylee?

Turns out in life, there aren't any home bases. Just time bombs waiting to go off at every turn.

Mel tapped her arm. "Jason was in looking for you," she said apologetically. "He wants you to call him a-sap."

She squared her shoulders and walked through the room, then ducked behind the counter. Cindy Lou caught sight of her when she turned to get clean pint glasses from the shelf. "Oh, hey! Jason was just in looking for you."

"Yeah, I heard." She crossed her arms and stared darkly at her assistant manager.

Cindy Lou pulled two beers from the taps. "What?"

"Did you—are you going to go work for William if he opens a restaurant next door?"

One of the beers slipped out of Cindy Lou's hand and crashed to the floor. Broken glass scattered everywhere and cheap draft beer slicked under the rubber mats.

"Son of a biscuit!" The bartender jumped away from the pool of beer and slid the remaining full glass across the bar. "Sorry, Billy, just give me another minute on that other one."

Mel hurried over with the mop and Janet picked up the dustpan and sweeper. Within minutes the floor was clear and Billy's second beer was delivered.

Cindy Lou's back straightened and she crossed her arms as she turned to Janet. "He offered me a pretty good position, but I haven't come to any decisions. Yet."

"I guess here's where I'm supposed to say that I want you to do what's best for you . . ." Cindy Lou screwed up her face and started to turn away before Janet added, "But in all honesty, I don't. I want you to stay here with me, and if we need to talk about giving you a raise, switching your schedule around, then that's what we'll do." Janet nodded gruffly and pivoted, but not before seeing Cindy Lou's lips lift in a grin.

She was going to keep orderly whatever part of her life she could just then, no matter the cost.

A hand reached out across the bar to cover hers, and she snatched it back reflexively, then let out a low chuckle.

"Oh, hey, Dad. I didn't see you th—"

Sampson wrapped his arm around the woman sitting on his left. "Janet, this is Kaylee. We've been waiting for you."

Her vision blurred, narrowing down to tubes of elongated color surrounded by black on all sides. The woman smiled tentatively, and she found herself shaking hands and asking—her voice too loud, overly friendly—how Kaylee's flight was.

The woman must have answered—her lips certainly flapped —but Janet only heard blood rushing through her ears, her heartbeat thundering in her chest. Her father said something, he touched her hand again, and she looked down at their fingers. Sound roared back unexpectedly.

"Where'd you sneak off to tonight?" From behind her father, O'Dell materialized out of thin air. Sampson Foster turned to assess the newcomer, and he didn't seem to like what he saw.

"Hey there, fella, a little space, please?"

O'Dell rocked back a step. Cindy Lou's elbow dug into her side and Janet muttered, "Yes, I see. Drunk."

"So unexpected." Cindy Lou's voice was low.

"What was that?" O'Dell swayed as he looked between the women.

Rivera put his hand out on O'Dell's shoulder and reached past him to set an empty water glass on the bar. "Come on, big guy. Time to get home." Rivera grinned at the group. "Haven't seen him drink more than one beer in a night in the five years I've known him."

"Big deal," O'Dell said with a sly wink. "So I had two beers."

"Two beers?" Rivera asked.

"Okay, fine. Four, big deal."

"With shots in between, and now you're closer to the truth." Rivera held up his credit card. "Can I close out my tab?"

Cindy Lou found the slip and ran Rivera's card. O'Dell wedged past Janet's father and leaned across the bar, motioning Janet closer.

"What?" she asked warily.

"Come here." He grinned boyishly.

She took a step forward and smiled, likening O'Dell's expression to that of a four-year-old caught rummaging through the candy jar in the pantry. "What is it, O'Dell?"

"If you leave him, I'm ready."

She laughed. "Okay, I think it's time you take that ride home."

His eyebrows knitted together and he lowered his voice. "I'm serious." His lips moved in an exaggerated fashion, each word getting full enunciation. "I'm ready for you, when you're ready for a change. Whenever, okay? I'll be waiting."

"Oh, boy. O'Dell, say good night to the pretty ladies. Sir," Rivera said, looking at Janet's dad, "don't mind us, we're on our way. Home," he added when O'Dell looked back hopefully.

"G'night, y'all." O'Dell waved to the bar in general, and Rivera pushed him out the door.

"Hey! Rivera?" Janet hustled out from behind the bar and caught Rivera just before he got to the door. "Can you not tell O'Dell what I'm about to ask you?"

His lips turned up at the corners and he nodded. "Did we go back to middle school? Passing notes in study hall? Okay, shoot."

"Is there any way to tell if the heroin in Liv Birch's system was tinted orange?"

Whatever he'd been expecting Janet to ask about, it wasn't a dead body investigation. He shook his head, and his eyes, which moments earlier had been crinkled at the corners with a smile, lasered in on Janet with a sharp, cutting focus. "What?"

"When you were out at Liv Birch's house—was there, by any chance, heroin that had been tinted orange?"

He checked O'Dell's progress in the parking lot through the glass door, then turned back and squinted at Janet. "I can't discuss an open investigation with you. But . . . what's going on? Do you know something about . . . something?"

Janet glanced back and saw her father staring at her, his face a mask. "I just . . . I heard that some bad heroin made the rounds a while ago that was tinted orange. I wondered if the heroin that killed Liv could have been from that bad batch." Rivera's eyes narrowed to slits and her heart rate accelerated. His cop stare made her feel guilty and she rushed to add, "It just made me wonder how a new user, like Liv supposedly was, got her hands on heroin that hasn't been sold around here in over six months."

Janet jumped when O'Dell pounded against the door. "Rivera! Let's go, man. Or let's stay. But let's not do neither."

She barked out a laugh before Rivera's glare silenced her.

"Come see me tomorrow. We have things to discuss." He gave her his card and added, "Nine a.m. sharp, Janet."

"Shit," said Mel from her post by the door as they watched the pair of cops walk to Rivera's car. "You're in it now, girl."

"I always am," Janet said with a frown. "I always am." It was approaching two in the morning, and Janet felt like she'd been awake for days. Her father and Kaylee left with promises to meet for brunch the following day. She bused a table and deposited the dirty glasses by the sink. When a new customer approached, Janet forced a smile. "Hi, hon, you got here at the last minute tonight. We close real soon. Probably time for a shot, but not a drink."

The woman bit her lip and leaned over the counter. "Are you Janet Black?"

The skin on the back of her neck prickled. "Who's asking?"

"Dave told me I could find you here. There's something you should know about Eric Birch."

"Cheese and rice," Cindy Lou muttered, then reached up above the cash register to ring the bell. "Closing time, folks. Everyone clear out!"

CHAPTER TWENTY-FOUR

When the last customer left, Janet pulled two pints of beer from the tap and walked them over to the corner booth.

"Hayley, thanks for waiting."

The other woman fiddled with her earring but made no move to take the beer, so Janet set it down in front of her, then slid into the bench seat opposite.

She took a sip and waited, but the other woman didn't move. "How do you know Dave?"

Hayley barked out a laugh. "We're not friends, if that's what you're asking. I'm a—well, I was a client."

"A client?" It sounded like too classy a way to describe a heroin dealer and his customer. "How long you been clean?"

"A while."

"What happened?"

She pushed the beer aside. "Can I get a water?"

"Sure." Janet called to Cindy Lou. When the assistant manager delivered the drink, Hayley held up the beer to trade. "Sorry, I didn't realize—"

"It's okay, I'm in a bar, why would you know? When I quit, I just decided I might as well make a clean break from everything.

Well," she added, her brow furrowed, "I still drink coffee, but I'm thinking about switching to herbal tea."

"Because of the caffeine?" Janet made to take a drink from her beer, then thought better of it. She turned to place the pint glass on the empty table behind them and Hayley smiled.

"Yes. I tend to go to extremes. I'm just happy this time it's extreme sobriety." The women sat in silence while Hayley collected her thoughts. "It used to be just the opposite. I—I took whatever I could get my hands on. Beer, vodka, Everclear, then the hangovers were too much, so I moved on to pills, Oxy, Vicodin, whatever I could beg, borrow, or steal."

"What happened?"

"It got too expensive—"

"No, I mean, what happened to make you turn to drugs?"

"Oh." Her cheeks colored. "It's a long, boring story, and not the one I came to tell you about tonight."

Janet nodded. Her fingers twitched for the pack of cigarettes she'd given up eighteen months earlier. "So you started using heroin?" The woman sitting in front of her looked just shy of PTA president material.

"It wasn't supposed to be my path." Hayley took on a faraway look. "Sometimes you can pinpoint exactly what went wrong. Which path you shouldn't have gone down. That's what it's like for me, anyway."

Janet rubbed at her temples. There were many forks in the road she wished she'd never chosen, but none that left her shooting up heroin in the bathroom at a diner or a library study cubicle, thank God. "What was it? Which path?"

Hayley shook herself. "There were too many. But I'm choosing the right paths now; that's why I'm here. I'm going through the steps—righting my wrongs. But this one . . ." She worried her upper lip and rubbed her arm with enough force that Janet looked for a spark. "It's not even my—I mean, I guess I should have gone to the police when I heard about it, but it was after the fact, so . . ."

Janet's left eye twitched and she pressed the heel of her hand against the socket. Her staff had finished their closing chores, but Mel lingered by the door, staring at Hayley while she pushed the mop around the same stain that had been there for years. Cindy Lou wiped a stretch of counter slowly. Everyone was waiting for Janet to wrap things up with this stranger. "What can I do for you, Hayley?"

"Dave called me tonight—I didn't recognize the number or I wouldn't have even answered." Her accusatory glare landed on Janet. "I should have blocked his number months ago, but I deleted it from my phone—it felt more freeing, you know? Like, I'm deleting you, you don't hold any power over me. Big mistake." She glowered at her glass.

Janet turned to trade a look with Cindy Lou and blew out a breath. She didn't have time to be this woman's drug counselor. "And uh . . . why did Dave call?"

"He said I needed to tell you what happened earlier this year."

Janet's hand moved from her eye to her temple. "Why me?"

"I don't know, he said if I didn't come talk to you he'd make trouble for me."

"Hayley, why don't you tell me what happened, and together we can determine if it's important."

"Okay, but—keep me out of it, if you can. I—I don't want . . . I mean I worry that—"

"What happened?" Janet's patience was running thin.

"So most people try to get sober a dozen times before it sticks, did you know that? Took me one try. That's how determined I was. But I have bridges to rebuild. Twelve-step programs to take. And unfortunately debts to repay."

"Hayley." Janet's eyes flicked to the clock on the wall. "I'm sorry if this sounds cold, but I have an appointment at nine o'clock—*in the morning*—and that means I need to get home and have a long-postponed discussion with my boyfriend as soon as possible, so I can get to bed at a reasonable time." She was aiming for head-on-pillow at three but would probably have to settle for four. "So what did you do that has you eyeing the beer behind me like it's a goblet of water in the desert?"

Hayley stopped licking her lips and tucked her tongue guiltily back into her mouth. "*I* didn't do anything. But my—my friend"—she winced—"made some bad choices. Her cellmate offered her drugs if, after she got out, she'd tell some guy they'd slept together."

"Her cellmate offered her money to sleep with someone?"

"No, that's just it. She didn't actually have to sleep with the guy! Just had to *tell* him that they did."

Janet's brow furrowed. "Who's not going to remember if they had sex with someone?"

Hayley looked down at the table.

"What else did *your friend* have to do?" Janet would have bet money Hayley was talking about herself, the way her cheeks colored at the question.

"She had to drug him." She looked up through a curtain of hair and added, "But just a quick roofie in his drink one night, then get him to a hotel and undress him . . . I mean, it sounds terrible but—it's done."

"Why?"

"I don't know. I don't think my friend even knows."

Janet's eyes narrowed. "Who?"

"Some mechanic out of Island Home."

"Some mechanic?"

"The guy's name was Eric Birch."

Janet stood up from the table so quickly she banged her knee. She reached down and tugged on the other woman's elbow. "We've got to go to the police." When the other woman shrugged out of Janet's hold she added, "I've got a friend on the force, I'll stay with you while you fill out the report. What's your friend's name? Who did she share a cell with?"

Hayley's hand trembled when she reached up to tuck a stray lock of hair behind her ear. She stood up and backed to the door.

"No, I can't—I'm not even supposed to be in a bar, and I'm clean now, I can't go back to the police."

Mel moved to casually stand in front of the only exit. Janet would have smiled, but she was too worried. "What did he say?"

"Who?" Hayley looked at Mel and then the door, as if calculating the distance between the two and her chances of making a break for it.

"The next morning—what did Eric say?"

Hayley rubbed her elbow, and her face became thoughtful. "He was just kind of resigned to the fact that it had happened. He said something like, 'I can't believe it,' and he just lay there on the bed, not talking." She flushed and cleared her throat. "That's what my friend said, anyway. And she just . . . she just left him there."

"To get her drugs?"

"Well, yeah. I mean, that's why—that's why she did it." She looked up at the bar taps and after a moment of silence she said, "Only five beers on tap? What kind of place is this?"

Janet ignored her question. "Does your friend know she ruined a marriage? Eric and his wife separated right after that happened."

"I'm sure they'll work it out." Hayley waved her hand and inched toward the door again. "Marriages come together and fall apart all the time."

"But now his wife is dead."

Color drained from Hayley's face.

"She died from a bad dose of heroin. Her family thinks she was a first-time user."

"Bad luck," Hayley mumbled.

"Was it?"

The other woman frowned and pushed past Janet, who in turn shook her head at her bouncer. Mel reluctantly stepped aside.

"Hayley!" Janet held a card out to the recovering addict. "There's an investigation going on, right now. Is one of your steps to make things right? I'll come with you. Just call me, we can do it together, okay? It would be nice if the investigators had a better idea of everything that happened, you know? Hey, you never told me—who was she?"

"Who?"

"Your friend." Hayley shook her head and Janet tried another question. "All right, who was her cellmate? The one who offered her drugs to do that to Eric?"

"I—I should be going." She pushed the door open, then threw back one last word over her shoulder. "Sorry." Hayley walked out of the Spot and disappeared past the cones of light from the streetlamps overhead.

"You thinking what I'm thinking?" Cindy Lou sidled up next to Janet, her hands on her hips.

"Doubt it."

Cindy Lou continued as if Janet hadn't spoken. "I'm thinking that that girl seems one stressful situation away from being re*lapsed* instead of re*covered*."

Janet frowned. "Maybe. But I'm wondering who her friend is. If she even has one."

"Why would Dave want you to know that information?" Mel asked, now leaning against the end of the mop. "That's twice tonight he wanted to tell you something. Do you feel informed?"

"Hardly," Janet said. "In fact, I feel like I understand less and less about Liv's death."

"What are you going to do?" Mel asked.

Janet shrugged. "Nothing tonight. I guess I'll talk to Rivera about it tomorrow."

Mel nodded and they all walked out together.

Janet locked the door. She wasn't looking forward to going home, but she'd run out of other places to go. She swallowed hard, a chalky taste at the back of her mouth as she thought about facing Jason.

Cindy Lou smiled as she pulled on her coat. "That Kaylee sure seemed nice."

Janet shrugged. She'd hardly said two words to the other woman. But that would change tomorrow. Then she'd have an opinion based on more than the gut-clenching feeling that she was being pushed out of a spot at her father's side she'd only just come to terms with.

There life went again, giving her whiplash. She squared her shoulders. What was the point of planning when things always changed on you anyway?

CHAPTER TWENTY-FIVE

The house was dark when she drove up, save for a faint light that snaked through the front curtains. Someone was still awake—but was it Jason or his father?

Truthfully, Janet didn't feel like seeing either, but she climbed out of the car anyway.

A metallic smack from the kitchen work zone had her hustling through the house. "Hello?"

"Oh, Janet." William stopped hammering long enough to shoot her a disappointed look. "I was hoping Jason would be home soon." He turned back to a two-by-four brace and raised the hammer.

"That's a little—" The clanging of hammer on nail echoed in the small space and Janet had to wait until he stopped to speak again. "It's a little late to be working on that, William. We do have neighbors to think about!"

"Oh, I guess you're right." He sat back on his heels and looked thoughtfully at the wall they shared with the half of the duplex where Mel and Kat lived, then raised the hammer again. "They're not sleeping in the kitchen, so I think it's fine."

"William!" He dropped the hammer back down, his shoulders tight. "It's too late for hammering. You can pick back up tomorrow morning." They glared at each other until William stood and dropped the hammer heavily into his toolbox on the makeshift counter.

"Fine." He adjusted his pants and turned his back on Janet, focusing on his toolbox with unusual concentration.

Janet rolled her shoulders and turned to leave, then stopped and blew out a breath. "Why are you hammering at two thirty in the morning, William? Is everything okay?"

He tucked some stray nails into a container but didn't turn to face Janet. "Have you spoken to Jason tonight?"

It was Janet's turn to dance around an answer. "Not directly, no. We . . . well, we kind of played phone tag." Kind of, if you could call Janet's running away from Jason at every turn "tag."

"He's not very happy with me." From his profile, she saw William suck in his cheeks. "He . . . I guess he talked to his mom, and she's not very happy with how things went down. She never was, but apparently now she's ready to tell him about it. And . . ." He blew out a sigh. "Now he's not very happy."

"Why?" Janet leaned against the door frame.

"I . . . I messed up, I see that now."

"How? Was it about being in charge, like you said earlier? Was she tired of you being in charge?"

"She thinks marriage is a partnership, but it's not. It never has been. It's about managing expectations, setting boundaries for who's going to do what. I was in charge of our finances, but she wanted to change that."

He looked accusingly at Janet and she shrugged. She could hardly fault a woman for wanting to be informed of her own financial situation.

He scowled and slammed the toolbox lid. "She didn't like what she found."

"What did she find, William?"

"I cashed out our 401(k)." He picked up a rag and vigorously shined the end of a screwdriver. Janet didn't say anything and eventually he dropped the tool and glared at her. "To buy the boathouse, okay? She was furious." He dropped his gaze and muttered, "Didn't stop her from taking half ownership of the damn thing in the divorce."

"And rightly so," Janet said. "You didn't even consult her?"

"I shouldn't have to ask permission to do something with my own money."

"*Your money?*" And there it was. William had just given voice to the exact reason she wanted to own the Spot outright. His money. William and Faith had been married for thirty-some years, but all their money was somehow *his*. She pushed off the doorjamb, feeling totally justified in her insecurities about co-owning the Spot for the first time in weeks. She wanted her own money, so there was never a question about whether she could support herself.

"No, don't go. I'm headed to bed. If you see Jason, tell him I want to talk. He can't avoid me forever, we're in the same dang house!"

She nodded stiffly and watched him walk up the stairs. After William's door closed with a muted *thunk*, Jason appeared in the basement stairwell.

"Thought he'd never leave." He stopped several feet short of where Janet stood. "You've been avoiding me."

"Me?" She crossed her arms and leaned against the door again. "No . . ."

Jason's lopsided smile meant he recognized the lie but wasn't going to argue the point.

"I thought—well, I thought you were going to break up with me."

"And you weren't going to let me?"

She bit her lip. "Well . . . no."

His stern expression gave way and he chuckled and leaned against the plywood top of the makeshift island. "I know I could never win against you, Janet, I just wish you'd let me play the game."

"What do you mean?"

He flipped the screwdriver his father had been polishing in his hand before answering. "I mean, sometimes I need you—need to talk to you, need to hear your voice. Why would you assume I'm going to end things?"

"Well . . . you were angry with me. With good reason," she added with a frown.

"I don't like when you take unnecessary risks—yes, *unnecessary!*" he said when she started to object. "But I guess that's you, that's who you are. I won't try to change you, I just wish you'd take me into consideration when you make your choices."

"I do. Really!" she added at Jason's incredulous look. "That's why I tried to sneak out this morning, so you wouldn't worry."

He snorted but grew contemplative when he looked down at the toolbox. His phone chirped, but he didn't answer the call.

"You better get that." When he still didn't reach for the device, she added, "Didn't you say you'd be available around the clock for your new clients? What if they're testing you?"

He rolled his eyes but reached for his phone. "Get a drink. Put your feet up. We're going to talk. Tonight." He put the phone to his ear. "Brooks Security, this is Jason. Oh, hi, Nev, what can I do for you at . . . two forty-five in the morning . . ." He shot her one last look before he left the room and headed down to his office.

Janet blew out a breath but couldn't seem to release the tension holding her entire body rigid. He was coming right back —*to talk*. Though he'd said it wasn't a breakup conversation, she wasn't looking forward to taking a deep dive into their relationship just then.

The light on their home phone blinked, and Janet picked up the receiver to listen to the voicemail, happy for the distraction. The message was from Jason's dad. She almost pressed a button to save the message and hung up, but something in his tone made her stay on the line.

"J, it's your father. Blocking me on your cell phone? Really? That's what we've come to? Listen, son, I know you're upset, but this was a mutual decision between me and your mom. We both have time to be happier with other people. Don't you want that? I want to talk at the house tonight. Goodbye."

The message ended but she didn't put the phone down.

"Janet?" Jason walked back into the room, his lips pressed into a flat line.

Her poor Jason. Shaken to the core over his parents' divorce. It was a shock, of course it was. And he was reacting the only way he knew how: by locking down his own life when chaos was trying to swallow him whole. She understood the feeling. She wanted to know that life wouldn't change, too. They were just going about it in different ways.

Heat bloomed in her belly, and she walked toward him. He took in her changed demeanor and held out a hand. "Oh, no. You're not going to distract me from—"

She unbuttoned her shirt slowly and he looked away for a moment, but then, almost against his will, he turned back and licked his lips. She wasn't trying to distract him. She finally understood where he was coming from, and she'd never felt a stronger need to be with him.

"Janet, can we please just—"

She reached out and tugged his T-shirt up from his waistband and raked her finger up his stomach as she pulled the shirt over his head. He groaned and she smiled. "We have so much to discuss. After."

He grabbed her hand and hesitated for a brief moment before he turned and led her to the bedroom.

CHAPTER TWENTY-SIX

Janet woke up on the floor, surrounded by fluffy pillows and their down comforter. Her right foot rested on the mattress above, and Jason's arm lay under her head.

"What happened here last night?" she said, her voice low and throaty.

"Well, we didn't actually talk after all," Jason said, but he smiled lazily at Janet and added, "but I remember there was a ruler, a necktie, and some new, creative cursing."

Janet chuckled and sat up, pulling the comforter to her chest. "I'm ready to talk now, if you are."

Jason traced circles on the skin of her thigh. "I could talk, or I could do other things."

"I guess we should talk first. Then do other things." Janet twined her fingers through his on her thigh. "I'm sorry about your mom. Is she okay?"

"She will be." He rubbed his free hand over his face and leaned back against his pillow. "She got tired of my dad's Han Solo act. Said she never felt like his partner. Only his secretary. I mean, if you can't be partners with your *partner*—ugh. I get it."

"And are *you* going to be partners with your dad?" Janet's

brow furrowed. How would Jason feel about being his dad's secretary?

"I don't know. It's all going to come down to how much the building goes for. It's not exactly in a prime real estate area, you know? But it's probably too much. My own business, our business . . . plus another?"

Janet took a deep breath. "Well, I've been thinking about our business lately."

"How so?" Jason asked carefully. He sat up and fixed her with a steady stare.

"Well . . . I wanted to discuss buying you out of the bar."

"Buying *me* out?" he repeated slowly.

She didn't like the shadow that crossed his face and she rushed to explain away his concerns. "It's not that I don't love working with you, because I do . . . and I love how we do business together. I just think it's time for me to do something on my own, you know? And you own Brooks Security, right, I mean, we don't own that together . . . And I want to . . . I don't know, try and make it on my own."

"Do you want to be on your own in other ways?" Jason's face was a mask, expressionless.

"No! Not everything! Not anything else. I—I don't want anything else to change. At all, actually."

He let out a long breath and his brow furrowed. "So . . . Han Solo at work, but not in life?"

The corners of Janet's lips tipped up. Was this going to come out okay after all her angst about discussing it with Jason? "Right."

"Becoming a PI, meeting drug dealers . . ." Jason grinned. "That's textbook *Star Wars* stuff there."

"Oh—well the PI stuff is happening, for many reasons, but I'm going to try not to meet with that drug dealer again." She laughed lightly and snuggled into Jason's chest. "Twice was enough, *thankyouverymuch*."

He pulled his hand away. "What do you mean, *twice*?"

She bit her lip. *Oh, daiquiri.* "No, I mean—"

"Is that where you were last night, when you weren't answering my calls and texts?" All the warm-and-fuzzy left his expression. "Did you—were—I can't—" He spluttered incomprehensibly before clamping his jaw shut. "Janet Black. Did you meet with that drug dealer *again* last night and not even have the courtesy to tell me you might be killed?"

"I wouldn't put it that way," she answered evasively.

He stood up and threw his pillow back on the bed. "I cannot believe you. It's not even about having the manners to tell me what you're doing! How is this relationship supposed to work? If you think I won't like something, you just aren't going to tell me about it?"

"Well, it's not like you tell me everything about your business, right?"

Jason glared at Janet. "Don't turn this around on me!"

Two splotches of red at his cheeks spread across his face. Janet's breath hitched. She couldn't bear to look at the accusation in his face any longer. She picked some clothes up off the ground and stalked toward the bathroom.

Before she shut the door, Jason said, "I hope you realize that I am *never* the one who walks away. It's always you!" She slammed the door and threw her clothes across the small room. Her bra landed halfway inside the open toilet and she swore loudly. Her heart slammed against her ribs and she could hardly catch her breath.

He had some nerve.

But she turned her back on her own reflection and twisted the shower knob on. She couldn't stand to look at herself just then, either.

———

When she got out of the shower, Jason was gone, and she

harrumphed to the empty room that sometimes he *was* the one to leave.

Her phone chirped with a new message from a number she didn't recognize. Damn telemarketers. This one left her a thirty-second voicemail. Like she was going to order health insurance off the phone! Instead of ignoring the call, she sat on the edge of her bed and waited for the voicemail to play. She might even call them back just to file a complaint; that was the kind of mood she was in.

"Janet, it's Nell. I—I guess you need to get down here. To the jail, that is. I'm—I'm in jail."

"Cheese and rice!" Janet yelled at the empty room. She tapped O'Dell's name on her contact list, but the call went straight to voicemail. She shook her phone in frustration, then flew out of the bedroom and down the hall, only stopping to slip on her shoes at the door.

"Janet, can I have a word?" William stood at the kitchen door with a mug of coffee in one hand.

"No! Sorry, William, but there's an emergency downtown!"

"Everyone okay?" His brow furrowed and he lurched forward a step.

"No! I—I mean, yes, I'm sure she's fine, but no, everything's not okay!" Janet grabbed her keys and raced out of the house without a backward glance. Kat and Mel jumped in their seats on the front porch when the screen door slammed against the house. "Sorry!" she called over her shoulder, but didn't stop to check their reaction.

Her phone rang again as she parked outside the Knox County Jail. She glanced at the screen and groaned when the main line for the police department came up. Rivera! She was late for their nine o'clock meeting, but the homicide detective would have to wait.

If the jail had had more floors, the inmates would have had a lovely view of the Tennessee River. Instead, they likely stared at the back of another building's limestone and cinder-block walls.

Inside the jail, she ducked past a long line of friends and family snaking through the lobby. Tuesday was visitor's day at the jail.

Earning some angry looks as she cut to the front of the line, Janet said, "Where can I post bail?" The employee waved her over to another desk—this one without any line.

An unusually unhelpful woman refused to look up from her computer for several minutes. Just as Janet's urge to cup her hands around her mouth and yell loudly was about to take over, the clerk said, still without looking up, "Welcome to the Knox County Jail, how can I help you?"

Janet's lips pinched together at her tone. "Yes, I need to bail somebody out?"

"Inmate's name?"

"Nell Anderson."

The clerk's eyes sparked with real interest as she looked up from her monitor. "You with the old lady?"

"Uh-huh."

"She's a hoot. You her sister?"

Janet bristled and said archly, "If anything, I'd be her daughter, but no, we're not related. I'm a friend."

"Well, friend, she'll need five thousand dollars cash or a bondsman can put down ten percent."

"Five thousand?" Janet sucked in a breath and rooted through her wallet, looking for the right credit card. "Do you take Visa?"

The woman smiled. "Cash. Or property."

"Prop—" Janet's jaw dropped. "That's highway robbery! What's the charge, anyway?"

The woman tapped her keyboard a few times. "Looks like obstruction of justice and theft."

"What'd she get caught with?"

"Let's see, theft from a motor vehicle." The clerk grinned as she read over the information on her computer screen. "Booking sheet says she stole a rabbit's foot out of a cop's car."

"Why would she do that?"

"If she was hoping for luck, it sure didn't work."

"And you're telling me that her bond is set to five thousand bucks for allegedly stealing a rabbit's foot? That's ridiculous!"

"Not to the rabbit." The woman somehow kept a straight face.

Janet blew out a sigh and heaved her purse strap over her shoulder. "Well I—I don't have enough in my account."

"I'm not surprised."

Janet scowled. "So what happens now?"

"Now your friend has to wait for a hearing tomorrow morning. Thursday at the latest."

"Didn't you say something about ten percent down?"

She passed a sheet of pink paper across the desk. "We recommend three bonds offices, and they all open at eleven." She swiveled away from Janet to answer a phone that hadn't stopped ringing since Janet stepped into the lobby. "Knox County Jail, can I help you?"

Janet stepped off to the side and added an alarm to her phone to remind her to call the bonds offices at eleven. Then she tucked her phone into her pocket and crossed her arms. The lobby was crowded, the line of people checking in for visiting hours now dispersed through the room as each person waited for their turn with their inmate. She looked at her watch, then at the check-in desk. Why not?

"Inmate name?" The man smiled politely, his hands hovering over his keyboard.

"Nell Anderson."

He dutifully typed in her name and after reading his screen said, "I'm sorry, she's not cleared for on-site visitation."

"Why not?"

"She's too new. But you can schedule a video-chat with her."

The words were so unexpected, Janet only stared at the employee while they sank in. "What do you mean? Like, from my phone?"

"Sure, or an iPad or tablet. I can schedule you fifteen minutes starting in . . . half an hour. If you pay the registration fee, and the inmate's fee, it'll be about thirty bucks. Cash or credit card. Should I proceed?"

Thirty bucks or five thousand? No question. She slid her card through the opening in the bulletproof glass. "Sure."

He held up a sheet of paper. "Instructions on how to use the system." A printer hummed to life, and he reached down and peeled a sticker off the freshly printed page and stuck it to the sheet. "This is your pin number, enter it when prompted and you'll be connected with Inmate Anderson." He pointed to an open chair across the room. "It will probably take you most of the next half hour to get registered. Wi-Fi password's on the wall if your signal's bad."

He swiveled away from Janet and she blinked a few times before heading for the open seat. She felt like she'd entered an alternate reality; she was supposed to be passing a vodka soda across the bar to Nell, but instead she was preparing to video-chat with Inmate Anderson. Her phone buzzed in her hand. She declined the call from Rivera and instead opened her Internet browser. "This should be interesting."

CHAPTER TWENTY-SEVEN

An extreme close-up of Nell's face popped onscreen in full color at exactly nine thirty. The older woman squinted over the device at someone Janet couldn't see, and Nell said, "It's not working, Anita, I— Oh, there you are!" She smiled into the camera as if she and Janet were chatting from vacation spots. "Isn't this the coolest thing?"

At the dark looks from those seated around her, Janet dug a pair of headphones out of her bag and plugged them in as she walked out of the lobby of the jail into the cool day. "Very unexpected," Janet agreed. "Like a lot of things about this day."

"What a grand day in this grand life!" Nell glanced over the camera again. "Goodbye, dear Anita. Be good, and life will turn your lemons into grape Kool-Aid." Nell's sharp eyes followed someone Janet couldn't see for another moment, then she leaned close to the screen and said, "Anita's gone, we can talk openly now."

"Grape Kool-Aid? What was that about?"

"I'm trying to really work the senile argument. I had about four hours in the clink to convince them I'm just a sad, confused little old lady. I think it worked. I've got this guard eating out of my hand." Nell grinned. "Thanks for coming down, Janet. I knew I could count on you."

"What were you thinking, Nell? A rabbit's foot?"

Nell waved her hand dismissively. "I was distracted. I really just wanted to see if it was as soft as I thought it would be. So I jiggled the door handle for the car and it was unlocked! I wasn't going to take it, but before I knew it, it was in my pocket."

Janet snorted. As if she'd had no part in the decision to take it in the first place!

"Of course, it's unfortunate that the cop was so close. I didn't see him smoking a few doors away. I think he would have let me go but when I opened my purse to give it back he saw the wallet I'd taken from the dash." Nell sighed. "I'd left the money and cards on the seat—I just wanted the fake-crocodile-skin wallet. You don't see that much anymore. It's a collector's item!"

"Where did this happen, anyway?" Janet settled on a bench overlooking the parking lot and angled her phone away from the sky to minimize the glare.

"I was visiting Skylar, Liv's old friend from high school. That girl has had a rough go of it, let me tell you! You and Summer were right—she's been in a bad way for some time now. But she's really trying to make her sobriety stick this time. Said that she feels like she's running out of chances and doesn't want to blow this one if it's her last. I like that!" Nell nodded decisively. "I want to support her in her quest, so I dropped off a home-cooked meal. She lives in a halfway house, and let me tell you, it was a sad, sorry little structure if ever I saw one. Full of hookers and druggies. How's anyone supposed to get clean surrounded by people like that?"

"People who've been in jail, you mean?" Janet looked meaningfully at Nell, but the other woman ignored the jab. "So let me get this straight." Janet smoothed the skin between her eyes with the middle two fingers of her right hand. "You went to a halfway house to visit a druggie friend of Liv's from high school, then stole from a cop's car on your way home?" Nell nodded. "Was it a marked car?"

"Yes, dear, that's what was so exciting. Well, at least it was when I thought I'd gotten away with it." Her lopsided smile was wistful before she shook herself. "I didn't realize this until I got here, but Skylar has a guilty feeling about her. I'm surrounded by it now, so that helped me recognize it."

"Guilty about what?"

"Well that's just it! I don't know. But she was talking about my Liv, and her family, and I couldn't put my finger on it then, but now I see that she's feeling guilty about something. Can you check on her today?"

"Before or after I bail you out?"

"Oh, good—I didn't want to pry, but is that going to happen soon?"

Janet blew out a sigh. She didn't have time to check on Skylar, her plate was already too full. "I'll have to call a bondsman—looks like most of the offices don't open until eleven."

"I'd love to be home in time for my shows. Do your best, okay, dear? What was that?" She looked over the camera again, at someone in the room with her, then looked back at Janet. "Anita says the beeping means our chat session is almost over. Chat session, I like the sound of that, don't you? Like we're royalty or something. Oh, and Janet, I just wanted to add—"

But the screen went black, and Janet was left staring at her own reflection as she wondered what else Nell wanted to say.

She closed out the jail chat app—deciding not to delete it off her phone completely in case she needed to use it again—and dropped the device into her bag as she walked to her car.

With a sigh that bordered on a moan, Janet cranked the engine and pulled out of the lot onto the street. She drove along the river for a few blocks and then spent just as long looking for a parking spot by the police department, because like it or not, she was late for her appointment with a homicide detective.

CHAPTER TWENTY-EIGHT

Janet waited in the cold, stark lobby for what felt like a long time, and her patience was running thin.

"Janet?" She turned and found the homicide detective standing in an open doorway. "Thanks for coming."

"Sorry I'm late. I had a—a . . . well. Anyway." She ripped off her visitor badge from the jail after he'd noted it with his squinty eyes, then cursed the series of events that had started her day.

Rivera led her back into the bowels of the building. She'd visited the station before, when she and O'Dell had first met that summer, and her step faltered as they entered the maze of cubicles. She scanned the room for O'Dell.

Rivera glanced back but kept walking. "He's not here. Called off sick, if you can believe it! Hungover is more like it." Rivera grinned and Janet tried to smile back. "You've really done a number on him, ya know?"

"What? I—"

"I've never seen him like this about a woman."

"I don't think—"

"He knows you're not available, but he really likes you. Strange."

She frowned and stopped walking.

He turned to face her, and his cheeks puffed out when he caught her reaction. "Not strange that he likes you, just strange for him to dig in on someone who's obviously unavailable."

"Are you done?" she asked. His eyebrows shot up comically as she pushed past him. "I'm not here to talk about that. I'm here to discuss a murder investigation that hasn't even begun yet."

He pulled a chair over from a desk nearby and motioned for her to sit. "No. You're here because I asked you to come in." He stood over her; they were about the same height, only—surprisingly—his attitude was bigger. "Talk."

Janet crossed her arms but eventually moved over to the chair and lowered herself down, keeping her eyes on the cop, trying to read his expression. "I have information that Liv Birch might have been purposefully poisoned with tainted heroin." She looked flatly at the cop. "And I want to know if you're looking into that as a possibility."

"Nope." She pursed her lips, but he wasn't done. "That's not how this works. You tell me things. I don't have to reciprocate."

She scowled. "And I don't *have* to tell you anything. I'm not under arrest. But I can talk to the press. I can tell them that someone poisoned a suburban mom and the cops aren't even looking into it. Let's see what happens at the next city council meeting."

A hard smile crossed his face. "You know how many crazies call those newsrooms every day? Most are ignored."

Janet leaned forward. "I have the assignment editor's cell phone number at the NBC affiliate in town. You don't think she'll take me seriously?"

"How—"

"We can do this two ways, Rivera. I'd rather keep it on the down-low so you can investigate. But only if I know you're actually investigating!"

He scrubbed a hand over his face and blew out a sigh. "Yes,

we're investigating. Toxicology report came back, and Liv died from the same bad heroin that ran through town months ago. Coroner is holding off on classifying the death for now, but she says it could go two ways. Homicide or accidental death."

"What's the deciding factor?"

"The needle mark—it was in her right arm. She was right-handed, so it doesn't make sense."

Janet fell back against the seat. "It would have been in her left arm if she'd done it herself?"

He nodded. "So tell me, Janet. What do you know?"

Their eyes locked and Janet unconsciously sucked in her lips.

Rivera scrutinized her for several long moments. "Insurance company contacted us." When Janet nodded his eyebrows shot up. "You knew about that, too?"

"The million-dollar policy? Mm-hmm."

"They're withholding payment until our investigation is complete." He turned away and moved a stack of papers on his desk, then picked up a clipboard. "We think Eric—" His desk phone and cell phone rang at the same time, and he checked the screen on his device, then silenced the phone, but didn't answer either.

Janet blew out a sigh and leaned forward, resting her elbows on her knees. "Listen, I just spoke to someone at the bar last night—"

"Are you investigating this crime?" Rivera's voice rose up a notch and he leaned in so their noses were just inches apart. "It's not your place, and, Janet, it's not safe, either! O'Dell would want me to say this—and you need to hear it. You're just a local business owner, and you need to remember that. You don't want to get in the middle of a domestic situation here, especially when there are kids involved!"

"I'm not trying to get in the middle of things, people keep putting me there! There's a difference!"

"Walk away. There's no place for you in this case. None. And

I'll tell O'Dell if you can't keep some distance. He won't be happy."

Janet feigned interest in a tear in her jeans, but only so she didn't have to look Rivera in the eye. She didn't think she could keep her emotions in check for much longer.

Rivera's phones rang again, and this time he picked up the landline. "Rivera." He stared over Janet's head while he listened to whoever was on the other end, but then his eyes zeroed in on Janet with an unflinching focus that made the walls of her chest squeeze in uncomfortably. "It says what?" During the next pause, his jaw tightened, and the stare became a glare. "I'll be there in ten." He hung up the receiver and leaned back in his chair. "Homicide call-out." He made no attempt to move.

Why was he looking at her like that? Like she was hiding something. "Who?"

"*Why* is the question I'm asking. My responding officer says he found your business card on the vic. You got anything to say about Hayley Vourhaus?"

Janet sucked in a gasp. "Hayley is dead?"

"How do you know her, and why does she have your card?"

"I—I just met her yesterday. She wanted to tell me . . ." She bit her lip. Rivera's expression told her he was one facial tic away from grabbing handcuffs and throwing her behind bars. She didn't trust him any more than she trusted Dave the drug-dealing dishwasher. "I need to go."

"Yeah, me too. I need to see about a dead woman."

Janet gulped but stood and followed Rivera out of the office.

"Don't forget, Janet. Stay out of this. I'm calling O'Dell. He'll be in touch. Soon." Rivera hopped into his unmarked car. His tires squealed as he left the parking lot, but before he disappeared, she climbed into her own car and eased out of the lot after him. A woman who'd just come to the bar to confess her crimes was dead. Janet had to know how it happened, where it happened, and when.

Keeping Rivera in her sights, she tapped Dave's number on

her recent call list. With Hayley dead, Dave was either a suspect in the murder or the next potential victim. Her stomach clenched when the call went to voicemail. Which was it?

She dropped the phone down onto the seat and gripped the steering wheel tighter. First Liv, now Hayley. Who would be next? She was suddenly glad that Nell was still behind bars. Jail seemed a very safe place to be just then.

CHAPTER TWENTY-NINE

Janet followed Rivera all the way to the crime scene but stopped two blocks away and watched him brake hard at the police caution tape. She assessed the low-rent neighborhood from behind the wheel. Paint peeled off the sides of the clapboard houses, whose porches leaned precariously; it looked like there hadn't been a level building in the area for decades.

A growing crowd kept watch over the crime scene techs as they marked and bagged evidence. Rivera ducked under the caution tape and headed straight for a cluster of cops gathered on a porch. A lumpy black tarp covered a section of sidewalk between the house and street.

Janet climbed out of the car and edged into the middle of a group of strangers, shivering slightly at the cool fall wind. When Rivera scanned the crowd, she was glad for once that her five-foot-six frame was easy to hide. She breathed out a sigh when his gaze slid past, and the man next to her chuckled.

"You on the lam, little girl?"

She grinned. "Hard to feel innocent when you're surrounded by cops."

"Preach, sister. Preach." He tucked a small hand-rolled cigarette behind his ear and swayed from side to side. His neck stretched out elegantly as he tried to see beyond the police tape before he whistled low between his teeth. "Hayley got herself into quite a mess, now. Quite a mess."

"What happened?"

The stranger was careworn, with baggy clothes and a persistent menthol smell that wafted from him as he moved. He rubbed his bald head. "No idea. I just heard it was Hayley. Shame. We all thought she was gonna make it. Just goes to show you never do know. These halfway houses—shoot. You just never know."

"Halfway house . . ." There must have been dozens in the city, but Janet squinted at the address, then pulled Nell's jail paperwork out of her purse. The arrest address on the booking sheet jumped off the page. This was where Nell had been just hours earlier, visiting Liv's old high school friend Skylar.

It was too late in the game for coincidence. She looked at the stranger with the cigarette. "Do you know someone named Skylar?"

He looked down at her with a grin. "No wonder you ain't feeling innocent! If you know Skylar, chances are you done something wrong." He whistled again and turned back to the crime scene.

"So you know her?"

"I know *of* her," he corrected with a shrug. "I know she's probably on her way back to jail now."

"Why?"

"She was Hayley's roommate. With a dead body, probie gonna do a drug test on her right now, and it ain't gonna come back good, based on how she been looking lately."

"Her probation officer?"

Her new friend nodded. "Either that or one of the cops'll just skip ahead and take her downtown themselves." He tore his eyes away from the crime scene to properly assess her. "Who are you anyway?"

"I'm—I'm nobody. I just met Hayley last night and then heard the news this morning—"

"Uh-oh, scram, girl. Cops are heading this way. I'm out. Good luck."

She looked up and sure enough, Rivera was cutting through the crowd like scissors through paper. The strangers around her melted away.

"You." Rivera pointed at the far side of the street, to the sidewalk opposite the body. As she walked, he asked, "What's going on?"

"I don't know—"

"The victim had your business card in her hand! A gunshot wound in her chest, your business card in her hand, and then you follow me across town to get to the crime scene. Care to explain?" Rivera's voice was controlled and even, but a steely glint in his eye made her feel queasy. "What's your connection with the vic?"

"Is O'Dell here?" she hedged, wondering if she could tell her story to a friendlier ear.

Rivera frowned. "I just spoke to him—he's at home, trying to suck down enough sports drink to feel human again." He shook himself and refocused on Janet. "Talk to me, Janet. Your choice —here, or downtown."

She felt her lips purse but looked over Rivera's shoulder at the body and said, "She came in last night. She must have taken my card from the holder on the bar—what do I know?" She avoided Rivera's eyes.

"Did she get a drink?" The question was casual, but Janet knew the game: try and trap her in a lie.

"Ummm . . ." She kept her gaze forward. Would Rivera believe her?

"Carson!" he barked, and a patrol officer hurried over. "Put her in my car."

"Rivera!" Janet huffed, but he was already walking away, and the patrol officer grabbed her arms. "Cuffs?" he called. Rivera nodded and she felt the slap of cool, unforgiving metal wrapping around her wrists.

"Goddamn it, Rivera!" she yelled.

Carson jolted her and when she gasped at the shock of pain that radiated up her forearm to her shoulder socket, Rivera yelled over his shoulder, "Careful, Carson. Gently."

"Sorry, ma'am, please step this way."

Mutinous rage roared up her throat as the cop led her to Rivera's car. First of all, *ma'am*? She wasn't fifty! He opened the door and tucked her into the backseat of the unmarked car, making sure she was inside before slamming the door and standing guard by the window.

She fumed in the seat, seeing red for what felt like hours. Eventually, though, she calmed down enough to focus on the yellow evidence markers, the blue crime scene tech uniforms, and even the black of the tarp covering Hayley's body. From her new seat, she had an excellent view of the crime scene.

The coroner's office arrived and moved the body onto a stretcher, then wheeled it right past Janet's window. Perfectly painted nails poked out from under the tarp and Janet looked away, not wanting to see anything else.

As the stretcher passed by, Rivera marched toward her, another woman walking in lockstep with him, her hands behind her back. When they reached the car, he opened the back door.

"Watch your head, Skylar. Just a few more minutes and we'll head downtown." Rivera winked at Janet before he slammed the door, locking her into the back of a cop car with Liv's old high school friend, and, apparently, the roommate of the murdered woman.

She stared at Skylar and thought again of that "before" picture. Skylar's hair was no longer greasy, but dark circles under her eyes stood out starkly on her pale, drawn face.

The other woman stared down at her knees.

"Skylar, I—I'm Janet. We met at my bar a few weeks ago? At Liv's . . . at her memorial gathering?"

Skylar blinked and slowly raised her eyes to Janet's. "I remember you. You're friends with Nell?"

Janet nodded. "What happened?"

"Is she okay? She got arrested here overnight. It must have been some weird misunderstanding, the cop said she stole from his car, but that just can't be—"

"You saw her get arrested?"

Skylar nodded.

"Why was she here?"

"Just checking in on me. I think with Liv gone she—she wants someone to take care of."

"Did she meet Hayley last night?"

"You some kind of cop?"

Janet felt one side of her mouth tip up as she held up her hands. "Cuffed in the back of a cop car? No, not a cop. Just someone the police don't trust, apparently."

Skylar snorted. "Join the club." Her fingers fidgeted, and she lowered her face to her shoulder to wipe at her cheek. "Damn handcuffs. At least yours are in front."

Janet shot her a sidelong look. "You clean?"

"Going on eight hours." She laughed bitterly and slumped against the door. "But I guess it's going to happen now, ain't it?"

Janet felt a flicker of unease and glanced out the window, locking eyes almost immediately with Rivera, who was staring at her from the porch. She shrugged but his eyes never left hers. She squared her shoulders and turned back to Skylar. "Did you talk to the police?"

"I ain't talking to no one. I'm not some kind of narc!"

Skylar turned farther away from her and Janet pressed her lips together, then took a deep, calming breath. "You can talk to me. I'm not a cop. I'm just a friend of Nell's, trying to make sure her grandkids are taken care of. Skylar?" She waited until the other woman faced her, then decided she had nothing to lose by asking some leading questions. "I spoke to Hayley last night. She came into the bar—my bar—to tell me what happened. With

Liv's husband." Skylar flinched, and the reaction bolstered Janet. Some color appeared on the other woman's cheeks, and she cast her eyes down at her feet again. "What do you know, Skylar? What do you know about what happened to Liv's husband? I think it might have to do with Hayley's death."

Skylar's eyelids pressed together and her head dropped back against the seat. She breathed out her nose and hummed something tuneless. The other woman knew something but was done talking.

CHAPTER THIRTY

"Did she say anything?" Rivera unlocked the handcuffs from Janet's wrists, and she rubbed her skin gently, then shook out her hands.

When she looked up, the cop was staring at her. "That wasn't cool, man. That girl is shell-shocked. And about to implode. Why'd you put her in the car with me?"

"She wouldn't talk to us. I thought she might talk to you."

"She did. She complained that she was feeling itchy and having her hands behind her back was killing her."

"She'll thank me next week. If her hands were in front, she'd be bleeding from a thousand scratch marks by now."

"Is she under arrest?"

"Janet, she's in the back of my car in handcuffs. What do you think?"

"I think that I was in the back of your car in handcuffs just a moment ago, so I'm actually thoroughly confused."

He smirked but remained otherwise silent.

"She's going to sober up in jail? That sounds fun for everyone." Janet looked back through the window at Skylar, who was now hunched over, her eyes closed, her body vibrating with an almost visible reaction to not getting her regular dose of heroin.

"You got anything to say? Anything that might help with this investigation?"

"Well . . ."

Rivera unconsciously flipped the single strand of the hand-cuff through the double strand with a metallic *ziiing*.

Janet swallowed hard. Was he preparing to arrest her? She bit her lip and his face tightened almost imperceptibly. She didn't trust him at all. "Are we done here?"

"Yes. Don't say anything yet, but we're going to bring Eric in for questioning. This thing with the insurance isn't adding up. Looks like Liv didn't take the policy out on herself."

She paused halfway under the crime scene tape when her breath caught. When she stood tall she said, "How do you know?"

"The signature on the forms—it's not hers."

"But why bring him in now?"

"You questioning how I'm running this investigation?" His chest puffed out, and he flipped the handcuff again. *Ziiing.*

She turned away from him and dialed O'Dell's number as she walked down the sidewalk. She might not have wanted to tell Rivera everything she knew, but she was more than ready to let a trusted ally like O'Dell take her information and run with it. The call went straight to voicemail, and she left a message asking him to call her back.

Before she stepped off the curb, a flash of color caught her eye across the street. It was her friend from earlier, the one with the hand-rolled cigarette. She ducked across the street and stepped onto his porch.

"Now I don't know what to make of you," the careworn man said. "You looked guilty as hell when that cop came over, and I thought you were done for in the back of that unmarked car—handcuffs and everything! But then you over there walking 'round the crime scene like you at home. Which is it, little girl? You guilty or a cop? Or both?"

"I'm not a cop. I'm . . . training to be a private investigator."

She knew the words were true as soon as they came out of her mouth.

"No shit?"

"No shit," she confirmed. "And today I'm looking into Hayley's death."

"I already told the cops that I don't know what happened, so you can just move on down the row, okay?"

"I'm not looking into what happened last night." He raised his eyebrows and she continued. "I'm interested in what happened all month, all year. How long have you lived here?"

"Always." He watched her for a long moment, then motioned that she should take the navy blue camp chair across from him. When Janet was settled he leaned back and said, "This block used to be nicer, you know? My grandmama raised me here, and when she passed, the house went to me. I try to keep it up, but it's hard, you know? Everything falling apart around me."

"Was that always a halfway house?"

He snorted. "Nah. Just in the last couple of years. Most of the women are nice. Really trying to make it, you know? But like I said, you just know by looking at some that it's just a quick pit stop before they head back to jail."

"I'm surprised you knew so many of them."

"Well, they here on my block, I'm gonna get to know them. My grandma always said people will treat you right if you treat them right." At Janet's expression he added, "I figure if they know me, they might rob someone else, you know? Skip my house and do the neighbor's."

She snorted. "What about Skylar?"

His lips mashed together and he shook his head. "Trouble. She didn't even look clean when she got here."

"And when was that, anyway?" Janet asked, wishing she had a notebook.

"Not long. Just a month? Maybe less?"

Janet sighed. Sounded like a dead end.

"Now, Hayley, like I said, I thought she'd make it. But you

know, you try not to let anything about these residents surprise you, because you just never know."

"Yeah?"

"Yeah. Most of them try to stay under the radar. Then sometimes you got the opposite, the alpha females who act like they queen of the street. This one lady, she was here not long ago; she tried to ooze charm and sophistication, but I kinda thought she might snap your neck if you didn't keep an eye on her."

"Who was that?"

"Can't remember her name exactly. Some kind of bug. Not one of those gross ones, either, something cutesy like Ladybug, but that wasn't it, either." He scratched his jaw, then shook his head. "Anyway, never was so glad to see the back of someone as the day she left."

"And where did she go?"

"My money says she'll be back behind bars before the year's up, but I heard she was working on a new career. New job. New beginning, you know?"

"Sounds like it was a good time to make a change."

"You know what, you're right. In the end, maybe she was lucky; sometimes it's time to make a change but you don't feel like you can—don't have time, don't have the will, don't have the means. But I bet she had nothing to lose, no reason not to start over. Huh."

Janet thanked him and stepped off the porch just as an alarm beeped on her phone. The bonds office didn't open for another hour, so she looked down at the screen, confused.

PI Test. 30 minutes.

New beginnings? Her gaze hardened when she looked up and found Rivera glaring her way. She was all about them. O'Dell wouldn't answer his phone, so she decided to reprioritize her day. And she had half an hour to make it happen.

CHAPTER THIRTY-ONE

When she walked into the office building downtown, she followed the signs to the PI testing room and took a seat in the sparsely decorated space with just a minute to spare, earning her a dark look from the exam proctor.

Only one other person was ready for a life of glory as a private eye. A ragged brown hoodie obscured his face, but he grunted in acknowledgment when the test giver placed a stack of papers in front of him.

When she dropped the exam in front of Janet she stepped back and raised her voice as if addressing a room full of people. "My name is Elaine Simmons. I will be giving the exam that you must pass in order to receive a PI license in the state of Tennessee. I am an administrative assistant"—she glared at Janet and her cohort in turn—"so do not argue with me over the fairness of the questions. I have no say whatsoever in how this exam is made!" When neither test taker spoke, her face softened and she said, "You have thirty minutes to take the exam. Notes are not allowed, nor are Internet searches on phones or computers. You may begin." She clicked a stopwatch and moved to a table at the front of the room.

Janet found a pencil buried in the depths of her bag and got to work.

The questions were taken directly from the two books she'd read, many of them from the first line or two of the main chapters. Janet looked up at the halfway point of her exam. The other would-be PI chewed the end of his pencil, staring forlornly up at the clock on the wall. Elaine scrolled restlessly through Facebook on her laptop, her eyes darting between the computer and her two charges every few minutes.

With fifteen minutes to go, Janet held the completed exam out to Elaine.

"The minute this test gets in my hand, your answers are considered final," the woman said, not taking Janet's exam. "There's no going back."

Janet nodded and laid the papers in front of Elaine. As she headed out the door to the lobby, she couldn't help but agree. There was no going back.

———

Janet tried O'Dell's cell phone again with no luck. Her back ached from the uncomfortable plastic chair in the lobby. At the end of the half hour, the other PI candidate and the proctor walked out of the exam room.

Elaine took one look at Janet. "No. No, I just can't do anything about it, I'm afraid. I told you that once you handed in your forms, your answers are considered—"

"Yeah," Janet interrupted. "I just wondered when you grade the tests, and when we find out if we passed."

"Oh." The woman looked at Janet as if she didn't believe her. "Well. I usually grade them right away and then email the results to the county admin and—well, and you."

Not wanting to go home, Janet sidled up next to Elaine. "Can I just wait here in the lobby?" Elaine sucked in her cheeks but didn't answer. "How about this. If it's bad news, just email me. If

I passed, come on out and let me know." She looked at Elaine with a question in her eyes.

The other woman wrinkled her nose. "Well . . . I guess that would be okay . . ." She looked at the door again as if it were an escape hatch, then glanced at the man in the hoodie. "Sir—did you want to . . . ?"

The man wearing a hoodie grunted out a no, then climbed into a waiting elevator car.

"He was a little more uncertain about the test," she said, almost to herself.

Janet cleared her throat. "I'll wait right here, for the next"— she looked at her watch—"twenty minutes. If I haven't heard from you, I'll just head home."

Elaine shrugged and took the papers through a locked door.

Janet took out her phone and held in a sigh when she saw the screen was blank. No missed calls. Her stomach clenched, and she shoved the phone back into her purse. She'd been so focused on passing on the new information to O'Dell, she'd been able to ignore her fight with Jason, but now, in the sparse, quiet lobby, their fight came roaring back. She owed Jason an apology. But could she change her ways? Include him in her decisions? Or was she just like William? Feeling justified in making the right choice for her, no matter what it meant for Jason?

"No," Janet answered herself, then smiled sheepishly when a woman three seats over got up and moved to another row.

Janet stared dejectedly at the wall opposite, but not for long. Elaine was back in the lobby but she wasn't alone.

Gary Donaldson smacked a roll of paper against his opposite hand. "You passed, but that doesn't make you a PI, you know."

"Thank you, Elaine," Janet said, ignoring Donaldson completely. "It was so nice of you to fast-track the results for me."

"Janet, it was my pleasure." Elaine smiled back so broadly that Janet suspected she wasn't a fan of Donaldson either. The admin took the papers from Donaldson and handed them over.

"You got one hundred percent correct! First one to do that in years, right, Gary?"

Donaldson grunted. "It's just the first step, though. Now you have to apprentice with an actual private investigator."

Janet nodded. "Yes, I've got some appointments set up already, thank you."

Gary sneered but couldn't seem to think of anything to say. He turned on his heel and marched back into the office space.

"I didn't know you knew Gary." Elaine tilted her head to the side as she took in the color rising in Janet's face.

"I don't, really," Janet replied. "He just—he's the one who inspired me to take the test."

Elaine crossed her arms and continued to stare. "He's not been the same since he and his wife divorced."

"What do you mean?"

"He—" She hesitated. "He's perfectly *polite*. But you kind of get the feeling he's not, you know?"

"He's rude?"

"No . . ." Her eyes narrowed. "Do you really have a firm to apprentice with?" she said, seeming to change subjects.

"Not yet," Janet admitted. "But I'll find one."

Elaine looked down at her hands and shuffled the papers she was holding until they were perfectly aligned. "Just stay away from Quizz Bexley," she finally said, then added with a small smile, "Apprenticing with Quizz would really piss Donaldson off. Good luck."

Janet watched her walk away. What was Elaine trying to tell her? She glanced down at her bag, resting on the floor near the chair. After digging out her phone, she found Bexley's number online. Someone answered on the first ring.

"I'd like to make an appointment with Quizz Bexley. Tell him it's about Gary Donaldson's wife."

Without a pause, the woman said, "She can see you in thirty minutes."

CHAPTER THIRTY-TWO

Quizz Bexley's office was small and exploding with *stuff*. Overflowing boxes were stacked everywhere, even under the chair the private eye offered to Janet. Towers of loose papers and file folders appeared on the verge of cascading off of tables and desks with any potential breeze. The lamp to Janet's right perched on a stack of legal notebooks the color of lemon juice.

"What do you know about Renee Donaldson?" Quizz Bexley was short, slight, and pale, with a shock of purple hair that looked like the end of a Q-tip. She wore black clothes and purple glasses.

"Not much, actually," Janet admitted. "I really wanted to know what you know about her husband." Quizz stared at her, nonplussed. Janet's gaze didn't waver and she added, "Seems like it must be a tough gig, being married to that guy."

Quizz's eyes narrowed. "I wouldn't know."

A silent standoff ensued, and Janet finally leaned forward, resting her elbows on her knees. "Listen, I just passed my PI test, and the moderator suggested I call you."

"Why?"

"I'm not really sure." When Quizz stared at her, Janet thought back to her interaction with Elaine. "She noticed

Donaldson being . . . well, kind of a jerk, and she offered up your name."

"What'd you do to Donaldson?"

"No idea," Janet answered. "How about you?"

Quizz grinned and leaned back in her chair, crossing her arms behind her head. "I turned down his business a couple of years ago. Domestics can get hairy real quick, and I didn't like the feel of the guy."

"How so?"

"He came in with this big song and dance about how he thought his wife was cheating on him. These people, they think I'm just dying for their money. They're wrong," she said when Janet raised her eyebrows. "I'm not going to deliver up a woman to a violent guy—not that Gary Donaldson is violent." She raised her hands, palms out. "I don't know that. But you've gotta be careful, okay?"

Janet pushed herself back so she, too, leaned against her chair. "So what happened?"

"Turns out he and his wife were legally separated. She was dating someone. I backed out of it as soon as I saw the paperwork. Not my business."

"Who was she dating?"

"Huh?"

"Gary Donaldson's wife. Who was she dating?"

"Some cop. Guy named O'Dell."

Janet blinked with her new awareness and scrambled for a question to ask to cover her shock. "So you . . . you pick and choose which cases you'll get involved in?"

"Absolutely . . ." Quizz started to wax philosophic about which cases to take and which to pass on, but Janet couldn't hear anything except a buzz slowly building in her brain behind her right temple. O'Dell had dated Donaldson's wife when the couple was separated, and Donaldson clearly wasn't over the sting.

Was he taking his frustration out on Janet to get back at

O'Dell? It seemed a stretch at the very least, but then again, O'Dell had made it clear he liked her. Was it so difficult to imagine others downtown knowing—the news slipping around the building to any interested ears? Donaldson deciding to exact his revenge on O'Dell by coming down hard on Janet?

Donaldson wasn't interested in *her*. He wanted to get back at O'Dell, through her. Was there even an anonymous complaint, or just a Donaldson complaint?

A slow grin spread across her face. O'Dell owed her. He'd have to sign off on her PI application now; she'd see to it.

"What are you smiling about?" Quizz snapped.

Janet blinked and refocused on the woman in front of her. "I'm in."

"You're in what?"

"I'm in for this apprenticeship. Just a few questions."

"Why does it seem like you're interviewing me instead of the other way around?" Quizz squinted and grabbed the arms of her chair for support.

Janet motioned to the piles of paper scattered around the office. "Looks to me like you need the help. And free help? You just hit the lottery, lady."

Quizz snorted. "True. You passed step one in the training program. Be observant."

"No offense—" Janet started.

"This'll be good."

"But what can you do as a PI that I can't do as a regular, curious person?"

"No doubt the Internet has changed the life of the private detective. I used to make half my earnings on easy background checks; now anyone can do them from the privacy of their own home. But it all takes time. And that's something a lot of people don't have these days—or at least they can't see giving up their Netflix time for something else. So they still pay up and I do the work."

"Mostly online?"

Quizz nodded. "Sure, but there's still some real-world work. Sometimes the computer only takes you so far. Then you gotta pick up the phone, go to an office."

"Huh." Sounded like just being a regular person and having someone pay you for it.

"I know. My sister is disappointed with the reality, too. When you get boots on the ground, though, you'll get much more information than the cops ever will. Certain neighborhoods, nobody's gonna talk to the police. But they don't mind talking to me. You just gotta be discreet."

Based on Janet's very limited time at the crime scene that morning, she knew Quizz's words to be true. The neighbor had told *her* about Hayley and the halfway house, not Rivera. Not the patrol officers on the scene, not the other detectives.

"All right. Let's do this." Janet checked her phone but the screen was blank.

"It's gonna cost you."

Janet's head snapped up. "Cost me? What—like money?"

"Time." The PI had an intensity about her that was exhausting. "As you can see, I'm backed up—way up. I need to know I can count on you for the duration of the apprenticeship. That I —what?" Her lips pushed out and she inhaled a long breath.

"It's just that I already have a case I want to work on."

"Why am I not surprised?" Quizz ran a hand through her hair. "Go on. Tell me about it."

"It's a murder investigation—actually, I think now a double murder investigation, and—"

"I'm going to stop you right there. That's definitely level-two apprenticeship. I was thinking I'd start you on an identity theft case that I just can't get to—"

"After the murder case, I'd be happy to take that one on." The two women stared at each other. Quizz's lips tilted up after a moment.

"I *think* I'm going to like you. Someday."

Janet grinned again. "So you'll help me?"

"Oh, *you* need help?" She tried to smother a laugh, but it chortled out, then she grabbed her belly and doubled over with a guffaw. When she sat back up she wiped a tear from her eye. "I think you just managed to hire me without a retainer and with no hope of payment for me. I guess that means you passed step two: convince and connive your way to success." Quizz locked her fingers behind her head and laughed again.

"How many steps are there?" Janet's forehead wrinkled and she wondered what exactly she was signing up for, apprenticing under this woman.

"I'll tell you when you need to know. Now, tell me about these murders."

CHAPTER THIRTY-THREE

The silence stretched so long that Janet wondered if one of Quizz's many skills was sleeping with her eyes open. She cleared her throat and Quizz grunted.

"I'm processing. Give me a minute."

It had taken Janet more than half an hour to explain everything about Liv and Hayley's deaths to the private eye, including a few trail-offs and more than once having to go back and fill in missing information. Quizz hadn't taken a single note but had fixed Janet with a nearly unblinking stare for the entire recital.

The clock behind the PI ticked, and no matter how many times she checked her phone, no new emails or text messages popped up, leaving Janet only one option: to stare at Quizz.

The other woman finally rubbed her temples. "We'll start with a background check on Dave."

"On Dave? The dishwasher?"

"The drug dealer, yes. He has a connection to both victims. Let's see if anything—or anyone—else connects them." Quizz tapped some words into her computer. "Do you know his last name?"

Janet shook her head.

"No worries." She picked up the phone on her desk and then

looked at her computer screen and dialed a number. In a raspy, deeper-than-normal voice she said, "Looking for Dave. He in?" A pause while young Poppy, no doubt, gave a long, convoluted answer to a simple question. Quizz rubbed her temple again and said, "What's his last name?" Pause. The cadence of the voice on the other end of the line picked up and Quizz's eyes widened. Without another word, she slowly moved the phone away from her face and hung up; Poppy's high, chatty voice only cut off when the receiver was back in the cradle on the desk. "Jesus."

Janet smirked. "She's a teenager."

"Yeah, I got that loud and clear." She tapped some keys on the keyboard and hit enter. "Dave *Martelle* apparently didn't show up for his shift this morning, and the teenager's father made her wash some of the dishes in his place."

"She wasn't a fan?"

"Mad as a hornet about the whole thing. Asked if I knew where he was, and could I go get him and bring him to Plaza Eats to do his job."

"Go get him? From where?"

"His apartment at River Crossing." She tilted her head up to look at her computer screen through her glasses. "It's nowhere near the river, by the way. Talking to her was better than reading a search results page."

"Are we going to go get him?" Janet asked, glancing at the wall clock again.

"No! But now we have his last name. I'm going to cross-search him with the other players. We'll see what comes up."

"Which other players?" Janet threw herself back against the chair. "I can't believe being a PI is all about using Google."

"Tut-tut. I'm using LexisNexis. Ever heard of it?"

Janet shook her head.

"Insanely expensive but so worth it for research. I can cross-search your buddy Dave with everyone else and a nice list of information will come up that may or may not be helpful." She sat up and moved her glasses up her face so she could properly look at the screen without hurting her neck. "I got a few hits here, let me see . . ."

Tired of waiting on Quizz to reveal anything, Janet whipped out her phone to do her own search on Dave Martelle. Over twenty thousand results, and almost all of the ones on the first page were about a baseball player. "Ugh." She bit her lip and tapped the arrow going to the second page. More baseball news.

"Bankruptcy filing about six years ago. Divorce granted the next year. Looks like some outstanding student loans and a lien filed against his car. Whew. This guy's a real winner."

Janet scrolled up and down her screen, unable to find any of Quizz's information. When she looked up, the other woman was grinning.

"I'm telling you, LexisNexis is the way to go. I pay hundreds a month for access, but it's so worth it in saved time."

Janet dropped her phone back into her bag. "Who'd he divorce?"

"Nnnn . . ." The sound issued from between Quizz's lips while she read the screen. "Woman by the name of June Martelle —née Hughes."

Janet's head went fuzzy with the information. "What? Dishwasher Dave used to be married to a woman named *June Hughes*? Could this be a relative of Summer's?"

"Already checking." Quizz tapped more keys and a sound hummed out from between her tongue and teeth while she scrolled through the search results. "Not a relative. Summer herself. June Martelle filed for a DBA permit—'doing business as'—in Knox County about eight months ago when she opened a counseling business. Summer Hughes Family Counseling is the business name."

"That's—that's Liv's friend. The one who's been so helpful since she died." Her head spun as she tried to make sense of Quizz's words. "That can't be right—she's . . . she's so . . . refined, and professional. There must be another Summer Hughes. The

Summer we're talking about would have never been married to *Dave!*"

"Another Summer Hughes who used to be named June Martelle?" Quizz looked at Janet over the rims of her glasses. "There are no coincidences in life. Only unknowns. And now we know something about Summer that we didn't a few minutes ago."

"But she told me that she, Eric, and Liv all went to college together."

"They were friends in college?" Quizz asked.

Janet started to nod but then stopped. "No. She didn't say that." She blew out a sigh. "She actually said they all went to Community, but they only recently made the connection." She jumped up from her chair to pace the small office. "I'd been assuming they were old college friends, but she made it clear that none of them graduated from Community."

"So she got her degree somewhere else." Quizz peered at Janet, nonplussed. "Let's see if she has any other aliases." *Clackety clack clack.* Quizz's fingers flew across the keyboard now. "Oh-ho! June Martelle, a.k.a. June Bug Martelle." More tapping, then, "And she did five years with the state for heroin use and possession."

"June Bug," Janet repeated slowly, thinking of her conversation with the neighbor outside the halfway house. Ladybug . . . or June Bug.

The women locked eyes over the stacks of files and legal folders.

Quizz frowned. "Quite a coincidence. And her ex still deals heroin?"

Janet nodded.

"And Liv died from a heroin overdose?"

"Yes, and Dave sent Hayley—a former customer—over to my bar to tell me about a scheme involving Liv's husband . . . and now Hayley's dead."

"Is Dave a good guy or not?" Quizz got to the heart of the

matter. Janet shrugged. "What's your gut tell you?" Quizz
pressed.

"That he's a good, bad guy. Does that make sense?"

Quizz tapped her chin. "Hayley was murdered this morning.
Now Dave's a no-show at his job today. Are we worried?"

"No," Janet answered quickly, but prickles of unease marched
up the back of her neck and settled at the base of her skull.
Quizz raised her eyebrows, and Janet looked down to find her
knuckles tightly balled, the skin stretched so tight it was white.
"Okay, yes. I guess I'm worried."

"Then let's go." Quizz stood and grabbed a light jacket off
the back of her chair. She swiped a key ring off the desk and
headed toward the door. "You follow me out to his place."

Quizz opened the door and looked back at Janet, who was
still sitting in the chair. "You coming?"

She jumped. "Yes. Sorry—it's just a lot to take in."

"Sounds like there's more coming, so make room."

Janet pushed up from the chair and followed Quizz out of
the office, digging around in her bag for her phone.

Liv was dead from tainted heroin that she may or may not
have injected herself with. A woman who knew something about
an effort by a third party to break up Liv's marriage with Eric
was now dead, and Dave, a person connected with everyone,
hadn't shown up for his shift at work. Was she worried about
Dave? Yes. But she was also worried about the other people
connected to Liv.

Nell was in jail—that seemed a good, safe place for her just
then. Eric? She wasn't sure about his role in anything yet, but she
worried that if he was innocent, he might be targeted. And the
kids—the kids were vulnerable. She tapped a name on her
contact list as she walked out of Quizz's office.

Her dad answered on the second ring. "We're just leaving for
the restaurant, are you already there?"

Brunch! She'd completely forgotten. "Dad, there's—well,
there's kind of an emergency."

"What do you need, Janet?" Her father's gruff voice was both concerned and soothing.

"I—I need you, to check on a family for me. I—I'm worried about the kids."

After a short pause her dad said, "What's the address?"

Just like that. No questions, no grilling, just a dad willing to help out his daughter. A breath she didn't know she'd been holding whooshed out of her lungs and she slumped against the wall. "Something's going down in this murder case, Dad. Can you get to the kids, check on their dad? Just . . . stay with them until I can get to you."

"You'll meet us there?"

Us. Janet cringed. Kaylee! She'd forgotten about the other woman.

"Yes, but I have to check on something first. Be careful."

She tossed the phone back into her bag and hustled out to the parking lot behind Quizz, but her heart felt sluggish, like it couldn't push her suddenly-cold blood through her body. "You have the address?" she called.

Quizz was already behind the wheel, her window down. "Head north, away from the river." She watched Janet climb into her car, and when she'd rolled down her window Quizz shouted over the two engines. "He's probably fine. Most killers don't strike multiple locations in one night."

If the words were meant to comfort, they missed the mark. Janet's tires squealed as she peeled out of the lot after Quizz, and a horn blared as she turned onto the road with barely enough room.

Was Dave a good guy? They were about to find out.

CHAPTER THIRTY-FOUR

Quizz slowed her car and pointed at a small crowd gathered by a shabby, tattered play structure to the left of the dilapidated row houses.

Janet eased into the parking spot next to Quizz and the women walked toward the small group in time to hear someone say, "Dare you to touch him." They traded looks and sped up. Quizz held out an official-looking badge and said, "What's going on here?"

Four boys, no older than twelve, jumped and looked guiltily over their shoulders. "We didn't do it, ma'am."

Janet's nose wrinkled again at the term, but Quizz took it in stride. "Step aside, boys. Step aside." The boys parted down the middle, revealing a man lying in a heap, his feet resting awkwardly under the bottom of the slide.

Janet leaned over the body. The skin on his face and neck was tinged blue; his lips were dark purple. His eyes stared blankly to the sky. It was Dishwasher Dave.

Janet sucked in a sharp breath. "I guess he was a good guy."

Quizz's brow furrowed and she whipped out her phone and dialed 911. Janet's phone was out, too, but she dialed a different set of numbers.

"What?" O'Dell croaked into the phone. Janet hesitated, and he added, "I'm not hungover, if that's what you're thinking."

"No, I—" Uncharacteristically at a loss for words, Janet cleared her throat.

"Janet, what's wrong?"

"The, uh—" Her voice warbled, so she cleared her throat again. "Dishwasher Dave is dead."

"Whaddyamean?"

It came out as a single word, and she could feel him perking up by the second.

"Quizz and I—"

"Who's Quizz?"

"This PI I'm working with. Anyway, we got worried when Dave Martelle didn't show up at work at Plaza Eats—you remember, Liv's restaurant?"

"Yes, I remember."

"We came to talk to him at his apartment, and he's dead."

"Who's out there? Rivera?"

"No one yet, we just found him lying on the ground!" She craned her neck to see all of him and added, "Looks like a gunshot wound." A black stain bloomed out from a small opening in his chest.

"Jesus Christ."

"I know."

"Don't move. I'm calling Rivera, I'll be right there."

The underlying edge in his voice did the opposite of comfort her, but she and Quizz locked down the scene until the first police cruiser arrived. It was her old friend Happy Handcuffs, and she frowned back at him when he recognized her.

"Don't look at me like that. O'Dell and Rivera are already on their way."

His eyebrows shot up, but before he could say anything, Quizz said, "We'll wait for them by our cars. Thank you, officer."

Because more people were pouring out of the apartment

complex to investigate, he was too busy controlling the crowd to stop them, but he didn't look happy as they walked away.

"You stay here to talk to the cops." Quizz jangled her keys. "I'm going to check on Eric and the kids."

"My dad should be there."

"But he doesn't know what's going on. Uninformed is the same thing as unsafe in a situation like this. I'll fill them in. What's the address?"

Janet recited it and swallowed hard.

Quizz patted her shoulder. "I'll call you when I get there."

The purple head disappeared into her car. Moments later, Quizz backed out of the lot and took off down the street. Janet's chest felt tight, and her head pounded. They said things like this happened in threes . . . Liv, Hayley, Dave—was this the end? Or was it about to start over again?

———

"So that's when you decided to check on Dave Martelle?" Rivera scribbled into his notebook, but his eyes never left Janet's face.

"Yes, we—well, I was worried about him."

"Why? Were you friends?"

"Friends? No." Janet started to laugh, the absurdity of the day wearing her defenses down. Rivera scowled and she forced the smile off her face. "I met him with O'Dell at Liv's restaurant. He . . . he seemed really down about her death, and I guess . . ." Janet stopped, not sure how to keep herself out of trouble. O'Dell drove up and she breathed out a sigh of relief—until she saw his expression as he climbed out of his car.

"Janet!" His roar echoed across the lot.

"Shit," she muttered, and Rivera moved in front of her. She peeked around his shoulder and said, "Feeling better?"

"Step aside, Rivera. I want to talk to her. Now."

"You'll have to wait. I'm in the middle of an interview. Cruise is cataloging everything found with the body. See what you can find out."

O'Dell pointed wordlessly at Janet, then at Rivera, then growled and threw his hands up before stalking off toward the body.

Janet let out a relieved breath and Rivera squinted after him. "He's worried about you, that's all."

"Well, I'm worried about him! Sheesh."

He asked a few more questions, but she dodged most of them, checking her phone screen with mounting worry.

"Something more important than this?" Rivera asked.

"It's just—" The phone buzzed in her hand and she looked down at the text from her father, then sagged against a nearby car.

Family fine. I'll stay with them for now.

"What?" Rivera cocked his head to the side.

"The kids. They're fine. Liv's kids are fine. It's fine."

"You seeing a connection here—between all of this?" He waved his hand in a circle. Before she could answer, O'Dell was back.

"Did you know about this?" He held up a silver compact in his blue-gloved hand, and Janet sucked her cheeks in. The letters L and A etched in the center of the circle identified it as Liv's. "You know the last person to have this? Eric! I released all Liv's possessions from her work locker that we didn't keep as evidence back to him. And now it's here? On a dead body? Like a calling card?"

Janet shook her head. "You think Eric did this? Then left his wife's compact on the body? O'Dell, you've got this all wrong—"

"You calling a BOLO?" Rivera asked, ignoring Janet.

O'Dell was already reaching for his radio. "Attention all units, be on the lookout for Eric Birch, white male, mid to late thirties. Suspect may be armed and dangerous. Arrest on sight, arrest on contact." He rattled off Eric's home address and his business name, glaring at Janet the whole time.

Janet stared at the ground while he repeated his message. She made a split-second decision not to set him straight. If Eric *wasn't* involved in the new murders, then he very well might be the next target. Maybe the best place for him right then was in police custody.

The cool metal slapping against her wrists was a shock. "What the—"

"Park her at my desk until I get there," O'Dell snarled. He pivoted and marched back to his unmarked car before she could articulate any words.

She stared after him, speechless, then turned to Rivera when he cleared his throat. "Am I under arrest?"

Rivera scratched his head. "No . . . not yet, anyway. Will you please accompany me downtown for questioning in the death of Dave Martelle?"

"No, thank you." She held her wrists out and raised her eyebrows.

Rivera frowned and crossed his arms. "Then, I guess you *are* under arrest—"

"Okay, fine," Janet exploded. "I'll come downtown. Don't add something to my record for kicks, Rivera! Cheese and rice! What's O'Dell got on you, anyway?"

Rivera snickered. "'Cheese and rice'? Haven't heard that in years." He led her to his car and opened the back door. "O'Dell's got nothing on me. We're friends." He put a hand on top of her head and guided her down to the bench seat. "Just like you two are."

She scooted sideways until she was completely in the car and held her hands in front of her face, assessing the metal bracelets. "Friends? Not for long."

CHAPTER THIRTY-FIVE

For the first half hour that she was chained to O'Dell's desk, Janet sat up, alert and ready to discuss things rationally and calmly with her supposed friend.

Now, at half past two in the afternoon, she was sprawled uncomfortably back in the cushioned office chair, the fingers in her cuffed hand long since numb, her bladder uncomfortably full, and her patience incredibly thin. She'd been sitting at O'Dell's desk for going on three hours.

A commotion at the front of the detectives' section forced her upright, and she watched O'Dell walk in and deposit Eric in an interview room. Eric's wide eyes were blank, his expression empty. It wasn't panic, necessarily, more like a confusion so overwhelming his brain had decided to shut down completely.

When O'Dell reemerged and headed her way, Janet tilted her head back against the chair until she was staring up at the ceiling again. "Cheese and rice."

"You hungry?"

She refused to look at O'Dell, so she continued to stare at the exposed ductwork above. "No. Tired, uncomfortable, and irritated, but not hungry."

O'Dell pulled out his chair and unlocked her handcuffs before he sat down.

"Thank you." Janet rubbed her wrist, now looking over his head at the back wall.

"Your dad and his fiancée are with the kids, along with some woman named Quizz? I'll have to call Children's Services soon . . . but thought I'd talk to you first. Nell is in jail?"

Janet nodded but still refused to look O'Dell in the eye. He blew out a noisy sigh and rubbed his head. She lowered her gaze and took in his sweaty brow, pasty complexion, and bloodshot eyes.

"You look like shit."

"Gee, thanks," he snorted, but grabbed a sports drink from his desk and twisted off the top.

"And you've got this wrong. All wrong."

His shoulders tensed. "How so?"

She pursed her lips. "There was no calling card. Eric threw a bunch of Liv's things away at the restaurant; I don't know why, but he did. Dave took the compact out of the trash can. He showed it to me last night. Tucked it into his pocket like it was important. I think he really liked Liv and felt bad that she died."

"Felt bad, or felt guilty?"

"Okay, you're right. Guilty—but not because he killed her. I think he had an idea of who did, though." O'Dell's eyes narrowed, but before she could continue, before she could tell him all about Summer's actually being June Bug Martelle, Rivera walked in.

"You want me to start on him, or are you taking lead?"

Janet said, "Would you just wait a minute—"

O'Dell held up a rigid hand and glared at her. "Together," he said to Rivera. But before he walked away, he reached into his lower drawer and pulled out a box. He set it down gently on his desk, then glanced around the empty office and said in a quiet voice, "Whatever you do, don't look through this, Janet. Keep your prying eyes to yourself." He drilled her with a meaningful stare, then, with a smirk, he laid a set of blue latex gloves next to the box before he turned and met Rivera in the aisle. "Let's do this." The two men disappeared into the interview room without a backward glance.

Janet, however, couldn't stop looking all around the room. Her stomach clenched as she studied the box O'Dell had set out for her. Was she supposed to look inside or not? With one more sweep of the space, she stood and slid the plastic tub closer.

On regular masking tape, O'Dell's messy scrawl labeled it "Liv Birch Locker." She pried the lid off and peered inside at a jumble of makeup, papers, and notebooks. Warily, she snapped on the gloves and pawed through the evidence in a murder investigation.

She wondered how O'Dell had decided what to leave for Eric and what to keep.

She flipped through a small binder that was a piece of artwork in its own right. The fabric cover unzipped to reveal a long line of colorful gel pens, tucked into small elastic loops, and as she flipped through the planner in the front, it was clear Liv had taken great joy in scheduling her family's life. Brendon's activities were written in forest-green ink, Andrea's in deep purple, baby Bonnie's in neon pink, and Eric's in a shimmery gold. Liv's own schedule was outlined in dark blue. The planner was stuffed with old shopping lists, a few library checkout receipts, and to-do lists, and behind the planner, a spiral-bound notebook was clipped into the three-ring binder. Children's scrawls in bright blue crayon filled the front and back of a few pages. Gibberish, at first glance, but it pulled at Janet's memory. There was something familiar, something patterned about the way the letters filled the space. Not that the child couldn't spell, more that they'd deliberately put specific letters on the page in a certain order, with regular spaces and punctuation.

Flipping forward a few pages, Janet found the same code written in the sure, steady hand of an adult, with pen. It was part of the last entry in the planner. There was also a phone number

and then, in a different color ink—and more hastily scrawled—
were the words, "Bonnie knows everything."

Janet tapped the numbers into her device and a bored voice
answered after two rings.

"Law offices of Thornton & Brown, how can I help you?"

She disconnected. A commercial featuring an ultra-serious
voice talking over video of an unhappy couple came immediately
to mind—in fact, the jingle would be in her head for days again:
*"Need a divorce, don't stray from the course. Thornton & Brown
Attorneys!"*

She looked around to confirm she was alone and then took
the notebook to a copy machine at the back of the room.

With the warm copies stuffed into her coat pocket and the
original notebook back in the evidence box, she snapped on the
lid and threw the gloves away.

She needed to find out if Liv's kids could break the code of
their mom's final journal entry, but she had no car—hers was still
at Dave's apartment building.

She opened O'Dell's top desk drawer and found his key ring,
then walked to the edge of the office and pointed his key fob at
the window. A beat-up blue Taurus winked at her when she
clicked the unlock button, and she grinned and headed out the
door.

CHAPTER THIRTY-SIX

"I'm headed over. Don't let anyone in but me." Janet braked hard at a light; she wasn't used to O'Dell's car, and the controls felt touchy. She eased off the brake and carefully engaged the gas pedal to turn right at the intersection.

"Quizz is here." Sampson lowered his voice. "She's a strange bird. Keeps walking from window to window, like she's expecting an invasion."

"Good."

"What does that mean?"

"Just—I'll explain when I get there."

Sampson hung up and Janet swerved as the door of a car parked on the side of the street was flung open. "Pay attention," she admonished herself. Crashing a car that was technically stolen wouldn't help anyone just then.

During the remainder of the drive she followed all the traffic laws, and at a particularly long red light, she noted how clean O'Dell kept the interior of his ride. A few gum wrappers had been shoved into an empty paper cup perched in the cup holder. The carpet was clear of dirt and leaves. Even the car manual and registration were kept neat and orderly inside the glove box.

When she finally pulled up at Liv and Eric's house, she made sure the papers she'd copied at the police department were in her pocket and headed up the front walk.

Janet shot a final glance at the street before heading in, then plastered on a smile and turned to face the room. "Brendon! Andrea!"

———

"You know how some people can speak pig latin really well?" Brendon looked at Janet, the expression on his eight-year-old, still-chubby cherubic face earnest, and she tried to nod but couldn't do it.

"Pig latin? No, I guess I've never heard anyone speak it *fluently*."

He leaned to the side and caught his older sister's eye. "Show her."

"Hat-way re-ay ou-yay alking-tay bout-ay?" Andrea said, as quickly as Janet could have said the words in English. The twelve-year-old grinned.

Janet's eyes went wide. "Are you kidding with that?"

"It was the same for me and Mom with the code." Brendon's chest puffed out. "She taught it to me when I was trying to plan a birthday surprise for my dad, but it was so cool, we spent all of last summer doing scavenger hunts around the house with it." He frowned and fell silent, then added in a quieter voice. "It was fun."

Janet gave both kids a moment to collect themselves. "So how does it work?" she asked gently, looking down at the paper. "It's not written in pig latin?" Surely she hadn't missed such an obvious pattern?

"Nah. It's way easier." He leaned forward and lowered his voice. "But it's a secret. Let me see it, and I'll read it to you."

"Um, I don't know if that's such a good idea." Janet scrutinized Liv's journal again. "What if it says something inappropriate?"

"Nah. No secrets in this house, believe me," Brendon said. Andrea nodded, and Janet handed the pages over to Brendon.

He studied it for several long moments, then looked up. "Excuse me, Mrs. Bexley? Can you take Bonnie to the kitchen, please? She's probably ready for a snack."

"'Nack?" their littlest sibling said, looking up from her puzzle with a smile. "'Nack!" She stood, clutching a worn and shabby stuffed animal, and wobbled into the other room. Quizz followed but shot a curious look back at Janet.

Sampson wandered closer and stood behind Kaylee, who was seated across from Janet.

Brendon recited slowly, "'Adultery is grounds for divorce, but in Tennessee must wait ninety days to file.'" He read the phone number for the law office that Janet had called earlier. Then he handed the first page over to Janet and read the line from the second page. "'Skylar says he was drugged. Don't trust Summer.'"

Brendon squinted at the final line, written in regular old English. "'Bonnie knows everything.'" He looked up. "What does that mean?" He passed the pages to Janet's outstretched hand.

Janet scrutinized the letters again and frowned. Now that she knew the message, the code became clear. Every other letter was bogus, put there to distract from the real word. In this case, "adultery" was written "ratdhuwlbtqevrry."

"Surprisingly clever." Sampson squeezed Kaylee's shoulder and smiled at Janet. Andrea reached for the paper, but Brendon smacked her hand out of the way.

"Not everyone here needs to know the code, okay?" Brendon's eyebrows rose and he grinned at his older sister.

She rolled her eyes. "Bren—you could just practice pig latin, and you'd be good at it. It's not like I'm not telling you how to do it!"

A short wrestling match between the two ensued, but Janet

was too busy trying to order the events of the past several months.

Eric had confessed his affair to Liv. She had planned to file for divorce, and had started making plans to that end, but then at some point Skylar told her that Eric had been drugged. Skylar's name muddied the waters. Who'd actually drugged Eric? Hayley? Skylar? And on whose orders? Whatever Liv had heard, it was enough that she didn't trust Summer anymore. But why? Why would Summer want to force a breakup between them? She claimed to not even like Eric.

She read over the note again. How could little Bonnie have known about all of this? And just how much could an eighteen-month-old really retain?

Janet looked over at the little girl as she and Quizz walked back into the room. She had a cookie in her hand, along with drool and a smattering of crumbs trailing down her chin.

Janet turned back to the journal entry. It was dated just a day before Liv died.

One day after learning that Summer may have been trying to break up her marriage, Liv had died with drugs in her system, tumbling down the steps with a full laundry basket headed toward a broken washing machine.

Janet rubbed the back of her neck and looked up to find her father staring at her.

"What do you want to do, Janet?" he asked.

"Lock the doors! No—wait. We're leaving. Everyone, we're going to my house. Now." She whipped her phone out of her pocket and pressed a name on her contact list.

"Can you meet me at my place in twenty minutes? Bring the dummy."

"Not nice!" Bonnie looked up at Janet with wide, accusing eyes.

"You'll see," Janet said with a wink. "That's the only name for him."

The large group trooped out of the house just as the sudden roar of an engine announced a new arrival. Summer waved as she slowed to park. Before her car came to a complete stop, though, Janet scowled and picked Bonnie up, then stood in front of the remaining two kids. Sampson, sensing the threat, stopped with a wide stance and held the kids back with his arms outstretched.

Though her heart rate quickened, Janet held Summer's gaze, her body as rigid as the sides of a keg.

The other woman's mouth pressed flat, and her eyes narrowed.

"Don't come any closer!" Janet called.

Summer's eye twitched, but she forced a smile onto her face and rolled down the window. "I brought a new book for Bonnie!" She put the car into park but didn't move to get out.

Janet frowned. "Stay right there. I'm calling the cops!"

Summer's eyes narrowed, her mouth twisted into a sneer, and she hit the gas; her car roared down the street, leaving behind the smell of burnt rubber and gasoline.

"Should I call 911?" Sampson asked, his phone out, his fingers hovering over the numbers.

Janet sighed. It was all out in the open. Dave's murder. Hayley's death. Summer's role in the entire series of events. The only missing link was whether Eric was involved, but just then, Janet didn't care. She only cared about keeping Summer away from Nell's family. Keeping Nell's grandchildren safe.

"No—the last thing we need is a beat officer getting involved." She pictured Happy Handcuffs showing up at a third incident with Janet in a single day, and knew it wouldn't end well for her. "I'll head downtown after I get you guys settled and let O'Dell know myself."

She shifted Bonnie over into her car seat—the child was nearly asleep, and even as Janet struggled with the seat belt, Bonnie blinked slower and slower until finally her eyes didn't open again. As she gently closed the door, an icicle of uncer-

tainty rammed down her throat, making it difficult to swallow.
Had she just upped the stakes? Was it enough for Summer to cut
and run, or had Janet just pushed Summer to a new level of
urgency? Because surely the other woman knew she was out of
time. But what if she had no intention of abandoning her
plan now?

CHAPTER THIRTY-SEVEN

An unexpected shriek split the air shortly after Janet opened the door for Mel. "What in God's name—"

"Bonnie, what's wrong?" Kaylee rushed over to the smallest child.

A tsk issued from Andrea, but the oldest sibling didn't look up from her perch on her chair, her nose buried in a book. Quizz and Janet locked eyes, but before Janet could offer up any solutions to quiet the noise, Mel knelt down by the little girl. When Bonnie's voice cut off in the middle of a wail, Andrea looked over the top of her book, her eyebrows raised.

"Mine?" Bonnie's lip trembled, but she swiped her shirtsleeve past her nose and looked at what appeared to be a key chain in her hand.

"Yes, just for you!" Mel stood up with a smile and began rearranging the furniture in the main room.

Bonnie traced the pink metal outline of a cat's face with her short, stubby fingers. The cat's round eyes were sized for adult fingers to fit through, and the ears were just pointy enough to look dangerous in the right situation.

"It's not technically a weapon. It's fine." Mel pushed the couch to the back wall, then stood up and brushed her hands together. "And hey—better than listening to that scream, huh? Janet, if you lay those mats down, I'll move the dummy over here, and we can get started."

Mel had Andrea's full attention now, and Brendon's, too. "What are we doing?" He studied the naked torso of a man, perched high on a metal pole, and grinned. "Why is that thing here?"

"This is Bob, the self-defense dummy. Janet wants all of you to learn a few simple self-defense moves, and since that happens to be one of my specialties—"

"Self-defense? What about *offense?*" Janet squinted at her bouncer.

"This is not the right crowd for offense," Mel said with a frown. "Self-defense is where we start."

Mel pointed to the mat, and before Janet joined the kids, she pulled Sampson aside.

"Dad, I need another favor. Can you and Kaylee go rescue my car? I had to leave it at a crime scene . . . it's a long story," she added when his eyes lasered in on her face.

"There seem to be a lot of long stories from you today."

"I'm driving O'Dell's car now, but that won't last. Can you and Kaylee drop mine off downtown, then meet me back here?"

"No problem, kiddo. Just tell me where to go."

She gave him Dave Martelle's address. As she watched him and Kaylee drive away, a faint smile crossed her lips. He was still on her team.

"Janet? You joining us?"

She nodded and moved to the end of the line next to Brendon.

"The goal of everything you're about to learn is to get away and get to safety, so that's what we'll be working on. Say it with me: get away, get to safety."

The kids parroted the phrase back to Mel; Bonnie's small voice finished a few seconds after the others.

"We'll start with the arm chop. Kids, if someone—now, not

your nana or your dad"—Mel laughed, then, perhaps realizing both people were in police custody, she choked before recovering—"but anyone who shouldn't be is grabbing you, this is what you do." She demonstrated a swift upward swing of her arm. "That will break their hold where it's weakest, at their thumb and fingers. Now you try."

As the kids' arms swooped up and down several times, Mel secured a padded arm brace around her forearm with three Velcro straps.

"Brendon, if I grab you here, what do you do?"

Nell's middle grandchild tentatively moved his arm up, making contact with Mel's padded arm with a soft *thunk*.

"Don't hold back!" she challenged.

Brendon grinned self-consciously. "I don't want to hurt you!"

"You won't."

Brendon's eyes narrowed. "Okay. Grab me again!" When she reached out this time, he used both arms to swing up, breaking Mel's hold almost immediately.

"This is dumb," Andrea said. She sauntered over to the chair and picked up her book. But her face was red, her breathing choppy, and before Janet could try to bring her back to the group, Mel shook her head slightly.

"Whenever you want to, jump back in, Andrea. Okay, Bonnie." She turned her attention to the smallest. "What are you going to do?"

As the little girl answered, Jason walked through the front door.

"What's—" He stepped back out of the house to check the address above the door, then tilted his head to the side as he assessed the scene. "What's going on?"

"Jason, you remember Nell's grandkids? They're going to be here for a little while."

"Here? Wh—" He broke off when he saw Janet's face and followed her into the kitchen when she excused herself from the exercises.

"What's going on?" he asked when they were alone.

"Let's see if I can sum it up . . . The kids' father is downtown, being questioned by police in two overnight homicides; Nell is in jail, accused of stealing a cop's wallet out of her car; and I think the kids are in danger, so I'm going to keep them with me until the police find and arrest Summer."

Jason managed to keep his face impassive. "So you took my advice and stayed out of it, that's good to see."

"Jason—"

"No, I get it. They needed you, that much is clear. How long do we have the kids for?"

A lump rose up in her throat and her eyes filled inexplicably. She swallowed hard and turned away. *We . . .* The single word held more meaning than an entire storybook. "Uh . . . well, I'm not sure. I'm hoping a bondsman can get Nell out with just ten percent of her five-thousand-dollar bail, but I—well, I still want them to stay with us. I don't trust Summer, and I want to make sure the kids are safe."

"Okay."

She turned to face him, and his lopsided grin widened when he saw her watery eyes. "We're going to be okay, Janet. You know that, right? Real couples have disagreements and fights. They just stick around to work through them because it's worth it."

She sniffed loudly and looked up at the ceiling.

"You're worth it. We're worth it. At least *I* think so . . ."

Her nose tingled but she forced herself to look at Jason. "I—"

"The auction was this morning." At Janet's blank look he elaborated. "The county real estate auction? My dad didn't get the restaurant."

Before Janet could hide her relief, Jason spoke again. "My mom bought it out from under him."

Janet's jaw dropped. "What? Does she have—I mean, she wants to run a restaurant?"

He chuckled. "No, I think she just doesn't want my dad to."

"Wow."

"And I've been thinking. I want you to feel secure, to know that you have options. And if that means you buy me out of the Spot, that's what we need to do. I never want you to feel trapped or stuck."

"Jason, I—" But her throat constricted again, and she had to look away.

"We'll call a lawyer as soon as this business"—he motioned toward the family room—"is settled and start the process. Because I love you, and I don't want you to feel like there are strings attached, you know?"

She couldn't speak, and when she finally looked over, Jason reached out to stroke her arm. "What?"

"You're gonna cry, darlin', and it's okay."

"I am not!" she snapped, but wiped her eyes and nose, too. She chuckled and so did Jason. "I don't deserve you." She walked forward and wrapped her arms around him.

"You do. And I deserve you. It's a good match."

Quizz popped her head through the kitchen door. "Your phone kept ringing, so I finally answered it." She held the device out and plopped Janet's purse on the plywood table between them. "It's Detective Patrick O'Dell."

Janet took the phone gingerly. "Hello?"

"Where'd you go?" Without waiting for an answer, he added, "Rivera and I are done talking to Eric, but we're gonna park him for a few hours. Give him time to think things through. Time for you to ask him some questions if you want to."

She looked at her watch. "I'll be there in ten minutes." She clicked off before O'Dell could answer.

"We'll keep an eye on the kids. You go. Sounds like there's work to do." Jason squeezed her arms and released her.

She pulled her purse across the plywood counter and plunged her phone down into the bag. Her hand hit a slick, rubbery surface. She dug around and pulled out a silicone mold she'd last seen at the bar. "What the heck?"

"Is that the ice wedge mold?" Jason asked. "Why do you have that here?"

"I have no idea. It went missing from the bar days ago." She studied the small black tray. "I just pulled this purse out of my closet this morning—haven't used it in weeks. How . . ." Her phone rang; Detective O'Dell's name lit up across the screen. She tossed the wedge back into her bag and shrugged. "Thanks, Jason!"

As she hurried out of the room she heard him say, "So who are you?"

"I'm Quizz Bexley, PI. Janet's apprenticing under me."

"Is she, now?"

Janet caught his eye as she closed the door. He winked.

CHAPTER THIRTY-EIGHT

"What's going on?" Janet stepped between O'Dell and his desk and gently laid the keyring on the surface. O'Dell narrowed his eyes when she grinned up at him, but he couldn't seem to figure out what was making her smile.

He glanced from her to the evidence box. "I thought you'd stick around to discuss . . . things."

She crossed her arms. "I had urgent business to attend to."

"We don't have to be adversaries in here, Janet. We can work together."

"Does that mean you won't twist what I say to suit your investigation—you're actually open to listening to my well-reasoned theories about what happened?"

He stepped back, a new look on his face. "Partners?"

She flinched, knowing Jason wouldn't like the sound of that. "Colleagues, in a way, yes."

"Rivera and I already talked to Eric. You want to hear my thoughts or talk to him yourself?"

She wasn't about to give him the goods on Summer now and risk losing her chance to interview Eric. They locked eyes and he grinned.

"I'll wait out here, take as long as you like. If he asks for a lawyer, come out immediately, okay?"

"He hasn't asked for a lawyer yet?"

O'Dell shook his head. "It's what has me and Rivera so puzzled. The guilty ones either don't ask for one because they think it'll make them look guilty—then they don't really say anything of value—or they ask for one before they say hello, because they know they're screwed. But this guy . . . he doesn't seem to know what he knows." O'Dell shrugged. "Good luck."

She pulled open the door and Rivera, sitting at a desk in the corner shuffling papers, looked up, then nodded and went back to his papers. Eric half-stood from his chair and motioned to the empty one across from him; Southern hospitality, even here in the police interview room. After she'd taken the seat, he folded his hands in front of him and leaned forward. "Your dad is with my kids—thank you for that. But where's Nell? Did she make it? She wasn't answering her phone."

"Oh, ah . . . right . . ." Janet hesitated. "The kids are at my house for now. Nell is . . . well, she got busted stealing from a cop's car. But don't worry—" Eric's hands clenched and she finished quickly, "I've got a call into a bondsman, and we're just waiting on the paperwork to come through. She should be at my house and with the kids by dinnertime."

"What happens if she's not?"

Rivera spoke without looking up. "Then we'll have to call DCS. They'll place the kids in temporary custody until family court takes up the matter."

"What?" Eric gasped, and half-stood, then froze uncertainly, clearly realizing he was stuck in the interview room.

Janet patted his hand reassuringly. "She'll be out. I'll make sure of it." She glared at Rivera, but the cop wasn't moved.

Eric sank back into the chair and rubbed a hand roughly across his face.

"The kids are okay. When I left them they were playing a fun . . . game . . . with plenty of responsible adults." She guessed that learning self-defense could be considered fun. "Anyway, I wanted to ask you a few questions."

"You're not the only one. I keep asking how long this is going to take, I need to check on Bonnie. I think she's getting an ear infection, the way she was rubbing her ear." He glared at Rivera. "But they 'don't have a timeline,' whatever that means."

Janet grimaced. It meant the cops were waiting for Eric to trip up—get caught in a lie—so they could arrest him. He wasn't going anywhere any time soon. Instead of saying that, though, she said, "I found Liv's notebook. Her planner?"

Eric's head whipped up. "Where?"

Rivera looked over, too, his eyebrows raised, and Janet lowered her voice. "I came across it, and found a note—written in code, actually. Did Liv do that often?"

One side of Eric's mouth tipped up. "She and Brendon were two of a kind." He shook his head and stared at the wall behind her. "He's really struggling."

Janet shifted in her seat. When Rivera cleared his throat and tapped his wristwatch, she leaned forward. "The note said that when—that when the affair happened, that you were drugged."

"None of that matters now. She's dead! It doesn't matter!" Eric's anger flared and Janet flinched. Rivera's feet thunked off the desk to the floor and he reached for the handcuffs at his belt but didn't stand.

"It matters, Eric, because the note also said that Summer can't be trusted. Did Liv explain that to you? Why Summer can't be trusted?"

"N—no, I don't know what you're talking about. Summer was a good friend to her there at the end—"

"I don't think your wife overdosed on her own, just like you didn't cheat on her."

"What—what do you mean?"

"I mean there's one common person involved in all your troubles, but what the cops want to know—and what I'm here to find out—is what you knew and when."

"What are you—what are you talking about?" Bubbles of spittle collected at the corners of his mouth and his pale face turned red. "What did I know about what? My wife is dead! My kids no longer have a mother, and I'm over here drowning in decisions! Who will watch them while I'm at work? Who will read to them at night? Who will get Brendon to soccer when Andrea has to be at rehearsal at the same time? All I know is that I can't do it all! I can't do it alone! I—I never wanted to—" His voice cracked and he pinched his lips together.

Janet nonchalantly rested one foot against the flat edge of the table between them, but her focus lasered in on Liv's widower. "Eric, did you have anything to do with Liv's death?"

"How can you ask me that?"

"Answer the question!"

His hands plunged into his hair roughly. "I can't even think about it."

"That's not an answer!" she pressed.

Rivera's eyes followed the action, but he didn't move.

"It's my fault—it's all my fault that she's dead." Still grasping his head, he dropped his elbows down to his knees, his eyes closed in defeat.

Janet knew, from their earlier conversation at the Spot, that Eric thought that his affair had driven his wife to use drugs—but saying, "It's all my fault," in front of a homicide detective wasn't good. "You mean that you blame yourself, Eric?"

"Of course I do! If I hadn't had an affair, she'd still be alive."

A quick look at Rivera's face confirmed that Eric was digging a hole, and she had handed him the shovel.

She needed him to state, unequivocally, that he wasn't involved with Summer, before she dropped a bombshell on Rivera about Summer's true identity.

She cleared her throat. "Were you having an affair with Summer?"

"No—God, no! I told you, I'd only spoken to her once or twice before Liv died. I didn't want anything to do with Summer when Liv was alive. She was working against me from day one." He groaned, now staring down at the floor. "I don't know what changed when Liv died, but Summer wanted to help. She did help! Then she disappeared, too, and it was almost worse, having to figure out life again."

"Did you know—" Janet faltered, aware that this particular bit of information might be hard for Eric to hear. "Did you know that Summer spent five years in prison?"

"Pri—what? No, that can't be right." He looked at Janet, wide eyed, and when she didn't smile, when her gaze didn't waver, he gasped. "For what?"

"Drugs." Her gaze slid to Rivera. "She used to go by the name June Bug Martelle."

Rivera jerked forward in his seat and shoved his stack of papers to the side. His fingers pounded over his laptop keyboard and he groaned. "What's she got to do with this?"

Janet turned to the cop. "You know her?" He didn't answer, just stared at his computer screen.

When Rivera snapped his laptop closed and stood, she followed him out the door, leaving Eric sitting at the table muttering, his hands still roughly grabbing tufts of hair.

In the main office space, O'Dell joined them at the door. "What happened?"

"Your girl here just connected some dots I didn't even know were out there, that's what."

O'Dell turned to Janet. "Tell me." It was a command.

Rivera turned his eagle eye on Janet as well. "I'd like to hear this, too. How did you figure out this friend of the family, Summer Hughes, is actually June Bug Martelle?"

Janet dug a folded-up paper from her back pocket and held it out. O'Dell snatched it from her. "This is the DBA form she filed last year when she opened a counseling office."

"Who is this?" O'Dell scanned the paperwork, then looked back up at Janet.

"June Bug spent a few years in lockup on drug charges,"

Rivera answered. "Got out about a year ago." He motioned that they should follow him to his desk.

Janet's face twisted as she walked through the office. "Is that allowed? I mean, can she counsel other people without disclosing her past?"

O'Dell looked at her sharply. "How did you even know who she was? Her arrest would have happened long before you moved here. Heck, it was before I moved here, too."

"Research," Janet said simply. "I also know she lived in the same halfway house as Hayley and Skylar. I know she used to be married to Dishwasher Dave. And I know she's currently worming her way into Liv's old life."

Rivera plopped down at his desk and then turned his computer screen toward the group. "June Bug's mugshot."

Janet kept her jaw from dropping by biting her lip. There was Summer, only without the put-together hair and makeup. No rosy cheeks, no perfectly applied lipstick, no sophisticated demeanor. Instead, the woman who gazed back at them from the screen was sickly thin, with smudged, bloodshot eyes and a hollow stare.

It brought to mind a similarly ravaged face she'd seen recently. "Did she ever share a jail cell with Skylar?"

"Skylar who?"

Janet looked up at the ceiling, searching her memory for a last name. "Skylar . . . Rowen, I think?"

Rivera's brow furrowed, and he attacked the keyboard, typing commands into the system. "No, they served time in different prisons."

Janet hummed out a breath. "What about Hayley? Any connection you can see in her file with Summer?" She'd never really believed Hayley's story that it was a friend involved in the drugs-for-drugging-Eric scheme anyway.

Rivera frowned and spent a few minutes poking around Hayley's records. When his frown deepened, she stood and leaned over his shoulder to read the screen with him. After a moment, Janet sucked in a loud breath. "Summer and Hayley were roommates at the halfway house?"

Rivera lifted one shoulder and dropped it. "According to the file, yes. They overlapped by a few months. Summer got out early." He rubbed his jaw and added in an undertone, "She must have had a great lawyer."

O'Dell, peering over Rivera's shoulder, said, "And Hayley clearly didn't. She was in that halfway house almost two years."

Janet's stomach clenched. Hayley had said her supposed friend had shared a jail cell with the woman who masterminded the plan to drug Eric. Two years in a halfway house had probably felt like jail.

She crossed her arms. "So Summer's friend Liv, Summer's ex-roommate Hayley, and now Summer's ex-husband, Dave, are all dead."

"But Eric is very much alive." Rivera turned to face O'Dell. "Who's to say they're not both responsible?"

"That seems to be the last question, doesn't it? Will prosecutors want to charge them together?" O'Dell stroked his chin and looked critically at his colleague. "What do you think?"

"I think it's muddy enough that I don't want to be the one deciding. We'll present the evidence. They'll make the call."

Janet threw her hands up. "What are you talking about? Charge them with what?"

O'Dell turned to Janet. "The Knox County Prosecutor announced months ago that her office is going to go after dealers and suppliers when their customers die. If they can prove that Eric and Summer provided Liv with the drugs that killed her, they'll go to jail."

"Listen; Eric's a broken man, but broken because his wife is dead, not because he gave her the drugs!" Janet felt heat rising to her cheeks and she took a deep, steadying breath. Losing her cool now wouldn't help anyone.

"This fits a pattern." Rivera crossed his arms and scrutinized Janet. "He *said* it's his fault that his wife is dead! Prosecutors can take that and run with it. It doesn't matter if he meant for her to die. But if we're looking at the big picture here, Janet, after finding out about the affair, Liv could have thought that her life, as she knew it was over! And if drugs were in the house, it might not have been a big leap to think the only way to feel better would be to try them. And where did those drugs come from? That's the only thing prosecutors will care about! And that's homicide, second degree."

"No! Eric feels guilty—yes—but only because he thinks he drove his wife to use drugs over his affair." Rivera shot her a look that said her words were only serving to prove his point more. She groaned. "This all traces back to Summer—to June Bug! She was married to the drug dealer who was peddling bad heroin. She must have saved some—then convinced Liv to try it, and she . . . fell down the stairs? I don't know, but it has to be Summer."

O'Dell frowned. "Don't forget that Eric's skipped out on the drug test we asked him to submit to twice. Would have been an easy way to clear his name."

"So he's busy! Not a crime." She could tell by the set of both men's jaws that she wasn't going to be able to convince them of anything just then. She grabbed her bag from O'Dell's chair.

"Where are you going?" he asked.

"Home." It wasn't a lie; she would eventually get there. It just wouldn't be her first stop.

O'Dell grabbed her arm. "Stay away from Summer. I don't know if Eric's a part of this, but clearly Summer is. I'm putting an APB out on her. I want her arrested on sight. We'll bring her in, see what she knows. You leave Summer to me, got it?"

"Gladly, O'Dell. She can't be far—we saw her when we left Eric's house an hour ago."

"What?" O'Dell roared. "Why didn't you tell me?"

"I just did!"

O'Dell turned his back on her and picked up his two-way radio. Rivera shot her a disappointed look and she knew she needed to leave before she said something that would get her in trouble.

She hurried out of the police station and scanned the street. Kaylee and her dad had left her car at the edge of the public lot closest to the police department, with two crisp dollar bills tucked into the change tray that would get her through the toll-booth and on her way. She found herself reflexively looking over her shoulder and in the rearview mirror until she got out of the cramped lot. She wouldn't feel safe until Summer was behind bars.

CHAPTER THIRTY-NINE

Janet drove across downtown, to a building that was becoming all too familiar. She ducked down behind the wheel when Donaldson stalked out of the side door toward the parking lot, and she didn't climb out until she'd lost sight of his car in the side-view mirror.

O'Dell and Rivera were focused on finding and arresting Summer, but Janet wanted to get to the bottom of whether Eric was in on the plan. Only two people could help with that—and she wasn't going to go anywhere near Summer.

No, she wanted to talk to Liv's divorce lawyer. She could only guess that Liv had hired someone at Thornton & Brown; after all, Liv had scribbled the firm's number on the last page of her notebook.

She entered the building and headed up to the third floor, then walked down the hallway and pulled open the heavy oak door to the office.

A young man behind the reception desk lowered the microphone on his headset but didn't look up from his computer. "Welcome to the law offices of Thornton & Brown, how can I help you?"

"I . . ." Janet's lips pinched together. How was she going to get past the receptionist? "I just have a quick question for the lawyer who's—" Before she finished her query, the receptionist lifted one hand from his keyboard to push a stack of papers toward her.

"Here are the intake forms, we require a twenty-five-hundred-dollar retainer to open a case, and of course that doesn't guarantee a win. You can step over there to fill out the forms, or take them home with you."

Twenty-five hundred dollars was a lot of money—certainly more than Liv could have afforded . . . but since she was here, she figured she might as well ask. "*I'm* not looking for an attorney, I'm here for . . . I wanted to talk to the lawyer representing Liv Birch. Her name is, uh . . ." She suddenly knew that Liv's final note could never have referred to her young daughter. She looked down at the business card holder perched at the edge of the desk and scanned the offerings. At the top of the tiered stand were cards for Gen Thornton and Rebecca Brown. Down a level she read the names Daniel Jones and Jill Riley, she kept going down a few more levels before—ah! There it was. "Bonnie Kerben. I need to speak to Bonnie Kerben, please."

The receptionist eyed her doubtfully. "Do you have an appointment?"

"Yes." Janet turned her stare up to haughty. "I was told to come in at one o'clock."

"Well you missed that, didn't you?" He smirked.

"Funny how your time isn't your own when you're dealing with homicide detectives." She smiled archly and looked pointedly at her watch. "Is she still available?"

His lips scrunched together. He couldn't tell whether Janet was full of it, or someone more important than himself. She decided to try and tip the scales toward important.

"Listen, if she wants to call my office to reschedule, that's fine, but I'm headed to a conference tomorrow—"

"Let me just call back there and see. What's your name?"

"Janet Black. Thank you." She turned and walked to a wall of artwork and pretended to admire the cheap, reframed prints while straining to hear what the receptionist said into his headset.

"I don't know, she says—I mean yes, I asked, but. . ." There was a long pause while whoever was on the other end spoke, then, "Well, I can ask her, or you can. I mean, why don't I just send her. . . okay, good. Thanks." He disconnected and called Janet over.

"Mrs. Kerben will be right out to get you."

"Thank you."

She continued to stand, hovering by the art wall, until the door at the far end of the lobby opened several minutes later and a young, fresh faced woman walked out, a curious expression on her face.

"Mrs. Black?"

"Bonnie, thanks for seeing me."

The lawyer inclined her head slightly at Janet's confident tone, and then dropped back a step to hold the door open for Janet. "I'm the first office on the left."

Once they were both seated around Bonnie's desk, the lawyer swept her long, dark hair away from her face, and settled back into her chair. "What can I do for you, Mrs. Black?"

"Did you represent Liv Birch?"

The other woman's face tightened almost imperceptibly and her hands spread out along the desktop. "What?"

"Liv Birch? Did you represent her?"

Bonnie tilted her head to the side. "I'm sorry, but we can't give out information on any clients." She picked up a pair of glasses that had been resting next to her computer mouse and began to polish them with a cloth, her focus on the task complete. When she looked up, she'd found her poker face. "Who, exactly, are you?"

"I'm friends with Liv's mother."

"Well, like I said, we can't confirm or deny the identity of any of our clients." The woman eyed the phone console sitting inches from her right hand and then placed the glasses on her face before leveling Janet with a dismissive stare. "Was there anything else?"

"She's dead," Janet blurted out. "Liv, I mean. Did you know that?"

"What?" Bonnie's eyes widened, her fingers clenched the cloth she'd been using on her glasses.

"She died nearly a month ago under suspicious circumstances. And her family is in trouble."

Bonnie's fingers flew over the keyboard and after a moment, she flung a hand up to her throat as she read, her lips moving along with the words on her screen. "I see now. Here's her obituary—I—I had no idea."

Janet pulled the photocopied journal pages from her back pocket and unfolded them on Bonnie's desk. "Liv wrote this just before she died." The lawyer's face scrunched together as she looked over the lines of code. "I know it's hard to make out, but this right here"—she pointed to the last line—"you can read that one just fine. It says, 'Bonnie knows everything.'" Janet leaned closer. "I know a lot about what happened, but I'm not sure I know *everything*. Think we can compare notes?"

Bonnie's face paled, so that it was whiter than the paper between them. "I—I don't think that would be appropriate . . ."

Janet waited until Bonnie looked up. "We have a problem. Right now, Liv's widower is sitting across town in police custody. My friends are watching Liv's kids, because their grandmother is in jail. The police are looking for Summer Hughes, a woman who claimed to be friends with Liv but who I suspect might have had a hand in her death. And before Eric gets charged with playing a part in his wife's death, too, and Liv's kids end up in state custody, I want to know if you have any information that might help them—might help *him*."

Bonnie closed her eyes for a long moment. When she opened them back up, her expression was pained. "I'm not sure what to do here . . . my role. . . I mean, I need to do what's in her best interest . . ."

"What's in her best interest is to make sure her kids are taken care of right now."

Bonnie looked back blankly for what felt like an eternity. She finally nodded almost to herself. "Yes . . . help the kids . . ." The lawyer studied her computer screen for a moment, collecting her thoughts. "She was supposed to come in to sign the divorce filing, but when she got here, she'd changed her mind. She told me she'd just learned new information, and wanted to stop everything."

Janet leaned forward. "Did she mention Hayley or Skylar?"

"Skylar, yes." Bonnie grimaced. "Skylar had told her what I consider to be a pretty far-fetched story about someone drugging Eric..." Bonnie rubbed at her brow roughly.

"What?" Janet asked.

"I'm a divorce lawyer! This whole thing was veering so far off course. But Liv had a name—"

"Summer?"

"Yes," Bonnie said with a frown. "We looked Summer up in the county database and discovered that she'd done time in prison under another name." Kerben looked over. "You can imagine how angry Liv was, I'm sure. This woman had been babysitting her kids!"

"So...what? What happened then?"

The lawyer shook her head back and forth a few times before speaking. "I told her she needed a different kind of lawyer to move forward. She wanted to talk about filing a civil suit against Summer. Calling the police and filing a criminal complaint. She said the divorce was off, and that's the only kind of law I practice these days. I told her to go home, discuss things with her husband. Then I'd refer them to the appropriate kind of lawyer."

"When did you last see her?"

Kerben leaned forward and tapped her keyboard, then squinted at her screen. "September fourteenth."

"The day she died." Janet looked down at the paper in her hand. The last, ominous phrase was added just hours before Liv had taken her last breath. "When you didn't hear from her again, why didn't you call? Check on her?"

Kerben looked over Janet's head and frowned. When she spoke, her voice was low. "I—I guess I was happy to think she was moving on. This was like a bad soap opera, lots of drama, and she had no money to pay for the next steps."

Janet narrowed her eyes at the lawyer, but before she could say anything, her phone buzzed with a new text from Quizz.

I'm out. Too much noise. Jason is here.

"I have to go—Liv's kids need me." She stood up and walked to the door, but turned back before leaving. "Her husband might be charged with killing her. You'll need to tell the police what you know." Kerben didn't react, and Janet spun on her heel and stalked out of the office and down the hall. She ignored the receptionist's syrupy, "Have a great day," her mind buzzing with information as she stepped on the elevator.

Just before Liv died, Nell's daughter had decided to call the divorce off, maybe even confront Summer with what she'd found out about Eric's supposed affair.

But what did Summer want? It was the final piece of this strange puzzle that had so far left three people dead, and from all Janet could tell, Liv's supposed friend was doing her best to blow up Nell's entire family. But why?

Janet left the elevator mentally exhausted, but there wasn't time for a break. She was late for an appointment at the jail.

CHAPTER FORTY

A crushing weight pressed down on her chest and she felt help-less standing in the jail lobby, tapping her fingers uselessly against her thigh as she waited for the bondsman to show. Kids at her house. Bodies piling up across Knoxville. And here she was, stuck downtown, waiting to spring Nell from lockup. A fourth check of her watch confirmed that the bondsman was still late.

"Janet Black?" A husky voice came from her left, and Janet smelled menthol cigarettes before she turned to find a woman in cargo pants with short brown hair. Her lips were flanked by deep wrinkles, like perfect parentheses, and the unlit cigarette dangling from them straightened when she smiled. "I'm Brighton Levine."

"Brighton Levine? You're the bondsman?"

"Bondswoman, if we're being technical. I've got the paper-work, do you have the credit card?"

Janet held out her Visa and Brighton tucked her cigarette behind her ear, then swiped the card through a reader attached to her phone.

A receipt printed from a small black plastic canister, and

after tearing the paper off, Brighton placed the device back in her bag.

"Do you have an office?" Janet eyed the bag and wondered what else was in there.

"Just my car. All the action takes place out and about. Not too worried about a sixty-eight-year-old woman jumping bail, though." She reached into her bag. "Hate to tase old people, anyway. Their hearts—too fragile."

Janet frowned when the other woman caressed the Taser—she almost seemed excited by the prospect—but she took the paperwork anyway. It wasn't like she could choose someone else to do business with at this point.

"It'll take about twenty minutes. Go ahead and get comfortable."

Janet sighed and after watching Brighton head to the desk, she left the jail lobby for the cool sunshine outside.

―――――

"Here."

Nell sauntered out the front door of the prison as if she'd been inspecting the facility, not spending time inside of it. She held out an envelope to Janet and sat down on the bench next to her.

"What's this?"

"I'd forgotten about it until they gave me my possessions just now. You know they do a strip search even for overnight bookings? That was unexpected."

Janet grimaced and inspected the letter, still clutched in Nell's wrinkled hand. "That's for me?"

"It's from that drug dealer guy. He came to the house—"

"Dave? When?" Janet snatched the envelope out of Nell's hand and turned it over, looking at each side for clues.

"Last night. I was going to drop it off to the bar after my visit with Skylar, but obviously things came up. . ."

"What house?" Janet's stomach dropped, and she swallowed down an acidic taste, like she'd just thrown up.

"Liv's ho—Eric's house, really."

"He came to Eric's house to leave me a note?"

"Well, no. He was looking for Eric, and when I told him he wasn't there, he got all twisted out of shape. Said he had to talk to Eric, but there wasn't time. Then he asked if I was going to see you soon, and when I said yes, he left a note for you."

"What's it say?" Janet asked, a feeling of desperation creeping in.

"As if I'd read another person's note," Nell harrumphed.

"Nell."

"Okay, fine. It says, '*Watch out for Summer.*'"

Janet's chest squeezed tighter still. "Nell, Dave is dead."

"What? Such a nice young man . . . well. He could have been, at least. What happened?"

"Shot to death near his apartment."

"No!" Nell sucked a breath in through her teeth and shook her head. "What do the police say?"

"Nothing, yet. Can you think of anything else about his visit? Anything important?"

"He was real agitated when he first arrived, but he calmed considerably—almost like he'd come to accept something."

"What?"

"What am I, a psychic? I have no idea, I'm just saying he seemed calmer when he left than when he got there."

Janet slid a finger under the flap and shimmied it open, unfolded the letter, and frowned.

Watch out for Summer. Then in smaller letters at the bottom of the page, *Bitch is crazy.*

Janet looked up. The second line could have referred to Summer—or Nell.

"What else happened?"

Nell looked over Janet's head and smirked. "I took his phone."

Janet's head dropped forward into her hands. "How—you know what, never mind. He had no idea?"

"I saw him search his car in the driveway, but he didn't come back in." She shrugged. "What can I say?"

"Where is it?"

Nell unzipped her purse and pawed around in the massive bag before finally pulling out an old flip-style phone. "Drugs must not pay the bills like they used to, huh?"

"It's a prepaid phone. Cheap, disposable. That's probably why he didn't come back in for it. He probably had another ready to go." She pulled her hair back from her face with her free hand. Dave had had Hayley come talk to Janet and at the same time left a note for her, warning her about Summer. Just hours before he'd met his own death, he saw death coming—but for whom?

"Nell, a lot of things have happened since you were arrested last night. I don't think any of us will be safe until the police can track down Summer. You're coming to my house—the kids are already there."

Nell's brow furrowed, but she climbed into Janet's car without a word.

Summer Hughes had already knocked off Liv, and now she'd tried to cover her tracks by killing Dave and Hayley. What else was she planning? Were any of them safe?

Janet wasn't going to take any chances until she knew the answer.

CHAPTER FORTY-ONE

The house was as close to destroyed as Janet had ever seen it—and that included when she and Jason had torn out the old kitchen last year.

Every pillow and cushion was gathered in the family room, the sturdier pieces tilted upright against each other, forming a tunnel along the base of the couch that led to a larger fortress in front of the TV. The blanket from Janet's bed was draped over the biggest cushion-room, and regular flashes of light made their way out of the opening, along with giggling and hoots of laughter.

"You're home!" Jason rushed to hug Janet and threw an arm around Nell and gave her a squeeze, too. "I'm going to run to the . . . to the store. We're out of . . . Uh . . ." He patted his pockets and pulled out a list. "Batteries. Gotta get more batteries. And kid's Tylenol. Bonnie's been pulling on her ear . . ." He winced when a crash issued from the fort. "Your dad and Kaylee pushed back their flight—they'll stop by tomorrow on their way to the airport. Quizz left about half an hour ago. You might never see her again. And I need to—just some quiet somewhere, if I could—"

"Get out of here, Jason. Thank you so much."

Relief flooded his face, and he grabbed his keys from the hall table and backed out of the house.

After he left, Nell peered into the fort, then squinted when a flash of light hit her square in the eyes. "Hey, kids!"

Another shriek from the fort. Janet wasn't sure they'd heard their grandmother.

Nell raised her voice. "Kids! Quiet down!"

A beat of silence, then the loudest burst of laughter yet. A cushion tilted, dangerously close to falling in, but it was quickly straightened from inside, and the laughing resumed.

Nell stepped back and sagged against the door frame, her face red, her breath labored. Janet had filled her in on her suspicions about Summer on the drive over, and rather than galvanizing her, the news seemed to have drained Nell of her remaining energy.

Janet stopped picking up puzzle pieces—where had they come from, anyway?—and walked over. "It's okay. Let them wear themselves out now, maybe everyone'll sleep better tonight."

Nell tried to smile, but it died about halfway to her lips. She pushed herself away from the door frame and took a step forward, then stumbled.

Janet caught her arms and steered Nell over to the couch, then stopped short. There was nowhere to sit.

Amid loud protesting, she picked up the two closest cushions from the tunnel and added them back to the furniture, then she helped Nell sit slowly.

"You need a break!"

"Well I can't take one, and neither can you! Not until O'Dell finds *that woman*."

"Nell, you're exhausted. Go lie down in the guest room. I'll take them to get ice cream." Janet held up a hand to stop Nell's protesting. The other woman was wilting right in front of her. She needed to rest, and even if it was only an hour of silence, it would do Nell good. "I insist. You take a break, and we'll bring back dinner, too."

Nell raised another feeble protest, but Janet already had the keys in her hand. "Come on, kids. Let's go get some ice cream!" The cushions broke apart, falling flat as the blanket sailed overhead. A herd of children galloped to the front door. Bonnie burst into tears and before Janet could ask what was wrong, Brendon stopped and ran back. "You're not last, Bonnie, see, I'm behind you now!" The youngest Birch child immediately cheered and the group trooped out the door ahead of Janet.

"They're amazing, aren't they?" Nell asked weakly from the couch. "I'm not going to be able to do my daughter justice. I just don't have the energy."

"You're here," Janet said, a lump rising in her throat. "That's all that matters. You're here, and you'll do your best. Can't ask for more."

"Of course I can. But it doesn't do any good." Nell leaned back heavily against the newly restored sofa cushion. "Bring me back some mint chocolate chip, huh?"

"Sure." Janet locked the door behind her, then, after making sure Bonnie was latched in, she got behind the wheel. "All right, kids. My mom used to take me to get ice cream on special occasions. What should our special occasion be today?"

"Childhood, as we know it, is over?" Andrea crossed her arms and looked mulishly at Janet through the rearview mirror.

Brendon groaned. "Nice, Andy. Nice." He turned to Janet. "We get to miss school tomorrow?"

Before Janet could tell them that there was no way they were staying home from school, Bonnie piped up from behind her.

"It's Thursday?"

"It's not—you know what?" Janet decided correcting the toddler was pointless. "Yes!" She cranked over the engine and grinned. "Yes! Ice cream for Thursdays!" She slowed to turn at the corner and glanced at Andrea. "And you're still a child. Despite what you've been through this last month, there is lots of fun ahead for you."

But Janet's optimism was short-lived. She hadn't planned

well, and the first ice-cream store they went to was closed. Bonnie threw up in the backseat before they got to the second. Janet climbed out of the car at a light and found a full roll of paper towels in the diaper bag. She ignored the honks and did her best to soak the vomit up off the carpet.

By the time she turned the car into the parking lot of a convenience store, she separated a fifty-dollar bill from her stack of cash and set it aside for a full auto detail. That left them with ten bucks for ice cream.

Andrea watched her brother and sister while Janet washed her hands in the bathroom, plastering on the sunniest smile she could muster as she headed back out to the main store. "Did everyone order?"

Bonnie wailed unexpectedly, and the sound drilled right down into Janet's brain, pulsing behind her right ear. "What's the matter with her?" Janet asked.

Bonnie's sobs ratcheted up to a new, unheard-of level, and she crumpled slowly to the floor. Janet's eyes widened, even as she wanted to plug her ears with her fingers. The child was saying something, but the words were muddy; they sounded like a coffee machine in the last gurgles before the brew is ready.

"Andrea?" Janet looked to the eldest sibling.

She was already checking under tables. "It's Baby Turtle."

Sure enough, the super-soft, extremely well-loved blanket with a head was not attached to Bonnie's right hand.

Janet picked up the stack of coats and searched through them. Bonnie's wailing grew louder, punctuated by occasional hiccups and coughing fits that left the child breathless. Snot ran down her nose and into her mouth. Before Janet could find a napkin, the little girl ran her sleeve across her face, smearing it into her hair. Janet's face contorted with disgust.

"It must be in the car!" Andrea said, glaring at Janet.

"It's not in the car, I just cleaned it from top to bottom!"

"Uh-oh," Brendon said, sitting on a chair with his feet propped on another.

"What?"

"I think it's at home."

"In the fort?" Janet asked, a sudden lightness in her chest. "Bonnie, honey, we'll just eat our ice cream and go right back home to get him."

"Her."

"Her. We'll go right back home and get her."

"Not *your* home," Brendon said. "Our home. I haven't seen Baby Turtle since we left our home this morning!"

They all thought back to the packing and leaving. Bonnie had fallen asleep as they left the house, and had slept in her car seat right though the ride to Janet's. The little girl had become upset right as they'd arrived at Janet's house, but Mel had come to the rescue with the self-defense key chain. Bonnie must have been so enthralled with the strangers and the pillow fort that she'd forgotten Baby Turtle. Until now.

Bonnie had stopped crying, but only to catch her breath. As if on cue, she opened her mouth wide and started screaming again.

"Did you guys want to order something or . . . ," the girl behind the counter said, and looked accusingly at Janet.

She rushed the group through ordering, but it was all wrong. The ice cream was too cold, Brendon's fell off the cone and splattered onto the floor, and Bonnie continued to lie rigid on the floor, her hair wet from the tears that streamed down her face.

"Let's go."

"We'll need a scoop of mint chocolate chip to go." Janet handed the employee her credit card.

"And then we'll stop by the house to get Baby Turtle?" Andrea asked.

"No, we'll just have to distract her. Look, she's already quieted down." Bonnie struggled to sit up and looked around, her eyes wide and glassy from the recent tears. "I think she's going to be okay."

Andrea crossed her arms over her chest. "Three. Two." Janet

wrinkled her nose. What was up with this kid? "One," she finished, and Bonnie wailed anew.

Janet jumped at the onslaught of noise. "We can't go to your house. You know that."

"I heard you tell Grandma Nell that the police are out there looking for Summer, and she knows it. She's not going to show up at our house. Besides, we only need to grab Baby Turtle and leave, then we'll be gone."

Janet took another look at Bonnie, who'd flung her little chubby arms over her eyes and stopped yelling to take another deep breath. "She'll calm down, won't she?"

"She'll keep going until she passes out. Then she'll wake back up and start all over again."

Janet crossed her arms and stared out the window. It was still daylight, and they could be in and out of the house in five minutes. Probably better to do it now than wish she'd done it at three in the morning.

"Okay, guys. Let's go get Baby Turtle."

CHAPTER FORTY-TWO

A gust of wind pushed them up the front walk, and Janet scrambled to find the key, buried in the depths of her bag. When she finally opened the door, she turned to block the kids from entering.

"We have five minutes. I want you to spread out and find Baby Turtle. The one who does gets . . ." She scrunched up her nose, trying to think of a fitting reward, until Brendon interrupted.

"Extra TV time tonight?"

"Yes! Extra TV time," Janet agreed. She held the door open for the children, then twisted the dead bolt after they were all inside. She wasn't going to take any chances, even if they *were* only going to be in the house for five minutes.

Bonnie tottered next to Janet, then used one leg to lever herself up onto the couch. She'd stopped crying as soon as she'd learned they were going to get Baby Turtle, but her face was still streaked with tears and snot, and the little girl was clearly exhausted.

"Baby Turtle," she whimpered.

"Shh, hush, baby. We're going to find it." Janet crouched low to look under the couch. When she stood up, she rubbed her hands up and down her arms. The cold weather outside had followed them in. She glanced around the room and found the thermostat. Though it was set to seventy-eight degrees, the room only registered at sixty-two.

A chill snuck up her spine that had nothing to do with the temperature. She walked back to the couch and picked up Bonnie. "Come on. Let's go find your brother and sister."

Janet walked up the stairs slowly, shifting the baby's weight so that she could see the steps. Just as she reached the upper level of the home, Brendon rushed out of a room, a triumphant grin on his face. "Got it!"

Bonnie took the stuffed animal and laid it out carefully on Janet's shoulder before snuggling in. A small, happy purr hummed from her chest.

Brendon stuck his tongue out and Janet turned to see his older sister. Andrea rolled her eyes. "You get more TV. Big deal."

It was warmer up here, and the house seemed secure. A quick check confirmed that all the windows were closed. So why was she still feeling so jumpy? Janet tried to shrug off the sense of unease. "Okay, great job. Let's get going."

She led the way back downstairs, and on the latest pass through the family room, the gaping black hole of the basement door beckoned her closer. Cold air blew up the steps and smacked her in the face when she reached across the opening to close the door. Her heart beat faster and she bit her lip. "Hello?" She set Bonnie down and turned to the older children. "Andrea, Brendon, keep an eye on Bonnie while I go and check the basement."

The baby howled anew, and Janet jumped at the sudden noise. "What now?"

"Take me!" she wailed.

Janet swallowed hard. "Fine! Just, shush, now. You two go get buckled up. We'll be right out." Bonnie waddled closer and Janet picked her up, then flicked on the overhead light in the stairwell and headed down. It was like entering the walk-in cooler at the bar, and Bonnie snuggled in closer, her hot breath leaving a trail of goose bumps along Janet's neck and down her back. She shivered and Bonnie giggled.

"'Gain!" She breathed hard onto Janet's neck.

Janet shivered again for pretend this time, and the little girl's peal of laughter ricocheted around the enclosed staircase. One final step, and the space opened up to the large rec room.

"Mom-mom." The little girl pointed solemnly to a spot on the floor.

Janet gulped and sidestepped where Liv's body would have lain weeks earlier. Her eyes moved around the basement, then zeroed in on the problem. The door to the backyard, beyond the laundry machines, stood wide open.

As soon as her fingers made contact with the wooden door, it whooshed closed with a terrifyingly loud *bang*. Bonnie whimpered and Janet twisted the dead bolt and the small lock on the doorknob for good measure, then whirled around to face the room. It was still empty. Nothing seemed to be out of place, but as she stood there, the feeling of dread she'd had since walking into the home came into sharper focus.

In the cool, open basement, she realized what was missing. A floral scent had been at the tip of her nose upstairs. Her brain hadn't even really registered it until she got to the cool, clear air in the basement.

"We need to leave right now." She tried to keep the panic out of her voice, but that smell distinctly reminded her of the disgusting rose-scented fragrance Summer had been wearing when they went to lunch, and Janet hurried across the room.

The staircase was ominously dark, and Janet hesitated before putting her foot on the first step. She'd turned that overhead light on just minutes earlier. Now it was off.

Perhaps sensing her strain, Bonnie was quiet. The child's grip around her neck was borderline uncomfortable. Breathing hard under the effort of carrying her, Janet hustled up the stairs, only to skid to a stop on the top landing when she sensed a flash of movement. She gasped and fell back a step as pain sliced down her free arm, her mind simultaneously processing the pain, calculating the closeness of the top of the stairs behind her, and scrambling to figure out how she could protect Bonnie from whatever threat lurked.

Summer stood to the side of the basement door, a tiny pocketknife in her outstretched hand. It might as well have been a machete. Janet had nothing in her arms but a child, and she knew then, with a conviction that surprised her, that she'd do anything at all to protect Bonnie.

Summer sneered and slashed the knife closer to Janet's midsection. "Give me Bonnie," she said, looking greedily at the child, "and I won't hurt you." When Janet glanced at the blood dripping down her arm, Summer added, "Any more than I already have."

Janet tightened her grip on the child. Summer's ensuing laugh was the least cheerful thing she'd ever heard.

"You don't even like kids!" Summer turned her attention to Bonnie. "Come here, sweet pea!" she crooned. "I will take care of you." She held her hand out and her eyes sparkled as she looked at Liv's youngest daughter.

Bonnie stuck her tongue out and the cooing that had died on Summer's lips turned into a howl as her knife slashed forward.

"I will not lose now!" Summer's nostrils flared as she faced Janet again. "I have worked too hard for this to end now, when I'm so close to what I want."

Janet couldn't tear her eyes away from the other woman, but she needed to know—where were Andrea and Brendon? Safe? Dead? Oh, God, why hadn't she listened to Jason? To O'Dell? "Why are you here?"

"I came to get what's mine. What I've worked so hard to get for these past six months."

"What did you do? What did you do to Liv?"

Summer's eyes glittered dangerously as her fingers tapped

against the knife. "Don't we all deserve to be happy? To enjoy life?"

"I think we get what we deserve." Janet turned her body to the side to shield Bonnie in case Summer struck again. But her arm throbbed, and the fingers in her right hand were starting to tingle. Her eyes darted around; the living room seemed empty. Had the other kids made it outside to safety? Would they stay there?

"You're right, we *do* get what we deserve." Summer nodded, and the crazy spark in her eyes intensified.

"Liv trusted you with her kids—at least, she did for a while. But she was on to you at the end. Did you know that?"

"No!" Summer snapped. "She didn't know what to believe at the end, she was confused. But she was too close to the truth. Just like you are now!"

The counselor was veering off the rails, and Janet didn't want to end up at the bottom of the stairs like Liv. She needed to calm the situation. "What happened to you, Summer? You seemed to have it all together when I first met you, but I know you served time in prison. What happened that got you so far off track all those years ago?"

Summer backed away, stopping when she bumped into the back of the couch behind her. "What happened?" She bit her lip. "I've spent a lot of time thinking about that over the years. What happened." She laughed, but there wasn't any humor in the sound. "It was... it was a dumb, run of the mill car accident. A broken ankle. No big deal. But the doctor prescribed morphine for the pain." Summer shook her head, still unable to believe her luck so many years later. "Morphine, for a sore ankle! That was it. I was done."

"What do you mean? You got—addicted to the pain meds?"

"Yes, and once the prescription ran out, I got my fix other ways."

"Is that how you met Dave?"

"That's exactly how I met Dave." She spit out his name like a swear word. "So he was my undoing—and in the end, what saved me." At Janet's questioning look she elaborated. "He sold me out to the cops to avoid going to jail himself. I sobered up behind bars—had no other choice, obviously...but still, he owed me. I guess now we're even." Her grim smile made Janet shiver.

"What does that have to do with Liv? With her kids?" Janet asked, trying to keep Summer talking. She needed time—time to find a way out of this mess.

"My sentence was almost over, I was almost free after serving my time." Summer's eyes glazed over, as if in her mind she was back in the courtroom—back in jail. "My counselor told me I needed to visualize where life went wrong so I could fix it."

"And what did you come up with?" Janet's eyes darted around the room, looking for something to use as a weapon.

"A date. It was the last normal thing in my, at that time, normal life. A date with Eric. We'd met up at a coffee shop. The accident happened as I drove myself home. So, obviously, Eric was the answer. When I got out, I found him. Of course by then he was married. Liv remembered me from our time at Community. But Eric? He didn't remember me.

"Here he was, the key to the last time I was happy—*and he didn't remember me at all?*" She blinked back to the present day, back to the room, the knife, the baby. "That's when I realized, I didn't want *him*—just a chance to start over with a family I missed out on having. Of course Liv was in the way of that. Eric was, too."

She folded the knife in and out of its handle; the repeated click seemed to count off the number of people Summer had killed.

Click. Liv.

Click. Hayley.

Click. Dave.

Click. Brendon? Andrea? Janet took in a shaky breath. Maybe herself?

"You worked for a long time on this plan, didn't you? But

how did you work things out with Hayley? To set the divorce in motion?"

Summer frowned. If Janet knew, it was possible that others did, too. Police. Prosecutors. She shook her head and refocused on her current prey.

"You forget what a small town this is. I don't know how I forgot that, but I did." She rubbed her eyes. "Hayley was my roommate in that hellish halfway house. I was ready to be on my own, but not everyone there was. When we met, Hayley was still drooling at the memory of drugs. I just planted the idea that I could help her if she helped me. She jumped at the chance, okay? Jumped.

"But I didn't realize—how could I have?—that Hayley would get assigned a new roommate who'd been friends with Liv in high school. Hayley must have told her what she'd done for me. And Skylar was going to ruin everything! Tell Liv. And I had Liv eating out of my hand by then! I'd convinced her to get the life insurance policy that will make this new way of living so much easier after Eric goes to jail and I become the children's guardian. You should have seen the way she was sobbing when she signed the forms. 'My life is over.'" Summer's face contorted into an awful rendition of crying. "She was weak, and she knew it."

"So that's why the signature looked like a forgery." Janet's head pounded in time with her oozing wound. Liv was so devastated to be planning her new divorced life, she could hardly sign the form.

Summer's eyes glinted, the knife glittered, and she kept talking, almost in a trance. "Some people never get rid of that hungry look. I thought Hayley wouldn't. But apparently her small errand for me left a bad taste in her mouth. Made her want to take the high road later. I couldn't have that! It wouldn't work!"

"Where did you get the drugs?"

Summer snorted. "You can get a roofie on just about any street corner—"

"Not the roofie for Eric. The bad heroin for Liv."

"I told you, some people are desperate to believe in second chances. Dave and I met after I got out. He'd been holding on to the tainted drugs for ages—debating whether he should go to the police and confess after those men died. I told him not to be ridiculous and that I would get rid of it for him. And really, in a way, I did.

"In the end, all of you knew too much."

Janet didn't like how Summer was referring to her in the past tense already, but before she could correct the other woman, Summer flicked the knife back to attention and advanced on Janet.

"Was Eric in on the plan?"

Summer halted. Her face scrunched distastefully. "Eric's too dumb to know anything. And he never will." The lines around her eyes smoothed out and she smiled. "He'll be in jail taking the blame for Liv's death. And little Bonnie is too young to understand what's happening."

"What about Brendon? Andrea?" Janet asked, holding her breath.

"Why would they know anything? I'll walk out of here with Bonnie and they'll never know what happened to you. Never."

Janet sagged against the door frame. Summer didn't know that the other children had come to the house with her that day. That meant they were safe—for now. So what was Janet going to do to keep them that way?

CHAPTER FORTY-THREE

Janet slowly lowered Bonnie to the ground and stepped in front of the child. Her arm throbbed; she felt each beat in her head, in her chest, even in her toes. She unclenched her jaw and tried to speak as if they were back at the restaurant in Market Square. Maybe if she remained calm, Summer would, too. "So what happened? Liv didn't suddenly decide to shoot up heroin, did she?"

"No, of course not." The other woman studied the knife handle, the mad humor gone.

"Did you just—" Janet looked sideways at the basement staircase and her stomach turned as hollow as the opening behind her. It was too terrible to think of doing that to another person . . . and yet. "Did you push her down the stairs in her own house?"

Summer looked up, her expression clinical. "She was making wild accusations after talking to Skylar. Liv was threatening to call the police! But Skylar's a user, and I told Liv she'd be crazy to listen to someone like that. I asked her to meet with me, to give me a chance to tell my side of the story." She snorted. "See? Second chances again." She glanced at the stairwell. "It was quick. I made sure of it. One little shove, then I followed her down with a syringe. It should have worked. A terrible accident. Such a tragedy."

Janet would have laughed at the gross miscalculation if her life wasn't on the line. "You didn't know the washer was broken, did you?"

"You plan something for weeks—months even—and something as dumb as a broken washing machine sends things spiraling out of control!" Summer groaned. "It was supposed to have looked like an accident—a missed step, sad but understandable when she was carrying all that laundry. How in the hell would I have known the machine was broken—or that a mother of three didn't deign to do laundry in her own house? But because of the damn broken machine, the police looked into things more thoroughly, and they noticed that little puncture in her arm, and I knew my plan was in trouble."

A flicker of something fired in the back recesses of Janet's brain. "And you planted the syringe in the bathroom trash can later, didn't you?"

"I got rid of the original—no one was supposed to know about it. But when they launched an investigation, I couldn't have the police think that Liv shot up on her own, could I? So I planted the idea with Nell that Eric could go to jail for giving Liv drugs. I had to make sure they locked on to Eric. So I put another needle in the trash can when I saw you and Nell drive up that day. Made up that lie about Crayons clogging the downstairs toilet, so Nell would have to go upstairs. It couldn't have been easier." Her smile made Janet's skin crawl. "With Nell's history of stealing, I knew *she'd* never get the kids, and there I was, being so helpful to Eric after his wife died. I was the one he'd turn to when he needed somewhere safe for the children. Me."

"There is no happily ever after for you. You must have realized that by now." Bonnie clung to Janet's legs, and she took a small shuffle step forward, to put some distance between the girl and the steep staircase. Unfortunately, that move also took her closer to a deranged woman with a knife.

Summer nodded, almost to herself. Her expression cleared, and she gripped the knife firmly again. "I am making my own happily ever after. No one is going to do it for me. I've learned that much since going to prison." Her tongue folded against the back of her teeth as she stared at the ultimate prize. Bonnie peeked out from behind Janet's leg and whimpered as Summer took a step forward.

Janet knew she had to act now and decisively, just like Mel had taught her. This wasn't self-defense; this was all about going on the offensive, and she'd only get one chance to keep Bonnie safe. To keep the other kids safe. She lunged forward. Summer's eyes widened slightly as Janet's arm struck out toward the other woman's windpipe.

Summer was fast—faster than a drunk customer ever would have been—and Janet's hand missed the other woman completely. She lost her footing and sprawled clumsily over the couch and rolled onto the floor.

Bonnie cried out, startled, and in the moment Janet looked back to check on her, Summer whirled around and kicked her in the ribs. Air whooshed out of her chest as if it were a burst balloon and she scrambled to get up, her injured arm affording her zero help as she tried to push off the floor.

Her brain felt fuzzy, the pain pulsing in time with her heartbeat, but she braced her feet and prepared to kick out, using all the power left in her body. Instead she jerked back when the knife whizzed by her face, so closely she could feel it graze her hair.

"Jesus!" Janet yelled. Anger bubbled up over her fear. Going for the face seemed well out of bounds.

Summer's miss meant she was the unsteady one now, and Janet's foot aimed for the inside of the other woman's knee. But again, Summer was too fast. She sidestepped the kick and swiped her elbow down on Janet's already injured arm. A crack echoed through the room—or maybe just in her head—like a gunshot. She dropped to the floor between the couch and coffee table, unable to move.

Summer threw her head back and laughed. The sound was unbalanced, raw, and ugly.

Janet moved her head, trying to find Bonnie, but from her vantage point, she could only see under the coffee table. The four legs—one with a sizable crack where the joint met the table —jutted down like tent poles, buried into the dirty shag carpet.

Liv's murderer leaned down, only stopping when her face was inches from Janet's. Her smile grew wide. She drew the knife back for one final blow but stopped when Janet said, "Was Dave angry when he found out what you used the drugs for? Is that why you killed him?"

Her eye twitched and the grin froze on her face.

"He liked Liv," Janet continued. "He wasn't happy that she died from his bad batch. The police know, Summer. They know. I made sure of it."

Summer's smile drooped until her lips finally pressed together in a flat line, and she stood up tall again, putting some physical distance between them. She raised one eyebrow and shrugged, forcing a slight smile back onto her face. "The police won't find any phone records connecting me and Dave in the last decade. You, on the other hand?" She grinned again. "You'll be the suspect, Janet. Not me. Don't you see? I've set it all up perfectly. You bought drugs from Dave, then met him on your own in a dark alley. Days later, he's dead?" She tutted. "Very suspicious, I think." She pushed her hair away from her forehead and stared hard at Janet. "I admit the police finding your body at Liv's house won't be ideal. But this can still work, I can still make this happen. You'll be dead and I can write the narrative! You . . ." Her wild eyes brightened as she tried to come up with a new plan. "You felt so guilty about Dave's death that you killed yourself! Yes, that's exactly what happened. I'll make sure of it."

Summer's over-bright eyes were hard to look at, and instead,

Janet focused on her lips, trembling with excitement. Liv's former friend had gone off the deep end, and the only thing that cheered Janet, albeit slightly, was that Summer was now entering *her* realm of expertise; subduing drunk and otherwise impaired people. One thing kept repeating over and over in her brain; *keep her talking.*

"How do you even know I met Dave—" As the pain numbed, Janet's brain started firing again, and she looked at Summer with new respect. "You planted his phone number in Eric's wallet, didn't you?"

"In his wallet?" Another peal of crazy town laugher split the air and from somewhere in the distance, Bonnie whimpered again. "I put Dave's number everywhere for *Eric* to find—I needed him to have a connection to a drug dealer for my plan to work. I wrote that phone number on the whiteboard on the refrigerator, a Post-it note next to the TV. And then somehow—Nell intercepts the one that was in Eric's wallet? Oh, that's just too perfect.

"Another unforeseen hitch in the plan. But in the end, it was still going to work out. I followed Dave to your parking lot, saw Nell make the buy. It was just more ammo to keep her away from the kids. *My plan can still work!*" Her eyes were bright; she leaned back down close to Janet's face again. "I'm sorry it has to come to this." There was real regret in her voice, and for a moment, Janet felt sorry for her. Sorry that she lived such a sad life, her happiness based on taking away from others instead of making her own. "Do you have any last words?" Summer looked down solemnly, her fingers twitching on the knife again.

"You won't be happy, Summer. You can't be. Not by forcing yourself into someone else's life. That's just not how it works. You can't make all the rules and hope that everyone just falls in line! You can only be happy by coming up with the rules togeth-er." Janet rested her head back against the carpet and turned away from the woman who was about to kill her. Bonnie's feet peeked out from the far side of the couch—the little girl was hiding. No matter what happened, she'd have nightmares for years to come from this day. Janet closed her eyes. "Life is change, Summer." She thought of Nell's words from weeks ago, and knew with surprising clarity that the older woman had been right. "You have to be ready to make those changes work for you, or make more changes until you get it right. What you're doing here? It will never work. You won't be happy, and neither will the kids."

Janet thought about Jason, about her dad and his new fiancée. She thought about Andrea and Brendon and hoped they were hiding or had left the house altogether. She thought about her bar, and her customers and employees there, who all felt like family. Cindy Lou, Nell, Elizabeth, Mel. And now here she was, lying prone on the floor in a dead woman's house, about to die on dirty shag carpeting next to a broken coffee table.

A spark of hope kindled in her gut as she studied the coffee table's cracked leg. She chanced a look at Summer, then, easily allowing the real fear she felt to color her voice, asked, "Where did Bonnie go?" When Summer's head whipped around, Janet reached up. Using her good arm, she grabbed the nearest leg of the coffee table and pulled with all her might. She'd heard it crack apart at the house a week earlier, and sure enough, as she gasped through another stab of pain, it snapped off in her hand. Summer turned back just as Janet stood and smashed the makeshift club down on her head. Hard.

Summer's last, predatory expression slid off her face as fast as her body dropped to the ground. The carpet muffled the sound of the fall, except when her head hit the unsteady coffee table with a thump. Summer lay on the floor, not moving.

"Better than a windpipe smash, and just as good as a goddamn beer bottle." Janet dropped the club next to Summer's unconscious form and slumped against the nearest wall. A smear of blood cut a sharp contrast against the white paint, and a steady stream still oozed out of the gash in her arm. She pressed on the wound, but the pain that seared up her arm left her breathless.

The front door blasted open on a gust of wind and faraway sirens sliced through the quiet room. Andrea stood at the threshold, holding a baseball bat in trembling arms.

Janet slid down the wall. "It's okay. We're going to be okay."

"I called the police," she said, still holding the bat aloft. "They're on their way."

Brendon appeared from behind her, just as a gentle snore came from the far side of the couch. Andrea bent down and laid a hand across Bonnie's forehead. "Baby Turtle works every time."

Brendon walked forward and leaned over Summer's inert body. His hand snaked out toward her coat pocket and he shoved something inside it before he backed up to his sisters.

"What are you doing?" Janet squinted, her vision blurry from pain.

"Just returning her pen. Grandma Nell took it by mistake a while ago, and I wanted to give it back."

Nell had said that one of the children had been putting items she took back in their rightful places—it looked like Brendon was that kid. He must have seen Nell take the pen and had just been waiting for the right moment to return it. Janet's head dropped back and she closed her eyes, and as her heart rate slowed, she listened to the wail of the sirens get closer.

CHAPTER FORTY-FOUR

The doctor frowned as her fingers probed the irritated and swollen flesh near the wound on Janet's left arm.

"Does this hurt?"

"Yessss," Janet hissed.

"Well, you're definitely lucky. The knife missed your major arteries, and the bones aren't broken." She snapped her gloves off and picked a tablet up off the table, then studied the readout from an X-ray image again. "The radiologist says we're looking at bone contusions on your distal ulna. That's going to be very sore for two to four weeks." She turned back to face Janet. "And it looks like you've got a pretty recent scar on the pointer finger of that hand. I'm sending our social worker in to talk to you, but you can talk to me, too, if you need help." She raised her eyebrows and waited for Janet to speak.

"Oh no—nothing like that—"

They both turned at a gentle tap on the door.

"You done in here, doc?"

The doctor looked between O'Dell and Janet, then tucked the tablet under her arm. "Maureen is very nice—trustworthy. She'll be in to talk in about fifteen minutes. Detective, she's all yours."

O'Dell stared out into the hallway for a moment after they were alone. "You've got quite a crew waiting for you out there. Your father's trying to get a court order to get past the nurses' station. I thought he was going to deck me out there."

Janet had to tamp down a grin. It was nice to have a father agitated on your behalf. The feeling died, though, when O'Dell moved closer and perched on the edge of the hospital bed.

"Summer is under guard at UT Medical Center across town. Grade-three concussion and a broken elbow. A judge is coming in to arraign her from her hospital bed on three counts of first-degree murder."

"The kids?" Janet winced when she tried to adjust her position and fell back against the bed with a groan. O'Dell jumped up and fluffed her pillow awkwardly before stepping back.

"They're going to be okay. Andrea and Brendon had just climbed into your car when they saw Summer walk around from the backyard. They ducked down to the floorboards to hide, and when Summer entered the house, they ran to a neighbor's to call 911. They had to try five different houses before someone answered the door, and even then, it took a minute for the stranger to believe that there was a crisis. Our cruisers were there within four minutes of getting the call for help. But if you hadn't been able to take care of yourself and Bonnie, we would have been too late." O'Dell's pale face looked haggard. Janet remembered that he'd started the day hungover, and things had gone downhill from there.

"Those kids are amazing."

"So are you."

When she glanced up at O'Dell, his cheeks turned pink.

Janet reached for a large Styrofoam cup of water on her table, but O'Dell got there first and gently guided the straw to her lips. She took a long sip and sighed as the icy water slid down her throat. "How is Skylar?"

"Skylar?" O'Dell placed the cup back on the table and perched at the edge of the mattress. "I'm working on getting her into an inpatient drug treatment facility. She says she's ready, for real this time, to try and get clean. I think everything that happened might just scare her straight this time around."

"What about Eric?"

"Released with no charges, after we got a call from a Bonnie Kerben." He plucked a small notebook from his pocket and studied the cover. "We should have—*I* should have listened to you from the start."

"You can make it up to me easily."

"Oh, yeah? How?" O'Dell leaned close, and even through her pain, Janet's heart rate increased.

"By supporting my PI candidacy in the next board meeting for the Tennessee Department of Commerce and Insurance."

O'Dell sat back and nodded slowly. "Yeah. I can see that. I'll do it."

———

After a week of recovery at home, Janet fled back to work, delighted to return to the Spot. She'd had too much of William, and his hammering and yammering. She was only going in for an hour, to see how the stitches in her arm would feel during a shift of bartending.

Janet slammed the car door, and as she approached the bar, a warm sense of belonging filled her soul. But when she opened the door, that feeling evaporated.

Cindy Lou stood next to Mel, both women grinning ridiculously at her. What was wrong with them? Then she saw William sitting next to Nell at the bar. Both with absurdly cheerful, brightly colored frozen cocktails at hand.

Janet scowled when she caught sight of the frozen margarita machine churning on the bar, taking up prime seating spots. She had been gone a week and someone had seen fit to change the very nature of her business into one that served happy little frozen drinks? What was the world coming to?

"Janet?"

Jason dropped down to one knee as soon as she looked toward the sound of his voice. Her father and Kaylee stood off to his left, smiling too. The blood froze in her veins, and her jaw dropped.

"Janet," he repeated earnestly from down low. He held something small in one hand, and even as she gasped, he lifted the blue velvet box up toward her.

Her heart felt weak, like she might faint. She shot an accusing look at Cindy Lou, who had the gall to smile bigger.

She didn't want to do this, not in front of a crowd, but if Jason was going to force the issue, she had no problem pushing right back. "Jason, stop right there!"

"Darlin'," he said, ignoring her completely, but before she could object again, he opened the box. A folded up piece of white paper was inside.

"What is that?"

He smoothed it flat against his bent leg. "Will you sign this, completing the sale of my half of our business over to you, and pay me one cent to make it official?" She didn't answer, just stared blankly into his eyes. "Will you continue to be your own goddamn obnoxiously independent woman, who also occasionally allows me to be the chivalrous, loving, and caring boyfriend I long to be?"

"Wh—" The sound puffed out of her mouth, but she didn't have enough breath to sustain an entire word.

"And when the bar is all yours, will you still let me drink here for free?"

She laughed, then gasped when the movement rocked her body and the wound in her arm protested the unexpected jolt. Jason looked expectantly at her, a pen in one hand, the sale paperwork in the other. She bit her lip and stepped forward, a wide smile spread across her face. "Yes! Yes, I will, Jason!"

He stood and slid the paper across the closest table. She signed with a flourish, then Mel signed on the witness line.

After the initial congratulations had passed, Mel pulled her aside. "This came for you in the mail today." She held out a white business envelope.

"Can you just throw it in the office? I'll deal with all the bills when I'm back full-time next week."

"I think you should take a look at this one now."

Mel held it up and the sender's address leapt off the page. Tennessee Department of Commerce and Insurance. She raised her eyebrows at Mel, who shrugged in return. "Want me to open it?"

Janet snatched it away and grumbled that she could open her own damn mail, *thankyouverymuch.*

She unfolded the letter and then smiled. "I've been awarded a temporary license to operate as a private investigator while I continue my apprenticeship with Quizz Bexley."

A small slip of paper fell out of the envelope. Janet bent to pick it up and gaped when she read the handwritten note. "This is from Gary Donaldson's admin." She scanned the note once and then a second time.

"Well?" Mel prompted.

"It says he's been placed on administrative leave for not following department procedures in my case." She looked up. "She says Donaldson made the anonymous complaint against me himself, based on a personal issue." She chortled out a laugh. "O'Dell owes me so big."

Before Mel could react, Janet's father walked over. He and Kaylee had hung back after Jason's "proposal."

"Congratulations, Janet," her father said, one arm still wrapped around his fiancée.

Janet grinned at Mel, then turned to smile at her father and Kaylee, too. "New beginnings for all of us this year." Jason hugged her carefully on her good side and she felt at home. "But let's not go crazy here. The margarita machine has to go."

Jason squeezed her tight. "Obviously."

Cindy Lou filled a rocks glass with the frozen drink and

passed it over. Janet took a sip. "I mean, that's just terrible." She took another, longer drink, then a third. "Really, really bad."

Cindy Lou grinned. "Sure, boss. I can tell how much you hate it."

"Oh, fine. It can stay—as long as you do, Cindy Lou."

"Then we're good." Cindy Lou smiled.

"Yes we are." Janet scowled. "Now get back to work, everyone!" As her employees—*her* employees—headed to different parts of the room, Janet couldn't keep the happy grin from her face. All was right with the world again—or at least her little corner of it.

A JANET BLACK MYSTERY

LAST CHANCE

LIBBY KIRSCH

LAST CHANCE

PROLOGUE

His hands trembled and the first match dropped to the ground, unlit. Swearing, he plucked another stick from the orderly row and swiped it roughly across the strike plate once, twice, three times. Nothing. *Stupid cheap party favor.* He frowned and dropped the useless match to the ground.

The sharp smell of gasoline burned his nose and his head was growing fuzzy from the fumes. He tore another match from the book and pressed his finger near the head as he pulled it across the narrow friction strip.

An initial spark of heat forced his finger back as the fire caught the end of the match. He held it up at eye level and watched the pulsing, blazing flame dance in front of his eyes. Then he assessed the chaos around him in the dark room—the blood, the blond hair, the mess—and a smile spread across his face.

They'd see. They'd understand soon.

He dropped the match and the sudden force of heat pushed him out of the room. Swiping the red bandana off the floor as he stumbled across the tile to the door, he ignored the banging from the walk-in cooler and tripped out of the building into the dark alleyway.

The parking lot lamps next door spilled light across his path, and he crouched in the shadow of the dumpster. He wouldn't stay here long, but he had time to wait. All he had was time.

The quiet night was broken as the roaring fire built higher and hotter, right in front of his eyes. When the building burned orange at the edges, when the heat was intense enough to make his eyes water, only then did he pick up his cell phone.

"911, what is your emergency?"

"Fire at the abandoned restaurant down on Retreat Road," he croaked out, both trying to mask his voice and because the smoke had gotten deeper into his lungs than he'd anticipated.

"What is the address of the fire, sir?" The dispatcher's dispassionate voice was the opposite of his own mounting emotions.

"I don't know the address. It's in the building next to the Spot. I think there's a woman inside."

"Why do you think that?"

He didn't answer. Just launched the piece of plastic and glass, metal and microchips into the flames.

Before the phone completed its arc to destruction *he* came. Running, yelling, looking like the hero he longed to be, he came.

"Oh no—what—how did this—" Jason's eyes were glued to the red glow coming from inside. He skirted the sides of the building, disappearing for a minute on the far side, before he came back into view. He found a hose, and cranked the spigot around, only to yell in frustration when he realized the hose wasn't connected, and the water shot uselessly to the ground before turning to steam.

As if a garden hose could stop his handiwork.

As Jason's hands flew up to his head, clutching his hair in horror, he slowly walked around the perimeter, as if in shock.

That's when the man watching made his way back into the burning building, taking care to lock the door behind him. There'd be no room for heroes today.

He caught sight of Jason's face through the flames as the

door closed. The last thing he saw was the red and white flashing lights of the fire trucks arriving.

It was too late, of course. Jason didn't know yet, but he would. It was only a matter of time.

He drummed his fingers against each other, still watching, always watching, from the relative safety of the kitchen; scanning the perimeter, watching the chaos that he'd unleashed.

Had he made any mistakes? He sighed. Yes, there were definite loose ends, but he had to hope things went according to plan. Would anyone notice the final piece of the plan as it came together? Surely not. Not with flames growling twenty feet into the air. Not with four fire trucks' lights flashing and spinning. Not with hoses connected and crowds gathering.

He waited until he was sure they knew. Until he could see the pain etched across Jason's face. Until he could see the terror in his trembling hands.

A team of firefighters gathered at the edge of the parking lot, coming up with their own plan. It was futile. You couldn't win against the initial surge of flames, the heavy, choking smoke. How long would it take to find them? Minutes? Hours?

He looked back at her limp, lifeless body. Her blond hair glowing red against the flames marching steadily toward her.

A blast shook the building, and the windows in the main dining room shattered.

"No, n-no. No!" Jason's cry echoed across the parking lot, sound trembling until it was sucked into the burned-out building along with Jason's hopes and dreams.

He shuddered against the heat, but felt a smile stretch across his face.

Jason deserved this.

Even Jason knew it.

CHAPTER ONE

One Month Earlier

The office was, predictably, a mess. The manila file folders stacked halfway up the wall listed precariously off center, and Janet Black carelessly rifled through one stack after another until she found what she was looking for and groaned.

"Really? Another identity theft case?"

Quizz Bexley adjusted her ball cap and grinned, her hair puffing out from the sides of her hat like purple wings. "Don't knock it. Those cases are our bread and butter." She adjusted the purple frames of her glasses. When Janet looked at her watch, Quizz said, "Oh no you don't. You owe me another hour today. Thirty minutes, at least!" she added hastily when Janet groaned again.

Janet threw herself down onto the couch and winced. The cushions might as well have been made of concrete for how much they gave when her body hit. She bounced more than sunk. She should be at her bar, the Spot, getting ready for a busy night. She *should* be preparing for her boyfriend's mother to arrive in Knoxville from Memphis for what was sure to be an exhaustingly revealing visit, crowding into the home they also shared with Jason's father—who they couldn't seem to shake after his parents had divorced and he'd moved in with them months ago for what was supposed to have been a week—maybe two—max.

Instead, she tucked her brown hair behind her ears and crossed one leg over the other, then flipped the file open across her lap and leaned back to scan the forms inside.

"Who investigates ID theft anyway? I mean, you just get your money back from the bank, close that credit card and move on with your life, right?"

"Sometimes. But what happens when the thief continues to use your social security number to get new credit cards?" Quizz asked.

"Jerks."

"Exactly. Jerks that we investigate and turn over to police."

"If we can stay awake long enough." Janet rubbed her neck and then grabbed a highlighter from the table and passed the bright yellow ink over the most salient information on the papers in front of her. When she'd gleaned all she could from the credit form, she headed to her own computer to type up some notes on the case.

Soon the only sounds inside the small, cramped office were keys tapping and Janet's stomach grumbling.

She jumped when the shrill ringing of the phone cut through the air. Quizz swiveled away from her extension, her laptop balancing on her knees, so Janet reached across the small space to pick up the receiver.

"Hello, Bexley and Associates."

Quizz snorted. The company name was actually Bexley Investigations, but Janet was in the early stages of her apprenticeship to become a PI, and the approval of her permanent license hung on her finishing the required hours with a qualified pro. If she was going to be here, working for free, she hated to feel like a secretary answering the phone, so she embellished the name when she answered.

She grinned at Quizz while the person on the other end of the line stumbled through their own greeting.

"Yes, hi. Uh—umm, hi. I'm looking for Janet?"

"This is Janet with Bexley and Associates. How can I help you?"

Quizz smirked and got up, then motioned to the door, and likely the bathroom at the end of the hall.

Janet settled into her uncomfortable seat. Whatever was waiting on the other end of the line had to be more compelling than a two-week-old identity theft case. After all, some of the most interesting things in life were difficult to explain succinctly. This could be good.

———

Quizz walked back into the office twenty minutes later to find the phone still pressed firmly to Janet's ear. She had three pages of notes scrawled on a yellow steno pad on the desk.

"Yes ma'am. I think we can really hit the ground running on this one and make a difference for you."

Quizz's brow furrowed and her eyes narrowed. Her nose wrinkled; in fact, her whole face shrunk by two inches in circumference as Janet watched, bemused.

"How many missing persons cases have we solved?" Janet repeated the client's question and looked at Quizz, her eyebrows raised.

Her mentor's eyes widened comically and she groaned. "None. We don't take missing persons cases."

Janet turned away. "Not many, ma'am, but we're a small firm and devoted to helping in cases like yours."

"Cases like whose?"

Janet peeked over her shoulder and saw Quizz advancing on her.

"We don't do missing persons cases. Period. We don't have the manpower."

Janet covered the mouthpiece, but it was too late. The woman on the other end of the line sniffled and said, "Who is that? Is that true? No—n-n-no missing persons cases?"

"It *was* true," Janet said. "But our firm recently doubled in size, and we're now more than happy to take on this kind of case."

"Oh, thank you." The woman blew her nose, and when she came back on the line her voice was steadier. "And you'd like which documents again?"

"We'll need anything you think might be relevant. Medical records, police reports, just bring copies of it all to me by close of business today, okay?" Janet glared back at Quizz when her boss popped a hand on her hip. She kept her voice soft, though, when she addressed the grieving mother. "I look forward to meeting you in person. Hopefully we can bring Lola back home."

"Lola?" Quizz said when Janet had hung up. "We don't do missing persons cases, especially not for girls named *Lola*." She shuddered visibly and dropped into her seat with a *thunk*. "You may be slowly taking over, but I do still get a say in some things."

"This case is special."

"Why? Because the mother sounds sad?" Quizz shook her head. "Well, I hate to burst your bubble, but they're all sad. The mothers, the fathers, the brothers. Even the dogs—you've never seen a sadder set of relatives than those of a missing girl."

"Yeah, but this is completely out of character for her! She's a star student, not some girl who'd up and take off with a boyfriend! I think she's in trouble."

Quizz's brow wrinkled again. "No one can sell a case like a mother, Janet. You don't know what's true yet and what the mother only *hopes* is true. So, I'm sorry, no dice. We're not taking the case."

Janet packed up her bag silently but turned back to Quizz before leaving the office. "I want to help."

"Missing persons cases are lose-lose," Quizz groaned. "Always have been. Most missing people don't want to be found. Also, there's no money in it! ID thefts—they pay the bills."

"But a solved missing persons case could put us on the map."

"But only if we find her!"

"And we will!

Quizz blew out a sigh as Janet twisted the knob and walked through the door. "I know you're not used to it, but I am the boss in this office. My word is the word. I know *that*, at least, is something you understand. And I'll tell the mother that myself when she comes in later today."

"No you won't!" Janet grinned. "I'm having her meet me at the bar. That's my domain."

The last sound Janet heard before the door slammed shut was Quizz laughing incredulously, and Janet thought, admiringly. Maybe.

CHAPTER TWO

Janet pulled up to the Spot and parked at the back of the smaller side lot. Walking over a grassy embankment, then across another parking lot, she gave the abandoned restaurant next door a dirty look. The buildings were 200 feet apart—and sometimes that felt like a long way; other times it felt stiflingly close. She turned her back on the eyesore, then made her way leisurely into the bar. They'd opened an hour ago, and sure enough, a few regulars were already parked inside.

Her eyes lingered on the frozen margarita machine whirling away on the main countertop in the middle of the room and she frowned. Jason's mother had bought the monstrosity when Janet had been home recovering from an injury, and though it was growing on her—helped in large part by the fact that margaritas had become one of their most lucrative drinks on the menu—she still didn't like how much space the machine took up.

"Hey, boss, how's it goin'?" Cindy Lou sipped sweet tea from a long straw. Her bleached hair was pulled half back that day, and long false eyelashes batted every time the assistant manager of the bar blinked. She wore short shorts and an ultra-tight V-neck T-shirt. The entire outfit left very little to the imagination, but

Janet assumed it sparked plenty of dreams for Cindy Lou's target audience.

Past Cindy Lou, Mel came out of the bathroom, still rubbing her hands on a paper towel. She tossed the wadded-up paper into the air, banked it off the side of the Beerador—a seven-foot tall bottle-shaped refrigerator that sat behind the bar—and the towel landed in a trash can.

"Two points." Mel nodded and reached into one of the many pockets in her cargo shorts. She typed something into her phone and dropped it back into the pocket.

If Cindy Lou was dressed to impress, Mel was dressed to get stuff done. The bouncer's Doc Martens and shorts were work-horse pieces, and her loose, boxy T-shirt gave her plenty of room to move around without feeling restricted. She wore a ball cap on her head with the garishly bright University of Tennessee colors and logo.

"Just got off the phone with Nell," Cindy Lou said, propping her hip against the countertop. "She was sorry to miss you but wanted me to tell you two things. One, no one better be sitting in her seat."

All three looked over to Nell's regular barstool and Janet grinned to see it was empty. No surprise at that hour, but she loved that her most loyal customer considered it *her* chair.

"And, two, she's having a great time on the cruise with her grandkids and son-in-law."

Nell had gone through a difficult period last month, and she needed some time away to bond with her family. Janet's heart felt happy at the news, but she was distracted by the customer sitting near Nell's seat.

"Booker, what are you doing here?" The traffic cop perched on a seat just two away from Nell's regular spot. He was a regular but wasn't usually in so early.

He grinned and spread his arms wide. "I'm the official scout for the FOP dart tournament."

"Oh, yeah? And is the Fraternal Order of Police interested in having it here?"

He nodded and Cindy Lou squealed.

"I knew adding those dartboards was a good idea. Didn't I say that, Janet?"

"Well, hold up." Booker scratched his head. "We usually serve a buffet of sorts at the tournament. Bosses don't like when all we offer is alcohol, you know?"

"Oh." Cindy Lou's shoulders drooped, but only for a moment. "We'll order pizza. And wings! It'll be great!"

"Can you quote me a price, Janet? Looks like around twenty in the tournament and their dates." Booker drained his beer and tapped the bar with his palm. "By the end of the week would be great."

As he left, he held the door open for another customer. The woman who walked in was a stranger; her short, wiry yellow hair was frizzy at the ends and stuck out in every direction. A shawl draped over her bony shoulders, and even as she stepped inside the bar, she pulled the garment tighter around her thin frame as her eyes squinted to adjust to the low lighting inside.

"Pick any table." Mel walked forward with the laminated drink menu and a smile.

But the woman didn't move; instead her brow furrowed and she planted herself more firmly in her spot.

"I–I'm looking for Janet Black?"

"Well, you found her." Janet walked out from behind the bar. "What can I do for you?"

"I'm Misty Bridges. We—we spoke on the phone earlier today?"

"The missing girl's mother?" Misty nodded and Janet steered her to the corner booth. Once they were seated Janet said, "I wasn't expecting to see you so soon."

"I thought, well, I had your attention...You know they say strike when the iron is hot and all that." The woman fidgeted with the end of her sleeve, and Janet noted that the yarn there had started to fray.

"You don't know what it's been like, these last few days. Police say she ran away, but I know that's not true. That's not my Lola, at least not—" She bit her lip as if she'd said too much and fell quiet.

"I was surprised I hadn't seen anything on the news about it. Or social media. These days someone's dog goes missing and the community finds it before nightfall."

Misty blew out a sigh and her lips pressed together in a thin line. "Dogs are lucky. People...not so much," she said under her breath.

Cindy Lou arrived. "I brought a sweet tea for you both. You need anything else, Janet?"

When the other woman shook her head, Janet sent Cindy Lou away. Once they were alone again, Janet leaned forward. "So, who are you working with at Knoxville Police Department?"

Misty took a worn, folded business card out of the pocket of her cardigan. She smoothed it out and slid it across the table. *Detective Kay Smith, Knoxville Police Department.* Janet knew a few cops over at the department downtown, but she didn't know this one.

"What does she say?"

"Well, not much, I'm afraid." Misty covered her mouth with one hand and Janet had the feeling she was trying not to scream. "She said they would start asking around, talk to Lola's friends, her teachers, see if anything stuck out. But right now they're not calling it a missing persons case so much as a runaway teen."

"That's a much different level of investigation."

"Not nearly the manpower we want—we need! It's just this one cop asking Lola's math teacher a question. It—it's just not—"

The door opened and a beam of sunlight cut into the dark space, landing directly in Misty's eyes. She squinted, and her words cut off as she shielded her eyes with one hand. She clearly recognized the man entering the bar. Her shoulders drooped ever so slightly. She forced her eyes wide. "Paul, come meet Janet. She's the woman I told you would find Lola."

CHAPTER THREE

"I'll do what I can," Janet said, twenty minutes later, "but it sounds like a difficult case."

Misty stared, unblinking at Janet, but Paul was already up and out of his seat.

"Let's go, Misty. We're late." He walked through the door without a backward glance. The chimes that jangled when the door closed felt inappropriately cheerful.

Misty slowly pushed herself up from the bench seat, and took her time closing her cardigan sweater over her chest. She crossed her arms over the fabric to keep it in place, then turned her eyes back to Janet. "You'll call Detective Smith?"

Janet nodded. "Right away. How'd you hear about Bexley and Associates?"

"A flyer came in the mail a while ago. The name stuck in my brain, I guess." Misty's lips once again pressed into a thin line and the corners tugged down before she turned and left the bar.

Janet stared at the doorway until Cindy Lou tapped her on the shoulder.

"I don't like that Paul fellow. What a drag." She shook her head and stirred her tall sweating glass of sweet tea with a black straw.

Janet cocked her head to the side. "You do know their daughter is missing. Was he supposed to tap dance here and do a show for you?"

Cindy Lou's hands fluttered in the air, brushing off Janet's sarcasm. "You know what I mean. He looked irritated to have to deal with this, instead of worried about his daughter." She frowned. "I don't like him."

Janet turned to the bar and deposited the still-full glasses of sweet tea and cardboard coasters onto the counter. She had to agree with Cindy Lou. Misty was exactly what you'd expect the worried mother of a missing teen to look like. Paul, on the other hand, appeared to have more important things on his to-do list than hunting down a wayward teen. But before she could say as much to Cindy Lou, the chimes rang again, indicating a new customer had walked in. Janet frowned; it was too early for so many people to be coming into her bar. This was supposed to be a quiet time—time to get organized for the night ahead.

Cindy Lou greeted the customer, but whatever the woman said in response left her assistant manager saying, *"Oh,"* as if she'd just found out she read the wrong book for a class report.

Janet turned to see who had entered. A nondescript woman with dark hair wearing a lumpy business suit and holding a white plastic clipboard in her hands walked past Cindy Lou and stopped two feet away from the bar.

"Are you Janet Black?" Her eyebrows disappeared under her bangs as she waited for Janet's response.

"Who's asking?"

The woman frowned. "He said you're a piece of work." Before Janet could ask who "he" was, she continued. "I am Amelia Turner with the state's Alcoholic Beverage Commission. It has recently come to our attention that you do not serve food at this establishment. Is that correct?"

Janet already didn't like Amelia Turner, her pointy nose, or her disapproving expression. But there was no sense hiding the fact that they didn't have a kitchen.

"We certainly do serve food." Cindy Lou's voice came from behind the visitor, and surprised Janet enough that she had to hide her smile behind a cough.

Cindy Lou crossed her arms under her ample chest and raised one eyebrow as she assessed Amelia Turner with a frown.

Amelia reached forward and gingerly slipped a sticky menu from the slot on the counter. Her eyes scanned the front, then flipped it over. "Blank on the back. I see five beers listed, and that's it." She glanced over at Cindy Lou. "Where exactly is the food menu?"

Cindy Lou smirked as if she was winning the argument. "We serve trail mix. And refill the bowls all the dang time."

Amelia grinned lightly and made a note on a clipboard. "According to section 554 – 215a, any establishment that serves beer, wine, or spirits is required to also have a full-service food menu."

Cindy Lou sidled up next to Amelia, who in turn took a step away. Undeterred, Janet's assistant manager leaned forward. "Well, Amelia Turner from the Alcoholic Beverage Commission, I am happy to tell you that the Spot has been grandfathered in for the last twelve and half years to that new state requirement. I remember when our old owner, Bernie, read the article that he didn't have to build the kitchen." She glanced over at Janet. "Was pissed as hell that he'd spent money on architecture plans for the addition, but ultimately saw it as saving a fortune on the project."

Janet's jaw almost hit the countertop. She'd never heard Cindy Lou sound so knowledgeable. But Amelia Turner didn't share her wonder.

The state flunky looked down at her notebook before turning to address Janet. "Was there, or was there not, recently a sale of this establishment?"

A shot of unease slid down Janet's throat and lodged into the base of her neck, making it difficult to swallow. She noted that Cindy Lou's smile disappeared as well.

"That is true." Janet and her boyfriend, Jason Brooks, had purchased the bar together several years ago, but Jason had recently sold his half of the bar to her at her urging. She wanted to own her own business, be her own boss, report only to herself. And she'd been absolutely certain it was the right choice up until twenty seconds ago.

"The state of Tennessee passed a resolution three months ago stating that any transfer of liquor license—even between existing owners—would nullify the clause that had grandfathered your businesses in up to this point."

Cindy Lou's jaw hung slack. She wrinkled her nose. "What are you saying?"

"I'm saying the Spot has thirty days to come into compliance with the laws of the state of Tennessee that govern alcohol sales and distribution, or your license will be revoked and the business will need to close." Amelia Turner tore a few sheets out of her notebook and slapped them onto the counter between herself and Janet. "Here is the relevant information and my contact number should you have any further questions." She looked around the bar and her eyes softened. "It looks like a nice place, but my boss is adamant that I address this issue immediately."

She turned to leave the bar when Mel stepped in her path.

"Who exactly is your boss?" Though Mel's smile was friendly, Amelia shuffled back a few steps before answering.

"As it turns out, I have a new boss. He just moved over from another department. His name is Gary Donaldson."

Mel pushed the door open and held it for Amelia. "You have a nice day."

"And you, as well."

When the bearer of bad news was gone, the three women gathered at the bar.

"Gary Donaldson?" Cindy Lou moaned. "Why can't that man just leave you alone?"

Mel crossed her arms. "You need to call O'Dell."

"I know." Janet frowned. "And I will...soon."

Detective Patrick O'Dell was a homicide detective with the Knoxville Police Department, and he and Janet had a semi-complicated relationship that he wanted to expand, and she was happy to keep exactly where it was. It turned out O'Dell and Gary Donaldson had a colorful history—that started when O'Dell went on a few dates with Donaldson's ex-wife. Now the state employee had been making it his business to try and put Janet out of business as a strange way of getting back at O'Dell.

However, just then the last thing she wanted to do was engage with the most engaging cop she'd ever met. Recent history had shown her that having O'Dell nearby didn't help her relationship with Jason, so for now, she'd trust her gut and try and figure things out on her own.

CHAPTER FOUR

Janet handed the papers to Jason, then leaned back against the couch cushion in the family room and crossed her arms over her chest. Her lips pursed, and she made a herculean effort to smooth them out. She'd gotten home a few minutes earlier but hadn't been able to relax since Amelia Turner's visit to the Spot.

Jason scanned the sheet. The *whirr* of William's power drill droned in the background. Three seconds on, then five seconds to reload a new screw, then three seconds on again. It was surprisingly relaxing compared to some of the hammering that had been issuing from the kitchen in the last weeks of the renovation project.

When Jason looked up, his eyes searched Janet's. "How long do we have to come into compliance?"

Some of the tension leached out of her shoulders as she leaned forward to rest her elbows on her knees. The simple fact that he'd said "we" was enough to remind her how much she loved the man sitting in front of her. "Thirty days." She reached up and rubbed her neck. They should have used a lawyer to handle the business sale, instead of printing forms off the Internet. Cutting corners always ended up costing you more in the long run. She should know that by now.

But Jason only shook his head. "That can't be. It must be thirty days to show them you're planning to come into compliance. They can't expect a full addition and renovation of the space in thirty days. It'll take that long to get a contractor in there to give us a quote."

Whirr. Pause. *Whirr.*

She relaxed even more, and the knot at the base of her skull eased up. She hoped he was right. Janet looked over Jason's shoulder through the open kitchen door. "Is that the last set of upper cabinets?"

Jason turned to glance at the space. "Can you believe it? Eighteen months without a kitchen, and Dad said he should be ready to install the oven by the weekend."

Janet smiled in spite of her sour mood. As much as Jason's father tended to grate on her nerves, she couldn't complain about his work ethic. In the six months since he'd moved in with them, he'd managed to lay a cork floor, install all the base cabinets, and was now almost done with the upper cabinets. They'd probably call in a specialist for the countertops and sink, though they hadn't broken the news to William yet.

If only he could find his own place to live after the divorce so easily.

Before Janet could comment, there was a light tap at the door followed by the doorknob turning with a squeak. A cheerful voice sang-spoke, "Knock, knock!"

Janet stared wide-eyed at her boyfriend and he winced back apologetically before jumping up to greet his mother.

"Come on in, Mom."

"She just did," Janet muttered under her breath as she stood.

Jason and Faith hugged in the entryway. A headband pushed her graying blond hair away from her face, but a few disobedient strands stuck up, and she reached up to smooth them back into place after the hug.

Her full lips, so similar to Jason's, were currently pulled down into one of those happy frowns some people managed to do, and her brown eyes looked adoringly up at her only son.

"How's my favorite Jason?" Her gaze drifted over to Janet's and her smile-frown deepened. "And the lovely Janet Black. How are you, dear?" She crossed the room and pulled Janet into a hug, then settled onto the couch across from her and patted the seat next to her for Jason. Her son obliged, resting an arm across his mom's shoulders and giving her a squeeze.

"It is so lovely to see you both. I sure won't let so much time slip by between visits again." She shot a dark look over her shoulder when the *whirr* of the drill punctured the air. She and William had gone through a bitter divorce recently, and Faith had purposefully kept her distance with her ex living in her son's house. Even though Faith was quick to tell anyone with an ear that she couldn't stand William, in the past, she'd taken special care with her appearance when they'd all gotten together. Janet was surprised to find her looking wind-swept and scattered. The details of why were quickly explained.

"I am so irritated with my hotel. I booked an open-ended reservation—" Janet cringed, "—and when I went to check in today, they said they can't actually do that! If I'd have known, I would have booked somewhere else. What with that big Comic-Con starting next week, there won't be any rooms available if I need to extend my stay!"

"Lots to do with the restaurant, then?" Janet asked in what she thought was a diplomatic voice, but she must have missed the mark based on the look Jason shot her.

"Oh, honey, you just have no idea! When I bought that place at auction, I thought there'd be a little bit of paperwork and that'd be it. Boy, was I wrong." Faith shook her head.

"Well, you're not alone in your troubles," Jason said. "Janet was just telling me that the state is trying to screw her over. Again."

Faith's expression darkened. "Language, dear," she admonished, but still turned to Janet with concern. "What do you mean? What's going on?"

Before Janet could explain, William came out of the kitchen rubbing a bandanna roughly across his forehead. "Well, that's done." He stopped short when he saw Faith. "Oh, I didn't know you were here."

The skin around Faith's eyes tightened and she smiled stiffly. "William. I see you're hard at work. Don't let me stop you."

"Never have. Never will." William's expression turned triumphant as Faith's lips pulled down into a genuine frown.

Jason hopped up and started backing out of the room.

Unbelievable.

They'd discussed just the night before how his penchant to leave before his parents could dig into an argument often left Janet in an awkward position. He'd agreed not to do it again, but now that he was backing out of the room, he refused to make eye contact.

"Sorry to leave you guys so quickly, but my break is over." Janet glared across the room. He owned his own computer security business, his break was as long as he wanted to make it. He caught her eye and glanced down at his watch belatedly, then looked up with a grin. "Big job just came in from Memphis. Might have to travel that way at the end of the week. Okay if I stay at the house, Mom?"

"I was just in Memphis," William said, a smug smile on his face.

"Why's that?" Faith cocked an eyebrow.

"Visiting Connie. She's got a beautiful place there. I've always thought that Memphis is a great city, haven't you, Faith?"

Faith turned her back on her ex-husband, clearly not interested in hearing about his new girlfriend. She smiled at her only son indulgently. "Of course, dear. Spare key is where it always is."

Jason nodded and then disappeared.

William and Faith, avoiding each other's eyes, instead stared at Janet.

She cleared her throat. "So, Faith, what's the word on the business license?"

Jason's mother had bought the abandoned restaurant next door to the Spot at a public auction several weeks earlier. Or as William liked to say, she'd bought it right out from under him. Now she was waiting on the business license to come through before moving forward with her plans to re-open the long-closed restaurant. It had been known as Old Ben's place for as long as Janet had lived in Knoxville, but the former owner had moved to Florida several years ago and had stopped paying property taxes. Now it was strange to think about someone else owning and operating the business under a new name.

"Nothing yet, and I'll tell you what, it's driving me crazy." A life-long southerner, Faith would never let her frustration spill over the surface. Her face was as sunny and cheerful as if she'd just learned she was going on vacation. "But enough about me—"

"No kidding," William said.

"What's all this?" Faith motioned to Janet's paperwork lying on the coffee table as if William hadn't spoken.

Janet went over the highlights—or lowlights—of the new situation with the liquor license at the Spot.

"And all this happened because Jason sold you his share of the business?" Faith narrowed her eyes and Janet frowned. It was all her fault, really. It had been her idea to own the business outright. Her idea to have Jason turn his shares over to her. Her idea, all of it. Her fault.

William headed toward the pair but couldn't bring himself to sit in the open spot next to his ex-wife. Instead he hovered in between them so that Janet had to crane her neck uncomfortably to look up at him. "So what are you going to do?"

"We did some digging in the office and found the old architectural plans for a kitchen addition. I guess we'll move forward with that. I mean, what's another fifty-thousand-dollar loan when you already owe so much?"

"Darlin', sounds like you need an interior designer." Faith straightened her skirt and crossed her legs primly at the ankle.

William guffawed. "Janet does not need your help with this, Faith. She's probably already got it all planned out."

Faith's expression darkened and she leaned back against the cushion to get a better look at her ex. "You have no idea what Janet needs. She probably needs *you* to finish the kitchen, that's what she needs."

William crossed his arms. "She needs a little space in her own house. That's what she needs."

A laugh exploded from his ex-wife, short and choppy. "That's rich, coming from you. How long have you lived here now?"

Janet stood up, but Jason's parents didn't even notice. By now they were deep into their regular argument, each trying to one up the other while also trying to prove how invaluable they were to their son's life. She backed out of the room and gently closed her bedroom door.

She kicked her shoes off and laid back against the pillows on her bed. As much as she hated to admit it, she hadn't thought much beyond getting the actual kitchen built. But Faith was right. She would need someone to design the space, help her figure out what kind of plates to buy, silverware, heck, even pots and pans. She sat bolt upright. She was going to need to hire a chef, maybe waitresses, too.

The cost for this project kept doubling every time she considered it.

The dates on the mini-calendar on her nightstand from a local realtor pulsed with each second. Thirty days wasn't long to figure out all of this while running a business and looking for a missing teen.

She texted Cindy Lou to put an ad up for the chef position, but the unsettled feeling in her stomach didn't abate.

It felt like the beginning of a bad joke—a business owner sets out to hire an architect, a builder, and a chef...

She had no doubt that in the end, *she'd* be the punchline.

In reality, she needed even more than those contractors and employees. She sure as hell wasn't going to bring Faith into that hot mess, though. Never in a million years did she need the chaos at home to enter her work life, too.

CHAPTER FIVE

"So what's this girl's name again?" Quizz tucked her car keys into a purple fanny pack, then twisted the pouch around so it rested on her butt. She looked up, and upon seeing Janet's scrutiny, said, "What?"

Janet hadn't seen a fanny pack in use since she'd left her small hometown in Montana many years ago. She shook herself and focused on the question. "Her name is Lola, and she's a senior here at Boulder Ridge High School."

"You have a good picture of her?"

"Mm-hmm. Lola's mom gave me one." It had been six days since Misty hired Janet—and Quizz—and she'd spent the bulk of her investigation so far doing online research. Lola didn't leave much of a footprint—which was unusual for a teenager these days. Facebook was a dead end, and Lola didn't have an Instagram or Twitter account.

But now that school was back in session after an oddly placed early winter break, Janet was ready to talk to the people who might have known Lola best: her classmates.

Janet held out a five-by-seven school photo of the girl. Her blond hair was loose around her shoulders and a small grin revealed a mouth full of metal. "It's from two years ago, but her mom swears she's hardly changed. Just got her braces off."

"What do the police say?"

Janet shook her head. "I don't know. I put a call into the detective who was assigned to the case but haven't heard back."

"What about your contacts? You put in any *other* calls?" Quizz drilled her with an unblinking stare, but again Janet batted the question away.

"Just waiting on the detective in charge of this one." They stared at the school building, quiet at this time of day. "This feels weird." Janet motioned to the parking lot then turned to face her mentor. "You sure we can't just go in and ask for help at the office?"

The lines of disbelief that formed on Quizz's face were all the answer Janet needed, and she held up her hands in defeat, but the other woman spoke anyway. "The rules at a school are unlike those you'll find anywhere else. Getting into the building is a pain in the ass. But asking an admin to talk to a student?" Quizz ran a hand through her hair and shuddered visibly. "Might as well ask the principal to chop off an arm. Too many hoops to jump through." Quizz looked down at the picture one more time. "She kind of looks like you."

"She's blond and seventeen. Are we looking at the same picture?"

"I mean the eyes. And her nose, maybe. Ahh. Here they come."

Janet leaned back against the front panel of the car. She didn't have any experience with kids or schools, so she wanted to let Quizz take the lead on this one. But after the first two students headed out of the building toward their cars, then a few more, a virtual flood of people exited the building. The women split up, heading in opposite directions, each with a picture of Lola.

A blond girl—preppy—stared at Janet with a question in her eyes as she approached.

Janet held the picture out as her greeting. "Do you know Lola?"

The girl shrugged. "Sure. I mean, the school's not *that* big."

"Her mom reported her missing. I'm trying to figure out where she might have gone."

"Yeah, police were here asking the other day." The girl crossed her arms over her chest and looked around again, clearly nervous.

"Anything new come to mind that you forgot to tell them?

The girl glanced behind her and lowered her voice. "I don't know anything, but that girl back there? The one with brown hair and, like, way too much eye makeup? They're pretty close."

Before Janet could say "thank you" the blond was in her car, firing up the engine, cell phone pressed to her ear. Janet stepped out of the way and then headed toward the brunette with a friendly smile.

"I hear you were friends with Lola." The first girl was right, this one wore way too much makeup, each eye ringed with enough black pencil and smudged shadow on the upper lids to make a panda jealous.

The girl's dark lids narrowed. "Am."

"Excuse me?"

"I *am* friends with Lola. You said '*were*' like it's past tense."

Janet cringed inwardly at her slip. "You're right, of course. I'm Janet Black with Bexley and Associates Investigations. Lola's parents asked me to look into her disappearance."

The girl snorted. "Oh, her parents did, huh?"

"Well...her mother did most of the talking," Janet clarified. "Did Lola and her dad not have a great relationship?"

The girl looked to her side and when she saw they were alone she stepped closer. "Did you meet him?" Janet nodded and she scoffed. "He's not her father. Paul's been dating her mom for a few months now. What kind of PI are you that you didn't even know that?"

Janet made a mental note of that bit of information and asked another question. "Do you think she ran away?"

The girl closed her eyes and ran a hand through her hair. By the time she opened her eyes, liquid had pooled at the corners and she stared at a spot just above Janet's head. "Honestly, I don't know. This isn't like her, but she hasn't been herself lately..." She clamped her lips and shook her head slightly.

"Ever since when? Did something happen?" The girl had something to hide, but Janet couldn't quite read her body language. She was holding something back. Was she worried she might get Lola in trouble? Was she worried *she* would get in trouble? Janet decided to press the issue. "What's your name?"

"I'm Amanda Rhodes."

"Listen Amanda, Lola's parents—I mean, her mom—is worried, and with good reason. Good things don't happen to teenage girls that go missing. If you know anything, now's the time to say something. No one's looking to get anyone in trouble. We just want to bring Lola home, you understand?"

Amanda's shoulders sagged as if the weight of the world had suddenly become too much. She sucked in her bottom lip and looked down at her toes. A new batch of students poured out of the building, their voices carrying across the asphalt parking lot. Amanda tensed, glanced behind her, and started moving away from Janet.

"I've gotta go. But if I were to pinpoint when things started going weird for Lola, it would be when she started dating Matt."

"Matt? I haven't heard anything about a boyfriend. Is he a student here? What's his last name?"

Amanda shrank farther away, and Janet tried to soften her voice. "Just a last name, Amanda. That's all I need. I don't have to tell anyone we've even spoken."

"I can't. I wish I could, but I don't know."

"So—not a student here, then?"

Amanda shook her head. "She met him online. That's all I

know. Well, that and I didn't like the guy. Overbearing asshole if you ask me."

"Hold up, did you meet him?"

"No—just...just based on what Amanda told me about him. He didn't want her going to parties. I mean, she missed Larissa Jenkins' birthday party, and her parents hired an actual band to play!" Her cheeks turned pink and she took a step back. "What do I know, though, right? She said it was love. Listen, I've got to go." Whatever Amanda's plans had been for lunch, she had obviously changed them. She pivoted on the spot and hurried back into the building without a backward glance.

Janet followed and shoved a business card into Amanda's hand. "Call if you think of anything. Sometimes even small details can make a big difference."

"Please step away from the student." An official voice rang out across the parking lot and even though Janet was many years removed from high school, she still froze, her shoulders tense, as a bowling ball settled into the base of her stomach. She turned and found a thin stooped man with an impressively authoritative expression facing her. "This is private property and you are not allowed to even *be* here without prior authorization, and you certainly may not speak to my students. Follow me into the office. The police are on their way. They'd like a few words."

CHAPTER SIX

What was it about sitting in a principal's office that made you want to shrivel up and die? Janet sat slumped in an uncomfortable chair in front of the principal's desk. Quizz seemed to find the whole situation amusing, and she'd somehow made friends with the receptionist. While Janet sulked, the other two women chatted amiably about hair dye and the usefulness of Kool-Aid as an accelerant in the process.

But Janet felt the injustice of the situation and sat glowering across the desk at the principal. He was completely unaffected, and in fact, the worse Janet's mood shined through, the happier he became. He'd started humming five minutes ago.

"I just want to point out—again—that Lola's mother hired me to look into her disappearance."

"So you've said." The principal clearly didn't believe her, and he eyed her like she might steal his paperweight if he looked away for even a moment.

"While we're waiting, why don't you tell me a little about Lola? Do you have any guesses where she might have gone? What might have driven her to want to leave?"

"Ms. Black, I'm not going to answer questions from anyone

except the police detective who's charged with investigating this case."

She threw herself back against her chair, disgusted. Curious students slowed as they passed the office window, but Janet hardly saw them, her vision clouded by anger. It took a moment for her to realize that the buzzing in her head was actually the front door buzzer, indicating someone wanted access to the building. Janet glanced over to the black-and-white security camera monitor and nearly gasped aloud when she recognized Detective O'Dell. Surely they wouldn't send someone so senior for a small case of school trespassing? His grinning mug, though, said just the opposite.

The receptionist buzzed him in and within seconds he crossed the threshold into the office. Janet hadn't laid eyes on him in weeks, and she unconsciously licked her lips as she drank in all six foot two of him. Nothing had changed, from his strong, muscular shoulders, to his close-cropped sandy blond hair, and those sparkling, mischievous green eyes which currently twinkled down at her.

"Principal Adler, nice to see you, sir. I heard we've got a problem here. Ladies? What's going on?"

Principal Adler stood up with a welcoming smile. "Detective O'Dell, didn't think we'd see someone so high-ranking here, but delighted to hear the department is taking things seriously."

O'Dell smiled good-naturedly at the principal's slightly condescending tone and widened his stance. "I heard the call-out come over my radio. Since I was in the area, I told the dispatchers I'd handle it personally." His eyes twinkled again and Quizz clicked her fanny pack back into place as she stood from the chair by the receptionist's desk.

"Thought we were on okay ground in the parking lot, but now that I know the rules, we'll know what to do next time. Detective, let's roll."

Despite Janet's grumpy mood, she had to hide a laugh at Quizz's ability to stay cool under pressure. Playing dumb was a great excuse to get out of almost anything—at least, the first time.

"Ladies, follow me. We'll head downtown to sort things out."

Quizz turned away, but not before her irritated expression belied her calm demeanor.

The two women waited by the front doors while O'Dell and Adler discussed a school resource officer who wasn't up to snuff, according to the principal. O'Dell finally led the way outside. Quizz and Janet peeled off toward Quizz's car when O'Dell turned, a hand out toward his car.

"Oh no. Someone's got to come with me downtown to make this look good, otherwise old Adler will raise hell at the next City Council meeting."

"I drove here, so I'm out." Quizz jangled her keys in the air and sidestepped away from the other two.

Janet scowled, and a grin stretched across O'Dell's face. "Looks like it's you and me, Janet. I'll even let you sit in the front seat, how's that?"

Janet marched in front of O'Dell, secretly glad he wasn't going to make her sit in the back. She waved goodbye to Quizz, then climbed in next to O'Dell.

They both stared forward until the silence between them stretched too long. When she turned to face him, she found he was still grinning at her.

"Oh, shut up."

He chuckled. "Admit it, you were happy to see me when I walked in that office."

Janet grinned despite her best effort to keep her face smooth. He chuckled again, and she finally relented. "Okay, fine. I was glad to see you."

He started up the engine with a celebratory laugh. "Hot damn, I'd say that's progress."

Janet buckled her seatbelt. "You're not really taking me downtown, are you?"

"Might as well come with me. Heard you been asking around

about that missing girl. Why don't you talk straight to the source?"

"You mean Detective Smith?"

O'Dell nodded.

"She hasn't been returning my calls. She in today?"

"You bet. She's in and she's expecting you. I radioed earlier to let her know I'd be bringing you downtown. She's nice, you'll like her."

Janet tried not to feel the flutters in her belly when he took one hand off the steering wheel and rested it just inches from hers. *I have a boyfriend, I have a boyfriend*, she repeated to herself, but she didn't pull her hand away.

She'd gotten to know O'Dell well over the last few months, though not as well as he'd have liked. Despite his interest, Janet was committed to Jason, so she batted down her every inclination to flirt with the attractive man next to her.

"How's business?" he asked, keeping his eyes on the road.

"Which one?"

"You pick."

She grinned. "Well, as you can see, I'm hitting it out of the park with my PI apprenticeship."

He chuckled and chanced a quick sidelong look at her as they approached a red light.

"Cops called on you at a school? If we're putting that in the success column, then I have to wonder, what constitutes a failure?"

Her face heated under his scrutiny, and when she turned, their eyes locked. "I guess an actual arrest." The silence stretched between them, sparked; electricity zinged out from their connection.

"Green light." She motioned with the hand not resting close to O'Dell's out the windshield.

"I wish." He sighed and eased his foot off the brake.

Janet cleared her throat, cleared her mind. "In other news, we'll be making big changes at the Spot."

"Oh yeah, why is that?" O'Dell pulled his hand away and shifted his body so that he was closer to the door.

"Well, our old friend has changed jobs." She said Donaldson's name and O'Dell's eyebrows raised.

"I heard he got kicked out of the Commerce Department after *someone* lodged an anonymous complaint against his conduct," he said, his expression leaving no doubt that he was the one who'd filed the complaint.

Janet sighed. Funny how things like that could backfire. Everything had unintended consequences. Her need for independence was going to cost her tens of thousands of dollars in a new kitchen. O'Dell trying to right the score between him and Donaldson meant a new threat from the ABC.

"Turns out he got hired with the Tennessee Alcohol Beverage Commission. And guess who is suddenly not in compliance?"

O'Dell cringed. "Oh no, I feel very responsible for this all of a sudden."

"As you should." Janet bit her lip. "But mostly I blame Donaldson."

"Asshole." They said the word in unison, then both laughed.

O'Dell reached over and squeezed her arm, then moved the gear to park. His touch zinged across her arm and settled into the base of her stomach. She sucked in a quick breath of air that was louder than she'd intended.

O'Dell's lips tipped up at the corners. "We're here."

Janet had never been so relieved to get out of a cop car.

CHAPTER SEVEN

O'Dell led the way past the receptionist down an ugly long narrow corridor of the police headquarters building in downtown Knoxville. Janet nodded to a surprising number of officers she'd gotten to know over the last several months, ever since O'Dell had turned the Spot into the de facto hangout for off-duty cops.

There was Riviera, the homicide detective, along with Booker, and another traffic cop named Mary Stafford.

But O'Dell's steps didn't slow as he weaved his way past all those desks into a section of the department she'd never entered before. Bulletin boards lined the hallways and the haunted, hollow eyes of dozens of missing children followed their every step. Were the empty rectangles hopeful—a found child—or sinister—a dead child? Before she could ask, O'Dell slowed and tapped with his knuckles at an open door.

"Kay, I told you I'd bring Janet by? Well, here she is." He held his hand out into the office and Janet squeezed past him to enter. The flush that colored her cheeks wasn't lost on Detective Smith. Her eyes narrowed briefly before she stood. "Thanks, O'Dell. I'll bring her to you when we're done."

O'Dell's lips pursed and he studied Janet one last time before he turned and left the small space.

Smith's eyes traveled to Janet and she smiled faintly. "Heard a lot about you. Have a seat." She motioned to a cold, hard, uncomfortable-looking seat.

The chair met all of Janet's expectations and then some. She shifted so that her right butt cheek took most of the pressure.

"So, you want to know about the Bridges case." She looked up and Janet nodded. "There's not much to share, unfortunately. This is actually the worst kind of case to come in. Mom thinks she's been snatched, school thinks she's a runaway. And we have no evidence to support either theory. It's hard to know where to go from here." She folded her hands across an open case file. "I got some three dozen runaways, and at least half the families are convinced their child would never leave. It takes some digging, but we usually find out that yes, they would."

Janet rubbed her hand across her chin. "So what happens? The case is over before it's even started?"

"Not technically. We do what we can, which unfortunately is very little."

"What about TV? Can't you call the news? Have them feature this case on the evening newscast?"

"Unless it's a missing white mother or a child under ten, they're not very responsive. We talk to the family, talk to the neighbors, talk to the friends at school." She leaned back in her chair and tilted her head to the side. "O'Dell said you were out at the school today. Not a chatty bunch, at least that's what I found."

Janet sighed and leaned back in her seat too, then jolted forward when her back protested the lack of support. Her eyes traveled the walls of the office, the dozens of kids staring at her from their posters on the wall. She glanced at Detective Smith, took in the small crow's feet around her kind but intense eyes, and wondered how anyone could do a job like this around the clock.

"I talked to one girl, a friend of Lola's."

Smith hinged forward and ran a finger down the open case file until she found the information she was looking for. "Amanda?" Janet nodded. "She tell you about this boyfriend? This Matt fellow?" Janet nodded again and Smith ran both hands through her hair. "It's been a dead end for us. Can't get a line on any of her social media habits, her Facebook account was practically empty, and no emails to anyone other than teachers and her mother. We haven't found any connection to anyone named Matt, except some poor kid in the chess club who vaguely knows Lola, but had never talked to her." Her eyes narrowed and that intense gaze sharpened. "Did Amanda have any new information? Or just the theory?"

"No, nothing new. Just got the impression she didn't like *Misty's* boyfriend any more than she liked Lola's new boyfriend."

Smith shrugged. "Show me a teenage girl who doesn't complain about the predominant father figure in her life, and I'll show you a winning lottery ticket."

Janet bit her lip, but a chuckle slipped out anyway. She certainly had experience in not liking her dad when she was in high school. They'd come a long way since then, but back then she likely would've sounded like any other teenage girl complaining about a father.

"There's not enough time in the day for my caseload, so I'm happy for the extra set of eyes on this. Stay away from the school, or you'll end up back here without O'Dell as your escort. Lots of kids from Boulder Ridge High hang out at a place called 'the Annex.' It's over behind the horse farm off Liberty. I hear Friday nights are pretty hot there. You might get more information out and about than when they're buttoned up at school." Smith stood. Her time with Janet was up. "I'll walk you back to O'Dell. I'm sure he'll want to say goodbye."

O'Dell's crush on Janet might have been the worst-kept secret in the entire Police Department. Janet slunk along behind Smith to O'Dell's desk.

He escorted Janet out of the office.

"I got a few minutes. I can drive you home, or to work?"

"The Spot, thanks." He smirked, and she knew *he* knew she didn't want Jason to know they had been together. They drove in comfortable silence to the bar and when he stopped the car, he turned to face her. "Would it be okay if I come in later today, or will that cause trouble?"

The flutters in her chest were back, but she tried to ignore them. "We'd love to have you, O'Dell." He searched her face for a long moment before nodding, almost to himself. She let out a breath and recognized the truth in her words. She wondered if O'Dell did as well. He was like a magnet to her, and even though she was committed to her relationship with Jason, she couldn't seem to shake the feeling that she wanted to keep O'Dell close.

"All right. Then I'll see you soon."

The words held a promise that Janet hated to investigate. So she didn't, choosing instead to pretend like it was no big deal.

She watched O'Dell drive away and jumped when someone laid a hand on her shoulder.

"Who was that?" Faith must have come from the shadows of the building, and Janet wondered what she'd been doing lurking outside the bar.

"Oh, Faith. I didn't see you there."

The other woman's eyes narrowed, and she looked from Janet to the disappearing taillights of the detective's car. "Are you in trouble?"

"Probably." Janet smiled and stepped lightly toward the main door to the Spot. "In fact, Faith, I almost always am."

CHAPTER EIGHT

Inside, Faith linked her arm though Janet's and steered her toward a stranger sitting at the corner booth.

"Janet, after our conversation last week, I took the liberty of calling an old friend in the construction business. This is Bruce Hobak of Hobak Designs."

Bruce unfolded his lanky six-foot-plus frame from the bench seat and shook Janet's hand. His grip was firm and warm. He motioned that the ladies should sit across from him, and Janet tamped down irritation at being invited to sit at a table in the bar she owned.

"We might have a great fit here, Miss Black." He ripped the tops off two sugar packets and poured them into a glass of tea. He didn't speak again until he'd stirred it, set the spoon down on the empty wrappers, and took a sip. "I had a big cancellation this week, and Faith tells me you already have some plans drawn up for a kitchen expansion. We might could help each other out. Your small expansion here would keep my crew busy and stay mostly on schedule with our next job, and you'll get your kitchen built and ready to use by the city's deadline."

Well, you couldn't say it any better than that, Janet thought with a smile. If he'd added a bless-your-heart somewhere in there, it'd be all the southern lingo she could handle.

"That will give us a chance to get the rest of the building up to code."

"The rest of the building? What do you mean?"

"You need fire extinguishers and fire doors at all points of entry." He looked around the space and wrinkled his nose. "I don't see either?"

"Well, of course we're up to code!" She shot Cindy Lou a look. The other woman surreptitiously wrote a note on the pad by the cash register. Janet could only imagine what it said. "Buy fire extinguishers and fire doors." She tallied the additional cost and felt her chest tighten before she pushed down her frustration and dug around in her purse. "What about the necessary permits?" Janet smoothed out the wrinkled paperwork from the city on the edge of the table, then scanned the official language in the complaint, looking for the required permits. "How long do they take to get?"

"I've got contacts in all the relevant departments. Shouldn't take but a day, and we can start work without them."

"You can?" Janet looked up doubtfully at the contractor, and thought about Gary Donaldson, likely doing his best behind the scenes to derail any of her plans coming into compliance. "I don't know, I've got a guy with the city who's not a big fan—"

"Well then, this really is your lucky day," Bruce interrupted. "I've got big fans everywhere. We'll be fine. Can I take a look at the drawings? That'll help me come up with a more accurate quote for the project."

Janet excused herself to find the architectural plans in the office. Bruce spoke like he was an hour away from digging up the parking lot for the foundation. Janet hadn't even contacted a bank yet to see if they'd entertain the idea of loaning her money for the project! But she supposed it didn't hurt to have a plan in place, in case things went well. She found the roll of papers in the closet, tucked them under her arm, and headed back out to the main room, slowing as she approached the corner booth again to listen to Bruce and Faith's conversation.

"Candy'll be so sorry to hear that, Faith. We always did love working with you two. So William's still back home in Memphis?"

Faith covered her mouth when she saw Janet approach.

When she didn't answer, Janet spoke up. "No, Jason's father is here in Knoxville, too."

Bruce looked confused, but Faith smiled. "I'm sure he'll want to help out, Bruce. You know Jason's dad loves construction projects."

Bruce's eyebrows shot up and his mouth opened, but Faith beat him to the punch.

"He'll do the outside and I'll do the inside." She patted the spot next to her on the seat. "Did you find the plans, Janet?"

Janet tried to keep her eyebrows from meeting in the middle. She felt like *the plans* were being made right there in the booth without her, and she didn't like it one bit.

"I'm not sure if they make sense. Like I told you last week, Faith, the former owner of the Spot had them drawn up. I have no idea what something like this will cost, and if it's even an option for me right now. I'm a little cash poor after taking over the business completely."

Faith nodded dismissively. "Well dear, there's opportunity cost with every chance for growth, and that's exactly what this is. Now, Jason might not have told you, but his father and I have done many projects together. William is great at the construction side, and I, of course, excel at bringing out the—the hidden beauty of a space." Her gaze swept the Spot uncertainly before she focused on the main bar area like she was accepting an unspoken challenge to her abilities as an interior designer. "No matter how buried it might be."

"Why you lookin' at me, Faith?" Cindy Lou called from behind the counter.

Janet coughed out a laugh, then nearly choked when Bruce slipped a sheet of paper in front of her.

"Based on the drawings, the total job will be about $150K, from start to finish. That includes digging out a basement under the kitchen, which will not only be great for storage, like in this drawing, but it'll also give us the room to run utilities out to the new space. Talk to Jason, and his dad—but get back to me at this number by tomorrow, and I'll do a walk-through with actual measurements to get you a proper quote." He slipped a business card on top of the construction estimate and stood. "Faith, nice to see you. Give William my best. Candy and I are pulling for him."

Faith hid a cringe behind a cough and walked Bruce out. Janet studied them as they walked away. Had Bruce just boldly told Jason's mother that he and his wife were taking William's side in the divorce? She got up from the table and walked toward Cindy Lou with Bruce's dirty glass and trash. People in the south could be so strange.

———

"So, what do you think?" Faith walked lightly back into the bar several minutes later and took a seat across from Janet, who was restocking the Beerador.

"I think it's more money than I have to spend."

"But you have to do it, Janet! The state can close you down without a kitchen. Is that what you're going to let happen?"

Janet rolled the tension out of her neck before turning to face Jason's mother. "I can't spend money I don't have, Faith! And I also can't take the first offer that comes my way."

"Truth." Cindy Lou picked up where Janet had stopped with the Beerador, and Janet grinned, glad that someone had her back.

"I mean, there's got to be a better way. I'm going to have to hire a chef, and probably a waitress or two—"

"Plus buy tableware, silverware, serving trays—all the same things I'll be getting for my restaurant." Faith ticked more items off on her fingers. "You'll also need to come up with a menu, set up an account with vendors to buy the food on a regular basis, and then print new menus." Jason's mother gazed out the east windows, her eyes connecting with the roofline of the abandoned building she'd bought at public auction. "But you've got to do it, Janet. It's like I told William last night: if you want to attract a limo crowd, you buy a limo, not a used RV."

Cindy Lou and Janet exchanged a look. Janet grinned and Cindy Lou swatted her with a dishtowel. "How long are your permits supposed to take, Faith?" the assistant manager asked. "Shame your pal Bruce can't rush *your* applications through."

"It's a completely different department." Faith heard the defensiveness in her own voice and hurried to smile. "He works with building and zoning, not business and permits."

"Still, seems like there'd be some overlap." Cindy Lou clunked the final bottles into the massive refrigerator and pushed the door closed. "Wonder if he'd try for you, anyway?"

"I asked him to do just that before he left," Faith confessed. "Fingers crossed. I had no idea this would take so long. Then again, it wasn't clear at auction just how many liens there were against the property, either. It's been a paperwork nightmare, that's the truth."

"Do you trust Bruce?" Janet asked, thinking about how he'd openly declared himself Team William just moments earlier.

"More than I trust myself." Faith stood and walked to the windows, looking out across the parking lot toward her restaurant again, and repeated quietly, "More than I trust myself."

CHAPTER NINE

"Where are you going?" Cindy Lou was elbow deep in the refrigerator chest behind the bar, trying to rescue an earring that had dropped inside.

"I'm going to check out used RVs."

Cindy Lou snatched her hand out and shook it vigorously from the cold but didn't look up from the cooler. "Dagnabit. I knew the earring back was bad this morning, why I didn't..."

Janet grinned and headed out of the building, checking her phone for an address as she walked to her car. Faith had left to inspect her building again, and now her blond head was barely visible through the windows of the abandoned restaurant.

The search results page finally loaded on her phone and she scanned the list. Another few taps loaded directions onto her device. She climbed into her car and fired up the engine, then twisted the heater dial down to low, because a tiny spark of excitement warmed her from within. If this worked out, this could be a cheap, easy solution to her kitchen problem, and as a bonus, would irritate Faith enough that she might wash her hands of the Spot and focus on her own restaurant instead.

The used car dealership was only a few miles away from her, off MLK Boulevard. She eased into the lot and scanned the offerings. She was looking—not for a used RV as Faith had mentioned—but for a used food truck. Surely there was an affordable option somewhere in Knoxville that no one wanted anymore.

A young man wearing a brightly colored Polo shirt and a blue sports coat strode toward her with a grin, the winter sunshine glinting off his slicked-back hair. Was it wet, or had he just used lots of gel? She'd know in just a few more steps.

"Hi-welcome-to-Krazy-Kam's-Kar-Lot-I'm-Dean-what-are-you-looking-for-today-I've-got—"

It was clear he wasn't going to take a breath anytime soon, so Janet cut him off. "You got any food trucks?"

"F-food trucks?"

She felt a slight uptick of satisfaction that she'd managed to silence Dean, at least for a moment. She tilted her head to the side and waited.

He looked back to where an older version of himself stared through the open doorway of the business office. The older man gave him a quick thumbs up and smiled encouragingly. Dean's head swiveled back and he took a loud, deep breath.

"Ma'am-we-don't-have-any-food-trucks-but-we-do-have-trucks-in-which-you-can-eat-food-and-sometimes-that's-all-you-really-need—"

"Is that your dad in there?"

Dean sucked in his cheeks. "Yup."

"First day on the job?"

"How'd you know?"

"You left the tags on the suit jacket." She pointed to his right armpit, and he swiped the paper sales ticket with his left hand.

"Bah. I thought the Polo shirt was enough, but Dad said if I *look* like a pro, I'll *be* a pro." He shrugged. "What can I say?"

"You know of any places that might specialize in used food trucks?"

He shook his head. "Nah. Let's go ask my dad." He turned

and his shoulders drooped as he led the way to the small shack in the middle of the parking lot.

"Dean Kamstetter, nice to meet you." The wrinkled version of his son pumped Janet's hand firmly up and down several times before pulling her closer. "How'd he do out there?"

She smiled. "Legendary. He's going to be great."

Dean Senior smiled. "What can I do you for?"

"She's looking for a food truck." Young Dean was busy trying to cut the tag off his jacket without cutting the fabric, and his tongue pushed out between his lips as he focused. "I said we don't have one, but you'd know where she can go."

"Don't have one? Don't have one?" Dean Senior's voice rose an octave and his son dropped the scissors and looked up at his dad, his nose wrinkled.

"I think I'd notice a food truck parked around here!" He tipped the tag into the trash can and crossed his arms, but his face was oddly engaged, as if waiting for something exciting to happen.

"You must have missed it because it's so gorgeous, so clean, so amazing, that you probably couldn't look at it long enough for your eyes to register what it was." Old Dean wiped at a sheen of sweat on his forehead, then prompted his son with a quick head jerk.

"Well, where is this thing of beauty, then?" the young one asked.

Old Dean's mouth moved right along with his son's as he asked the last question. They were trying to play Janet, but why?

"Let's see this magnificent beast." Janet walked out of the small office first and scanned the lot. Plenty of beat-up Buicks and Fords, but nothing that resembled a food truck that she could see.

The Deans were close behind and the elder breathed out, "There."

She turned to where he was pointing, and across the street,

parked in the shadows of a mechanic shop, an ancient-looking food truck clung to life.

She took an involuntary step back. "Does it—I don't know, does it work?"

"Does it work? Son, tell her about it."

Still trying to fish the other half of the plastic fastener out from the inside of his jacket, Young Dean jumped and shrugged the suit back up over his shoulders. "Dad, don't sell her that piece of crap. I'm sure there's a nicer one somewhere—"

"Son! First rule of business, give the customer all the information and let *them* decide what to do!"

Dean Junior sighed and crossed his arms. "What's your name?" His father nodded approvingly.

"Janet."

"Well, Janet, the engine of that there truck has been partially rebuilt, but when the mechanic went out of business, the work on the engine stopped completely. It might coast downhill a bit before completely stopping, but the engine won't do a thing."

Janet squinted at the beast. It was bright red, with *Timmy's Tacos* painted in mustard yellow across the front, under windows that were closed tight. The boxy vehicle was the same size as a UPS truck, and she mentally tallied the distance between here and her bar. Less than two miles. According to Dean, the truck would never make it.

"Bring her over, Dean, show her the amazing inside of that gorgeous giant!" Senior practically shoved his son toward the abandoned mechanic shop, throwing a set of keys toward him before he turned back toward the small office, muttering, "All you gotta do is *try* for the sale, and my kid wants to try to *lose* the sale, jeez."

"Well, come on." Young Dean led the way across the street. Janet slowly lapped the truck, while the salesman wrestled with the lock on the door.

When he pried it open, he motioned grandly that she should go in first.

She tentatively poked her head in. Dusty, grease-splattered aluminum, streaks of black grime, and a questionable odor met her when she was fully inside the vehicle.

But.

But the set up would easily allow for one chef plus another employee—a cash register operator—to move around each other and work. Under the patina of neglect, she could see good bones inside the cooking equipment. The fry baskets could easily be replaced, but the stove and cooktop had been lovingly maintained.

She climbed back out. The tires were nearly flat. The passenger side rear tire might have a rotten spot that would need to be addressed before she could even attempt to get it towed.

Dean clucked his tongue but waved encouragingly at his father, who'd taken out binoculars to keep tabs on the sales pitch.

He turned his back on his old man. "It's in rough shape. That rear tire is shot. I don't know if you saw the rusted-out fry baskets, but those would be easy enough to replace. I don't know. It's a risk. What do you think?"

"Does the generator work?"

"Let's check." He walked around to the back and pulled the doors open. They both studied the generator for a long moment, then Dean flipped a switch and turned a key. Nothing happened. "Could be out of gas?"

She frowned. She didn't need the generator; after all, she could just run some kind of extension cord from the bar out to the truck, but Dean didn't need to know that.

"How much?"

His eyebrows shot up and he stuttered for a moment before regaining his composure. "Sticker there says ten thousand."

"How much, Dean?"

He rubbed the back of his neck and his lips moved soundlessly.

"The engine doesn't work, the tires need to be replaced.

Insides are in a bad way. Generator might be busted...I'll give it to you for five."

"Five thousand?"

She crossed her arms. She'd gladly tow the truck to the Spot for another 250 bucks, and not lose a minute of sleep over saving herself $145,000 and a year-long renovation headache. She also couldn't wait to see Donaldson's face when he heard the news.

Dean looked over at his old man, who even from across the street was vibrating with excitement. "I've got a friend who does custom paint jobs. You mention my name, he'll give you a discount."

"Eat at the Spot."

"Excuse me?"

"Oh, that's what I would have your friend paint on the truck. Eat at the Spot."

"Nice."

Janet patted the side of the truck, and a bolt that kept two panels of siding together popped loose. She snatched her hand back, and Dean rubbed the back of his neck again. "Four thousand," he blurted out, his expression hopeful. "And how about this, we'll tow it anywhere you want for free." He stuck his hand out and waited.

A slow grin spread across her face. She was coming into compliance with the law for less than five thousand dollars, Faith would be appalled, and she couldn't be happier. She reached out and grabbed his hand.

"You've got yourself a deal, Dean."

CHAPTER TEN

The next day, Faith sat in the corner booth with Jason, occasionally shooting disgruntled looks across the room toward Janet.

"Whoo boy. She ain't gonna get over it, is she?" Cindy Lou pushed a flyaway hair off her forehead with the back of her hand and then finished slicing a lemon. "It's like she'd already planned how she was gonna to change this place and can't believe it ain't gonna happen."

Faith's brow furrowed and she leaned toward her son. Whatever Jason said coaxed a smile from the older woman, and Janet turned back to her job behind the bar.

The Spot had just opened for business. Thanks to a rush job, the food truck was at the paint shop getting a fresh coat, and with that situation settled, Jason was supposed to be helping her break into a cell phone she'd just acquired. Misty had breathlessly brought it in the day before after finding it stuffed between Lola's mattress and the wall in her room. While she waited for Jason to wrap up with his mother, she turned to her assistant manager.

"Did you post the ad?"

Cindy Lou rinsed the cutting board off and slid the knife into a small wooden block on a shelf under the counter. "Not yet. I thought I'd wait until the truck came back—make sure it all works, you know? But then I'll post it online—say we're looking for a full-time cook, familiar with fry baskets and flan."

"Flan?" Janet chuckled. "We won't be serving flan here, I can promise you that."

"I figured that would help weed out the losers." Cindy Lou added, "Plus I was going for alliteration."

Janet finished pouring vodka into a new bottle. "Hmm, then maybe fry baskets and fettuccine? Nah, even that's probably not likely. Oooh, I know, fry baskets and frozen burgers." It was Cindy Lou's turn to chuckle.

Janet tossed the empty bottle into the recycling bin and screwed the cap on the now-full bottle and set it back on the shelf before turning to study her assistant manager. "What's wrong with you?"

Cindy Lou massaged her lower back and pushed her hips out with a grimace. "I threw my back out yesterday and feel like I'm going to break clean in half."

"What were you—wait, don't answer that."

Cindy Lou's wicked smile was all the confirmation Janet needed that the injury wasn't sustained on her own.

"I'm gonna do some stretches in the office. Be right back." Her blond head bobbed—slightly off-kilter—around the bar and disappeared into the back office. Janet wiped down the prep area, then tossed the dishrag into the sink and called to her boyfriend.

"Jason?"

He half-stood, then leaned across the table to kiss Faith on the cheek before heading her way.

"Just trying to smooth over the disappointment." His low voice suggested a funeral, but he winked to show he didn't agree with his mother's grave assessment of the situation. He held his hand out for the phone. "Sorry this took so long. Let's take a look."

"Work's been really busy for you lately, huh?" She headed

around the counter and took a seat next to him while he set up his laptop. Lately, he spent more time in his basement office than out of it.

"Yeah, it's that big job from Quali-Corps. I knew it would be a beast, but I didn't know it would be *this* busy."

Quali-Corps had offices in all the major cities in Tennessee, and snagging them as a client had been a major coup for Brooks Security.

"What can I do?"

"Just keep being patient with me." He caught her hand in his when she held out the phone, and he stroked her palm lightly with his thumb. "I'm looking to hire help—it's too much for me to do on my own, and then hopefully we'll be able to see each other during daylight hours again."

"Help? Like an employee?"

"Exactly. Since I'm not at the Spot as much, I thought I could handle everything, but it's intense. I probably have enough work for two or three full-time employees, but I figured I'd start with one and see how it goes. I mean, the job's not for everyone, you know? Working out of a home basement."

"Well, maybe it's time to upgrade office space, too?" Janet swiveled her seat around to face her boyfriend.

His lips tilted up at the corners. "Yup. Time to upgrade, time to expand—and no time to do either." He dug through his bag and pulled out a small clear tackle box of coiled cords, then ran his finger across the lid until he found the right one. "This should do it."

"You think you can hack into the phone?" Janet studied the cell phone. "Misty said it's not Lola's normal cell phone, so she's not sure what to make of it."

Jason plugged the phone into his computer and tapped a few keys. "I've got a great code-breaking program here. It'll be pretty easy on this old phone. Looks like a four-digit password—no fingerprint or face recognition ID, no problem." After a few more keystrokes, he sat back. "Should only take a few minutes.

Where'd she get this thing, anyway? Her mom said it's not the one they bought her?"

Janet's nose wrinkled. "Right. Misty asked the police to trace Lola's iPhone, and they tried immediately, but they said it must be turned off. It's not pinging off any cell phone towers anywhere. Then she found this one tucked between the mattress and the wall—and I think she's trying to convince herself it belongs to the cleaning lady or something."

The computer beeped, and Jason looked down. "We're in. Password is fourteen eighty-seven...shall we?" He held the phone up and Janet leaned across the space to get a better view. "Okay, let's see...the messaging app is completely empty." He tapped a few more icons and shook his head. "If she used this phone, she sure didn't use it very often."

Janet reached forward and tapped the photo icon. "Let's see what kind of—Oh God! What the—" She flinched away from the picture and simultaneously snorted out a laugh.

"What?" Cindy Lou materialized in front of them.

Janet grabbed the phone from Jason and twisted it around so her assistant manager could see.

She whistled low. "A dick pic? In all my years, I will kill my son if he ever sends one of these to a girlfriend."

Cindy Lou leaned in closer, making Janet chortle anew. "Just can't get enough, can you?"

Her nose wrinkled. "No, believe me, while this is an impressive representation, it's not the best I've seen. But I'll tell you what, I've never seen a birthmark like that. On his stomach? It looks like the Hawaiian Islands! With his belly button in the place of the one island, what's it called?" Cindy Lou sucked on her teeth while she thought. "Kauai? Why are you looking at me like that?"

Flustered, Janet tried to come up with something that wasn't as offensive as saying she didn't think Cindy Lou would have known the names of the islands.

"I'm smarter than I look," she said, flipping a grin before she turned away.

Faith appeared on the other side of the bar. "And why is that, Cindy Lou? You don't need to impress men with your chest when your mind is so sharp. That's sexy, too."

Janet turned to share a secret laugh with Jason, but he was already packed up. He shot an apologetic look at Janet as he shrugged into his coat.

"Sorry, I've got to go. I'm so behind—gotta meet with a potential hire, and then get back to work." He squeezed her shoulder, grabbed his tackle box of cords, and headed to the door.

"Jason!"

She didn't think he was going to stop, but after a few faltering steps he turned back, his face oddly blank.

"The phone?"

"Oh." He set his bag down on the closest table and forced a chuckle. He dug into the bag and gently set the phone down with a frown before hiking the bag over his shoulder again.

Janet watched him leave, an unsettled feeling in her stomach. Had she offended him by laughing at the sexting photo?

She collected the phone, noting absently that Mel looked similarly concerned by the turn of events, then she ducked into the office, determined not to get sucked into another long conversation with Jason's mother. The last thing she heard before she closed the office door was Faith chattering on about Cindy Lou's many assets.

CHAPTER ELEVEN

The shriek of the tow truck's backup alarm split the air in two-second bursts, and though Janet pointed toward the building the driver didn't adjust the wheel.

"Over—no—closer to the wall." She cupped her hands around her mouth and shouted, "Closer!"

The driver rolled his window down and squinted at Janet. "What?"

"Closer to the building! I want just enough room to walk behind the truck to plug it in—that's all!"

"Why didn't you say so?" The driver grumbled, but pulled forward and cranked the wheel around. With some kind of reverse-engineering magic, he positioned the food truck into place. By the time he disconnected Janet's new rolling kitchen from his tow dolly, the front bumper was exactly three feet to the right of the main entrance, and twelve to eighteen inches of daylight shone between the top of the truck and the roofline. The truck's rear bumper lined up with the end of the building, and if she stood between the exterior wall of the Spot and looked toward her new food truck, she could just make out Faith's sad empty building across her parking lot, up the grassy embankment, then at the end of Faith's parking lot. Several hundred feet separated the buildings, but Janet had to wonder what would happen when they were both serving food. Competing with Jason's mother for business? She shuddered at the thought.

After the tow truck drove away, she stood alone in the parking lot, studying her new acquisition.

"How's your missing girl case coming?" Faith stood at the back of the building. She must have come out the back door and walked around to see the food truck with her own eyes.

"Oh... it's..." Janet hesitated, not sure what she should share with Jason's mother.

"I overheard Cindy Lou say something about Hawaii. You don't think she's gone on vacation, do you?"

Janet shook her head. "No, nothing like that. We—well, we don't know much, to be honest. I haven't been able to figure out much more than the police."

"The phone?"

"Dead end." Janet looked away, not wanting Faith to pry into every single facet of her life. Faith didn't need to know about the sexting picture—especially when Janet hadn't even decided whether to tell Misty about it. Lola's mother needed to know that there was a good chance Lola had voluntarily gone off with a boy. But the fact was, they must be close. Kids in high school didn't have many resources to stay hidden for long. She hoped it was just a matter of waiting them out, and then being able to deliver Lola back to her family.

Faith rounded the food truck without looking at the offensive vehicle, then came to a stop next to Janet. "You know, some outdoor seats would be nice here." Faith smiled tentatively from where she stood in the open doorway to the Spot. "I know you don't want—or need—my help with anything, Janet, but I'd say some nice tables, even just one or two, would be a really lovely thing for your customers."

Janet grimaced, but smoothed her expression before turning to face Jason's mother. "I—I think that's a great idea, I just—I don't have time to get that organized." She made a mental note to order several new trash cans to set outside.

Faith's eyes lit up, but she looked away. "I might have some time while I'm waiting for my permits to come in." She walked in front of the truck and assessed the space. "It looks like we could take a ten-foot square area here, and mark it off with a simple pergola—Erm..." She bit her lip when Janet frowned. "I just mean some nice, ahh, smallish off-set umbrellas for shade, you know, so it's comfortable to sit here and eat, even in the summer months." She turned to Janet, her expression hopeful. "Don't you think?"

Janet took in Faith's expression, her lively eyes, her upturned lips, and realized—however crazy it was to think—that Faith would take joy from helping Janet with this small job. And if she could allow herself to give up control—just a little bit—for Jason, that it seemed the least she could do.

She blew out a long, quiet breath, and then turned to Faith with a smile. "Okay, Faith. Go for it."

"Really?" Faith's eyes sparkled, and Janet gulped.

"But just a small budget, Faith. I mean, less than a thousand bucks. See what you can do, okay?"

"Oh, you're going to love it, Janet! I think we can do some really exciting things out here, and yes—I do surely love a good budget as a place to start."

Start? Before Janet could get Faith to clarify, she was off and running, talking about materials and suppliers and spacing. Janet backed slowly into her bar, only chuckling when Faith didn't notice that she'd left. She had a feeling she was going to regret allowing Faith to "help." Then again, how much trouble could the woman get into with only a thousand-dollar budget?

She'd soon find out.

CHAPTER TWELVE

When Janet got into work the next morning, she was fighting off a funk that threatened to take over her attitude for the day. They'd been out of coffee grounds at home, so she'd had to stop by a coffee shop and pay five dollars for an extra-large brew that was bitter and too hot to drink, anyway.

By the time she pulled into the parking lot of the Spot, her attitude took a turn for the worse. An excavator blocked the back half of the lot along with a dozen construction workers. She squeezed her eyes shut, but their orange vests pulsed brightly against the back of her eyelids; the endless drone of a jackhammer drilled right down into her brain.

She looked at her door handle—did she want to risk it? Of course not; she was going to call this day what it was—a total loss. Janet eased the gear shift into reverse, but before she lifted her foot up from the brake, she spotted Faith, weaving between the workers, no doubt offering helpful tips and tricks. Unbelievable!

Janet shifted into park and smacked Jason's name on her cell phone with unnecessary force. The call went straight to voicemail. She disconnected without leaving a message and then climbed out of her car so fast that coffee slopped out of the small sip hole in the flimsy paper cup and landed on her thigh. She swore when it sunk immediately through the denim and burned her skin.

Tut-tut-tut-tut-tut. The jackhammer was relentless.

"Faith!" she shouted, but it wasn't loud enough to compete with the construction equipment. She walked forward and raised her voice. "Faith! What the hell is going on?"

A smile stretched across the older woman's face as she raised her hand in greeting. "Isn't this fabulous, Janet? Come see what we're doing!"

Janet squared her shoulders and stalked toward the construction zone. She zigzagged past several orange barrels and came to a stop inches from Faith and her friend Bruce Hobak.

"What is happening?"

Bruce motioned to his crew to stop, and blessedly, the area plunged into silence.

Janet stared at Faith as she motioned to the small crew of workers. "I greenlighted a one-time one-thousand-dollar expenditure for picnic tables, don't you remember?" At Faith's innocent expression, she turned to point at the food truck—now covered in a thin layer of dust. "No kitchen addition. Food truck." Her words were rudimentary at best, but Janet worried if she added any adjectives, she'd start swearing at her boyfriend's mother, and she might not be able to stop.

Faith smiled as if she were about to deliver a winning lottery ticket. "This one's on me, hon."

"*On you?*" Janet repeated. "What are you talking about? What are you doing?"

Bruce Hobak turned toward Faith. "What's this? You said everyone was on the same page."

Faith's back stiffened, but she gamely kept the smile on her face. "Bruce, you keep right on doing what you're doing. Janet and I just need to have a little girl talk. We'll figure this right out." She winked at Bruce and then motioned that Janet should head into the Spot.

Janet looked incredulously between Faith and Bruce and back to Faith again. *Girl talk?* The last thing that would settle this—this usurping of power over Janet's business plan by Faith —was girl talk. But Janet stalked ahead of her boyfriend's mother into her own bar. As the door closed, the jackhammer came back to life and Janet pivoted, ready to launch into Faith, but the other woman spoke first.

"You don't have to thank me, Janet. I wanted to do this. For you."

"Thank you?" Janet had never heard her voice get so high, and she took a deep breath to calm herself. Once again Faith was faster.

"That food truck is a stopgap solution, hon, but I respect your decision to save money now with a cheap, temporary thing. And though I want you set up for long-term success, Jason's father convinced me that this is your call." She sighed, then brightened perceptibly. "So I decided to really throw myself into the patio plan."

"What *patio plan?* You mean the picnic tables?"

"Well, that would have worked, sure, but to really own the outdoor eating space, I thought we could do so much better. That's why I called Bruce in for the project. You're going to really love what he's come up with. And like I said, it's my gift to you."

Janet cleared her throat. "I cannot accept this gift, Faith." She worked hard to keep her voice level and calm. "This is not something for which I can pay you back. And not only is this too much, but I don't want it!"

Faith's eyes shifted from bright to crafty. "You can't not like the plan, Janet, you don't even know what it is!" She laughed lightly. "Come on out and Bruce can show you the plan he drew up for me—er, us—last night!" Faith's expression hardened. "This is clearly the way forward, Janet. If you don't see that now, surely you will by the time the project is complete."

Janet's hands flew to her hips and she opened her mouth, but before words could come out, William walked into the Spot.

"What's going on out there?"

Faith smiled brightly at her ex. "I'm helping Janet to really own the outdoor eating scene in Knoxville. By the time Bruce is done..." She turned back toward Janet and said, nonchalantly, "... which, by the way, hon, today is demo day, but then his crew can't come back for a few weeks for the building part. I told him that would be just fine, and ultimately, this schedule will get us across the finish line just a bit earlier." She smiled and looked up through her lashes at William. "And you should see what Bruce came up with, William. Really gorgeous stuff out there."

As Janet fought off the temper tantrum that was building in the base of her stomach, Faith asked William, "What are you doing here, anyway? I thought you had plans with Connie."

"I was supposed to, but..." He fiddled with the top button of his shirt, then blew out a sigh. "Well, she's stopped returning my calls."

"Oh." Faith turned away, so only Janet could see her smile. "Well, I'm awful sorry to hear that, William."

He grimaced. "I'm sure you are."

"What were you supposed to do, anyway?" She'd recovered control of her expression and faced her ex-husband, looking appropriately disappointed for him.

"She's been wanting to try a hike down at High Ground Park."

Faith couldn't stop herself from asking, "Since when do you hike?"

William flinched, and the ensuing pause was so long that Janet looked up, distracted from her bad mood.

"Janet, will you excuse us?"

Faith scoffed. "We do not need to discuss my reaction to your girlfriend, William. If you don't want to see me smirk, then don't bring that woman's name up in front of me."

William stepped closer. "It's not that. I—I got a phone call, and I thought you and I should discuss it."

Faith sucked in a quick breath. "Is everything okay?"

"I'm not sure. That's why I thought we should talk."

Faith froze, only her eyelids blinking repeatedly. After a long moment, she wiped her palms on the seat of her pants and led the way to the corner booth without a word.

When they were both seated, they turned to stare at Janet. Suddenly she felt like an intruder in her own bar.

"I...I guess I'll go talk to Bruce."

"Ask him to show you the finished plans. It's going to be gorgeous, Janet!" Faith did her best to recapture her earlier haughtiness, but Janet thought her voice sounded thin and worried.

As she walked to the door, and before the rising construction noise hammered too far into her brain, she turned back to look at Jason's parents, now huddled in the corner booth, heads together. What were they up to? And where was Jason when she needed him? These were *his* parents causing her trouble, and he was missing in action again.

She looked down when her phone chirped. It was a text from Quizz.

Where are you? You need hours this week.

She brightened marginally. She'd much rather go to Quizz's office than go over construction plans. She waved off Bruce's attempt to call her over and instead headed for her car. What better way to take out her angst over her boyfriend's mother than doing some legitimate investigative work?

CHAPTER THIRTEEN

"Okay, so now the question becomes, what are you going to do about it?" Quizz's heels plunked down on her desk and she assessed her apprentice over the rim of her glasses.

Janet tilted her head to the side and squinted at the printout in her hand. "I guess I need to go to the cafe where the bogus charge was made?"

Quizz nodded. "Exactly. Ask the clerk there if they'd recognize the person who used the stolen card. Thankfully the perp was dumb. They made a huge order from a small shop. They'll be more likely to remember who made the charge than if they'd just bought a coffee and a muffin."

Janet tucked the papers into her bag and headed to the door when Quizz spoke again. "I wasn't expecting you to come right in—I thought you were working today at the Spot?"

"I needed to escape." Quizz pushed her glasses up her nose and stared. Janet sighed and added, "Jason's mother is trying to take over my business."

Quizz's rueful smile turned mischievous. "I know the feeling. What's the latest on the missing girl?"

Janet filled her boss in on the cell phone and the picture. Quizz whistled low. "What did the mom say?"

"Nothing yet. I'm going to wait to tell her until after I head to that hangout spot Friday night. I'm hoping I can get some information from the kids on the boyfriend."

Quizz nodded. "All right. Well, good luck at the coffee shop. Don't forget, identity theft cases pay the bills! Call if you run into any problems."

Janet left the office with a promise to do just that.

———

The coffee shop was small, tucked away in an alley between store fronts, but Janet found it easily enough. Inside, several dozen potted plants softened the exposed brickwork. Some crept up from the floor and countertops, others twined down in spirals from hanging pots.

The clerk on duty, Amber, had a short, perky pixie haircut, and she was cheerfully unhelpful; over-large brown eyes exuded disappointment through her cat-eye glasses at not having the right answers to Janet's questions.

"I really am sorry, but like I said, I just started working here last week. I can call Brenda? To see if she remembers that order? But I don't know if she would, all these weeks later. You know what I mean? We take a lot of orders every day. Lattes and americanos, flat whites and everything in between."

Janet grimaced. "Well, I'd assume this order might jog her memory. I mean," she looked down at the fraudulent charge on her client's credit card statement, "how many times does someone order ten gallons of coffee and ten dozen muffins? Do you even have a bakery on site?" She glanced around the small space doubtfully.

"Oh, no!" Amber trilled at the thought. "We get them from our supplier, Jenny's Bakery. I can't imagine why someone would order that many muffins from us! The markup alone would have bought an extra dozen if they'd gone straight to Jenny's!" She looked up guiltily. "Although of course you can't beat the convenience of having everything you need all in one place."

"Okay. Let's call Brenda." She was done with Amber, and maybe the other employee could shed some light on the case.

Amber shot an apologetic look at Janet when an actual paying customer came in, and Janet stood off to the side, staring broodingly at her phone. Jason was out of town working on his new client's enormous caseload but had assured Janet that he'd hired someone to help him out. It was a local computer security expert, Mike, who'd luckily been able to start immediately.

Jason said he'd be swamped for a few more days while he got Mike up to speed on the project, but after that, he promised to help out at home more—and keep his parents in line.

Janet wasn't sure that would happen, but she'd be glad to have the chance to actually see him on a regular basis. She dismissed a text from Cindy Lou (*Crisis at the Spot. Need you here now*) and dialed his phone. The call went straight to voicemail again, in a way that meant he'd either declined the call or had his phone turned off.

She sighed, thinking about yet another crisis at her bar, and turned to look around the coffee shop while Amber's customer made the apparently agonizing decision of whether to get an iced coffee or a hot one.

"Are you muttering?" A woman stood at her elbow, one eyebrow raised.

Janet cleared her throat. "I might have been." She stepped farther aside. "You go ahead—I'm not waiting to order."

"I work here—so if you're not waiting to order, what are you doing?"

Janet stepped back and assessed the newcomer. "Are you Brenda?"

She nodded.

"Super. I'm with Bexley and Associates," she handed over a business card, "and we're looking into a credit card theft case for a client."

"Are you a PI?" Brenda asked.

Janet nodded. "Mostly. I'm hoping you might remember the person who charged a large order just last week. Several dozen muffins and gallons of coffee."

Brenda assessed her through narrowed eyes. "What do you mean, 'mostly'?"

Janet snuck a look at Amber, thoughtfully answering a question about the different kinds of nut milks available, and realized she missed her blankness. "It means my associate just handed me this case this morning, and now I'm trying to get to the bottom of who stole money from my client's account. Does the order ring any bells for you?"

Brenda's narrowed eyes relaxed and she nodded. "Sure. He's actually become quite a regular. He usually sits right at that table by the window."

Janet looked over, but the seat was empty. "When did you last see him?"

The new barista's lips scrunched together and she looked down at the floor. "Hmm...maybe last week? I know he hasn't been in this week yet, because I started upping our muffin order with him as a regular customer, and I just had to throw a bunch away yesterday." She bit her lip and looked up. "I feel terrible about this, but I knew he wasn't Karla. He said Karla was his wife, and the card never got declined, so I honestly didn't think anything of it."

Janet stepped closer, ready to take advantage of Brenda's chatty, informative nature. "So who was he? Did you ever get a name?"

"Sure..." She grimaced. "Why are the handsome guys always thieves or cheaters? Ugh." She shook her head and squared her shoulders. "His wallet fell out of his back pocket right after he started coming in and I saw his driver's license. Not Karla. That's when he told me about his sick wife." She shook her head again angrily. "The ID said William Brooks. Do you need me to file a police report or anything?"

Janet stared at the other woman like she'd just started speaking a new language. "Did you say William Brooks?"

"Uh-huh. Real handsome, tall. I could probably help a forensics sketch artist come up with a pretty good mug shot—"

"That won't be necessary, thank you." Janet backed away. "I'll be in touch if I need anything else." She walked numbly out of the shop into the cool shaded alleyway and caught her breath. There could absolutely be another William Brooks. But tall and handsome...and named William Brooks? She cringed. Why was Jason's father stealing credit cards and using them to drink coffee and eat muffins? And what in the hell was she supposed to do with this information? Call the cops on her own semi-permanent house guest?

"Jason," she growled, and dug her phone out of her bag again and tapped his name when it came up on her screen. "If you don't answer this time, I will personally see to it that—"

"Janet! How are you, darlin'?"

"You're there!" she said, so shocked that he'd finally answered the phone that she forgot her anger for a moment.

"I know, I'm sorry it's been so crazy—again—but Mike is almost up to full speed, and then we'll really be cooking with gas. This job is bigger than they thought—"

"Jason, wait." She filled him in on the stolen card and then waited through a long pause on the other end of the line.

"Can you give me a bit to figure things out?"

She bowed her head and breathed out a quiet sigh. "Will you talk to him? I don't want to get in the middle of this, but Jason, maybe he's not doing so well with the divorce and he's just acting out?"

"Maybe."

"Or, and I don't want to pry into his business, but he's gotta be in financial straits. I mean, divorce is expensive, and he bought that stinker of a boathouse that he can't even live in until spring, but I'm sure he's already paying on it—"

"I said I'll take care of it, okay?" Jason snapped.

She bit her lip and stared at a seam in the sidewalk. This was uncharted territory, and she didn't want to overreact, but...

Jason sighed. "I'm sorry. This is just a stressful time. I promise, I'll look into it. I—I've got to go."

Before she could answer—or reply at all—he disconnected. She slipped the phone into her pocket and marched toward her car, when her phone buzzed against her butt. She grabbed it and tapped the screen without looking. "It's okay—I'm stressed, too, okay?"

"What are you talking about?"

Not Jason. She pulled the phone down and frowned. "O'Dell, sorry, I—I thought you were someone else."

The detective's voice was clipped, short, when he spoke again. "We've got another missing girl. Smith wanted me to call you and let you know."

Janet's eyes snapped up and scanned the street, as if she might see the girl if she looked fast enough. "Does she think it's related to Lola?"

"Yes."

O'Dell's single-word answer sent chills up Janet's spine. "What do you need me to do?"

"Just hang tight. I'll be at the Spot in ten minutes."

Janet dropped her phone into her bag and hustled to her car, wiping beads of sweat from her brow even as she smiled. If O'Dell wasn't *already* at the Spot, then at least for once, the crisis at her bar that Cindy Lou had texted about earlier had nothing to do with police.

CHAPTER FOURTEEN

When Janet pulled up to the Spot, the situation outside had taken a surprising turn for the worse. Not only was half the lot inaccessible due to the large construction vehicles and the workers, but an overflow of cars crammed into the other half. It was only one in the afternoon—way too early to be so overrun with customers.

She wedged her beat-up car into a non-spot so close to the excavator that if the construction vehicle moved even an inch it would demolish her ride.

Good riddance, she thought, glaring at the setup. Bruce probably had enough insurance to rebuild her entire bar if things went wrong.

She approached the building and counted fifteen people waiting listlessly in a line that bloomed out from the front door.

"They're not ready to start yet," a voice called from the back of the line.

Janet's head swung around. A scrawny guy glared back at her as she walked into her bar.

"Why are those people waiting outside?" Her eyes swept the room. William was gone, but Cindy Lou and Faith were there, along with one customer. "Why is everyone waiting outside? Are we open or not?"

Cindy Lou adjusted her bra strap and avoided eye contact, only lifting one shoulder and dropping it back down.

Janet lowered her voice as she got closer to her assistant manager. "What's going on?"

Cindy Lou raised her chin toward the corner booth. Faith clutched a clipboard and seemed to be taking notes as the man across from her spoke in fits and spurts. She strained to hear the conversation and then narrowed her eyes when she caught a stilted recital of the man's work history.

"What is she doing now?"

"Interviewing," Cindy Lee muttered out of barely opened lips.

"Interviewing who?" Janet's voice was loud. And when Faith and the stranger looked over, she spoke louder yet. "Who are you interviewing, Faith?"

Faith and the stranger locked eyes for a moment, then stood and shook hands. He left, and Faith looked longingly after him before sucking in a deep breath and heading toward Janet.

"I'm interviewing for the new cook position, of course." Faith looked up at Janet with wide, innocent eyes.

"Whose cook?" Janet crossed her arms over her chest and narrowed her eyes. But it was lost on Faith, who was happily checking off lines on her clipboard.

"For your cook. I know *you* don't want the job, based on what Jason and William say happens in your own kitchen. Am I right?" Faith looked up at the sound of Cindy Lou stifling a gasp. "What? Am I wrong?"

"Faith, while I appreciate..." Janet tapped her foot and tried to unclench her jaw, but she couldn't think of a single thing she appreciated about Jason's mother just then.

Faith grinned victoriously. "This shouldn't take me but a day, Janet. I've got a whole process set up here. Got some great candidates from the ad I posted online. We should have some-body up and ready to start by the first of the month."

Cindy Lou jabbed Janet in the side with her elbow. It was just what Janet needed to snap out of her shock at Faith's complete lack of boundaries.

"This is completely unnecessary."

"I know, but you don't have to thank me, Janet. I've been doing this for a lot longer than you have, and I know—"

"You misunderstand me, Faith. This is completely unneces-sary because I have already hired a chef."

"A *chef?*" Cindy Lou asked, the surprise in her voice colored with awe.

"That's right." Janet nodded slowly, the idea taking shape with every passing second. "I—I've already hired a chef. And he'll be ready to start in the food truck as early as tomor-row." Janet nodded and uncrossed her arms, but her fingers wouldn't stop fidgeting as she wondered how she was going to make her last statement true. "And that should bring us into compliance, at least with serving food, with plenty of time to spare, while I figure out what to do about our parking lot."

Faith's shoulders slumped before she straightened her back and dropped the clipboard down to her side. "I had no idea. I wouldn't have gone to all this trouble—"

"Yes, please don't...ah, go to this trouble again without checking in with me first."

Faith stepped back as if Janet had pushed her, and after a long moment, she tucked the clipboard into her bag.

"Well, I guess I'll let you tell everyone outside there's not a job. Boy, will they be disappointed! I better go check in with Bruce. He might need my help with decisions outside."

Janet and Cindy Lou watched silently as Faith headed out the back door into the alley. For the few seconds the door was open the sound of jackhammers filled the air, then muted again when the door closed.

"So. Who are you going to hire?" Cindy Lou asked, a sly smile on her face.

"I guess I'm gonna run outside while Faith isn't looking and ask those job applicants who can start work tomorrow."

"It's okay to let her do this for you. Gives her something to do, keeps her out of your hair at home...I don't know, it sounds like a win-win to me."

Janet shook her head. "That woman has no boundaries. If I don't shut her down now, who knows where it'll end."

Cindy Lou shrugged and went back to prepping the bar. At the same time, Janet crept to the front door and peered through the glass until she spotted Faith. When the other woman walked around the back of the building with Bruce, Janet ducked outside and called the remaining job applicants over.

"Thank you all so much for coming on what I can only imagine was short notice—"

"I saw this job posting last week! What do you mean, short notice?" It was the same scrawny man who'd yelled at Janet when she'd walked in her own bar just minutes earlier. Janet frowned but was glad for the information. It was good to know that Faith had been planning to hire a cook for Janet for a week, long before she got to Knoxville—and long before she presented Bruce Hobak's services as a win-win. That woman was a schemer, and Janet would have to keep close tabs on her for the remainder of her time in Knoxville.

She cleared her throat and addressed the group in front of her. "My name is Janet Black and I am the owner of the Spot. Who is available to start tomorrow?"

Amidst the general grumbling, the scrawny man from before said, "The ad said the job would start on the first of the month! I wouldn't have wasted all this time coming out here to this crappy part of town if I'd have known tomorrow was the start date." As many turned to leave, one man slowly raised his hand.

"I can start today, if you need me to."

"It wouldn't be until next week. I was just weeding out the

applicants." Janet frowned, not realizing she'd weed them out so thoroughly with one question. "What's your name?"

"Cameron."

"Well, Cameron, call me at this number in twenty minutes. I can't talk to you now." She looked over her shoulder and saw that Faith and Bruce were still out of sight behind the building. "I want to ask you a few questions before I make this job offer official."

Cameron's brow wrinkled and he looked around uncertainly. "Can we just do that now?"

"I'm sorry, we can't. It's complicated, but if you'd like the job, call me in twenty minutes."

She watched him walk away, wondering what else Faith might have set into motion from Memphis. But she didn't have long to think, because as Cameron drove away, O'Dell's car pulled into the lot.

CHAPTER FIFTEEN

O'Dell stared across the bar—but not quite at Janet. More like at her shoulder. He refused to make eye contact. "Are you seriously telling me that you don't care that Lola's best friend has been missing since last night?"

Janet pursed her lips and stared back, willing O'Dell to meet her eye. He didn't. "I'm telling you that Amanda Rhodes's parents haven't hired me to look into her disappearance. What's Smith doing, anyway? Why are you working this case?"

"Everyone steps up for a missing kid, Janet. We're not all so heartless."

She blew out a sigh. "I'm not heartless! I just have a full plate. I haven't even really dug into the Lola Bridges case yet—a fact that Quizz won't let me forget. And I'm up to my ears in staffing issues here, plus a new state investigation! I mean, if we all stick to our own jobs, we'll be much happier in the long run."

O'Dell stuffed his hands into his pockets and frowned. "I just never thought I'd wonder what kind of person you were. Huh." He shook his head as he backed away from the bar, then nodded tersely at Mel—who'd just arrived for her shift—and Cindy Lou. "Ladies."

Janet groaned. "Dammit, O'Dell! I'm not heartless. I just

don't have time to do Smith's job. And you shouldn't be doing it, either!" she called.

His step slowed and he glanced back at her. "Come on, Janet. Help a guy out, huh?" His wheedling tone was so unexpected that a grin spread across her face.

She laughed, although, based on how Cindy Lou's nose wrinkled, it might have sounded more like a giggle. The thought brought her up short and the smile vanished from her face. "Why do you think I'll be able to help, anyway, O'Dell?"

"You can speak their language. I'm a cop—they'll go running from me. Smith, too. But you? You're like their cool older sister. I mean, you own a bar—you can get alcohol whenever you want. That's some serious credibility in their eyes. I want to use you shamelessly to get some intel on Amanda. These first few hours can be really important in finding someone—young girls especially." All the humor left his face. "You hope it's their choice to be out of communication, but that's not always the case. In fact, it's *often not* the case."

A knot of genuine concern balled up in her stomach.

Cindy Lou nudged her in the side. "I can handle things 'til you get back, boss. Get outta here. Go find that girl."

Janet tucked her ID into her back pocket and tossed the rest of her purse on a shelf under the bar. "Fine. Let's go, O'Dell— but you owe me."

Their fingers brushed when they both reached for the door at the same time. He cleared his throat and motioned that she should go first. "I'm pretty sure you still owe me from over a year of investigations here, but sure. I owe you."

———

"I met her."

O'Dell looked over, his eyebrows drawn together.

"Amanda. I met her out at the high school, asked her about

Lola. She seemed genuinely confused about where Lola could be. Also made it sound like the boyfriend was no good."

"What'd she say?"

"Just that she'd never met him, but didn't like how Lola described him." She shrugged. "Not much to go on, huh?"

O'Dell shook his head.

"So what happened?"

"Parents said they last heard from her yesterday morning, when she left for school. She sent a text at the end of the day like usual. Nothing seemed out of the ordinary, but she wasn't home when her mom returned from work. Mom went through her room and noticed that her overnight bag was gone—and her school backpack hung in the closet instead. So she definitely planned to go somewhere."

"Boyfriend?"

O'Dell flicked on the turn signal and headed north through town. "Uh-huh. He's from another school, and his parents haven't seen him since yesterday, either."

"Oohhh." Janet nodded knowingly. "So they're together somewhere...planning their future? Ugh. Kids are so dumb."

"No—they're naive. Big difference."

A billboard advertising the zoo, just a mile ahead, touted their new cage-free enclosures. For some reason the sign made her think of Jason's father. Did he feel caged in after the divorce? Trapped? They passed the beautifully manicured zoo entrance, with tall, yellowed grasses swaying in the late afternoon breeze. It would be terrible to feel that way...but breaking the law? Doing what basically amounted to petty theft for free coffee and muffins? She pressed her forehead against the window, her eyes glazed, barely seeing what they passed as she wondered when Jason planned to talk to his dad. Or if.

"Hey—you still there?"

She blinked back to the car. O'Dell's hand rested just inches from her thigh, as if he'd reached out to tap her and thought better of it at the last minute.

"Oh, sorry. Just thinking."

"When you answered the phone earlier, you said 'It's okay. I was stressed, too.' Are things okay?"

She looked away from O'Dell out the window again. He was always so observant when it came to her. It was nice...and also stifling.

O'Dell took the on ramp onto 40 East, and she turned back to face him. "Where are we going?"

He smiled, recognizing that she wasn't going to answer him. "A friend of Amanda's thinks they might be holed up at a motel in Kodak."

"Then why didn't you just go?"

"You think they're going to open the door to a cop? Never. And I can't go breaking the door down—kids might die of shock. No, you go in, act like housekeeping or something, and talk to them. Get them to come home. Their folks are worried. They probably can't see past tonight, you know?"

"I am not the right person to talk to them about a responsibility to their parents, O'Dell! I wouldn't even know where to begin!" Janet's mother had been dead for years, and she'd only connected with her father recently, after a lifetime of thinking that he'd abandoned her mother when he found out she was pregnant. He'd tracked her down recently and claimed her mother had never even told him she was pregnant.

"Do your best. Pretend it's your kid, Janet. I'm sure something will come."

When the motel loomed large in front of them, she turned to her partner for the day. "And if I manage to talk sense into these two idiots, what then?"

"Then you bring them out and we take them home."

"No charges?"

"They're minors. We'll let their parents take care of punishment."

Janet thought about that while O'Dell went inside the office to get information from the front desk. He was out a few minutes later with a key and a smile.

"The housekeeping cart is on the second floor. The manager said it's all yours. They're in room 215."

She crossed her arms. "You seem to be enjoying this a little too much. Why isn't Smith here? This case is right up her alley."

"Kids have only been gone fifteen...twenty hours. Not a missing persons case yet. But Mr. Adler asked if I could help. What can I say? I wanted to."

"Mr. Adler? You mean the school principal who wanted to have me arrested? Great. So glad to be doing *him* a favor." She harrumphed but snatched the key from O'Dell and climbed out of the car. "Ridiculous. Housekeeping, my ass. I'm about to walk into two teens boinking each other with nothing more than a cart of towels to cover my eyes."

"Do your best, Janet. Talk some sense into them."

She huffed up the metal staircase to the second floor and swiped the housekeeping cart from the nearest hallway. Since when was she ever the voice of reason? She was just as likely to be the one gallivanting off with her boyfriend under her mother's disapproving glare as the one trying to end a secret tryst.

Nevertheless, she reached out and knocked on the door to room 215. A muffled giggle was followed by a warbly voice saying, "No—no thank you. We're good."

She pinched her lips together and knocked louder this time. "Open up," she snarled, then cleared her throat and tried to lighten her voice. "Uh, building maintenance here. There's a problem with the uh...plumbing in the bathroom. Should just take a minute." She inserted the key into the lock and entered the room.

The drapes were drawn, the room dark. "Amanda? I have a message from your mom. Can I talk to you for a minute?"

CHAPTER SIXTEEN

At a red light, Amanda caught Janet's eye from the backseat through the rearview mirror. "Would you say my mom is super pissed, or more like...super worried?"

Janet looked to O'Dell to answer. He shifted sideways with a frown. "Did you hear your boyfriend's dad?"

Amanda swallowed hard and nodded. "Uh-huh. He was really angry."

"Right." O'Dell faced front again when the light turned green and eased off the brake. "I think your mom is going to be more worried."

Amanda pressed her forehead against the window. "I'm sure the anger will come later."

Janet snorted. "Well, I mean, you did leave your mother's house to get laid, without having the courtesy to leave a note, call, let her know you were safe, and now you have the *gall* to complain that she might be angry? Uh...yeah! She's pissed. Of course she is."

"Janet," O'Dell admonished, and reached out to touch her leg.

She smacked his hand away. "O'Dell! I'm serious. Can this girl try and put herself in her mother's shoes?" She craned her neck around to look at Amanda. "Imagine that *you're* at home after school one day, and your mom never comes home from work. No call, no note, nothing—just a complete no show. Would you be able to fall asleep, not knowing what had happened to her?"

Amanda closed her eyes and her bottom lip trembled, but Janet didn't let up. "Or maybe you'd call the cops? Her friends? Maybe you'd start with her boss, to ask if she knew what happened?" Janet's face felt hot and her voice was too loud, but she couldn't rein in her emotions as she rounded on the teen in the backseat. "Would you try the hospitals to see if they had any accident victims? Call the highway patrol for the same reason?"

Unshed tears shimmered in the teenager's eyes when she opened them, and O'Dell shot Janet a look. "What? You told me to act like she's my kid. And now suddenly I'm pissed!" O'Dell stared ahead and she shrugged. "I'm just saying, she better go in there groveling for forgiveness."

Janet wrinkled her nose, Amanda continued to stare out the window, and O'Dell looked at her like she'd lost her mind. She squared her shoulders and caught Amanda's eye through the mirror. "Don't do drugs."

"Huh?" Amanda's wide eyes stared at her blankly from the backseat.

O'Dell snickered and she glared at him. "Isn't that just always good, solid advice?"

They pulled up to Amanda's house and the teen tried to shoot out of the car, but there weren't any handles in the back and she groaned and threw herself against the seat. "Can *she* stay in the car, please?"

O'Dell hid a chuckle behind a cough. "No, we'll both escort you inside, in case your mom has any questions."

His shoulders shook with unaired laughter and Janet ignored him completely as she stood and opened the back door.

Amanda climbed out of the car and made to move past Janet,

then stopped and searched her eyes. "She was lonely. Like, really, terribly lonely."

"Who?"

"Lola. You asked me back at school the other day if there was anything I wanted to tell you that might help bring her home. Her mom just started dating that loser Paul, and wasn't spending any time with her. And I...well, I guess I abandoned her at the same time with my new boyfriend. I didn't mean to, it just—it happened." She looked over her shoulder when O'Dell cleared his throat. "Anyway. I just wanted you to know that. She might have decided to leave because there wasn't anything keeping her here, you know?"

Amanda sniffled loudly and then squared her shoulders and walked stiffly up the front walk.

The front door flew open and an unexpected figure ran onto the porch and down the steps.

"Mrs. Bridges?" Amanda said.

Lola's mother hugged her. "Oh, Amanda! We've been so worried!" Her eyes darted behind her to the cop car parked on the street. "Is—we thought that you might not be alone..." She dropped her arms down to her sides. "Was Lola with you, too? You can tell me. I won't be mad at her, I promise!"

Amanda's face fell, and she stammered down at the sidewalk. "I'm sorry, Mrs. Bridges. I don't know where Lola is."

Misty covered her mouth with her hand, her eyes bright, and nodded rapidly. "Of course not, dear, I don't know what I was thinking. Get in the house, your mother's been sick with worry."

Amanda glanced at Janet one last time and then walked with heavy steps up to the porch. O'Dell followed. Before they disappeared inside, a woman cried out, "Mandy! Oh, thank God!"

The circle of light that cut across the dark night shrunk to a mere sliver before disappearing completely as the front door swung closed.

Suddenly, Janet found herself alone with Misty, both women teetering on the edge of an emotional breakdown.

"I thought—I-I hoped that Lola might be with her. Maybe they'd planned just to get away for a few days. You know how kids are—they like to do things in groups, and I...I guess..." She shook her head violently and crossed her arms over her chest, as if physically holding herself together. When she looked at Janet again, her face was closed off, hopeless. Her eyes shifted to something behind Janet as she said, "No news, then?"

Janet shook her head. "I'm going to the Annex Friday night." She tried to clear the emotion out of her creaky voice with a cough. "Amanda thinks that Matt, the guy Lola might have been dating, hangs out there. I thought we're more likely to get some answers on their turf, you know? Away from school."

Misty stepped closer to Janet and reached out to touch her arm. "Are you okay, dear?"

"Of course—yes, I just...thinking about you and Amanda's mother...it just—I'm fine."

Misty's lips pressed together and her breath stuttered in. "You'll keep us posted?"

"Of course. I'll call you as soon as I find out anything new."

Lola's mother nodded again and walked past Janet down the walk to a car parked across the street. Janet watched her drive away, filled with a new resolve to bring Lola home.

"What happened back there?" An hour later, O'Dell put the car in park and turned to face her; the overhead lights in the parking lot of the Spot cast a yellow glow on the lower half of his face.

"What do you mean?" Janet studied her folded hands, resting on her lap.

"Well...you got pretty animated with Amanda."

"Uh-huh."

"So...who did you lose?"

She leaned against the head rest and blew out a sigh. "I bounced around a lot after high school, and a few years ago, I'd moved back in with my mom. We kept out of each other's way, mostly. But one night she didn't come home from work. I found out later that she'd had a heart attack while driving home." She turned to look at the front door of the Spot. "It took days to find her. The car went into a ditch—it was completely covered by overgrown scrub brush. They were..." Her breath caught and she sniffed loudly. "They were long days."

O'Dell reached out and placed his hand on hers. "I'm sorry, Janet. That must have been very difficult."

Her nose tingled and her eyes felt full from unshed tears. "God, this was years ago, but something about tonight just brought it all back for me. To do that to someone on purpose? No one should have to lay in bed at night wondering where her family is."

"You helped bring Amanda home." O'Dell squeezed her hand. "And hopefully we'll do the same for Lola."

She frowned—she hadn't managed to do anything for Lola's mother yet.

"Do you want me to walk you in?"

She moved her hand from under O'Dell's and shook her head. "I'm fine. Good night, O'Dell."

He sighed and leaned away. "Good night, Janet."

CHAPTER SEVENTEEN

"I feel like we all should've had a say in this hire." Cindy Lou's big blue eyes looked at Janet reproachfully as she signed for a delivery at the cash register. Several days had passed since Janet had returned Amanda to her house.

The bar had been open for an hour, but it was still early, and no customers were there—although that was perhaps due to the raucous noise from the construction crew outside.

Now that Bruce Hobak's employees had finished digging up the area of the parking lot where the covered eating area would go, a dozen workers gathered to assemble the framework for the pergola addition. Hammers, both manual and powered by batteries, were going non-stop.

"I mean, it's like adding a member of the family. Don't you want to know what we think about him?" Cindy Lou opened a pair of scissors and sliced open the tape holding the cardboard box closed, then lifted out another box, heavy by the way she moved.

"What's that?"

"I think..." She opened the interior box and squealed. "Yes! I thought so!" She grinned and lifted out a bright red fire extinguisher and added, "I got two! One for each exterior door!"

Janet rubbed her temples and took a deep breath, then poured herself a vodka. She picked up the soda wand, but when two pneumonic hammers hit at the same time, she placed the wand back in its cradle, opting for a lime wedge instead.

Cindy Lou walked the larger extinguisher out and set it down by Mel's usual seat by the door, then came back and eyed the back door doubtfully. "I'm not sure where to put this one. It doesn't look like there's room to hang it because of the juke box."

"Let's just put it under here for now," Janet said, shoving the bright red canister under the bar. "And thanks. I'd forgotten all about what Bruce said."

"Luckily you've got me, lurking in the background taking notes." Cindy Lou grinned. "So...about Cameron..."

Janet smirked. "I know we are a small staff, but I really think he's going to fit in with everyone here."

Mel stopped taking chairs off a table nearby and turned. "Where did you find him again?"

Faith turned the page of her newspaper loudly and didn't look up, but Janet could almost see her ears tuning in to the conversation from a few seats away.

Janet bit her lip, unwilling to admit that she'd hired him from Faith's pool of potential employees from a few days earlier. She squared her shoulders and got up from her stool. "What's important is that he'll be here any minute. And I want us to welcome him into the Spot family."

"The Spot family?" Cindy Lou tilted her head to the side. "I like that."

A jingle caught everyone's attention. Amidst the chaos in the parking lot when she'd first met Cameron, Janet hadn't really taken stock of her new employee. So the man who walked into the bar was shorter than she'd remembered, barely five-foot-six, and had stocky, wide shoulders and slim hips. His white blond hair caught the light just as the door swung closed behind him and when Janet stepped forward, she saw Cindy Lou looking longingly at his naturally pale hair.

"Cameron, nice to see you. I'd like you to meet a couple of your coworkers. This is Cindy Lou, my assistant manager," the two nodded at each other, "and this is Mel. She works the door for us on busy nights, and sometimes helps out at the bar when we're in a pinch."

"She's your bouncer?"

As Cameron assessed Mel critically, the bouncer leaned forward and rested her chin on top of her hands, which were folded on top of the mop handle.

A short stand-off between the two followed, which finally ended when Mel pushed the mop roughly around the floor without taking her eyes off of the new cook. "I could bounce you or anyone else out of here whenever I want. Don't you forget it." Her eyes narrowed and she stared at Cameron until he looked uncomfortably away.

Janet forced a laugh. "We've got a real nice crew here, Cameron. I can't wait for you to get to know everyone." She shot a look at Mel, who only pursed her lips in response, and pushed Cameron back the same way he'd just walked through the bar.

"I didn't mean to—"

"Never mind. She'll be fine."

"I've just never heard of a girl bouncer."

"She's *a woman*, and I said I understand. But I'd say it's time for you to open your mind."

Cameron looked taken aback, but Janet straightened her back and continued to guide Cameron out the door. This was her first hire in ages, and she was hanging a lot on it being successful.

"Here it is." She gestured grandly to the food truck. The new layer of red paint didn't entirely cover the old logo, the letters for Timmy's Taco Truck still raised slightly against the rest of the panel. "What you think?"

"I guess I'm wondering where Timmy is?" Cameron

scratched his forehead and his eyes settled on a rusty spot of the frame by the front tire.

"You and me both. It's my truck now, and you mentioned on the phone you are familiar with fry baskets. I think that's all the expertise we need for this job. Let's head in and check out the set up."

She pulled out her keyring and unlocked the back door to the truck, then motioned that Cameron should go first.

Janet climbed up three steep steps to get into the truck and immediately crossed the small space inside and forced open the service window. Every surface, even the floor, was made of stainless steel. Cool air drifted into the small interior, and dust motes danced in the early afternoon sun.

Cameron drew a fingertip across the closest counter. "Pretty dirty."

"And that's why I'm giving you a few days to clean the inside, test everything out, and let me know what I'll need to purchase to get things up and running by Saturday. That's going to be our grand opening of the restaurant."

"What's it going to be called?"

"What?"

"Are you renaming the place now that you'll be serving food?"

"Huh." Janet leaned back against the nearest countertop, stumped. "I hadn't thought about it." She tried to shift, but her back pocket was now attached, via some unknown sticky splotch, to the counter. She twisted her hips to break the seal, then ripped a paper towel square from the roll hanging behind her and draped it over the sticky spot. When she looked back up Cameron was eyeing the door like it was an escape hatch. "You got something in mind?"

"Sure. Cameron's Canteen."

Her brow wrinkled and she tried to come up with a diplomatic way to say, "Who the hell do you think you are?" Before new words came, a sly grin lit up his face.

She chuckled. "If we make any changes, it'd be something like

Janet's Joint." He ducked his head and she led the way out of the truck. "Come on. You'll need to fill out some forms and then you can get to work. I have a bunch of cleaning supplies left over from a situation with the Beerador a while ago. You can start with those." She led the way through the bar and into the office and pointed at a bank of small lockers on the wall adjacent to the door.

"The locker on the top left is open. That's where you can put your stuff when you get to work every day. We have a strict no-phones policy when you're on the clock. I'm not paying you to play games or text with friends. If you don't have food to cook, there's always going to be something that needs cleaning. If you can't find something to do, I'm more than happy to give you a job."

Cameron nodded, then took the seat Janet motioned to and picked the pen up from the desk. "Come on out when you're done and we'll get you set up out there."

She let the door close with a bang and sidled up to Cindy Lou. "Well?"

"Well, what? You hardly let us say two words to the man before you ushered him to safety."

"I thought Mel was going to break him in half."

"Could have if I wanted to!" the bouncer called from across the room.

"Well, don't! We need him."

Cindy Lou leaned in toward Janet and lowered her voice. "That woman has ears like a damn moth!"

"A moth? Don't you mean a bat?"

"That'd be like saying someone is as strong as an ox."

"What's wrong with that? Ox are strong, right?"

"An ox is the third strongest living animal. You should say strong as a gorilla."

"Right again!" Mel called with a grin.

Janet shook her head, then looked around the space, still empty of customers. "Where's Faith?"

"Oh, she left in a huff about five minutes ago. Muttered something about all her hard work not being appreciated anywhere she goes." Cindy Lou popped one fist on her hip and shook her head. "You'd think she might take the hint, but I'm guessing she's gonna keep right on 'working hard' for you, hon."

Janet grimaced. She had no doubt Cindy Lou was right.

"What's this?" Janet picked an envelope with her name on it up off the bar.

Cindy Lou's brow furrowed. "I don't know. I'd swear it wasn't there just a minute ago."

Mel put the mop away and cruised closer. "That lady from the other day dropped it off. Asked for you, but said she couldn't wait."

"Misty Bridges? The missing girl's mother?"

Mel nodded and Janet tore the envelope open. Inside, a new, more recent picture of Lola. This one was a candid shot, with a group of friends in the background.

Amanda sent me this, and I wanted you to have a copy. Today is Lola's birthday. Thanks for all your help bringing my baby girl home.

A sliver of guilt slid down Janet's throat, making it hard to swallow. She hadn't done much since Misty had hired her. But that would change tonight at the Annex. Janet's plan took shape in her head.

"Mel, can you show Cameron where the cleaning supplies are? Tell him to take a few hours today to scrub out the truck, and then have him write out a list of supplies he'll need. I can pick everything up tomorrow morning."

"No problem, Janet." Mel rubbed her hands together in a way that made Janet worry for Cameron.

"Go easy on him, okay?" she admonished, then grabbed her purse from the shelf under the bar. She peered inside the massive bag and made sure Lola's phone was there, then she dug her keys out.

Cindy Lou turned at the jangle of noise. "Where are you going?"

"To the Annex."

Mel planted her elbows on the bar and leaned forward. "Isn't that a high school make-out spot? What, ah...who are you meeting there...and does Jason know?"

Janet smiled without humor. "Not that he'd have time to meet me anywhere lately." She moved out from behind the bar and headed toward the door. "I'm going to find out who Lola's boyfriend is, and see if his friends know where he might be. He and Lola have been gone for too long."

CHAPTER EIGHTEEN

The sun was already setting in the cool late-winter afternoon, but it was still too early to find anyone at an outdoor hangout spot, so Janet made an unscheduled stop by Quizz's office.

Her mentor's feet rested on her desk, and she leaned back in her office chair and looked up with a grin when Janet laid out her evening plans.

"You want to take me to the Annex?" Quizz smiled. "I think at some point you got the wrong idea about me, Janet." She chortled at her own humor, but made no attempt to move from her desk chair. "I don't think so."

Janet leaned against the door jamb. "There's something creepy sounding about a woman in her thirties roaming around Lookout Point alone. But *two* women in their thirties?" She wagged her eyebrows comically. "Totally legitimate, right?"

Quizz picked up a pen and clicked it open and closed a few times while she thought. "You think you'll find this Matt guy there?"

"No, but I think we'll finally find some of his friends, learn more about him—where he lives, what grade he's in, where he hangs out. And all of those facts might help us track him and Lola down."

"Police haven't been able to identify him."

"Right. But what kid's going to talk honestly to police—especially when they think their friend is going to get into trouble? Not many. But we're just a couple of cool chicks." She tried to use O'Dell's logic to make her argument, but Quizz wasn't buying it.

"We're going to stick out like sore thumbs, and someone will probably call the cops on us for even being there."

"No way. No one's supposed to be there. If anything, we'll just ruin the night for some super cool kids who won't feel comfortable smoking their weed or drinking their illegally purchased beer in front of us."

Quizz clicked the pen slower and slower until she stopped altogether. "I hate cool kids."

"Right? They're the worst."

A wide grin stretched across Quizz's face. "Yes," she hissed. "Why didn't you open with that? I'm in. Let's go ruin the night for some cool kids!"

"It's not exactly Lookout Point, is it?" Quizz eyed the ramshackle barn warily. Only the thumping bass to an unknown song made it out to the road where they stood. The rundown structure was lit in the distance by car and truck headlights and a campfire.

"I guess the darkness is part of its charm."

"Just part of it?"

"Hmm, good point. It might be *all* of the charm." A breeze blew across the field and Janet lifted her nose into the air and sniffed. "Well, that and the weed."

They left the car alongside the road, figuring they'd have better luck approaching the teens on foot. Closer to the barn, figures came into sharper relief, and the familiar tune of an old punk rock song took shape.

"Looks like two groups—you want to split up?" Quizz asked.

"Then we're right back to creepy old single lady wandering amongst the teens."

"Together it is. Follow me." Quizz made her way to a scrawny teen hunched over an open laptop. When he saw them, his eyes darted down to his computer; his fingers snaked out and soon a new song echoed from the speakers.

Quizz cocked her head to the side, listening. "Is that '*Warning*' by Green Day?" His double take was comical. "We're not cops, okay? Not here to arrest anyone." Nearby, engines fired, a stampede of people intent on leaving.

"Not cops?" the boy asked, eyeing a set of car keys on the table next to his computer.

Quizz reached out and covered the keys with her hands. "Nope. PIs. Just want to talk. Can you tell your people to abort the exodus?"

He grinned appreciatively, then tapped a button and a different song replaced the last. He produced a microphone from the table and announced, "False alarm. Back to business." Then he looked at the two women. "Don't screw me over, okay?"

Janet sat down on a folding chair across from him. "What's your name?"

"Kyle Bronstal."

"You all go to Holderside High?" He nodded, and she held Lola's picture out. "You know Lola Bridges?"

Kyle leaned in and studied the picture, then shook his head. "Never seen her. She a freshman or something?"

Janet shook her head. "No. She goes to Boulder Ridge, but she's supposed to be dating some kid named Matt from your school."

He shrugged. "Don't know any Matts."

Quizz frowned. "Not police, remember?"

Kyle lifted one shoulder and dropped it. "Fine. There's a Matt in that truck over there—but I'd make some noise as you approach, unless you want to see all of him, you know?"

"Why are you up here all alone?" Janet asked.

He shrugged again. "Lookout. Plus I like to mix the music. It's kind of my thing." He looked up at Janet. "You sure she's not your daughter?" He motioned to the picture with his chin. "She looks just like you."

She pressed her lips together, more offended than she should be that this kid thought that she was old enough to have a seventeen-year-old daughter.

He donned a pair of headphones and turned his attention back to his computer.

Quizz shot Janet a look that said, *you owe me so big*, then led the way to the truck.

Janet was relieved to see that the vehicle was not, in fact, rocking, but she still cleared her throat and coughed as they approached. She tapped on the passenger-side window. "Looking for Matt?"

A girl stared at her without moving.

Quizz had gone around the back of the truck and now knocked on the driver-side window. "Hello!"

The pair sunk down in their seats, trapped, and then both windows lowered automatically.

"Hey, listen, we weren't doing anything wrong, okay, and you can tell my mother that when you drop us off. Don't impound my truck, man. Last time it cost two hundred and fifty dollars to get it back and my dad was supper pissed—"

"We're not cops!" Janet said loud enough that Matt's girl-friend flinched and shrunk away from the window. "We're looking for this girl. Do you know her?"

The girl's eyes narrowed and she crossed her arms over her chest when she looked from the picture of Lola to Matt.

"I don't know her, Wendy, I swear!"

"Unbelievable!"

Janet jumped out of the way when Wendy shoved her door open and stalked toward the circle of light around the barn.

"Thanks a lot," Matt said with a frown.

Quizz wrapped her hands around the window frame and leaned in. "Listen, Matt, I don't have a lot of patience for teen angst. This girl, Lola, is missing. You know anything about her?"

He threw his hands up. "Don't know her! Never even met anyone with the name Lola, okay? God!" He threw himself back against the seat and pulled a face.

Quizz and Janet's eyes locked through the cab of the truck. The kid seemed put out that his girlfriend was pissed, not because of anything to do with Lola.

"Are there any other Matts at your school?"

Matt stared ahead with a pout, but Janet had nowhere else to go. She would happily wait him out. He must have sensed it, because he blew out a loud breath. "I don't know. There are, like, a ton of Matts, aren't there? It's not exactly an uncommon name."

"Any of them dating Lola?"

He shrugged, and Janet lost her temper. She reached into the cab of the truck and picked up a wine bottle. "I'm sorry that we messed up your plan for the night—which I'm guessing included wooing your girlfriend with a swig of Strawberry Hill Boone's Farm straight from the bottle and hoping she forgot about the smell of pig shit in the air so you could get to second base, but we're looking for a missing girl, and her parents are worried. Now, look at this picture and tell me what you might know!"

Matt's cool-guy attitude dropped like a rock and he shrunk away from Janet, a look of defeat on his face. "I'm sorry about this girl, but I don't know her. Ask Kyle. He knows everything about everybody at the school."

She whirled around to look for the DJ, but the table was empty. He was gone.

CHAPTER NINETEEN

Janet bolted down the poorly lit path toward the main road. When the light from the barn had all but disappeared, she caught sight of a hunched figure, moving fast.

"Kyle!" she called. "Kyle, just a few more questions!"

Quizz huffed and puffed behind her, trying to keep pace. "Suddenly you're an Olympic-caliber sprinter?" she muttered.

But the sprint was short-lived, because up ahead, Kyle tripped over a loose rock and fell to the ground, his bag of electronics flying off of the path into the dark mass of unmown pasture grass. He swore colorfully and creatively and when Janet finally reached him, clutching the stitch in her side and gasping for breath, he looked up at her, rocking back and forth on his haunches.

"Do you have a flashlight? Where's your cell phone, dammit? I've got to find my stuff!" He crawled forward on his hands and knees, reaching out blindly for his beloved electronics.

By then Quizz had joined them, loudly hacking as she caught her breath. Janet held her phone up, lighting the closest section of the field. Soon Quizz did the same. After he'd collected his belongings, he stood and clapped dirt off his pants.

"Thanks." Kyle clutched his messenger bag to his chest and

took an unsteady breath. "Took me two years working at McDonald's to save up the money for this stuff."

Janet and Quizz kept their cell phone lights trained on the path in front of them, and they took a more leisurely pace to the road.

"Where were you going?" Janet asked when they finally got to the line of cars parked on the shoulder. She followed Kyle to his car, a beat-up Ford Escort, and memorized his license plate in case he ran off again.

"I know you said you weren't the cops, but I'm not really supposed to be out tonight. I don't know, it seemed like as good a time as any to just head home." He unlocked his car and gently set his bag down in the backseat. "Did you find anything out about your girl?"

Janet shook her head. "Matt said that he didn't know her." Kyle made to get into his car, but she held out a hand. "Matt also said that you might know if any of the other Matts at Holderside were dating Lola."

Kyle made a face. "Matt doesn't know shit. Excuse me, but it's true. He's thinking of Kyle Richardson. That dude is always up in everybody's business. I'm the music guy, right? The tech guy. I don't have time to get into everybody's personal relationships. Jesus," he added under his breath, "I'd make time for my own relationship first."

Quizz snorted and Janet had to force the smile off her face as well.

"So you're a tech guy?" She rummaged around in her bag, finally pulling out Lola's cell phone. "My boyfriend's a tech guy, but something struck me as I was out here tonight. We are old, and *old* and *tech* go together about as well as Matt and Wendy, am I right?" Kyle snickered and she continued. "So can you take a look at this phone, tell me if you see anything that Lola's mother and I might have missed?" She punched in the password that Jason had discovered earlier at the bar then handed the unlocked phone over to Kyle. He swiped through the screens, then made an appreciative sound in the back of his throat.

"Yep, here it is." He held the device out so Janet could see the face of it, then pointed to an innocuous-looking app.

"What are you showing me—she liked maps? What does that have to do with anything?"

Kyle shook his head. "It *looks* like a maps app, but this is actually an app of subterfuge. It's like a Snapchat you can hide from parents. Parents are so tech dumb that she probably didn't really even need to have it on her phone, but it's kind of fun."

He tapped the app open and Janet was less than impressed when a familiar-looking directions page filled the screen. She shrugged. "So...what am I looking at, exactly?"

Kyle grinned and nodded. "I don't know, maybe I was wrong. Even when it's open you're not seeing it."

Janet's eyes narrowed and she took the phone from Kyle's outstretched hand and held it close to her face. That's when she saw it. In the upper left corner of the directions page, a small transparent envelope icon faded in and out. "Right here?" She pointed to the icon. He nodded, and she tapped it with her finger. Suddenly the interface of the app changed completely, and a chat session opened with one question:

Continue chat with Matt?

"Bingo," Quizz breathed, reading the screen over her shoulder.

Janet held the phone out like it was a bug. "Argh! What do I do? I don't want Matt to know that I have Lola's phone!"

She slid the phone into Kyle's hands like it was a time bomb. He tapped the screen three times rapidly, then handed it back to her. "Here's their conversation thread." He swiped up and whistled low. "Looks like they'd been talking a lot. Hey, I've really got to go. My mom's going to kill me. I said I was going to work, but McDonald's closed an hour ago."

Quizz thanked him, because Janet's head was bowed over Lola's phone. The screen glowed brightly in the dark night, and

Janet scrolled down to read the last few lines between Lola and Matt.

"He asked her to visit him..." She scrolled up. "Looks like a couple of weeks ago. Ugh, he said, 'I can't stand being apart.' Is this guy even in high school?"

"I'm guessing not." Quizz sighed.

"Oh my God, he wants her to get on a Greyhound bus—"

"A Greyhound? To where?" Quizz asked sharply. "I thought Matt went to another school in Knoxville. Is he from another town—another state? Oh, Jesus, this is going to mean informing the FBI if she moved across state lines. I never should have let you take this case—"

"Hold on, hold on..." Janet continued reading the messages until she found the answer. "Memphis. He asked her to meet him at a restaurant in Memphis."

"Well, I guess that's better than a motel. But what are we supposed to do now?"

Janet looked up from the phone and squinted in the sudden darkness until she found Quizz. "I guess we're going to Memphis."

"I don't have time to go to Memphis!"

"Tomorrow. We'll have to leave tomorrow. This can't wait."

CHAPTER TWENTY

"I cannot believe that you talked me into doing this." Quizz shot a disgruntled look at Janet before hiking the strap of her bag over her shoulder. "Our client's sure not going to pay for this. I'm not going to pay for this. So who's going to pay for this? Remind me again?"

"We're going to mark this down as a business expense and you'll get a big fat tax break for the year." Janet turned toward Quizz. "Hey—it'll pay for more advertising!"

"More? What are you talking about? I don't do any advertising. Who's got money for that?"

"Oh—I thought...Hmm." Janet had remembered Misty Bridges saying she'd found Quizz's agency through an ad, but she must be mistaken. She looked up to compare the departure time on the overhead board to the time displayed on the digital ticket on her phone. "Looks like we have forty-five minutes until we board."

"And remind me again why we're not driving?"

"Because then we'd have to get a hotel room and pay for gas and more meals. I think we'll end up coming out ahead here, especially flying standby like we are."

Quizz's silence was tacit acknowledgement that Janet had

found a great price on their tickets. After a moment of silence, she said, "But we'll have to rent a car."

"I got a great deal on a crappy car. We're all set."

"But then we can't split up! And we only have six hours on the ground."

Janet stared at Quizz for a long moment. "Well, you know what they say."

"What?"

"Teamwork makes the dream work."

Quizz chuckled and started walking toward their gate. "Come on, Black. Let's get this over with."

———

The flight was uneventful and within three hours they were sitting in their rental car while Quizz called up directions on her phone.

A smile ghosted her lips, but she didn't look up when she said, "I can see why you got a steal on this car."

"Turns out they don't give deals on Mercedes or BMWs."

"Guess not. At least it's clean."

The old Chevy Metro was indeed clean, the vacuum tracks still visible on the upholstery in the backseat.

"Can you turn off the heat? I'm starting to sweat."

Janet fiddled with the controls, but all she could do was change the air from hot to cold—there was no way to turn it down from full blast.

"Now we know why it was on sale."

Janet cranked her window down, hoping the cool winter air might counteract the intense heat blowing from the registers, and put the car into drive. "Which way?"

"Looks like Monahan's, the restaurant where Matt and Lola planned to meet is just northwest of where we are now." Quiz studied the map on her phone and added, "We'll need to go north on 55."

They were quiet as Janet navigated the unfamiliar streets, with Quizz occasionally adding directions to the voice on her phone's map program until they got into the correct neighborhood in South Memphis and started looking for parking.

Quizz turned in her seat to face Janet. "I hate to be blunt—"

"No, you don't."

"But how are we going to get a line on this guy—are we going to ask the other customers if they know a dude with a Hawaii-shaped birthmark near his belly button? I could be wrong here, but we might get the cops called on us. Especially if this guy's a minor." Quizz shivered, despite the heat blowing on them.

"I brought Lola's picture along. I'm hoping we'll get a hit on her before we have to resort to the birthmark." Janet handed a spare picture of the girl to Quizz.

Her mentor grumbled but kept her mouth shut until they climbed out of the car. "I'll work the front of house. You head around back and see who's chatty in the kitchen."

Janet raised her eyebrows, but Quizz didn't look back as she disappeared into the front of the restaurant. Alone outside, Janet gingerly made her way to the alley between buildings and peered around the corner. Though it was daylight, this wasn't the kind of neighborhood she'd usually care to wander through on her own. The smell of day-old grease hung heavy in the air and she stepped over a puddle of questionable liquid as she headed toward the back of the restaurant

A screen door hung crookedly on its frame. Meat sizzled, metal spatulas clanked on the griddle, and Janet stopped to listen to the short bursts of speech that issued from within. "Lucy, order up! Jonesy, order up! Got to get this food 'fore it gets cold, now. Order up, order up!"

Footsteps pounded toward the door, and Janet leapt aside to avoid getting smacked as the screen slammed against the brick wall.

The cook had a cigarette clutched between two fingers in his right hand and a lighter in his other. "Entrance is around front."

She nodded but didn't move, and his head tilted to the side. "What are you doing out here?" He stopped just a foot away from Janet and kept an eye on her while he lit his cigarette.

"Getting clogged arteries just by proxy." Janet leaned closer and looked hungrily at the cigarette. She'd quit smoking years earlier, but still loved the smell.

The cook grinned and held the stick out toward Janet. "You need one?"

Janet blew out a slow breath and leaned away. "No. Thanks, though. I'm looking for someone. A girl from Knoxville's gone missing—maybe came here." She reached into her purse and pulled out Lola's picture. "You recognize her?"

"Nope." He took a deep inhale.

"Can you look at the picture before you answer?" Janet stepped closer. "She's only fifteen. Her mom's worried, man."

He took another deep drag, then cut his eyes sideways at Janet as he exhaled. "Fine. Everybody looking for someone lately. Give it here." Janet put the picture in his outstretched hand and watched his eyes as they scanned Lola's face. "Maybe."

Her eyes narrowed and she tried to squash down the flicker of excitement in her gut. "When?"

"I don't know. There was a girl. Maybe a week ago? She mighta been here with Matty—but like I said, I don't know. She was blond, that's about all I could say for sure."

"Matt! Yes. We're looking for him, too. Do you know him? Last we heard he asked this girl to meet him here, at this restaurant."

The cook blew out a slow breath that had nothing to do with his cigarette. "Shit. He's one weird dude. How old you say she was?"

"She *is* fifteen. How—how old is Matt? Is he in high school?" As soon as the question was out of her mouth she knew the answer was "no." The cook looked to be in his thirties. No way he'd know a high schooler dating another high schooler by name.

"Lola." He rolled the name around in his mouth and then looked over at Janet, a question in his eyes.

"Yes—yes, that's her name. Did you meet her?"

"I don't know, man. A lotta chicks come and go up there, okay?"

"Where? What's Matt's last name?" Janet pulled out a notebook and was still feeling around the bottom of her bag for a pen when the cook smacked his lips.

"I don't know. I mean, I don't hardly know the dude, okay?"

"But you might have seen her? What did they order? You're not going to get in trouble! We just want to bring Lola home. So what's Matt's last name?"

The cook tossed his cigarette down onto the uneven asphalt and ground it out with his heel. "My break's over. They didn't come into the restaurant—at least, not that I know of. I saw them heading up there." He pointed to a rickety fire escape ladder that looked like it hadn't passed a city inspection in decades. "I only know Matt because sometimes we out here taking smoke breaks at the same time. His apartment's up there."

He looked sidelong at Janet again before disappearing back into the kitchen.

Janet texted Quizz, and minutes later the other woman rounded the corner into the alley. "I'm glad you got something. The hostess couldn't seem to get past my being a PI to actually answer any questions. Do you think Lola's up there?"

"Only one way to find out."

Quizz nodded and followed her to the base of the ladder. "Let's do this."

CHAPTER TWENTY-ONE

The fire escape creaked when Quizz placed her foot on the bottom step and she looked back at Janet with a scowl. "You do not inherit my business if I fall off this ladder and die. You hear me?"

"Loud and clear, boss. You want me to go first?"

"No. I want you to be my soft landing if the metal fails."

Janet started to chuckle, but as she heaved herself onto the ladder behind Quizz, it shuddered and screeched and the laugh died on her lips. "There goes the surprise factor."

Quizz looked up from the steps at the two large windows facing the alley. "I don't think surprise was ever in the cards."

By the time they completed the dangerous journey to the first level of the fire escape balcony, all the blood had drained out of Quizz's face, leaving her pale. She crept closer to the apartment wall and only acknowledged Janet's "You going to knock?" by reaching out with a shaky hand toward the metal fire door.

Janet narrowed her eyes. "Are you scared of heights?"

"Of course not." *Knock, knock, knock.*

The sound was timid, and when nothing happened, she tried again, pounding loud enough that the cook downstairs stuck his head out of the screen door and yelled, "You tryin' to wake the dead?"

Janet breathed, "God, I hope not."

She took her lock pick set out of her bag and went to work on the doorknob, Quizz barely moving to the side, so that the woman was breathing down her neck. "A little space, please?"

When Quizz didn't move, Janet looked up to see that the other woman's face was still pale, and now a sickly sheen of sweat covered her forehead.

"I'm not scared of heights. I just..." She sighed. "I just don't like it that much. Now move," she snapped. Janet stepped back. "There's a reason I'm called the mentor, and you are called the apprentice." She turned her back on the railing behind and straightened her shoulders, as if leaving her fears behind. She set her oversized shoulder bag down by her feet, unzipped the main compartment, and pulled out a crowbar.

With a splintering crack, they were in. The cook shook his head and scurried back inside the kitchen. Quizz used her elbow to push the door open and Janet peered over her shoulder into the dark room beyond.

"Don't touch anything." Quizz snapped on a pair of gloves and reached into the apartment, feeling along the wall for a light switch.

As soon as she flicked it, a blue-white overhead light illuminated the entire space. Janet took in the entire small efficiency apartment with a glance. What she saw kept her glued to the metal landing outside.

In a low voice, Quizz said, "Oh my God."

Janet's eyes didn't know where to land. The kitchenette took up the back wall; the refrigerator and a foot-long stretch of chipped linoleum countertop led to the undersized two-burner stove. But it was the small lacquered wooden table that left her wide-eyed and unblinking. A stack of old VHS tapes took up half of the table. Three rolls of duct tape were stacked with precision next to them, with two great strips of the silvery tape hanging off the close edge of the table and fluttering in the slight breeze coming through the open door. Several zip ties jutted through the jagged plastic opening of a package, and as Janet finally stepped into the apartment, she couldn't help but wonder to what use the rest of the package had been put.

"Ugh." Quiz pulled her sweatshirt up to cover her nose and mouth. Janet looked down at her useless V-neck, wishing she could do the same. The smell of spoiled milk or meat made her think no one had taken the trash out for days.

"What's this?" Quizz stepped close to the wall leading to the bathroom and passed her gloved hand over what looked like brown paint splatters.

"Paint? Dried blood? I can't tell."

Janet grimaced. Had a crime happened here? She looked down at the duct tape and zip ties as she wondered. That's when the first VHS cover came into focus. She cringed.

"Oh my."

"What?"

She lifted her lock pick up—still gripped tightly in her hand—and used it to tip the top VHS case over, revealing another porn tape underneath. "There must be twenty different movies here."

Quizz frowned. "What is this place?"

Both women continued to catalog the space.

The only other place to sit—or sleep—was a futon, shoved against the adjacent wall and covered with piles of clothes.

Beyond that, a narrow wooden door stood half open just three steps away. "Bathroom?" Janet's voice was barely more than a whisper.

"Think it's empty?" Quizz's voice was also low.

Janet's heart rate quickened at the thought of what might be lying on the other side of the door. Was there a bathtub? Was it occupied?

She raised her face and sniffed the air. Nothing could compete with the smell of spoiled food. She took a few cautious steps forward and, following Quizz's lead, used her elbow to push the bathroom door open. Her eyes swept the tiny space and she slowly raised one hand to cover her mouth.

Behind her Quizz held up her phone. "Do I call 911? What's in there?"

"Nothing. But this bathroom hasn't been cleaned in months." It wasn't until the words left her mouth that her shoulders slumped forward in relief. She backed away from the bathroom and when she turned, she found Quizz staring at her, a funny expression on her face.

"What? It wasn't until I saw the bathroom was empty that I realized how worried I was that we'd find Lola here, dead!" Janet heard the warble in her voice but couldn't help it; you could hardly fault someone for feeling jittery in a stranger's apartment with duct tape, zip ties, and the smell of decay.

"No, it's not that." Quizz's eyebrows drew together and she searched Janet's face for a long moment, then picked a picture frame up off the coffee table at her thigh. From where they'd entered just inside the door, a pile of laundry had obscured their view of what sat on the table. But now that they were across the small apartment, a framed picture—a big one at that—seemed to take up all the surface area.

It was a silver decorative frame, almost a foot tall, with white matting surrounding a professionally taken eight-by-ten picture. Quizz handed her the frame. Dread cracked like an egg over the top of her head and slid down the back of her neck until her body convulsed with a bone-jarring shiver.

Her legs felt weak, like jelly, and she placed the frame carefully back on the coffee table, setting it down next to a stack of bills. Her eyes zeroed in on the top page. It was an electric bill, but that's not what caught her attention. The customer name, listed right above the PO Box address, was William Brooks. She slipped the paper out from under the picture frame and, hands shaking, tucked it into her bag, then backed away from the futon, away from the blood splatters, and out of the apartment into the bright winter sunshine outside. Quizz followed her out and pulled the door closed as best she could with the splintered wood and broken lock.

After they made their way back down the rickety ladder, Quizz stepped in Janet's path, forcing her apprentice to look her in the eye. "What's happening here? What's your connection to this Matt guy?"

Something bad was going on, but there was no way she was going to tell Quizz that *Jason's father* was paying the light bill at that duct tape-zip tie-porno house apartment...but that wasn't all. She swallowed down the acidic taste at the back of her tongue and looked up at the apartment door with a grimace.

"Janet, we don't know who he is, but he's got a framed picture of you next to his bed. I don't know where we go from here. Do you?"

CHAPTER TWENTY-TWO

At the airport, Janet excused herself to the bathroom. She needed a minute alone to think. They had a problem, and Quizz only knew the half of it. Why was Jason's dad renting that shitty apartment, and why did it look like a frat boy's dark sexual fantasy had played out there? And why did he have a framed picture of *her* next to his bed?

The obvious explanations were too ridiculous to even consider, and yet...was it possible that William was involved in Lola's disappearance?

She thought back to his behavior—not just since Lola went missing, but in the weeks before that.

He'd been moody, difficult—on edge. But she'd chalked it all up to Faith's looming visit, and the emotions dredged up from a decades-long marriage ending in anger.

But what if it was more? What if he'd been unable to adjust to his new reality?

And what about this Connie woman he'd been dating? No one had met her or seen her during his entire alleged relationship. Did she even exist?

What if she didn't—what if Connie was just a front for Lola? She shuddered. Someone knocked on the stall door.

"You okay?" Quizz's voice was tinged with concern.

Janet cleared her throat. "Yup. I'm almost done." She reached back and flushed the toilet for show, then walked out of the stall and washed her hands.

"What's going on?" Quizz leaned up against the hand dryer and studied her.

"Nothing. I mean, that apartment was just jarring, you know? What do we do now?"

Quizz frowned. "I don't think it's enough to call O'Dell with. I mean, the cook didn't even know for sure if he recognized Lola —and there wasn't any sign that she'd been inside that apartment. Plus, we broke in...so...I think we keep this to ourselves for now."

Janet nodded, her throat suddenly dry. That was fine with her, because at this point, any kind of investigation might lead police right to her own house. A rush of hot fear and cold dread ran through her at the same time, leaving a trail of goose flesh up and down her arms. She rubbed them roughly and avoided Quizz's eye in the mirror.

"Flight's about to board." Quizz looked at her watch. "I'm going to buy some Red Hots. You want anything for the flight?"

She shook her head. After Quizz left, she pressed her hands against her temples, trying to steady her mind. Out in the terminal, she found a quiet corner and called Jason.

The call went straight to voicemail, but just hearing Jason's strong, steady voice was a comfort. "I can't take your call right now. Leave a message, or please call my associate, Mike, if you need immediate help."

How could she possibly summarize her last three hours in a voicemail? "I need you to call me. Like immediately! I'm in Memphis about this missing girl case, and...something strange came up with—" Her voice faltered and she fell quiet. It wasn't exactly voicemail material, accusing his father of child abduction and possibly murder, was it? "Just please call me," she finished weakly.

"Who was that?" Quizz was back, chomping on the cinnamon candy, her cheeks already red from the spice.

"Just trying Jason again."

"No luck?"

Janet shook her head.

"What's going on with him?"

"What do you mean?" she shot back.

Quizz's eyebrows met her hairline and she chewed the candy in her mouth thoroughly and swallowed before answering. "I just mean he's been MIA lately." She studied Janet, clearly noting her jumpy, defensive tone.

Janet forced herself to relax. Quizz didn't know. Jason didn't know. Only *she* knew about William's connection to that apartment. "He's been really busy with a new job." Quizz went out of focus as her brain made a connection. Busy with a job in Memphis, in fact. Huh.

"Now boarding flight 5039 to Knoxville. All silver medallion passengers, welcome aboard."

Quizz popped another candy into her mouth and then pulled her boarding pass up on her phone. "Never been so happy to leave a place, you know?"

They barely spoke on the trip home. The only words Janet uttered were to the flight attendant when she ordered a vodka straight up with lime. She was headed home—to the home she shared with Jason's father. Did she confront him, or wait for Jason? And just how long would Jason keep her waiting, anyway?

———

Not ready to face her house or William, Janet dropped Quizz off at her office and then drove to the Spot. The bar was crowded; the parking lot was full, and even the street was lined with cars for blocks. Janet ignored the construction barrels and drove around the caution tape to park alongside the Dumpster in the back alley.

She ducked past Mel and spotted O'Dell and Detective Smith at the bar. Seeing the other cop set Janet on edge even further. Smith was actively looking for Lola, and now she had information on the case. Information that she wasn't going to share with police just yet. Her body tensed as she approached the pair.

O'Dell smiled when he caught sight of her and stood to offer Janet his seat. Smith didn't move, but kept a steady, if not completely unfriendly, stare on her face.

Janet didn't sit. She locked eyes with Cindy Lou and leaned across the bar to order a vodka with lime. "Make it a double, Cindy Lou."

Janet felt Detective Smith's eyes boring into her and she resolutely continued to face forward, downing half her drink in one gulp. *Steady,* she told herself.

O'Dell continued to hover at Janet's elbow, and Smith finally leaned forward and tapped her on the arm. "Have a seat, Janet."

"No thanks."

Smith and O'Dell exchanged a look, and the other woman stood. "I've got to go to the bathroom. I'll be back in five minutes."

They watched her walk away, then O'Dell pulled Janet into the open seat and sat lightly in the seat next to her. "What's going on, Janet? You seem jumpy or something."

She needed to talk to someone about what she'd discovered in Memphis, but chatting with a police detective probably had consequential side effects. She took a small sip of her drink, already feeling the warm flush of the alcohol branch out from her chest. "O'Dell, what are your job requirements?"

He looked blankly back. "What do you mean? I investigate murders and then arrest people. What's not to understand?"

"No—I mean, if you hear about a..." Her voice faltered, and O'Dell's brow wrinkled. She plucked the lime wedge from the rim of her glass and squeezed it over her drink to keep herself focused and calm, then tried again. "If you hear about a possible crime, do you have to move it up the chain? Or can you sit on it for a while?"

He scooted his stool closer. "What's going on?"

"Seriously, O'Dell, if I tell you something—"

"Can I just say that if *you* know something about a crime and don't report it, *you* could be found guilty of a crime."

"What?" Her eyes darted up to the cop, but she couldn't take the weight of his stare, and she looked back down at her drink. It was empty. Dammit.

"And the same is certainly true for me. I'm a mandatory reporter. However..." He fiddled with the label on his beer bottle, then downed the remainder of his drink in three great gulps. "However, I'm willing to listen to something as a friend, not an officer of the law." He leaned closer. "What happened?"

She met his eyes and saw nothing but raw truth gazing back at her. She could trust him. But before she could launch into the story of what she saw in Memphis, Detective Smith was back from the bathroom.

Instead of waiting for O'Dell to stand up from her seat, Smith slid onto his lap and wrapped her arm around his neck. "So, Pat, are you done here, or do I need to go back to the bathroom?"

Janet's shock at seeing the two of them *together* must have come across, because a flush rose up O'Dell's face. "Janet...I, ah, I wasn't sure if you knew, but Kay and I have been dating for a couple of weeks now."

"And I intend to make sure Patrick doesn't get in any trouble." Detective Smith looked at Janet with a smile that didn't quite reach her eyes. "Can we help with anything, Janet?"

Janet stood and backed away from the stools—from the happy couple—and forced a smile onto her face. "Yes, of course. I—I hadn't heard, so...that's great news. Really, really great." *Jesus, stop saying great.* "We're done here. You two have a great night." She cringed and then turned, walking fast along the bar before ducking under the service area. She didn't breathe again until she was standing next to Cindy Lou, their backs toward O'Dell and his girlfriend.

"Crazy-good business tonight!" Cindy Lou looked over to Janet as she waited for two pints to fill at the taps. "Cameron's doing a great job out there—but God, the paper plates sure fill up our trash cans fast. Faith was in here, talking 'bout having Bruce add an outdoor kitchen to the lanai plans? You'd better keep her on a short leash, huh?"

Janet didn't answer, just stared around her bar with flat eyes. She'd never felt so strange and out of touch with her own business as she did just then. Like she shouldn't even be there. But the alternative—going home to face William—was even less appealing.

Cindy Lou babbled on, too busy to notice Janet's mood. "Everybody sure does seem to love the food. I think you were right to keep the menu simple. Hard to mess up a cheeseburger, ya know? It's funny, ain't it? You get so used to how things are, you can't even see that change is a good thing sometimes, huh?"

"Yeah. Change is so great." Janet turned away from a customer's order and instead filled her own glass. Whether she liked it or not, change was here. She pounded the shot and poured herself another, the action finally catching Cindy Lou's attention. Her assistant manager frowned, but Janet ignored her.

Change was here, all right; she just never imagined she'd be navigating the changes on her own.

CHAPTER TWENTY-THREE

The last customers left only after Mel flipped the overhead lights on full. With a grumble, the group of girls walked out into the night, a white cloud of breath following them through the parking lot.

"Finally!" Mel twisted the deadbolt after them. "I'm beat, Janet. Okay if I leave the mopping until tomorrow? I'll come in early." She looked hopefully across the room.

"That's fine, Mel. Thanks for all your hard work. See you tomorrow."

When the bouncer was gone, Cindy Lou set the glasses she'd been cleaning down on the drying rack and turned to face Janet. "You ready to talk yet, or you wanna keep brooding silently over there like dad-gum Batman?"

Janet hardly smiled at the joke.

"Well, now I know it's serious. Are you okay, hon?"

She couldn't exactly spill the secret of William's Memphis apartment to Cindy Lou, but she was touched that her longest-tenured employee cared enough to ask. "I guess I'm just feeling kind of...adrift."

"Because Jason's been gone so much?" Cindy Lou nodded sagely. "It's a change, isn't it? Weird when it's the change you

wanted that's making you feel so alone." She picked up two more
dirty glasses and turned back to the glass washer in the sink. "I
think this new setup's just going to take some time to get used
to. I don't know." She tossed a smile over her shoulder. "Does it
help or hurt having Jason's family breathing down your neck?
You'll never be alone as long as William's living in the upstairs of
your house."

She laughed lightly and turned back to the glassware, but
Cindy Lou's words sent a chill down Janet's spine. The last thing
she wanted was to go home and face William on her own. How
could she possibly be alone in the house with him and not bring
up his Memphis apartment? But did she really want to know why
there was porn, duct tape, and zip ties? Or find out why he even
had that apartment at all?

No wonder he couldn't afford his own place in Knoxville—he
was already paying for a place somewhere else.

She closed the lid on the condiment container and slipped it
onto the middle shelf of the Beerador, thinking. Maybe asking
William some questions wasn't a bad idea. After all, what would
Jason know? He'd been busy for the last seven or eight days,
hardly home, barely checking in.

Her stomach clenched just thinking about an interview. Then
again, it clenched thinking about not asking him, too.

She and Cindy Lou walked out to the Dumpster with the last
two bags of trash. A light spilled out the food-truck window
onto the dark pavement.

"Cameron?" Janet called. She'd forgotten that the cook was
even there, let alone still working.

He stuck his head out the window and smiled. "Just cleaning
up out here. Busy freaking night."

"How'd it go in there?"

"Good. We ran out of buns with about an hour to go. I just
used lettuce leaves and called them our low-carb special, and no
one really complained too much."

Janet snorted. "I guess we need a process for keeping track of how much to order of everything. You should have let us know in the bar about the problem. Maybe Mel could have gone out to buy more from the grocery store."

"Yeah—there's really no way to get anyone's attention. I could hardly stay on top of the orders as it was! I would have texted, but I had to put my phone in my locker, you know?"

"Hmm." Janet pulled a face as she considered Cameron's dilemma. With him outside, removed from the bar, it really didn't make sense for him to not have any way to reach them except for leaving his post—which was far busier than she'd expected. "I guess I either need to run a phone line out there, or have you keep your cell phone, huh?"

He smiled and ducked back into the truck. Seconds later he pulled the windows closed and the lights flicked off as the back door opened. "Do we lock it up?" he asked.

"I'll get it." Janet stepped forward with the key ring.

"Let's go get our stuff and get outta here, Cameron." Cindy Lou yawned and pulled the door back open. While Janet was in no hurry to leave, everyone else clearly was, because before she could make it back inside the building, Cindy Lou and Cameron were already out the front door and gone for the night.

———

Mel and Kat's half of the duplex was dark when Janet drove up, but her side looked like a midnight madness sale at the mall. Light shone through the blinds from every window, including her bedroom.

The bass of music greeted her as she walked up to the front door, and when she pulled the door open, the heavy smell of cinnamon wafted out of the kitchen, mostly covering a sharp ammonia scent that lingered in the front room.

William dropped a scrub brush into a bucket when she stepped in and mopped his brow with a cloth. "Whew. I'm beat, how about you?"

She looked blankly at the freshly scrubbed windows. "Were you...cleaning?"

"Funny how something hits you and you've just got to get it done that minute! That ever happen to you, Janet?"

"Uh...sure."

"Is that Janet?" Faith called from the kitchen.

"What is Faith doing here?"

William grunted as he climbed down from the stepladder. He carried the bucket of cleaning water to the sink in the minibar— but before he hefted it up to drain, he changed his mind and plucked a rocks glass from the shelf, then turned the faucet on all the way, cranked it over to the hot water side, and pulled out a bottle of whiskey along with some other ingredients.

"I got the oven set up in there today, and I told Faith she needed to make sure it works! She's making cinnamon rolls, and I just decided this minute to make a hot toddy to celebrate. You want one?"

Janet flinched when the chef's knife sliced down into a lemon with a *whack!* Juice sprayed the mirror in a pattern not unlike the blood spatter in the Memphis apartment.

"N-no thanks, I'm just about ready to turn in." Suddenly she didn't want to ask him any questions. About anything.

He shrugged, a suit-yourself expression on his face, then added some steaming hot water to his mug. He shut the faucet off, then twisted the cap off a bottle of whiskey and slugged some into the already steaming liquid. He stirred in honey straight from the squeezy bear and then pinched a lemon wedge between his finger and thumb before dropping it into the mug.

He lifted the cup to his lips. "Mmm." He took a long sip and then cruised to the couch and looked up at Janet, still frozen at the threshold. "How was business tonight?"

Janet admonished herself to *get it together* and walked stiffly to the couch across from him and took a seat. She made a conscious effort to relax her body. "Good. Surprisingly busy, actually." Faith walked into the room with a plate of fresh rolls and set them on the coffee table between Janet and her ex. "We ran out of hamburger buns, if you can believe it."

Faith pulled a roll apart from the rest and sat next to William. "Maintaining the right balance of wholesale ingredients is one of the hardest parts of running a restaurant."

Janet took a deep breath and tried to ignore Faith's superior tone.

"Well, it's a big learning curve for us this week, but the food truck worked amazingly well," she embellished with a smile, feeling no remorse. "Another day or two, and we'll have paid off the truck completely. Won't be able to say that about the outdoor dining addition, will we?" She pressed her lips together. This was not the start she'd planned in the car on the drive home. Riling Faith up would not result in getting answers to any of her questions about Memphis and William. She pressed her shoulders down and tried for a friendlier tone. "Anyway, there are definitely some bugs we need to work out— including how much of what to order. Maybe you'll be able to help me with that, Faith? You certainly seem like an expert in that area."

Faith tried to hide her satisfied smile in her pastry but failed. "I'd be happy to help, Janet. All you need to do is ask."

Janet suppressed a sigh. She felt like she'd just done that, but Faith wasn't going to capitulate so easily. Before she could say something else she'd regret, she turned to William. "Quizz and I made a quick trip to Memphis today."

He choked on his hot toddy, and the next several minutes were spent cleaning sticky honeyed whiskey off the table and leather couch. When all was quiet again, she tried again.

"Yes, we had a tip that whoever Lola was dating might actually be from Memphis."

"Any luck?" Faith's eyes never left her cinnamon roll; her focus on pulling the layers apart was unlike anything Janet had ever witnessed. And it might have been her imagination, but it sure seemed like Faith's body went rigid with her question.

"Uhh...not exactly. Just a dead end that left a lot of questions, you know?"

"Well," Faith replied briskly, "I guess a dead end is better than a dead body."

"What?"

"I-I—I just mean that dead ends are a kind of closure unto themselves, aren't they?"

"To be honest, it all made me think about Connie." Janet turned to face William again. His face, moments ago red from his coughing spell, had drained of color.

"What about her?" he asked with genuine surprise.

"Isn't she from Memphis? When are you going to see her again?"

"William, didn't you tell her?" He shook his head but didn't speak. After several long moments, Faith blew out a breath and said, "William and Connie broke up. He said he just didn't see it working out, you know, in the long term."

"Well...it's a shame we never got to meet her," Janet said as diplomatically as possible, even as her insides squeezed as if she'd turned into the honey bear.

"Whatever are you talking about?" Faith asked, relaxing back into the couch. "I'm glad we didn't waste any time on her, to be honest."

William chuckled, though it sounded forced to Janet's ears. She excused herself as soon as she was able, and found when she was alone in her room, she couldn't quite catch her breath.

A bloody apartment with William's name on a bill, and now he'd apparently told Faith that he and Connie had broken up.

Was that true? Or was Connie dead?

She covered a scream when a sharp knock issued from the other side of her door.

"Janet?" William asked.

She crept to the wood separating her from Jason's father as quietly as she could, and then pressed the toe of her sneaker against the lower corner of the door, knowing that simple physics would be on her side if William tried to force it open.

"Uh-huh?"

"Just wanted to let you know that Jason called—he said he's busy as all get out, but will try and call you tomorrow at the Spot."

"O-okay. Uh...thanks, William."

"Good night."

"Good night."

His footsteps echoed on the floor as he made his way back to the couch. She didn't move from her spot—instead, she leaned forward until her head rested against the unforgiving wooden doorframe. She was exhausted, but probably wouldn't sleep a wink. She'd never be able to turn her brain off, to stop from wondering whether she was living with a killer.

CHAPTER TWENTY-FOUR

Janet hardly slept that night; every time a floorboard creaked, she was convinced that William was sneaking around the house, doing something bad. And somehow, even though Janet had been holding her phone all night, Jason managed to sneak in a call that went straight to voicemail. She was convinced he was avoiding her, using a technology trick to keep her phone from ringing. But why?

She must have drifted off to a hard sleep sometime after five in the morning, and she awoke to the shrill ringing of the landline in her room, late-morning sun slanting through the curtains.

She reached blindly for the receiver. "What?"

"I hate to call you with this problem right now, Janet, but we've got a real situation here at the Spot." Cindy Lou's breathless voice had Janet leaping out of bed.

"What? What's happened now?" She clutched her chest and searched the floor for her pants from the night before, hopping into them and just barely keeping her balance. "Are the cops there? What's wrong?"

Cindy Lou gasped. "Oh, good Lord, no! It's just that—you know we're hosting that big FOP dart tournament tonight? Well, I told Cameron to come in early, and don't you know, he's two darn hours late! I can't get ahold of him. I don't know what to do. But there's got to be a load of prep work for tonight and someone needs to get started."

Janet fell back against her bed with a groan. Planning gone awry for the Fraternal Order of Police dart tournament was not a crisis—at least, not according to her new sliding scale for disaster. No blood? No psycho killer? No crisis. "I'll be right in. Call Mel and ask if she can come in early. I'm sure he just overslept." She buttoned her jeans and plopped back down onto the mattress. "Hopefully he'll show up, but I'll be in soon, too." Janet hung up with a frown, then pulled on her T-shirt and tucked her cell phone into her back pocket as she walked out of her room.

"Jesus, Mary, and Joseph!" she yelped, when she came face to face with Jason's father. His arms stretched high over his head, and an awful expression contorted his face. She leapt back and managed not to scream, only because as his arms dropped, it was clear he was stretching—not launching an attack. "What are you doing? Did you—" She looked behind William at the blankets and pillow stacked on the couch. "Did you sleep out here?"

"Faith decided it was too late to drive back to the hotel, and I thought I'd give her the bed and sleep down here."

"But there's another guest room upstairs—"

"We didn't want to cause extra laundry for just one night, you know?"

"Oh...sure." She slunk past him to the kitchen—absentmindedly admired her new working stove—and then dumped some grounds into the coffee machine and waited while it percolated. Was she nuts? How could Jason's father—so polite that he didn't want to make extra dirty laundry—also be a part of that house of horrors she and Quizz found in Memphis? There must be another explanation, but she couldn't for the life of her figure out what it might be.

She wanted to keep Jason's parents close, keep an eye on them, monitor their behavior. Suddenly, she knew just how to make that happen.

"William! I might need you and Faith to help out in the food truck tonight!"

———

"This really was a great idea, Cindy Lou." Janet surveyed the huge crowd and watched as Mel carted a new keg out from the back cooler. "Right in there, Mel, thanks."

She moved the empty keg onto the cart after Mel heaved the new one into place. The five dartboards that Cindy Lou had purchased at a real-estate foreclosure sale for peanuts hung on the back wall of the bar, and the twenty people who'd entered the tournament mingled with the other patrons as the tournament got underway.

"Finally don't have to worry about the cops showing up, huh?" Cindy Lou asked with a smile.

Janet chuckled, but the sound died on her lips when William walked in the alley door.

"I can't get the damn stovetop to keep the heat!"

Janet made to move out from behind the bar, but Faith stood up with her hand up. "I'm on it, Janet. William, let's go."

She watched Jason's divorced parents chat comfortably as they made their way back outside.

"They sure have come to an understanding recently, haven't they?" Cindy Lou stared after them as she wiped a glass with a dry towel and set it back on the shelf. "I wonder what changed?"

Janet looked thoughtfully at the door through which Faith and William had disappeared. "It's almost like they're going to get back together."

"I've got to hand it to Faith," Cindy Lou said, tapping her lips with a finger, deep in thought. "She sure does have him by the balls, don't she? Like, she swept into town and suddenly he's ended things with his girlfriend and is giving up his bed so she can sleep comfortably? She's got it."

"What?"

"That enviable ability to hook a man." Cindy Lou sighed and then snapped to attention when a customer asked for a frozen margarita. She winked at Janet, then looked across the bar. "No problem, sweetheart. One fantastic frozen margarita, coming up."

Janet's phone buzzed. She looked at the screen and groaned inwardly. Quizz wanted to talk. But before she could answer the call, O'Dell tapped her hand.

"Can I have a word?"

She slipped her phone into her pocket—she'd call the PI back later—and grabbed a pint glass, avoiding O'Dell's eye. "Sure. Need a drink?"

"N-no. I'm good, thanks." He held up his beer bottle and she felt her cheeks heat up at the mistake.

"Oh, okay. So...what's up?" She set the pint glass down and assessed the other customers at the bar to see who was ready to order.

"I guess I just wanted to explain about Kay and me—"

"O'Dell! You don't have anything to explain. I mean..." She scrubbed the counter between them with a wet rag. "I'm dating Jason. You're free to date anyone you want."

After a long pause, he hummed out a sound, then said, "Okay, we won't talk about it." He reached out and touched her hand, forcing her to stop scrubbing and look up. "But I also wanted to follow up with you after last night. You wanted to tell me something?"

"Oh—no. It's fine. Everything's just fine." She pulled her hand away, and filled a glass with beer, just to give her something else to focus on.

"Are you sure? Because you can still count on me as a friend, Janet. I'll always be a friend to you."

She set the full pint glass down on the bar and stared at the thin layer of foam on top. O'Dell was a friend...and she surely felt like she needed someone to talk over everything she'd uncovered lately. She looked up and stared into his engaging bright green eyes. She could trust him; of course she could. She opened her mouth, but someone else spoke first.

"What are you drinking, hon?" Detective Smith came to a stop by O'Dell's side. "Ooh, I'll have the same, Janet. Pat, did you see Rivera got two doubles and then a dang bullseye? You've got to watch his next turn. Come on." She held her credit card out for Janet. "I'll just start a tab. Thanks." She linked her arm through O'Dell's and took the bottle before pulling O'Dell away.

Janet turned her back on the happy couple, but there wasn't time to worry about O'Dell, because Mel materialized at her side.

"I think you need to get out there to the food truck, Janet. I don't want to say they're going to kill each other...but they've got sharp knives, hot oil, and a lot of poorly resolved anger issues."

"Are they fighting?"

"No, but they're backed way up, and don't seem to be handling the stress very well."

Janet hurried through the crowd inside the Spot and climbed into the back of the food truck outside. Faith stood at the griddle with two dozen burger patties sizzling away. Meanwhile, William hoisted a basket of black fries from the hot oil.

"Dammit, Faith, I told you to tell me when the timer went off. I can't hear it over everyone shouting orders at me. Now we've got to toss all this oil 'cause it'll taste like burnt food!"

"Well, I can't hear the timer when you're over there yakking away with the customers like we ain't got five hundred things to do back here, *William*!"

"Hey guys. Looks crazy out here. What can I do to help?" Janet stepped between the two.

"Oh, she wants to help now, isn't *that* delicious," Faith muttered, tossing cheese squares onto half the patties.

"You leave her alone, ya old hag. Janet," William's eyes sparkled as Faith sucked in an injured breath, "we need another bag of frozen fries. I set them in the ice machine when we came in from the store this morning. Can you go get them?"

"I'm on it," Janet replied, ignoring Faith completely. She skipped back down the steps and entered the Spot through the alley door to avoid the crowds.

O'Dell smiled at her, but she pretended not to see him as she headed for the walk-in cooler. Kegs were stacked two tall right by the door, and she had to pick her way past even higher stacks of cases of bottles to get to the ice machine along the back wall. "What a mess," Janet grumbled. Cameron must have moved things around earlier in the week when he'd been prepping the food truck. She'd have to tell him—if he ever came back in—that part of his job was to leave the cooler as neat as he found it. She stepped around a messy pile of broken-down boxes and reached out to lift the lid of the ice machine when she pulled up short. An open hand rested on the concrete floor at the base of the machine. The skin had an unhealthy bluish pallor that left a smattering of goosebumps across her shoulders. Janet's eyes moved along the lines of the woman's outstretched arm, the blond hair, the camisole and jeans.

The blond hair.

Was it Lola?

She reached out to touch the wrist, but the skin was icy.

Whoever she was, she was dead.

CHAPTER TWENTY-FIVE

Janet stumbled back toward the door, then stopped and turned back. She crept forward again and lifted a lock of hair that covered the woman's face. Small crow's feet stamped the outer edges of the woman's eyes, her thin lips were parted slightly, and a drip of blood came from the ear closest to the ground. A small puddle of it pooled just below her chin, and the blond hair on that side matted into the blood.

Definitely not Lola. But there was something oddly familiar about the woman's face.

She backed out of the room and walked directly into O'Dell's chest. He grabbed her by the shoulders to steady her. "Whoa there! You okay?" Janet turned around and locked eyes with the homicide detective.

"Yes, Patrick, of course she's fine," Detective Smith snapped from somewhere to Janet's left. "It's your turn, come on. You're holding up the tournament. I'm sure Janet has things to do tonight."

But O'Dell didn't drop his hands. "Janet? What's wrong?"

Suddenly she was shivering uncontrollably, and it had nothing to do with the temperature. "B-b-body. There's a body."

"What body?" O'Dell asked.

"Patrick, really!" Smith snapped.

William stuck his head inside the door just feet away. "Janet? You got those fries? I got a dozen hungry cops out there just a-waitin' on you, now!"

Janet looked at William, then back at O'Dell. Her lips felt tight, as if she couldn't move them, but with everyone looking at her, she forced the words through. "There's a dead woman in the cooler."

"What'd you say, Janet?" William stepped all the way into the building, and his lips tilted down into a frown. "Who's dead?"

Janet pointed wordlessly at the door to the walk-in cooler, and William made to charge in.

Smith's arm shot out, nearly knocking William off of his feet. Her earlier irritation was immediately replaced with cool, calm authority. "Janet, where exactly is the body?"

"Against the back wall. By the ice machine."

Smith pushed William against the wall and O'Dell dropped Janet's arms and stepped around her, then pulled open the door to the walk-in cooler. The cops nearest him put their darts down, somehow aware through body language alone that the tone of the night had shifted dramatically.

"Secure the entrance," someone said.

Janet made a half-hearted attempt to head to the door when Smith barked, "Not you! Stay there."

Rivera propped the door open with his foot as O'Dell disappeared into the dark interior.

He was back out less than a minute later, his cell phone pressed to his ear. "Homicide at the Spot, down on Retreat Road. Rivera and I are already here, but I'll need an evidence crew as fast as you can get them here." He slipped the phone into his pocket and then lifted something in his other hand. His eyes squinted as he read off the small rectangle. "The victim had an ID in her back pocket. Connie Hutchings." He looked to Janet. "Do you know her?"

"Connie," Janet repeated slowly, and couldn't keep herself

from turning to look at William, still pressed up against the wall by Smith.

"Connie?" His ragged breathing almost swallowed the name.

"Is that your girlfriend?" Janet couldn't keep the accusation out of her voice.

The lights flicked on across the room, and the people farthest away from the cooler squinted around, confused.

Smith pushed William to the corner booth. "Who is she?"

William's already pale face drained of any remaining color. "She was my—my girlfriend. I mean, kind of. We'd been taking a break."

"Is that right? And why's that?"

"Well, she'd stopped returning my calls, but also, well...Faith thought it was best."

"And who's Faith?" Rivera asked, his voice calm, friendly.

"My ex-wife."

"And where is she?"

Janet didn't like the direction of this line of questioning. "Hey, Rivera—"

Smith stalked forward and grabbed Janet's arm, steering her toward the bar, away from William, away from Rivera. She still heard William's answer.

"Well, she's in the food truck, just like I was."

Rivera nodded to another cop and he headed for the door.

"What's going on here?" Janet asked, shaking free of Smith's grip and turning to face the cop. Smith was unusually short, and it felt satisfying to stare down at someone for a change.

The cop smiled humorlessly. "What's going on is that your future in-laws are the best suspects we've got in what looks like a murder investigation. Take a seat. You're not going anywhere, either."

———

Because her calls had gone unanswered for days, she sent a text message to Jason.

Dead body at the Spot. Police questioning your parents. CALL IMMEDIATELY.

Seconds after hitting send, a text came in from an unknown number.

This is Mike. I'm contacting Jason ASAP. Hold tight.

"Hold tight? What the—"

"Hold what?" O'Dell appeared by her side, his eyebrows drawn together.

Janet tucked the phone back into her pocket. Had Jason turned his phone over to his colleague? She'd have to investigate that question later. She looked up at O'Dell. "Nevermind. What's going on?" She motioned to William, still sitting in the corner booth. The color had returned to his face, but his vacant gaze was unsettling.

"Something's not right here, Janet. Why would he be holding back?" O'Dell crossed his arms over his chest. "Do you think he'd protect Faith?"

"You think Faith killed Connie?"

O'Dell rubbed a hand roughly across his face. "Too early to say. But she's completely unaffected by the death, and William's acting strange."

Janet looked across the bar at the other corner booth. Faith sat at the table, studying her nails.

"Any idea yet on when Connie was—" She pressed her lips together, unable to finish the question.

"The temperature inside the cooler complicates the timeline. The coroner doesn't want to say until she gets the body back to her lab. But best guess—around twelve to twenty-four hours."

So when Janet was lurking around a Memphis apartment, Connie—from Memphis—was likely killed.

O'Dell cleared his throat and sat down next to her. "I need to ask you a few questions."

"Shoot."

His eyes narrowed.

"I just meant go ahead."

"When was the last time you were in the walk-in cooler today?"

Janet blew out a sigh. "I was in there before we opened today, but just grabbed a couple cases of Bud closest to the door. I'm not sure I would have noticed if Connie was—if she was already lying back there."

"What about last night?"

She shrugged. "Cindy Lou or Mel might know more. I'm sorry."

He nodded. "I believe you."

Some of the tension leached out of her shoulders and she slumped over the table, until O'Dell's next question caught her completely off guard.

"Where was William last night?"

"At my house. I was tossing and turning all night and heard him working in the kitchen on and off."

O'Dell's mouth tilted up on one side. "Still not done?"

"So close I can taste it. There was a measuring issue with the countertops and they had to be sent back. We're just waiting on them and we'll be ready."

"So what was William working on?" The question was casual, but Janet felt the intensity behind it.

She looked up from her hands and narrowed her eyes. "He's still working on the cabinet trim and baseboard pieces. He can only do so much at a time because of his knees."

"Arthritis?"

Janet nodded.

Q'Dell made to stand. "Please thank Mel for us. She corralled all the customers inside and kept them from leaving until we could take down everyone's names. She was a real lifesaver."

"You heading out?" Janet stood with him. They were close. O'Dell didn't step away when she moved next to him, and she instinctively looked around for Smith.

"She left. And yes, I'm leaving, too. Not enough evidence to bring anyone in, but we'll make sure William and Faith know they're not to leave Knoxville city limits."

Janet nodded. They weren't going anywhere, anyway.

As O'Dell pushed away from the table and headed over to talk to Faith, her phone buzzed and she took it out of her back pocket to see a final text from Mike.

Can't reach Jason. I'm coming in tomorrow. I have some questions.

Janet set the phone down on the table and slid it away from her like it was a grenade about to go off. Was Jason missing, too? It seemed the only reasonable explanation for why he wasn't calling her back, or responding at all to her last text. But Mike was coming in. What did he have to say to her that he didn't want to say over the phone?

She tried to steady her breathing, but could only manage short, shallow gasping breaths. It didn't feel like there was anywhere safe to go tonight. Janet rested her head on her folded hands on the table.

Another night in her house with Jason's parents, who may or may not have killed Connie in cold blood and then dumped her body at the bar. Suddenly, William's story about having an inexplicable urge to clean her windows left her feeling cold and clammy. Was the reason behind the cleaning so innocent? Or was there something else to hide?

CHAPTER TWENTY-SIX

Faith rolled her suitcase to the bottom of the stairs and turned to look accusingly at Janet. "This night has been one of the worst in my life!"

"Pretty bad for Connie, too," Janet muttered, hanging her coat in the closet by the door.

When she turned back around, Faith's sharp eyes matched the tone of her voice when she said, "What?"

Janet stalked across the room and headed for the minibar. Last night she hadn't felt safe in her own home. Tonight, she was officially pissed off. She was angry with Jason for disappearing when she needed him most. She was angry with his parents for acting shady when she needed stability. Hell, she'd take plain sanity just then. "I said it was a pretty bad night for Connie, too."

"Oh." Faith bowed her head and took a step back. "You're right. How thoughtless of me."

"William, what happened to her? What happened to Connie?" Janet narrowed her eyes and studied his reaction.

Jason's father's expression darkened. "I have no idea, Janet. And you'd better watch who you're asking what."

William moved to the bar and Janet had to step out of his

path—she wasn't at all sure he wouldn't bowl her over if she didn't. She and Faith ignored each other, both women watching him fix a large pour of bourbon.

After he placed the bottle back on the shelf, Janet cleared her throat. "I haven't talked to Jason tonight. Have either of you?" Again, she watched both of their faces like a hawk. She wanted —no, needed—to believe that none of them could get ahold of him.

"Nope," William said slowly after he'd drained his glass.

"Nothing here, either," Faith added.

William put his glass next to the sink and turned around. "When I talked to him yesterday, he said he was still in Memphis for work. Weren't you just there, too?"

Janet didn't answer. She felt adrift; as far from Jason as she'd ever been—and not just physical distance. She'd never felt so unconnected emotionally from him, either. What was he up to?

"You never said what part of town you were in, Janet." Faith's tone made it clear she thought Janet had let her down with the omission.

"Some kid at a local high school helped me crack into that missing girl's cell phone, and she'd agreed to meet her boyfriend at a place called Monahan's Restaurant."

Janet studied Faith's oversized red suitcase and stepped forward. "Bummer about the hotel not having a room for you anymore, Faith. Want me to bring your bag upstairs for you?"

When Jason's mother didn't answer, she looked up and found Jason's parents staring at each other. The tension between them took her breath away. She didn't like the way Faith was looking at William—anger, mixed with fear and anxiety—and she didn't want to be anywhere near it.

Janet grabbed Faith's bag and made her escape.

She ignored the dust bunnies that swirled around her feet on the steps, her heart heavy. Life felt out of control, and she hated that feeling—it reminded her of her wayward younger years, when she was angry, rudderless, and irresponsible. Now she was a business owner with a boyfriend, but the same internal chaos swirled up inside of her.

She dumped the bag into the empty guest room and headed back down the hall. Tense, angry voices floated up the stairwell.

"Where is my son, William?" Faith's terse whisper meant she was trying to be quiet, but the soundwaves bounced along the wooden floors and drywall like they were being amplified by speakers.

Janet froze at the top of the staircase.

"I don't know where he is," William answered, and Janet had to strain to hear him. "But we do know that Jason's looking into things. It's going to be okay."

"How can you say that?" Faith snapped. "I've never felt like things were worse!"

"Not now, Faith!" William whispered, then he called up the stairs, "Janet, need any help up there?"

Her cheeks flushed with the feeling that she'd been caught, but she clomped heavily down the stairs and beat a hasty retreat to the safety of her bedroom with an unconvincing excuse about being exhausted—even though her body vibrated with nervous energy. After she closed her bedroom door, she stood just inside her room, her ears straining to hear the rest of Jason's parent's conversation.

It wasn't long before they continued with their conversation.

"...can't be the problem..."

"...But what if that's what he's looking for?"

William's low bass got lost in the HVAC system, but Faith's pitch was just high enough that it was easier to hear through the door.

"We said we'd washed our hands of him. And we have to hold firm to that."

Whatever William said in response angered Faith.

"We're not abandoning him. You know how he is! You can't reason with him. He's safe as long as he can keep his spot at the home. He's safe there!"

William's voice raised in accordance with his temper. "I'm telling you it's all quite suspicious. And I think that's what Jason's looking into. He didn't go to Memphis for work, no matter what he's telling us. And that must mean he's worried about her. And I am, too. Look what happened to Connie—and we weren't even serious. Jason *loves* her! What do you think he's going to do about that?"

Faith shushed him and the floorboards creaked as the pair made their way upstairs.

Janet leaned against the wall in silence for a long time. By the time she wearily made her way across the room and dropped into bed, she knew two things with certainty. Faith and William knew —and maybe Jason did, too—who'd killed Connie, and they weren't going to tell the police a thing.

———

"Inspection day," Janet said as soon as her assistant manager walked in the door. "What are our odds?"

Cindy Lou plopped her bag down and then propped her hip against the countertop. She tilted her head to the side and, ticking them off on her fingers, listed out her thoughts. "*One* murder case is now open here, *two* fry baskets melted right into the hot oil last night in the food truck when Faith came in to see what was taking William so long and the cops pulled both aside for questioning and no one remembered to turn the heat off until smoke started billowing out of the windows, *three* of the food truck tires are now completely flat, and *four* people might have gotten food poisoning from the frozen interior of the burgers that Faith served." Her eyes narrowed and her lips crowded to one side of her face. "So I'm thinking we have a shot."

Janet's brow furrowed.

"Oh, I'm sorry, did I say we had a shot? I meant we have no chance in hell of passing this inspection."

Despite her foul mood, Janet smiled. She'd never heard Cindy Lou cuss before. "What has you so riled up?"

"I was in the darn walk-in cooler twice yesterday *with a dead woman*! I sure wish people would get their act together around here. You can't go shoving dead bodies into this bar! That's twice now! What is wrong with people?"

Janet had to agree; they'd had more than their fair share of death at the Spot. But there wasn't time to question the universe just then. The inspector's appointment was coming up in just half an hour.

"Did you call the clean-up company?"

"Yes, and they said we get the frequent customer discount. Ten percent off for repeat clients."

Janet's nose wrinkled. "So we'll be able to open today?"

Cindy Lou crossed her arms and nodded. "The medical waste crew will be here in fifteen minutes."

"And we've got thirty minutes to clean up that food truck. Since Cameron seems to be a no-show—"

"Again!"

"Would you mind keeping an eye on the bar while I head out and assess the damage?"

"No way!" Cindy Lou said. "I am not staying in this bar alone. You stay here, *near the murder closet*. I'll go clean that darn truck."

"Uh—you're going the wrong way!" Janet called after her when she went in the opposite direction of the food truck.

"I have to put my bag away first!" She flounced off into the office with her bag. A minute later, she was back. "Janet?"

Her tone caught Janet by surprise and she looked over. "What now?"

"I think you'd better come see this."

Janet glanced at her wristwatch and sighed. They didn't have time for any other surprises, and frankly, she didn't have the energy for anything else just then. But she followed Cindy Lou into the small office space. Cameron's locker door tilted open.

"I didn't mean to open his locker, but you know how sometimes if you slam one of the doors, the others kinda open up? Well, I just put my purse into my locker, but I was a little irritated about how this day is starting off, so I might have closed my door with more force than normal."

"So? Just close it back up, Cindy Lou. It's not the end of the world." She reached forward to do just that, when a wisp of blond hair made her snatch her hand back. "What the..." She leaned forward and lowered her voice to a whisper. "What's in there?"

Cindy Lou shook her head hard. "I'm not touching anything."

Janet groaned and, swiping a pen off the desk, she nudged the locker door open.

"Good Lord," Cindy Lou breathed. "Is that the next victim?"

CHAPTER TWENTY-SEVEN

"Are you going to call Cameron?" Cindy Lou asked when Janet picked up her cell phone. They were back behind the bar, and by unspoken agreement weren't going to separate again.

"No." Janet's lips pinched together and she tapped O'Dell's name, then waited impatiently for him to answer.

"If you're calling for an update, I'm not at liberty to discuss anything with—"

"No. I'm calling with information," Janet interrupted.

"What kind of information? I know you'd like to believe that Faith and William are innocent, but just because they're Jason's parents doesn't mean we're not going to take a long hard look at their possible involvement."

"It has nothing to do with them. My new cook Cameron is a no-show at work again today, and Cindy Lou and I happened to look in his locker, and we found a lock of blond hair in a little baggie, and a picture of a blond girl. I just thought...well, with Lola missing, and Connie dead...it sure seems like someone's going after blonds."

"Do you have Cameron's contact information?"

Janet relayed his cell phone number and his address, as he'd marked down on his employment papers.

"And the picture—the hair?"

"I'll keep it safe for you here behind the bar." Janet gingerly picked up the zip-top bag, then shoved it and the five-by-seven picture on a shelf below the counter.

While she did that, O'Dell heaved a great sigh. "It probably won't do us any good, especially since you moved it from his locker, but we'll run some tests on the hair at least; rule out Connie and Lola."

Janet grimaced but nodded.

A silence between them stretched, and she turned away from Cindy Lou.

O'Dell finally spoke. "Are you all right?"

"Mm-hmm. Just been a crazy week."

He barked out a laugh. "That's one way to describe it. I'll swing by Cameron's place, see if he's home. If he is, I'll bring him into the Spot. We can both ask him a few questions, okay?"

"Sounds good." Janet's breath hitched as a surge of emotion hit her, and she blinked quickly to clear it away. O'Dell—though just a friend—was a lot more reliable than Jason lately. She hated to wonder why that was.

She disconnected and slipped the phone into her back pocket. When she turned around, Cindy Lou was studying her intently.

"I know this isn't my place, but if you're going to make a change, do it now. He's not too interested in that Smith lady, but he might be if they spend more time together. You know?"

"Don't be ridiculous, Cindy Lou." Janet squared her shoulders and grabbed a spray bottle. "We'll wait for Mel to get here to do the cooler—"

"Praise Jesus!" Cindy Lou chirped.

"That means we have time to wipe down the tables right now." Evidence techs with Knoxville Police hadn't cleared the scene until after four that morning. It had been far too late to clean anything. But now they had to get ready for a full night of business.

The bell over the door jangled, and a gorgeous brunette walked in.

"Hey, hon, we're open, but barely. Food service doesn't start until...later." Cindy Lou finally came up with a time frame that was technically true.

The woman moved like a cat, slinky and sure of herself. She glided past Cindy Lou and came to a stop by Janet. "Are you Janet?" Her voice was like an FM disc jockey: low, throaty, sexy.

"Who's asking?" Janet immediately felt on the offensive. She ran a hand through her hair—which she'd washed, but let air dry on her way into work that morning. The woman standing opposite her looked like she'd just had a professional blowout, with contoured makeup and designer clothes.

"I'm Mike. I've been working with Jason, and I have some questions for you."

"*You're* Mike?" Cindy Lou's voice cut through Janet's shock and she snapped her mouth shut. She ripped her eyes away from the goddess in front of her when Cindy Lou spoke again. "What in the hell is wrong with Jason?"

Janet nodded along with Cindy Lou's question, wondering the same damn thing when Mike cleared her throat delicately.

"I haven't been able to get in touch with him for days. He hired me, trained me briefly, then set me loose on a project and I haven't seen him since. I just don't feel comfortable with the setup."

Janet snorted. "I'm right there with you, *Mike*."

Mike's eyes narrowed. "It's short for Mikaela, but I've gone by Mike since middle school. You got a problem with that?"

Cindy Lou stepped between them. "No. No problem here. I'm afraid Jason's not here. We haven't seen him for days, either."

Mike's expression hardened. "Well, he's missed my first pay day, and I'm not inclined to keep working for him. I'm in high demand in this area, if you want the truth—"

"I believe it," Janet muttered.

"And I don't take lightly to being treated this way." She tossed a 9x12 yellow clasp envelope down on the table between them. "Here's some information I found interesting. You can tell Jason I expect to be compensated properly if he expects to keep me as a contractor." She pivoted and stalked out of the bar.

When Janet recovered enough to look at Cindy Lou, the other woman was fanning her neck with the envelope. "Is it me, or was that woman H-O-T hot?"

Janet's lips twisted into a snarl. Janet didn't like it one bit that Jason hadn't fully explained the hire. The factual omission stung worse than an outright lie.

Cindy Lou nudged Janet's shoulder with her own as she picked up her spray bottle and cloth. "I guess now we've got to figure out where in the heck Jason is! He's not here, he's not with Mike, so what's he been doing while the world crumbles down around us?" Cindy Lou's head jerked up as she realized that she'd spoken out loud. "Oh, I mean, well, you know what I mean, boss. I just...where is he, right? I'm sure he'll be back home with you soon enough. And really, good news that he *wasn't* with Mike, right? That's got to be a good thing. I wouldn't want my man near that man-eater if she was the last computer expert in the world!"

Janet winced and turned away from Cindy Lou. She sprayed cleaning solution on a table and swiped at it angrily. Where *was* Jason? His father mentioned that he'd been in Memphis when Janet was there. Was he still there? Was he ever coming home?

Her phone buzzed and she ripped it out of her pocket—but it wasn't Jason. O'Dell's text was short and to the point.

Taking Cameron downtown. Meet us there.

Well, at least she'd get answers to one question today.

CHAPTER TWENTY-EIGHT

•

Janet clutched the zip-top bag with the picture and hair in one hand and scrolled through her phone with the other. There wasn't even a seat in the waiting area of the downtown police department, so she leaned up against the wall. O'Dell had never minded keeping Janet waiting in the past, and today was no different.

When the door that lead back to the detectives' section finally opened, it wasn't O'Dell who stepped through.

Smith, though small, looked down her nose at Janet. "Let's go. He's waiting for you in the back."

Janet brushed aside the urge to stay right where she was and followed Smith down the hall. "Anything new on Lola?"

"Nothing. We've re-interviewed all of her friends, the principal, her teachers, her parents. Everyone knows about a boyfriend, but nobody knows who he is."

Janet's step slowed down until she was several doorways behind Smith. She needed to tell Smith about Matt, about Memphis, the apartment, William. "Ummm...the boyfriend—that's the kid everyone's calling Matt, right?"

Smith looked over her shoulder at Janet. "That's the one. Doesn't seem to go to any nearby schools, either; at least, not that we've found. This way, Janet." She pushed open a door on their left and walked in.

Janet followed slowly, still mulling over how she needed to proceed. But this was going to be tricky, and almost anything she shared could lead to William going to jail. Maybe Faith, too. Did she really think them capable of murder? Her lack of sleep the last two nights were a testament to how unsure she was.

"Well?" Smith stared at her expectantly.

"Uh—sorry. What was that?"

"Did you bring the picture and the hair?"

Janet reached into her bag and pulled out the items from Cameron's locker.

Smith assessed the picture quickly, then scrutinized the hair, her nose scrunched. "Not Lola, but that's the only thing I know."

"How can you tell just by looking at it?"

"Lola dyed her hair. This is untreated hair." She looked up with a grin. "My mom was a hair stylist. I spent a lot of long days at the salon with her when I was growing up."

Janet nodded stiffly and Smith took the evidence and left the room. When she was alone, Janet frowned as she surveyed the space. The room was plainly furnished: a small table, a large dark window, and two hard plastic chairs. She sat down and crossed her arms, realizing belatedly that she was more put out by Smith's anecdotal story about her childhood than by being alone in a police interview room. She didn't like knowing anything that made Smith seem more human. She didn't like to think about why that was.

When the detective came back empty-handed, Janet asked some questions rapid fire. "What are we doing here? Is O'Dell going to bring Cameron here? This room won't hold all of us, that much is clear." Even just the two women in the small room made for a tight squeeze.

Smith pressed a button on the underside of the table, and the dark window lit up to reveal the room next door. "O'Dell thought you could watch him interview Cameron from in here."

Cameron sat at an identical table and chair setup in the other room. He leaned back in his seat, aggressively chewing a wad of gum, and Janet had to wonder how long he'd been sitting there. "We're ready," Smith said into her walkie-talkie.

Moments later, the door in the other room swung open and O'Dell walked in. "Sorry to keep you waiting. We sure do appreciate you coming in on such short notice."

"No problem, man. But I don't have a lot of time. I missed work the last two days, and I really need to go in today and grovel, you know?"

"As it turns out, I did know about that. We had a situation at the Spot last night—"

Cameron's groan cut O'Dell off. "The dart tournament? Oh, man, I'd completely forgotten about that dang thing until just now." He groaned again and ran his hands roughly through his hair. "I'm sure I'm totally fired." He groaned again.

"Where were you?"

The cook sprawled back in his chair, one arm hanging down by his side, the other still grasping a tuft of hair at the crown of his head. "Unbelievable. Family problems will come looking for you, no matter how far you try and get away, man. I was just dealing with some family drama. It's over now, but not soon enough, man. Not soon enough."

O'Dell nodded sympathetically. "Your parents? Siblings?"

"My parents. I had to run to Memphis for a crisis that just never seemed to end."

O'Dell's eyes flicked over to the two-way mirror, and Janet's gut clenched. Cameron had been in Memphis?

"Where in Memphis were you?"

"My parents live in Cooper-Young. I just got back last night —but late. Too late to go into work."

"Probably for the best," O'Dell said, leaning against the table on his elbows.

"Oh yeah? Why's that?"

"Janet found a dead woman in the walk-in cooler."

"What? Holy sh—I mean...was it someone...was it someone they knew?"

Cameron's voice shook on the last word, and Janet and Smith both leaned forward instinctively.

"It wasn't a stranger, that's for sure. While we were investigating the scene, we found this in your locker. Care to explain?" O'Dell held out the lock of hair and the picture.

The color drained from Cameron's face. His lips pinched together, and he suddenly became interested in a rip in the knee of his jeans. When he looked up, his face was set, his expression grim. "Am I under arrest?"

O'Dell leaned back in his chair, crossed his arms over his chest, and rubbed his lips with his hand. "Is there a reason you think you'd be under arrest?"

Cameron didn't take the bait. With a screech of metal against tile, he pushed his chair back and stood. "You know where to find me, obviously, but I have to go. I'm late for work."

O'Dell nodded, but didn't move, just watched Cameron walk around the table and out the door.

Janet crept to the door and eased it open in time to see a patrol officer disappear around the corner with Cameron, headed out toward the lobby.

O'Dell stepped into the hall and looked past Janet. "What'd you think?"

"I think he's hiding something, but not anything to do with Connie Hutchings' death," Smith said succinctly from behind her.

"Agreed." O'Dell's gaze sharpened as he focused on Janet. "You?"

"I'm not sure I want to be at the bar with him. Something didn't add up there. Whose hair is that? Who's the girl?"

O'Dell shrugged. "Maybe he'll tell you." He held up the zip-top bag. "I'll have this tested, see if we get a hit in the system. But I agree with Smith—this has nothing to do with Connie."

Janet frowned, but before she could answer, a commotion at the end of the hallway made all three turn.

Lola's mother fought her way through the door into the detectives' section. "You!" She pointed at Janet, her expression torn. "You told me you'd keep me updated! But I just heard—I just heard that there was a body found at your bar. A blond girl, that's all anybody's saying. Was it my Lola?"

Smith stepped forward, around Janet and O'Dell, reaching out toward Misty. "Mrs. Rivers, you should have called. We don't have any news of Lola." When she got close, Misty gripped her arms for support. "Come with me, ma'am."

They disappeared down the hallway, leaving O'Dell and Janet staring after her.

"Surprised she hasn't turned up, yet," O'Dell finally offered.

"Yeah. Me, too."

"Doesn't bode well, does it?"

"No." Janet turned toward the exit. "It doesn't."

CHAPTER TWENTY-NINE

O'Dell escorted Janet out to the lobby, and they stood together by the front door, O'Dell not turning to head back inside, Janet not walking away.

"Tell Misty to come to the Spot when she's done here, okay?"

O'Dell nodded, searching her face for something.

Janet gulped under his scrutiny. "You looked over when Cameron mentioned Memphis. Why?"

"Quizz called me. Said there's something going on there."

"Did she tell you what happened?"

O'Dell shifted, then looked down at the ground to watch the toe of his loafer scrub a black mark off the tile. She didn't think he was going to answer—he just kept looking at the damn tile floor—but he finally blew out a sigh.

"She told me enough that I can see that you're connected somehow. I don't know how, but you are. So I'm working some back channels down there, keeping everything on the down low until I know that you're safe."

Janet blinked. "But what about Lola?"

"Whatever happened to her already happened. And I'll work to make sure that her family finds justice. You're my priority now."

The words hung heavy in the air as Janet tried to make sense of what he was telling her. He thought Lola was dead. He thought Janet was in trouble.

"Where's Jason?"

She blinked again, hating that he kept catching her off guard. "I wish I knew. He's been MIA for over a week now. Just a few text messages and voicemails so I know he's alive."

O'Dell frowned when she opened the door. "Be careful, okay?"

She drove to the bar, feeling unsettled. She wasn't in danger. Obviously if William was going to kill her, he'd had ample opportunity over the last five months of living in her house. But what was driving him? And what was Jason's role in all of it? What did Faith know? What was Cameron hiding? Was anyone else at the Spot in danger?

Cindy Lou waved happily from behind the bar when Janet walked in. "I canceled the kitchen inspection because of unusual and unplanned chaos. That's actually one of the reasons listed online—and boy, does it fit our situation! They said they can push it back for a week, but they'll just pop in when they have time in their schedule. Hopefully we'll have a chance to get those new fry baskets in!" She lowered her voice. "The walk-in's all cleaned up, too. I wrote a check from the office account and put the receipt in the lockbox. Now there's a business expense you didn't plan on using twice. Bet you get audited." She shot a sympathetic look over the bar and Janet mustered up a smile.

She sent Cindy Lou home to get some rest before they opened for business later that afternoon.

But when she was alone, she couldn't settle into any task while she waited for Lola's mom to come in.

Finally the bell over the door jingled, but it wasn't Misty who walked in.

"Let me just set a few things straight with you right now." Quizz cracked her knuckles as she glided to a stop directly across the bar from Janet. Her lips curled as she spoke. "You are not a PI. You are not legally allowed to investigate anything on your own without me. *You are an apprentice*, and that means you have to do what I say or go find another PI dumb enough to try and mentor the one woman *on the planet* who already knows everything there is to know about everything!"

Janet tried for a conciliatory smile. She must have failed, because Quizz's snarl deepened.

"I have left you no fewer than four messages, demanding that you call me back. Have you called me back?"

Janet meekly shook her head.

"No, you have not!" Quizz pounded her fist against the bar with each word. "I have information that is pertinent to your missing-girl case, and if you cannot find the time in your *very busy schedule*," she looked scornfully around the dead empty bar and paused for effect, "then I suggest you make the time to prioritize the case that you signed my firm up for *on your own and without consultation from me*, so that we can find Lola and move on to taking cases that will make us actual money to keep the lights on at Quizz Bexley Investigations. *Do I make myself clear?*"

Janet blew out a slow breath and nodded. "Yes."

Quizz blinked. "Yes...you understand?"

Janet nodded again. "Yes, and I'm sorry I've been out of touch. It won't happen again."

"Oh." Quizz slapped the bar with her open hand and pulled out the barstool she'd been hovering over. "Good. I'm glad we've got that straight."

Janet poured the other woman an iced tea and set it on a coaster. "So what's the news?"

Quizz took her time stirring the ice cubes around in the tall skinny glass and taking a long, steady sip before answering. "I got some information about that apartment in Memphis."

"Oh yeah? What?"

"Not so fast." Quizz tilted her head to the side and studied the tightness around Janet's eyes. "What's been keeping you so busy?"

Janet set about making herself a Long Island iced tea, needing to keep her hands busy so her brain wouldn't lock up with information overload. "Well...let's see...Jason's father's ex-girlfriend was killed...and her body was left in the walk-in cooler. The new cook I hired has a weird obsession with blond girls and keeping locks of their hair...so *that's* nothing to worry about, obviously. And my boyfriend has been MIA for so long that his new employee Mike—who's pretty much the most gorgeous woman I've ever seen, by the way—came into the bar to tell me she's quitting. So, you know, just a regular week, really."

Quizz sat frozen with her lips still clamped around the straw. "You haven't heard from Jason? In how long?"

"I guess it's been..." Janet looked at her watch, as if it was minutes or hours she was dealing with. "Yeah, going on a week now."

"And not a word?" Quizz breathed.

"An odd message here and there, but my texts are going unanswered and he won't pick up when I call. So yeah. Something's going on."

Quizz shifted uncomfortably in her seat and stirred the ice cubes around her empty glass.

"More tea?"

"No. No thanks. I'm not sure how to say this, Janet, but... well, that apartment in Memphis? With the porn and the duct tape and zip ties?"

Janet kept her eyes on the cocktail shaker. She poured in vodka, then rum, but even as she tried to distract herself with the task, her stomach clenched. She was certain that she didn't want to know what Quizz was about to say, but she nodded anyway, and the PI continued.

"I made some calls to some contacts I have in Memphis after we got home. Let me tell you, nobody wants to talk about anything until they know why you want the information. I finally connected with the real-estate firm that owns that building."

Janet's vision went hazy, but she picked up the tequila and gin and poured them in at the same time. "Uh-huh?" Her voice hitched on the short syllables and she cleared her throat roughly. Quizz leaned forward and tried to catch her eye. Janet refused to look up.

"Well, here's where things get strange. Apparently that unit failed inspections several years ago because of the fire escape— no surprise there. So as far as their records indicated, no one's allowed to live there—the unit was supposed to be empty."

Janet twisted the cap off the triple sec and glugged some into the shaker, then squeezed in some simple syrup. She shook the whole concoction, then poured it into a tall glass filled with ice, added a splash of coke and a lemon wedge, and sucked half of it down through the straw before setting the glass carefully on the countertop and looking at Quizz for the first time.

"And?"

"It took some smooth talking, but I finally got a helpful person over at MLGW."

Janet's nose wrinkled.

"Memphis Light, Gas, and Water."

"Oh. Good idea." Janet was momentarily distracted from the mounting sense of dread, impressed with Quizz's investigation.

Quizz's chin jutted up. "They're not supposed to share customer information, of course, but I can be very persuasive when I want to be." Her proud expression slid off her face as quickly as it had appeared, and she seemed to brace herself for what was coming. Janet did, too. She already knew the answer, but what would happen when it was out in the open? Who else would they have to tell?

"And did they tell you who was paying for the power?"

Quizz shook her head, then reached across the bar, pushed the straw aside in Janet's Long Island, and took a pull straight from the glass. "The customer information was missing—in fact, my source was blown away, because the name had been wiped clean out of their database." Janet's mouth went dry, but Quizz wasn't finished. "But here's where things get really strange. They made a note in the system that someone else called, asking for the same information. Janet, Jason Brooks called two days ago asking about that apartment. How is Jason involved in this?"

Quizz searched Janet's face, but Janet was saved from answering when the chime over the door jangled.

"Janet, Quizz, thank God you're both here!"

CHAPTER THIRTY

Misty crossed the bar and fell into a seat next to Quizz. Her boyfriend, Paul, hovered behind her, resting his hands on the back of her barstool. "Detective Smith told us all about the body here. And I just feel awful. I didn't realize that your family was suffering a loss, too."

Janet winced at the assumption that she'd been close with Connie but didn't want to correct the other woman and lose the sudden surge of goodwill.

Quizz saved her from having to create a narrative.

"Mrs. Bridges, I'm sure you're frustrated by the lack of progress in your daughter's case."

"We are!" she said, including her boyfriend. "We just can't believe that nobody knows anything! I mean, her friend made it twelve hours before they were found out. I can't help but think it doesn't—" Her voice caught, but after a moment she soldiered on. "It doesn't bode well for Lola."

"As I told you on the phone after you first met with Janet, these cases are tricky at best, and downright awful and intractable at worst. We're doing our best, and following up on leads, but at this point, like Smith has surely told you, there's just not much to go on."

"What about the phone? Did you get anything from the phone? Detective Smith wasn't happy that I gave it to you and not her, but I told her that you seemed to be taking it more seriously than her department. I don't know, maybe it was a mistake."

Janet came out from behind the bar and took the seat on Misty's other side, forcing her own turmoil over her boyfriend's possible involvement in a murder to the very back of her brain. "Mrs. Bridges, we are doing everything we can to find your daughter. Quizz and I have been following up on leads since last week. We were able to crack Lola's password and discovered that she'd been exchanging messages with a guy named Matt. They planned to meet up in Memphis."

Misty sucked in a gasp and her hand covered her mouth. "No! Why would she do that? How?"

Janet stared over Misty and Quizz's heads. That was a good question, and one Janet had skipped over in her haste to go to Memphis and investigate. Would the girl have gone? She didn't have the funds to fly, didn't own a car. Minors couldn't buy bus tickets on their own.

"The reason we haven't been in touch is because we just can't tell if she went or not," Quizz said, covering for Janet's silence. "We showed her picture all around, and the good news—at least, we think it's good news—is that no one really recognized her. The closest we got was a cook at a nearby restaurant remembering a blond girl—hardly definitive. Maybe she never left town at all."

"But if she's still here, why wouldn't she have gotten in touch? It doesn't make any sense!"

Quizz's head dropped and Janet cleared her throat. "All I can promise is that we'll keep working on finding Lola, Misty. We'll keep looking for your daughter."

Paul held a handkerchief out to his girlfriend and she clutched it against her eyes for a brief moment before heaving a great sigh and pushing back from the bar. "Thank you. I guess that's all we can hope for."

After the couple left, Janet sagged against the bar. It was too much. Her business in chaos, her personal life turned upside down. Trying to find a wayward teen was going to push her over the edge. Janet turned to Quizz. "I want off this case."

Quizz's eyes bulged, and blood rushed to her face. "I don't give a great goddamn what's going on in your personal life. You just sat here and promised Misty that you would work to find Lola. And that's exactly what you're going to do!"

Quizz swiveled away from Janet and stalked to the door. "I want an update on what you've done to find Lola tomorrow. My office, nine a.m. *sharp!*"

———

By the time Cindy Lou got back into work an hour later, the door to the bar was locked, the lights were off, and Janet lay across the small uncomfortable threadbare couch in the office with an ice pack over her eyes.

"What are you doing?" Cindy Lou crossed her arms and leaned against the doorframe, just a shadow, illuminated from behind by the bar lights she'd flicked on when she crossed over to the office.

"Sulking." Janet's head pounded. Her heart felt like it was shrinking in her chest. She didn't know what to think about everything that had happened over the last forty-eight hours.

Why was Jason looking into that Memphis apartment? Was it a good sign? It meant he surely knew—or at least suspected—that his father was involved in Connie's death, and maybe Lola's disappearance, too. But then why wasn't he back home, telling her what was going on?

But worst of all, Quizz thought she was going to keep working on the missing-girl case? Janet couldn't keep going in so many directions at once. Not only did she not have any brain space left for someone else's crisis when she was so fully mired down in her own, but she was failing at nearly everything she attempted! Misty needed a pro—not an amateur.

Cindy Lou interrupted her internal struggle with a reminder that even more chaos was coming. "Hey, don't forget the FOP rescheduled the dart tournament for this weekend."

"What?"

"I thought you might have forgotten. Friday night? I told them we'd pay for the pizza, in light of...well. Just seemed the least we could do, you know?"

Janet must have groaned in response. She pressed a hand over the ice pack covering her eyes and wished she was anywhere else. But Cindy Lou was determined to cheer her up.

"You need a trip to the salon. I've got the perfect girl for your hair. I'll make the appointment. Let's go."

"No." Janet didn't move from the couch. A blowout was not going to make her feel better—and more importantly, she didn't *want* to feel better. She *needed* to feel all these terrible things swirling around her body in order to figure out what to do next.

"You're not going to just lay there like a sad sack."

Janet groaned, and Cindy Lou glided over and pulled her up with surprising ease for someone in three-inch stilettos. "Let's go. You'll be able to think better after a conditioning rinse."

"Cindy Lou! No! I'm not over here moping. I'm processing a lot of shit right now. William might have k—" The words died on her lips. Impossible. She just couldn't see it happening. Now, Faith...that was another story, but what did it all mean? She groaned again and Cindy Lou jumped back like she'd been shot. "Sorry! Sorry, I'm—I just..." She looked around the small space and suddenly felt like she was stuck inside a pinball machine. If she had to stay inside the Spot for even a minute longer, she was going to explode. But she couldn't go home. Jason's mother and father were there. What was their connection to the Memphis apartment, to Connie's murder?

"Fine. Let's go."

Cindy Lou jumped again, this time in delight, and she clapped her hands together as she steered Janet out of the office, through the bar, and toward her car in the parking lot.

Janet slid into the tiny red convertible. Maybe Cindy Lou was right; maybe she'd be able to think better in a place where she wasn't surrounded by memories of Jason, by his smell, his touch. She rode in silence, which allowed Cindy Lou to ramble on without interruption about everything from her son Chip to her cat Bubbles.

When they arrived at the salon, Cindy Lou ushered Janet in like she was a celebrity client. She and the stylist put their heads together for what felt like a long while, and then the stylist, Tracey, instructed her to lay back against the sink while she put on a conditioning treatment that would "make your hair shine like this morning's sunrise."

Janet almost backed out then, but Cindy Lou sighed in pleasure as she took the seat at the sink next to her while Tracey walked away to collect the product. A different younger girl came back a few minutes later and introduced herself as the intern. Cindy Lou's headphones were in, her eyes closed. Some new age music wafted toward Janet and she shuddered. She'd rather have silence than listen to that.

The intern got to work on Janet first, squeezing something out of a tube and rubbing it all over her head. Her eyes watered, and an unfamiliar sharp smell tingled her nose. "Do you have headphones, too?" the intern asked.

Janet nodded and reached into her bag. Maybe her brain could work out a way that it wasn't Jason's family who'd killed Connie and lured Lola to Memphis. She cued up a heavy metal song and zoned out to the drum beat as she prayed that some other scenario would come to her. Anything that might mean the people she loved were innocent.

CHAPTER THIRTY-ONE

"I am so incredibly, terribly sorry." Tracey met Janet's eyes mournfully through the mirror, then shot a look that could kill at her intern. "I was clear that Tammy was to work on Cindy Lou, as she's a return client, and I was going to work on you. Then I got a phone call from my daughter's school, and I'm afraid there was a mix-up."

Janet tilted her head to the side and took in the new color of hair on her head. It wasn't blond...more like orange at the tips and just *without* color near the crown of her head. "I—I still don't understand. What happened?"

Tracey shuddered before answering and Janet flinched. It must be bad if Tracey didn't even want to utter the words.

"Cindy Lou just loves that white blond hair that so few people naturally have. So on Cindy Lou, we do a bleach treatment, then pre-tone and she's good to go."

Janet looked blankly back through the mirror, but she could see the color that was so clearly missing from her hair now rising in her cheeks. Her natural brown hair was ruined. Was this woman saying she couldn't get it back? Before she could ask, Tracey spoke again.

"So the reason I was gone for so long that *this*," she pointed at Janet's head, "was allowed to happen, is that after I got off the phone with my daughter's school, I discovered a situation with our color wheel."

Janet's brow wrinkled. What did that have to do with her?

Tracey covered her eyes with her hand and took a deep breath. "The shades from light auburn all the way to black are ruined. One case exploded, and now we just can't trust any of them—"

"What are you saying?" Janet roared. "Get my hair back to brown! It can't be that hard!"

Tracey bit her lip. "Well, that's just it. We're out of color. I can make you blond, but I can't do brown—not until we get our new shipment of color in next week. Maybe in two weeks. It just depends on our supplier!" she added hastily when Janet let out an aggrieved groan.

"Blond! How is it that you have the product to do that?"

"Well, that's just it; the blond contains bleach, and they're packaged in stronger materials, so they're just fine. No exploding packets. But everything else has to be sent back to the manufacturer. Not safe to use."

"Not safe—not safe—" Janet spluttered, but Tracey didn't stop long enough for her to really get going.

"So what we'll do," Tracey plodded on gamely, "is a second round of bleach to get the color evened out." She took a lock of Janet's hair into her hands and peered at the roots. "Definitely needs a treatment, and a pre-tone, and then add a really gorgeous yellow undertone to give you some depth of color." She looked up with a smile. "I mean, really, a lot of women would pay a ton of money for this—ah—obviously, we'll be doing it for free because it's not what you initially requested, but don't be surprised if you decide to stick with it in the end." Her smile slid off her face when she took in Janet's mutinous expression and she beat a hasty retreat to the color station.

Words failed Janet completely. Cindy Lou had taken her headphones out around the halfway mark of Tracey's explanation and she smiled brightly. "Everybody goes blond eventually, Janet. It was just your turn." She rested her head back against the sink basin and closed her eyes. "Sounds like you'll be here for hours. Don't you worry, hon. I'll head right into the Spot when I'm done and get everything up and running. I'm not the assistant manager for nothin', after all." She stuck her headphones back into her ears and fell quiet, a small smile on her lips.

"William, Faith, I wasn't expecting you two to come in today." Janet walked nonchalantly past Jason's parents and headed behind the bar. She tried to ignore the deafening silence that met her greeting, along with the four sets of eyes she felt were glued to her head.

She grabbed a rocks glass and filled it halfway with the sticky, syrupy frozen margarita and held the icy glass against her forehead for a moment before taking a small, refreshing sip. "I hate to say it, but you were so right about this machine, Faith," she called to Jason's mother across the room. Faith's brow furrowed, and Janet grimaced and looked down at the tiny beads of frozen drink, then swirled them around her glass before taking another sip. She closed her eyes and then tilted her head back, reveling in the cool liquid making its way to the back of her throat.

"Well, I think it looks great," Cindy Lou said, her voice as syrupy as the drink now sliding down to Janet's belly. "I mean, really, really like...not exactly *natural*, you know, but like you spent a whole lot of money on the job."

Mel barked out a laugh. "Cindy Lou said there was a crisis, but I didn't realize it was a...I mean, a *life* crisis."

"This is why I came in?" Quizz's plaintive whine was enough to finally draw Janet's eyes away from her glass.

"I wouldn't call this a *life* crisis, Mel." Janet tried to brush off her disgruntled feelings. "It's a mistake that I have to live with, but not for long."

"Are you going to change it?" Cindy Lou asked, dismayed.

Janet ignored her. She didn't blame Cindy Lou for her hair, but she didn't want to chat things over with the woman, either. Instead she looked at Quizz. "Why are you here?"

"I'm asking myself the same question."

Mel chortled, "I called her and Jason's parents in after Cindy Lou said—and I quote, 'The shit is about to go down.'"

"I really thought you were going to murder Tracey. I mean, I know that you knew it was that intern's fault, not Tracey's, but the look you had in your eyes! I've never seen anything like it."

Janet threw back the rest of her drink, then squeezed her eyes closed and pinched the bridge of her nose when the freeze headache struck, like a dagger was cleaving her head in half. When she blinked back to awareness fifteen seconds later, her eyes landed on Faith and William, heads bowed together at the corner booth. Faith's hands moved animatedly above the table, and William's expression dropped into a scowl.

Janet's heart lifted—were they fighting? Were things back to normal? But before she could celebrate, William dropped his head into his hands and Faith reached forward to stroke his shoulder. The pair stood and walked quickly to the exit. "We'll see you at home, Janet," William called.

Faith stopped and turned to look at Janet. "I don't think it looks too bad, hon. I'm sure we'll all get used to it."

Mel chuckled as the pair walked out into the parking lot.

Janet turned away and met Quizz's eye. The PI had seen the strange touching scene between Jason's parents, too, and wasn't going to let it lie.

"I just got off the phone with a friend of mine in Memphis. She's with the Shelby County Sheriff's office. She told me that Connie's family reported her missing eight days ago, but they hadn't actually heard from her in a couple of weeks."

"Hmm. That lines up with when William said she stopped returning his calls."

"Are you sure?"

Janet's nose scrunched up as she searched her mind. "Well, no. I guess not. I mean, he told us that Connie'd stopped returning his calls—that was back when I hired Cameron, maybe... a week, week-and-a-half ago? I heard William tell Faith that he was ending things with her. I guess I just assumed that they talked that day and officially ended things. But...well, I don't know if that happened."

"What did he say *exactly*?"

"Faith said it was time to end things. William said, 'Don't worry, it's taken care of.'" She looked up at Quizz, her eyebrows so close together they were practically touching. "But he didn't mean—I mean, there's no way he meant that he ended *her*."

Quizz didn't answer, only took a long, slow sip of her sweet tea.

Janet rinsed out her sticky glass and set it in the dishwashing sink. "When did her family last see her?"

Quizz looked down at her notebook. "Just over two weeks ago."

Janet's stomach dropped, like she'd just noticed a deer in the road and wasn't sure her car was going to stop in time. "The sixth? That's the same day that Faith arrived in Knoxville. That's the day she drove in from Memphis."

CHAPTER THIRTY-TWO

Quizz left, and Cindy Lou, complaining of a stomachache, went home, too. So only Janet and Mel were working for the few customers who sat sprinkled throughout the bar.

Because there wasn't a huge need to check IDs at the door, Mel was doing an inventory count in the walk-in cooler. She walked out with a clipboard in one hand and a bottle of beer in the other. "We're just about where we should be. I'm celebrating by drinking this bottle, so now we're one short of what we should have." She clapped the clipboard down onto the bar and twisted the cap off her beer in the same second. She took a slug, her eyes never leaving Janet's. "What's going on? Kat and I haven't seen you around the house in a while. Or Jason, for that matter."

Mel and her partner Kat lived in the other half of the duplex that Janet and Jason owned. The unit was a mirror image of hers, and the women usually chatted over morning coffees or anytime they sat on the porch. Not lately.

"I don't know." Janet absently continued dusting the liquor bottles on the shelf next to the Beerador and stared off into space.

"Is there anything I can do?"

"I wish there was. But it doesn't seem like there's anything anybody can do."

"I gather that Jason's acting strange?"

Janet snorted. "That's an understatement. I haven't heard from him in over a week. He's hiding something, Mel, and I don't know what."

Mel shifted on her feet and studied the peeling label on her beer bottle. When she looked up, her expression was pained. Like she didn't want to say what she was thinking.

"Spit it out." Janet wasn't in the mood for games.

"It's just—I mean, how much do you know about Jason?"

"Well..." Janet set her rag down and crossed her arms. "I mean, I've been dating him for years, his father lives with us, his mother's practically moved in. I feel like I know him really fucking well."

Mel nodded, unaffected by Janet's misdirected anger. "That's good. But I mean—do you know anything about his past? His history?"

Janet's arms flew up. "Of course I do!" She pinched her lips together and dropped the dusting rag, then wiped her forehead with the back of her hand. She closed her eyes, her hand still resting against her head. When she pried her eyes open again, Mel was taking another sip of her beer, and after a minute Janet sighed. "I mean, no. Not really much at all."

"Maybe that's a good place to start?" Mel walked away, and Janet stared after her until she disappeared into the walk-in cooler.

———

Her shift at the Spot had never felt longer. Business was slow, but not slow enough to close early. She and Mel easily handled the crowd, but when it was finally time to go home, closing down the bar took twice as long without Cindy Lou's help.

Despite O'Dell's best guess, Cameron hadn't come in begging

for his job back, so Mel had manned the fry baskets and griddle for the three people who ordered food.

"I guess it's time to hire a new cook, huh?"

Janet grimaced. The last thing she cared about was hiring another cook to work at a food truck she didn't want that hardly any of her customers were ordering from. "I guess I should have let Faith make the hire in the first place."

"Hey, one less thing for you to worry about, huh?"

"Sure."

Mel grinned.

"What?"

"You just don't want anyone to think that you need help. Nobody does it all on their own, you know. That's no way to live."

Janet dumped ice into the sink from the lower compartment of the condiment container, then closed the lid and set the whole thing on the lower shelf of the Beerador. "Sure, sure. I know. I'd just *rather* do it all myself. Other people only end up letting you down. Easier to not let them step up in the first place."

"Ouch!" Mel grabbed her heart dramatically.

"Oh, Mel, you know what I mean. I'm completely happy to rely on you for all bouncer- and friend-related issues. Let's start right now, with this trash can." She laughed when Mel groaned.

"That's not what I mean, and you know it. But I did toss the lettuce and tomatoes out there. They were way past their prime." Mel heaved the trash bag up out of the can and tied the ends closed. "Hardly worth having the food available if none of the customers are going to order anything."

"No lie," Janet said, adding *buy produce* to her list of tasks on the notepad by the cash register. "I wonder when they'll come for the inspection. I hate having to be ready all the time. I guess our menu isn't enticing enough." She ran a finger down a copy of the closest menu. *Hamburgers. Cheeseburgers. French fries.* "I mean, what else could we add that won't break the bank? Hot dogs?"

Mel shrugged. "What about those fried cheese stick things? They can't be too expensive."

Janet wrote it on her list so she'd remember to think about it the next day, and the two walked out into the dark parking lot together. Mel tossed the trash into the Dumpster while Janet locked the door. "See you at home!" Janet called.

"I'm heading to the grocery store," Mel corrected. "Kat says there's no food in the house."

"It's three in the morning! What kind of food do you need?"

Mel laughed. "I don't know. I only know if it's not there, I'll be starving until morning."

Engines started up and Janet flicked the radio off so she could think on the drive home. Since Jason wasn't answering calls or texts, she was going to work on William and Faith as soon as she got home. Wake them up, if necessary. After all, they were staying in her house. It was time to stop being polite and start being herself. She smiled grimly at the thought.

Ahead of her, Mel turned off toward the twenty-four-hour supermarket, and she idly wondered while she waited for the light to turn green what midnight feast Mel was planning.

When she turned down her street, it took her an extra minute to notice that Jason's truck was in the driveway. She turned off her engine and sat in the dark as her exhausted body tensed up and a hot flush worked up from her belly. When she realized she was girding her loins, stalling for time, she launched out of her car and up the front path to the door. She twisted the handle and pushed, but the door was bolted shut.

She fished her keys out of her bag and jabbed the correct one into the lock. It didn't work.

She pulled the key back out and inspected it—definitely the right one. She tried again, and nothing happened.

Janet pounded her fist against the door.

Bam, bam, bam.

"Jason, are you in there?" She tried to keep the anger from

her voice, but didn't think she succeeded, especially when her fist hit the door even louder the second round of knocks.

When the door finally flung open, Jason stood at the threshold, a scowl on his face. Her heart fluttered, and despite her anger with him, her own body couldn't hide how glad she was to finally see him.

"Your key won't work. I changed the locks."

"You—you what?" She looked at him blankly, confused by his words, his expression. She was supposed to be the angry one —not him.

His scowl deepened, and he stepped forward, forcing her back down the front steps. His broad shoulders filled most of the doorframe, so that she could barely see around him into her house.

"Move, Jason! You have a lot of explaining to do! Where have you been? Why haven't you been returning my calls?"

His jaw locked, and he crossed his arms. "You can't come in. In fact, you need to leave. Mom packed your stuff today." He motioned to the side of the porch, and Janet gasped when she saw three suitcases stacked on top of each other. "Goodbye, Janet."

A sudden chill settled in the base of her stomach. Jason was kicking her out of the home they owned together?

Her face froze, and after an indeterminate amount of time, she reached up and touched her lips, parted in shock.

Jason had been gone for weeks, out of touch, not communicating, and now he was telling her that she had to go? She had to leave?

She shook her head, trying to make sense of the very few but confusing words that Jason had uttered. She was out, *but his parents were in?*

Her boyfriend stared at her, his face a mask, completely void of emotion. She reached out toward him tentatively and he didn't move away. Then, with a strength that surprised even her, she put her hands on his chest and shoved him out of the way and stalked into her house.

"My belongings don't fit in three goddamn suitcases, Jason. And you don't get to kick me out. This is my house just as much as it's yours."

•

CHAPTER THIRTY-THREE

The silence inside the house was palpable. It felt like a bass drum beating in Janet's heart, her ears, her head. She prowled around the main room, passing Faith, William, Jason—but no one would even look her in the eye.

"Where have you been?" She glared at Jason, but he only stared at the wall behind her, unblinking. She swung her gaze over toward his parents. "What about you two? What are you up to at all hours of the day and night, heads together at the bar? You're up to something. What?"

Faith stared at Janet—not with confusing anger like her son. It was another emotion that simmered just under the surface, one that Janet couldn't quite name. William stared at the floor; whereas Jason and Faith's faces were red, William's was pale. Like he'd just learned some terrible truth.

"I don't understand, Jason. This is my house! This is my—" Her voice broke, and she couldn't get the words out. She couldn't say that this house and everyone in it just then, were her life— her family. She could no more leave them than she could cut off her hand.

Faith's face twitched. William—pale already—turned a shade

of light green, and he swayed on his feet. Only Jason remained impassive, staring at her, completely unmoved.

"You have to go, Janet." His lips pressed into a flat line, and the muscles in his arms—crossed tightly over his chest—were strung tight like a bow.

Janet's eyes narrowed. "I'm not leaving. You can leave. In fact, you can all leave! But I'm staying."

"Go!" Jason's yell was so unexpected, so loud, that she and Faith jumped. He moved toward her, propelling her toward the door before she could command her own feet to stop moving. And even then, he physically lifted her over the threshold and barred her from walking back in. "Go, Janet. Go now. Please." His voice broke on the last word, and it was that sound—the emotion that seeped into his voice that broke her out of her own rage. Her shoulders dropped, and she leaned toward Jason. His eyes were tired, sad, like he'd just learned something awful.

She reached out and rested her open palm against his chest. He didn't move away, and she took a shaky breath. "Jason, why? What are you doing? I don't—I don't understand what's happening. Where do you want me to go? It's—" She shook her head, then motioned to the darkness around her. "It's three in the morning! Just let me stay. Let me help you work out whatever's going on. Jason. Please." The crinkles around his eyes softened; he reached up and pressed his hand into hers, and her heart lifted. He looked like he might be thinking about letting her in, might be considering telling her what in the hell was going on.

But then, red and blue flashing lights lit up the street behind her, and a voice called into the darkness. "Janet?"

Jason's eyes hardened, and he pushed her hand away from him. "Your ride's here. Goodbye, Janet."

And with that, he closed the door in her face. The last thing she heard was the *thunk* of the deadbolt sliding into place.

———

O'Dell tossed her bags into his trunk, then hustled around to the driver's side of the car and climbed in. He looked at Janet, pale, fighting off tears, and then closed his door and started up the engine. "Uh...where to?"

Janet took in a deep breath through her nose and then blew it out her mouth. When she looked over at the cop, he quickly looked away. "Why are you even here?" she spat out.

"Well." He shifted in his seat, still staring at the road ahead. "Jason called me about fifteen minutes ago. Told me I needed to come get you."

"What?" she exploded. "And you listened? Since when did you two become friends?" O'Dell didn't answer, and she forced herself to turn and face forward, then took a minute to calm herself down. "I'm sorry. I'm not angry with you. I'm just—God! I'm just angry!" She took another deep breath and focused on modifying her tone. She couldn't find friendly, but managed to drop anger. "What else did he say?"

O'Dell looked at her sideways and cleared his throat. "He said that you'd need somewhere to stay, and that I should come pick you up. Now—now wait just a minute," he added quickly when Janet's thin grip on composure started to slip. "Not like that. He said you were going to need a friend. And we're friends, aren't we, Janet?"

She pressed her fingertips to her eyelids. No matter how many deep breaths she tried to take, she couldn't seem to fill up her lungs with enough air. "I'm not sure I'll be able to sleep tonight, O'Dell."

"Well. You'll need somewhere to stay, anyway, and I have a guest room all ready for you. Can't be wandering around town at this hour. Nothing good happens after midnight, that's the truth."

She nodded. Couldn't argue with that after the last thirty minutes of her life.

"Here comes Mel," O'Dell announced. Sure enough, Janet's

bouncer was headed their way, grocery bags clutched in her hands as she made her way toward them.

Janet rolled down her window and tried for a smile. "Hey."

"What's going on? I heard yelling, then I saw O'Dell, and damned if that didn't make me more worried. No offense." She looked past Janet and frowned. "If you need a place to stay, Janet, our guest room is open."

Janet blinked back what could only be tears, finally making their way to the surface. How could she be suffering through the greatest emotional turmoil of her life and find out, at that exact same time, that she had somehow acquired some really great friends, despite her best efforts to be cranky and mean?

As she considered Mel's offer, Jason opened the door and stared out at them. She wasn't close enough to see his face clearly, but she could feel the anger rolling off him in waves. He was waiting for her to leave—waiting for her to be across town, not just across the thin drywall separating their unit from Mel's house next door.

"No, thanks, Mel. I'll head to O'Dell's place. He's been kind enough to offer me his guest room while I figure out what...what I should do next."

Mel nodded soberly and stepped back onto the sidewalk, hitching the bags up higher in her arms. When O'Dell put the car into gear, she called to Janet, "Hey. I'll see you at work tomorrow."

Janet nodded and watched her in the sideview mirror until she shrunk into nothing. Mel was telling her that while her home life might be exploding into a fireball of disaster, nothing else had changed. Janet could still count on her. She reached out, without looking, and grasped O'Dell's hand.

"Thank you."

He didn't answer, just squeezed her hand as he drove through the darkness.

CHAPTER THIRTY-FOUR

Sunlight squeezed through the blinds and Janet buried her head deeper under the covers. O'Dell had shown her to the guest room and left her alone—but not before looking at her worriedly like she might dissolve into a pool of emotion.

When the bedroom door had closed, she'd thought she might do just that. But in the end, a sense of overwhelming so deep and complete enveloped her, leaving her unable to feel anything at all.

Eventually she'd kicked off her shoes and crawled under the covers. But now her brain was turning on along with the day, and she groaned, her throat dry and scratchy. She poked her head out and saw a bottle of water on the nightstand. She chugged half of it down, then leaned back against the pillows. She hadn't been in a state to notice anything the night before, but now, in an effort to not think about her life or her boyfriend (*ex?*), she studied her surroundings.

No doubt she was in a man's house. The bedroom set was made of dark wood, the walls were painted a smoky blue, and the only decorations were two hockey sticks crossed into a "x" hanging across from the window. Cheap mini blinds that weren't closed all the way were to blame for letting in those cheerful rays of light, and Janet was eyeing them suspiciously when a light tap on the door interrupted her investigation.

She made to pull the covers up, then realized she was still fully dressed from the day before. So she climbed out of bed, ran a hand through her hair, and opened the door.

O'Dell smiled at her like they were at a funeral. "How—ah... how ya doin'?"

She smiled thinly back. "No one's dead...so that's a start."

He held out a mug of coffee. "You like it black, right?"

She blew on the surface as a sudden chill started at the base of her spine. She wrapped her hands around the mug. O'Dell noticed her discomfort and stepped past her into the room, opening the closet adjacent to the hockey sticks. "You need another blanket in here?" He pulled down two and tossed them on the bed. "I'm sorry. I should have gotten you more set up in here. I just—I mean, it was all pretty last minute, and—"

"How last minute? When did Jason call you, anyway?"

O'Dell looked down at the floor. "It was just a few minutes before I came to get you."

"You were just—what? At home? And he called you?"

"He called me on my cell."

"How did he have that number?"

"I was going to ask you." O'Dell rubbed the back of his neck with one hand and took a sip from his own mug. "I sure didn't give it to him."

"Neither did I!" Janet's brow furrowed. "You were at home?"

"No. And apparently neither were you. He, ah...he said you would be on your way home, and I should get there in fifteen minutes." O'Dell turned away from her and busied himself with reorganizing the extra sheets in the closet. There was something else, something he wasn't saying, but he was happy to ignore her completely. Of course, Janet wasn't. She stepped closer.

"What? What aren't you telling me?" He didn't answer and she took the fitted sheet out of his clumsy hands and shook it out, then started gathering the corners together. "What does Smith think about me being here?"

He shrugged, and his eyes narrowed as he watched her hands. "What are you doing there? I've never understood how to fold these damn things."

She lowered her hands. "O'Dell. What does Smith think?" She finished folding the sheet and handed him the tidy square packet.

He looked at her like she was a magician. When she crossed her arms, he grimaced. "I explained to her that we were just friends."

Janet raised her eyebrows. "And?"

He took the sheet from her and shoved it back onto the shelf along with the rest of the unfolded crumpled-up set. "And...she didn't really care for the plan. So...we broke up."

"I—I'm sorry. She knows...I mean, surely she knows that nothing's going to happen here." She stared hard at O'Dell. "Nothing." She didn't want there to be any expectations. His eyes darkened and she backpedaled. "I just mean—argh!" She turned away and stalked to the other side of the room. "I shouldn't even be here. I don't know why Jason arranged this— this thing! It just—I mean, nothing about it makes sense! I should be at a hotel. This is—it's not your problem—"

"Calm down." O'Dell's commanding tone did the opposite of soothe her.

"I am calm," she snapped. "And I'm leaving."

"Stop! I don't know what's going on with your boyfriend, but he made it clear to me that he didn't want you on your own."

"What?"

"Whatever's going on, he thinks you need protecting."

"That's bullshit. I don't need—"

"And for some reason, he doesn't feel like he can do it, but I can. And I will," he added grimly. "Now let's go get breakfast."

He stalked out of the room, and Janet fell back onto the bed, feeling more confused than ever. So Jason thought she was in danger, and was happy to push the job of keeping her safe onto somebody else without even discussing it with her? She was so irritated that she couldn't even begin to think about eating. O'Dell pounded on the door. "Let's go. I'm starved."

"I am not a child," she muttered to herself, "who needs to be coddled."

"Now!" O'Dell barked in his cop voice and she jumped up from the bed and hurried to the door.

"Dammit! Stop doing that!"

He grinned and tossed a hat to her. "It's cold out there. Better bundle up." He walked down the hall ahead of her and she smiled against her will. She *wasn't* hungry, but she might as well eat. She'd need energy, strength, for whatever lay ahead.

She must have been in a haze the night before, because now she walked through O'Dell's house as if for the first time. The short hallway opened up into the main room. A television took up most of the far wall, and a cluster of black leather theater seats formed a half-circle facing the screen. An old barn door, hanging on casters across a heavy steel bar, was open, revealing a small but tidy kitchen. Janet's eyes zeroed in on the coffee pot, gleaming under an overhead light on the countertop, and she took another sip from the mug still clutched in her hands.

"I'll drive." O'Dell tossed back a grin. She always thought he was handsome, but here in his element, with day-old whiskers and a casual T-shirt stretching across his chest, she felt a stab of guilt that she was responsible for his relationship ending.

He didn't bother locking up when they left the house, and as he navigated the streets of Knoxville, she found herself wondering what had happened to make Jason race home, only to kick her out and ask his least favorite person to watch over her. What had Jason found out while he'd been in Memphis? What scared him enough to send her packing?

She was determined to find out.

CHAPTER THIRTY-FIVE

"Have you ever been here?" O'Dell eased into a spot on the street and pulled open the change drawer next to the steering wheel. "Ah! Four quarters. That should do it if we don't dawdle." He slipped the quarters into his palm and opened his door. "You coming?"

She squinted at the restaurant across the street. "Morning Glory? Is it any good?"

"You ever heard of a Dutch Baby?" Janet shook her head. "It's like a cross between a pancake and eggs. Greatest thing I've ever tried. But you gotta wait for it—I'll put the order in right when we get in, and we should be fine."

"I'm not even hungry," Janet said, realizing it was true as the words left her lips. Her stomach was so full of confusion, there wasn't any room for eggs—or anything else for that matter.

"You need food. You have a busy day ahead of you." O'Dell walked around the hood of his car and opened her door.

"I do?" She felt sluggish, like her brain couldn't make any decisions. She hated that feeling.

"You do." O'Dell steered her across the street by her elbow and then held the door to the restaurant open. "You have to see what your boyfriend's been up to."

She leveled O'Dell with a stare. "And how am I supposed to do that? You know Jason! He can get phone numbers without asking for them. He can tap into computers near and far. What can I do?" O'Dell greeted the hostess and followed her to their table, and Janet finished talking to herself as she followed him. "What can I do, for real, except pour drinks and be irritated with people?"

"What was that?" O'Dell waved the menu away and instead, placed an order for two Dutch Babies and a pot of coffee. "You want juice, too, or anything?" Janet shook her head and he took his time moving utensils around after the hostess left. "Janet. You have work to do today."

Her shoulders dropped. "I can't do anything, O'Dell. I don't even want to."

He spread the paper napkin across his lap and rested his elbows on the table. "You have to find out what Jason's working on. What he doesn't want anyone else to know."

Janet blew out a sigh but waited for the busboy to fill their waters and walk away before responding. "There's nothing I can find out that Jason wants me to know—and obviously he doesn't want me to know anything, which is why he kicked me out of my own house."

"Janet." O'Dell shook his head. "You're not thinking this through! Jason's not worried about anyone else. He's sure as shit not worried about me. He's not worried about Detective Smith. But you—he knows that you can figure this out if you stay close, and he's not going to let that happen. So what can you do that we can't?" She shrugged again. "Well...figure it out. And then do it. I mean, think! His father's girlfriend goes missing—winds up dead—right as he starts acting strange, aloof. It might be connected." He drained his coffee and then picked up the carafe to refill it. "Happy to help if you need it." He looked up earnestly. "I'll always be here for you."

She blinked when tears sprang up unexpectedly. His horrified expression was enough to drive them away, but he handed her a napkin and looked across the restaurant while she composed herself.

"Thank you. For everything. And I'm sorry that I've managed to mess up things between you and Smith."

"It wasn't serious. It was probably time to end things anyway."

"Why?"

He leaned back, but his eyes never left Janet's face. "I just wasn't really ready to dive in with anyone right now."

"Oh." He held her expression and her stomach did a flip-flop that had nothing to do with hunger. She looked down at her lap. "You deserve to be happy, O'Dell."

"I know." She looked up in time to see a sly grin cross his face. "I will be."

She was saved from having to answer by a cackle of laughter from the other side of the restaurant. Her eyes narrowed. She'd know that laugh anywhere. "Cindy Lou?" O'Dell shrugged and she scanned the room. Had her assistant manager gone home sick the day before only to be enjoying a cozy brunch this morning? The laugh rang out again.

It sure didn't sound like someone recovering from an illness.

Her eyes zeroed in on Cindy Lou at a booth across from the kitchen. Her employee was wearing full makeup and a bright sunny outfit that attracted all the light in the room. But it was the cowlick on the back of the head of the man across from her that had Janet leaping up from the table.

She stalked across the room, nearly taking out an unsuspecting waiter with a full load of plates on a tray over his head.

"What's going on here, Jason?" Janet snapped as she came to a stop at the edge of their table, crossing her arms and staring down at the table full of half-eaten biscuits and gravy, eggs, and bacon.

Cindy Lou's big blue eyes looked up and the laugh died on her lips. "Oh, hey, Janet."

"Hey? Hey? What's going on, Cindy Lou?" Her voice was

louder than she'd intended, and her assistant manager flinched slightly. She could hardly bear to look at her boyfriend, but when he remained silent, she was forced to turn her eyes on him. "And what about you, J—" The man sitting across from Cindy Lou was not Jason. "Oh my God, I'm so sorry! I thought you were..." In a panic, she looked back at Cindy Lou, whose confused expression turned sunny again.

"Janet, I'd like to introduce you to Jeff—" She touched her lips and another laugh trilled out. "I can't believe I'm going to say this, but I don't even know your last name! Oh my stars, isn't that so embarrassing?"

Janet couldn't take her eyes off the man sitting across from Cindy Lou. It wasn't Jason, as she'd been so certain from her table, but it was easy to see how she'd made the mistake. This stranger, Jeff, had the same coloring and the same cowlick in his hair. But this man's features were more delicate, his lips thin and unfriendly. Cindy Lou's words finally wormed their way into her brain, and instead of apologizing, she felt herself getting angry all over again.

"What do you mean you don't know his last name? Did you just meet this morning?"

Cindy Lou blushed and looked down at her coffee. "Well, no...although I think we got to know each other a little better this morning, Jeff, wouldn't you agree?"

Janet threw her hands up in the air and a girl sitting alone at the adjacent table picked up her book and scrambled away from them toward the exit. "Unbelievable! Cindy Lou, when are you going to learn that you can't hop in bed with any man who wants to? You don't even know his last name!"

"I know, but like I said when we met, there's just something so familiar about him—"

Janet snorted. "I'll bet. It's called his big, giant d—"

"Janet!"

She jumped at the closeness of O'Dell's voice and turned to face him. "What?"

"Let's leave Cindy Lou alone to enjoy her breakfast. I think it's time for us to go."

He grabbed her under the elbow with a firm grip and steered her out of the restaurant. He stopped and faced her out on the sidewalk. "What is wrong with you?"

"What's wrong with me? She's in there with another stranger, doing God knows what—"

"I think we all know what they did, and she's a grown woman. She doesn't need you judging her just because you disagree with her life choices."

"Well, that's just—I can't—" Janet spluttered into silence, hating how obnoxiously reasonable he sounded. She turned back to look through the window.

"You really cleared it out in there," O'Dell grumbled. "But we were only halfway to our Dutch Babies; you'd have never made it."

She squinted at the empty table next to Cindy Lou's.

"Leave her alone," O'Dell barked. "Stop staring at her like that."

"No—it's not that."

The change in her tone—no longer uptight and angry—was enough to pull O'Dell out of his breakfast lament. "What?"

"The girl—I think the girl sitting next to them—the one I scared away? I think that was Lola."

CHAPTER THIRTY-SIX

A phone chirped from the depths of O'Dell's pocket and he winced when he read the screen. "It's Kay—Detective Smith. I've got to take this." He held the phone up to his ear and turned away from Janet, heading toward his car.

Janet took the opportunity to head back into the restaurant to see what she could find out about the girl who looked so similar to Lola.

Cindy Lou and the stranger were gone, a waiter clearing their half-eaten plates away as Janet approached. But the girl from the next table had come back! She was digging around in her wallet, staring at her bill. She looked up when Janet stopped, and her eyes went wide. She leapt up, spilling her coffee across the table in her haste to get away. She didn't look back as she hustled out of the restaurant, with Janet hot on her trail.

"Lola!" she called, certain the girl in front of her was an exact match for the picture in her purse. "Lola, wait! Your mom is so worried about you!"

But the girl shot a terrified look back at Janet that was so fearful, so frightened and panicky, that Janet froze in her tracks. She watched the girl run across the street and flinched at the screeching tires of a car that narrowly avoided slamming into her.

Lola didn't slow down, just shot one last scared look over her shoulder as she disappeared between buildings.

O'Dell stood uncertainly at his car, his cell phone grasped in one hand, one foot in the car, the other on the pavement as if he hadn't been able to make up his mind on whether he should get out and chase after the girl or not. "Who is that?"

Her frown deepened as she thought back to Lola's look of terror as she ran away.

"I think—no, *I know*—it's Lola. She looked like she was terrified—of...of me!"

O'Dell's voice was clipped, short, when he spoke. "Stay here. I'm going after her."

As she watched him disappear into the same alleyway, her brain made a connection that had been missing up until just then. As Lola ran away, she didn't just look haunted. She looked hunted, like an animal running from a hunter in the woods.

What had made the girl so terrified of Janet? Or who?

———

"No trace at all?"

"None. It was like she just disappeared," O'Dell answered, slowing at a light before turning right.

"I don't like it," Janet said.

"We don't even know that it was Lola. In fact, the more I think about it, the less sense it makes. Why would she be here in town—on her own, I might add—and not let her parents know?"

"It was her." Janet stared out the window, her voice low. "I know it was."

"Well." O'Dell shrugged, and kept driving.

Janet glanced over. "You can just drop me off at my car. I don't want to take over your life."

"I think that's already happened," he said, but he didn't

frown, just said it matter-of-factly. "And I'm not worried, so don't you be worried."

Her chest felt tight, and she turned away from the detective. O'Dell was being so nice, but she knew that this wasn't fair. She'd roared into his life the night before like a hurricane, ruining his relationship, messing with his weekend. And she knew—she wondered if he did, too—that she'd blow out just as furiously as she blew in.

"Looks like a party," O'Dell muttered as he pulled up to the house. Mel and Kat stood on the front walk, in the middle of an animated discussion that stopped as soon as they saw Janet climb out of the car.

"I decided I'm not leaving." Janet attempted to smile when the women looked over, but it felt more like a grimace when it made it to her face. "I mean, after all, I pay for half. Jason can't just kick me out."

Neither woman responded, and Janet turned away from their confused faces to find the door to her house standing wide open, the inside so dark, the open door looked like a yawning black hole.

"What—" She raced up the porch steps and gasped, not daring to cross the threshold. The furniture was gone. Even the pictures had been taken off the walls.

The house was empty. Deserted.

"What happened?" She whirled around to face Mel.

Her bouncer shrugged. "That's just what Kat and I were discussing. I have no idea. We were home all night and didn't hear a thing."

Kat looked unhelpfully back, then bent down to pick a wine-key up off the cement path. She held it out to Janet. "Is this yours?"

Janet dug her hands into her pockets, refusing to take it— refusing to believe that the only possession she had left, besides three suitcases of clothes at O'Dell's house, was a cheap wine key from a shitty bar in Montana.

O'Dell had been hanging back by the car, but he pushed off the passenger door and walked past the trio, heading right into Janet's place. He was only inside for a couple of minutes, but not a word was uttered until he came back.

"Everything is gone." He looked past Janet and asked Mel, "Where did they go?"

Her lips were pressed into a thin line and she shook her head back and forth.

Finally, Kat spoke. "We don't know. We were home all night and didn't hear anything, until the moving van fired up and pulled out this morning before six. If I hadn't looked out the window and watched the taillights disappear, I wouldn't have known that they were here at all."

"What was the moving company?" O'Dell was in full detective mode now. He slipped a notebook out of his back pocket, but Kat shook her head. There wasn't anything to write down.

"It was dark—and—and hard to see. And, you know, the truck was really dirty. I didn't see the name—or maybe there wasn't a name. I'm so sorry, Janet." She looked back and forth between O'Dell and Janet, not sure who she was apologizing to.

"We didn't connect the dots until just now—we were heading out to the store and saw the door standing open. That's when we realized what must have happened."

"We were just about to call you when you pulled up."

Janet turned away from them all, unable to control the emotions swirling up inside her. Shock, embarrassment, humiliation. For all three of them to be here with her at a time like this was terrible. There was nowhere to hide.

"So he—he took all of your stuff?" Kat shook her head. "I didn't see that coming from him."

Before Janet could answer, a van pulled up and rumbled to a stop, blocking the driveway. A worker from the gas company climbed out of the vehicle and hitched his pants up as he walked around to the sidewalk. He surveyed the crew gathered in the drive. "You folks heading out?"

"Why?" O'Dell asked, and Janet was grateful to have someone else ask the questions. Her brain was too overwhelmed to even get a single word out.

The gas employee took a pack of cigarettes out of his front shirt pocket and lit one before answering. "Starting in about thirty minutes, we'll have a crew out here rerouting the gas line for this property. The whole structure's gotta be evacuated for at least seventy-two hours."

Mel looked wordlessly between her house and her partner. It was Kat who spoke. "The entire structure?"

The gas worker dug a clipboard out of the passenger seat of his van and ran a finger down the paper, mouthing words silently. "Yup. Says right here the work begins at ten a.m., and the entire structure will need to be vacated for approximately seventy-two hours." He looked up and added, "You know, until the job is complete."

Janet finally came out of her stupor. "Who booked this project?"

He referenced his clipboard again. "The property owner." He sucked in a breath and the end of his cigarette glowed red. "Asked for a rush job. Said it had to get done now. Jason Brooks?" The employee looked up, a question in his eyes. "If we need to cancel now, it's going to cost you a cancelation fee. It's out of my hands so late in the project timeline."

Janet turned and apologized to her renters. "I'm sorry you two are getting wrapped up in this. I'll pay for your hotel until this is settled. Why don't you go pack bags and meet me up at the Spot for lunch, okay?"

After they hurried into their home, Janet climbed into O'Dell's car.

When he fired up the engine, his jaw was tight. "I never thought Jason would play you like this, Janet. I'm really sorry that this is happening."

But for the first time in twenty-four hours, hope kindled in

Janet's gut. O'Dell looked at her expression and frowned. "Why are you smiling?"

"Jason is telling me it's not safe to be home." Her smile faded and her voice dropped until she was almost whispering. "He also doesn't want Mel and Kat caught up in whatever's about to go down...and that means he doesn't know what's going to happen. And that's why he made me leave, too. What's he so afraid of?" She stared out the window, hoping her brain might figure out what she was missing—what clue she'd overlooked or forgotten about.

O'Dell shook his head. "Don't give him so much credit. He's hiding something. You think he's trying to keep you safe—but that's clearly not his only priority, or else he'd be sitting here telling you and me what he's so worried about. What he thinks might happen." He sped up to make a light that turned yellow up ahead. When they were through the intersection, he glanced at Janet. "And he's not doing that. So you have to ask yourself, why? What's more important than keeping you safe?"

Janet's frown deepened. She wouldn't have put it that way, but now that O'Dell had, the question hung heavy in the air. Family. She knew that Jason must be trying to protect his father. But why? And what did William have against her? Was she in danger? She had a feeling whatever was about to go down would be over in seventy-two hours. Would Jason figure things out in time? Would she even make it through to find out?

CHAPTER THIRTY-SEVEN

Janet fired up the generator outside the food truck and even managed to turn on the grill, O'Dell offering helpful tips like, "You'll want it hot, but not too hot," and "Should you clean that before using it?"

Finally, when he said, "Should you defrost the burgers before you put them on the grill like that?" she shooed him out.

"Why don't you get drinks ready for everyone?" she said, then locked the door behind him. When she was alone in the food truck, she blew out a sigh and rolled her neck from side to side, stopping to stare up at the ceiling. Jason thought something bad was going to go down, and he wanted to keep her safe. But why was he protecting his father? Was William guilty of murdering Connie, and brainwashing Lola somehow? Family or not, would Jason protect a killer? She shivered, just as O'Dell tried to open the door.

"I smell burnt meat. Hey—is this door locked?" He jiggled the handle again. "Are you paying attention in there, Janet?"

She shook herself and slipped the patties off the grill, unlocked the door, and then turned the knobs on the control panel all the way to the right just as O'Dell pushed the door open and walked up into the truck. His nose wrinkled when he saw the black patties. "Well...I guess they're only burned on the one side?" He reached past Janet and, with a fork from the counter, flipped the top patty over and grimaced. "I'm sure it's not as raw as it looks." Then he added in an undertone, almost to himself, "We'll be fine."

Janet grabbed a bag of buns from the shelf and turned away from O'Dell to assemble the sandwiches. "Mel and Kat here yet?"

"Just arrived. They're sitting inside."

O'Dell picked up the plate of food and headed down the steps and out of the truck, leading the way into the bar. Mel was behind the bar. She looked up when Janet and O'Dell walked in. "I'm making Long Islands—you two want one?"

Janet nodded, but O'Dell shook his head. "I'll stick with soda, thanks."

"Where did you two end up?" Janet asked when Mel came back to the table with a tray full of drinks.

"Nowhere yet. We'll check in somewhere tonight. Figured we'd just kind of hang out today." Mel bit her lip as she studied her burger and grabbed the bottle of ketchup from the middle of the table.

"Maybe salt, too?" O'Dell said, shaking enough on his burger that it would float in water.

"Yes," Mel breathed, taking the shaker when he was done.

Kat pushed her plate aside and leaned over the table. "We're staying close. Something's not right, Janet, and we don't want to go too far until we figure out what, you know?"

Before Janet could object, O'Dell said, "I agree. None of you are safe—at least, that must be what Jason thinks. And until I know why, I want you all close."

Janet harrumphed and took a huge bite of her burger. The patty was mushy on top and so crispy on the bottom that her teeth struggled to cut through the burnt side. She forced herself not to gag on the texture as she again attempted to bite through the meat.

O'Dell turned to face her. "Janet, what aren't you telling me?"

She twisted her mouth away from the burger and the bite tore off into her mouth. She forced the meat to her back molars and they managed to break up the burned food. She swallowed hard and then downed half her drink before her mouth was clear enough to answer. "What are you talking about?"

"Something happened when you and Quizz went to Memphis. She's on her way in, but I thought I'd give you the chance to tell me first."

She closed her eyes. It wasn't just her who was in danger now. Jason was worried enough that he and his parents had moved out of the house in the dead of the night, while also making plans to keep her, Mel, and Kat away. But there was no hiding the Spot. They were all like sitting ducks there at the bar. Jason knew it, and frankly, William did, too. She couldn't keep the information from them any longer. They might all be in danger.

While she was working over how to tell everyone what she'd known for weeks now, what she'd been keeping to herself— perhaps being criminally silent—the door opened and Quizz walked in.

"Something smelled kind of good in the parking lot, but now that I'm inside, I'm changing my mind. It's like bacon crossed with a fire alarm, you know? Just exactly that." Quizz squinted at the table and adjusted her glasses.

Mel bravely dipped one edge of her burger and bun into a pool of ketchup and cracked her neck before taking a bite. O'Dell, the half-eaten burger in front of his face at eye-level, said, "It's not too bad, really. Considering."

Janet moved her chair over and pushed her plate away. Quizz took a chair from the next table over and squeezed it between Janet and O'Dell. She was glad for the added physical distance between them before she said what she was going to say.

"Where's Cindy Lou?" Mel looked around the bar after Quizz asked the question, as if the spunky bartender might appear suddenly from a dark corner.

"She's supposed to come in at three today."

"So, Janet?" O'Dell set his burger down on the plate and wiped his hands on a napkin. He fixed her with an unblinking stare and asked again, "What happened in Memphis?"

She fidgeted with her utensils. Her throat felt too thick to talk, and she swallowed a few times as too much saliva filled her mouth. "Quizz and I were looking for Lola's boyfriend, Matt. And we found...well, a house of horrors, really."

"That's an understatement." Quizz shifted Janet's burger farther away from her with a grimace.

"What else?"

Janet dropped her hands down into her lap and looked up at the people—her friends—gathered around the table with her. "I found a bill on the table as I was leaving. It was the light bill. The customer name—the person who paid the bills for that apartment? It's William Brooks. Jason's dad."

O'Dell's stare was unwavering, but Janet sensed a shift in his expression, too, as disappointment merged with anger. He shoved his plate aside and stood quickly, his phone pressed to his ear. "Yes, this is Detective Patrick O'Dell, calling in a BOLO for a possible murder suspect. Suspect's name is William Brooks."

CHAPTER THIRTY-EIGHT

O'Dell spent the better part of the next twenty minutes pacing in the parking lot. He swept back into the bar, rolling his neck, and asked Janet and Quizz several more clipped questions about their Memphis trip and the apartment.

Before Janet could answer any of them, Quizz stepped forward. "Here's the address of the apartment, along with the name of the cook who said he knew Matt." She took a packet of papers out of her bag and flipped past the first page. "This is the ID number for the MLGW employee who told me about the account information vanishing for the apartment in question, and this last page..." She held the packet out toward O'Dell. "This is a copy of the picture of Janet that we found in that apartment." Quizz turned toward Janet. "It's from your Facebook profile. I made a copy and blew it up to the same size that we found in the apartment."

"Thanks, Quizz. Glad someone is willing to be so forthcoming. Excuse me." O'Dell left the building without a backwards glance at Janet.

Janet gathered the plates from the table—including Mel's, even though she was still gamely trying to eat the burger—and dumped the trash in the can behind the bar.

She must have been staring at the trash can for some time, because she didn't hear anyone walk up and flinched when a hand patted her shoulder.

Kat's face was full of concern when Janet whirled around. "It's going to be okay, but not if you keep operating like you're on your own. We're here. O'Dell is on your side. And Jason's not just abandoning you, even though that's what it might feel like."

"Hrmph," Janet muttered, hating how Kat's words lifted her spirit just a touch. "I know he'd never abandon me, especially now...but it sure does feel that way."

"It's happened before." Mel ran a toothpick gingerly across her gums and dug out a tiny bit of blackened burger. "Remember after Ike died? But that time he left us a pretty clear clue. I wonder why he's keeping us in the dark this time?"

Janet nodded, remembering the computer he'd set up in their kitchen, cued up to surveillance video that helped her figure out part of a murder that had happened at the bar several months ago. She wrinkled her nose. "Yeah, but that time he disappeared because he couldn't compromise a customer..." Her mouth froze open on the end of the word, and a lightbulb went off in her head.

Back then, he hadn't wanted to compromise a paying customer, but he'd left the information out so Janet could put it all together.

She gasped, and it was Kat's turn to flinch.

"Oh my God! The folder!"

"Huh?" Kat said.

But Janet blew past her without a word and barreled toward the office.

Just the other day, Jason's employee, Mike, had dropped off a folder of information supposedly for *Jason*. Janet had been so irritated by Mike's gorgeousness that she'd tossed it down in the office without a second thought.

She pushed the door open—and there it was. The yellow clasp envelope sat just where she'd left it on her desk. She carefully slid her finger under the flap, jiggled the seal loose, then sifted through the sheaf of papers that fell out onto the desk.

On top was the full bill from MLGW. It was only when Janet saw that it was three pages long that she realized she'd only seen the first page in the Memphis apartment.

The full bill included the payor's name, former addresses, and Social Security number. William Jefferson Brooks, 4444 Jones Parkway, Memphis, Tennessee.

But that couldn't be right. William had last lived with Faith, and their house wasn't on Jones Parkway. She flipped her computer on and did a reverse address search.

Quizz ambled into the room and came to a stop behind her. "What are you finding out?"

"I'm checking William's former addresses to see if anything stands out." Janet waited for the results page to load. "It looks like William Brooks's only other address was on Jones Parkway."

"I guess that makes sense, right?"

"Well, it would, but that's not the house Jason grew up in. It's not the home William moved out of when he and Faith got divorced."

"Oh. So that doesn't make sense...unless..." She waited until Janet met her eye. "Is it possible that he's kept a secret double life for years?"

Janet's vision went blurry as she considered the possibility. Would it be such a shock to find out that William had been living a lie for so many years? His former lover had been murdered. What else didn't they know about him?

Mel knocked on the doorframe but stopped just outside the office. "Hey, Janet? Your construction guy is here, asking about the parking lot project...I just don't know what you want me to tell him..." She looked apologetically at her employer. "I mean, I can send him on his way, but...You know it'd be nice if they would pave over the nonsense out there so everyone can park in the lot again..."

Janet blew out a sigh and pushed away from the computer. "It's fine. You're right."

She hurried out to the bar. Bruce waited by the door with his hat in his hands, an uncomfortable expression on his face.

"Hey, Janet, sorry for interrupting."

"No problem, Bruce. What's going on?"

"Well, Faith has us adding a thirty-foot pergola with full electric, plumbed for an outdoor kitchen, but I just wanted you to sign off on the project before we got started." His hand rested on the architecture roll, unfurled on the closest table. "Seems like she's not communicating with you as well as I'd have expected."

Janet attempted a smile for the first time in what felt like days. This was her chance—her opportunity to make the outside exactly how she'd imagined it from the beginning—just a small area offset from the main lot by some raised planter boxes with room for tables and umbrellas. But she looked down at the plans and bit her lip. It would be gorgeous. Faith had a good eye for this kind of thing, no doubt. Her shoulders drooped and she forced her lips up.

"Faith's paying?"

"She pre-paid for the whole project."

"All right, then. Let's do it." Janet peeked around Bruce out the front door and saw a full team of orange-vested workers milling around in her parking lot. "Let me send you out with some sweet teas for the crew. Sound good?"

"Sure. Thanks."

She led the way to the jug of tea on the bar. "How many?"

He held his hands up with his fingers spread wide. "I guess ten—nah, just make it an even dozen."

She nodded and pulled a stack of plastic cups down from the shelf.

"That's some great tea," Bruce said conversationally. "You usually don't find anyone who's not from Tennessee can make it so good. Where'd you learn?"

"Oh, this is all Cindy Lou! She's got a whole process and

doesn't let me anywhere near it." Janet focused on the amber liquid streaming from the spout of the carafe as her brain made a connection she didn't realize she knew. Bruce certainly seemed to have known the Brooks family for some time. If he was in the mood to chat, she might as well take advantage of it. She looked up and smiled. "How's it going out there?"

Bruce picked up a stack of lids from the bar and started adding them to the cups as Janet handed them across. "No major surprises, that's the good news. But these jobs take time. We'd like to have the plumber and electrician out to lay the pipe work and lines today so we can get on with re-laying the asphalt and setting the posts on the same day. That'll save you some money." He grinned and started stacking the cups two high to transport outside. "Well, Faith, anyway."

"Here," Janet said, handing him a tray and then adding six cups to her own. "What's your connection to Faith and William? I never did remember to ask Faith how she knew you!"

He chuckled. "I did some work for the Brooks family when I was just starting out in Memphis. Years ago. Jason and William had been sharing a room, and apparently they were close to tearing the whole house apart. Faith wanted another bedroom added on so they could spread out."

Janet fumbled with the door as she looked back at Bruce. "Jason and William were sharing a room? Why? Were he and Faith having trouble even back then?"

A laugh rumbled out of Bruce. He stopped walking to balance his tray but continued to chuckle as they walked out of the dark bar into the waning afternoon winter sunshine outside. "Not William Senior! William Junior. Jason's brother."

"Jason's brother?" Janet felt like a parrot the way she was repeating everything Bruce said, but she'd known Jason for going on three years, and he'd never once mentioned a brother. Had gone so far, in fact, as to tell her he was an only child.

"What happened to him? William Junior, I mean?"

"Oh, he's still there in Memphis, last I heard." The twinkle in

Bruce's eye faded, and his smile flattened into a thin line. "Those were happier times, that's for sure."

The construction crew gathered around her and Bruce, and soon she was walking back into the Spot with two empty trays and a looming migraine. Jason had a brother. But something bad had happened; that much was clear from Bruce's demeanor. Why hadn't Jason ever brought it up? Or his parents? What were they hiding?

CHAPTER THIRTY-NINE

"Did anyone hear from Cindy Lou today?" Janet looked at the clock again, and a knot of worry settled in the base of her stomach. Her assistant manager's shift was supposed to have started at three, but it was now quarter past four, and she hadn't called and wasn't there.

"Nope." Mel frowned. "It's not like her to just not show up. Did you call her house?" Janet looked down at the ground and Mel pressed her. "What?

"Well, I...I saw her this morning."

"Oh, good." Kat smiled and patted her on the shoulder. "I'm sure she's just running late." All three turned to look out the door at the cloudless clear blue sky. After a moment, Kat turned back to face Janet. "Did she look okay? Mel said she went home sick two days ago."

"She..." Janet gulped. She felt guilty just thinking about how she'd spoken to Cindy Lou that morning. "I saw her this morning, at a restaurant."

"What did you do?" Mel folded her arms across her chest and stared hard at Janet.

"Well...she was with a man—she didn't even know his last

name, and I...I might have gotten a little...uh...judgmental with her."

Mel frowned. "She's a grown woman, Janet. Why do you feel the need to cut her down all the time?"

Quizz came out of the office before she could answer the unanswerable, holding the sheaf of papers from Jason's employee. "Hey. I think there are two William Brookses."

Janet nodded. "You're right." Through the lump in her throat, she filled in Quizz, Mel, and Kat on everything—from her investigation at the coffee shop to what she'd learned from Bruce about Jason having a brother. When she was done, Quizz's short purple hair stood straight up from the number of times she'd run her hands roughly through it.

"So let me get this straight. Your boyfriend has a brother that you didn't know about." Janet nodded. "It now seems likely that that brother was living in the apartment we visited in Memphis, which also means he could be dating—or doing something with —a minor named Lola *who we are charged with locating*, and likely is responsible for the illegal charges you investigated at the coffee shop earlier this month."

Quizz stopped to take a breath and Janet nodded slowly. How did the coffee shop fit in? It didn't make sense.

But before she could really consider the question, Quizz continued. "William Brooks *Senior's* last known girlfriend was killed and left for dead in your bar, and now," Quizz looked down to read something from the papers in her hand, "and now, we don't know where to find William Jefferson Brooks *Junior*? Am I missing anything?"

A clunk of noise echoed in Janet's brain as Quizz's last words thunked into place. William *Jefferson* Brooks Junior.

"This morning—Cindy Lou called the man she was with Jeff. I—I was angry with her because from across the restaurant, I thought she was sitting with Jason. So then I stormed across the restaurant, and O'Dell tried to stop me, but—but it's so clear now...so...terribly clear!"

Jeff's hair was the same color as Jason's, and he and Jason shared the same cowlick at the back of their head. And even though she'd dismissed Jeff's appearance as being different from Jason's, the resemblance was there. She knew it. "I think Cindy Lou was with Jason's brother this morning!"

Kat's face was pale when she spoke. "And now she's a no-show for her shift here? We need to find her. She could be in danger."

Janet already had her phone pressed to her ear. Someone picked up on the first ring, but it wasn't Cindy Lou.

"Hello?" Cindy Lou's son had moved home after almost failing out of UT Knoxville during fall semester.

"Chip, it's Janet. I'm looking for your mom. Is she there?"

"No. I—wait. I thought she was with you at the Spot?"

Janet felt that same pulsing worry in her chest from earlier. "She had the day off yesterday—how'd she seem then?"

"I didn't see her. I thought she was at work yesterday."

"I'm sure she's fine." The words sounded hollow to her own ears, and Chip didn't seem reassured, either.

"I have class tonight. Should I—" He cleared his throat. "I feel like I should stay here in case she needs me."

"Chip, you go on to class. I'll have your mom call you on your cell when she gets into work. I'm sure she's just running late."

He seemed relieved that Janet had taken charge of the situation and agreed to check in with her at the break time for his class. She gripped her phone tightly at her side and looked at her colleagues in the Spot. "We need to find her. If she's with Jason's brother, she's not safe."

"Where do we start?" Quizz asked uncertainly. "We know about his apartment in Memphis, but we don't know where he's staying here in town."

"But I bet Jason does." She tapped Jason's name in her contact list with force.

"He's gone, Janet. He left in the middle of the night and he's not going to answer your call now." Quizz looked sadly at her apprentice, but it was Kat who answered.

"Jason left to keep Janet safe—and he kicked us out of our side of the house because he must have been worried about us, too. He'll answer."

Janet was glad Kat was so certain, because just then, she was doubting everyone and everything in her life.

After five rings, her call went to voicemail.

She hung up, refusing to leave a message. When she looked up at her friends, her colleagues, their expressions mirrored her own pain and confusion.

She squared her shoulders, but before she could come up with a plan, her phone rang in her hand.

She turned away from the prying eyes in front of her. "Jason Brooks, you have some major explaining to do."

"I know, but there's no time."

"No time? No time? I can't believe you have the gall to say—"

"Mom's missing. I think my brother took her. I wanted you to know that I called O'Dell and told him that Dad and I are coming downtown to talk."

CHAPTER FORTY

Janet nudged her way into the interview room slowly and held out a hand when Jason made to stand. "Don't—just...Don't." She waited for him to look at her. He didn't. "You could have told me," she finally said. "I could have helped you."

He shook his head. "No one can help with this. That's the problem. When he's off his meds, he's so unpredictable. So angry. I wanted to bring him to us—let him know that he was still our priority. But—" He looked up, his eyes imploring her to understand, "I had to keep living, you know? We've spent a lot of time and money on making sure he's okay. And I put my life on hold so many times—and was happy to do it. But at some point, you've got to live your life, and let him live his. I just never—I didn't think it would come to this."

Janet threw the manila folder on the table between them. "Your employee got some info. It might help."

Jason reached out to take the folder and opened it slowly, as if it might bite. He scanned the top sheet, then the second. His eyes widened and he flipped back to page one. "How did she find this?"

"She said she's the top security hacker in the state. And she's pissed that you didn't pay her last week."

He grimaced. "I was kind of busy."

"Apparently, so was she." Janet tilted her head to the side. "Why didn't you tell me Mike was a woman?"

He looked up at her, his eyes wide. "It never occurred to me that you didn't know."

She frowned. "Working with Mike at all hours of the day and night and you didn't think I should know?" His eyes squeezed together slightly—but it was enough to confirm to Janet that he'd purposefully kept the information to himself. "That's what I thought."

"It's not a big deal. I'm not worried that Cameron's your new hire."

"And I didn't tell you his name was Brenda!"

"I didn't make up her name! She goes by Mike!"

Tap, tap. They both leaned back at the knock on the door.

"Hello? Janet, Jason, are we on a tight deadline or not?" O'Dell crossed the threshold and set his laptop down across from Jason.

Janet felt heat rise in her cheeks; she'd forgotten that he was watching from the room next door. She squared her shoulders and faced Jason. "What do you know? And don't leave anything out."

Jason paled, and the determined expression slid off his face like melted wax, leaving behind a mess of emotions she'd never witnessed in him before.

"So William's younger than you, huh?" O'Dell's sad smile said it all.

Jason nodded slowly. "I was six when he was born."

Her heart hurt just listening to his broken voice. No matter how hard he tried, big brother couldn't stop this runaway train. William Junior had done too much—made too many mistakes for Jason to help him now.

O'Dell must have felt it, too, because his voice was low, his tone softer when he spoke again. "You tried your best, Jason, but now it's our turn. So either you can tell us where to start, or we'll consider you a co-conspirator. Your choice for the next five minutes. My choice after that."

A somberness came over Jason. He folded his hands on his lap and looked down for a long moment before answering. Finally, he flinched, as if he'd come to some internal decision, some forgone conclusion that he could hardly face.

"He's been in trouble before, but nothing like this. Nothing so violent. But he—he's out of chances, you know? We were so lucky to get him into the facility—so, I mean, if this thing with Lola and Connie—I mean, if it *wasn't* him, if it was a terrible misunderstanding—it would have ruined things going forward, you know?"

"Why?"

"Huh?" Jason looked up, confused.

"Why was it lucky that you got him into the facility?"

"There were some... issues after high school. He...he couldn't really make the transition into life, and he had...problems."

"What kind of problems?" Janet asked.

"Legal problems." O'Dell turned his laptop around so the screen was facing Janet.

She squinted to make out the words. "Assault—"

"He hit a guy, but not on purpose. He just lost control for a moment." Jason's set face dared her to disagree.

"Battery—"

"Look, the guy was making fun of him. What kind of asshole makes fun of a kid with an illness?"

"*Felony* assault?" Janet waited for Jason's explanation. It didn't come.

"That was—that was when we got him into Liberty Meadows. It's a special facility, and they really know how to—how to handle Jeff. It's been a great place. I don't know why he wanted to leave."

"This is all from his adult record. Any juvie problems?"

Jason's lips clamped. He only shook his head—but not in a

way that made Janet think he was answering "no." Just in a way that meant he didn't want to face the question.

"So what happened? Why is he doing this now?"

"Best I can piece together from talking to the staff at Liberty, my parents' divorce shook him. My dad leaving Memphis was another blow. Then, when Mom came here, too—I think he snapped." Jason pressed his lips together and looked at his folded hands again.

"Don't hold out on us now. There's no time. Tell us what you know." O'Dell turned his computer back around with his hands hovering over the keyboard, ready to take notes.

Jason blew out a breath and nodded slowly. "My dad got a call from Liberty Meadows that Jeff had become unpredictable. That he'd been caught trying to flush his meds—was causing trouble for other residents. Nothing serious, but enough that Dad was worried. Before he could get there, Jeff was gone."

"When was that?" Janet asked.

"It was right after you learned the Spot needed a kitchen. Dad got the call from Liberty Meadows, and I started working online to try and track him down. We hoped to keep it simple— find him, alert Liberty Meadows, and they'd get him back on track. We thought if I got involved right away, it might make him feel like we'd ganged up on him. We—we didn't know how far gone he already was."

"Did you know about Lola?" Janet heard the anger in her voice, but didn't apologize.

Jason didn't answer.

"Did you know about the secret app on her phone?"

He looked away.

"Jason!"

"When I saw the birthmark on that sexting photo, I knew that Jeff was involved. I copied Lola's phone onto my hard drive so I could investigate. That's when I left for Memphis to track him down. The apartment was empty by then. Jeff was gone. Then Connie was killed, and I—I didn't want to believe it. I figured there was another suspect. There had to be!" Jason's voice had gone brittle, and his pale face was tinged yellow, like he might get sick. "But I was wrong. It was him all along."

Jason ran his hands roughly down his face, then pulled some folded papers out of his back pocket. "This is what I know." He tossed the papers across the table.

O'Dell flipped it open. "What am I looking at?"

"It's a rental agreement. It's under my name, but I had nothing to do with it. It must be him. That's where you'll find my brother—and maybe my mom...Lola...Cindy Lou." He stared down at the floor again, his whole body bowed over as if he could no longer bear the weight of what was happening.

"When did you find out where he's staying?" Janet asked, one hand pressed against her chest. Was it possible all three women were still alive? What would the police find inside that apartment? She shuddered, images of duct tape and zip ties flashed across her brain. If his place here in Knoxville was anything like his place in Memphis, it would be a miracle to find anyone had survived.

Jason's head dropped down into his hands. "Just this morning. Mom said she was going out to get coffee, but Jeff must have gotten in touch, convinced her to meet him. When she didn't come back—didn't answer her phone—we got worried. Then I had a breakthrough with some malware I'd installed remotely on Jeff's cell phone through an email." His eyes flicked up to Janet's, then sunk guiltily back down, and he fell silent.

Detective Rivera pushed his way into the room and stared down at Jason, his hands on his hips.

"We just need to approach him with caution—I don't know what he's capable of—"

"Well, unfortunately, we do," Rivera interjected. "One murder and now at least three missing women—that's just what we know of! Let's just pray they're all alive—because we know exactly what he's capable of."

Rivera snatched the papers out of O'Dell's hand and spoke

into his radio. "SWAT call out. Gather and prep—wait to move out on my command."

Jason started. "The SWAT team? More people are going to die if you go in guns blazing. There has to be a better way. A smarter way!"

"This guy's dangerous, Jason. If we've got to take him out to rescue the women, then that's what we're going to do. There's no other way," Rivera said.

Janet steeled herself—she owed it to Faith, to Lola, and mostly to Cindy Lou to do her part to help bring them home. "What can I do?"

"Nothing," Jason and O'Dell spoke together, but Rivera's eyebrows raised as he appraised Janet.

"Come with me."

Without a backwards glance, she turned and followed him out the door.

CHAPTER FORTY-ONE

"The worst part of any SWAT situation is going into the house blind. We'd much rather have Junior come out to us. Safer for everyone that way." Rivera stood in a conference room in the heart of the police department downtown, surrounded by men and women in black SWAT gear. The men and women painted black and dark green paint on their faces as they listened to their commander.

As Rivera spoke, an enlarged map glowed behind him from a projector screen onto the white board at the back of the room. "Janet, that's where you come in—"

"I must state, again, that I completely object to this kind of use of a civilian. It makes much more sense to go in and get him than to put another person at risk." O'Dell stood glaring over the room from the corner; his lips barely moved when he spoke.

"Noted and dismissed. Again." Rivera hardly paused in his instructions. "You'll be standing by, Janet, using the phone to get William's attention. We suspect that he's desperate to talk to you —as he's not been able to take out anyone Jason cares about yet." He winced when O'Dell growled. "Poor choice of words, but you know what I mean. You are not to go into the house, but if the phone doesn't work, we'll put you on display outside."

Janet nodded. She was going to get the women out of there one way or another, but she didn't plan to share that with Rivera just yet. O'Dell seemed to know, though, and she pulled at her collar under his heavy stare.

As the team broke apart and headed for the parking lot O'Dell came up from behind her, breathing down her neck. "I'm staying with you, Janet. And I'll attach handcuffs to your wrists if that's what it takes to keep you safe, you hear me?"

"O'Dell, please. I'm not out to play hero tonight. Of course we'll stay together."

"Oh." He stepped back an inch but continued to look at her suspiciously. "I'm glad to hear you sounding so sensible." He pulled her arm and she turned to face him. They both stopped walking. "Cindy Lou, Faith—they might not even be alive, Janet. We're dealing with a sociopath. Nothing is certain except uncertainty."

She nodded, but didn't agree, at least not completely. Jason saw some redeeming quality in his brother, and that meant that somewhere inside, maybe *deep inside* when he wasn't taking his medicine, he had something worth saving—even if that was only so that he could spend the rest of his days in a facility. She was going to make sure that happened, if only for Jason. He'd helped her out of enough tight spots that she knew she owed him. Even if he didn't want her anywhere near his brother.

"What are you thinking?" O'Dell was close again, obviously not trusting her despite her words.

"I'm just worried about everyone," she answered truthfully. "Are Jason and his dad under arrest?"

"Jason just left. I told him to keep his distance, that we'll arrest anyone at the scene who's interfering with our operation."

"Why'd you let him go?"

O'Dell frowned. "We can't charge him, and we can't continue to hold him if he decided he wanted to go. Which he did. William Senior doesn't know that, but Jason did."

"So William's just...sitting there? Wondering if his ex-wife is alive?"

O'Dell's lips pressed flat. "At least he's safe there. Not everyone can say the same."

"She going with you?" Rivera called from his car.

"Yes!" O'Dell called back.

"We'll stage three blocks away. Then we'll move in to make the call."

Janet took in the information and her eyes swept the parking lot, looking for O'Dell's car. She spotted it alone at the end of the lot—the nearest car some dozen spots away. "You sure do worry about your car...which is great, but unusual, given its condition."

The blue Crown Vic was old and beaten up, with nicks and scratches that another car wouldn't have survived.

O'Dell patted the top with affection. "That's why I've got to be so careful with her. She won't survive much more." He glanced over at her and she swatted him.

"Don't look at me like you look at your car. I'm not that old and weathered, okay?"

O'Dell snickered and climbed behind the wheel. "Get in. Let's get this over with so I can make sure you're around tomorrow and the next day, too."

She grinned, glad for anything that lightened the mood, and walked around the front of the car. She saw Jason's truck out of the corner of her eye and it felt like her soul grinned. Of course Jason was going to watch over her. Whatever else was going on in his life, that hadn't changed.

"Are you ready?" O'Dell asked lightly, but his jaw was tight, his shoulders stiff.

She nodded, an uneasy feeling washing over her from the inside out, and O'Dell pulled out of the lot, headed for William Junior, for Cindy Lou, for Faith, and maybe for Lola.

———

By the glow of the streetlamp, Janet read her watch. Just after six o'clock, but the sky was cloudy and the early winter sunset had already plunged the area into total darkness. A chill that had nothing to do with the cool winter air slid down the back of her neck and settled into the base of her spine. She shivered, and O'Dell looked over, concerned.

"You don't have to do this, you know that, right? This isn't your job."

"I know, O'Dell. But it's the quickest way to end this, and that's important."

He frowned, but nodded, too, and she tuned back into what Rivera was saying to the team.

"After Janet makes contact on the phone, she will glean as much information as possible from Suspect One on where he is in the unit." He pointed to a board behind him with a hastily drawn rendering of the apartment floor plan, taken from the owner of the unit, now standing alert next to the detective. "As soon as Janet gives us the signal—"

He waited, and only when O'Dell poked her in the ribs did she blurt out, "Do you need any food?"

Rivera glared at her before nodding. "That's when we know he's in the kitchen and it's safe for us to move in. If at any time we get word that victims are in pain, injured, or otherwise in bad shape, then we move in immediately on my command." He stopped and surveyed the team assembled in front of him. "Any questions?"

Janet half-raised her hand as if she was back in a classroom. "I'm feeling a little underdressed. Do I need a bulletproof vest or anything?"

"You are not going anywhere near the scene, so there's no reason for you to have anything on other than your regular clothes," O'Dell growled loud enough for Rivera to nod approvingly.

"All right." Rivera's gaze swept the group one more time before he clapped his hands together. "Let's go get this guy."

A whoop of noise rose from the assembled men and women, and everyone broke apart and took up their posts around the perimeter of the building and up the back stairs under cover of darkness.

Rivera walked over and held a cell phone out toward her. "Are you ready, Janet?"

She quenched the sickening feeling in her stomach and squared her shoulders. "Let's do this."

CHAPTER FORTY-TWO

Her palm was sweaty, and the phone slipped down, just her fingertips catching it at the last minute.

"Got it?" Rivera glared and she gulped audibly.

"Yup. Sorry."

O'Dell opened his mouth but shut it before any words came out. His glare was enough to remind her and Rivera that he didn't like what they were doing. His grim attitude bolstered her own, and she wiped her palm off on her jeans and then gripped the phone tightly.

"Dialing," she said softly as she pressed the keypad, reading the numbers off a notepad Rivera held out. She held her breath. "It's ringing," she said, and Rivera pushed his fingers up to his lips. She nodded and pressed her own lips together. The call went straight to voicemail. She relayed the information to Rivera and he reached over to end the call.

"Try again."

She dialed the numbers a second time, and before she could whisper to Rivera that the call had rung through to the other end, a voice spoke.

"Who's this?"

Her eyes flew open, and when a bitter taste flooded the back of her mouth she realized exactly what she'd gotten herself into. There was no script, no help. Just her, a cell phone, and a madman. And several lives possibly hanging in the balance.

"This is…Janet. I—" She locked eyes with O'Dell. "I heard you've been looking for me."

A long pause met her declaration and Janet thought she might have lost him. But then he spoke.

"I've been watching you, that's true. Looking for you. Trying to meet you."

"Well, you should have stopped into the Spot to say hi."

"Jason has that place locked down. I could never get in unnoticed."

O'Dell raised his eyebrows and she shrugged. How could she explain what was being said without giving herself away? "Your dad is worried about your mom."

"I'll bet."

"Can I talk to her?"

"No."

"Is she okay?"

Rivera leaned in, as if certain he'd be able to hear Junior's answer through the line. But it wasn't going to be that easy. Of course it wasn't.

"What does Jason think?"

"Jason?" Janet was surprised by the change in topic. Was Junior worried about his older brother? Or did he want to impress him? "Of course he's worried, too."

"Where is he?"

"I don't know. He…he broke up with me. Did you know that?"

"Bullshit. He's just trying to keep you safe. Worked so far, didn't it?"

"Do you want to hurt me, William?"

No answer.

"Why? Why are you so angry?"

"You haven't seen angry yet." Another chilling statement, but

Rivera was getting impatient. He glared at her and she bit her lip, then blurted out, "Do you have Cindy Lou?"

"You surprised me. At the restaurant this morning. I wasn't expecting to see you."

"You surprised me, too. From across the room, I thought you were Jason." She gulped; would the comparison make him angry? He didn't speak, so she asked him again, "Is Cindy Lou with you?"

"Not exactly."

Janet's breath caught. What did that mean? She didn't want to risk his wrath by asking, so she switched gears. "Is your mother alive?"

He snorted. "Of course. I wouldn't kill my own mother. She was just in the way, so I put her to sleep while I finish the job."

"Asleep? Not dead?"

He sighed "I'm bored with this call. Goodbye."

"Wait!" But only silence met her cry. She looked down at the screen—the numbers timing the call length ticked onward. Despite his silence, Junior was still on the other end of the line. She motioned O'Dell closer and held the phone between their heads. "Junior?"

"Don't call me that!"

"What should I call you?"

"Jeff! My name is Jeff."

"Right. Jeff, what are you going to do? You have to know this isn't going to end well, right?"

"I know." His voice was suddenly small, frightened.

"Then what are you going to do?"

"I guess I wanted to talk to you."

Relief flooded O'Dell's face. She felt it in her bones, too. Talk. They could do that. They *were doing* that. "I want to help you, Jun—Jeff. How can I help?"

"Where are you?" The mini blinds on the windows in the apartment above moved, a triangle of light now visible from the street below. "Are you out there with the police?"

O'Dell's face tightened. Janet felt the shift across the cell phone signal. What did Jason's brother know? She cleared her throat. "Um, yes. They thought I could help."

"Are you protected?"

"Well, that's a funny question, seeing as you know I'm with the cops. Of course I'm protected."

"I'm not stupid!" he roared. "Don't treat me like I'm stupid!" Heavy breathing shallowed out to a small cough. A deep sigh. "People always underestimate me. I hate that."

The streetlamp under which they stood suddenly went dark. Just coincidence. It had to be. But O'Dell must have felt the same uncertainty that roared up Janet's throat, because he clicked the safety off of his gun and held it stiffly at his side. She looked nervously around. There wasn't any movement from inside the apartment, but then the streetlights all down the block extinguished at once, plunging the team into complete and utter darkness.

She gripped the phone tightly in her fist, and when Junior spoke again, his voice was slick, slithery. "Oh, Janet. I've been waiting for you. Now I can see that it was worth it."

An explosion of sound and smoke fired from nearby, then another and another. O'Dell shoved her to the side and she stumbled down the ledge of the sidewalk onto the street and fell down onto the ground, dazed.

"Go!" Rivera roared the command, but it was too late. The chaos of the darkness and explosions rendered the SWAT team useless, their coordination completely destroyed.

O'Dell helped her up and pushed her down the street, away from the chaos, away from the dangerous madman who wanted to hurt her. The night was black, the smoke was chokingly thick, and O'Dell's gloved grip was painfully tight.

"Jesus H. Christ, O'Dell, I'm not going to run away from you! He's a lunatic!"

O'Dell turned to face her—only it wasn't O'Dell.

"What—"

"Move. Now." The man pushed her hard—shoved her—away from the SWAT team, away from safety, and she tried to plant her feet, but he was stronger, and he lifted her almost completely off the ground. She looked wildly around, but couldn't see through the thick smoke, could only tell they were getting farther away from her crew, from her team, because the sounds of battle were getting quieter. Her head finally swiveled away from the SWAT team behind them and she looked ahead to see where they were going.

"Junior?" she gasped, as his crushing grip on her shoulder blade threatened to break bones.

"Don't call me Junior!" he roared, and her legs shook at the raw anger in his voice. She stumbled and would have fallen if Jason's brother's grip on her collarbone hadn't tightened. She gasped at the fresh pain that shot through her shoulder and down her arm, and no matter how hard she tried, she couldn't stop moving forward, even though she saw where they were headed.

"No—no, no, no. I am not getting into a van without windows. Nothing good happens in a van without—"

But he opened the back door and before she could react, he lifted her effortlessly. She kicked, fought with everything she had, but he easily overpowered her. The fact would have been infuriating if she hadn't had other more pressing issues to deal with.

He tossed her into the back of the van like she was a snack cooler. If only she could have absorbed the impact of the landing as easily.

The jolt of hitting the metal floorboards took her breath away, and before she could reconcile the pain in her head, elbow, and hip, Jeff slammed the back door, plunging her into darkness. She struggled to sit up, and as she writhed around the unforgiving metal floorboards, her elbow landed on something bumpy. She felt around with her hands and found herself situated between two lumpy rolls of carpet. Her fingers danced over the rough edges of the frayed material as the van began to move. Her hand shot out to steady herself, and then she flinched when her skin touched someone else's skin.

She wasn't alone in the van after all.

She tried to yell, but it came out more like a gasp. "What is happening?"

But it was no use.

The bodies lying next to her didn't seem able to answer.

.

CHAPTER FORTY-THREE

The van rumbled along, Janet increasingly uncomfortable by what she didn't know about her situation. Where was Jason's brother taking her? And who else was along for the ride?

"Are you okay?" she whispered to the dark rolls on either side of her. "Can you hear me?"

There was no answer.

Her hands skittered along the floorboards, searching for anything that she could use as a weapon. Passing over the lumpy carpet roll on her right, her fingers stretched to the cool metal side of the van without luck. To the left, her search was rewarded by something sharp slicing open her finger.

Janet gasped and raised the finger to her lips, sucking off the blood.

After a moment, though, she leaned over the carpet roll. Whatever had been sharp enough to cut her was sharp enough to cut someone else. She squinted, waiting for passing headlights to help her see.

Finally, a beam of light shot through the front of the car and lit up the interior enough for her to make out what had injured her. Her stomach dropped when she saw it—just a rusted out spot of the interior wall of the van. Not a weapon at all. Disappointment slid down the back of her throat like acid, and settled uncomfortably in her stomach.

Eventually the van slowed to a stop, and the driver's door opened with a click and then slammed shut. Footsteps crunched around the side of the van.

Janet climbed to her feet and balanced in a low crouch, her arms bent and ready to rocket out. She knew she'd have just one shot to overpower Junior, to escape; but when the door opened, he struck first, as if he knew she'd be waiting for him.

His fist connected with her right eye and the side of her nose. He might as well have used a stun gun on her; she fell back, immobile, both eyes watering and stinging, her breath gone.

After the ride in the back of the dark van, the light behind Junior felt as bright as fireworks. With her eyes still watering, she had trouble keeping them open at all. Before she could recover, Junior grabbed her ankles and pulled her roughly forward along the floor of the van, and jabbed her in the neck with something sharp.

"What was that?" she yelped.

He didn't answer, but she saw a flash of metal at his side, before it disappeared into his pocket. She reached up to touch her neck and wiped a drop of blood away from her skin. A panic, unlike any she'd ever felt, swept through her bloodstream and a shiver rocked her body.

"Was that a needle? What did you give me?"

When she kicked out, he jabbed her so hard in the kidney that she couldn't mask her gasp. He chuckled, then pulled her roughly out of the van and tied her wrists together behind her. She stood on shaky legs, unsure what he might do next.

Dammit. She tried to calm herself, to take in her surroundings. If she was going to have any chance of escaping, she needed to keep her wits about her; figure out where she was.

He shoved her forward. The contact helped snap her out of the growing sense of panic. But still, her legs felt unusually weak, her brain foggy. Gravel crunched underfoot, then the jangle of a keyring. She shook her head to clear it and recognized the brown metal door in front of her. The back entrance to Old Ben's restaurant. They were so close to the Spot if she turned, she could see it.

Her brain sparked with awareness. If she yelled, someone might hear her. But suddenly, her vision went sideways, then Jeff grabbed her under her arms. Had she fallen? Her joints felt loose, her mind out of focus.

She smelled day-old grease and burned hamburger, and an image of her food truck flashed across the back of her eyelids.

Why were they here?

Junior set her down on the floor, but her legs couldn't support her. Her knees felt weak and her vision—still blurry from the punch—went hazier yet.

"Why, Junior? Why...why are you... doing th..." But she couldn't finish her question. Instead, consciousness slipped away.

———

Sometime later, a pounding woke Janet from a very bad dream.

"Och." Keeping her eyes tightly shut, she gingerly reached up to touch her head. *Bam. Bam. Bam.* The pounding was slow, steady. "What is that?"

She blinked her eyes open and sucked in a sharp breath. Where was she?

The space was dark and smelled funny, like the inside of an old locker room. And it was hot. So hot that beads of sweat trickled down her arms; her shirt stuck to her skin.

"Fuuuuck."

"Cindy Lou?" Janet lurched forward, remembering everything that had led up to this moment in one horrible flash. "Cindy Lou, is that you?" She reached out toward the voice and held back a sob.

"I reckon so, but I feel like someone hit me with a sledgehammer. Where are we?"

"We're inside Old Ben's restaurant." Janet glanced around the dark space. "I think we're inside the walk-in cooler."

Janet ran her hands over the other woman's head. No bumps, no blood. "Do you know what happened to you?"

"I honestly don't." Her nose wrinkled and she looked up and searched Janet's face. "I saw you at breakfast—that happened, right?"

Janet nodded.

"Then we went back to Jeff's place and the last thing I remember is he gave me a cup of tea." She shook her head and winced. "But that doesn't make sense, does it?"

"He must have drugged you."

"But why?"

"It's a long story. Have you seen Jason's mother?"

Cindy Lou looked around the cramped room slowly. "No, hon, I sure don't see her."

"No—I meant—never mind." Janet stood and tried the door. "Locked."

Cindy Lou coughed. "Man, I would kill for some water right about now. My mouth is like the dang-Sahara."

Janet continued to search the room, her hands skimming the walls, they were almost too hot to touch.

"I'll tell you what, if we're in the cooler, the designer did something wrong. It's hotter than blue blazes in here!"

Janet blew out a slow breath, trying to force her brain to work. Junior had tossed them inside, but when? How much time had elapsed?

"Hey!" Janet banged on the door with her fist. "Hey! Let us out!"

Cindy Lou joined in, but no amount of banging brought Jason's brother back to them.

Cindy Lou rubbed her knuckles and leaned against the door. "Is he gone, d'ya think?"

"I don't know." Janet wiped beads of sweat from her face and snapped her shirt away from her stomach.

"Do you smell that?" Cindy Lou asked, coughing again.

Janet nodded slowly.

"Smells like...a campfire or something. But with burning tire thrown on top. What is going on, Janet?"

"I think..." Janet swallowed, hardly able to utter the words. But with the heat, the smell, and what she'd mistaken for a fan earlier, it seemed the only explanation. "I think the restaurant is on fire."

"No." Cindy Lou shook her head. "No way. Maybe he's just makin' us a snack...or...oh, dear." Cindy Lou pointed to the ventilation slits at the top of the insulated walls. Smoke seeped into the room. They needed to find a way out of the building.

A sudden blast of noise knocked Janet off her feet. Cindy Lou screamed.

"Shh!" Though her ears were ringing, she thought she heard a scrabbling of noise at the door.

Janet leapt back up just as Junior stormed into the tiny space. He grabbed her arm. In a panic, she tried to shrug out of his grasp, but his grip was iron-like, so tight she felt a bruise blooming under his fingertips.

"Let go of me!" Panic rose up her throat, choking her, along with the heavy smoke now pouring into the small space. But he was stronger, and his grip didn't falter. When she tried kicking out at him, he slapped her across the face. Hard.

She hadn't been expecting it—which made it hurt all the more. But it also knocked some sense into her, and her panic disappeared along with the feeling in her jaw. This kidnapping had just ventured into bar brawl territory, and that knowledge hit her in the face almost as hard as Junior's open hand.

When he pulled his arm back again, she was ready. Just before his palm made contact with her face for a second time, she dodged to the right and used his momentum as a weapon, pulling against him with all her might, then shoving his body forward when he lost his balance. When he stumbled, he lost his grip on her arm. She brought her knee up with as much force as she could muster, and felt, rather than heard, his nose break against her kneecap. He gasped in pain, and she took the opportunity to strike. Her elbow swung down against his head with a crack that she felt all the way to the tip of her pinky finger. He dropped down to the ground, his face hitting the cement floor with a sickening smack. Cindy Lou crawled over to him and pried one eye open. It lolled like a pinball.

"You knocked him out cold!" She looked up in awe.

But instead of feeling galvanized, Janet dropped down onto her knees, suddenly hardly able to catch her breath. Hyperventilating when it was all over, how ridiculous! She raised her head in search of cooler, more oxygenated air.

Cindy Lou tottered to her feet, swaying with the effort. She poked her head out of the cooler and yelped. "We need to get out of here!"

Another blast of noise rocked the entire structure. Janet couldn't hear anything over the roar of the fire. *Think!* she admonished herself.

Though Junior was a killer, he was also Jason's brother. How could she live with herself if she left him here to burn to death? Also, he was likely the only one who knew where Lola and Faith were—if they were dead or alive.

"This asshole is going to owe me so big," she growled. Light from the fire illuminated the inside of the cooler, and she made her way back to where Junior lay on the ground. "Help me, Cindy Lou!" she cried, and together, they managed to lift the upper half of his body up, but Janet couldn't find purchase to get his nearly 200 pounds of dead weight up over her shoulder.

"It's never gonna work, hon. Just leave him—you have to leave him!"

"But then we might never know what happened to Faith! To Lola!"

Cindy Lou grabbed Janet's arm and pulled. "I don't care right now! If we don't get out of here, we'll never get to wonder what happened to anyone. Janet, we're out of time!"

Another coughing spell grabbed hold of Janet, and when she caught her breath, she stumbled toward her friend. "Follow me!" she called over her shoulder, and stepped out into the main part of the kitchen. The heat was intense—but just from one side. Propane tanks lined up like soldiers from the wall of the walk-in cooler through the kitchen into the main dining area. Janet turned the other way and headed past the dishwasher station and toward a metal door. She hoped it led to safety.

She twisted the knob and pushed against the door, but it didn't budge.

"Come on, Janet! Together!" Cindy Lou joined her at the threshold, and they pushed, hit, and kicked at the door. Nothing happened.

Suddenly, the metal surface shuddered with a *thunk* of noise. The women looked at each other and leapt back.

"Someone's here! Someone's out there to help!" Cindy Lou cried.

The door shuddered again, but the lock held steady. A third chop of noise and whatever had been holding the door locked broke loose, and the heavy metal slab swung open.

An axe-wielding fireman stood before them, and even in their precarious situation, with a fire raging behind them and choking smoke overhead, Cindy Lou ran a quick hand through her messy blond hair and smiled. "Boy, are you a sight for sore eyes, mister!"

Janet shoved Cindy Lou past the fireman. "There's a man back there. He's—uh, he's knocked out in the kitchen!"

She hurried out into the cool refreshing air and didn't look back.

CHAPTER FORTY-FOUR

Janet stumbled out of the burning building, gasping for air and squinting against the sudden bright flashing lights from the fire trucks. She doubled over and took huge gulps of air, never appreciating oxygen more than she did just then.

A medic led her and Cindy Lou forward, out of the way of emergency crews still trying to get a handle on the fire. As they walked past a truck, she caught sight of Jason and O'Dell, standing next to each other at the edge of the parking lot.

Jason's hand clutched his chest like he was trying to keep his heart inside of his body. His open mouth looked frozen in mid-scream, and the soot on his face had settled into the fine lines around his eyes.

O'Dell's rigid stance relaxed as soon as he caught sight of her, and his mouth moved, maybe saying her and Cindy Lou's names before he smacked Jason on the shoulder and jogged toward them.

Jason didn't move—he stood as far from her as the property would allow.

Her focus shifted to O'Dell. When he reached them, he pulled them both into a hug, then stepped back and dropped his gaze, but not his hands, which squeezed her shoulder tighter. "I will never forgive myself, Janet. You were ripped away from right under my nose! I don't know how he did it!"

"It wasn't your fault, O'Dell." Janet reached out and lifted his chin. "I thought you were pushing me away to safety. I didn't realize it was Junior until we were halfway to his van." She shuddered. "It's all my fault." O'Dell didn't look convinced, but Janet had more pressing issues than his guilty conscience. "Faith? Lola?"

He shook his head. "Nothing yet. We thought they might be with you."

All three turned to face the building. And it might have been her imagination, but the flames looked smaller. Less intense.

"I don't know. They weren't in the cooler with us, but they might be somewhere else in there." Janet's stomach dropped again. Were Faith and Lola in there? Dead? Alive? Dying even as she took great gasping gulps of clean air into her own lungs?

A group of firefighters emerged from the restaurant, holding a gurney between them. Janet recognized the beanie covering the patient's head. "Junior."

"He was in there? That just doesn't make any sense." O'Dell's frown deepened. "What was his plan? To die in there with you?"

Janet couldn't even find the energy to lift her shoulders in a shrug. It *didn't* make sense, but then, nothing about Junior's actions in the last month had made sense. She looked back to where Jason had been—but he was gone.

"His mom's still missing. I'm sure he's worried." O'Dell squeezed her shoulder once more before dropping his hand. "We'll need to talk to you both—take official statements. But first," he held his phone out to Cindy Lou, "you should call Chip."

"Great balls of fire! Chip!" Cindy Lou grabbed the phone and turned away from O'Dell and Janet to dial the phone. While she laughed and cried into the phone with Chip, the scene commander gathered the firefighters near one of their trucks. The fire was winning, and O'Dell murmured in Janet's ear that they were going to probably change from attacking the fire to regrouping, finding a new strategy.

A third explosion rocked the building. Janet flinched against the noise, and O'Dell pulled her farther away from the restaurant. "It's propane tanks," she said. "They were stacked between the cooler and the restaurant. I think Junior's plan was to level the building and everyone who was in it."

"But why?" O'Dell scratched his head. "And why Cindy Lou?"

"What do you mean? Why any of us is the question!"

He turned to face Janet. "Jason told us that Junior was angry that the family had abandoned him in Memphis, that they'd chosen Jason, in a sense, by all moving to Knoxville. So in his anger, and more importantly, off his meds, he decided to target each family member. He killed Connie to get back at his dad. He took you to get back at Jason. But why Cindy Lou? You know?"

Janet chewed on her lip as she watched the firefighters break apart and surround the restaurant again. "Cindy Lou really admired Faith—" O'Dell snorted and Janet's shoulder slumped. "Okay, you're right. It was probably just another route to get to me." But her guilt over Cindy Lou's involvement in Junior's plan took a backseat when she looked at the burning building again. She sucked in a gasp loud enough that Cindy Lou looked over from her phone call.

"What?" O'Dell moved closer to Janet and grabbed her shoulders again, shaking her slightly when she didn't answer.

'She shrugged him off and an animal-like sound came from somewhere—maybe her own throat—as she ran toward the building. Toward Jason.

"What the hell is he doing?" O'Dell said when he caught sight of Jason, wrapping a bandana around his face, simultaneously cowering against the heat and stepping through a broken window into the inferno.

"Jason!" She tried to lunge past a fireman, but O'Dell held her back.

"Jesus, Janet—no. *No!*" He grabbed her from behind and

locked down his grip. Her fingernails scratched at his neck, but O'Dell gently pulled her back, away from the building. The seconds passed like hours—everything moving in slow motion. Even the water was sluggish as it left the hoses, hardly making it to the building—to the fire—to Jason.

But just before she turned away, defeated, there it was— movement from within. Jason emerged from the orange glow of the center of the building, bent in half, lumbering toward the window, toward safety, the limp form of a person resting over his shoulder in a fireman's hold.

"Jesus," O'Dell breathed and dropped his hold on Janet to hurry forward and help, but a firefighter got there first and eased the body from Jason's shoulder.

Janet crept up behind O'Dell, drawn like a moth to the flame, even though she didn't want to know who Jason had found. Lola? Faith? Alive...or dead?

Jason stopped to cough, his face soot-blackened, his voice barely more than a croak. "Is she alive?"

Janet looked down at the ground. Faith lay crumpled—and it might have been her imagination, but she swore the older woman's chest rose up and down.

Before she could make sure her eyes weren't playing tricks on her, an EMT team pushed them all aside. The woman slipped an oxygen mask over Faith's face, then she and her partner lifted Faith onto a gurney and hurried away.

Only Jason's labored breathing punctured the relative silence.

Janet reached out to touch his shoulder, but when he flinched, she dropped her hand. "How did you know she was in there, Jason?"

"My brother," he said the word like a curse, "left a clue for me. I almost missed it. I almost didn't get to her in time." He choked back a sob.

"What clue?"

He didn't look up from the ground, but through barely moving lips he answered. "Her scarf. He left Cindy Lou's bandana, your jean jacket and Mom's scarf by the door. I didn't realize it was a clue until you and Cindy Lou came out. I almost missed it. This is my fault." His shoulders stiffened and he walked away into the night without a backwards glance.

O'Dell's radio crackled to life. He murmured something back to whomever was on the other end. Janet stood, staring into the darkness where Jason had disappeared.

She jumped when he tapped her on the arm. "What do you think?"

Janet wiped her eyes and turned to face her friend. "I'm sorry, O'Dell. What?"

"I said, Junior's regaining consciousness. Rivera's going to interview him in the hospital. Do you want to come?"

She wanted to curl up in bed in a dark room and never face anyone again. But that clearly wasn't an option, and she did have a job to finish. Find Lola. And that meant going with O'Dell to see the one person who might have some answers. She steeled her resolve. "Let's go."

"What about me?" Cindy Lou wailed.

"You'll take an ambulance," O'Dell said. "They'll want to make sure you're okay after everything that happened."

She nodded and followed an EMT toward a waiting ambulance.

O'Dell reached out for Janet's hand. "Ready?"

"Ready."

CHAPTER FORTY-FIVE

"What's going on?" Janet asked as they passed the hospital entrance and instead took a turn down an unlit path.

O'Dell smiled without taking his eyes off the road. "Rivera said the press is gathered at the emergency entrance. So we're taking the service road to a side entrance. A patrol officer will open the door for us."

He slowed the car as they drove past the hospital helipad. The chopper sat motionless on the pavement, waiting, no doubt, for the next car crash or shooting victim who'd need immediate evacuation to the hospital.

O'Dell eased the car into park but didn't turn off the engine. "I don't know if you should come into the room or not."

"What are you talking about? Then why did I come—why did you invite me along?"

"Honestly? Because I didn't want to leave you alone out there. You've been through a lot. I want to keep you close."

Her eyes filled unexpectedly and she turned away. Across the grassy yard, a pilot climbed up into the helicopter. The blades started to spin and soon, the rest of the flight crew spilled out of the hospital, gearing up for some kind of emergency.

"Life will never be the same," she said slowly. "Jason's family will never be the same. I don't know how we come back from this. But I do know that there's still a missing piece—Lola. And if I can help find her, if I can help shake Junior's tongue loose, then that might be the only thing I can do tonight. The only thing that might help me feel better about this whole lousy day."

O'Dell heaved out a sigh. "You're not allowed to actually shake his tongue loose. You know that, right?"

She smiled grimly. "Let's go."

Out on the pavement, O'Dell clicked the key fob to lock his car and motioned that Janet should follow him. He spoke into his radio and the side door opened just as they approached.

"Detective." The patrol officer nodded as they walked past, then resumed his guard duty by the exit. They took the elevator up to the third floor, and O'Dell led the way through the maze of hallways, past a nurses' station, and finally slowed at a room guarded by another cop.

That officer spoke into the radio clipped to the epaulette on his uniform, and less than a minute later, Rivera came down the hallway from the opposite direction.

"Any updates?" O'Dell asked.

"I just left Faith—she's fine," he was quick to add when a sound escaped Janet's mouth. "Some smoke inhalation, so they're keeping her overnight for observation, but the doctor said she shows no other signs of trauma."

"Impossible," Janet said, remembering her unconscious body sliding from Jason's grip after he'd rescued her from the fire.

"She says the last thing she remembers is that Junior called her, and said he was in trouble—that he needed her help, and only her help. So she gave William and Jason the slip and took an Uber to his apartment."

"The apartment where the SWAT team met?"

Rivera nodded. "When she got there, he offered her some tea. That's the last thing she remembers before waking up in the ambulance on the way here."

"Are there drugs in her system?"

Rivera shook his head. "No trace of anything. But if he used some kind of roofie on her early this morning, it would be out of her system already. He's smart."

O'Dell frowned. "That's probably what he did to Cindy Lou, too."

"And me." Janet reached up and rubbed the spot on her neck where Junior had jabbed her with a needle. "So what about Lola? She's been gone for weeks, but I swear I spotted her at breakfast yesterday—sitting right next to Junior and Cindy Lou. So how's he been keeping her, if he's not drugging her and he didn't kill her—what the hell is going on?"

"Time to find out." Rivera pushed open the door to the patient room.

William Jefferson Brooks Junior's bed was half-inclined, so that he wasn't flat but wasn't sitting up, either. Janet wondered if he'd turned away from the door when he heard it open, or if he'd been facing the window for a while.

Rivera cleared his throat, but Junior didn't move. The only acknowledgement that he knew they were there was the fluttering of his eyelids.

"You like to be called Jeff?" Rivera asked, his voice calm, pleasant, as if the man before them hadn't just tried to kill himself and three others.

"It is my name. So I guess so." His voice was soft but steely. Like his anger simmered just under the surface.

O'Dell edged slightly in front of Janet but didn't block her completely. The movement caught Junior's attention, and a spark of recognition kindled in his eye as he turned to face his visitor.

"You." He looked at Janet appreciatively, then said, "How's the identity-theft business going lately?"

"Huh?" The question was so unexpected that Janet was distracted from the much larger issues at hand. "What are you talking about?"

"Coffee, muffins...I wasn't sure how big I'd have to go to get your attention." When her brow furrowed, his lips pressed together into a bitter smile. "How disappointing. You didn't figure it out? Not as smart as they said, then. Hmm."

His expression jarred her brain loose, but she was still confused. "The credit card theft investigation? At the coffee shop? So that wasn't your father then, but...who cares?"

"I wanted to get your attention, but that firm you're working for is slow. I filed the theft complaint with Bexley and Associates weeks before you finally looked into it. I got tired of waiting for you."

"You? What do you mean *you* filed the complaint? We were investigating for some lady named Karla."

"There is no Karla. I made her up, opened a fake credit card account, and then hired you to investigate."

"But...why?"

"I'd heard a lot about you, Janet. I wanted to see you for myself. But Jason had your bar locked down. Your home was... inaccessible, though I continued to try. In the end, it only tipped my parents off that I was...interested."

Janet froze—remembering Jason's father randomly deciding to do a deep clean at her house just the other day. "The windows?" she asked.

Junior nodded. "Just a little love message to let you know I was coming."

"And they knew? They knew that you were out there and dangerous, and they didn't warn me?"

"It's like they don't trust you at all." Junior's somber face was worse than his chilling grin.

"All right, pal, we're not here to go over your greatest hits. We want Lola. And when we get her, no one's going to care about anything you do ever again, you got that?" O'Dell's hard smile would have made many people stand down. But Junior wasn't like many other people. His gaze never wavered from Janet.

"Where's Lola?" Janet's throat felt raw from the smoke, but she faced her kidnapper head on. His smile made her skin crawl.

How she'd ever thought he resembled Jason was beyond her. There wasn't any kindness in those cold, calculating eyes.

"Where is Lola? That's a great question." He turned back toward the window, then murmured, "Tick tock."

Janet sucked in a loud breath and grabbed O'Dell's hand for support. "Tick tock? What does that mean?"

Junior blew out a slow steady breath and repeated himself.

"Is Lola in danger? Is she alive? Tell us where she is!" O'Dell barked.

Rivera held out his hand, a warning. "We can help you, Junior, but only if you help us, you understand?"

"It's Jeff, you asshole."

After a lengthy silence, Janet and the two cops headed to the door. At the sound of movement, Junior turned and caught Janet's eye. "Tick tock for Lola. And tick tock for Jason." Then he started laughing, and the crazed, joyless sound echoed around the small cold room.

Janet stumbled backward, away from Jason's brother, out into the safety of the hall.

Rivera gently closed the door on Junior, and he, O'Dell, and Janet gathered in the hallway.

"Chief's coming down to deal with the media. Turns out someone tipped them all off about this 'fire-revenge plan.' That's what they're calling it."

"What do you think? Does he know where Lola is?" Janet asked.

"She's not at the apartment. SWAT is still going over everything there, but there's no sign of struggle. No sign that Lola was ever there." Rivera rubbed a hand roughly over his forehead. "Plenty of other things—like a computer that had hacked into the city's electrical grid...but no sign of a missing teen."

Janet crossed her arms over her chest, trying to ward off the chill that bloomed deep in her core. "It's a game for him. A game he's still trying to win."

"The game's over, Janet. And I think we have to come to

grips with the fact that Lola's dead." O'Dell gripped her shoulder and squeezed. "Maybe he gave her too much of the drug that he used on Cindy Lou and his mother. Maybe he dumped her body before we even got to his apartment tonight. It'll all make sense soon—someone will find the body. They'll call it in. There's nothing we can do until that happens."

She nodded, not believing anything O'Dell said. It wasn't over. Junior's words proved that he was still in the game, and he was still planning on taking Jason down.

O'Dell and Rivera had their heads together, talking about who was going to file which part of the report that would span several locations, multiple victims, and a recalcitrant suspect unwilling to confess.

She cleared her throat and held out her hand. "Can I have your keys, O'Dell? I need some air."

CHAPTER FORTY-SIX

If O'Dell thought she was only heading outside for some fresh air, he was more tired than he was letting on. Janet climbed into his car, cranked over the engine, then showed unusual restraint by easing slowly down the poorly lit path instead of laying rubber on the road.

Before she turned at the corner of the building, the lights on the helipad came up full. She rolled her window down and heard the *thwack-thwack-thwack* of the chopper's blades. Wind kicked up and pushed her car forward as the helicopter prepared to land. Had they saved someone, or were they too late?

She wondered the same thing about her own rescue mission.

Junior had given Janet a clue—a clue that Lola wasn't the only one in trouble. Janet wasn't going to sit by and wait for his twisted plan to come to an end.

She didn't think Lola was dead. She didn't think Lola was missing. She thought Lola had been a partner to Junior for weeks. It was the only thing that made sense in the completely senseless series of events of the last forty-eight hours. And that meant that Jason was in grave danger.

Out on the main road, she sped up, racing toward the Spot as if a life depended on it. Jason's just might.

Faith's restaurant—what was left of it—still smoldered next door.

The irony wasn't lost on her. The abandoned building next door was alive with activity—flashing lights from the fire trucks, emergency crews milling around, a fire line ringed by curious spectators. Meanwhile, her bar appeared dead and deserted.

She turned away from the circus and fumbled for her keys. She needn't have bothered. The front door was unlocked.

The sharp smell of gasoline greeted her when the door whooshed open unexpectedly.

"Freeze."

She flinched when the cool metal of a gun touched her temple. "Lola. I thought I'd find you here, I just didn't expect you to be preparing an arson."

"I'm just doing my part of the plan, just like Jeff asked. Besides, you don't fool me!" Her voice quaked. "You're the dangerous one! Jeff showed me pictures of how you've been stalking me at my school, my house. He said you were dangerous."

Janet knew it was critical to stay calm. Lola was terrified. Janet needed to show her she was not the enemy. But her heart beat so loudly in her head that she couldn't remember anything except the fact that a gun was inches from her forehead. She took a shaky breath and tried to make eye contact. Lola refused to look up. Janet spoke anyway. "Your mother hired me. She's worried about you. She wants you back home."

"Lies!" Lola pushed the tip of the gun against Janet's head, her hand trembling. "She didn't care about me when I lived in her house; she sure as shit doesn't care about me now that I'm gone."

"You're wrong, Lola. She's terrified for you. She misses you. She wants you to come home."

"She doesn't want anything other than her boyfriend. She's made that clear."

Janet's queasy stomach lurched, and she swallowed hard. "If

you really felt that way, you would have told her you were going. By disappearing, you ensured that your mother would care. You know that's true. It's terrible that you felt abandoned. It's awful that you felt so alone. But you have a mother who loves you. What you're doing now—arson? It's a crime, Lola. Jeff knew it was wrong, and so do you. It's not okay, Lola."

The teen didn't answer, but the tip of the gun pushed against Janet's head with more force.

"When did you learn that his name was Jeff?" Janet tried to keep her tone conversational. As if she wasn't talking to a girl with a gun.

"Huh?" Lola's over-bright eyes blinked, and she refocused on Janet.

"It's just—well, I guess I was wondering..." Janet cleared her throat. "It seems like when you first met him, Jeff went by a different name. Matt. Why?"

Lola licked her lips and her eyes darted around the bar. "He's had to hide who he really is for ages. People—they just don't understand him. And that's made life really difficult for him."

Janet took a slow, quiet breath. "It's really awful when people don't understand you, isn't it?"

"Don't belittle me, please."

"I'm not. I know how you feel—how Jeff must have felt." Her mind raced—was it time to act? She'd never had a gun so close to ending her life. She might only get one chance. Was this it? The fact that she didn't know made her think it wasn't. She cleared her throat again. "Where's Jason?"

"Jeff said...he said Jason's a criminal, and that we can't be happy until he's...uh...out of the picture." Her voice caught; her hand trembled again and she swallowed hard. It sounded like a sob. "I—I—I don't know..."

"Then what? What are you going to do then?"

"We're going to go away. Live together. Love each other. Start —we're just going to start over."

"You could have done that anytime over the last month.

Why did Jeff have to kill his family first? Burn down two buildings first? Think, Lola. Is that the plan of a good person?"

"Kill people? No. He didn't..." Her lips moved, but no more sound came out. Lola was lost, rudderless. Janet knew exactly how that felt.

"You're a minor, Lola. Police will take that into consideration. But Jeff—he's in real trouble. You should know that. Police are talking to him now, and it's not going to end well. He kidnapped me, my friend, and his own mother. He tried to kill us in the fire next door."

"No, that can't be. He was just going to burn down that deserted building. And I'm supposed to do the same thing here to prove my love to him. Then we get the insurance money and leave this crappy town. We can finally be together."

"Think, Lola! Neither of these buildings belong to him! The only way he'd get insurance money for them is if his entire family —and me—was gone."

The two women stared at each other. Lola was the first to look away.

"You're lying. Jeff said you were sneaky like that."

Janet shifted gears. "Who's idea was it for Jeff to sleep with Cindy Lou?"

Lola shook her head. "More lies! They didn't sleep together. He drugged her after he brought her back to his apartment. She only thought they hooked up."

"But why?"

"Because he..." she faltered, and the gun started to slip from her hand, so she brought her other up to support it. "He wanted more information on you and Jason."

"Why?"

"I don't know, okay?" she wailed. "I don't understand everything, I just know that we want to be together, and he had to take care of some things first."

Janet saw nothing but fear in the younger girl's face. Without Junior running the show, the girl had no idea what to do.

Janet chanced a quick glance around the room. Her office door was propped open, but the rest of the space was dark; she could barely make out where the back booths ended and the walls began. Jason wasn't here, but if Janet played her cards right, she just might keep Lola from burning down her business.

"Lola," she tried again. "Jeff is under arrest. There's not going to be a chance for the two of you to go away together. But you still have a get-out-of-jail ticket here; tell me what Jeff's plan is—for Jason. What is he going to do to his brother? We all know it wasn't your idea—" Her cell phone buzzed in her pocket and it might as well have been an actual buzzer in the room.

"Is this a trap?" Lola said, lowering the gun down to her side. "Are you going to arrest me?"

"I'm not a cop—I can't arrest anyone." She slipped her phone out from her back pocket and held it up for Lola to see. "But I'm friends with a cop, and I stole his car to get here. He probably just found out, and now he's worried about me. Should I answer the phone, Lola? Tell him that we're okay, but that we need help?"

The girl's face crumpled and she dropped her head into her hands, folding into herself. Her rounded shoulders started to shake with her tears. She nodded. "Yes, please."

"Okay, hon. Okay." She answered the call.

"Jason's here to check on his mom," O'Dell said mildly. "Imagine my surprise when I went to bring you back inside and found you'd taken off with my car."

Relief flooded her veins and she blew out a loud breath. Jason was safe. With any luck, she could save her business, too. "I'm at the Spot with Lola. We need help."

"At the...Rivera! Keys!" O'Dell barked, his voice directed away from the phone. "I'm coming for you, Janet. Is everything okay?"

"It is now." Janet took the gun from Lola and tucked it into her back pocket. She saw a box of matches on the bar and grabbed them with her free hand, wanting to put them somewhere safe—somewhere far away from Lola.

"I'll be there in five minutes, ten at the most."

Janet set her phone down on the bar, the tension that gripped her chest loosened for what felt like the first time in hours. She blew out a slow breath and rolled her head from side to side. Jason was okay. She was okay. They were going to be okay.

But then, from behind her, a small snap of noise. When she looked over, a tiny orange-red flicker of flame lit Lola's face. The fire at the tip of the match danced and undulated, illuminating Lola's distress.

"It's over. There's nothing left for me now," Lola whimpered, and she dropped the match over the gasoline-soaked carpet.

CHAPTER FORTY-SEVEN

Besides a few bonfires in her younger years, Janet had never been one to seek out fires. She didn't light them in their fireplace at home; she didn't even use a charcoal grill, opting instead for the propane model off the back deck.

So, despite how she'd spent her night, locked inside a walk-in cooler surrounded by fire, she was unprepared for how quickly the fire from Lola's match spread.

It dropped from Lola's outstretched hand as if in slow motion, floating more than falling to the ground. The flames spread before it even hit the carpet—the fumes strong enough to ignite seconds before it would have hit the floor.

Lola stood rooted to the floor, watching the fire spread around her, transfixed. The heat and smoke quickly moved at lightning speed with the flames, and soon, Janet couldn't see anything except the red-orange fire as it snaked out along the carpet, lapping the bar.

Janet paused long enough to note the irony of a full team of firefighters being only hundreds of feet away—but not close enough to help her until it was undoubtedly too late.

"Lola! We've got to go." The girl didn't move. "Now!" Janet shouted.

The teenager stumbled backward—but not to make her escape. Instead, fire licked up the legs of her pants, greedily feeding on the gasoline that must have splashed onto her clothes as she prepared to burn the bar down.

"Dammit," Janet muttered. Her vision clouded, but she remembered the fire extinguisher Cindy Lou had bought. She jumped over the bar and felt along the shelves until her fingers hit the cool metal surface. That's when she saw them—four propane tanks, lined up between the Beerador and the entrance to the bartender area: the same kind of tanks that had been inside the abandoned restaurant next door. "Dammit!" she said louder, taking the extinguisher up to eye level, trying to figure out how to activate the life-saving foam.

She sprayed it at her feet to cover the path of the fire so she could find her way back to Lola. Screams of fear—maybe pain— led her around the bar back to Jeff's girlfriend. Janet flooded them both with the extinguisher and pulled Lola toward the door.

"Help!" She called across the parking lot as soon as they hit the fresh air. "We need help!"

The fire next door was burning itself out. Teams of emergency responders gathered on the outside of the building, waiting out the flames, but no one turned. They were too far away.

She deposited Lola on the pavement by the Dumpster and headed back toward her bar. She wasn't going to stand around and watch her business burn to the ground. The second fire extinguisher next to Mel's spot by the door could help. But she also needed to call 911.

Janet cursed her inability to think clearly—then charged back into the bar for the fire extinguisher.

The situation inside had deteriorated rapidly in her absence. Fire now raged in the front of the space. The Beerador gleamed an impressive silvery-red in the fire. She grabbed the extinguisher from the hook and ripped out the safety ring so she could press the handle down. The small amount of retardant that came out was no match for the gasoline that Lola had poured.

She doubled over with a coughing fit. By the time she caught her breath, she saw there was no hope. Flames jumped over a metal stool and caught the corner booth like it was made of kindling. The acrid smell of burnt plastic stung her eyes, and as the smoke grew thicker, she felt behind her, knowing she had to stay calm—not panic—if she was going to find her way back out of the building.

She thought she'd only taken one step inside, maybe two, but with the choking smoke and oppressive heat, she'd lost her bearings. Panic fluttered at the base of her stomach. Then, O'Dell crashed into the bar, a halo of light from the parking lot nearly blinding her. His strong, steady arms pulled her back—away from the fire, away from her bar.

"What were you thinking?" O'Dell screamed, ripping the fire extinguisher from her hands and pushing her toward the back of the parking lot. "You could have died in there! Are you crazy?"

"I just thought if I could get to the other extinguisher, I could stave off the flames until firefighters arrived."

"Did you call them?"

"N-no—" She doubled over when another coughing fit wracked her body, finally dropping to all fours when her shaky legs gave out.

O'Dell must have picked up his phone or two-way radio, because he spoke with his official-sounding cop voice, directing fire crews one address to the west of where they were gathered. "Need ambulances for two people. One with smoke inhalation, the other with burns."

Janet looked over at Lola, lying prone on the ground. She'd kicked her shoes off, but her pants still smoldered where they hadn't burned off completely. Janet was no doctor, but the girl looked to have some moderate burns on her calves and lower legs. But still, she was lucky.

They both were.

She tried to catch her breath, but a rush of emotion left her more breathless than the fire. She looked up at her bar and the tears spilled over, coursing down her cheeks, dripping uncomfortably off her chin. She rocked backward, sitting down hard on the pavement, and cried.

Once again, O'Dell's strong, steady hands reached out, this time gently, as he pulled her close. "I've seen you stoically face so many things. Murder, death, your boyfriend breaking up with you. But this breaks through, huh? It's going to be okay, Janet."

She rested her head against his chest and closed her eyes. It wasn't just a building—the Spot was more than that. It was her livelihood. A physical embodiment of her independence, her power. And it was gone.

CHAPTER FORTY-EIGHT

Never had Janet been in a room with so many people and had it be so quiet. The table in the conference room at the downtown police department was full. Two chairs at one end were empty, but the rest of the spots were filled with Janet, her employees, and Jason's family. Hardly anyone made eye contact as O'Dell and Rivera walked in, shuffling paperwork and taking their seats at the head of the table. It had been a week since the Spot, among other things, had burned to the ground.

"Thanks for coming in today. We wanted to go over the results of our investigation with you before we release it to the press at a two o'clock press conference." Rivera looked at his watch, as if counting down the minutes until he could head home for the day.

"Janet, as you know, firefighters were able to save the western shell of your building, but as I understand it, almost all of it will have to be rebuilt?" Rivera looked up, a question in his eyes.

She nodded. "Only the Beerador survived. Insurance will cover the cost of rebuilding completely, and we should be able to reopen by summer."

O'Dell leaned forward. "Mr. and Mrs. Brooks, you've met with prosecutors?"

"Yes." William's voice was clipped. He wasn't going to offer up any other pleasantries.

"They tell me they're moving forward with felony murder, kidnapping, attempted murder, and arson charges against your son, along with a number of lesser charges related to the events over the last month. He'll be arraigned tomorrow."

Faith bit her lip but nodded, not looking up from the table.

O'Dell cleared his throat. "Cameron? You wanted to say something?"

Janet turned in surprise to look at her cook. She hadn't been sure why O'Dell had invited all her staff. Looked like she was about to find out.

Cameron cleared his throat and fidgeted with the zipper on his jacket. "I..." He cleared his throat again. "I just wanted to clear something up. About the blond hair you found in my locker?" His cheeks flushed pink, but he straightened his shoulders and stared right at Janet. "My younger sister ran away a few months ago. She and my parents didn't see eye to eye on many things, and she hasn't been in touch since she left." He took a deep breath and hurried through the rest of what seemed to be a rehearsed speech. "I—I worry about her, and try to keep her close to me."

"A lock of her hair?" Mel said doubtfully.

"It's all I have. She left a note and her picture for me. She must have cut her hair before she left, because I got that out of the trash can—like she'd just chopped off her ponytail. It was still connected at the elastic band. Anyway. It's not as creepy as it looks. I guess I just wanted you to know that." He hunched back down into his chair and folded his hands in front of him.

"What about your parents?" Mel asked. "Are they looking for her?"

"No. And that's why I moved out and needed a job. If they don't want her, I don't want them, you know?"

A moment of silence as everyone at the table processed that. Janet had to wonder why families were so complicated.

O'Dell tapped the corners of his papers together and made to stand up, but Janet cleared her throat.

"What about Lola?"

"I'm afraid we can't release any information about any minors involved in the case." Rivera frowned. "But you'll find out more as we get into the legal proceedings. She's agreed to testify against Junior."

Both cops stood to leave. "Thanks for coming in, everyone. We'll be in touch if we need anything else." O'Dell raised his eyebrows at Janet, and she gave him a small smile. He nodded and left the room.

"Janet?" She turned to find Jason at her side. He winced when she stiffened, as if she'd punched him in the gut. "Can we talk?"

She nodded, and he led the way out of the building to a quiet alcove overlooking the parking lot. "So...good news about the insurance. The Beerador survived?"

Janet stared at a particularly ugly SUV as she answered. "Yup. The fire actually left it shinier than ever. Everything else, though —destroyed."

"And you're going to rebuild?"

"Of course. The new building will have a full-service kitchen, too. Insurance should cover the whole thing."

"So no more food truck?"

"Oh, no, we'll get another one of those, too—but the new one will be drivable. We can take it to festivals and add beer taps. Listen, I don't have time to chat, actually. I've got to meet with the architect to finalize the rebuild plans." That was a lie, but she couldn't bear to stand there making small talk. "What do you want?"

"I, uh...I know that I owe you an explanation."

"You don't owe me anything, Jason." Her voice was wooden. She didn't care.

"That's where you're wrong. I owe you everything."

"Fine," she snapped. "You owe me everything, and you

trusted me with *nothing!* But worse than that—you left *me* vulnerable, because you didn't tell me what was going on."

"I thought I was protecting you! I thought if I could just figure out what Jeff was up to, I'd keep you out of it, and get him back into his home, and we'd all be okay. I thought I was doing the right thing! You have to know that I didn't know—"

"When did you know?" Janet interrupted him. "When did you know that Jeff was involved? What tipped you off?"

"The password to get into Lola's phone."

"What? How?"

"It's Jeff's birthday. Of course, I wasn't sure then, but when we saw the picture with the birthmark—that's when I knew without a doubt that he was involved. But I thought—I hoped—that I'd be able to track him down and no one would be the wiser."

She snorted. "Epic fail."

"I know." Jason shook his head. "He was one step ahead of me the whole time. I think he'd been planning it for months. The apartment in Memphis, meeting Lola. Did you know he's the one who suggested Quizz's agency to Lola's mom?"

"How?" Janet looked incredulously at Jason.

"He sent her a postcard he'd made up to look like an ad. Just to get her to call you guys. To get you involved."

"Wow. That's—that's...diabolical."

"I agree. I'd never seen that side of him before. I don't know, maybe I just didn't want to. But you have to know, I'd have never guessed he was capable of doing what he did. You have to understand—I was only trying to protect him. Protect my little brother." His voice was thick, his lips pressed into a thin line, and he stepped away from Janet. "So I just wanted to let you know that I'm going away."

"Away? What do you mean?" Janet wasn't ready to forgive him, but she wasn't ready to never see him again, either.

"I—I let a lot of people down, and I just need some space. Some space to figure it all out."

"You're leaving?" He nodded. "*You're* leaving. That's usually my move."

His short, choppy laugh held no trace of humor. "I'll miss you. But I get it if you don't feel the same. I wouldn't."

"Jason—" She stopped. She didn't know what to say, so she didn't say anything. Just watched him walk away.

———

Alone with her thoughts on the landing was a terrible place to be, so Janet drove to the Spot. She didn't know why—there wasn't anything there anymore. Even the Beerador was gone. She'd had a storage company pick it up for safekeeping until her new building was ready.

To her surprise, another car was waiting for her in the parking lot. Janet's forehead wrinkled when a woman stepped out onto the pavement. She had a familiar look to her, but it wasn't until she shrugged out of her puffy jacket and Janet saw her lumpy business suit underneath that a name came to the tip of her tongue.

"Amelia Turner?"

"Janet Black." The other woman fumbled with her clipboard. "Today is the day of your inspection with the Alcohol, Tobacco, and Firearms Bureau...but...Well, I've had people go to extreme measures to avoid a fine, but this seems over the top." She frowned and turned her kind eyes back to the burned-out shell in front of them.

"What happens now? Do we get some kind of deferment?"

"Are you rebuilding?"

Janet nodded.

"Then of course. We'll coordinate with the city on your necessary permits and codes. When you're ready to open, call for a final walkthrough." She handed her card to Janet. "Glad you're okay. Take care."

Janet watched her drive away, and an incredulous grin forced its way onto her face when a sleek black convertible slid into the lot and parked in the handicap spot by what used to be the front door.

Nell climbed sprightly out of her car. "I'm gone for a few weeks and the world ends?" Nell's silvery-white hair was tucked into a chignon, and her overcoat was open, revealing a black velour sweat-suit underneath.

"Nell! We've missed you."

"I think I'm glad I was gone!" the older woman said, assessing the ashes and blackened remnants of the building. "Is everyone okay?"

"They are now. And we're going to rebuild."

"Good," Nell said with a decisive nod. "But where do I get my vodka soda until then?"

Janet chuckled. "How was the cruise?"

"It was something else, Janet. You could be as alone or together as you wanted to be, you know? Just depending on where you went on the ship. Kind of great."

"Hmm." A buzz started to build at the back of her brain.

"What's Jason think about this?" Nell asked.

"I don't know. Well—I mean, we're kind of...taking a break right now. I'm staying with a friend while I figure out what's next." O'Dell had been kind enough to offer her his guest room permanently.

Nell launched into a series of questions but didn't give her time to answer any of them before the next one rolled forth. Janet finally held a hand up.

"Nell? What did you say the name of the cruise ship was?"

"Why?"

"I have no home to go back to, my business is totaled, and I won't be able to work for months. Now might be the perfect time to get away." *From everything*, she added in her head.

Nell narrowed her eyes and dug into her coat pocket, eventually holding out a crushed and folded brochure. "Great time to go, Janet. They're having a buy-one-get-one-free deal for the next month." Nell slung her purse back into her car, then stopped and turned to look Janet full in the face again. "You got someone in mind to join you?"

The buzz in Janet's brain turned into a fully formed idea. "I have just the right person, Nell. Thanks."

The older woman clucked her tongue with one final look at the missing building, then climbed back into her car and drove away.

It wasn't often that you could manage to run away from everything that was causing you trouble in your life and call it a vacation, not complete avoidance.

Janet picked up her phone and called an old friend. "This is going to sound crazy, but hear me out..."

Thanks so much for reading the first three books in the **_Janet Black Mystery Series_**! Help get the word out about the series by leaving a review. Reviews help other readers and the authors, too.

ABOUT THE AUTHOR

Libby Kirsch is an Emmy award winning journalist with over ten years of experience working in television newsrooms of all sizes. She draws on her rich history of making embarrassing mistakes on live TV, and is happy to finally indulge her creative writing side, instead of always having to stick to the facts. Libby lives in Michigan with her husband, three young children, and Sam the dog.

Connect with Libby
www.LibbyKirschBooks.com
Libby@LibbyKirschBooks.com

facebook.com/LibbyKirschBooks

twitter.com/LibbyKirsch

amazon.com/author/libbykirsch

bookbub.com/authors/libby-kirsch

goodreads.com/libbykirsch